DEVIL MUSIC

DEVIL MUSIC

A NOVEL

CARLY OROSZ

LOGSINE LABS PRESS

CHAPTER ONE

SERVITUDE

WHEN LANCE ANNOUNCED THAT he had fallen in love, no one paid much attention. Lance fell in love at least three times a month, each time with a different pretty girl who had no interest whatsoever in being his girlfriend. He would pine over her for a week or so, and then fall out of love just as quickly when the next pretty girl came along. To those who knew him, Lance's claim that he had fallen in love carried about as much weight as a lion's claim to have become a vegetarian.

So when Lance rushed into Mr. Warwick's study babbling about being in love for the second time that June, Cain, who was in the next room, turned up the radio to drown out his voice. Yet he could still hear Lance ranting to his father, and he could understand most of it.

"Hey." Steve poked his head through the door. "What's Lance carrying on about? I could hear him all the way in the kitchen."

"New girlfriend." Cain rolled his eyes. "I think her name is Michelle."

Steve snorted. "Again? I give 'em three days."

Steve was Mr. Warwick's other son. He was younger than Lance, fifteen years old, and Lance was seventeen. Steve was thin and dark, whereas Lance was big, beefy and sandy-haired. Steve was level-headed and intelligent, whereas Lance was impulsive and often stupid. The two brothers even had dramatically different tastes in fashion. Lance liked loud Hawaiian shirts, and his tastes for specific styles frequently changed to accommodate whatever clothing happened to be popular at the moment; Cain vividly remembered the tantrum he had thrown last year when Mr. Warwick refused to buy him a Members Only jacket. Steve gravitated toward plain black or white T-shirts and didn't particularly care what his classmates thought of his outfits. In fact, Steve was much more like his father than Lance was, but Lance was clearly Mr. Warwick's favorite child. Cain didn't pretend to understand it; but then he was a demon, and as Mr. Warwick liked to remind him, what did demons know about the stranger points of human emotions? As Mr. Warwick's servant, Cain was not in the position to say anything anyway.

Lance had apparently finished his tantrum; the study door slammed, and his angry stomping echoed through the hall. After a moment of silence, Cain heard Mr. Warwick calling him to the study.

Steve made a face. "I think my dad wants you, Cain."

"Mmm." Cain already knew his master wanted to speak with him; the dog collar around his neck had jerked even before Mr. Warwick called out. "Wish me luck."

He stumped off down the hallway—clumsily—because Mr. Warwick insisted that he wear an old pair of Lance's shoes in the house so his hooves wouldn't scuff up the expensive hardwood floors.

Mr. Warwick was seated behind his desk. He was a tall man with piercing gray eyes and long, elegant hands. The records of the various corporations and government agencies to which he sold his services listed his occupation as "scientist" or "consultant." However, anyone who had seen him at work or caught a glimpse of the odd books lining the shelves of his study would realize at once that it was neither consulting nor science that had made him the fourteenth richest man in America and prematurely silvered his hair. He looked up as the door to the study opened.

Cain paused in the doorway. "You wanted to see me, Master?"

"Yes. Come in, Cain." Mr. Warwick's sharp-nosed, brooding face was even more brooding than usual. "Lance thinks he's found the girl of his dreams…again."

"Does he, Master?" Cain repressed a sigh of annoyance.

"He does," said Mr. Warwick. "Michelle, this one's name is. Apparently, she's from out of town, visiting family in the city. He was just in here, complaining bitterly because she wouldn't give him the time of day. It's a pity, really, that he falls in love and gets rejected so often. He's such a sensitive boy."

Cain thought that Lance was about as sensitive as a lump of granite, but he wisely kept his observations to himself.

"Lance is angry with me now because I refused to use my power to help him win this girl over." Mr. Warwick shook his head. "I love my son, but I'm finished with wasting my precious energy on love spells for all the silly girls he'll fall out of love with in a week's time. Still, I hate seeing him in so much pain. I don't know what to do, Cain. I really don't."

Cain said nothing. He knew from experience that he

3

wasn't expected to provide answers or advice; he was expected to stand and say as little as possible while Mr. Warwick vented and bounced ideas off him, as if he were no more than a favorite dog or a photograph of a long-dead relative.

"I'm sure Lance will be over his infatuation in a few days," he went on, sounding a little reassured. "Until then, though, he'll be miserable and angry. Then, of course, there's the danger that this little episode will be repeated in the future. It's high time I had a talk with Lance, man to man, about girls and dating." He raised his eyebrows quizzically. "Do you think he would respond to that, Cain?"

"I think he would, Master," Cain lied. Mr. Warwick had been having the same man-to-man talk with Lance two or three times every month for the last five years, and Cain seriously doubted that yet another repetition of it would make any more of an impression on Lance than all the others had. If anything, it would make him even more sulky and short-tempered and convinced that the girls who sensibly wanted nothing to do with him were stuck up and didn't know what they were missing.

"Yes, I think he would too." Mr. Warwick nodded. "The sooner the better, I say. Lance will be eighteen soon; it's high time he stopped chasing flighty, loose girls and started looking for a nice one."

Most of the girls Lance chased were perfectly nice, in Cain's opinion; it was Lance who was flighty, loose, and most definitely not nice.

"Yes—the sooner, the better," said Mr. Warwick. "I won't be around forever, and I do hope Lance will take over the...family business...one day. He's been making such great strides in his lessons."

Cain nodded in feigned agreement. Perhaps Lance was indeed making great strides in his lessons, but Cain had certainly not noticed them. The few traces of his father's abilities that Lance had inherited were less than impressive, and Lance was too impatient to learn to use them properly.

"I'll feel much more confident about his readiness once he's married and settled down and has an heir of his own on the way. I had such high hopes when he took a shine to Clarissa; the Babbitts are a fine—and *very* wealthy—old New York family. It's too bad he lost interest in her so quickly."

Cain said nothing and stared at the floor. He had been shocked the first time he had heard Mr. Warwick talk about breeding his son, and the fact that the old man only spoke of Lance's crushes in terms of their value as breeding stock for passing on the Gift—the rare ability to channel magic—disturbed him even more. The subject still made him very uncomfortable.

"Too bad indeed." Mr. Warwick frowned. "Still, I suppose it's just as well. Clarissa is pretty enough, but she's such a *mundane* little thing that I doubt any child that came out of her would have the Gift no matter who the father was. Besides," he smirked, "I've had the dubious pleasure of working with her parents. Senator Babbitt would be quite useless if it weren't for his deep pockets, and his wife is a horrible shrew. They'd make wretched in-laws. Don't you think so, Cain?"

Cain became even more uncomfortable. Mr. Warwick was always polite to his female clients' faces, but his bland façade always melted away as soon as they left. He even referred to his own late wife—when he spoke of her at all— as "the traitor." Cain had never met Mr. Warwick's wife, but

5

Steve's few fuzzy memories of her were pleasant ones. Cain had no idea why the old man hated her so.

But it wouldn't do to let Mr. Warwick see his discomfort. Any sign of dissatisfaction on his part could bring on a scolding, or worse. "Yes, Master," he said in the faintest hint of a resigned tone.

Mr. Warwick didn't seem to notice. If anything, his expression became a bit more cheerful. "Yes, I'm sure that's the best thing to do. I'll wait until Lance has recovered a bit, and then we'll have a nice talk. I'm sure he'll come to his senses this time. You may go now, Cain."

"Yes, Master."

"Oh—and Cain?"

"Yes, Master?" Cain paused in the doorway.

"Turn that damned radio down. I can barely hear myself think in here."

"Yes, Master."

Steve was standing in the hallway as Cain emerged from the study. His head was tipped back, and he was pressing a bloody towel to his nose.

"Hey, Cain." He grimaced. "Can you help me out here? His Royal Spitefulness caught me on the way back to the kitchen and decided to take it out on me again."

Almost from the day Lance learned to walk, he had been taking out his frustrations on Steve. As Mr. Warwick was too busy to notice, Steve had always come to Cain for comfort and pain relief after their one-sided fights. Cain, in turn, went to Steve to vent after Mr. Warwick talked down to him or took the fireplace poker to his back for failing at a task. Steve was the closest thing he had to a friend in the human world.

"Of course. Come and sit down in my room."

6

Steve followed Cain to his bedroom and sat down on the edge of the frayed, rickety bed as he had done many times.

"It doesn't look broken." Cain watched a fresh trickle of blood drip from Steve's nose as he removed the towel. The fragility of Steve's human body amazed and worried him. Cain's thick scales protected him from most injuries like those that Steve sustained in minor tussles with Lance. Even Mr. Warwick's occasional beatings did little damage, though Cain always made a point of pretending that the beatings hurt him more than they actually did for fear that his master would dream up harsher punishments. "That's good. There is a lot of blood, though. This may take a while."

Steve nodded gingerly and sat back. He winced as Cain placed three fingers against the bridge of his nose and concentrated. Cain couldn't heal wounds exactly; but if he was careful, he could stimulate the body's natural healing mechanisms to work at an accelerated speed. It was a delicate job, but Lance's frequent temper tantrums had given him plenty of practice. In two minutes he had managed to stop the blood flow, and Steve looked much less uncomfortable.

"Thanks." He wrinkled his nose and gave an experimental sniff. "You know, you'd think I'd be better at avoiding Lance when he's pissed about something by now."

"I think he's just gotten better at finding you."

"That's probably true." Steve sighed. "You're lucky you're bigger than he is, Cain. He'd never have the balls to try and beat you up even though you aren't allowed to fight back."

"Maybe not." Cain scratched at his collar thoughtfully. It was true that Lance had never actually hit him, but he could recall several occasions when he could distinctly feel him *wanting* to hit him. It was bound to happen one of these days. "Still, there are times when I'd rather be hit than listen to the old man complaining about how the whole world is against his dear son."

"What did he say this time? The usual?" Steve made a derisive grunting noise in the back of his throat.

"The usual. 'These stupid, fickle girls don't know what they're missing, Cain! It's a shame. Lance is such a sensitive boy.'" Cain imitated Mr. Warwick's voice mockingly. "I don't know whether his Lance-worship makes me want to laugh or cry, and the worst part is that I'm not allowed to do either."

"You've got more self-control than I do." Steve rolled his eyes. "I wouldn't be able to keep a straight face. Or I'd just throttle dad."

"A slave collar is good for self-control," Cain began. As he spoke, he felt it again—the collar gave a sharp jerk, as if someone had tugged an invisible leash around his neck. In this way, he always knew when Mr. Warwick wanted him even when he couldn't hear him calling. It was also the charm that bound him to Mr. Warwick in servitude until the old man released him or died. He hated it, but there was nothing he could do to change it. The black leather drew tight around his neck like a noose whenever he even thought about tearing it off.

"Speaking of which," he said wryly, "your dad's calling me again. Let's hope he wants me to help him put a curse of impotence on Lance."

"Fat chance." Steve grinned. "Like the idea, though. I think I'll try that once I learn enough magic."

Cain lay in the early evening twilight, listening to the

distant, comforting buzz of the Warwicks' muffled conversation at the family dinner table. Mr. Warwick had excused Cain from serving them today, and Cain had already eaten his dinner of raw ground beef in his room. He was never allowed to eat with the family because Mr. Warwick found the demon diet of raw meats undignified. Cain preferred to eat alone anyhow. If Mr. Warwick didn't give him enough food, which he usually didn't, Cain could sometimes sneak out his window to snatch a pigeon or a small rodent from the backyard. He often wished that he could venture into the woods outside the neighborhood in search of larger game, but his collar wouldn't allow him to travel outside the confines of Mr. Warwick's property without his express permission. Hunting came easily to Cain—a skill, he guessed, that he had learned in his previous life—though he had no memory of his life before servitude.

Mr. Warwick often wiped Cain's memory. Cain suspected that it was one of the many ways in which Mr. Warwick kept him in check. As a result, Cain was always excited and somewhat anxious when he was sent to do errands. Every time, he felt as if he were encountering the outside world for the first time.

In the last five hours, Cain had flown to the Peruvian Andes to gather rare mountain lichens that Mr. Warwick needed for a specially ordered flying ointment, stopped in El Salvador to slip a poison too vile to contemplate into the wine glass of a progressive-minded politician whom Mr. Warwick had been hired to assassinate, and passed into Mexico to pick up a flint knife, cruelly sharp and inlaid with an exquisite turquoise mosaic, which Mr. Warwick wanted for purposes of his own. He had also had orders to spy invisibly on Lance's new crush for an hour or so. He had learned nothing new about Michelle except that she was visiting her Uncle Walter and Aunt Janice in Yonkers, that she was pretty and brown-haired, and that she was intelligent enough to have recognized immediately that Lance was bad news. He told Mr. Warwick everything but the last point. Each errand had been both terrifying and exhilarating for Cain. After dinner, he knew Mr. Warwick would wipe his memory of all of these events. He savored them while he could.

Cain switched on the ancient radio that sat on the milk crate he used as a bedside table. He squinted up at the grimy little window with its threadbare yellow curtains, hovering on the edge of sleep and dangling his feet over the footboard of the lumpy old bed—not that he had much choice, for the bed was too short for him. The last notes of a song he had been half-listening to faded out on the radio, and the opening chords of Killing Medicine crackled through the speakers. Cain perked up. Killing Medicine was one of his favorite songs.

He closed his eyes and listened. The band—he had never been very good at remembering band names (was it Lion of Judah, maybe?)—had a lead singer with a voice unlike any Cain had heard before. It veered effortlessly between smooth baritone and shrieking tenor, moaning an arcane tale of betrayal and anger.

The guitarist launched into a complicated solo. Cain sighed and began to relax. He liked the mournful, distorted wailing of electric guitars. It reminded him of something from before he was captured, something he was no longer permitted to remember...

His eyes flew open.

A mountaintop in the Outside. We flew here together, my

tribe and I. I shivered in the snow as they lined up—tall creatures, hoofed and scaled like me, but darker somehow, trailing black wings behind them.

The memory was fading already, as all memories of life before his capture inevitably did. He fought to hold it.

They turned their faces to the sky and began to sing.

The collar started to sting. Cain dug his long, sharp nails into the mattress and closed his eyes tight, straining against the inevitable.

Such singing! Cain thought. *More tones than I could count, perfectly mingled and overlaid...and sad, so deeply sad. A mourning song. A song that seeped into veins and deadened nerves...*

A sudden, painful burst of light erupted against the inside of his eyelids, and the memory was gone. He let out a snarl and squeezed the mattress in helpless anger. The collar bit him as his claws left fresh punctures in the already tattered fabric.

Michelle went back home to California two days later. Lance was gloomy and irritable for two days more. He beat Steve up three times, talked back to his father and earned the first cross word Mr. Warwick had said to him in months, and threw a shoe at Cain, who had failed to bring the Coke he ordered upstairs in what he considered a timely manner. By the end of the second day, he was grumbling sullenly about Michelle being too stuck up to give him a chance. He seemed on the verge of writing her off and moving on to another girl.

The next few days were normal enough. Mr. Warwick wiped Cain's memory of his previous errands, but he allowed him to keep the memory of spying on Michelle until the matter was "resolved." He also sent Cain to Ontario to pick up a pound of witch hazel. The boys sat through Mr. Warwick's attempts to teach them the basics of sorcery. Steve wasn't half bad at it, but Lance was a hopeless cause. One day, Mr. Warwick came home in an exceptionally good mood.

"Some rich televangelist met him for lunch today," Steve explained when Cain asked what was up. "Seems he's offering dad a lot of money to help him fight this freaky underground cult that, like, kidnaps people and sacrifices them in demon-worshipping rituals and stuff."

As he did laundry that afternoon, Cain wondered who these mysterious demon-worshipping humans were and what in the world they thought they could accomplish by kidnapping other humans and sacrificing them. He sighed as he inspected a stain on one of Lance's shirts.

If these people exist at all, he thought with a bit too much enthusiasm, *they're probably very angry with Mr. Warwick and ready to give him a solid beating for enslaving one of their "gods"*...

The collar tingled ominously. He pushed the idea out of his mind and started on a spell to remove the stain.

There was only one thing out of the ordinary: Lance kept talking about Michelle.

He wasn't grumbling about her alleged coldness anymore either. Instead, he was sighing over what he saw as her more pleasant attributes.

"She had the most amazing hair," he gushed at the dinner table one night while Cain was in the kitchen tidying up. "It was always so perfect. And that figure! I'm getting hot just thinking about it."

"Lance," said Mr. Warwick as he helped himself to more

mashed potatoes, "don't you think you should forget this Michelle person? She's gone now, and she wasn't good enough for you anyway."

"I know she's not good enough for me!" Lance brought his fist down on the table, launching a minor eruption of peas from his plate. "That's the whole problem! She's not good enough for me, but I'm in love with her anyway."

Cain rushed into the dining area and started cleaning up the mess with a wet rag.

"I was afraid this would happen someday." Mr. Warwick shook his head sadly. "I was always afraid that you would fall in love with a girl who wasn't good enough for you, and she would break your heart. You're too sensitive, Lance."

Steve and Cain exchanged a disgusted look over the table. Cain knew that if Steve had started whining about being in love with a girl who didn't love him back, Mr. Warwick would tell him to get over it and to stop bothering him while he was eating.

Lance poked his untouched potatoes sulkily. "This wouldn't have happened, you know, if you'd just given me help when I asked for it. She'd be eating out of my hand right now, and my heart wouldn't be broken."

"I admit that," said Mr. Warwick. "But you see, Lance, love spells are expensive to make and even more expensive to undo. I really didn't want to act until I knew that this was the real thing."

"It *is* the real thing!" Lance squirmed with frustration. "I told you that, and you didn't believe me."

"Tell you what, then. We'll wait a while, and if you're still in love with Michelle after a certain period of time— say, two weeks—then we'll start talking magical solutions."

Lance was pacified and began to dig into his food.

"Good boy." Mr. Warwick smiled, and then glanced at his empty cup. "More coffee, Cain."

Cain balled up the dirty rag and went to get the coffeepot. He knew from experience to show no interest in the outcome of the argument, but he couldn't help feeling sorry for Michelle.

Steve and Lance went to the beach the next day. Cain, of course, was not allowed to go.

"Meet any pretty girls today, Lance?" Mr. Warwick asked pointedly as the boys came home.

"Plenty." Lance glared at his father. "They were all bitchy, uptight college girls, though. I can't stand it when a girl knows more than me. Michelle is smart, but at least she's decent enough to hide it."

"A fine quality for a young lady to have," admitted Mr. Warwick.

"She wouldn't have to hide it if you would make a little effort to raise your IQ above the single digits," muttered Steve as he rummaged for a cold drink from the refrigerator. Lance was sulking too deeply to hear him.

The days crawled by, and Lance showed no sign of moving on to a new unwilling girlfriend. Mr. Warwick called Cain into his study on the evening the two-week deadline expired.

"Well, Cain, Lance has certainly proved himself. He's never been in love with anyone this long," he said, sounding as if Lance had fawned over her for two years instead of two weeks. "I'd still rather not resort to using spells, but I don't see any other way to keep my promise. The only question is how to do it. I don't want something so powerful that I'd have trouble undoing it should Lance decide he doesn't want her anymore, but the lesser ones aren't good for much of anything but a simple crush."

"Yes, Master," said Cain unhappily.

Mr. Warwick frowned. "Of course, the effects are strengthened if the victim already has fond feelings for the intended object. If only there were some way to make this Michelle fond of Lance to begin with—some way that didn't involve magic."

"Master?" Cain swallowed nervously. Speaking out of turn was risky, but this time he felt that he had to say something. "Ah…doesn't Michelle live in California?"

"She does." Mr. Warwick drummed his fingers on his desk. "We'll need some excuse to bring her back to New York…"

"What if…I'm sorry, Master, but…what if…she doesn't want to be with Lance anyway because he lives too far away? It *is* a long way for a human to travel." Cain stared at the long-necked blue vase that sat on the corner of the desk. It wasn't much of a defense, but he was afraid to come across as insubordinate.

"What a quaint idea, Cain." Mr. Warwick chuckled. "Distance makes little difference to young people in love— though I wouldn't expect any demon to understand love since you all have limited ability to overcome baser instincts."

He cast a jaundiced eye over Cain's bare chest and arms.

"I'll wear a shirt tomorrow, Master," said Cain unhappily. He had hated the squeezing and scratchiness of human clothes since the first hours of his capture. It was a hot day, and he thought that wearing pants was a perfectly adequate compromise.

"Good." Mr. Warwick smiled. "Anyway, I suppose you are at least right that the distance is inconvenient. I'll overcome it somehow. I just need a little time to think."

The time Mr. Warwick took to think annoyed Lance greatly, and he took his frustration out on Steve in increasingly bloody ways. Cain was too startled to react when Lance slapped him with an open hand for burning his toast at breakfast. Lance rarely came close enough to touch him because he was a little afraid of the blue demon ever since he was seven years old and suffered a nasty bite after he pulled Cain's tail.

"Whoa, Lance. Take it easy!" yelled Steve from the safety of the other side of the table. "It's not Cain's fault that dad's too cheap to replace our piece-of-shit toaster."

"Shut your mouth, Steve," growled Lance. "Stupid animal had it coming to him. He needs someone to teach him a lesson."

Cain shuffled over to the sink without a word and willed himself to start unloading the dishwasher. As much as he would have loved to leap on Lance and give his other arm a matching bite-shaped scar, the momentary satisfaction wouldn't be worth the vicious choking he knew he would get from the collar. He had hardly felt the slap through his scales anyway.

Mr. Warwick had lunch with a client that afternoon. While he was away, Cain and Steve sneaked into his study to search for a love-ending spell. Unfortunately, love spells tended to be most effective as potions. Although Lance was a poor magician, he did have a minor talent for sensing and detecting magic, especially the kind of magic found lingering on potion-contaminated food.

16

Cain pushed yet another dusty tome aside. "Well, there were plenty in that book, but they were all potions. He would smell them from a mile away."

Steve groaned. "Why do love spells always have to come in potion form? At the rate Lance is going, I'll be beaten to a pulp or dead before dad stops brooding over work and turns his full attention to the Michelle problem."

Cain began to flip through another book with no success. "I feel sorry for the girl too. She has no idea what she's about to be dragged into."

"True. She might at least civilize him a little, though— Oh, shit!"

Cain followed Steve's gaze to the door. The handle was turning.

"I thought dad was away at some kind of meeting," Steve hissed.

"He was," Cain whispered back. "He must have gotten home early. Well, on to the emergency plan."

They scrambled to opposite ends of the room. Cain closed his eyes and concentrated on reducing his size until he was small enough to crawl into the space between the wall and the last book on a shelf. He hated to shrink himself—it caused a crushing, breathless sensation that made him feel as if he had been stuffed into a thick paper bag and stomped upon—but it was a quick and effective way to hide. Steve hunched in a corner and rattled off a spell of invisibility, one of the first spells he'd learned, and one he had used many times to escape from Lance.

It wasn't a very good emergency plan. They left books scattered all over the floor, and though Steve's invisibility spell was more than enough to fool Lance, Mr. Warwick could probably see through it if he put the proper effort into

17

detecting hidden magic or looked in just the right place.

Mr. Warwick swept in, and Cain held his breath as he moved in the direction of the pile of books. Fortunately, he didn't seem to notice them. He walked silently to his desk and leaned there with a casual air. A moment later Cain and Steve both saw why he assumed this stance: he had company. Mr. Warwick's companion was a big man in an expensive-looking blue suit. He paused in the doorway, peering suspiciously into the study as if he feared that dozens of bloodthirsty murderers were lying in wait among the books.

"Come in, Reverend Breen." Mr. Warwick made an inviting gesture. "You see, there are no dried bat wings or toads in cauldrons in here—just books—like your study at home. I assure you that what I do is perfectly legitimate and respectable."

"It does look that way. But there is something uncanny about it." The minister's words were spoken slowly, in a sonorous tone, and slightly over-pronounced as if he were trying to hide a Southern drawl. His steely, olive-colored eyes narrowed as he leaned toward the shelves—perilously close to Cain's hiding place—and inspected a book with a collection of arcane glyphs engraved on the spine. "Still, my congressman-friend recommended you pretty strongly. Says you singlehandedly took care of that dangerous Communist firebrand Aurelio Cáceres somehow, and that if anyone could give us an edge in our battle against this awful cult, it's you. Knowing what you do, though, I had to come meet you myself and make sure…" He looked uncertain.

"That I'm not a Satanist myself?" Mr. Warwick chuckled, not at all insulted. "You have nothing to worry about—I assure you. I detest black magic of any kind."

For someone who detests it so much, thought Cain contemptuously, *you certainly use it a lot*.

"That's good to know." The Reverend Breen didn't sound entirely convinced. "Are you willing to help us, then?"

"I don't see how I could pass up the opportunity," Mr. Warwick replied in his most sickeningly faux-sincere business voice. "Your cause is a good one; the pay is excellent; and I do believe that this assignment will be much more challenging than anything I have ever encountered. I do love a challenge, Reverend Breen."

Cain wondered if Mr. Warwick knew that he was being hired to fight people who didn't exist. He did sound excited at the thought of hunting demon worshippers, but Cain had known him long enough to recognize the placating smile plastered on his face. It was the same smile he flashed at clients when he thought he could send them on their way with a vial of perfectly ordinary sugar water tinted with green food coloring instead of the powerful potion they ordered.

"Good, good." The minister sat down heavily in the antique oak chair that faced the desk. "Now, if we can get down to business. What exactly do you intend to do?"

Though Cain couldn't quite see him anymore, he suspected that Mr. Warwick was sitting behind his desk with his fingers pressed together, fixing the minister with his most intense and sphinx-like stare. Mr. Warwick liked his clients to feel uncomfortable; their discomfort made it easier for him to remain in control of their interactions.

"I intend," he said finally, "to fight magic with magic."

The minister winced visibly at the word *magic*, but said, "Go on."

"You say that these Satanists have escaped justice so far because they use their powers to mask the evidence of their crimes and keep ordinary law enforcement officials away from their meeting places, do you not? I know how these things can be done."

"And you know how to keep them from being done, I hope?"

"Of course." Mr. Warwick's voice grew more serious. "But I cannot do it on my own. I'm just one person, after all, and there are thousands of them—thousands upon thousands. If you want me to be able to make any difference at all, I must have help."

"What kind of help?" asked the minister with more than a hint of suspicion in his voice.

"People with…special training," Mr. Warwick replied. "People who can do the kinds of things I can do. People who can go out into the field, as it were, and be my operatives. If I have enough of them working for me, and if I am given enough time, I am quite sure that I can manage to bring the whole organization down from the inside."

"That sounds like excellent news," said the Reverend Breen nervously. "But I have to ask, where would you get your…recruits? We aren't expected to provide them, are we? I would rather not have anyone in my ministry getting involved in…in that line of work. No offense."

"None taken," said Mr. Warwick calmly. "I understand your objections, and I assure you that I already have people in mind who have nothing to do with your church. You need not be involved with the training process either; I'll oversee that myself. I just need you to provide me with enough money to run it and enough space to work."

"That sounds reasonable," said the minister. "I am

curious, however. How exactly does one go about training for your *program*?"

"It is a rather complicated process. I'm afraid you would find the technical points very boring, but basically what I do is..."

To Cain's disappointment, he lowered his voice so they could no longer hear what he was saying. This tactic was another favorite trick of Mr. Warwick's: he'd awe his clients by whispering information to them, giving them the impression that they were being let in on wonderful and highly privileged mystical secrets. He could see the minister shifting in his seat as the conversation went on.

"That sounds awfully drastic," he said at last.

"It's the only way, I'm afraid," said Mr. Warwick sadly. "You know what kind of people we're up against. And you must remember that you wouldn't have to be involved in it—not directly anyway."

"What about the legal issues?" the minister asked. "This sounds like it's in the gray area at best..."

"I've dealt with the law before," said Mr. Warwick. "The law won't touch me."

There was a long silence, and then the minister said, "Very well. I'll consider your offer."

"Excellent." There was a shifting sound, and Cain guessed that Mr. Warwick had stood up. "I'll show you out."

The Reverend Breen got out of his chair with a great noise of upheaval and effort. He turned slowly to the door, and Cain thought he looked as if he deeply disliked whatever Mr. Warwick had told him. Mr. Warwick glided around the desk and began to show the minister out. Cain held his breath as he paused to frown at the pile of books on the floor; but he apparently decided to deal with it after he had seen to his guest. He continued out of the study, the minister following in his wake. The door closed, and there was silence.

Cain hopped cautiously down off the bookshelf. He had barely finished expanding to his normal size when Steve materialized beside him.

"God!" Steve's face was pale. "That scared the shit out of me. I thought dad was supposed to be gone all day."

"Me too." Cain shuddered and picked at his collar. "Let's get out of here before he comes back."

They scurried out of the study without replacing the books, having decided that Mr. Warwick would be even more suspicious if he came back to find the study clean. Once they were safely in Cain's room, they turned on the radio at full volume to mask their voices in case Mr. Warwick was listening.

"Wow," said Steve. "That Reverend guy—Brent? Bryant? I forget his name—seems pretty serious. I wonder if there really is a cult out there."

"I don't think so," said Cain. "If there were people who really *worshipped* demons, why would they let anyone put a slave collar on me and mess with my memories?"

"Maybe they're scared of dad for some reason," said Steve, his eyes full of worry. "Maybe dad expects us to help him fight them, as some sort of test to see what we've learned or something?"

"I wouldn't worry about it." Cain sighed. "What is it your dad always says about those televangelist people? That they're a gang of hypocritical, sanctimonious, money-grubbing..." he paused, trying to remember all the complicated words Mr. Warwick was so fond of using.

"Bloviating, mendacity-minded frauds?" Steve volunteered. "Yeah, he comes home ranting about some televangelist friend of Mrs. Babbitt's every time he has a meeting with the senator. I'm surprised he made it through a whole lunch with that preacher guy without being an ass to him."

"Exactly," said Cain. "I don't think he's going to do anything to help the minister. I think he's just going to let the minister think he's helping."

"Oh!" Recognition dawned in Steve's eyes. "You mean like the fake beauty spells he started giving to Mrs. Babbitt after she called him her husband's glorified assassin when she thought he wasn't listening? Yeah, that's definitely something he would do. But still, why would the minister lie about something like this? It's a pretty big and crazy thing to lie about."

"Yeah," Cain agreed. "I have no idea why anyone would lie about something like that. But I'm not the best person to ask. I have no idea why humans do a lot of things."

Mr. Warwick brooded in silence for the rest of the day. It made Cain uneasy; the old man was usually annoyingly cheerful after landing a lucrative deal. This time he sat at the dinner table glaring at his pork chops. He even went so far as to snap at Lance to stop whining and to be patient, for he was already doing everything he could. Steve and Cain exchanged worried glances as he pushed his half-eaten meal aside and slouched off to his study without another word. The scattered books weighed heavily on Cain's mind as he cleared Mr. Warwick's dinner plate.

Two hours later, Cain felt a tug at his collar as he lay in his bed rehearsing good explanations for the mess. He switched off the radio, set his teeth, and wobbled his way to the study.

Mr. Warwick was sitting behind his desk, most of his attention focused on the paperweight suspended in the air four inches above his outstretched palm. He looked, if it were possible, even more disgruntled than he had at dinner.

"Cain," he said curtly. "I need you to go to Los Angeles for me tomorrow."

Cain blinked in surprise and relief. It was a tentative relief, however; Mr. Warwick was still clearly in a temper about something.

"Yes, Master," he said in his meekest tone. "What do you need me to get for you?"

The paperweight barely wavered as Mr. Warwick's eyes bored into it.

"It's not for me," he said at last. "It's for Lance. I need you to bring Michelle to him."

Cain raised an eyebrow, convinced that he couldn't have heard correctly.

"I...ah...beg your pardon, Master?"

"I need you to bring Michelle back to New York for Lance." Mr. Warwick's tone was suddenly gentle, but Cain wasn't fooled; the paperweight was beginning to vibrate, reflecting his irritation.

"Now, now, no need to look so shocked, Cain. I don't mean for you to swoop in and carry her off against her will. You must convince her to come of her own volition and give my boy another chance—without using magic, of course. I'll take care of that part. You just be kind and attentive to her, and praise Lance often. *Beg* her to come back for another visit. Use all the charm you have. She'll be bound to come around eventually."

Cain's tail curled nervously around his knees. It had not

24

taken him long to realize that most humans found the sight of a seven-foot-tall, scaly blue demon with curved black horns and fangs distinctly less than charming.

"But I don't have any charm, Master," he muttered.

"Nonsense. You're charming enough in your human form." Mr. Warwick smiled, and the paperweight gyrated furiously.

Cain groaned. It was true that he could take human form easily enough, but he rarely bothered. He had always found it terribly uncomfortable, and somehow he could never avoid making himself look so striking that he stood out almost as much among humans when he was in human form as he did in his natural shape.

"I'll take human form, then," he said in resignation. "But Master...I hope I don't sound like I'm trying to get out of work, but...Well, I don't see why you want *me* to do this. I'm not very good at this kind of thing." Contrary what most humans seemed to expect of demons, Cain had absolutely no talent at tempting anyone into anything. He had regularly failed even to tempt Lance and Steve to come in from the snow for hot cocoa when they were both younger.

Mr. Warwick's smile instantly turned to a frown. His hand shot up, snakelike, and snatched the paperweight from the air.

"If you had been paying attention when you were spying on Michelle, you would know why I need you to go," he hissed. "But you weren't. You failed to give me one important detail: her last name. It's Breen. Does that sound familiar?"

"I..." It did sound familiar, but the absurd unfairness of being blamed for not finding out Michelle's last name distracted him. He had assumed that Lance would at least bother to find out the last name of the girl he was supposedly in love with on his own.

"She's the daughter of Nathaniel Breen." Mr. Warwick's eyes narrowed. "The *Reverend* Nathaniel Breen, who just so happens to be my biggest client right now."

"Oh. I see, Master." Cain tried his best to look abashed.

"There's no doubt about it," growled Mr. Warwick. "I had a meeting with him this afternoon, and what do you think he brought up in the conversation? His darling only daughter, Michelle, who was just in New York visiting relatives and ended up being followed for days by some dunderheaded love-struck local boy." He looked furious at the very memory of hearing Lance described this way. "I can't tell you how much this revelation complicates things, Cain. The good minister was leery enough of me already. I had to bring him back to the house to show him that I don't work out of a deep, dank dungeon. Thank God we didn't run into you; I don't think I ever would have convinced him to come back. If he ever found out that Lance is Michelle's love-struck local boy...I can't look as if I was involved in this arrangement, Cain. You must convince Michelle for me, as quietly as possible."

"I'll do it, then, but...but I still don't understand how I'm supposed to do it, Master," said Cain desperately.

"Use your imagination!" Mr. Warwick shot him an exasperated look. "Pretend to be a friend of Lance's who has come to put in a good word for him, or convince her that her aunt and uncle want to see her again. Become a movie star if you have to! I really don't care as long as you get the job done. This girl wouldn't be my first choice for Lance, to be perfectly honest, but she does at least seem to have a good reputation and a decent background. And most importantly, she's held his interest longer than any other girl. That must be a good sign."

"Yes, Master." Cain sighed. "Is that all?"

"Not quite." Mr. Warwick pressed the tips of his fingers together. "I found a pile of books lying on the floor of my study when I came home this afternoon. You wouldn't happen to know anything about that, would you?"

"Steve wanted help studying, Master," said Cain meekly. This statement was the truth, more or less; Mr. Warwick couldn't prevent him from lying, but he was more than capable of punishing him for it.

"Hmm. Well, just clean up after yourself next time." Mr. Warwick turned gloomily to the window. "Good for Steve. I do wish Lance would study more. He has the potential to be great if he would only apply himself."

Cain almost said "Hah." Luckily, he remembered where he was in time, and just said, "Yes, Master."

Cain lay awake, staring at the darkened ceiling in tense, set-jawed concentration. A few frayed memory fragments had emerged from the empty stretch of impenetrable darkness in his mind, which stood in place of all the recollections of life before his capture. He juggled them as they shifted in and out of his grasp, trying to get a good look at them before they vanished again.

I spoke another language before I knew this one. It's gone now, swallowed up in the past, but bits and pieces come back sometimes. Havah *was food and* raii *was fire;* kema *was yes and* amo *was no. My whole tribe spoke it. We called ourselves* Malakim, *or Fallen Ones. Never demons. I was not a demon until my master captured me and gave me that name. Now it's the only name I know.* Nath samakh, *my tribe would say. That is the way of things...*

The sudden headache came, and the memory was lost again. Cain blinked away the ghostly blue aura that danced against his vision. It was perfectly circular with a five-pointed star in the middle. That same symbol always exploded in his mind's eye after he stopped remembering. He had no idea why he saw it or what it meant, but he hated it almost as much as he hated the collar.

Cain switched the radio on with a sigh. He still hadn't the slightest idea how he was going to find Michelle, let alone convince her to come all the way across the country for the sake of a boy she had known for all of two days and detested.

He wasn't even sure he wanted to convince her; but that made no difference. What he wanted did not matter, and it would never matter as long as Mr. Warwick lived. He was his master's demon. He had to follow orders, whether those orders involved collecting rare herbs, poisoning someone who had never done him any harm, or procuring a girlfriend for loathsome Lance. He scratched at his collar as guitars wailed angrily in his ears.

CHAPTER TWO

CARNICERÍA

THIS ISN'T GOING TO work, thought Cain unhappily as he stared into the hall mirror.

His transformation into human form was less than convincing. Most people who simply glanced at him as they passed in the street would mistake him for a normal—albeit unusually tall and pale—young man. But he wasn't going to the city to pass strangers casually in the street. He was supposed to be charming a young woman into coming all the way across the country with him.

Cain didn't know much about human women, but he was fairly certain they did not automatically find huge, unkempt men with odd, piercing blue eyes and unruly mops of wolf-like black hair trustworthy, especially when those men showed up on their doorsteps in California and tried to persuade them to come all the way to New York for a date with a boy they hated. Even if he got lucky, he was sure the deal would be off as soon as Michelle noticed the series of bulges down the left leg of his pants where his tail was painfully concealed or looked closely enough at his hair to see that its extravagant scruffiness was concealing horns. There was nothing else he could do to hide either of these

29

features; they always stayed unchanged no matter how he transformed himself.

Then, too, there was the collar. It hung around his neck, black and spiky and ugly against Cain's ivory-colored human skin, making him stand out even more. He shifted awkwardly on human feet that felt as big and clumsy as fallen logs while he waited by the front door for last-minute instructions.

A small explosion rocked the kitchen, and little plumes of smoke rolled out the door. Over the tinny buzz of the fire alarm, Cain heard Mr. Warwick's voice saying, "Another good try, Lance, but you keep forgetting to focus properly. It's as important to direct your spells as it is to steer a car; you wouldn't want your car to go off the road and hit a tree, would you? You need to start remembering those steps, especially when you're working with fire. Well, I think that's enough for today."

Lance slunk out of the kitchen, grumbling to himself. His face and hands were dusted with ash. Cain glanced through the door and saw Steve glaring resentfully back and forth from the flames of the five candles he had lit without incident to the melted remains of Lance's candles.

Mr. Warwick swept into the hallway, silencing the fire alarm with a snap of his fingers.

"I think today's lesson went well," he said. "It'll take me all day to remove those scorch marks from the kitchen table, but at least Lance is actually producing results now."

"Yes, Master," said Cain. He couldn't argue that Lance had produced results.

Steve made a please-kill-me-now face at him over Mr. Warwick's shoulder.

"I think I'm ready to go now, Master," he said, trying

not to smile.

"Hmm…Yes, I think you are too." Mr. Warwick walked in slow circles around him, inspecting his disguise. "Pity we can't do anything about the horns. Still, you did a good job of hiding them."

"But I look like a black dandelion, Master." Cain raised an eyebrow in disbelief; he would have bet a chance at freedom that his ridiculous bouffant would have been the first thing Mr. Warwick criticized.

"So you do, but that's not a bad thing at all. Big hair is very fashionable among young people nowadays." Mr. Warwick shook his head in bemusement. "You should see some of the young ladies at the boys' school. You'll fit right in."

"Yes, Master," said Cain doubtfully. "Any last-minute instructions?"

"Yes." Mr. Warwick frowned. "You are *not* to use magic. I mean it. The last thing I need is to have Nathaniel associating Lance with anything uncanny and refusing to let his daughter have anything to do with him."

Cain nodded, wondering how he was going to survive. "What if there's an emergency, Master?"

Mr. Warwick considered his question. "I suppose you can make an exception if extraordinary circumstances arise. Just take care not to do it where the Breens can see you. For day-to-day living, I expect you to act like an ordinary human. For that, you'll need this." He pressed a handful of bills into Cain's hand. "That is all. Any other questions before you go?"

"Do you know where I can find the Breens, Master?"

"I believe Nathaniel just moved into a mansion in Beverly Hills." Mr. Warwick's lip curled with contempt. He despised people who flaunted their wealth. "You'll find her there."

Cain thumbed through the stack of money. It was more than he had ever seen in one place, but it was certainly not enough to buy the house next to the Breens. "But Master, *how* am I supposed to—"

"Figure it out for yourself." Mr. Warwick shooed him out the door. "And remember, no magic unless it's absolutely necessary. It isn't just the Breens I'm worried about. The world outside is dangerous. It's 1982, an age of science. People would probably haul you off to a laboratory to experiment on you if they saw you casting spells. I speak from experience, you know. Even in my lifetime, I've had to deal with more and more such people over the years."

Cain wondered how many times Mr. Warwick had given him this exact speech before he left on one of his errands. He glanced back at Mr. Warwick, and he thought he saw an odd expression of paternal worry in his eyes. After years of having been bullied and bossed and treated like a pack animal by the old man, Cain was surprised by Warwick's expression, more surprised than he had been in a very long time.

"Goodbye, Cain." Mr. Warwick smiled, and now his affection was unmistakable. "I know this assignment may seem a bit overwhelming to you, but you'll find a way. You've been a good servant to me. I'll miss you very much while you're gone. Goodbye and good luck."

He stepped back inside with a final encouraging nod. Cain watched the door shut behind him. He would never, ever understand humans if he lived among them for a thousand years.

The afternoon was sunny and cloudless. Cain paused for a

moment to look back at Mr. Warwick's house with its neat white-columned façade and roomy front porch, distinguished but deceptively simple compared to the newer mansions that surrounded it. It suddenly occurred to him that he would probably miss it in spite of himself; it wasn't exactly home to him, but it was safe and familiar.

The door opened again as he turned to go. Cain sighed and prepared for more confusing bits of parting advice from Mr. Warwick, but it was not Mr. Warwick at the door. It was Steve.

"Oh, it's you." He smiled in relief. "I hoped you'd come and say goodbye before I left."

Steve stepped resolutely through the doorway. "I haven't come to say goodbye. I'm going with you."

"Going with me?" Cain stared at him. "Why on earth would you want to? I'm going to Los Angeles." Cain knew he would never feel at ease in any of the big human cities. He imagined that the relentless crowds and noise and foul air would make him downright sick with anxiety. The very thought of having to live in Los Angeles for any length of time filled him with trepidation. It staggered his imagination that anyone might actually *want* to go there.

"You're going to LA!" Steve gave him an exasperated look, as if this declaration were somehow self-explanatory. "*That's* why I want to go."

"I can't take you, Steve," said Cain apologetically. "I have to do this on my own."

Steve began to climb down the front steps. "I wouldn't get in the way, I promise. Please take me with you, Cain! I've never *been* anywhere. Dad almost always leaves me behind when he goes on his stupid business trips, and all the ones he took me on were to totally boring places. I want to go to Hollywood and see movie stars and lie on the beach, not sit around in some hotel room with Lance while dad goes to meetings. *Please*, Cain."

"You know I have to do what your dad says, Steve, and he didn't say anything about taking you with me."

"He didn't say you *couldn't* bring me, did he?" Steve pouted. "He wouldn't care if I went anyway. He's too busy worshipping Lance to notice anything I do."

"Steve, that's not true," said Cain weakly. "He'd be very upset if I took you all the way across the country without his permission."

"No he wouldn't." Steve kicked at a clump of grass. "He'd probably give you a reward for getting rid of me."

Cain hesitated. He was seriously tempted to take Steve with him. It would be comforting for him to have a familiar face around, and it would be good for Steve to get away from Lance and Mr. Warwick for a while. But he had no idea how he was going to take care of himself in the city, let alone another person as well, and if something should happen to Steve because of his inexperience…that would be worse than any punishment Mr. Warwick could devise for him.

"I can't take you, Steve," he said. "You have school to think about. And your dad really would be *very* worried and angry if he woke up tomorrow and found you gone."

"I'm coming with you," said Steve firmly. "My mind's made up. You can't stop me."

"Maybe I can't, but Lance can." Cain crossed his arms with an air of challenge. "What do you think he'll do if I shout to him that I'm trying to go pick up his girlfriend for him, and you're holding me up?"

He knew that Lance was probably sulking somewhere

because Steve had outperformed him in their sorcery lesson, and aching for an excuse to beat Steve up. It was mean to threaten him, but it worked. Most of the bravado drained from Steve's face, and he backed up a step.

"I'm sorry, Steve," Cain shouted over his shoulder as he waved goodbye. "If I'm still in Los Angeles over Christmas break, and if I have found a decent place to live, I'll get in touch with your dad and try to convince him to let you visit me for a few days."

"I'll come on my own." Steve planted himself firmly on the lawn, as if to show Cain he was very serious. "Whether dad says I can or not. Just you wait and see."

"I'll send you right back home if you do."

"You can try." Steve squared his shoulders defiantly as Cain turned and walked up the street alone. "But I'll just come right back. I *hate* it here."

The patch of woods behind the country club was the most secluded place in the neighborhood. Cain struggled over the high brick wall, cursing Mr. Warwick's lack of foresight in the question of how he was supposed to get to Los Angeles. If he had just been allowed to remain a demon until he arrived in the city, he could have flown there over the course of a few days. The heavy, earthy human body he was forced to clump around in muted his powers. If he wanted to use magic of any kind now, he would have to find a quiet place where he could slog uninterrupted through a complicated and troublesome series of human-made spells. Surely there weren't many places he could do these incantations in a big, crowded city. Maybe this was exactly what Mr. Warwick intended: to force him to show as little evidence as possible of his true nature for the entire mission.

Once behind the wall, he bumbled through the undergrowth until he came to a place where five trees grew together in a tight ring. He barely managed to squeeze inside the small space, but he succeeded. He did not want to be seen doing this spell; the few people who passed him on the street on his way there had already given him plenty of strange looks.

Carefully, with a good deal of shifting to avoid protruding branches, Cain knelt on the ground in the posture of a runner poised to begin a race. He took out the amulet Mr. Warwick had given him—a pendant of polished silver in the shape of an arrowhead that had a single, glinting seawater-colored stone in the middle—and carefully laced the strip of leather on which it was strung through the fingers of his left hand. Once it felt secure, he raised his arm to the west and began to chant.

The incantation was a hybrid, an ear-twisting mix of words from Old English, archaic German, and several Native American languages that required a good deal of focus and discipline to say in the correct order. He also had to concentrate on holding onto a vivid and detailed mental picture of his destination, which was a difficult task because his mind's reference points for Los Angeles were all cribbed from the battered twenty-year-old guidebook Mr. Warwick had shown him the night before. Cain was so intent on doing this spell correctly and on forcing his stunted power to the surface that the sudden wrenching tug of fast, upward movement startled him.

He opened his eyes but had to close them again right away to quell his protesting stomach. The earth spun away beneath him at a sickening rate of speed. Or maybe, the earth was actually above him, or off to one side of him. Cain had difficulty determining directions while he was travelling this fast, and he seemed to be spinning as he went. The silver arrowhead wavered from side to side in front of him as it cut through the screaming air into the unknown territory beyond.

Then, as abruptly as the journey had begun, it ended. Cain slammed into something solid. Green stars exploded all over his field of vision as he cracked his eyes open, and his first attempt to stand sent a wave of nausea through him. He doubled over and retched.

After a few moments, the stars shrank to dissolving sparks, and the nausea subsided. Little by little, Cain was able to stand up and get his bearings.

He was standing in the middle of a broad sidewalk lined with tall palm trees. The sun was high above him, shimmering through a haze of thick gray air. More humans than he had ever seen along a single street crowded around him, jostling and pushing past him. None of them seemed to notice that he had just fallen from the sky into their midst, but a lot of them were giving him nasty looks for blocking their paths. He took the hint and began to maneuver his way through the crowd in search of an open place to rest and think. It took some time before he managed to force his way out of the river of people and into a green park.

There were several slatted wooden benches among the park's neat pink-and-blue flowerbeds. Cain sat down on the only unoccupied one, trying to show no sign of pain as his cramped tail screamed in protest, and tried to devise a plan.

He knew that Michelle lived in Beverly Hills and that he was somewhere in Los Angeles. That was all. Mr. Warwick had not provided him with any real instructions as to how to navigate the city. The old man clearly trusted that he would be able to figure everything out for himself once he got there, as he must have done on so many other missions. However, the task was going to be significantly more difficult with the hindrance and limitations of a human body thrown into the mix. How was he supposed to find anything if he wasn't even allowed to fly? Perhaps he could ask one of the humans in the park for directions, but with the apprehensive looks some of them were giving him, he wasn't entirely sure it would be a good idea to approach them.

Someone tapped him on the shoulder. Cain started, looked up, and found himself staring into the face of a uniformed police officer.

"Move along, now," said the policeman in a gruff voice. "This isn't the place for loitering, kid."

Cain looked down at his clothes, which had gotten torn up during the trip. The policeman must have mistaken him for one of the homeless wandering the streets. He stood up and shuffled meekly back into the noisy jumble of moving bodies on the sidewalk. He had no desire to irritate Mr. Warwick by getting arrested before his first hour in the city was up.

Within minutes he was hopelessly lost. His unfamiliar human's-eye view of the city confused and disoriented him, and the jostling crowds carried him far out of course—if he ever had a course to begin with. The little green street signs that stood on the corners meant nothing to him without a map to put them in context, and they only added to his growing sense of confusion. Also, the layout of the city made no sense to him. Cain was suddenly walking through a maze of warehouses, when a moment before, there had been a row of cozy-looking townhouses on either side of him.

Next, he found himself in an area of low-rent apartment buildings, and then in a cluster of sleek corporate offices. Big billboards peppered the landscape, advertising Pepsi and cherry-red Mustangs and a beautiful amber liquid in a dainty glass bottle labeled "Opium." The advertisements were so colorful and attention-grabbing that Cain stopped several times to look at them, even though his frequent stops slowed his progress through the city.

As the sun dipped low in the sky, he stumbled into a neighborhood with bright murals of various Mexican saints and heroes painted on the walls. He was very hungry, as he hadn't eaten since breakfast. He saw a low stucco shop with a sign that read CARNICERÍA out front. He wasn't sure what the word meant, but he smelled remnants of cooked meat in the air. When he looked in the window, the shop appeared to be closed. Chairs were stacked on tables, and the lights were off. Cain was about to move on when something caught his eye: a movement in the alleyway by the dumpster. The dumpster was enormous and industrial-looking, covered in a scarred coat of army-green paint. Upon closer inspection, Cain could see dozens of gaunt brown rats scurrying around it. Cain eyed them with distaste as he approached. They looked like they would be mostly hair and bone with little edible meat, but a fresh-killed rat or two would at least tide him over until he found a place to stay.

The rats disappeared into the trash bin. With less effort than he thought it would take, Cain pushed the lid open. A few dozen rats wiggled out of the tangle of trash bags. To his astonishment, the dumpster was full of raw meat— mostly scraps and organs—but Cain could comfortably eat it, and it was better than rats. He picked up a heavy thighbone, pried a squealing rat from the exposed joint, and began to strip off the last bits of edible meat. As he finished and picked up another one, the shop's back door opened.

Cain's head snapped around, and he saw a heavyset woman standing in the doorway. Her long black hair was pinned up in a messy bun, and she had a harried expression on her face. A trash bag hung from one of her hands, the thin plastic bulging with the weight of the animal parts inside. She paused at the door when she saw him, and her eyes wandered from the bone in his hand to the blood on his mouth. To his great relief, there seemed to be no fear in her eyes. She gave him a look of mingled pity and disgust and began walking toward the dumpster with a brisk, no-nonsense gait, muttering as she half-heartedly kicked at the rats that swarmed around her ankles.

Without thinking about what he was doing, Cain reached up to brush the hair out of his eyes.

The woman stopped in her tracks, and he knew right away that she had seen his horns. Her eyes bulged in terror; all the color drained from her face; and the bag slid out of her hand. Rats scampered out of her path as she spun on her toes with astonishing speed and fled back into the shop, leaving the bag where it lay, screaming over and over again something that sounded like *el Diablo*.

Cain didn't understand Spanish, but he assumed that whatever she was screaming was not a good sign. He stared after her, cursing his carelessness. He quickly hopped off the dumpster, picked up the forgotten trash bag, and searched for fresher and better meat to eat on the go. He grabbed a handful of fresh scraps and shoved them in his mouth when he heard a noise at the end of the alleyway. He turned. People were gathering at the exit of the alleyway. There were about a dozen of them, and as they packed into the narrow space, they seemed numerous and threatening. The woman from the shop was up front, leading the group, which included a tired-looking man with a mustache who seemed to be her husband, and a man wearing the cassock and collar of a priest. She was talking in a fast, panicked voice to the priest.

Cain felt as if the ground had dropped out from beneath him. He disliked priests almost as much as he disliked cities, though he could never quite explain why. He suspected that some priest-related incident from his early life had been traumatic enough to slip past the spell Mr. Warwick had laid on him to block his access to pre-captivity memories. Or maybe, he simply found their black robes and dour scowls unnerving. Whatever the reason, he gave priests a wide berth whenever he could.

But this priest wasn't scowling. He squatted down beside Cain, frowning, and examined him for several minutes. Cain wondered if he should speak. He was unsure how to act around authority figures other than Mr. Warwick. However, the priest didn't seem to expect him to say anything. So he sat in patient silence while the priest turned his head from side to side, poked at the uneven place where horns grew from skull, and peeled back his lips to look at his teeth as if he were a horse for sale. Then the priest seemed to make up his mind, and stood up.

"Mrs. Delgado," he said in a droning, tiresome voice, "I don't think that what you have here is the Devil or any other evil spirit. I think he's a perfectly human teenage runaway with an unusual deformity."

The woman from the shop relaxed a little, but she did not seem entirely convinced. "But *Padre*, he was eating raw meat," she said in accented English. "You see the blood on his face. How can he do that if—"

"I do see." The priest seemed to be suppressing a sigh of annoyance. "And I think there must be a perfectly logical explanation for that unfortunate situation too. No, no, listen to me. If you didn't know where your next meal was coming from, Mrs. Delgado, wouldn't you eat any food you could find, even if it were something that most people would find completely inedible? I think this young man has a stomach hardened from years of living on the street, eating whatever was available to him. I wouldn't be surprised if he had some mental defects as well. Really, he's more deserving of your pity than your fear. Now, if you'll excuse me, I have a sermon to write."

Mental defects? thought Cain. *Do I really look that terrible?* He was about to correct the priest when another thought occurred to him. If he pretended to be less intelligent, then people might be less afraid of him. He did not want to be run out of town by a mob who thought he was evil and dangerous. So, Cain remained silent.

The priest shouldered his way back through the crowd. One or two people followed his example and left, but most of them stayed where they were, staring with uneasy eyes.

Cain tried to ignore them and eat, but he was getting more and more uncomfortable. Most of the people watching him were wearing highly visible silver crosses or medals of various saints, and several of them did not look completely convinced that Cain wasn't the devil. Their eyes bored into him as his trembling hands tried to pick meat scraps off a rib.

There was a shout from the crowd, and a little girl in a faded blue dress squeezed out between two old men's legs. She was holding something rectangular and yellow to her chest. Cain thought she looked about as old as Steve had been when they first met. One of the old men tried to grab her shoulder, but she squirmed out of his reach.

The girl scurried toward Cain before anyone else could make a grab for her, holding the yellow thing out proudly as if it were an expensive gift, her black eyes fixed on him in eager curiosity. Cain noticed the horrified looks on some of the adult spectators' faces and tried to shuffle well out of the girl's path.

It was no use. The girl walked resolutely up to him and knelt down on the pavement. She set the yellow thing down—he could see now that it was a Styrofoam tray—and began fumbling with the thin plastic that encased it. Several worried voices ordered her to come back, but she ignored them.

A woman in a faded pink blouse pushed through the front row of spectators, the three full grocery sacks in her hands bouncing and bobbing wildly. She broke free of the crowd, took a few steps toward the girl, and then froze. Cain guessed that she was torn between rescuing the girl and staying as far away from him as possible.

The woman dropped her bags, held out her hand, and said something in a frantic whisper. The girl didn't look up; she was busy trying to push away a rat that had leapt onto the Styrofoam tray and seemed quite reluctant to abandon whatever food it held.

Cain very carefully set the rib down on the pavement, watching the girl struggle with the rat as her mother took a small, reluctant step closer. He sensed that he was being tested somehow. It was an unpleasant feeling, considering he had no idea what he could do to make the grim-faced crowd relax and leave him to go on his way.

The mother swallowed nervously, took a deep breath, and shuffled forward another inch. The girl had lost her struggle with the rat. She fell back, whimpering and clutching a nipped finger, as it sauntered off with the long strip of meat it had pulled from the package.

Cain let out a low growl. After ten years' worth of guarding and caring for Steve, he had developed some strong protective impulses toward human children. Without thinking, he pounced, and rat bones cracked between his teeth.

The dead rat flopped into Cain's lap, and he realized what he had done. Mr. Warwick had made it clear on many occasions that his hunting methods were considered barbaric to humans. A chorus of appalled gasps rose from the crowd. The girl's mother clapped her hands over her mouth, and her eyes widened in horror. The girl herself stopped whimpering and blinked at the dead rat for a moment. Then, as if she were giving a treat to the family dog, she picked another strip of meat out of the package and tossed it to him.

Cain hated being treated like a dog, even by a small child, but he caught the meat and ate it to appease the crowd. The girl's mother shot forward in a sudden burst of courage and whisked her daughter away.

The crowd stayed where they were for the rest of the day, talking in low voices and staring at him while the woman from the shop and her husband argued about something with increasing intensity. They lapsed in and out of Spanish at random intervals, making it difficult for Cain to follow the argument.

"But he didn't hurt her, Delfina," said the man. "He could have, but he didn't—didn't even look like he wanted

44

to hurt her. He just seems lost and hungry to me."

The woman cast a terrified look at Cain. "But he's a devil, Arturo. We can't let him stay. I'll call the exterminator in the morning..."

"The *Padre* didn't think he was a devil," said her husband. "We can't call the exterminator. He wants too much money. And if the rats are still there when the health inspector comes back...This devil-boy could be a gift from God, Delfina. All he'll want for it is a meal..."

They switched to Spanish again, and Cain stopped listening. He toyed with the idea of asking them to stop calling him a devil, as it was vaguely insulting, but he decided against it.

He intended to move on as soon as the crowd dissipated, but they stayed well after sundown. The woman from the shop did disappear briefly, but she returned right away with an armful of threadbare brown blankets. She plopped them down by the dumpster and pointed to them, barking an order to Cain in a voice made stiff with fear. Cain was taken aback. He really wanted to leave and find a hotel, but he knew how quickly a crowd could turn into a mob. He crawled obediently over to the blankets and curled up on them. Even with padding, the concrete was uncomfortable, but he was tired enough by now that he had no trouble falling asleep.

As soon as Cain opened his eyes and stretched his aching limbs the next morning, the woman from the shop— Mrs. Delgado, he assumed—was standing over him. She wore an apron with greasy, bulging pockets and held a broom, which she brandished at him like a spear as he sat up.

A clamor of excited voices caught his attention. He

turned and found himself facing a real crowd—fifty people or more—all packed into the little dead-end alley as tight as a cork in a wine bottle, cutting off any chance of escape. Afraid that an attempt to push through them would be interpreted as viciousness, Cain flattened himself against the wall and hoped that they would all leave if he made himself unimposing and uninteresting.

Mrs. Delgado took a small scrap of meat out of her apron pocket. She shook it at Cain, snapping something in Spanish. Then, when he did not respond, she tried again in English.

"You want it?" She held the meat closer. "You want it, yes?"

Cain eyed the meat, wondering if this scenario was another test. It was a scrawny little piece of gizzard, but his dinner had been meager enough that it looked absolutely delicious. He moved toward her to get it, and cleared his throat to thank her, only to receive such a hard poke in the chest from the broom handle that he nearly toppled over backwards.

"No!" Mrs. Delgado shook the broom at him. "Kill rats first."

Cain was shocked. Mr. Warwick had often shoved him around, but he expected that type of treatment from his master, not from a complete stranger. And what did Mrs. Delgado mean? Did she really want him to kill the rats?

Cain blinked stupidly up at her. He couldn't have heard that right; it was his impression that humans—with the notable exception of Lance—generally disapproved of killing small animals for no particular reason. The crowd's reaction to him last night had certainly been far from favorable.

Mrs. Delgado seemed exasperated by his inaction. Her foot tapped the pavement in short, impatient strokes, and some of the carefully controlled fear in her eyes was replaced by amazement. Cain guessed that she was amazed that he was so dense.

"Kill!" She pointed the broom at a nearby rat and mimed a crushing motion with her free hand. "Like yesterday. You can do this, yes?"

Of course Cain could kill the rat, but he wasn't here to serve Mrs. Delgado. He looked at the crowd, at Mrs. Delgado, and then back to the rats. He sighed. He didn't know how he was going to complete his duty to Mr. Warwick if he didn't get out of here soon. His instincts and quick reflexes did their work; the rat died without a sound. He spat out the carcass and, not sure what he was expected to do with it, laid it gingerly at Mrs. Delgado's feet. She looked disgusted, but handed over the meat. Before he could swallow it, she pulled out another scrap.

"Another one," she barked, holding the meat over his head as if he were a dog. "Now!"

Cain didn't really want any more meat. He just wanted to leave. He seriously considered speaking up, but when he opened his mouth to say something, the crowd flinched in unison. He dodged another poke from Mrs. Delgado's broom. Apparently some humans could live with the vicious, indiscriminate murder of small animals after all. Cain continued catching rats. Sooner or later, he knew the crowd would get tired of the spectacle, and he could continue on his way peacefully.

Mrs. Delgado shouted orders at him and jabbed him with her broom, growing bolder as he repeatedly complied without any sign of anger or aggression. The work was surprisingly grueling and tedious.

A little before noon, something interesting happened: most of the surviving rats fled the alley, and Mrs. Delgado sent him to poke under the dumpster in case he had missed one while she sifted through the considerable pile of corpses with the tip of her broom, as if counting them. Peripherally, over the noise of the crowd and the street beyond it, Cain heard a familiar man's voice shouting, "We're going to be late. I *forbid* you to go in there, Michelle! Your head is full enough of silly fantasies as it is. Come back RIGHT NOW!"

He automatically looked up upon hearing the name *Michelle*, but he saw only the same staring crowd. Before he could turn his attention back to the dumpster, a couple of women in the front row were forced apart, and Michelle Breen slipped through the gap between them.

Cain sat up girder-straight, too surprised to be embarrassed at being caught grubbing around in a rat-infested alley by the girl upon whom he was supposed to make a good impression. His eyes wandered over her as she walked toward him. He wasn't surprised Lance had fallen in love with her; she had everything a man would find attractive, from her long, slender legs, to the silky brown hair that hung halfway down her back.

Michelle kept walking, well past the invisible barrier that the rest of the crowd had set between themselves and Cain. Several people were griping because she had pushed her way through, and several more called in tense voices for her to get back to safety. She ignored them and knelt down on the pavement.

"Hi there!" Her deep brown eyes met his, and her pretty lips broke into a friendly smile. "You must be the reason all those people are packed into this alley."

Cain reached up shyly to wipe his sticky face. Pretty human girls rarely, if ever, took any interest in him. He was aware of how savage he must look to her now. He wanted to look away, but somehow, he found that he couldn't. There was something about Michelle that commanded his attention, and he was glad that she was looking at him even if she saw him with blood on his mouth.

"You've made quite a sensation, you know." She had a bright, breathy voice; she sounded like she was sixteen or seventeen at the most. As she spoke she leaned forward subtly, as if to show off her well-developed figure and prove she was older. "I asked some guy out there," she pointed to the crowd, "what was going on in the alley, and he said the devil was killing rats for the butcher. I thought he was messing with me. Say, what's your name?"

Cain couldn't answer. He stared at Michelle, completely captivated. While spying on her from a distance in New York, he had not realized that she was this pretty and soft. He wanted to take her hands in his, to run his fingers through her hair, and to breathe in the smell of her skin. His collar tightened as he thought about Lance's love interest in this inappropriate fashion.

"Don't want to say in front of everyone? Can't blame you for that either." Michelle smiled sadly, misinterpreting his silence. "People must be asking you rude questions all the time. You should tell them to go away. How you look is none of their business." She glanced at the pile of dead rats and flinched. "I guess the rat thing is kind of weird, but hey, you've got to make a living somehow, right?"

Still shell-shocked from meeting Michelle in this unlikely place, Cain managed a very small nod.

Michelle nodded back, satisfied. "I know what it's like

to be different, you know. My daddy moved us here from Tennessee in the middle of my sophomore year, and I was the new kid. It didn't help that I was interested in things the other girls weren't interested in. All year long those kids stared at me—like I wasn't a person worth getting to know, just some kind of animal that was put there for their amusement. Same way everyone here is gaping at you like an idiot, and no one even notices how handsome you are."

Cain gave her a skeptical look. Michelle laughed.

"But you are!" she assured him. "Haven't you ever seen yourself in a mirror? Those eyes are amazing. And your hair is nice and thick and glossy. If you'd just wash it and comb it out, it would really be in style. Plus you look like you'd be pretty tall standing up. Most girls like tall men. I do myself. Seriously, you could be in the movies if it wasn't for those horns. Or maybe…" she paused thoughtfully, "maybe you could anyway. They make a lot of horror movies with demon characters nowadays."

Cain blushed, the warmth spreading over his cheeks and down his neck. He knew he was in trouble. He liked Michelle. How was he going to deliver this beautiful creature to Lance?

There was a great sound of shifting and confusion from the crowd behind them. A huge man burst through the packed bodies like a charging bull.

"Michelle!" he called in a big, booming voice full of authority. "Get away from that thing right now! I have to get to the conference."

Cain looked up and recognized the Reverend Breen from Mr. Warwick's study.

"This *thing* is a human being, Daddy!" Michelle straightened up indignantly. "And I was reaching out to him, like you always say I should reach out to the less fortunate."

The minister shook his head. "I didn't mean you should strike up a conversation with every filthy bum you find on the street. And you certainly shouldn't be saying the things I just heard you say to that dirty kid. Come on now; we have to get to the conference."

Michelle hung back. "*You* have to get to the conference, Daddy. I'm going to sit around the church and be bored. Can't I explore the neighborhood a little? You said you were bringing me here so I could see how people from other cultures lived."

"You had plenty of time to look on the way here." The minister seized his daughter's arm in a steely grip and began to drag her back through the crowd. "I don't want you wandering all over this dirt-poor, crime-riddled place alone and unprotected. The only reason *I'm* here is because the dratted interfaith dialogue conference is being held at their church, and I thought it would be good for you to see the squalid conditions these people live in—make you more empathetic. I would've never brought you if I'd known you'd start making friends with some urchin off the street..." He shot Cain a venomous look, as if Cain had deliberately made Michelle come and talk to him.

Michelle let out a long-suffering groan when her father resolutely turned on his heels, as if to indicate his word was final. As soon as he was out of earshot, she quickly added, "Sorry about him. He always does this, you know. Tells me I spend too much time in my room and pushes me out into the world to explore, and then as soon as I find something worth exploring, he jerks me back and tells me it's dangerous. I swear, I'll have to run away if I ever want to have anything that even *looks* like a life..."

Her voice faded as she followed her father. Cain got a glimpse of the spike-heeled black boots she was wearing under her modest pink dress, and she was lost in the crowd.

The crowd murmured with indignation that the minister had described their neighborhood as dirt-poor and crime-ridden. Cain understood how they felt; the minister clearly thought he was not worth Michelle's time and attention. However, he should have been happy; Michelle's appearance in this unlikely place suggested that she would not always be hidden, as he had expected, behind an impenetrable fortress of gilded gates and security guards. She had shown no sign of discomfort in his presence even though she had definitely caught him at the worst possible time. She also seemed discontented enough at home that it should be the easiest thing in the world to convince her to come away with him, if only on the promise of taking her someplace where her father couldn't boss her around. He might be out of the city before the end of the week. He would have been happy and relieved beyond measure had it not been for one little thing.

Suddenly, Cain couldn't stand the idea that Michelle was to be Lance's girlfriend. To his dismay, a small seedling of longing had sprouted in him; he liked Michelle too much to surrender her to Lance. He hoped the feeling would go away when the shock of meeting her so suddenly subsided, but it stayed and grew stronger as the day went on and more people came to stare and feed him raw meat. By the time the last stragglers wandered home to bed, he couldn't even think about Lance being with Michelle without longing to re-sprout his claws.

Chapter Three

Only in Los Angeles

BY THE TIME THE crowd dispersed, and Cain was free to leave the little alleyway, he no longer had the desire to continue on his mission. In fact, he had no desire to do anything. A cloak of moroseness settled over him, a pall he could not seem to shake.

Cain's feelings did not change as the days passed. He worried that his long absence would make Mr. Warwick suspicious, but he could not will himself to leave the alley and pursue Michelle on Lance's behalf. Days became weeks, and the collar seemed to tighten and pinch his neck to remind him of his long-neglected duties. He stubbornly stayed where he was, making no move whatsoever to find Michelle.

Meanwhile, the people of the neighborhood gradually caught on to the practical possibilities of a strange horned boy who could dispose of rats and mice as efficiently as any cat. Various neighbors crept into the alley and attempted to lure him off to their pest-infested yards and shops with scraps of meat. Like Mrs. Delgado they did so fearfully at first, but they gained confidence when it became clear that Cain was not interested in hurting anyone. Under normal circumstances, Cain would have been offended by their treatment. However, he decided to put up with it, to continue to play the role of a mute, deformed boy because anonymity was a relief. These people were not aware of his magical powers, so they could not exploit them. He was not expected to carry out sinister errands—except killing a few rats here or there. And Cain did enjoy having so many opportunities to hunt—a luxury rarely afforded to him in Mr. Warwick's household. The meat the people gave him as a reward became more delectable with every rat-battle he won. Plus, Mr. Warwick would never think to look for him in such a place—so for the moment, Michelle was safe.

Still, Cain was irked when shawl-swathed grandmothers tossed chicken breasts at him without a word after counting out the mouse corpses he had laid at their feet, and he was outright discomfited when he heard Mr. and Mrs. Delgado talking about him in Spanish right over his head as he tried to eat. Even the pudgy toddlers who sneaked into the alley to climb all over him and pull at his hair and horns while their mothers chatted with Mrs. Delgado in the shop seemed to see him as a very large and dirty toy.

They took to calling him *el animal*, in the same spirit of affectionate disgust they displayed when they watched him eat his unconventional meals. Several times Cain considered talking to them, if only to tell them that he *did* have a name; but they seemed so comfortable with his silence that he could not bring himself to do it. He had never dreamed that so many humans would ever be fond of him.

Rumors about the wild-eyed devil-boy who lived in an alley behind a butcher shop and ate raw meat spread to other parts of the city. People found excuses to wander into the quiet little Hispanic neighborhood in groups of three or four. Some of them were quite bold—to the point of marching into the alley and standing over Cain as he ate. He was not terribly surprised when a sharp jab in the shoulder roused him from a light sleep one evening. He looked up from his pile of blankets and found himself facing a man he had never seen before.

The man was sallow and scrawny. His lank black hair was slicked back with more grease than it needed. He wore polished leather shoes and an orange and green suit and tie made of much nicer material than the clothes most people in the neighborhood owned. But the color combination—which Cain thought Mr. Warwick might have described as "eye-sodomizing"—and the odd way the suit fell on his crooked frame ruined the effect. He watched Cain for a moment, bouncing warily on the balls of his feet, his sunken-but-bright black eyes gleaming. Then he shuffled closer and leaned in as if he wanted to say something.

The door banged open. The man flinched and stumbled back with a guilty air.

"What are you doing here, Jodido?" Mrs. Delgado advanced into the alley, brandishing her broom. "I told you never to come around here again."

The sheepish look on Jodido's face mingled with a flash of resentment.

"My name is Nicanor, you know," he muttered. "So I'm not allowed to be curious now? I'd heard you and Arturo got yourself some kind of rat-catching devil-thing, and I just wanted to get a look at him…"

His reply seemed to infuriate Mrs. Delgado. She leapt in front of Cain, holding her broom like a sword.

"You were pushing!" Her voice was shrill with anger.

"Just like you try with all the kids who don't know better. But I won't let you—not on my property. If I ever see you here again, *Jodido*, I'll break your face."

"Er...pushing?" Jodido shifted in discomfort, avoiding her eye. "No, not me. That'd be a waste of time. I mean, does that dirty *coño* look like he has any mon—"

"Go away!" roared Mrs. Delgado.

"Okay. Okay. Fine." He fled at an awkward hop-skipping gait, muttering as he ran. "Bitch. I saw an opportunity to expand my business, and I ran with it. So what? Don't know what your problem is..."

Mrs. Delgado stared after him for a minute. When she turned around, she was still quaking with rage.

"Can you believe him?" she said, shaking her head incredulously. "I tell him not to come here, and he comes anyway—in broad daylight!"

Cain said nothing, but he did allow himself an incredulous glance at the sky. He wouldn't exactly have called the early evening dusk "broad daylight."

Mrs. Delgado was fuming too hard to notice. "The police should have cleared him off the street ten years ago if you ask me. Him and his drugs...Oh, *animal*, I'd rather have a hundred of you than one of him. You may be a devil, but at least you don't hurt people."

Then she did something very strange. As Cain stared at her, trying to puzzle out how on earth Jodido thought someone who looked like a penniless street urchin could possibly "expand his business," she put out an arm gingerly and ruffled his hair.

"You can stay here as long as you like, *animal*," she said. "I won't let anyone bother you."

Mrs. Delgado was as good as her word. From that day

56

on, she chased away the most blatant rubberneckers. Cain was amazed that such a squat little woman could be so formidable when she chose, and he was fervently glad that she was on his side for the time being.

So he didn't pay much attention one afternoon when a woman watched him from across the street, leaning on a shopping cart. He simply glanced at her briefly and looked away, waiting for Mrs. Delgado to shoo her off.

The woman swung her cart around and began to cross the street. Cain heard the wheels creaking over the pocked, uneven pavement. He quickly fixed his gaze on the drab gray wall in front of him, trying to make himself uninteresting.

The woman advanced with calm, resolute steps. She paused in front of the alley, giving the handle of her cart a practiced downward push to get the front wheels up on the curb, and rolled up to the dumpster. She stopped directly in front of Cain and leaned against the cart, looking down at him with an expression of friendly interest.

"Hi there, little devil." She chuckled kindly. "Enjoying the City of Angels so far? Too bad they couldn't offer you better accommodations, but at least they've been feeding you well."

Cain stared up at her, taken off guard. No one in the city had really talked to him since Michelle. Still, he caught himself and played the same game he had with the Delgados and their neighbors; he tried to be utterly quiet and submissive, showing no sign of human-level intelligence.

"No need to pretend to be voiceless for me." The woman flashed a conspiratorial smile. "I know that you can talk. I have it on very good authority in fact."

As hard as Cain tried to stare dumbly up at her and

pretend he didn't understand, he found himself nodding almost against his will. There was something compelling in her wrinkled brown face and deep, soft black eyes.

"That's better," she said approvingly. "But I'd like to hear your voice. I know that you can talk, and I know you have things to say. You'll say them sooner or later. You must—even if old man Warwick tries to keep you mute."

Cain stiffened. He had been ready to dismiss her speech as the ramblings of a disordered mind, but her mention of Mr. Warwick gave him significant pause. He thought he felt the collar shifting against his skin too, reminding him of its presence. Could this scenario be something set up by his master, as a trap or as a test?

"I don't know what you're talking about," he whispered in a voice grown low and hoarse from disuse. "Mr. Warwick is good to me…"

The woman sighed. "In his own way, I suppose he is. But you're not some domestic animal to be satisfied with the cold comforts of food and shelter after a day's mindless labor. The blood of angels is in your veins—and the blood of humans too. From the first, you get the urge to sing fierce songs, in praise or in defiance. From the second, you get your desire for the freedom and dignity you deserve. You never really gave up that desire, did you, after the old man slipped that collar around your neck? If you had, you wouldn't still be resisting."

Cain sat hunched and wary, taking in every aspect of the woman's appearance. She was ancient, appeared to be from an indeterminate race, and was dressed in clumpy men's work boots, a multicolored, stitched-together skirt, several sweaters and jackets, and a grimy blue bandanna that covered her matted hair. Her rusty cart was filled to the brim with boxes, blankets, various discarded gadgets, and, unexpectedly, a large dog with silky white fur. Its liquid-sapphire eyes peered curiously at him over a mountain of rumpled pink fabric. He decided that this woman was not a trap. Mr. Warwick would never take on a form like hers. He was too proud.

"I don't *always* resist, you know." It never hurt to be cautious. "I have no idea why I'm resisting this ti—" The collar cut him off with a choking jolt of pain as he admitted his willful dissent. "I mean I'm not even sure it really is resisting. I'm just taking a really long time to complete my mission."

"Don't apologize for yourself." A touch of annoyance crept into the woman's voice. "You have been rebelling and defying your master, whether you realize it or not, every day for the past ten years. Your master hasn't silenced your voice; he has only muffled it, and it's time for you to take it back now."

A shiver of hope ran through Cain before he could repress it. The collar tightened sharply to remind him of his place. He clutched at his neck and stared meaningfully up at his visitor.

She seemed to understand. "Oh, I know you can't be direct about it. You'll have to find hidden ways—as you learned to do so quickly—and I can point you in the direction of the most hidden way. A few blocks east of this neighborhood there's a shop. In the window of the shop there's something you've wanted for a long time. You should have enough money to buy it."

"What is it?"

"I suspect you'll know it when you see it. Understand that it is *very* important it finds its way into your hands,

Cain. It'll help you regain your voice and possibly your freedom as well."

"Who are you?" he demanded. He had been disconcerted when this woman knew of his true nature and of his servitude to Mr. Warwick, but the fact that she knew his name was too much. "Why are you so interested in me? What does it matter to you if I'm free or not?"

The old woman turned to leave. She paused, giving him a deep, unreadable look over her shoulder.

"I'm interested," she said quietly, "for a couple reasons. First of all, a very good friend of mine asked me to watch over you while you were in the city."

"Who?"

"No one you know, honey. Then there's the fact that I object to what Warwick did to you on moral grounds. I can't stand the thought that he'd keep a slave at all, let alone shut an angel in a cage…"

"I'm no angel." Cain kicked at a pile of dry chicken bones near his foot.

"Maybe not." Her voice hardened. "Your father was one, though, and that fact alone should be enough to make the old goat afraid to look you in the face. As for who I am, I'm not really anybody. I don't use my name in public. I just go by the nicknames folks give me."

"What do they call you, then?"

"People here've been calling me Lotus Blossom. They think I'm Asian."

Cain looked curiously up at her. Her skin was a bit darker than that of Mr. Warwick's few Asian clients. "Are you?"

She seemed amused by the thought. "I'm not, but I don't tell them different. What does it matter? Come to think of it,

they've started shortening the name and calling me Crazy
Loti, and I'm not crazy either. Trust me; it doesn't make any
difference what other people call you."

The cart's wheels creaked, and she was lost around the
corner.

A moment later, Mr. Delgado bustled out the back door
with half of a rack of ribs and a few undersized steaks
balanced precariously in his arms. Cain ate in silence and
drifted off to sleep beside the dumpster, unable to banish the
promise of freedom from his mind.

Cain might have been able to dismiss the events of that
afternoon as a dream brought on by the strain of his long
resistance to Mr. Warwick's orders. It had certainly seemed
very dreamlike when he had awakened at dawn. He spent
the morning patiently letting two little girls crawl all over
him while their mother chatted with Mrs. Delgado outside
the butcher shop. The priest walked by the alley and glanced
at them. Cain was startled to see jealousy and annoyance in
his expression. What could possibly make a priest jealous of
him?

He continued to lie on his bed of old blankets in the
evenings, thinking about Michelle as he fell asleep. The days
began to blend together again in the comfort of this routine.

Everything seemed normal again, except for the fact that
Cain was seeing Crazy Loti everywhere.

Every time he looked up, she seemed to appear,
wheeling her cart balefully past. More than once he noticed
her standing among a group of tourists who had come to
peer surreptitiously at him. She did not approach him or
speak to him, but she did look more and more impatient as
the days went by. Cain tried not to notice her presence, but

he was beginning to feel uncomfortable, and without quite knowing why, he also felt a little guilty.

One afternoon as he picked the last bits of meat from a shoulder blade, wheels clattered over the cracked pavement of the alley. Crazy Loti stood over him, leaning against the handle of the cart in the posture of a teacher who had walked in on a misbehaving class. The white dog popped up and gave him a disapproving look. He prepared himself for a scolding.

But the scolding never came. Crazy Loti smiled in a sly, conspiratorial way as she leaned toward him.

"Michelle," she said in a voice heavy with meaning.

The bone slid out of Cain's hand, forgotten.

"Michelle?" He tried and failed to sound calm and uninterested.

"The loudmouth preacher's pretty daughter." Loti smiled. "You liked her, didn't you?"

"I guess so."

"I think it's more than a guess." Her eyes glinted. "I think you like her very much. And I think you want her to like you too."

"I have orders: bring her back for Lance." Cain couldn't keep the resentment out of his voice this time. "What I want doesn't matter."

"Maybe." She sounded vaguely disappointed, as if she expected more from him. "But it's not your fault if she chooses you over Lance, is it? The old man doesn't have a slave collar on *her*. You just need to get her attention. The thing you need will get her attention all right. A few blocks east, remember. And I want you to go tomorrow. No more dawdling."

She dragged the cart around almost without effort and

began walking resolutely away. Cain heard her whispering to the dog, "See, sweetheart, I told you he'd do it when offered the right treat. No need to fuss anymore…"

"Can you at least tell me what the thing is?" he called to her. "Or what kind of shop it's in?"

"Like I said, you'll know it when you see it," Crazy Loti called over her shoulder.

This is a bad sign, thought Cain as he scanned the storefronts of the dozen or so dingy little shops along the narrow street. The mere idea of getting attention from Michelle had been enough to send him off on a fool's errand for a human stranger.

He also hoped that he might find something to shake off the hated collar, and a general sense of restlessness and curiosity had been growing in him since his first day in the city. Yet his feelings for Michelle had tipped him over the edge; Michelle was the reason for his first open defiance of Mr. Warwick in ten years, and he was almost certainly going to get in trouble.

At least he wouldn't get in trouble today. Cain had been up and down both sides of the dingy little side-street twice, and he had seen absolutely nothing that he had wanted for a long time, and very few wares looked like they had a chance of impressing Michelle. He was about to turn around and make his way back when one storefront caught his eye.

He had missed it the first time because it was so small and so far off the road—built into what had once been the garage of the old house that now housed a beauty parlor. It was so covered with garish, cheaply printed flyers that the glowing neon sign that read "SECOND-HAND INSTRUMENTS" only showed faintly through the layers of flimsy paper. The rummage store was the least likely of all the trashy boutiques on that road to have caught Cain's attention, and he would have passed it by without another thought if he hadn't seen the guitar.

It nearly filled the whole front window of the store, gleaming and new, crowding out the tarnished flute and dented bongos that hung on either side of it. Compelled, Cain moved closer. It was easily the most beautiful instrument he had ever seen—sleek, swallow-tailed, and black enough to backlight his staring, wild-haired reflection in perfect detail against the glass.

He laid a hand against the window for a moment, sighing longingly. A guitar was definitely something he had wanted for a long time, but he doubted very much that Mr. Warwick would let him have one. The old man seemed to find the sound of the radio annoying enough as it was.

But there wasn't any harm in looking, was there?

Cain opened the door and stepped through. If there wasn't any harm in looking, there wasn't any harm in getting a closer look.

The interior of the shop was dusty and cluttered. Battered saxophones, violins, and drums bristled from every inch of the walls, and the glass cases under the counter were crammed full of more rust-eaten instruments. The one clerk on duty shot him a weary glance and immediately turned his attention back to the trumpet he was repairing. Cain guessed that it was common for street people to wander into shops in this part of town.

Cain stood unmoving by the window, staring at the magnificent guitar, wondering how it would feel in his hands, how it would sound. He had not realized how much he missed the tinny wail of music over the radio in his room, but now the longing to hear good music welled up all at once.

Five minutes passed, and the clerk began to cough impatiently. Cain sensed that he had overstayed his welcome and reluctantly prepared to go. It was too bad, really, that Mr. Warwick wouldn't let him have a guitar...

But then, Mr. Warwick had never *said* he couldn't have one.

In fact, Mr. Warwick had said he was to live as a human while he was in the city—and there was nothing to stop a young human man with enough money from purchasing a guitar of his own.

"I'd like to buy this," he blurted.

"It's a grand," said the clerk dubiously.

Cain laid the money on the counter. The sly, greedy expression on the clerk's face told Cain that he probably should have haggled, but he didn't care. He hastily ducked out of the shop. He had just turned onto the street to make his way back when he started remembering again.

I was in the ancient, unchanging depths of the Inner World. I squatted on the rough black rock below one of the torches my tribe used to bring something like daylight into the unbroken darkness of the deep places. Someone knelt beside me, drawing symbols on the rocks with luminous pale green chalk. I saw them take shape, slowly ...A...S...R...C...P...N...Z...

Cain frowned.

That can't be right. Why would someone draw humans' letters in the Inner World? We had our own language, we Malakim, and we wrote it in pictures, not symbols for sound...

The memory was slipping away now. Cain concentrated

harder, straining to make out more details. Had one of his recollections of watching Steve make chalk drawings on the driveway been trapped accidentally behind Mr. Warwick's barrier?

No. Chalk from the Outside doesn't glow like that. Besides, the other person started talking to me, and the voice was not Steve's. She had a girl's voice...

Suddenly, the headache hit, and the star-and-circle of light wiped the image away. He was standing on the street, frustrated and confused and unable to recall why he felt that way. The weight of the guitar's battered case tugged at his arm.

The sun dipped toward the west, and a cool breeze sprung up from the direction of the sea as Cain began to trudge back. He put a hand up to protect the structure of his carefully disheveled, horn-concealing hair. The collar was uncomfortably tight, but fortunately not much more so than it had been when he was doing nothing more defiant than sitting in the alley wasting time.

The sun had dipped out of sight behind the houses and buildings by the time he found the alley again. Mrs. Delgado was the only one who saw him return.

Mrs. Delgado watched from behind the dumpster as her *animal* crept home. He plopped down on his tattered wad of blankets and opened the mysterious black case he had brought with him. Her old lingering suspicions began to reawaken when he brought out a guitar that looked like it cost more than what the shop made in a month; but when the mute devil-boy laid the instrument across his knees and ran his hands over the strings with an expression of intense concentration on his face, she found the sight so charming that she ducked silently off to fetch her husband.

Cain plucked at the strings, unaware of the fading light or the knot of people chuckling from the entrance to the alley. He knew that something was wrong: hard as he tugged, the guitar produced only flat, muted notes. He knew he was not playing incorrectly. Lance's toy acoustic guitar had provided him with enough practice, when he had been able to sneak into Lance's room to play it, and before Lance had broken it in a fit of childish rage over being expected to do homework. Something important was missing.

Electricity, he thought suddenly as he began to perceive the Delgados and their friends chuckling fondly at adorable *el animal*, trying to play an electric guitar without that essential ingredient. He was missing electricity. In his excitement and his haste to buy the guitar and get back to the alley, he had completely forgotten that he would need a power cord.

He drummed his fingers against the dead strings. A close inspection of the guitar yielded the receptacle for the plug. Not that it would have mattered if there had been a cord to put into it; the alley had no outlets.

Then again, maybe electricity wasn't necessary if another energy source were available. Slowly, carefully, he drew a magical force from inside himself, channeling it into the guitar. The collar constricted violently, but Cain ignored it. He had come too far to give up now.

The spectators began to straggle back home. The Delgados were bidding good night to their friends and neighbors when a single note rose from the alley, high, clear, and startlingly pure. They scurried back and stared in astonishment at Cain, their own sweet, silent *animal*, sitting proudly with his fingers resting on the trembling strings.

A great deal was made of Cain's newly discovered talent that night. Quite a few of the neighbors gave in to their nagging belief that the devil was among them and began to mutter fearfully about demonic miracles. The priest was fetched and made to listen to ten minutes' worth of Cain's enthusiastic—if discordant—playing. He listened irritably, for he couldn't help but be jealous of the fascination the devil-boy held for the people of his parish. Plus, he had been awakened from a sound sleep. He told the expectant crowd that he had no earthly idea how an electric guitar could be played without any apparent source of electricity, but he was sure it wasn't a miracle, demonic or otherwise. Half the crowd backed nervously away from Cain once the priest left, unable to discard their suspicions; the other half, mostly the Delgados and their closest friends, nervously praised his cleverness and told each other what a good thing it was that their poor *animal* possessed such a wondrous talent to make up for his many outrageous defects.

Though none of them knew it yet, a murder had taken place in the city.

Dr. Deborah Brown was patiently listening to the square-jawed police detective, Ted Sullivan, ramble on about his kids as he opened the door to the viewing area. She was surprised at the appearance of the boy in the interrogation room. He tugged nervously at the sleeves of the worn gray jumpsuit he was wearing. He had a thin, nondescript face and oily yellow hair. His mud-colored eyes were fixed on some distant point beyond the cinderblock walls, and the odd intensity in them created the illusion that he was aware of the two people watching him behind the one-way glass window.

"His name is Michael Anderson," said Ted, finally getting to the task at hand. "Long story short, we responded this afternoon to reports of a stabbing in Glendale, and we found a woman named Arlene Anderson bleeding from at least twelve wounds to the arms and torso. She named her son as her attacker before the ambulance took her away—said they'd been fighting. He'd fled the scene by the time we got there, but a patrol car found him under an overpass an hour ago. He was still wearing the same bloody clothes. Still carrying the knife too. Luckily, Arlene is in stable condition. She's in surgery now."

Dr. Deborah Brown gave him a questioning look.

"Honestly, it sounds like a straightforward case of domestic violence and assault with a deadly weapon," she said.

The detective stared through the window. A strange expression passed over his face.

"That's not all. When he was picked up, he was standing over a dead body—that of a white male about eighteen years old. We haven't identified him yet, so we don't know if Michael knew him."

"You think Michael killed him?" Dr. Brown turned her gaze back on the boy in the interrogation room. She couldn't help but be perversely amazed as she studied his scrawny arms and sickly pale skin; he looked far too tiny and frail and meek to commit such violent crimes.

"It's possible. The coroner is working on the body right now. The strange thing is…the boy didn't have any stab wounds-just a few shallow cuts." He shook his head. "We really need your help interrogating this kid, Deb. He swears up and down that he doesn't remember what happened."

"Does he now?" Dr. Brown tried not to sigh. She had been hoping for something more interesting than an amnesia defense.

The detective seemed to know what she was thinking. "Look, I know that lots of suspects 'don't remember' what happened. But something about this case feels different. This Michael Anderson isn't all there, and he's not faking it. I don't know what it is, but…there's something *off* about the kid. Those weird eyes of his…Deb, I think he might be an MPD case."

"Weird eyes aren't a telltale symptom of Multiple Personality Disorder, Ted." She resisted the urge to roll her eyes in annoyance. This was the third time in the last month that she had been called in to evaluate a supposed Multiple Personality Disorder case. Come to think of it, more of her civilian clients were complaining of MPD as well—ever since Dr. Cora Hammond had cadged that interview with Lana Willis on *About Town*. Now multiple personalities were as much a fad in this town as any new dance move or fashion accessory, and sensible mental health professionals such as herself risked career suicide if they dared to suggest that MPD might be just a tad overly diagnosed. "I'll see what I can do, though."

The detective gave her a grateful nod and stepped aside to open the door for her. Michael Anderson looked up as she came in. Dr. Brown noticed that he flinched and balled up his left hand when she came close, but his gaze remained steady.

"Hello, Michael," she said softly. "My name is Deborah, and I'm here to help you."

Michael made a tiny noise in the back of his throat and

pulled his fist closer to his body.

She tried again. "Detective Sullivan called me in. He says something bad happened, and you don't remember it. I can help you remember, if you let me."

Michael said nothing, but he kept staring at her. Dr. Brown hid a shiver of uneasiness; she was beginning to understand why Ted had thought something was "off" about the boy. While he was drawing in his arms and slumping his shoulders, making himself as small as possible, the fear and discomfort that were etched on every line of his face and body contrasted sharply with the quiet intensity of his gaze. It was as if his eyes belonged to someone else, and she found it disconcerting.

"It's all right if you'd rather not remember what happened," she went on, concealing her growing unease. "But I think it would be best if you at least tried. You could get in trouble if you don't remember..."

Michael took a deep breath and partially unclenched his fist. Dr. Brown leaned forward eagerly.

"I was under a bridge." His voice was as whispery and dry as a discarded corn husk, yet it had a hint of depth to it that commanded attention. "There was something in my hand—something cold. My clothes were wet. There was a man lying in front of me." He opened his hand and stared at his palm. "He was dead."

"Good, good." Dr. Brown glanced at the open hand. There was some sort of thick scarring over the palm—a sign of childhood abuse, maybe? "What happened before that? Do you remember how you got under that bridge?"

Michael shook his head, still staring into his palm. He shifted in his seat and appeared to be on the verge of saying something—then his back stiffened, and his jaw clenched.

"Michael? Are you all right?"

His head snapped up. There was a wild light of panic in his eyes.

"She's dead!"

"Who's dead? Tell me who's dead, Michael."

Michael had begun to sweat and tremble. He stood up abruptly, knocking over his chair. Dr. Brown flinched at the loud clatter it made against the concrete floor.

"It was my fault." He spoke in a clipped, fevered voice, staring at a point somewhere on the ceiling. "It was my fault it was my...my...My mom woke me, shook me out of it. 'Stop this! It's a sin, Michael, a sin...'"

His eyes rolled back in his head, and he slumped against the wall, flailing. The door burst open and Detective Sullivan ran in.

"Ted, wait!" Dr. Brown saw the handcuffs and pepper spray canister in his hand and leapt up in alarm. "He's having a seizure!"

As if on cue, Michael went limp and slid to the floor. He lay still for a second, crumpled like an old dust cloth. Then, as the detective reluctantly stopped in his tracks, and Dr. Brown stood up to examine the inert boy, a violent convulsion ran through his body, and his head snapped up.

The next few seconds seemed to happen in slow motion. Dimly, she saw Michael lunge for and hurl the upturned chair. It glided in a lazy arc before plowing into the detective's chest. His gasp of pain sounded far away. Michael dodged past him and half-leapt, half flew over the low table, his hands outstretched like talons. He moved so quickly that her attempt to get out of his way felt like a swim through syrup. She managed one step to the side before he barreled into her.

The shock of it pulled her back into reality. Michael's skinny hands pinned her wrists to the wall with astonishing strength. She tried to twist free of him, but to no avail. Even when she panicked and kicked him in the shin, his grip didn't weaken for a second.

A lusty grin passed over Michael's face. He stared at Dr. Brown with eyes so dilated that the brown in them had disappeared under the shining black of the pupil. A thin, shrieking laugh burst from his lips.

"Why so fearful?" His voice had become deeper and louder. It took on a feverish tone as he spoke. "Why so sad and scared? This is a day for rejoicing! You should be singing and laughing!"

The door banged open, and three more policemen scrambled into the room. They were on top of Michael in seconds, prying his hands loose and dragging him away from his captive. Dr. Brown shuddered with relief as her wrists came free.

"The Beast has come!" Michael arched his back like a cat as two officers struggled to put him in cuffs, and his face twisted into a rictus of deranged joy. "The Dark Lion is among us. He shall stand against the Righteous Man, and he shall triumph…"

"Are you all right, Deb?" Detective Sullivan lumbered up to her.

"I…I think so."

"Good. I'm so sorry." He patted his ribs gingerly. "I knew that kid was off. I didn't think he was *that* off, though. I never would have left you alone with him if I thought he'd attack you like that."

The other policemen had managed to get Michael into handcuffs, but they didn't seem much better off for having done so; he lunged forward like a dog drawing a heavy sled up a hill, digging his feet into the floor against their attempts to drag him off. Even with the three of them pulling together, they seemed unable to budge him further than a few inches. Dr. Brown stared at them, rubbing her bruised wrists. To her astonishment, she found herself wondering if Ted had been right. Of all the seizures and psychotic breaks and unexplained changes in demeanor she had witnessed in her patients, Michael's was the first one that truly looked anything like the emergence of a destructive alternate personality.

"It's all right," she murmured. "It's a hazard of my job, really. Listen, Ted, if it's all right, I'd like to do some more work with this Michael Anderson."

"I was hoping you'd offer, actually. We need to know if he's competent to stand trial."

"Trial?" Michael cackled. "No, there'll be no trial for me. I've got blood on my hands. I'll walk free. It's the innocent who are tried and judged."

Detective Sullivan glanced at Michael with a shudder, and lowered his voice. "This case just got a lot more complicated, Deb. Arlene Anderson is dead."

Dr. Brown stared at him.

"When, Ted? I thought you said she was in surgery…"

"She died on the table. We got the call from the hospital a minute or two ago, right before the kid seized up in fact."

"*Right* before he seized up?" The image of Michael staring into his palm flashed into her mind. She began to form another question, but a loud metallic snapping sound interrupted her train of thought.

Michael had broken the handcuffs' chain in half. He writhed like an angry snake in the arms of the increasingly desperate policemen, flailing and punching, the useless cuffs jangling on his wrists. One of the officers was nursing a black eye; another clutched a bruised shin. Then, just as the least-injured officer managed to force Michael's hands into a fresh pair of cuffs, Michael went rigid and stared at the ceiling.

"These are the days of the Dark Lion." He murmured the words in a distant and dreamy voice, as if he were on the verge of falling asleep. "He will set us free."

This declaration seemed to mark the end of Michael's fit. He went limp, and the maniacal expression faded from his face. His eyes darted unhappily around the room, and he seemed distressed to find himself in handcuffs, but he let the police escort him out the door quietly.

Dr. Brown watched him slink off, massaging her aching wrists. She always tried hard not to form quick judgments of any patient after one meeting, but she couldn't shake the feeling that Michael had the potential to be one of her oddest cases.

Chapter Four

Dying to Make It

CAIN NOTICED THAT THE people of the Hispanic neighborhood were fascinated by his playing. Crowds formed at the entrance to the alley when he practiced, murmuring excitedly about miracles or darkly about witchcraft. Children who were old enough to know that he was doing something impossible crept up close to him and scanned the guitar for hidden power cables, dodging their mothers' attempts to pull them back.

During one of these gatherings, Cain noticed the neighborhood priest at the back of the crowd. Cain swore that the priest's face darkened with jealousy. That Sunday, Cain heard rumors that the priest had preached a sermon about the danger of valuing devotion to earthly heroes over devotion to God. He wondered if the priest was targeting him.

After a few days, the crowds stopped coming. The novelty of seeing the electric guitar played without electricity wore off, and Cain found himself reduced to the status of an ordinary teenage boy teaching himself to play a loud instrument. Annoyed housewives took to running out of their houses and snapping admonitions at him in Spanish

76

whenever he tried to tune up, and many brooms and aprons were shaken in his face if he dared to ignore them and play on. Even the Delgados started to show signs of impatience.

Cain took the hint and settled on another place to practice, an old industrial district half a mile north of the neighborhood. Few police patrolled the maze of abandoned factories and warehouses, and the many homeless who clustered around trash barrel fires in rusting buildings never complained about his playing or even seemed to notice him much.

One night it began to drizzle while he played. Cain considered forcing his way into one of the derelict buildings, but decided against it. Whenever he tried to practice inside one of the warehouses, the distorted echoes which bounced incessantly around their cavernous insides interrupted the flow of his music. Instead he took refuge on a side street between two warehouses, under a fire escape through which no rain could penetrate due to the thick layer of sodden paper, dirt, rotten plant matter, and rat carcasses that daubed every inch of the mesh. He strummed through a series of notes half-remembered from various songs on the radio as he huddled there, so intent on stringing them into a coherent tune that he barely registered the squealing of car tires a few yards away. He also missed the sound of heavy feet clumping against the pavement until someone stepped into the beam of the single streetlight.

Cain looked up. Three young men in khaki pants and pastel-colored polo shirts glowered down at him, swaying unsteadily, their hands balled into tense fists.

"Here's one, Rick," said the pudgy redhead to Cain's left. "I told ya it'd be easy to find one here."

"Good." The muscular blond boy stepped forward,

rubbing his hands together in anticipation. "Let's blow off a little steam, shall we?"

The tall, bony one held back. "What're we gonna do, Rick?" he asked. "We're not gonna…"

"For God's sake, Travis," said Rick in a sort of drunken stage whisper that Cain was clearly not meant to overhear. "For the last time, we're not gonna kill anybody. We're just gonna slap him around a little bit, teach him a lesson for gunking up our streets. Then we'll let him go."

Cain's heart drummed in a frantic rhythm as he took stock of the situation. Three big, strong young men, all obviously drunk and out for his blood for no apparent reason. If he were in his true form, he would have a decent chance of fighting them off, but he was trapped in a human body and bound by its limitations. Together, the three men were more than a match for his advantages of height and weight.

"Hey, street kid." The one called Rick was advancing with measured steps, a bloodthirsty glint in his eye. "Gonna ask me for spare change?"

"Come on, Rick, George, let's get out of here." Travis backed up a step with the jerky movement of a spooked horse. "We'll get in trouble…"

"No we won't, Travis." George pushed him forward with a big hammy hand. "Don't wimp out now. I wanna have fun."

"You *always* think the dumb shit Rick dreams up is fun," muttered Travis in the ghost of a rebellious growl, but he allowed himself to be pushed forward and assumed a half-hearted fighting position.

"I really don't want any change," Cain broke in, making a pitiful attempt to diffuse the situation. "You don't have to bother with me."

"Oh, but we do." Rick slammed a heavy fist into the palm of his other hand as if testing its weight for Cain's face. "See, we're students at UCLA—putting ourselves through without scholarship money. Do you know how much work that takes? George and I—we're both working shitty jobs for wages that barely cover tuition. Travis is working two jobs to get by."

Travis shifted and made a noncommittal noise.

Rick went on. "See, kid, the fact is that while we break our backs at real jobs, people like you do nothing. Nothing at all. You just sit in the street, beg for money, and live off the state. We pay for you to do that; that's our tax money, our hard-earned wages. That pisses me off. Don't it piss you off, George?"

"Yeah," grunted George.

"Don't it piss you off, Travis?"

Travis shrugged, avoiding Cain's eye.

"Sounds like the vote is unanimous," growled Rick. "Nothing personal, street kid—you were just the first bum we saw. Course, we might be able to make a deal if you hand over that fancy guitar. You probably stole it anyway."

They advanced in unison, fists up. Cain decided that the situation had definitely escalated to an emergency and scrambled to his feet.

The drunken bullies paused for a moment in what appeared to be dismay when they saw how tall he was—as he had hoped they would. Cain needed time to draw his painstakingly summoned magical energy out of the guitar and focus it into a spell that would temporarily disable his attackers. But Rick and George seemed all too conscious of their superior numbers; they began to advance again almost immediately, pulling Travis with them.

Cain backed up desperately against the wall, the ponderous human spell tangled into a hopeless snarl in his mind. His hands twitched and fluttered helplessly. His fingers brushed the strings without conscious effort, and a note of angry, cutting music tore from the guitar.

Rick's body jerked back violently. His feet left the ground, and he flew upward as if a giant invisible hand had swung down from the sky and smacked him into the air. George and Travis watched open-mouthed and round-eyed as he flew away from the fire escape in an arc, flipping and swearing all the way. He landed with a smack on the pavement fifteen feet away.

"Rick! Rick!" Travis tore away from blank, stupidly staring George and ran to his fallen comrade's side. "Rick, are you okay?"

It was a full two minutes before Rick staggered to his feet, apparently too drunk to feel the injuries the fall probably caused. He stared at Cain with terror in his eyes.

"I...how...he...*What the hell was that?*" he gasped. "The music...Get away from him, George. Quick!"

George needed no second bidding. He scurried over to Rick and Travis, casting nervous glances over his shoulder all the way.

Rick swayed back and forth where he stood, his knees bucking and trembling, his gaze flicking from Cain to the guitar. "That music...How did he?...He just...He threw me into the air without touching me! With *music*. The music did it somehow, but I..." His eyes grew even wider as he stared at the guitar. "Say, kid, what's that thing plugged into? It's not plugged in at all. But how...How is that even possible? How are you doing...Oh God, what *are* you?"

Cain stared back, almost as startled as Rick. The music had accomplished this feat; or, more accurately, he had accomplished it using the music as the means of conveyance. It had taken little more effort than it took to breathe, and it had produced much more spectacular results than the spell he had planned to use would have.

"Look, kid." Rick waved his hands in a frantic placating gesture. "We're really, really sorry. Swear to God we are. It was all a stupid mistake. It won't happen again. We'll go away and leave you alone now, okay?"

Rick, George, and Travis broke into a clumsy run in the direction of their car, knocking into each other and stumbling over each other's feet as they went. As he watched their comically exaggerated fear, a perverse desire for mischief entered Cain's mind.

Slowly, with careful, exacting movements, he began to run his fingers over the strings. They produced a steady crescendo of discordant sound, the full force of which Cain focused on the filth-covered fire escape.

"Oh shit!" Rick leapt up in panic. "He's doing more witchcraft stuff! Run!"

The three would-be attackers picked up their pace, failing to notice the black cloud rising from the fire escape or its steady billowing movement heading in their direction. Travis leapt into the back seat, ducking down as low as possible. Rick and George were fumbling with the front doors when Cain abruptly stopped playing the guitar. They turned toward him, confused for a moment.

Then the moment was over. The cloud of dust and decay that was no longer suspended over the car by Cain's will dropped down, showering them with dirt and desiccated rat corpses. Rick and George screamed and clawed at the air as if they had been sprayed with acid. Cain could see Travis through the grimy back window. His thin face was pinched with fear; yet he was also gradually beginning to shake with laughter at his friends' melodramatics.

Rick and George finally ripped the doors open and scrambled inside. The car tore off in reverse down the narrow street, knocking over an empty trash can and bouncing off the wall with a loud bang.

Cain watched them go. The collar pinched sharply to reproach him for getting carried away, but he barely felt it. The guitar rested in his hands, heavy and beautiful and humming with his energy. It had stopped drizzling, and the moon shone through a thin film of clouds overhead. He stared up at its ghostly glow as fierce pride welled in him. For the first time in ten years, he did not feel helpless.

As the length of his practice sessions stretched to engulf entire nights, Cain began to divide his daytime hours between sleeping and his pest-killing duties. He had difficulty sleeping during the day in the alley. When there wasn't some housewife shaking him awake with a demand that he chase pigeons off her roof or a gaggle of bored young children wanting to play, a delivery van would roll noisily up or Mrs. Delgado would toss a heavy load of refuse into the dumpster with a loud, resonating bang.

Early one morning as Cain caught a few precious hours of sleep before people started waking up and going about their noisy business in the neighborhood, he was rudely awakened by a boot poking into his ribs. He rolled over, clutching at the blanket-wrapped guitar case that he had taken to using as a pillow, hoping that whoever it was would give up and go away.

The poking continued, gentle but insistent. Cain still

wasn't risking speech, but he did allow himself a surly grunt.

"Come on, honey. Rise and shine," said a familiar voice. "You've got things to do today."

Cain cracked his eyes open painfully and squinted up at Crazy Loti, who towered above him in a sheath of blinding morning light.

"Don't lie there blinking at me now," she said cheerfully. "You have a busy day ahead of you. The sooner you start out, the better."

Cain groaned. "It must be seven in the morning."

"Nine, actually. Everyone else is on their way to work, and you should be too."

"I was up until three last night." Cain burrowed back into the blankets with a sullen groan. "I'm still tired."

"No one gets enough sleep in the city." Loti seized his shoulders and began to haul him upright. "Come on. Get up. You need to eat before you go to work."

She was strong and persistent. Cain went rebelliously limp in her arms, but she still managed to force him halfway into a standing posture before he gave up and got to his feet on his own.

"What's this all about?" he grumbled, rubbing his eyes.

"You need to eat and get your work for the day done early to get to your other job in time."

"What other job?"

She propelled him in the direction of the dumpster. "The one you start today, of course. Less talking and more eating."

Mrs. Delgado had put out a bag of fresh morning scraps for Cain while he slept. The bag was slim, but the nearly stripped bones, chicken skin, and organ fragments provided enough nourishment to get him going. Afterward, Cain headed to the post office and eliminated some mice that had been hiding in a dark corner of the mail room. The mailman paid him with a pound of ground beef. At the post office, another family asked him to clear a nest of rabbits out of their tiny side-yard vegetable garden. The rabbits, though a bit wiry, were enough to satisfy Cain as payment. Cain could see Crazy Loti out of the corner of his eye. She was watching him from a distance the whole time, stroking her white dog's silky head.

It was nearly four in the afternoon when they set out. With his guitar slung over his back, Cain followed Crazy Loti down a confusing and seemingly endless series of streets and neighborhoods. His uneasiness grew with each twist and turn.

"You said someone asked you to look after me while I was in the city," he said at one point, to break the silence that had prevailed for the past fifteen minutes and to distract himself from the steady and unsettling gaze of the dog. "Who was it?"

"Like I said, no one you know."

No one he knew? Cain marveled at the chaotic unpredictability of humans; during his time in the city, he had met three strangers who had wanted to hurt him for being poor, an entire neighborhood who wanted to feed and protect him for his value as a ratter, and now someone who desired to keep tabs on his welfare even though this person had probably never even seen him.

"Why would someone I don't know want to help me?" he persisted.

"Because of your master, mostly." Loti gave him a grim look over her shoulder. "Old Warwick has made a lot of enemies over the years. I should warn you right now, Cain, if you follow my instructions you'll be happy, but not until you've fought your way through enough trouble to last ten lifetimes. I hope you're up for the challenge."

Cain said nothing and tried to ignore the sinking sensation that was rapidly engulfing his insides. Because he was so distracted, he almost plowed into Crazy Loti when she stopped.

"We're here," she called back to him.

Cain looked around, wondering where "here" might be. It seemed to be a jumble of seedy clubs and cheap-looking apartment buildings—even dingier than the section of town where he had bought the guitar, if that were possible. It had clearly been a nice neighborhood once; most of the buildings were built from an attractive buttery-gold stone that looked somewhat like marble, and remains of gargoyles and intricate decorative stonework peeped from the buildings' eaves. Now, trash clogged the gutters, all the windows in sight were cracked or boarded up, and garish neon flickered from every corner.

"There we go." Loti pointed to one run-down old building with an especially ugly neon sign that partially obscured the stylized palm branches carved into its façade. "The Bayou Jewel. It used to be a jazz club, so I'm told, until the neighborhood around it went to seed and the rich folks stopped coming. Now young people come here to listen to new bands play."

Cain nodded, taking in its grand ruin in silence, unsure of what he was expected to do.

"Sit outside and play," Loti explained. "I'll come back to pick you up when I think you've played long enough."

"Sit *outside*?" he repeated uncertainly. He had been

under the impression that the bands played inside.

"For now, yes." She gave him a reassuring smile. "You'll get your chance to play inside someday, but not until you've done as I said."

She wheeled off down the dirty street without another word. The dog loped reluctantly after her, keeping its eyes fixed on Cain until it disappeared around a corner. Cain watched her go and then crept over to the club's grimy, flyer-covered wall and sat down. Slowly, he took out the guitar and began to play. A crowd of open-mouthed young people congregated around him, and he felt rather foolish until money started dropping into his open guitar case. By the time the last few stragglers went home for the night, he had amassed a decent-sized bundle of coins and bills.

"I told you that you'd do well for yourself here, didn't I?" Crazy Loti chuckled as she led him home.

Cain started to go to the club to play every few days or so. Crazy Loti accompanied him the first few times, but he soon memorized the route and started going on his own. Some of the extra money he earned on these nights he kept for himself, but he left most of it for the Delgados. Mrs. Delgado was moved to tears several times by the selflessness of *el animal*; however, some of her friends cautioned her to think about from where the money might be coming.

Meanwhile, Cain was becoming a fixture at the Bayou Jewel. He was a fairly competent guitarist by now. Plus, his horns and his magical talents made him wildly popular among the crowds waiting to get into the club, and his popularity convinced the manager and bouncers to tolerate his presence. For many patrons, a Saturday night visit to the Bayou Jewel was now incomplete without a glimpse of the devil-boy magically playing his guitar without power cords or amplifiers while old flyers fluttered around him like enormous butterflies or while multicolored shooting stars rained down on the sidewalk. Cain felt the bite of the collar whenever he added the special effects. Sometimes it was a light prickling, and sometimes it was an intense wave of agony. Cain could never predict which punishment it would deal out, and he suspected that there was a reason the collar worked that way; it was meant to keep him constantly on edge with the knowledge that even his most minor infraction might result in a jolt of debilitating pain.

Still, Cain kept on enhancing his performances with magic. The delighted looks on the faces of the people around him were well worth the discomfort.

It was an unusually cold September night. The club was closed and most of the patrons had gone home. A few small groups still staggered about the street, talking in loud voices about other parties to which they were heading. Cain ignored them as he packed up his guitar, but gradually he became aware of someone standing a few feet away, watching him.

He looked up. The stranger was leaning against the wall of the club. He peered at Cain from the corner of his eye, dragging slowly on the stub of a cigarette. He seemed familiar, but Cain couldn't quite place him.

"Hey," the strange young man said finally. "You're the kid who plays the guitar without electricity, right? That's a pretty neat trick."

Cain blinked for a moment; he had almost gotten out of the habit of expecting humans to address him directly. The only person who talked to him openly on a regular basis was

Crazy Loti. He nodded, still wondering where he had seen the man before.

"I could hear you through the walls back there while I was getting ready to go on. You're pretty good." The young man tossed his cigarette away and held out a hand. "Vincent Sweet. My band had a gig here tonight. We're called Heavy Metal Toxicity, and I'm the lead singer."

"I'm Cain." The handshake felt odd and awkward to Cain. Handshakes were one of those many human customs that Cain had observed again and again but never actually had an opportunity to practice. But Vincent Sweet didn't seem to notice his discomfort. "Just Cain."

"That's a great stage name. My band mates keep pestering me to make one for myself; they keep telling me my real name sounds too girly." He seemed more amused than offended by the thought. "But I can't settle on a good one. Say, where do you live?"

Cain thought that this question was an odd one to ask a stranger, but he didn't want to be rude. "A little east of here. Why do you ask?"

"That's good. My apartment is on your way. If you could walk with me..." Vincent shrugged apologetically. "I wouldn't normally ask someone I barely know, but my band mates are all headed off to parties, and I have to get up early for work tomorrow. And you know it isn't safe for us to walk alone at night anymore."

"It...it isn't?" Cain was more surprised at the word "us" than at the news of danger; Vincent Sweet was the first human besides Steve who had really treated him as a fellow human.

"You don't know?" Vincent ran a hand through his long, straight red-gold hair, his eyes widening. "Jesus, how could you not have heard? That serial killer took six of us already, and he'll probably take more before the police get off their asses and do something about it."

"Who's us?" Cain knew he could easily defend himself against a human predator, but it struck him as a good idea to know what profile of victim he fit, just to be prepared.

"*Us*, of course!" Vincent seemed genuinely astonished that he didn't know. "Guys like you and me. Young men in rock bands."

"Oh. But why would anyone want to kill us?"

"I have no idea. But you really didn't know? The last dead guy went missing *from this club*." An eager tremor ran through Vincent's voice as he said this, as if he couldn't help but find the situation a little exciting no matter how deadly serious it was. "I wasn't there when it happened. The guy was a drummer for some band I'd never heard of before. I think they were called *Danger* or something. My friend Izzy Unger is a drummer too, and he knew the guy. Anyway, Izzy says the guy left the club right after their set so he could meet his girlfriend, only he never showed up at her place, and a couple of kids found his body stuffed down a storm drain three days later. It was pretty nasty—covered with all kinds of weird cuts and burns plus some shit so twisted that the coroner wouldn't discuss it with his family."

Cain barely had to say anything for the duration of the trip. Vincent happily chatted away, elaborating on the latest gossip about the murders and putting forth his pet theories as to who was behind them. His boyish face lit up with a curious excitement as he prattled on. Vincent's grotesque fascination was off-putting to Cain at first, but Cain eventually decided that he probably wasn't intending to be morbid. He had an air of innocence about him. Cain guessed that he had not been in the city long and was still getting used to the frenetic pace of life there.

"Then again, that Breen guy could be behind it somehow," Vincent said in an offhand way. "He's the only one I can think of who hates us enough to do something that drastic."

"Breen?" Cain perked up at the familiar name.

"Geez, you *are* out of the loop, aren't you?" Vincent chuckled. "Nathaniel Breen is this unbelievably obnoxious TV preacher who thinks all rock n' roll is evil—especially the heavy stuff that we play. I wouldn't put it past him to try and kill us all off somehow. Of course, Breen would have to be smart enough to think of a plan like that, and I don't think he comes close to having that kind of intelligence. He thinks we're the leaders of some secret devil-worshipping cult. Do you believe that shit? As if we had time to be leaders of anything between practicing and writing songs and finding gigs and trying to make the rent payments. Anyway, this is where I live. Good night, I'll probably see you at the club tomorrow."

Vincent climbed the crumbling concrete steps to the third floor of his building. Cain watched him, trying and failing to sort out his thoughts. He stood for a moment, staring into the smog-obscured sky; then he turned and hurried off into the deepening dark.

Michael Anderson woke up in the middle of the night and saw his mother.

She was in his cell with him, shuffling around in her familiar faded blue dress. Her slippered feet glided without disturbing the thin film of dust on the concrete floor as she walked, but Michael knew that she was not a ghost. He sat up on his cot and watched as she extended her hand, dusting an invisible mantelpiece with an equally invisible rag. The rag materialized as he watched—first, it appeared wispy and transparent like a jellyfish; then it changed to a faded eggshell color; and then it solidified into its original canary yellow. The mantelpiece also puffed into existence like a piece of theatrical scenery emerging from the wings of a stage.

Michael's eyes followed the rag as it slid over the framed photographs, over the baby-blue veiled statuette of the Virgin Mary, over the folded flag from his father's casket, and finally over the steely gray granite of the mantelpiece itself. The scene unfolding before him was not real, he knew, but it was not a hallucination either.

Michael Anderson had visions of the past. He had seen carpenters and stonemasons erecting cities long since buried under the sands of ancient deserts. He had seen covered wagons trundling across the prairies and Model Ts rumbling down dirt roads. He had seen a sniper's bullet kill his father in Vietnam. These visions were vivid and immediate. He could smell them, taste them, reach out and touch them; they bled into his present reality and distorted his sense of time.

Sometimes, he had other types of visions. Occasionally, people went transparent when he looked at them, and he could see into their minds. He had not realized as a child that other people could not see the world the way he did, not until his mother had discovered his powers.

The vision shuddered and warped.

The fireplace sank into an indistinct, blood-red background. Arlene Anderson loomed over her son like a malignant beast, clutching a stark black coat hanger in her hand, her face twisted into a grimace of anger and fear. She drew back the hanger with agonizing slowness. Michael could not see himself—he never saw himself in his visions—but he knew that he was curled on the floor before her, shuddering in anticipation of the blow. Most likely, he was whimpering that he was sorry, begging her to not hit him, and swearing that he would never see things again.

Then things shifted, and Michael was alone in his cell, crouched on the floor.

He dragged himself back into bed, sighing in relief at the comfort and safety of the empty darkness. Tears squeezed from his tightly closed eyelids. His mother was dead, and he had killed her. He was alone.

He would rather be alone than tangled up in his visions.

In one of the crumbling apartment buildings near the Bayou Jewel, Vincent Sweet yawned, stretched, and rolled out of bed.

He prepared for work without much enthusiasm; the anticipation of an evening spent singing with his band was the only thing that enabled him to get through yet another day of draining oil and patching up cracked radiators in the mechanic's shop where he worked. At least the girls at the club seemed to find the stains on his hands sexy and masculine. Breakfast was a simple bowl of cereal, but he purposefully took a while to eat it because there were always so many broken cars that needed fixing.

When he realized he was late for work, he panicked. He hurried down the stairs, pulling on boots and a jacket as he stumbled and bumped and tripped his way down. He knocked over a young woman who had been standing at the bottom of the stairwell, glancing from the building to the piece of paper in her hand and back again. Vincent stopped to pull the young woman to her feet, apologizing profusely.

"No, no. Really, that's all right," she finally managed to shout over the torrent of oh-I'm-so-sorry-ma'ams and just-let-me-help-you-theres. "Actually, I'm trying to find someone. Do you know if a Vincent Sweet lives here?"

"I *am* Vincent Sweet." He raised an eyebrow in surprise, looking her over. She was trim and professional, with her hair permed and her nails tastefully manicured. Her business suit had imposing padded shoulders, and she was wearing a gold bracelet set with sparkling red stones. She was exactly the kind of person he would least expect to see in this neighborhood. He wondered if he was in trouble.

"Oh, good." The woman brightened. "I hoped I'd catch you before you left for work. I have a message for you from my boss at Daggerspoint Records."

"Seriously?" Vincent stared at her, feeling as if the wind had been knocked out of him. Every young musician he knew would kill to be noticed by someone at Daggerspoint Records.

"Absolutely." The young woman gave him a warm smile. "We had an agent in the audience at the Bayou Jewel last night, and he liked what he saw *very* much. My boss wants to meet with you, Mr. Sweet, and see what you can bring to the table."

Vincent opened his mouth to speak, but he could only push out the tiniest of joyful squeaks. A meeting with someone at Daggerspoint Records was something he had hardly dared even to dream of.

"Four o'clock today, if you can manage it," she continued with an understanding grin.

"Oh, yes. Yes, I can." Vincent nodded enthusiastically, and then he became serious. "Of course, I'll have to track down the guys first, but I'm sure they'll all jump at the chance—"

"Ah…yes," the young woman interrupted. About that, Mr. Sweet…My boss specifically requested to see *you*. Alone."

Vincent's smile began to fade. "My band mates can't come?"

"I know this may seem heartless," she continued. "But you must remember that we're a business, and our business is to pick up the best talent in the city. Your band mates are good from all I've heard, but they aren't the best. You are. With our help, you could be great, but you won't be great until you work with people whose talents match yours."

Vincent stared at her, torn. It didn't seem right to ditch them—but then again, what obligation did he have to his band mates? He wasn't particularly close to either of the two guitarists, and he and the bassist outright detested each other. But there was also Izzy, the drummer, his best friend who had grown up with him in Illinois. He wouldn't feel right leaving Izzy in his dust.

But then again, how many more times in his life would an offer like this come along?

"I'll be there," he said quietly. Izzy was his best friend; Izzy would want him to take this opportunity.

"Excellent. Here's my card." The young woman turned and began walking briskly away. "We'll all look forward to seeing you."

Vincent spent his morning at work in a happy haze, flashing wide grins at customers and singing as he tinkered with overheated engines. He punched out early against the wishes of his boss and hurried eagerly up the street in the direction of the Daggerspoint headquarters.

Heavy Metal Toxicity had to cancel their show that night when their lead singer failed to appear. He didn't show up the next night either, or the night after that, and his band mates gave him up for dead. Izzy the drummer was inconsolable and dreaded the day he would hear the unbearable news of a seventh body turning up. However, he had no need to be afraid; no body ever surfaced. But still, Vincent did not return. The terrifying rumors about the murders intensified, and began to spread to a wider audience.

Cain was strumming his cordless guitar in the cool autumn air, listening to the chatter of the crowd when he overheard the news about Vincent. He was very sorry (and felt a trifle guilty) that he hadn't managed to prevent the tragedy. Something happened that night, however, that drove the disappearance of Vincent Sweet from his mind completely.

For a moment, he thought he saw Mr. Warwick in the crowd. Cain was in the middle of a riff of his own invention—one that made a cold, blue fire lick harmlessly about the guitar—when the old man's familiar face popped out of the wall of people in front of him. Mr. Warwick's eyebrows were knit in surprise and disbelief. Cain jumped, hit the wrong note, and the flames suddenly glowed red. When Cain recovered, he looked in the same place, and the face was gone. Later on, he would convince himself that he had imagined it; but at the time, he was so shaken that he had to pack up and slip away early.

CHAPTER FIVE

THE OFFER

AS THE DAYS PASSED, Izzy Unger held onto a last ragged shred of hope that his best friend was still alive. One week after Vincent Sweet went missing, he slipped away from a party at the club, emboldened by a heavy dose of cocaine. He dragged a loudly protesting casual acquaintance along with him to help him retrace Vincent's every step. They passed Cain and charged up the rain-grimed street. When Izzy and his companion failed to turn up the next night, the club-goers and performers traded hushed gossip about a mysterious serial killer who targeted aspiring rock stars. They began to call the killer the Engineer. No one knew where the nickname came from—many people claimed to have coined it, even though they could not explain what it meant—but the mere mention of the word soon sent shivers of terror and excitement through the most jaded audience.

Several regulars claimed to have caught glimpses of this maniac in the shadows of the decaying neighborhood around the club.

"The Engineer was checking the place out again last night," said Skeeter Judd as he sidled up to his band mates at the bar. "I saw him on the corner across the street."

"No kidding, Skeet?" Skeeter's twin brother, Goober, looked up from his whiskey with an indulgent grin. "What did he look like?"

"Er..." Skeeter frowned. "He had real dark eyes, like almost black. Same color hair. Yeah. And he wasn't very tall, just sorta average height. I couldn't see his face 'cause he had a baseball cap pulled down over it. You know, I'm pretty sure I saw him on the night Vince was taken too, hanging around the stage door. I didn't think much of it then, but now I know he wasn't a fan. Poor Vince."

Goober nodded politely, trying not to laugh at Dog the drummer who was making faces behind Skeeter's back. The last time Skeeter had "seen" the Engineer, the Engineer had been a hulking six-foot giant with flaming red hair and green eyes, and Skeeter had personally chased him across five blocks only to lose him down an alley. Skeeter's penchant for tall stories was well-known around the club.

A few musicians didn't fully believe the tales and laughed at the possibility of abduction.

"The Engineer?" Jazz Brixton put his arm around a concerned female fan, pulling her closer under the pretense of comforting her. "Nah, no need to worry about him getting me, babe. I could take him down easy."

The girl needed no encouragement. She cuddled up to him and stared into his blue eyes, enraptured.

"Really, Jazz?" she whispered. "Everyone's saying he's, like, really strong. He'd have to be, to drag all those big guys off—"

Jazz interrupted her. "Everyone's been saying a lot of shit about him, and probably half of it isn't true. I guarantee you this Engineer wouldn't stand a chance against me. I'd throw him down and kick his ass right there in the street! Once I finished with him, he'd never darken the doorway of this club again."

"Oh, yes he would." Candi Jayne poked her head though the door to Jazz's dressing room. "You'd better pray the Engineer never attacks you, Jazz. He might go for your hair first, and everybody knows Jazz Brixton can't fight when his pretty hair gets messed up."

To Jazz's annoyance, his admirer giggled. He glared at Candi, tossing his considerable blond mane indignantly.

"Fine!" He pushed the girl away. "Laugh all you want. Fucking bitches. We'll see who's laughing when the Engineer comes around again. He'd better hope the cops get him before I do."

Jazz and Candi's band mate, Ty Thorpe, was sitting cross-legged on the hallway floor. He looked up from the newspaper he was reading, his eyes dark and serious.

"If the cops get him at all," he said in his quiet voice.

Jazz paid no attention to Ty. He pushed past Candi and flounced off angrily down the hall. The girl scurried after him in consternation, stammering a desperate apology.

Candi frowned. For several weeks now, the police had shown very little interest in pursuing the Engineer.

"It's disgusting, Ty," she blurted. "Nine people are dead, for God's sake!"

Ty stood up slowly and leaned casually against the wall, studying Candi with his perpetually calm black eyes.

"Nine?" he said. "Last I checked, the last three guys' bodies hadn't been found yet. They could still be alive."

"The way things are going, they're as good as dead," said Candi bitterly. "Someone should make the cops get off their asses and do something."

"That won't happen," said Ty. "Not as long as Nate Breen has breath in his body and big wads of cash to make friends in the PD."

Candi rolled her eyes. "Oh yeah. I forgot about Breen and his little imaginary-cult-busting hobby. I know he's got a lot of police on board his snake-oil train, but I'm surprised they've stayed on this long."

Ty shook his head.

"You'd be surprised," he said. "Breen may be a crackpot, but he's a damn convincing one. And you know...he might not be selling snake oil the same way some TV preachers do. I think that somewhere deep down inside, the guy's actually bought the line of bullshit he's selling."

Snatches of gossip about the Engineer traveled from patron to patron outside the club. Cain overheard it all and became increasingly uneasy and fearful. To make matters worse, he was sure that someone had been following him for the past five nights. He kept catching glimpses of a dark figure ducking into alleyways and hiding behind mailboxes or garbage cans on the other side of the street as he walked to and from the club. The unknown pursuer always kept to the shadows and never came close enough for Cain to make out his face. The stalker did not seem eager to follow him into the Hispanic neighborhood at first. But after the first few nights, the figure ventured into the neighborhood; Cain sensed someone watching him as he gnawed a thigh bone before settling down one night. When he looked up, a shadow flickered around the corner of the alley and was gone.

He became tense and excitable. The Delgados noticed the change and discussed it with their friends.

"I took some chicken gizzards out to my *animal* last morning," Mrs. Delgado told a group of regular customers as she mopped the floor. "The door shut really loud behind me, and he went straight up in the air. He really jumped—four feet at least! And he had a weird look in his eyes afterward—I swear I saw fire in them. It was so unlike him. I hope he's okay."

Mr. Delgado looked up from the pork loin he was carving and cleared his throat.

"Ah…you don't think he's…you know…going wild, do you? I mean, he already eats raw meat and doesn't talk and kills mice like a cat, so maybe…"

This possibility had been at the back of Mr. Delgado's mind for quite some time, but he had been afraid of mentioning it to his wife.

"That's ridiculous, Arturo!" Mrs. Delgado stabbed the mop into the bucket furiously. Several customers leapt back with bilingual curses as a small explosion of water soaked their legs. "*El animal* may not be right in the head, and his taste in food is kind of…different…but he's so gentle. You've seen him with the children—he's more patient with them than anyone I know! He'd never go wild."

One of the younger customers piped up. "I bet he's scared of the killer. I'd be too, if I were him."

"Killer?" Mrs. Delgado's hands tightened around the mop handle.

"I was talking to my boyfriend the other night," said the young woman who had spoken. "He tends the bar at this club where rock bands play, right, and he says that there's this guy who's been killing rock musicians."

She paused, blushing and swaying awkwardly as if she expected to be scolded or laughed at for spreading unfounded gossip, but the shop had gone silent.

"They've been calling him the Engineer," she went on in a wavering voice that slowly gained strength. "I don't know why. They think he takes his victims when they walk home at night after shows. The cops have found six bodies already, and three more are missing. And *el animal* plays outside on the street sometimes for money. I think I've seen him there a couple times...and I'm sure he can listen even if he can't say anything, and he hears people talking about it."

A low buzz of talk filled the shop. Mrs. Delgado whipped the mop out of the bucket and gave the floor a vicious swipe.

"What's this city coming to?" she muttered. "Some maniac murders nine young men in the street, and not a word is said about it on the news or in the papers! Well, this Engineer had better not come around here, and he'd better not mess with our *animal*. I'll deal with him if he tries. Just you wait and see."

Mr. Delgado picked up another pork loin, knowing that it was useless to argue with his wife when she was in one of her moods.

Cain heard their conversation through the open back door and appreciated their concern, but he wasn't reassured. The neighborhood itself felt safer, as people looked out for him there, but he couldn't stay in the neighborhood every minute of the day, and his stalker was following him more frequently now when he was out of it. He started to wonder what would become of him if the Engineer were to take him by surprise, and he could not get to his guitar in time. Even without it, he was still bigger and stronger than most humans; but size and strength might not count for much against a serial killer practiced at taking victims down quickly, quietly, and unexpectedly.

He found excuses to leave the neighborhood less often. The guitar seemed to tempt him to play it—the urging was almost to the point of physical pain—and he missed the frenetic chatter of the crowds at the club, but the close, dirty shelter of the alley felt safer.

Not that it always felt perfectly safe; on several more occasions, late at night, Cain had the distinct impression that someone was watching him from the deserted sidewalk outside the alley. Once, upon waking from a light, troubled sleep, he was certain he had seen a dark figure standing on the other side of the street. It was gone as soon as he forced his eyes to focus properly. He tried to convince himself that it was only a dream as he settled uneasily down again. He stayed asleep until sunrise—until he was jolted awake by someone laying a hand on his shoulder.

"Calm down, little devil," said Crazy Loti in a quiet but firm voice as Cain scrambled to his feet with a fearful yelp. "You know I won't hurt you."

"What do you want?" Cain asked in a voice much harsher than he meant it to be. "You scared me."

"There's no reason for you to be afraid, honey," she said gently. "Not yet, anyway. But that's not what I came to tell you. I came to tell you that the folks down at the Bayou Jewel miss your playing."

"Oh." At any other time, Cain would have been flattered, but now the news caused him more stress. "Well, I miss them too, and I'd really like to play again, but…"

"But you're afraid of the Engineer?" Loti gave him a sideways look, drumming her fingers on the handle of the cart. "Or maybe you still feel a little guilty about what happened to that nice young man at the club?"

Cain's face fell. He had hoped that no one else knew he'd been with Vincent the night before his kidnapping and was unable to prevent whatever gruesome death Vincent had suffered the next day.

"You know about that?" he said bleakly.

"I know everything that happens in this city," Loti replied vaguely. "It's my business to know. I also know that it's not your fault, if that makes you feel any better. There was really nothing you could've done to stop Vincent Sweet from falling into the Engineer's hands. He was tricked, and he went into the Engineer's lair willingly. Of course, he didn't know it was the Engineer's headquarters. That's how the Engineer gets his victims."

"You know how the Engineer gets his victims?" Cain snapped out of his self-pitying sulk immediately. "Does that mean you…"

Crazy Loti nodded.

"You know who the Engineer is?" he gasped as soon as he found his voice again. "You knew all this time, and you didn't tell anyone?"

"I just told you, didn't I?"

"You know what I mean!" Cain tossed his matted hair over his shoulder. "Why didn't you tell someone who could actually *do* something about it?"

"That's not my area." Loti shook her head sadly. "I oversee everything that happens in this city, but I can't get directly involved. I can only point people in the right direction and hope as hard as I can that they go that way."

"I don't know what you're talking about," said Cain angrily. "But couldn't you have made an exception? The Engineer has killed nine people so far, and he'll kill more soon."

"Still just six, actually." She sighed deeply. "Vincent Sweet is still alive."

"What?"

"Vincent Sweet is still alive and so are his two friends who went looking for him."

Cain felt as if he had been kicked in the gut. It had been more than two weeks since Vincent disappeared and a little more than a week since his drummer friend and that bassist had gone looking for him, and they never came back. He didn't want to think about the tortures they had surely been put through during that time, and he certainly couldn't imagine why Crazy Loti wouldn't do anything about it and then burden him with the knowledge of their fate as well.

"I have to go to the police," he said finally. "I have to, even if you won't. Just tell me the Engineer's name, and maybe they can still save Vincent and—"

"Honey, it's already too late for them." Loti put a hand on his shoulder. "You can't save them now; you can only try to get justice for them and for all the other young men who fell into the Engineer's hands. I can tell you how to begin, but you have to complete the task yourself."

"Do what by myself?" Cain sighed. "I don't see what a homeless boy who lives in an alley and eats rotten meat *can* do."

"You know perfectly well that there's more to you than that." Crazy Loti tapped the cart handle impatiently. "And there's plenty you can do. You can start off by following directions and not asking me questions I'm not allowed to answer. If you want vengeance for what the Engineer did to those young men, go to the club tonight and play. Play, and say yes to the first person who makes you an offer."

"What offer?" Cain asked warily.

"You'll know," Loti chuckled as she began to wheel away. "At least, I *hope* you can recognize an offer when you hear one."

"Well...yes, but...can't you at least give me something I can work with? Like the Engineer's name or address, for instance?" A few weeks ago, he had figured out how to play a chord that might, with the right direction, stop a man's heart; if he was going to have power that terrible, he might as well use it to make the city a nicer place.

"Sorry," she called over her shoulder as she vanished around the corner.

Candi sat down next to Jazz Brixton, who appeared to be in a foul mood. He sat at the bar, glowering at his untouched drink while two blonde admirers tried in vain to hold his attention.

"That kid is back again," he grumbled.

"Kid?" said Candi. Usually she walked away whenever Jazz started getting upset over something minor, but leaving wasn't an option right now. She might miss her friend Yuri, who had said he would meet her at the bar after the show. "Huh. I didn't see any kid."

"That kid with the stupid fake horns." Jazz took a sip from his whiskey, making a sour face.

Candi vaguely knew about whom he was talking; she kept overhearing club patrons talk about a horned devil-boy who played the electric guitar without electricity. She had never seen this mysterious street musician in action, and she was certain that Jazz hadn't seen him perform either. Most performers entered the club through a stage door on the other side of the building. She had no idea why Jazz had gotten so worked up over this person, but Jazz often chose the weirdest little things to throw snit fits over.

"Oh, yeah. *That* kid." She tried to sound noncommittal. "I didn't notice."

Jazz would not be put off. "He didn't show up for three nights in a row, so I hoped he was gone for good. Why don't the bouncers tell him to fuck off?"

Candi cast a longing glance at Ty, who was sitting a few seats down from her. She wished he would join the conversation. Ty wasn't much of a talker, but he had known Jazz for a long time and could shut him down quickly when he chose to do so. Unfortunately, Ty was going through one of his quiet spells right now. He nursed a barely touched gin and tonic, staring straight ahead with distant eyes. Candi knew that it was useless to try to get his attention when he was preoccupied like that. She wished Yuri would hurry up.

"I don't see why they would." She shrugged. "He's not hurting anything, and folks seem to like him."

"It's such an obnoxious gimmick." Jazz finally noticed that he had two miniskirt-clad women pressing against him, and he put his arms around them. "Isn't it, girls?"

Both the women blushed and nodded enthusiastically, though Candi doubted they really heard or cared what he said.

Emboldened by his new audience, Jazz continued. "The kid's guitar skills are pretty pitiful," he sneered. "If you can call them skills at all. He sounds like he's strangling the damn thing instead of playing it. He ought to show some respect for us *real* guitarists and stick to those cheesy magic tricks that he's actually halfway decent at doing."

Candi rolled her eyes. She should have known that Jazz's tirade was about the devil-boy's skills. Jazz fancied himself the best guitarist in the city, and the presence of anyone with even marginally better skills was enough to send him into fits of jealousy.

"Figures he would come back on the one night Bruce Arkin visits the club looking for new talent," said Jazz. "I bet he's hoping Arkin will be blinded by his smoke and mirrors and hand him a record deal on a silver platter. Well, I've got some bad news for him: they have standards over at Daggerspoint. They're not gonna be swayed by a pair of plastic horns from a cheap costume shop."

Skeeter Judd ambled up to the bar and squeezed in between Jazz and Candi, casually brushing his hand over the backside of one of Jazz's admirers.

"That's what he wants you to think," he said. "That the horns are fake, I mean. They're not. See, 'devil-boy' ain't just a nickname. Fact is, he's a real devil from real Hell."

Jazz glared at him. "Fucking fascinating. Now why don't you go tell someone who cares?"

"That's why he's so dirty and poor," Skeeter went on, paying no attention to Jazz. "He makes himself look that way, so he won't scare anyone. Some say he'd be red and scaly in his real shape, like those devils in cartoons. Some say he'd be a big fierce critter like a wolf or bear, with fangs and glowing yellow eyes. Maybe he'd be totally made out of fire, or even out of pure darkness." He lowered his voice. "One thing's sure, though; if you saw that devil-boy as he really is, you'd be scared—scared enough to go shit-crazy. Some sensitive folks might die on the spot."

Jazz made a guttural sound of annoyance, but nobody heard him. Skeeter could be a compelling storyteller when the mood struck him, and at the moment, it had struck him hard. His eyes glowed with enthusiasm, and his voice took on a rich, authoritative tone. Candi and the two blonde women were drinking in every detail, and even Ty shook out of his funk and looked in their direction.

"That's some creepy stuff," Skeeter continued. "But it's even creepier that no one knows why he's here, especially since that magic of his is real too—and believe me, he can do a lot more than set stuff on fire without burning it and make old beer bottles float. If he wanted, he could change all of Los Angeles into a cloud and all the people in it into birds. He could make the earth split open and the stars fall from the sky with one wave of his hand. If he wanted to rain death on the whole world, or make us all his slaves, there'd be nothing to stop him, nothing at all. But some say—good luck for us—that he doesn't mean us harm. That he's come to this earth with one man on his mind."

"Who?" said Jazz, now interested in spite of himself.

Skeeter grinned triumphantly.

"The Engineer," he whispered. "He's come to bring the Engineer to justice. That's why he chose this place to hang out—he's biding his time, waiting for the Engineer to walk into his trap. And when he does...oh, that'll be a day to remember! There won't be a place in the whole world for that low-down killer to hide. I just hope I'm there when it happens."

Awesome story, thought Candi as Skeeter continued his story. *Too bad it can't be true.* Yet she couldn't quite suppress the little shivers of excitement prickling her skin.

It was two in the morning, and the crowd at the Bayou Jewel was beginning to dissipate. Cain packed up quickly, not wanting to be the last one left on the street. Earlier that evening, the dark figure had been waiting in an alley just outside the Hispanic neighborhood. The figure had followed him again, always a few streets behind but unshakable as his own shadow. Cain had lost sight of the shadow in the confusion of people milling around the club, but he had sensed its presence the whole time.

That's the last time I follow Crazy Loti's advice, he thought as he wrestled the guitar back into its case. Playing outside the club hadn't gotten him anywhere. During the entire four long hours Cain had been sitting outside the door, not one person had made him an offer of any kind. Some of the club-goers seemed excited about some sort of special event, but he hadn't been paying particularly close attention to the chatter. He found the presence of his unseen stalker so unnerving that none of the club-goers' conversations had made an impression on him. The crowd quickly dissolved and drifted away. By the time Cain was packed and ready to go, he was almost alone in the street. He glanced nervously around as he prepared to walk home.

Someone coughed behind him. He wheeled around and found himself facing a man in a polo shirt and khakis.

"Easy does it, son." The man put up his hands in a placating gesture; he must have seen the fiery panic in Cain's eyes. "I'm not going to hurt you. I want to talk to you."

Cain inspected the newcomer warily. He was trim and tanned and had thinning but fashionably bleached hair. Cain guessed he was in his late thirties, but he had never been very good at estimating the ages of humans. The man had a jovial and relaxed air about him. He did not look like a killer, but humans were unpredictable that way. Sometimes, the most ordinary-looking ones turned out to be the most evil.

"About what?" he asked, trying to sound disinterested

and casual.

"About you, of course." The man smiled. "I've heard a lot about you. You know, it's a really great story: the homeless boy with incredible guitar skills became the Bayou Jewel's unofficial opening act. But the story gets even better, doesn't it? I understand that playing isn't all you do?"

"Oh, well, I just do some silly tricks to get the crowd's attention." Cain spoke hastily, fearful that the collar would punish him. "And I'm not that good. There are plenty of guitarists at the club who are a lot better—"

The man shook his head with a bemused chuckle. "Why so modest? I heard you earlier this evening, and you're great—a little raw, maybe—but you're pretty damn outstanding for someone who taught himself to play. Trust me; I'm in a position to know these things."

Cain blinked.

"You don't know who I am?" The man looked at him sideways. "I'm Bruce Arkin, president and CEO of Daggerspoint Records."

Cain blinked again. Bruce Arkin laughed.

"Well, kid, I'm exactly the kind of person every young musician like you needs to know. People like me make people like you famous." He stopped laughing and looked hard at Cain. "And to tell you the truth, you're exactly the kind of young musician every person like me needs to know. You've got the talent, and you've got something that sets you apart from the crowd. I never dreamed I'd have the good luck to find a real, honest-to-god demon that could play rock guitar."

"You know I'm a demon?" Surprisingly, the collar did not pinch as Cain gave away his identity, but he still winced. "I mean, I'm not really—"

"Come on, kid." Mr. Arkin grinned. "The horns alone are a dead giveaway. Don't try and tell me they're fake; they're way too realistic. Some movie studios would have difficulty creating those horns with top-of-the-line makeup, and you're an untrained homeless kid with no resources. And that awkward lump down your left leg is a tail, isn't it?"

Cain nodded, trapped. He was actually surprised that he had gone this long without anybody else noticing the poorly concealed tail. His tight jeans left little to the imagination.

"Thought so." Mr. Arkin nodded triumphantly and glanced again at Cain's tail bulge. "You know, kid, you really ought to cut a hole in the seat of your pants or something. That can't be good for your circulation. Anyway, we're getting off topic. I'd like to meet with you tomorrow and discuss getting a band together, and hopefully, we could put a record deal together after that. What do you say?"

Cain didn't know what to say. His "yes" was purely automatic, and he only said it because he suspected that this was the offer Crazy Loti had been talking about.

"Great." Mr. Arkin paused. "Say, kid, do you have a place to stay tonight?"

"Yes."

"A place indoors?"

"Well…no."

"Jesus!" Mr. Arkin stared at him. "You mean you've been sleeping on the streets where anyone can get at you, while the Engineer—you do know about the Engineer, don't you? Please say you do."

Cain nodded.

"Good. You know how dangerous it is out on the streets, then." Mr. Arkin frowned, scratching his neck. "Well, I guess if you've made it this long, odds are good you'll be fine for one more night. No need to take risks, though. You'd better come with me. The company owns a nice townhouse where we put out-of-town prospects up for the night sometimes; I can let you stay there for a few days."

Cain started to follow him, but then he stopped.

Mr. Arkin turned around. "What's wrong, kid?"

Cain just remembered something Crazy Loti had said about the Engineer—that he did not force his victims to come with him, but he charmed them into coming on their own. Mr. Arkin's offer sounded as if it would be very attractive to an up-and-coming musician. Plenty of young men had probably followed him just as Cain was about to do now, hoping that those promises would be fulfilled. Had Vincent Sweet been among them?

Mr. Arkin seemed to know what he was thinking. He sighed and shook his head. "No, I'm not the Engineer. I know I'm on the suspect list; maybe it was inevitable that I would be. But it's ridiculous. Why would I want to destroy my own livelihood? If I ever meet the real Engineer, I swear I'll kill him myself. He's bad for business."

Cain was not entirely convinced. He might have refused the offer and slipped back to the safe obscurity of the Hispanic neighborhood if he had not happened to look up at that moment. He froze at the sight of a figure standing in the shadow of a decrepit newsstand on the other side of the street; the figure was watching him.

"I know, kid." Mr. Arkin leaned toward him, speaking in a grim whisper. "Whoever that guy is, you're not the only one who's noticed him following you. I asked around at the club tonight. Lots of people have seen him; some of them tried to catch him once, but he got away. Trust me, I want to help you here, and it isn't safe for you on the streets. Unless you're immortal or something?"

Cain knew perfectly well that he was not immortal, even in demon form. He scurried after Mr. Arkin, casting a last terrified glance into the gloom-filled street.

Mr. Arkin's car was parked in the one reserved spot in the narrow, rubble-and-weed-covered lot behind the club. It was an old blue Chevrolet in good but faded condition, and Mr. Arkin drove it himself. Later on, after he had met a few more record company executives, Cain would realize that Mr. Arkin's vehicle choice was very unusual for a man in his position, but at the moment, he thought nothing of it. Mr. Warwick was probably five times richer than Mr. Arkin, and his car was a battered, old black Volkswagen.

The streets of Los Angeles were crowded and chaotic. Mr. Arkin maneuvered the Chevy through lanes of vicious honking traffic with aggressive grace, making an impossibly sharp turn here and slipping into a forbiddingly small space between two other cars there. Meanwhile, he carried on a conversation as if nothing else were happening.

"So, kid," Mr. Arkin said calmly as he drove over the curb to avoid a taxi that had cut in front of him. "It may sound strange, but when I was asking around the club about you, no one seemed to know your name. They just knew you as 'devil-boy.' But I'm sure that's not what you call yourself."

"No, it isn't. My name is Cain."

"Cain what?"

Cain gave him a confused look.

Mr. Arkin raised an eyebrow. "Don't you have a last name?"

"Oh." Cain shrugged. "I never thought I'd need one."

"Well, you will now." Mr. Arkin's brow knitted in

perplexity, as if he couldn't imagine how anyone could survive without something so essential as a last name. "I mean, even if you don't use it on stage, the company will have to put it on your paychecks. Let's see…What kind of last name would people expect a demon—*Damn!*"

He stood on the brakes as the car ahead of him came to an abrupt halt. Cain let out a surprised yelp.

"Sorry about that." Mr. Arkin regained his composure just as quickly as he had lost it. "Hey, look, landmark on your right."

Cain squinted through the window and saw a huge black building against the dark sky.

"San Juan de la Cruz," said Mr. Arkin. "It was a Spanish mission before Los Angeles existed, and the city kind of rose up around it. It's a gorgeous old building, and after all these years, it's still an active church—" He stopped, glanced at Cain, and seemed a bit flustered. "But I guess churches aren't really your thing, are they?"

Cain shook his head. He was indeed uncomfortable with churches, particularly grand ones like San Juan de la Cruz. Whenever he passed by one, or looked at one, a sickening, uneasy feeling seeped through him, worming its way out of the closed-off section of his mind…

My tribe left the Inner World sometimes. We wandered the human world under the cover of darkness to…forage? Study humans? I can't remember…but I do remember the many warnings not to stray from the group because of the dangers of the Outside. One day, I ignored those warnings and hung back. I saw a pretty building—a Greek basilica— and I wanted a closer look.

I remember taking it all in—the carved pews, vaulted ceilings, stained glass windows, and paintings of saints in bright robes of purple, green, saffron, and sky-blue. There were so many beautiful things I could hardly decide what to look at first. I darted up and down the aisle, drinking it all in. When I found the little wood door behind the altar, I was sure it led to something even more wonderful.

The door opened on a small room with nothing in it except some plain wooden benches and a metal table covered with melted candle stumps. I started to close it again, and then I saw the mural.

A stern bearded man was leaning on a long-handled spear, bearing down on it as he drove it into the throat of a small, prone female figure at his feet. She had the horns and tail of a Malakh, just like I did. The image was crude and garish, marred by white patches where the plaster had crumbled away. It looked cheap and ugly compared to the serenely beautiful saints in the sanctuary, but it felt…more honest somehow…as if I'd stumbled across some evil secret I wasn't meant to see.

I don't remember how my father punished me for wandering away from the group, though he must have. I only remember him explaining the mural to me—Wisdom and the Prophet of Falsehood, he said it was called—and warning me that I must hold it in my mind because that was how humans would always see us and would always treat us: as enemies to be tamed or stamped out.

"Cain?" Mr. Arkin gave him a worried look. "You all right?"

Cain nodded, staring up at the dark jagged outline of San Juan de la Cruz. He could feel the headache starting. He grasped desperately at the memory just before the star of light made it vanish again. He focused on the broken form of the Prophet of Falsehood and on the exotic Greek word his father had used to denote her...

"Pseudomantis," said Cain softly.

"Hmm?" said Mr. Arkin.

"My last name is Pseudomantis." Cain blinked away the star-shaped motes of light in his eyes. He no longer knew why he had picked the name, but the choice simply felt *right* somehow.

Mr. Arkin drummed the steering wheel thoughtfully. "What is that, Greek? It might be too much of a mouthful for the average fan to remember—then again, you never know. It does have that sort of semi-exotic, semi-Satanic sound that I think would be right for you. You know, I think it *could* work. Cain Pseudomantis. Huh. I don't think I could come up with a better name for a demon rock star if I tried."

The place Mr. Arkin had been talking about was in a clean, new-looking, little neighborhood of pink granite townhouses with brown-tiled roofs. Mr. Arkin parked on the street and led Cain to the last house in the row.

"The kitchen is to the left, living room to the right, and the bed, bath, and loft are up the stairs," he said cheerfully as he unlocked the door. "I'll send someone along in the morning with breakfast and a fresh change of clothes. Oh, and Cain?"

"Yes?" Cain yawned.

"I mean this in the nicest possible way," said Mr. Arkin delicately. "But please do take a shower."

Cain was sure now that Mr. Arkin was not going to harm him, and he was beginning to remember how pleasant sleeping on a real bed could be. The Delgados and their friends would probably be unhappy when they discovered that their rat-catcher was missing, but he couldn't do much to alleviate their worries right now. Cain also thought it was strange that the collar hadn't chastised him for being distracted from his responsibilities; however, it had remained silent for quite some time. Cain puzzled over the collar's unusual behavior as he got ready for bed, until he remembered something Mr. Warwick had said before he left: "Become a movie star if you have to! I really don't care as long as you get the job done."

Surely *movie star* translated into *rock star*.

He was following Mr. Warwick's orders, sort of, even if it wasn't in the way the old man intended.

Cain settled into bed with a sigh of contentment. This was going to be fun. The collar trembled indignantly as he fantasized about all the fun he could have in the city without his master holding him back, but it couldn't seem to muster enough evidence for a full-blown punishment.

CHAPTER SIX

OPENING ACT

MR. ARKIN'S ASSISTANT STOPPED by early the next morning. Cain found her in the kitchen when he stumbled down the stairs, still bleary from sleep. She yelped and flattened herself against the wall when she saw him.

"Breakfast for you," she said in a shrill voice, tossing a white paper parcel onto the table and then leaping back again as if she were trying to distract a hungry tiger. Her next words were so rushed and garbled that Cain had difficulty understanding her: "Mr. Arkin sent me. Anyway, there's more in the fridge. Call me if you need anything. Bye." She fled for the door, keeping her face turned away from him. Cain shook his head as he picked up the parcel. He couldn't help but find it upsetting when humans reacted to him that way. The contents of the package cheered him up: a full two pounds of raw tenderloin, much nicer meat than he had eaten in weeks. He finished eating just as Mr. Arkin himself came by to pick him up and help him carry his guitar out to the car.

"I hope you enjoyed breakfast," he said as they wove their way through a violent tangle of rush hour traffic. "I specifically instructed Chelsea to pick up the best cuts the shop had available."

"Oh, I did." Cain glanced at him. "But how did you know…"

"About your special diet?" Mr. Arkin chuckled. "Simple research. I always try to pay attention to my clients' cultural backgrounds and culinary preferences. Some businessmen don't think that sort of information is important, you know, and you wouldn't believe the trouble their ignorance gets them into."

Daggerspoint Records was headquartered in an angular building of glass and gleaming steel—about a forty-five-minute drive from the house. Despite the imposing appearance of its exterior, it was much more intimate inside. Most of the office doors in its halls were open, and Mr. Arkin greeted everyone by name as they passed. He led Cain down several halls filled with offices, and then they strolled down another, much longer and wider hall lined on both sides with ten recording studios. Only nine of them were in working order; studio 4B had a sign tacked on the door that read, "Closed for repairs." Cain lingered by the decommissioned studio for a moment, wondering what went on in those rooms. Mr. Arkin made a nervous sound in the back of his throat and herded him away.

Mr. Arkin's office was a big room with taupe walls. A fine old oak desk sat at the far end of the room, and two chairs stood in front of it. Cain thought that Mr. Arkin would seat himself behind the desk as Mr. Warwick always did, but instead, he straddled one of the chairs, leaning his elbows on the backboard in a posture of relaxed interest.

"Now, Cain," he said. "I'd like you to show me what you can do."

"Right now?" said Cain.

Mr. Arkin grinned. "Right now. Play your heart out. And don't be shy with the hocus-pocus either. I want to see what you can do in that area too."

Cain took up his guitar and began to play, shyly at first, but he became bolder as Mr. Arkin started to look more and more interested. He performed all the feats he had used to get the attention of the crowds outside the Bayou Jewel: making fire and lightning billow around his guitar, levitating books and papers off the shelf in the corner, and creating starbursts and fireworks that harmlessly rained down on the carpet. He also raised the empty chair off the floor. He made the carpet and curtains change color several times in a rapid kaleidoscopic swirl. He caused a pile of pens on Mr. Arkin's desk to leap up and sail around the room like a fleet of tiny golden missiles. Mr. Arkin looked thoroughly impressed by the time he had finished.

"Well, Cain, I don't mind telling you that you're even better than I'd hoped you'd be. With a little guidance, all those special effects combined with your guitar skills could make for one outstanding stage show." He poked the pens gingerly. "I must say, though, I'll try to avoid making you mad from now on. I don't want my own pen jumping up to stab me in the eye."

Cain and Mr. Arkin talked for another hour. Cain got the impression that the record company would choose worthy band mates for him. While they were searching, he would study to improve his "technique"—whatever that meant—and do any odd jobs the studio needed done. He suspected that this scenario was not the usual way of getting a band together, but he wasn't worried. Mr. Arkin seemed to know what he was doing. Only one thing bothered him.

When the hour was over, Mr. Arkin called a frightened-looking young woman in hospital scrubs into the room and told Cain that the company needed to take a blood sample before they could take him on.

"To check for a certain virus," he said reassuringly as Cain stared at him in shocked confusion. "One that always turns up in people with AIDS—some scientists think that it's the cause of the disease, in fact. We test all of our artists for this virus before they sign with us."

AIDS? Cain tried to remember whether he had ever heard of such a disease. Mr. Warwick had never allowed him to watch the news on television, and the old man always retrieved the newspaper himself and secreted it away in his bedroom, where Cain could not enter unless he was specifically invited. Cain's only approved exposure to "current events" came in the form of the newsreels which Mr. Warwick sometimes made him watch: slick little black-and-white films that showed cheerful American soldiers sailing off to defeat Communists in Asia and Russia, or a bullet-shaped white craft blasting magnificently into outer space, or senators in immaculate suits shaking hands with other, similarly attired senators. Mr. Warwick never hesitated to remind Cain that many powerful men like the ones in these newsreels were in his debt, and some even considered him a friend. They were far too busy running the most powerful and prosperous nation on earth to offer help or sympathy to a barely literate demon savage who claimed that Mr. Warwick was holding him in servitude against his will.

Unbeknownst to Mr. Warwick, however, Steve had quickly cottoned on to the idea that his father wanted to restrict Cain's exposure to the news. He had started collecting clips from newspapers and magazines to show to the blue demon when his father wasn't watching. From these scraps of paper Cain had learned that the hated Communists had driven the US army out of the jungles of Asia and had even beaten the Americans to space. He also discovered that dignified politicians in suits were not above accepting bribes or even stealing outright from their opponents. These tidbits of information did nothing to improve Cain's lot, but he was glad to know them anyway. There was a certain sense of power in knowing that he had access to facts that belied Mr. Warwick's idealized vision of the world, facts the old man could not take away because he had no idea that Cain had formed memories of them. Yet one concept that Cain could not recall having encountered in his illicit readings was that of a mysterious disease called AIDS.

"Now don't take this the wrong way," said Mr. Arkin in a placating tone. "I'm not accusing you of being gay. The problem is that AIDS isn't just a disease for gays. There's a reason they've stopped calling it 'gay-related immune deficiency,' you know—junkies catch it a lot, too. Lots of rockers are needle users—they shouldn't be, but they are—so we always do this test on new hires to be safe."

Cain blinked. He did remember a mention of this mystery illness now; a very brief one, from an article about the spread of disease in modern American cities. The author of the article had called it GRID.

The nurse took a deep breath and shuffled closer to him, brandishing the needle. Cain leaned away from her.

"I...don't think you have to test me," he said. "I'm not...I... can't get human diseases." Cain had caught flu from Steve once or twice, so this was technically a lie, but he doubted that lying would do any harm in this instance. His body could fight off infection twice as fast as a human body, and it certainly didn't sound as if he was at any risk of coming down with AIDS.

Mr. Arkin shook his head. "I'm afraid that doesn't matter. We have to do the test, for every musician we hire. I could be sued if I let you opt out. I'm sorry."

Cain shifted unhappily. The thought of that needle piercing his skin filled him with deep anxiety. But Mr. Arkin had been so kind to him, and the last thing he wanted was to get him in trouble. Besides, after listening to Mr. Arkin's enthusiastic chatter about the brilliant career he had ahead of him for the past hour, he wanted to be in a band—a real band—more than he could remember wanting anything before.

The nurse tentatively swabbed his arm with cotton. Cain swallowed hard and submitted with tensed muscles and gritted teeth to the unnerving bright needle. He felt faint and violated after it was done, and he failed to notice that the nurse seemed as terrified by the prospect of taking his blood as he was by the prospect of having it taken.

"Easy, Cain," said Mr. Arkin in a soothing voice as Cain climbed shakily to his feet and promptly fell back into his chair. "I know how you feel. I don't like needles either. Well, it's over now. Just try to forget it."

Cain did try to forget the experience, and for a long time, he succeeded.

Mr. Arkin wasted no time where Cain was concerned. The guitar lessons started the next day.

"I hope you realize how big a deal this is," said Mr. Arkin as he and Cain waited in his office for Ty to arrive. "Ty Thorpe isn't only the rhythm guitarist for Candiryde, impressive as that is, but he's also the last surviving member of Lion of Judah. Plenty of guitarists would kill for one lesson with him—let alone have him personally ask to teach them."

"He *asked* for me?" said Cain.

"Yeah. He made it pretty clear that he wouldn't take no for an answer." Mr. Arkin frowned thoughtfully. "It was the damndest thing. Usually he's Mr. Laid-Back."

Ty was a tall black man with slender hands and heavy-lidded eyes that made him look half-asleep. He gave Mr. Arkin a brief greeting and led Cain to one of the studios in the hallway without another word. Cain played a short tune for him, and he listened with such a somber expression on his face that Cain was terrified he hated what he heard. But when the strings fell silent, Ty perked up and leaned toward him in frank admiration.

"Damn, that's amazing," he said reverently. "Folks told me that you could play without electricity or amps, but I didn't believe them at first. It sounded impossible. Of course, that's not all they're saying you can do. I've heard…"

"Heard what?"

"Oh, mostly the things you'd expect people to say, like you can summon storms and earthquakes and turn people into animals."

"Well…" Cain studied Ty's face as he tried to work out a reply, wondering who "they" were and what else "they" had been saying about him. Ty didn't wait for him to speak.

"They say…" An eager gleam flashed in his eyes. "They say you can bring the dead back to life—that some of the Engineer's victims are walking around again because of you."

Cain stared at him in astonishment.

"Not true, huh?" Ty didn't sound surprised.

"I...I'm afraid not. Sorry. I'd bring the Engineer's victims back if I could."

"No problem. I guess I should know better than to listen to Skeeter Judd's stories." He sighed deeply. "We should get started."

To Cain's puzzlement, the first five minutes of the lesson consisted of Ty running out to his car and coming back laden with piles of coiled black cables and heavy boxlike contraptions. Ty stood over the mysterious devices in regal silence until Cain shyly asked him what all of it was.

"This," said Ty matter-of-factly, "is the way we humans play an electric guitar, with power cords and amplifiers. Now, let's get started, shall we?"

Cain shuffled reluctantly up to the pile of equipment. It seemed like a waste of time to bother setting up all this stuff when the magic way was so much easier and didn't require any legwork. He did manage to get everything set up to Ty's satisfaction eventually, but not before he had tangled his legs in the cords, produced several ghastly drawn-out electronic shrieks that slammed against his eardrums, and banged his shin painfully against the sharp corner of an amp. By the time the lesson was over, he never wanted to see another speaker as long as he lived.

The next lesson was a bit more pleasant. He had less trouble setting up the equipment; and once he figured out how to play his guitar without it yowling like an angry cat whenever he plugged it in, he made an intriguing discovery about the human method. It was less tiring. He didn't have to strain, pour energy into the guitar, or focus unwaveringly with the force of will needed to make magic do what he wanted. He had more leeway to properly focus on the music itself. Ty showed him how to produce sound effects and subtle changes in tone and pitch that he had not known were possible to create before, and he showed Cain a few chords that Cain had tried on his own but had never quite mastered. Mr. Arkin checked on his progress frequently, and he seemed to like what he saw.

Cain was assigned to open for Hellhound on Halloween night. Mr. Arkin personally helped him get ready, fussing over him like a nervous old grandmother and throwing out so many tips on beating stage fright that Cain, who had been perfectly calm before, began to feel definite pangs of stage fright. He felt like he might vomit.

"I guess the collar goes pretty well with this outfit," Mr. Arkin muttered as he inspected Cain's spiky stage attire. "Still, we should probably consider trying something different for other shows."

"Ah...about that..." Cain sat up straighter on the uncomfortable little makeup stool. "I can't take it off. It's...it's a spell that lets me stay in the human world."

"Oh. I see." Mr. Arkin hastily drew back his hands. "Better leave it on, then."

The performance itself went well. Cain's nausea subsided as soon as he began playing, and the audience seemed moderately entertained even though he wasn't the main attraction. Then, as he was playing the last note, he happened to look down.

Michelle Breen was there.

Cain blinked and stared, unable to believe his eyes. The young woman in the third row was wearing a pair of fluffy false cat ears and a tight black dress that revealed a great deal of flesh. She was hanging off the arm of a tattooed man who looked too old for her, but she was staring up at Cain with happy amazement in her mascara-and-shadow-smeared eyes. She was definitely Michelle Breen.

She nodded her head in the direction of the offstage door and flashed an eager smile at Cain. Cain swallowed nervously and hurried offstage.

Unfortunately, Mr. Arkin would not hear any talk of leaving early.

"These are your people now, Cain," he said firmly. "You have to mingle with them after shows, just like people who work in an office building have to mingle with their co-workers. That's how you get good contacts. Besides, what's a Halloween party without a real demon?"

And so Cain endured a very loud and long party backstage. No one seemed interested in talking to him. Indeed, half the guests found excuses to scuttle away whenever he came near them. He got a few minutes' worth of amusement from eavesdropping on a conversation that Hellhound's lead singer, Skeeter Judd, was having with a group of bemused young women. He was regaling them with the convoluted and highly improbable tale of his brother Goober's heroic foiling of a bank robbery; supposedly, Goober was armed with nothing but a rubber band and a handful of guitar picks. But because Skeeter blanched and shut his mouth the moment he noticed that Cain was listening, Cain didn't get to hear how the story ended. He ended up moping in a corner while people in superhero capes and plastic masks drank and threw up around him. Even though he was very bored, he did find some comfort in the thought that Michelle had probably gotten tired of waiting and had gone home by now. If he encountered her, he would have to resume his mission.

He wasn't about to finish his errand and return home just when life in the city was getting enjoyable. And he certainly didn't want to turn Michelle over to Lance.

"Well, that was fun," said Mr. Arkin as they made their way to the stage door. The several beers he had downed made his voice louder and merrier than normal. "Aren't you glad we stayed?"

They were the last ones to leave the club. The street was almost deserted. A few revelers much drunker than Mr. Arkin were staggering around and a woman in a black dress and fluffy cat ears was leaning in an impatient posture against the wall by the stage door.

"Hey, devil-boy," she shouted at Cain as he passed her. "I thought you'd never come out. I've been waiting for hours."

Cain froze at the sound of her voice.

Mr. Arkin grinned and slapped Cain on the back. "Well, well, Cain. Now I know why you wanted to leave early. Why didn't you tell me you had a pretty girlfriend in the audience? I could've gotten her backstage."

"That's not why I..." said Cain in a frantic whisper, wondering how he was ever going to explain the situation to Mr. Arkin. "It's just..."

"You want to be left alone. Of course. I understand that." Mr. Arkin staggered off down the alley. "Good thing the house is in walking distance from here."

"But I—"

"Use protection!" he bellowed over his shoulder before he disappeared around the corner. "You don't want to get some girl pregnant at this point in your career; trust me!"

Then he was gone, and Cain was alone in the alley with Michelle Breen.

"Remember me?" She smiled. "From the alley behind that butcher shop?"

Cain nodded.

"Good. You know, I came to the show without knowing that you would be here tonight." Michelle laughed. "I thought I was seeing things at first when you came out on that stage. I guess you took my advice to comb your hair, huh?"

"I guess so." Cain braced himself in anticipation; he thought that the collar would tighten to remind him of his duty, but it hung loose.

Michelle laughed. "And he talks! I thought you probably could speak, but I wasn't sure, and Daddy didn't give me enough time to find out. Well, now you can finally tell me your name."

"My name?" Cain was confused. "Didn't you see it on all those posters on the front of the club?"

"I saw the posters," said Michelle doubtfully. "They all said that 'Cain Pseudomantis, guitarist from Hell' was opening for Hellhound tonight. I seriously doubt that's your real name."

"Oh." Cain scratched the back of his neck. "Actually, that is my real name—except for the guitarist from Hell part. I've never called myself that."

"Really?" Michelle raised an eyebrow. "But who would—"

Her eyes widened as she caught sight of Cain's tail, which was protruding from a specially cut hole in his pants and waving happily in the free air.

"Oh God...that's...*real*?" She watched the iridescent blue scales glint in the dull glow beneath the stage door light, shaking her head in amazement. "I thought it was fake and a puppeteer was making it move from backstage or something, and all that crazy stuff you did…" Her mouth fell open as she stared at him. "It was *all* real, wasn't it? And you really are…"

"Yeah." Cain sighed. Well, that conversation certainly took care of the Michelle dilemma; now that the sweet, virtuous preacher's daughter knew his true nature, she'd want nothing to do with him, and he would never be able to bring her back for Lance. The thought made him strangely happy and sad at the same time.

"Oh…my…God," gasped Michelle, her eyes getting wider with every word. "That is so…so…sexy."

Cain stared at her.

"*What?*"

"Oh, come on!" Michelle gave him an incredulous look. "A heavy metal guitarist who happens to be a real demon? You're like the ultimate bad boy. Plenty of girls would kill to be with that. Trust me."

"Be with?" Cain backed up against the closed stage door. He had an uncomfortable feeling that they were both on the verge of doing something they really shouldn't be doing.

"Yeah." She moved toward him with an odd hunger reflecting in her eyes. "You know, I was kind of hoping to get lucky tonight, but my date left; he said he didn't want to wait outside the stage door for the opening act all night. I was thinking…there's no one here but us, and we're both dateless…"

Michelle was right; the last few stragglers had left, and there was no one to see her arms snake around Cain's waist. She levered herself up on her toes so her lips could press against his, and she gently pushed his jaws open so her tongue could slip in his mouth.

Cain had witnessed humans kissing before, but until then he had no real idea what it might feel like. He couldn't remember how his tribe used to show affection, but he had a feeling it was not in the same way. The warm, close wetness of the kiss was so startling that he acquiesced without protest. His actions became automatic; he barely registered them. His hands reached around Michelle's back to pull her closer as a strange hunger built inside him in answer to hers.

The collar contracted violently around his neck.

"Ow!" He pulled away from her. "I can't do this."

"Sure you can." Michelle tried to pull him back.

He dodged to one side, cowering away from her arms. "No, I can't. I've never…please, I just can't."

"If you've never been with anyone before, I don't mind," said Michelle a bit impatiently. "I'll show you what to do. It really isn't that hard."

"You don't understand. I can't." He backed away, trying not to look at her.

"What don't I understand?" Michelle put her hands on her hips. "Tell me what it is I don't understand."

"Please just leave me alone. *Please*."

He fled from the alley. The black whiskers painted on Michelle's cheeks trembled indignantly as she stared after him.

A cold night breeze blew in his face as he hurried away from the club, carrying with it a lingering stale scent of engine exhaust. The walk was not alleviating Cain's misery, which was rapidly turning into irritation.

What had Michelle been doing at that club anyway? He was sure that nice preacher's daughters weren't supposed to go to those types of concerts. They probably weren't supposed to dress in revealing clothes and wear heavy makeup either, and surely they weren't supposed to spend their evenings lurking around stage doors in grimy back allies, waiting to ambush rock stars with indecent advances.

Yet Michelle had been there, waiting for him in her skin-baring dress.

Mr. Arkin had forgotten that he had Cain's key. Cain was forced to take out his guitar and flip the lock with a quick, metallic *plink* of the E-string.

"I'll never understand humans," he muttered to himself as he closed the door behind him. "Not if I live *another* two thousand years. Nothing they do makes any sense at all."

Coffee swirled in the cup in Michelle's hand. She raised it to her lips and tried not to make a face. She couldn't show her distaste for the bitter liquid, not with her father sitting right across the table from her. He thought she drank coffee because she liked it. If he were to find out that she hated the stuff, he would probably start asking uncomfortable questions about why she needed a cup of strong coffee on certain mornings to help her stay awake in school.

The Reverend Breen sat pushing his half-eaten toast around his plate. Michelle watched him through the corners of her eyes. She could tell that he had been on the verge of saying something all morning, and it made her nervous.

"Ice cream social at school this Friday, Daddy," she said to break the silence.

"Hmm?" Her father looked up.

"It's for graduating seniors and their families. We could go."

Her father nudged his plate aside. "I can't," he said. "Groundswell is next week."

"That big conference in Texas? Didn't you go last year?"

"That's the one." The minister reached for his newspaper. "Sorry, sweetheart. Maybe we could go next time. You know how much they need me there."

Michelle frowned into her coffee cup; her mood soured. She had no desire to go to an ice cream social at her stupid school, with or without her father, but that wasn't the point. Sometimes it seemed as if her father was off at a gathering of fellow ministers every other week, and fundraising for his various anti-cult projects absorbed the rest of his time. The last real conversation she could remember having with him had been an argument over whether she was old enough to stay home alone while he was gone—and even that discussion had devolved into a lecture on the dangers of devil-worshipping kidnappers.

The minister bent to pick up a piece of paper that had fluttered to the floor. He unfolded it slowly, muttering something about the newspapers being crammed full of useless advertisements nowadays. Then the annoyance in his eyes changed to puzzlement. He squinted at whatever was printed on the paper for a moment, his mouth working silently; then he stared very hard at his daughter.

"Michelle," he said. "Where did this come from?"

Michelle looked up, startled by the quiet anger in his voice, and found herself staring at a torn flyer with a guitar-wielding horned man emblazoned against a background of red flames.

"Where did this come from?" her father repeated, shaking the flyer. "It isn't from the paper; it's ripped up and has glue on the back. *I* certainly didn't bring it into this house, and I'm sure the maid wouldn't have."

133

Michelle eyed the poster cautiously. She had a muddled memory of tearing it off the stage door last night in a fit of pique. But she had no idea how it had ended up on the table for her father to find; maybe all her late nights and coffee-fueled mornings were beginning to catch up with her. But she could worry about that later. She had to come up with a good explanation for that damned flyer's presence as quickly as her fuzzy head would allow.

"I saw it pasted to a wall near…the school. I'd never heard of the guy, but…well…with those horns, I thought…I thought you might want to use it for the Black Book." She sat back with a quiet sigh of relief, inwardly congratulating herself on the stroke of inspiration. Her father was always on the lookout for new material to add to his ever-growing dossier of evidence for the evil and depravity of modern rock musicians.

The minister opened his mouth and closed it again. He contemplated the flyer for a few more minutes.

"Yes," he said slowly. "I do believe I can use this information. Thank you for your help, sweetheart. I'll be doing some research on this…Cain Pseudomantis. But you must promise me something."

"What's that, Daddy?"

"Sweetheart, I want you to stay away from this man."

Michelle hid a twitch of surprise by taking a quick sip of coffee.

"What do you mean, Daddy?"

The minister shook his head. The flyer crinkled under his tightening grip.

"I know his type," he muttered under his breath, as if he were talking to himself rather than to his daughter. "How they lure people to them, to corrupt and use—"

"Daddy?" said Michelle, startled by the quiet intensity in his voice.

The dog barked in the next room. The minister put the flyer down and shuddered as if he were waking from an unsettling dream.

"I have to go let Abednego out." He sounded strange and distant. "You know where my files are, sweetheart. Just go up to my office and pop that...thing...into the Black Book, won't you?"

Michelle picked up the flyer and trotted out of the room, blinking in astonishment. Sadly, it wasn't unusual for her father to pass immediate judgment on someone's character based on a photograph, but his reaction had caught her by surprise. She had never seen him respond so viscerally to any rock star— even Jazz Brixton or the late JoJo Thorpe, and they had probably slept their way through more girls her age than there were people in the greater Los Angeles area.

The "Black Book" was a three-ring binder bursting with newspaper clippings, articles from music magazines, fragments of posters, and pages of hand-written notes. Michelle dragged it out of the bottom drawer of her father's desk with a grunt of exertion and plopped it down on the floor. She stole a last look at the flyer before slipping it into the binder.

"God, you're a sexy bastard," she murmured. "Even if you *are* a tease." She made up her mind to give the devil-boy another chance. Her father didn't usually single out rock stars for her to *specifically* avoid. She wondered why he felt compelled to warn her about Cain explicitly.

The morning dawned bright and unusually clear. Cain felt better once he had breakfast—a whole free-range chicken— and stepped out onto the low porch for a few minutes to enjoy a rare view of a smog-free sky. He sighed contentedly and relaxed.

Unfortunately, the feeling didn't last long. He saw Michelle Breen marching resolutely up the sidewalk.

"Oh, no you don't," she called out as he tried to slip back inside and pretend he hadn't seen her. "You stay right where you are, devil-boy. I want to talk to you."

Cain's half-second hesitation was a half-second too long. Michelle climbed the front steps with startling speed and stood beside him, arms crossed.

He tried to avoid her eye. "How did you find me?"

"I went to Daggerspoint to ask around," she said coolly. "Bruce Arkin was in the lobby talking to the receptionist, and he recognized me from last night. He was absolutely scandalized that you left your pretty girlfriend alone in a dark alley where she could easily have been raped or mugged, by the way. He'll probably come around here to scold you pretty soon."

"Thanks. Just what I needed." Cain sighed. "Now could you please tell me what you want?"

"I want to know what it is I don't understand."

"You wouldn't understand."

"You know what I don't understand?" Michelle tapped her foot impatiently. "How you could seem happy to see me last night, and be so cooperative for ten seconds' worth of making out, and then suddenly push me away and run as if I were some disgusting thing you never should have touched. You're right: I don't understand you at all."

"Please, go away, and don't ask any more questions." Cain backed up against the door. "I'm a danger to you. A really big danger. Please, just go away."

"You're a danger to me?" Michelle tried unsuccessfully to

suppress an incredulous laugh. "No offense, but offstage you're so timid I don't think you'd be a danger to an ant."

"I was sent to tempt you, all right?" A preacher's daughter ought to understand that concept. "But I couldn't go through with it, and that's why I have to avoid you. I'm sorry."

"Oh. I see." Michelle looked surprised. "Well, you were doing a pretty good job until you started sending mixed signals. Honestly, though, I don't know why the forces of Hell would go to the trouble of sending a demon to tempt me. I can be tempted into sin more easily than anyone I know."

"A human sent me," said Cain. "And I'm supposed to tempt you into a specific sin. You really don't want to know what it is."

Michelle swept past him into the house. "Oh yes, I do. I want to know every single dirty little detail. This is too exciting; it's not every day someone sics a demon rock star on me, you know."

"It's not that exciting," Cain protested, but Michelle ignored him, and he had no choice but to follow her inside and tell her as much of the story as he could without being strangled by the collar; it pinched a lot less than he thought it would, however.

"Lance Warwick?" Michelle's face scrunched in disgusted disbelief as soon as he had finished. "That big, ugly meathead who followed me around for two whole days even though I told him to fuck off and die a thousand times? His dad sent you to pick me up and bring me back to New York?"

Cain sighed. "Yep."

"Oh God, that's so creepy!" Michelle shuddered. "Well, now I know why Uncle Walter and Aunt Janice kept warning me that I should be nice to Lance for old Mr. Warwick's sake. So what will he do to me if I refuse to come back to New York with you?"

"It's hard to say." Cain could guess what Mr. Warwick might do, but he decided not to elaborate on his thoughts. She already seemed alarmed enough. "Actually, I think Lance has probably already lost interest in you. He can't hold any one girl in his mind for very long, and my collar hasn't been punishing me as much for disobeying orders, so—"

Michelle interrupted him. "That's horrible, you know that? Making another person wear a magic collar that tortures them every time they disobey some stupid rule…There should be a law against what he did to you! It's just *wrong*. Isn't there anything at all you can do about it?"

"Oh…Only Mr. Warwick can take it off," said Cain, taken aback by her concern. "But he won't ever remove it."

"He should be in jail," said Michelle vehemently. "Slavery is illegal in this country, you know."

"I don't think he cares."

"Neither should you, then." She moved toward him again, slowly backing him up against the wall as she had at the club. "Disobey him, for God's sake. Have some fun at his expense in the big city. If that damn collar starts hurting you, ignore it."

"I *can't*," Cain protested weakly as her arms locked around his waist again.

"My offer from last night still stands," said Michelle.

She pressed against him, nuzzling his neck. The faint smell of strawberries rose from her hair, and with it, another scent arose, one much harder to identify, but it was musky and exciting. Cain tensed as he breathed it in.

"Relax," she murmured into his collarbone. "You can do it."

"You don't understand," he gasped. "I can't disobey. I'm not allowed…" but his hands were moving of their own accord again, running down Michelle's back, under her blouse, and up again over bare skin.

Together, they stumbled their way to the couch. His pants came down and slumped uselessly around his ankles. Michelle bore down on him. Pleasant little electric shivers pulsed under his skin as she rolled against him. He was inside her now. The warmth intensified and he wanted to move with her, to pull her close, but he was afraid. He was so much bigger and stronger than Michelle; what if he hurt her?

Michelle seemed to notice his hesitation. She picked up his hands and pressed them against her breasts with an encouraging smile. A deep purr escaped his throat. He tentatively began to participate, pushing his hips against hers—gently, because he was still afraid of hurting her. The pulses of pleasure became stronger and more frequent, and Michelle didn't complain. Cain looked up at her anxiously, unsure whether she was enjoying this. Her face had a weird, contorted expression that made it difficult to tell, but the drawn-out sighing noises she kept making sounded happy. He let his hips move with more enthusiasm, and she shivered and groaned with what he thought might be satisfaction.

The collar pinched furiously.

Then the pulses consolidated, rushing through him in a sudden, limb-stiffening, breath-stopping, *wonderful* burst. The pain ebbed away unnoticed.

Outside on the otherwise empty sidewalk, Crazy Loti stood watching the door with a curious and fixed expression. Her dog hopped out of its rusty shopping cart bed and glanced up at her quizzically. She smiled, patted the dog's graceful white head, and nodded reassuringly, never breaking her gaze.

Cain did not see Michelle again for several days. Then one night a band called him to stand in for their sick guitarist, and she was waiting outside the stage door when the show was over.

"Sorry I haven't been around," she said as they embraced in the shadows of the alley. "It's gotten harder for me to sneak out. I think Daddy is starting to suspect something. He's been talking about taking the lock off the door so he can 'check on me' at night; if he takes down the trellis, I don't know what I'll do."

They met several more times that week, mostly at his place, but they met once at the Breen household itself. Cain was skeptical when Michelle suggested it. He remembered the nasty look her father had given him in the alley behind the butcher shop, and he doubted that his newfound minor rock star status would do anything to improve the minister's opinion of him.

"Don't worry," Michelle assured him. "I don't think Daddy actually remembers you from that alley. Besides, he's off at some evangelical conference in Texas, and he thinks I'm staying with my friend Leslie." She giggled. "If he were paying attention, he'd know that Leslie isn't real. But he isn't, and I have the house to myself all week."

The Breen house was a massive stuccoed structure with a red tile roof. Michelle's room was on the second floor, conveniently located above a roof ledge and the bougainvillea-swathed trellis that she routinely used as an escape ladder. The room was papered in soft pinks and creams, and all the furniture was decorated with feminine scrollwork, but Cain caught glimpses of leather and black spandex cunningly hidden among the frilly clothes in the closet. Stacks of records were also crammed behind the speakers and record player, and he suspected that these records did not belong with the genteel classical fare displayed on the shelf.

"Now that was a great way to kick off a whole week of freedom." Michelle ran a finger over the elegant black curve of Cain's left horn as they lay together in her bed. "Seven glorious days before Daddy comes back, and I have to start pretending to be a sweet, boring, good girl again."

"I'll trade places with you." Cain grimaced. "Tomorrow is a day off for me, but the day after that I have to be in some sort of music video."

"I'd trade places with you in a minute!" Michelle sat up and clapped her hands gleefully. "You get to be in an actual music video before you even have a band?"

"You mean you like music videos? Have you seen many?"

"You haven't?" Michelle was baffled. Most rockers she'd known would have been delighted by the prospect of a TV appearance. She was confused, and charmed, by Cain's apparent skepticism toward the concept of music videos.

"I haven't watched much TV at all," said Cain. "My master didn't let me watch TV."

"Never?" Michelle raised an eyebrow.

Cain paused. "Well, he did show me a few newsreels, years ago when I was still learning about the human world, and his younger son sometimes let me watch TV with him when his dad wasn't home and Lance wasn't around to tell on him. But we mostly just watched cartoons and the news together, not music videos."

"Your master sounds like a grade-A control freak," said Michelle. I'm sorry he made you miss out on so much.

Anyway, I think you'll have a great time. Music videos are lots of fun."

"But what exactly *are* they?" Cain asked. "Lance talked about them sometimes, and all I could picture was a videotape of the band playing the song."

Michelle nodded. "Your guess was pretty close to the real thing, actually. Most music videos just show shots of the band from different angles. Sometimes they'll throw in half-dressed pretty girls or scary monsters for effect."

"And humans find that entertaining?" Cain raised an eyebrow as if to illustrate his point. Michelle laughed loudly.

"It's weird," Cain continued. "Anyway, it's not so much being in the music video that bothers me; it's where they're filming it. They're shooting it in the sanctuary at San Juan de la Cruz."

"So, demons can't go into churches?"

Michelle felt his tail twitch nervously against her bare leg. "Oh, we can go into churches; churches are just buildings. The problem is that I don't *like* churches. Something bad happened to me in one when I was little, and I've been scared of them ever since."

"Hmm. That's unfortunate." Michelle thought for a moment. "But since you have the day off tomorrow, why don't you take some time to acclimate yourself to it? You know, go there and stay long enough to convince yourself that there's nothing to be scared of."

"I was afraid you'd say that. Mr. Arkin said the same thing."

"So what *did* happen to you in the church?" She gave him a reassuring pat. "Whatever it was, I promise you it won't happen to you here."

"I don't know." Cain frowned. "My master won't let me

remember my life before I was captured. But churches make me feel so creepy that I just know something bad must have happened to me in one at some point."

"He took away your memory?" Michelle was appalled. Cain's slave collar was horrifying enough, but the knowledge that Mr. Warwick had gone so far as to invade his servant's mind left her sick. "Damn, forget what I said about him belonging in jail—Old Sparky would be too good for him if you ask me."

San Juan de la Cruz had been a proud edifice in its younger days. Now the sapphire-blue skyscrapers across the street shamed it into dusty, crumbling obscurity. Its thick walls were built of pocked, soot-colored stones, making the space feel forbidding and unadorned. The interior was damp and poorly lit, and the garish green altar cloth and begrimed stained glass windows did little to counteract the general effect of colorlessness and gloom.

"There. It's all right." Cain forced himself to step over the threshold, drawing in his breath sharply. "Nothing to be afraid of here."

One of the primitive bulbs in the wheel-shaped metal chandelier above his head flickered insistently. At the front of the church, an old woman in a shawl knelt before a dusty, wax-smeared shrine; she glanced up briefly as Cain entered, and then she immediately went back to her prayers without batting an eye.

"No, nothing to be afraid of at all." He took a deep breath and clenched his fists as he began to hyperventilate. "It's just a building."

He clutched at a pew to steady himself.

"Yep, it's just a building." His eyes flicked nervously

about the dusty expanse of the room. "Just a really big, dark building." A big, dark building with murky shadows in the corners, and a musty smell in the air…

The door to the chapel opened, and a stooped, bald priest shuffled in to fuss with the dull candles burning before another shrine. He gave Cain a mildly disapproving look as he passed, eyeing his tight leather pants and long hair.

Cain spun around and beat a hasty retreat to the door. "Forget it! I can't do this. Mr. Arkin can find someone else to appear out of fake fire in front of the altar and drag the blonde girl out of the lead singer's arms."

A beam of sunlight streamed through the open door, golden and inviting. Just as he reached it, a dark figure stepped across the threshold and blotted it out. Cain panicked for a moment, remembering the unknown stalker who had followed him to and from the Bayou Jewel.

"Long time no see, Cain," said an all too familiar voice.

Cain froze, too surprised to be frightened.

"Lance? What are you doing here?"

"Dad brought me. He has business in the city." Lance stood blocking the doorway as if he were a guard at an army fortification; his arms were crossed, and his expression was stormy. "I told him I wanted to check up on you, to make sure you were still doing your job."

"Oh." Cain swallowed nervously. "About that…it's taking longer than I expected, but it's actually…going pretty well."

"Yes, it must be going well. I hear you're some kind of big rock star now." Lance glared at him. "That's just great."

"Thanks." Cain tried to sound meek and submissive. He knew that tone; it was the one Lance always used when he was barely holding himself back from hitting someone.

"How've you been?"

"Funny you should ask." Lance's voice was dangerously calm. "See, dad had a meeting yesterday, and I got bored waiting at the hotel for him, so I ran to the grocery store around the corner to pick up some snacks and a tabloid to read."

"Really?" Cain was astonished that Lance would actually choose of his own free will to read something.

"Really," said Lance. "And while I was flipping through this tabloid, I found a picture that didn't make any sense. But you must know all about night life on the Sunset Strip; I'm sure you can explain what it means."

Lance thrust a rumpled mass of cheap newsprint in his face. On the front cover was a candid photograph of Cain and Michelle by the Bayou Jewel's stage door, locked in a passionate kiss.

"I'm sure you can explain this!" Lance's voice rose to a scream. "I'm sure you can explain why this rock star—who looks *just* like you, by the way—is running his big, filthy hands all over *my* girlfriend! I'm sure you can explain why she's dressed like a cheap slut too!"

There was a caption below the photograph, but Cain was too shocked to read it. He hardly even registered Lance's growing anger. He was utterly stunned by the thought that anyone would care enough about his kissing a girl to stop and take a picture of it, let alone plaster it on the front page of a cheap gossip magazine.

"What the hell did you do to my girlfriend?" shrieked Lance. "You were supposed to pick her up and bring her to New York; it should have been simple. But I have to come all the way across the damn country to look for you, and this is what I find!"

145

The old priest must have sensed that trouble was brewing because he stepped timidly forward as if to diffuse the situation. One look from Lance sent him scurrying back into the chapel. Cain watched him go.

"Look at me when I'm talking to you, demon!" Lance dealt him a stinging slap across the face. "You turned my girlfriend into a whore, and now I'm gonna make you pay for it. I know I should probably just let dad handle it, but I've got something special in mind."

Cain heard an ominous clinking sound. Lance had produced a length of rusty bicycle chain, which he was in the process of wrapping around his knuckles.

"Please, Lance!" Cain retreated several steps, his hands automatically floating up to protect his face. "Just let me explain. It's not what you think."

Lance balled his hand into a fist. Cain flinched as the chain creaked.

"I'd change back to your real shape if I were you." Lance advanced with heavy steps, swinging his fist eagerly. "Those nice thick scales might keep you from losing too much blood."

Cain's eyes dilated with terror. He hunched over in a desperate attempt to wrap his arms around all his vital parts; he was certain that Lance would not hesitate to beat him to death. In his fear he did not notice that someone else had come through the door until that someone grabbed Lance by the shoulders, spun him around, and slammed him against a pew.

Cain's tensed muscles loosened, and he breathed a sigh of relief. The newcomer was nearly a head taller than Lance, and he was muscular. He ought to be able to subdue Lance quickly...if only he would do something more aggressive than stand there looking him calmly in the eye, holding his left shoulder in a firm but gentle grip. Cain knew perfectly well that a peaceful approach was the wrong way to stop one of Lance's tantrums; sure enough, the chain-wrapped fist was already poised to deliver a vicious punch.

The punch never came. Lance's fist froze in midair. A look of confusion crossed his face, giving way almost immediately to horrified panic.

"Don't touch me," he gasped. He was panting as if he had run up a steep flight of stairs on a hot day. "Mind your own business, asshole. No one asked you...asked you...to interfere..."

His voice trailed off. All the color drained from his face. His knees buckled, and he slumped to the cracked stone floor, flailing weakly and making little wordless sounds of distress.

The other man dropped with him, landing on his chest in a predatory crouch. His hand still gripped Lance's shoulder. Lance convulsed several times and was still.

"Lance?" Cain dashed up and poked the limp body with his toe. "Lance, can you hear me? Damn, what did you *do* to him? Will he be all right?"

The stranger let go of Lance's shoulder and looked up. When Cain saw his face, he completely forgot about Lance's predicament, and he could only stare in disbelief with his mouth and eyes wide open.

"Vincent Sweet?"

CHAPTER SEVEN

BAND MATES

THE YOUNG MAN CROUCHING over Lance did look very much like Vincent Sweet as Cain remembered him. He had the same glossy, red-blond hair, green eyes, and slightly upturned nose and the same light sprinkling of freckles along the cheekbones. Yet there was something different about him, something that Cain instinctively sensed and disliked. He emitted an air of hardness. His eyes were empty and cold. He also seemed to have an inner glow, an eerie, faintly electric sheen; maybe it came from the life he had apparently sucked out of Lance.

"Yeah." Vincent Sweet stood up. His voice was a low, ill-humored growl. "But don't you go calling me by that name anymore. I hate my name; it makes me sound like a homo. I go by my stage name now."

"Oh. Sorry." Cain coughed politely, wishing he had brought his guitar. "So you came up with a good stage name?"

"I did." He jabbed Lance with his toe. "It's Vampire Vince."

"How…appropriate." Cain gazed anxiously down at Lance, who did not appear to be breathing. "So…Vampire

148

Vince...tell me, what exactly did you do to Lance? Will he be all right? He is still alive, isn't he?"

"What the hell do you care?" An angry gleam flashed in Vampire Vince's eyes. "He tried to kill you."

Cain didn't like Lance, but Lance was his master's son; he was duty-bound to protect him, or at least, he was duty-bound to try to fix any damage that had been done to him.

"He just tried to beat me up a little. I don't want to see him *die* for it."

"Fuck. His energy tasted awful—all sour and spoiled." Vampire Vince spat contemptuously at Lance. "I go and choke it down to save you, and you thank me by going all soft, whining that I shouldn't kill him. What kind of demon *are* you? Mr. Arkin never warned me you were an ingrate. I can't work with an ingrate."

Cain had no idea what Vampire Vince was talking about, but there were more important things at stake at the moment. "Look, if it were anyone else, I would let you deal with him in any way you pleased. And I really am grateful that you saved me. But this boy happens to be the son of my boss."

"You're a liar. Bruce Arkin doesn't have a son. He's only got a daughter. I've seen pictures on his desk."

"Not Mr. Arkin. My *other* boss."

Vampire Vince's eyes narrowed suspiciously, and Cain began to feel desperate. "It's a long story, but I swear I'm telling the truth. I have another boss; this is his son; and as much as I'd like to kill him or allow him to be killed sometimes, I can't. I'd be in very deep and serious trouble if I did." He could feel the collar pulsing ominously as he spoke.

Vampire Vince did not look entirely convinced, but he shrugged.

"Yeah, he's still alive," he snapped. "Well, fine. I'll let

the little bastard live. His body should re-energize in an hour or two; he won't feel so good when he wakes up, but he'll be fine."

"Thank you. Thank you so much," said Cain fervently. "Now, if you could just stay here and make sure no one moves him while I get my guitar, I'd really appreciate it. It'll hardly take ten minutes and—"

"What do you need your damn guitar for?"

"To make him forget why he came here. If my boss finds out what happened, I'll still get in trouble."

Vampire Vince rolled his eyes. "Christ, why didn't you say so in the first place? I can fix that problem for you right now, and I don't need a magic guitar to do it either."

He dropped down on his knees and pressed his fingers against Lance's skull, in the area behind his left ear. Lance moaned and squirmed weakly. Cain watched in silent confusion as he poked in Lance's hair as if he were looking for lice.

"Now, if you could tell me what I'm looking for…Wait…Never mind; this must be it." Vampire Vince looked up at Cain. A rather nasty smile played on his lips. "Dude, you fucked his girlfriend? No wonder he wanted to kill you."

He drew his hand away, and with it came a spectral blue quiver of neural energy—a memory. Cain stared at it, fascinated. He knew all too well that spells to block memories existed, but he had never known it was possible to completely *remove* them. There was something hypnotic and compelling about that memory shifting and sparking in the air just above Vampire Vince's hand; he wanted to touch it, play with it, slip it into his own mind to see how it felt, even though he knew perfectly well that it belonged to horrible Lance.

But Vampire Vince was already stalking down the aisle, looking for another head in which to deposit the memory.

"Is there anyone else here besides the old hag?" he asked.

The woman in the shawl looked up from her devotions long enough to give him a haughty glare.

"There's a priest in the chapel, I think," said Cain.

"Perfect." He stomped up to the chapel and pounded on the door until the priest stepped cautiously out.

"Father, I've got a sin to confess," said Vampire Vince in a voice dripping with atrocious mock piety. "It ain't technically *my* sin, but I wish it were. It's pretty damn juicy."

He reached out and slapped the memory into the priest's head. The priest's mouth contracted into a shocked little O. He stared at Cain for a moment, confusion mingling with an alien jealousy, and then rage flared in his eyes. He fled into the chapel and slammed the door behind him.

Vampire Vince turned around and walked back toward the door. He was smiling now, but the smile looked like a malicious sneer.

Cain suppressed an earnest desire to turn and run as hard as he could. Ever since he had seen the new Vincent Sweet's face, a quiet nagging sense of foreboding had been growing in him. After what he had just seen, it was quickly intensifying into full-blown dread. The dead-eyed young man advancing on him had the most powerful talent for mind-stroking he had ever seen in a human; it was so powerful, in fact, that he suspected even Mr. Warwick would be impressed. Where had this immense power been on the night the Engineer had taken him? Had the trauma awakened it somehow?

"I love that part." Vampire Vince actually looked happy now. "The look in their eyes always kills me."

"That was pretty impressive," Cain admitted. "You can pull memories out of people's heads, just like that?"

"Yep." Vampire Vince grinned proudly. "I can take 'em out and put 'em back in too. I can also eat people's energy. I don't need to do it—I can live on normal food like everyone else—but the skill does come in handy when some asshole is antagonizing me and won't back off."

"Is that how you escaped from the Engineer?" Cain blurted.

Without warning, Vampire Vince's entire demeanor changed. Rage twisted his face. He hurled himself on Cain, his fingers curled and clawing. Caught by surprise, Cain had no time to take evasive action or fight back. Vampire Vince pinned him down on the floor next to Lance.

"I was *not* taken by the Engineer!" Vampire Vince shook Cain viciously as he shrieked, battering him against the cold stone. "Everyone thinks I was kidnapped for some goddamned reason, but I wasn't. I wasn't! Don't you understand that? Can't you get that through that thick fucking head of yours?"

Cain tried to shout that he was sorry, that he was mistaken and would never ask again, but he was being shaken so hard that he couldn't get the words out. Then, as suddenly as it had begun, the shaking stopped. He was pinned flat to the floor, aching and dazed. Vampire Vince was sitting on his chest, staring into his face.

"I'll tell you what." The rage was gone from Vampire Vince's face now; a cold smile had taken its place. "I'll take that silly rumor off your mind for you, so you won't have to fight the urge to spread it around anymore."

His hands locked around Cain's head like a muzzle. Whatever violation Cain had felt when the nurse took his blood in Mr. Arkin's office, this assault was a thousand times worse. Vampire Vince's fingers were inside his skull, poking through the folds of his gray matter, sizing up his thoughts as if they were items for sale at a supermarket. Cain couldn't move. He couldn't cry out. He could only lie there and watch his tormentor's face blur as tears of pain and fear filled his eyes.

"I could take more memories, you know." Vampire Vince's voice resonated through his insides. "Mr. Arkin told me all about you. Your magic is in your guitar, isn't it? Huh. Some fucking demon you are. My magic is all inside me. I could take every last thought in your head and leave you drooling on the floor with no idea who you are. You wouldn't be able to do a thing about it, would you? But that would be too much work, so I think I'll only take the nice thoughts."

Then—thank goodness—the invading hands withdrew. Cain's mind went blank with relief for a moment. Then he became conscious of Vampire Vince talking to someone in a whining, but still arrogant, tone.

"Oh, come *on*, Sammi," he was saying. "I wasn't going to hurt him—just scare him a little. He deserved it; he insulted me."

"Yeah, right," said a voice Cain didn't recognize. "Get away from him, Sweet, and don't let me catch you fucking with him again. What were you thinking, mind-raping your own guitarist?"

Cain sat up shakily, thinking hard; fortunately, no memories seemed to be missing. A curious sight met his eyes.

Vampire Vince had retreated and was now crouched behind a pew, peering over the top. Another young man stood in the doorway. He was slight and wiry, with a pleasant, cheerful face and spiky dark brown hair that looked as if he had styled it by sticking a fork into an electrical socket. He was pointing a single index finger at Vampire Vince, and Vampire Vince was staring at the finger as if he thought it might suddenly turn into a loaded pistol.

"Apologize to Cain, Vinnie," said Sammi.

"Fuck you, Sammi," muttered Vampire Vince without conviction.

"Vinnie!" Sammi made a swift stabbing motion with his finger. Vampire Vince flinched.

"Sorry, Cain," he said furiously under his breath.

"Project, Sweetums! The folks in the cheap seats can't hear you."

"I'm sorry, Cain."

"That's better." Sammi trotted over to Cain's side and steadied him when he began to wobble on his feet. "Here, take it easy. Sit down in one of these pews for a while. It'll take you a few minutes to recover. Sorry about Vinnie. He's the biggest asshole on the planet, but he really is a great singer. So, you must be Cain Pseudomantis."

Cain nodded, still too shaken to speak.

"Great!" Sammi seized his hand and pumped it enthusiastically. "Mr. Arkin took us to see you play a little while ago. I don't mind telling you that you kicked more ass than any guitarist I've ever seen. By the way, I'm Cipriano Guerrero, but my loyal fans know me as Sammi Amp. I believe Vampire Vince, also known as Vinnie Sweetie McSweetums, has already introduced himself."

Vampire Vince gave Sammi a venomous look. Sammi returned it.

"Anyway," Sammi continued, "Vinnie was impatient to

meet you, so he wandered off to look for you. I suspected he would make trouble like he always does, so I followed him. Good thing I did."

"Impatient to meet me?" This declaration surprised Cain more than anything. "Why?"

"Because we're your band, idiot!" shouted Vampire Vince in a tone of utter exasperation. "Me and Sammi and Izzy. Why the hell else would we ever want to meet you?"

"No insulting your own team, Vinnie," said Sammi. "Come on; let's get you to the house. We'll explain along the way."

"Yeah, let's get out of here." Cain was thoroughly tired of being in the church, and he was aware that Lance was showing signs of regaining consciousness.

They walked up the street together, two humans on either side of one demon. Vampire Vince moved with a steady, menacing lope, like a polar bear stalking a seal. Sammi Amp was full of a strange nervous energy; he trotted and scurried, his arms swinging, his eyes darting here and there and never resting on any one object for more than a few seconds. He smiled broadly the whole way. Vampire Vince didn't smile at all.

Michael Anderson was deeply agitated. Dr. Brown could see all the signs of discomposure etched in his body as she peered at him through the one-way glass: he had made himself smaller, folding his body in on itself so that his chin rested on his drawn-up knees. His right arm was pulled in as close as the handcuffs binding his wrist to the heavy steel chair would allow. Only his left arm hung loosely. She could see the scarred hand clenching and unclenching in a steady rhythm. His eyes were fixed on the floor.

"This can't go on, Deb." Detective Sullivan frowned at Michael, shaking his head. "You need to get through to him faster."

Dr. Brown tried not to give him an indignant glare. She had only had three sessions with Michael, and so far, he hadn't been anywhere near as fascinating as she had predicted he would be. He answered most of her questions with monosyllabic grunts, and he promptly shut down whenever the conversation turned to his mother or the scars on his hand. His fearsome alter ego had not returned, and she was beginning to wonder if the dramatic shift in his character had simply been a one-time outburst brought on by the shock of committing murder.

"I'm going as fast as he'll let me," she said coldly. "He's a hard head to get into."

"Is there any way to speed up the process? Hypnosis... drugs...anything?"

"Ted, I can't do a thing with him until he trusts me," she said. "Look, what's this about? I know you didn't call me away from a session with another patient just to tell me that I'm not working fast enough."

Detective Sullivan was silent for a moment, staring through the smudged glass. He took a deep breath before he spoke.

"I'm sorry, Deb," he said. "It's just that...Michael got into a little altercation with another inmate today."

"*What?*" Dr. Brown looked at him sharply. "I thought you were keeping him separate from the general population."

"There's only so much space in the protected ward, Deb. We had to free up a bed for another first-time offender who needed it more."

"Who did he fight with?" She bent closer to the glass, anxiously studying Michael. He looked too small and fragile to sustain a light slap, let alone survive a full-on brawl in the juvenile detention center where he was being held pending his trial.

"Oh, he wasn't fighting. The other kid kicked him in the face."

Dr. Brown gaped at him in disbelief. Michael's face was completely whole; he didn't even have a single suspicious red mark to suggest he had been struck.

"We had brought the other boy in a couple days ago on drug charges." Detective Sullivan sounded weary. "He's a member of the Calaveras gang. I think his name is Diego. Anyway, no one really knows how it started. From what I heard, the kid just jumped Michael in the exercise yard. According to the inmates and guards, Michael went down like a sack of bricks, but Diego is the one who ended up in the hospital."

"Surely Michael didn't put him there?"

"Well…" Detective Sullivan frowned. "He never actually touched the guy. But in a manner of speaking, he did put him there."

"I don't follow."

"The witnesses say that Michael got up a second later. His face looked like raw hamburger. And he gave Diego this cold, steady look, and said, 'Now that you've spilled my blood, I'll make you drink yours.' Then he walked off like nothing had happened."

Dr. Brown sighed. "You called me in because Michael threatened someone who assaulted him?"

Detective Sullivan cleared his throat impatiently. "I called you in because he appears to have followed through

157

with his threat. Deb, Diego is in the hospital because he has three ruptured ulcers in his stomach. Ulcers that ruptured the minute Michael turned to walk away. Ulcers that didn't show up in any of his medical records."

"I see," said Dr. Brown carefully. She was beginning to wonder whether the whole setup was meant as some sort of elaborate joke. "But Ted, you said Michael was bleeding after he was kicked."

"He was. You can still see the big bloodstain in the exercise yard."

"But now he isn't…"

"No, he isn't. He's already healed, Deb. His face healed up, just like that, right in front of the other inmates. Before he'd taken three steps, his face was clean and smooth, as if he'd never been injured at all." Detective Sullivan shuddered. "All the witnesses were pretty shaken up when we questioned them about it. They say it was just like…"

A faint clanking sound made them both turn their attention to the window.

Michael's feet were on the floor now, and his arms, both of them, hung at his sides. The handcuffs that had bound him to the chair sat on the table in front of him. He stared at them in terrified fascination, as if even he had no idea how they had come off.

"…like magic," Detective Sullivan muttered.

Dr. Brown nodded vacantly, gaping at the handcuffs. Even through the dirty glass she could see that they were not broken or manhandled like the ones from the night of his arrest had been; it looked as if he had simply slipped them off like gloves. He lifted his head. She started when his eyes seemed to meet hers. He visibly relaxed, and his lips curled into a timid smile. His gaze was as unsettling as ever, but this time it was deeper, more focused and—to her great surprise—weirdly calming. Her apprehension vanished, and she found herself fighting the urge to charge into the interrogation room and pepper him with questions.

"I'll see what I can do," she whispered, almost against her will.

Michael's smile broadened, and he leaned forward expectantly. She noticed a definite gleam of relief in his unblinking eyes.

Sammi talked nonstop as they walked along. From his rapid-fire chatter, Cain got the impression that he and Vince and Izzy were not only his new band mates, but they were also his new roommates. Apparently, they had all lost their homes for unspecified reasons.

"So I was only gone for a couple weeks," said Sammi, hopping along the edge of the curb with his arms out for balance. "I'd even paid my rent for the month on time. But when I went back to what used to be my apartment, I found the locks changed, and all my stuff was lying on the curb. I tried going to my asshole landlord about it—he was at the building at the time, harassing some other tenants about their cats or something—but he just made a face at me and rattled off some legal-sounding bullshit that I'm pretty sure he made up on the fly." His smile faded a little, and he gave Vince an apprehensive glance. "Something similar happened to Vince. Didn't it, Vinnie?"

Vince looked up from the crushed tin can he had been kicking along the sidewalk. His face was sullen.

"I wasn't kicked out," he muttered defiantly. "I *moved* out. One more minute in that shithole, and I'd have punched that bitch landlady's stupid face in."

"Sure, Vinnie. Whatever." Sammi sighed, and he seemed disappointed for a moment. Then he brightened again. "Anyway, that's how I lost my apartment."

Cain watched Sammi. He was truly amazed that Sammi could maintain such a cheerful air after discovering that he had been thrown out of his own home.

"But don't feel too bad for me." Sammi chuckled. "I found the greedy bastard's car parked out front and melted his tires. Of course, my revenge was pretty mild compared to what Vinnie probably did to his landlady when he found *his* stuff on the curb."

Vince coughed uncomfortably. "Hey, Cain," he said in a loud voice. "Is it true you eat a human soul for dinner every night?"

Cain's mouth dropped open in horror. He couldn't imagine *touching* something as sacred and intimate as another being's soul, let alone devouring it as if it were a juicy porterhouse.

"Vinnie!" Sammi rounded on Vince as if he were a misbehaving child. "Jesus, what's wrong with you? You can't just walk up to some guy and ask if he eats souls for dinner."

"He's not just some guy; he's a fucking demon." Vince kicked the can in Cain's direction. "Skeeter Judd swears it's true, you know."

Sammi rolled his eyes. "Yeah, well, Skeeter Judd swears it's true that Ty Thorpe lets his brother JoJo's ghost possess his body on Saturday nights so JoJo can keep on enjoying groupies and acid from the afterlife." He gave Vince one last exasperated look and turned back to Cain. "Anyway, we all might have ended up sleeping under a pile of newspapers in an alley somewhere if it weren't for Mr. Arkin. We're pretty damn lucky, you know. Most bands have to do all their own grunt work, and they have to fight to be noticed. But we...Well, coming up with our band name is the hardest job we'll have. Bruce Arkin has pretty much made us his personal project."

"Only because Cain Pseudomantis is his freaky little pet," muttered Vince.

"Oh, stop it, Vinnie." Sammi scurried up the front steps. "If it weren't for Cain, you'd still be singing for peanuts at the Bayou Jewel."

Cain started to follow him, but he stopped in confusion when he heard steady, rhythmic pounding emanating from the townhouse. Did he leave the radio on? It sounded awfully loud.

"It sounds like Izzy unpacked his drum set." Sammi grinned. "I bet we'll get lots of noise complaints soon. Well, let's go in and meet him."

The kitchen area was divided by a jutting countertop, separating the room into two equal parts: the kitchen and the dining room. The dining room area had once had a table, but now the table was gone, and a big, shiny, elaborate drum set stood in its place.

Izzy was behind the drum set, playing so violently and ferociously that his huge, thick, sweat-stained arms were a blur. His tawny hair whipped crazily around his face while his head jerked up and down. He did not seem to notice them standing in the door.

"Izzy!" shouted Sammi over the pounding of the drums. "Cain is here!"

Izzy continued playing. He showed no sign of having heard Sammi.

"Izzy! Cain is here!" Sammi shouted even louder. Izzy

still didn't answer. Sammi darted to Izzy's side and shook him by the shoulder, yelling in his ear, but Izzy shrugged him off and kept playing. Sammi threw up his hands in exasperation and returned to the doorway.

"He gets like this sometimes, you know. He really gets into his drumming, and he totally zones out. Well, he leaves me with no choice. I hate to do this, but what Vinnie does to get his attention is even meaner. Here I go."

Sammi raised his index finger, pointing at Izzy as he had pointed at Vampire Vince in the church. His body tensed. A crackling arc of blue electricity shot from the outstretched finger and hit Izzy squarely in the chest.

Izzy's arms flew out convulsively, and he leapt five feet into the air, shrieking in pain. His form began to waver and compress. By the time he landed, he had changed completely into an enormous, fluffy golden gibbon.

Sammi flashed Cain a conspiratorial grin. "See, that's why we were chosen to be your band mates: 'cause we're like you. We can all do something a little special."

"I'll say." Cain watched the gibbering monkey leap up and down on the drummer's stool, shaking its knobby little black fists indignantly at Sammi. "Now that you have Izzy's attention, aren't you going to change him back?"

"Change him…?" Sammi blinked at Cain, and then he laughed. "Oh, I see. No, man, I just provided the lightning; the transformation was all Izzy. You should see some of the things he turns into when he gets *really* riled."

The gibbon launched itself into the air with a final enraged shriek and caught hold of the chandelier. It swung there for a moment, and then it dropped onto the counter. From there, it turned into a golden retriever and ran toward them, spraying a trail of urine along the countertop. The dog tumbled off the edge of the counter and folded into a hedgehog, which balled up and rolled almost to their feet before it uncurled and expanded back into Izzy.

"Damn it, Sammi! That really hurt!" Izzy's forehead trembled, and his huge hands balled into fists while they pumped up and down for emphasis. "Sheesh! Why can't you just tap me on the shoulder like a normal person?"

Cain noticed that despite Izzy's big, bulky frame and imposing appearance, his voice was reedy and querulous, almost childlike.

"I tried." Sammi shrugged. "You ignored me. Sorry, Izzy, it was the only way to get your attention. And no, I won't try to take the drumsticks away from you. Vince says he ended up with a black eye the one time he tried that."

"Fine." Izzy's features briefly shifted into a facsimile of Sammi's. He copied Sammi's face perfectly. The only differences were the nasty expression on his face and a curious red birthmark resembling the word *dick* on his forehead. "Now, what's so important?"

"I told you three times: our new guitarist is here."

Izzy's demeanor changed immediately. His face lit up, and his hair turned a vivid shade of purple.

"Hey, Vince!" he bellowed gleefully. "Cain is here!"

"I *know*, stupid," snorted Vince. "I *brought* him here."

All the joy drained from Izzy's face. "I'm not stupid, Vince."

"Oh, yes, you are. You're the stupidest person I know."

"You're so mean to me!" Izzy pouted. "How come you're always so mean to me nowadays?"

Vince put on an expression of mock repentance. "You know, Izzy, I *have* been awfully mean to you lately. I'm sorry. I guess the truth of the matter is that I'm just confused."

"Confused?" Izzy frowned. "Why, Vince?"

"Because I'm a little…attracted to you, Izzy." Vince gave him a sultry come-hither look. "I'm hot for you. I really am."

Izzy backed up a step, and he literally turned green. "You…are?"

"Yeah. See, I never told anyone about this…situation…but I was born a girl."

"Oh God!" Sammi threw up his hands in disgust. "Not this bullshit again!"

"Really?" Izzy scratched his head, his discomfort lost in confusion. "But…you're a guy, Vince."

Vince nodded sadly. "I am *now*. See, my parents had me because they needed a big strong son to help them bring in the crops on the farm. But they had a girl instead. That was me."

"But…" Izzy clenched his head in his hands, trying very hard to remember. "I was friends with you then, and I never saw you in girl's clothes."

"My parents always made me wear boy's clothes. But that wasn't enough for them. They needed me to be big and strong like a boy. So one day, they told me they were taking me to the hospital to make sure my heart was healthy." A theatrical waver entered his voice. "I went with them without complaining because I knew that healthy hearts were important. But once I was in that hospital, they did all kinds of horrible shit to me; they gave me lots of shots to make my voice deep and my muscles big. Then they chopped off my tits and sewed a dick on me—just slapped it down there and sewed it on like a button. They didn't even put me to sleep for any of it."

Izzy listened with rapt attention to the whole tale.

"That's horrible, Vince!"

Sammi rolled his eyes. "No it's not, Izzy. Sweet is pulling your leg."

Vince ignored him. "You know the worst part, Izzy?" He reached behind his own head and pulled out a mass of glowing energy. "*These*. These are all my memories of being a girl."

"Ooh." Izzy reached out to touch the memories, but he pulled his hand back at the last second.

"Come on, Izzy. Vince is just shitting you." Sammi groaned in exasperation. "He was never a girl. Those are his memories of all the hot dogs he's ever eaten or something like that."

"You know what?" said Vince with sudden intensity. "If I were to put these memories in someone else's head, I wouldn't remember being a girl. I would think I'd always been a man."

"Yeah!" Izzy clapped his hands with delight. "Then you wouldn't be unhappy anymore."

"Exactly." Vince heaved a wistful sigh. "Oh, if only my best friend, Izzy, would volunteer to take these memories off my hands."

"Uh…me?" Izzy looked significantly less enthusiastic about the idea now.

"If only my bestest buddy, Izzy Unger, would step up and let me pop these awful memories into his tiny little brain! Then it would be Izzy who secretly wants to have babies. Izzy who hates everything he has between his legs and wants to chop it all off with a kitchen knife. Izzy who wakes up every night crying because he can never wear pretty pink dresses and put ribbons in his hair and kiss cute boys…"

Izzy turned into an orange cat and fled the room, squalling in terror.

"Fucking moron." Vince snickered as he popped the memories back into his head. "Got him again—second time today, in fact."

"Yeah, you're hilarious." Sammi shot him a sour glare. "Guess what, Mr. Comedian? You've just won yourself a job cleaning up Izzy's piss."

"What? Hell no!" Vince's lip curled in disgust. "Izzy can clean up his own piss."

"Izzy can't clean up his piss. He's hiding somewhere in God knows what form because you scared the living daylights out of him. Thanks to you, he'll probably piss there too."

"*You* clean it up, then," snarled Vince. "You startled it out of him in the first place."

"I was just trying to get his attention. You were being a dick to him for the fun of it."

"Make the rookie clean it up." Vince jabbed an accusing finger at Cain.

Sammi jabbed his own charged finger at Vince. "Clean up the damn piss, Sweetums. And don't just swipe a paper towel over it; use chemicals. We've gotta eat off that counter."

Subdued by the threat of electrocution, Vince set to work on the counter with violent passion.

"This is so gross!" he muttered as he squirted kitchen cleanser liberally over the whole counter. "Why the fuck can't Izzy learn to control his bodily functions no matter what shape he takes? We should start rubbing his damn nose in it."

"Do they…ah…always act like that?" asked Cain, who

had observed the whole scene in amazed silence.

"Usually." Sammi blew out a weary sigh. "Vince loves to torment Izzy that way. I've already heard too many stupid horror stories like that one to count. For some reason, Izzy gets really scared every single time Vinnie tells one. Maybe with all the shape-shifting he does, he's afraid of losing his identity or something. Say, can I ask you something?"

"Sure."

Sammi glanced at Vince, who was now fully absorbed in his rant against Izzy's animalistic habits and slashing a soggy paper towel over the fouled countertop.

"What did you say to Vinnie in the church to make him attack you?" whispered Sammi.

"Oh." Cain shrugged, embarrassed. "I mentioned that he escaped from the Engineer. I had no idea it would make him so angry."

Sammi nodded knowingly. "Let me guess: Vinnie said he'd never been taken by the Engineer, that he'd just hit his head and wandered around the streets without knowing who he was for a couple weeks, and that he was going to take that vicious lie right out of your brain so you couldn't spread it around."

"That's almost exactly what he said."

"Well, Vinnie was lying to you." Sammi rolled his sleeve up to the elbow and held out his arm for Cain to see. "Look."

His forearm was covered with half a dozen crescent-shaped scars. Cain guessed that the scars were from shallow cuts, and they were placed in a ritualistic, alternating pattern. A livid pink mark, from a deeper cut, scarred Sammi's palm; it looked like an angular symbol that Cain knew he'd seen somewhere before. Unfortunately, he couldn't remember exactly where he'd seen it or what it meant. "Izzy has these scars too, and so does Vince," said Sammi quietly. "We were all taken by the Engineer, but we were lucky. Apparently, the cops found us weeks after we were taken in different abandoned warehouses all over the city. We were naked and trussed up by our ankles like pigs about to be slaughtered."

"Apparently?"

"Yeah, apparently. I don't remember anything and neither does Izzy. We went out to look for Vinnie one night, and that's the absolute last thing we can recall before we woke up in hospital beds. He must have drugged us or something. But Vinnie…"

His voice trailed off. He watched Vince swipe the last bit of mess from the counter and storm past them in a flurry of imaginative maledictions. Once he had gone, Sammi continued.

"We think that Vinnie wasn't drugged. We think that he was awake, and he knew what was being done to him the whole horrible time. Mind you, we don't *know* that he wasn't drugged because Vinnie won't talk about what happened, not to us or to the police."

"And that's why he's so…" Cain could not finish his sentence. He shivered. Ever since he had seen the dead look in Vincent Sweet's eyes, Cain suspected that something truly awful had happened to him, but the incident at the church had made him wary of inquiring about the matter further.

"Yeah. I remind myself of that every time Vinnie pulls some shit so awful I want to kill him. I'd probably turn into a cold-hearted asshole too if I could remember all the cuts and burns and…" Sammi shuddered. "Well, I better not describe all the stuff the doctors found on and in our bodies after they found us; it might give you nightmares."

"And your powers?"

"We found out about them afterward." Sammi laughed. "I accidentally zapped some poor nurse who tried to put an IV in my arm. Izzy was so happy when they told us Vince had been found alive—they were best friends before all this shit happened—that he changed into a gigantic purple rabbit right there in the hospital bed. The transformation scared him pretty bad because he didn't know how he'd done it, and he couldn't figure out how to change back. But then he figured it out and liked it so much that I had to threaten to kick him out of our room if he didn't stop shape-shifting. The room started to feel really crowded when Izzy changed into the larger animals: tigers and horses and dragons and ostriches." His voice became serious. "Vinnie didn't find out about his powers until after we were all released and got together. Thank God. He'd probably have spent the rest of his life locked up in a straightjacket if they'd seen what he can do."

"Sammi!" Izzy shrieked from somewhere upstairs. "Vince has my memories of my first girlfriend!"

"Speaking of Vinnie, I have to go play mom again." Sammi scuttled into the front hallway. "I wish Izzy would stand up for himself, but he can't. He doesn't remember anything the Engineer did to him, so he doesn't understand why Vince acts the way he does, and he just wants things to go back to the way they were before. Vince thinks he's weak and walks all over him. And then Izzy tries harder to be nice to Vince, and *that* makes Vince pick on him more. It drives me fucking crazy. I swear, one of these days I'll…"

His voice trailed off into the distance as he stomped up

the stairs, steeled to confront Vampire Vince for the third time that day.

Cain stared after him, wondering if all rock bands were so eccentric. He had already decided that he liked Sammi and Izzy very much; however, he made a mental note to always have a ready hand on his guitar whenever Vampire Vince was in the room.

CHAPTER EIGHT

FALSE PROPHET

IZZY CLAIMED THE BEDROOM across the hall from Cain's. As if by magic, the room overflowed with magazines and car parts and rumpled clothes a few hours after they moved in. To Cain's consternation, Izzy's possessions began to creep out of the room and encroach on the rest of the house. Cain came downstairs the morning after move-in day and nearly sat on a battered old street sign that had been left on the couch. He picked it up and squinted at it, but the words "WOODCOCK LN" meant nothing to him. Sammi came down from the loft for a snack while Cain was turning it over in his hands.

"Izzy has a lot of weird crap, doesn't he?" said Sammi as he rooted around in the refrigerator. "I helped him haul twenty big boxes full of garbage up the stairs yesterday."

"But what does he *do* with it all?" Cain poked at the cluster of rusty metal canisters that Izzy had piled on the coffee table.

Sammi shrugged. "Dunno. He wouldn't let me throw any of it away, so maybe he's going to, like, make it all into some kind of crazy junk sculpture or something. Then again, I wouldn't be surprised if he's just a packrat. He's a nice guy, but sometimes he gets…confused. I wouldn't worry too—what the fuck?"

He pulled something black and angular out of the refrigerator. When Sammi turned around, Cain saw that the object was an ancient typewriter missing half its keys.

"See?" Sammi dropped the typewriter onto the counter with a grimace, tipped it up, and started scraping something off the bottom of it. "Man, he put it right on top of my sandwich too. Look, Cain, we'd probably be fine just throwing this shit away. I doubt Izzy's gonna notice it's gone."

A big yellow ferret bounded down the stairs. It became Izzy halfway through the kitchen door, and his face brightened at the sight of the typewriter.

"Hey, I've been looking for that," he said. "Thanks, Sammi!"

He swept up the typewriter under one arm and sauntered off. Sammi stared after him.

"Okay, so maybe he *would* notice the bigger things." He sighed and poked sadly at the flattened paper parcel that had been his sandwich. "Oh well, we can live with the clutter for a while. It's just until we all get back on our feet and find new places, right?"

Cain nodded. He considered throwing the old street sign away, but ultimately, he decided against it. Clutter or no clutter, he found it impossible not to like Izzy. He was one of the very few humans Cain had met who showed no sign of disgust at his unconventional eating habits. No one in the Hispanic neighborhood had ever managed to hand Cain a scrap of raw meat without briefly grimacing in disgust; and Mr. Warwick had never allowed him to eat at the dinner table. Izzy could lean casually against the counter and watch

Cain devour an entire pile of dripping red steaks without even wrinkling his nose. Sometimes, Izzy would sit and watch with a glow of fascination in his eyes as Cain plunked at his guitar, and once, Cain caught him trying out a pair of horns in the bathroom mirror. He found this attention unnerving until Sammi explained to him that he already had a modest following in the city.

"You know, man, I think Izzy admires you." Sammi chuckled. "That's a pretty big compliment, considering Izzy's older than you, and he's been playing longer than you have."

"Older?" Cain raised an eyebrow. "Izzy is twenty. I'm two thousand, give or take a few centuries."

Sammi let out a low whistle. "Damn, you've really been around that long? You look like you can't be much older than eighteen in human years."

"Sometimes, I feel like I'm only eighteen," Cain admitted.

Cain began to see other signs of Izzy getting "confused" as Sammi had warned. He would sometimes try to read the newspaper upside down or forget how to tie his shoes. More than once, he took a beer out of the refrigerator and the bottle opener out of the drawer and then stood staring blankly until Cain or Sammi opened the beer for him. He hadn't simply forgotten that he had taken them out, either, but he seemed to no longer remember what purposes the two objects served.

Late one night when Cain came downstairs for a drink, he found Izzy sitting behind his drum set and staring at his hands.

"I don't know," he muttered when Cain asked him what

the matter was. "I don't know what's going on all the time. Sometimes I try to think back and whole big chunks of the day are just...I dunno...blank. It's scary. It never happened *before*."

Cain had no need to ask him what he meant by *before*.

"Go to bed, Izzy." Ordinarily, he would have suggested that Izzy play his drums for a while—he always seemed so completely sure of himself when he was practicing—but the neighbors wouldn't appreciate the noise. "It's two in the morning. A little sleep might help you feel better."

"Yeah, I guess so." Izzy heaved himself up with a sigh of longing. "You know, it's too bad all the bars and clubs are closing up for the night about now. Nothing makes me feel better like talking to pretty girls after a few drinks."

Cain could only shake his head in amazement at his drummer's stamina. Izzy had gone to the clubs for the last three nights in a row, and Cain had gone with him the first night in a burst of eagerness to fit in with his new human friends. He had soon found that the club was a completely different environment when he wasn't separated from the crowd on a raised stage and concentrating on his music. The jostling and smoke and alcohol fumes and relentless noise had battered his nerves and rendered him slightly nauseated; he had lasted half an hour before he came down with a raging headache and had to slink back to the blessed silence and solitude of the house.

I know I'm having a vision of the near past; it's the night I killed my mother. The dark, malignant shadow of the overpass towering over me, and the lifeless body of the young man splayed on the sodden pile of rags and plastic where it was dumped.

"Tell me about your mother, Michael."

Michael flinched at the word *mother*. His upturned left hand clamped shut. He was in the gray room again, and the kind doctor was before him. He saw her watching the little shifts in the muscles of his face with minute attention. Her face betrayed no emotion.

Then, as Michael stared at her, she went transparent.

The interview had been going so well for her, he thought. *She'd got me talking about school, about drawing, and about the way I notice things: the tiny round mole on my classmate's neck, the slight limp in my other classmate's walk, and the way the sunlight pooled in the grass of my front yard. She likes that I remember these things. It impresses her. She sees me shutting down now, and it makes her anxious. She wants to get more questions in before the door closes.*

"You're not ready to talk about her," she said quickly. "That's all right; we can talk about something else for now."

Michael opened his hand and drew it up to his face, staring into the scarred palm.

He was not ready. He would never be ready, probably.

"She did this, you know," he said softly. "My mom."

Dr. Brown stared at him for a moment, too surprised to answer. Michael's mouth opened and closed again, and a little spasm of pain ran through his body.

"She started doing it when I was little." Michael's jaw tensed, but his voice was calm. He felt relieved to finally speak the words. "Mama made me soak it in water till it got soft. Then she'd scrub."

He set the hand palm-up on the table, letting her see the full extent of the injury: a mass of rough scars so thickly clustered and overlaid on his palm that the entire surface was a single, unbroken expanse of sickly white tissue.

"Why would she do this?" she whispered.

It hurts her to see my pain, thought Michael. *She aches for me.*

"The mark," said Michael in the same calm, quiet voice. "There was a mark there she didn't like. Said it was evil. Oh, she'd scrub hard...with soap and water...with steel wool and bleach." He paused, trying to remember what the mark had looked like. He couldn't. "She'd scrub it even after it was gone...and she'd hit me sometimes."

"Why would she hit you, Michael?"

Michael sighed and shrugged. Thinking about his mother was like holding a hot pan: he could only do it for so long.

Michael was transported to the vision again. *The murdered man's name was Jim Kellerman. He was only twenty-two years old. I've never met him, never seen his face before this moment; yet still I hear his voice in my head. It screams in pain. The screams echo through me, searing into the folds of my brain like a brand. Cars shudder and roar along the overpass, their horns howling mournfully in the hazy night, and Jim Kellerman cries for justice.*

Michael wrenched himself back out of the vision. He had to think about how to answer her question. He had to tell the truth, even though it hurt him.

"Because," he continued. "I see into people's heads."

A heavy load felt as if it had been taken from him. He had never told anyone about his curse before. He flexed and straightened his shoulders with a soft sigh of relief.

"What do you mean?" The kind doctor hid her unease very well. If he had not been looking into her mind at that moment, he would never have known that his words disturbed her.

"I've done it since I was little," he said. "I look at people and...know things about them. Or about things that happened to them. Sometimes I sort of...black out...and know things about people I've never even met. That's what I'm told, anyway; I don't remember much about the blackouts. Mom hated it. She tried and tried to make me stop, but I couldn't."

"I see." He saw her unease subsiding as she spoke. "That must have been very frightening. What kind of things did you know about people?"

Michael looked very hard into the kind doctor's mind. He wanted to tell her about his visions, about the night he had killed his mother, about Jim Kellerman. But he could see clearly that it would do him no good. *Delusions*, he could hear her think at him. *Schizophrenic hallucinations*. She would never believe him.

Anyway, he was not the right person to lay Jim Kellerman's soul to rest. He shivered as his mind's eye pulled up the image of the bloody knife in his hand. His own mother's blood. He still felt the wet heat of it on his skin. It had stained him forever, rendering him monstrous.

"I know things that people don't want anyone else knowing," he whispered.

Mr. Arkin's assistant left a small brown box along with Cain's lunch on the kitchen counter the next morning. It contained a yellowed notebook and four cassette tapes wrapped in a piece of paper. The notebook was full of crude drawings and notes written in spidery script. Cain flipped through it, but he was a very slow reader and the handwriting was so erratic that he couldn't make out more than a few words. The tapes were more promising; he had observed Lance playing tapes often, and he knew that he could play the music on them by slipping them into the little slot on the front of the stereo. After some fumbling, he managed to hit the right button.

"Hey, Cain." Izzy poked his head through the door. "That sounds nice. Did you record it?"

Cain shook his head. The tape contained a collection of rough, disjointed guitar solos. Between the solos, he could hear a man talking in the background, but his voice was so fuzzy that Cain couldn't make out what he was saying. None of the music sounded familiar, and he had no idea why Mr. Arkin sent the tapes.

"Oh." Izzy shrugged. "It still sounds nice, though. Hey, is this paper yours? I found it on the counter next to your lunch."

Cain looked up and saw Izzy holding the piece of paper in which the tapes had been wrapped. "Oh, that. It was in the box with the tapes. I guess Mr. Arkin's assistant must have brought it over with the meat this morning," Cain said. He had not actually seen Chelsea drop off the package. She had started dropping off his food very early, probably so she would be less likely to encounter him.

Izzy turned the paper over in his hands and squinted at it. "Huh. Well, it has some writing on it."

"What?" Sammi materialized from somewhere behind Izzy and pushed his way through the door. "Cain got a note from Mr. Arkin? What does it say?"

"Er…" Cain fidgeted and stared nervously at the floor. He was worried that Sammi would hand him the letter and ask him to read it. Mr. Warwick taught him the basics of reading, but had not encouraged him to develop his skills.

Even with the practice provided by helping Steve with his homework, Cain still found the whole concept of English letters difficult and alien. He could read, but whenever he tried he had to concentrate very hard to keep track of which letters represented which sounds and to combine those sounds into proper words.

To his relief, Sammi took the paper out of Izzy's hands and began to read it himself, silently moving his lips along with the words. A frown appeared on his brow. Suddenly, he tore his gaze away from the paper and looked hard at Cain.

"Where are those tapes?" he said.

Cain pointed to the edge of the coffee table where the tapes sat, startled by the intensity in Sammi's voice.

Sammi practically flew across the room. He swept up the tapes, knocking half of Izzy's canister collection to the floor.

"Holy shit!" He held up the tapes reverently. "Holy fucking *shit*! Do you know what these are?"

Cain looked to Izzy for guidance, but Izzy didn't seem to know what was going on any more than he did.

Sammi was almost dancing with excitement. "These are the lost Morningstar demos! Shit, I'm actually *holding them in my hands*. Man, I knew Arkin had some big plans for you, but I didn't know they were this big."

Izzy's eyes went round with amazement. He turned into a large orangutan and gamboled about the room, upsetting both armchairs and knocking the rest of his canisters off the coffee table.

"Morningstar demos?" Cain flattened himself against the wall to avoid a flying canister. "What are the Morningstar demos?"

"Hmm?" Sammi was already kneeling on the floor next

to the stereo, gazing up at the speakers as if they were holy relics. "Oh, they're the demos for the last album Lion of Judah was supposed to put out. They say Eddie Morningstar locked himself in the studio for three days straight to record this stuff, and he only left because Ty and JoJo dragged him out so he wouldn't starve. Everyone thought they lost these tapes."

"He had to lock himself in the studio to record?" asked Cain apprehensively.

"Nah," Sammi replied. "Eddie wasn't right in the head just before he died; he was talking to himself, obsessing over stuff, doing those kinds of things. I think he was on drugs."

Izzy found Mr. Arkin's letter. He changed back to human form and sat cross-legged on the floor, scratching his head as he read it.

"Mr. Arkin sent JoJo's notes too," he said. "We're supposed to make the demos into real songs."

"Real songs?" said Cain. "They sound pretty good to me."

Sammi snatched up the letter. "He says they're not finished. He wants us to piece together these guitar bits and add new parts for drums and bass, and—oh my god!" A shiver of joy ran through him as the music faded out and someone began talking in the background again. "Do you hear that? That's *his* voice, man! That's Eddie fucking Morningstar's voice!"

"This is awesome!" Izzy grinned. "Wait till Vince sees this stuff—he'll be so happy. Maybe he'll stop sulking in the loft and come talk to us."

It took Sammi an hour to persuade Vince to come downstairs and see what Mr. Arkin had sent them. He finally had to hijack Vince by finger-point. Vince slunk into the kitchen, flipped through the notebook, poked half-heartedly at the tapes, and read the letter. The sour expression on his face deepened into a scowl when he finished.

"Well, this is just great," he grumbled. "Arkin doesn't even trust us to write our own songs. He must get some kind of tax break or something for supporting our sorry asses because we'll never make it as a real band this way."

Assembling the fragmentary solos into a song with several parts was not as difficult as Cain thought it would be. Bits and pieces of the music wormed their way into his mind while he listened to the tapes; they floated there, coalescing into patterns as he reproduced them on his guitar. Sammi and Izzy were content to follow his lead.

Vince was not as easy to work with. He rarely passed up an opportunity to torment Izzy or Cain or to throw JoJo's notebook down and scream that he'd given up on extracting coherent lyrics from "that damn dead junkie's scribbles." By the time Sammi put a stop to his tantrum, everyone had gotten off track. Cain began to find the constant squabbles more and more stressful, and he was glad when Michelle dropped in for a visit one afternoon after they had all adjourned to the porch to supervise Vince's smoke break.

"Hey, devil-boy," she called up to Cain. "I heard a rumor on the street that you've been busy getting your new band together." She grinned up at the three young men staring down at her from the porch. "Is that true, guys? I assume you're Cain's band mates."

"We are." Sammi blinked. "Who are you?"

Cain spoke up. "This is Michelle. She and I have kind of been..." What was the term again? "...*seeing* each other since the night I played my first show."

Vince made a throaty sound of disgust as he crushed out

his cigarette. Cain wondered why he looked so irked and repulsed. Perhaps, Vince was jealous that a beautiful girl had come to see Cain and not him. Or perhaps, he thought it was disgusting that a human and a demon were seeing each other. Cain decided to ignore him.

"She's pretty, Cain." A dreamy grin broke over Izzy's face.

"She's all right," said Vince rudely. "But I like blondes better. The brunettes always want it way too much, and then they're not very good once you give it to them."

"I'm sorry you feel that way, but maybe it's just as well," said Michelle without batting an eye. "I don't like redheads much. They're always so slow to rise and so disappointingly short."

Vince went purple with rage. Only one thing seemed to be holding him back from pouncing: the sight of Sammi's finger trained on his abdomen.

"I bet your energy tastes like peaches and honey, you nasty little slut," he muttered.

Izzy started laughing. He must have finally got Michelle's joke. "She's funny too. She got you good, Vince."

"Shut up, Izzy," snapped Vince. "It's not funny, you big, stupid moron!"

"Sorry about Vinnie," Sammi called down to Michelle. "He's kind of an asshole. We aren't all like that; really, we—"

"What the...?" Michelle interrupted him. She was staring at Izzy. Rather, she was staring at the place where Izzy had once been, which was now occupied by a copy of Vince. The fake Vince was identical to the original Vince in every way except for the exaggerated, goblin-like grimace on his face.

"Izzy!" hissed Sammi in his ear. "What did Mr. Arkin say about showing off our powers in public?"

"Oops." Izzy took his own hulking form again. "Sorry, Sammi. Maybe she didn't see."

Cain noted the plain amazement on Michelle's face.

Sammi apparently decided not to dignify Izzy's statement with a direct response. "Look, no one is supposed to know what we can do until our first show." Sammi motioned Michelle inside. "But Izzy has already given himself away, and if you're Cain's girlfriend I'm sure you already know what *he* can do. We might as well tell you all about it. Just keep in mind it's a secret for a while."

"Powers?" Michelle whispered to Cain as they followed Sammi into the house. "Are your band mates demons too?"

"As far as I know, they're humans with special abilities," Cain whispered back. "Tell you all about it inside."

Vince went stubbornly quiet when they settled down in the living room, leaving Sammi and Cain to tell the story of how the band members discovered their powers. Izzy quietly changed into a cat and hopped into Michelle's lap as soon as all her attention was absorbed in the tale. He lolled there as she stroked him, purring a loud, percussive purr, a look of smug contentment in his half-closed eyes. Cain began to feel jealous.

"That's strange." Michelle stopped stroking Izzy. "The Engineer took you, and then you all found out that you had powers after you were rescued?"

"No," snapped Vince. "Sammi and Izzy were taken. I fell down some stairs and hit my head. I couldn't remember who I was for weeks."

"Whatever you say, Sweetums," said Sammi indulgently. Vince huffed and stomped out of the room.

"Vinnie was taken, actually," Sammi told Michelle as soon as Vince had left. "He has the same marks on his arms and hands as we do. He wants to forget about the whole thing and pretend it never happened. It's too bad; he's probably the only person in the city who can identify the Engineer."

"But don't you think it's weird?" Michelle ignored Izzy's attempt to paw her into paying attention to him again. "Some maniac kidnaps you to do God knows what to you, and you suddenly have powers after you get rescued? Do you think he somehow *gave* them to you, as some kind of experiment or something?"

"I'd considered that," said Sammi.

"I'd wondered about it too." Izzy frowned. "It doesn't seem like a good idea, though. I mean, *I* wouldn't torture people to give them superpowers. What if one of them remembered what I'd done and came after me?"

Michelle made a face. "Well, I'm not sure crazy serial killers usually make practical considerations like that. I bet Cain could shed some light on the subject, though. He knows a thing or two about magic."

Sammi and Izzy looked to Cain. "Izzy's right, sort of," said Cain slowly. "Magic isn't something you can just *give* to someone—you have to be born with the Gift. You can't even really change someone's powers or make them stronger; what you're born with is what you get." Mr. Warwick had been trying to find a way to improve Lance's meager talents for years, and he was never able to bolster them.

"But what about those stories about people who want to

become witches, and they sell their souls to…" Sammi trailed off. "No offense, Cain."

"I was wondering when someone was going to ask me about that." Cain sighed. "I know humans tell each other stories about devils all the time, but…well, to be honest, I can't imagine where they came up with that idea. *I* wouldn't go around giving magic to humans, not even if I could; I'd be too afraid they'd turn out like—" The collar squeezed his neck in warning, and he quickly changed what was going to say. "Er…that they'd do bad things with it."

"I'm pretty sure I wasn't born with magic." Izzy cocked his head curiously. "Why couldn't I use it before?"

"Maybe you didn't know you had it," said Cain. "Maybe the Engineer *did* give it to you, sort of, by scaring it out of you. It happens sometimes; my friend Steve used his magic for the first time when his brother locked him in the attic and told him the rats were going to eat him."

"*Weird.*" Michelle frowned. "You'd think more torture survivors would get powers, then."

"Yeah. It is weird." Sammi generated a large spark on the tip of his finger and watched thoughtfully as it drifted to the floor.

Five minutes before the next practice session, Vince started a vicious argument with Sammi over what to call the band. He backed down when Sammi lost his temper and threatened to give him something painful to think about if he didn't shut up. Then, when Izzy missed a beat halfway through the first song, Vince pelted him with a barrage of particularly vile insults and threatened to replace his memories of his mother with memories of the warthogs at the San Diego Zoo. Izzy ran up to his room and slammed the door behind him before Sammi could come to his rescue.

"Great. Now look what you've done." Sammi set his bass down with a sigh of exasperation. "Damn it, you *are* going to apologize when I've got him calmed down, Vinnie, and you're going to mean it too."

With Sammi gone, Vince turned his bad temper on Cain. He paced menacingly through the living room while Cain ran through some fingering exercises and tried to ignore him.

"So, Fido," said Vince. "What do you think that Michelle chick sees in you?"

Cain gritted his teeth and said nothing. He had scrupulously avoided drawing anyone's attention to the fact that he wore a dog collar, and Izzy and Sammi seemed to think it was nothing more than a fashion statement, but some instinctual gift for nastiness had allowed Vince to sense Cain's shame. He never passed up an opportunity to remind Cain of its presence, especially when Sammi wasn't around to hold him back.

"Come on, don't look so offended, Fido." Vince faked a yawn and stretched so that his hand passed within a few inches of Cain's head. "I want to learn your secret. I really do. How does an ugly asshole like you end up with such a hot little girlfriend?"

"I don't know." Cain gripped the neck of his guitar furiously, wishing he could muster the strength to use it. Ever since Vince had attempted to steal Cain's memories in the church, Cain had been itching to teach Vince a lesson, but he found he couldn't do it once his guitar was within reach again. He could also blame that weakness on the collar. Ten years in the service of Mr. Warwick and Lance had forced him into the habit of taking any abuse humans gave him without complaint or retaliation. He knew from experience that retaliation usually led to more pain and humiliation. "Maybe she finds me attractive."

Vince snorted with laughter. "Sorry, sorry," he gasped. "Yeah, maybe she does find you"—another snort escaped him—"attractive. Weirder things have happened. Maybe she's got some kind of sicko tail fetish or something. Or maybe she just needs glasses."

Cain ground his teeth, wishing Sammi would come back downstairs.

"Or maybe…" Vince gave Cain a sly look. "*Maybe* she has no choice but to find you attractive. Maybe you put a spell on her with that magic guitar of yours. Oh, don't worry. I don't blame you. A guy's gotta get pussy any way he can, right? I mean, there's no way you'd ever attract a hot little number like Michelle on your own *merits*." He gave Cain a deliberate and contemptuous looking over while he pronounced the last word.

Cain couldn't stand it anymore. "Look, Vince, I would love to chat right now, but I really should practice. If you wouldn't mind stepping out…"

Vince smirked.

"That's Mr. Vampire Vince, *sir*, to you," he said quietly. "Yes, I would mind stepping out. And you can't make me. Know why? Because I'm human."

Before Cain could move, Vince lunged at him and seized his head in his hands.

"I was pretty scared that day I went looking for you in the church." Vince's fingers curled and pressed; Cain could feel them rubbing against the edges of his awareness, threatening to invade his mind. "Mr. Arkin swore up and down that you were a real demon with real powers, and I didn't know what to expect—hellfire and glowing red eyes, I guess. I expected screams to greet you whenever you walked into a room. Then I get to the church, and I find the same homeless kid who used to play for pocket change outside the Bayou Jewel. I had thought the name was a coincidence!"

Vince's fingers pressed in a fraction further, just piercing the thin barrier between his consciousness and Cain's. "I didn't go poking around in your brain that day to be a dick, you know. I wanted to size you up, to find out what your weaknesses were. I'm glad I did. I learned something about the way the world works, and I think it's gonna be really useful to me."

He pushed savagely all the way into Cain's mind, not to gain information this time but to hurt and terrorize him. Cain let out a strangled scream. Vince bent over him and stared into his face.

"Demons have to serve humans, don't they?" He grinned repulsively while Cain made a weak attempt to free himself. "You've got magic more powerful than anything any human has, but you can't use it unless one of us tells you to use it. I know how the collar hurts you whenever you don't do as you're told. That's pretty fucking pathetic, but you know what? I like it. Let's test it out, shall we? As a member of the human race, I command you to go upstairs and turn Sammi into a—"

"Turn me into a what, Vinnie?"

Vince's hands withdrew, and Cain could move again.

"Mind your own damn business, Sammi," snapped Vince. "I wasn't telling Cain to actually *do* it. I was just asking if he *could* do it."

Sammi extended both index fingers without a word and

blasted two lightning bolts at Vince.

"Take one for beating up on Cain and plotting against me," he said while Vince crumpled to his knees. "And take another one for being a dirty liar and not even being good at it. For the last time, leave Cain the hell alone. Cain, man, why don't you stand up to him? That's the only way to keep him off your back."

"He can't stand up to me." Vince somehow managed to sneer through his pain. "He's nothing but a *slave*."

Suddenly, something snapped in Cain. He snatched up his guitar and directed a single cutting note at Vince, who immediately toppled again.

"What the hell?" Vince jabbed a finger into his thigh. "What did you do to me? I can't feel my legs!"

"It's a spell. I'll take it off in a minute." Cain stood over Vince, his arms crossed. "But there's something I want to tell you first. You're half right about the collar—it is a slave collar, and it does hurt me when I don't follow orders. But if you had been paying attention, you would know I don't have to obey *every* human who starts telling me what to do. I only have to obey the human who actually put the collar on me. I don't think that was you, Vinnie."

"Fine. It wasn't." Vince rubbed his legs. "I'm sorry, okay? Now give me my legs back, you big fucking circus freak!" He flinched as Sammi wagged a finger at him. "I mean, please."

"All right." Cain played a lower, gentler note. Vince relaxed and started to shift his legs. "But there is one other thing you should know. My human master forbade me from using some kinds of magic, but anything else is fair game." He ran his hand up the guitar neck, tapping rather than plucking the strings to produce an odd plunking sound.

"Do you know what? My master never said I couldn't teach Vincent Sweet of Los Angeles, California a lesson he would never forget."

"Oh, *fuck!*" Vince scrambled clumsily to his feet, all his swaggering bravado gone. "Get out of the way, Sammi!"

"It's no good running, you know." Cain increased the speed of his tapping. "I don't need to be touching you to make this spell work. I don't even need to be in the same room. You could run all the way across the city, and it wouldn't do you any good."

Vince made it halfway to the door before the plunking became a single concentrated note that hit him directly in the stomach. He doubled over with a shocked grunt and fell heavily to his knees. He sat where he had fallen for a moment, hunched and trembling; then he retched and vomited a handful of marbles onto the carpet.

Sammi snickered. Vince glared up at him and opened his mouth (probably to say something nasty), but three more marbles came up and choked off his voice.

"Not bad for a pathetic slave, huh?" Cain poked Vince with his toe. "You're lucky you caught me in a nice mood. The original spell makes the victim vomit pins, but I changed it up a bit."

Vince coughed and spewed more marbles.

"Next time, you won't get off so easy." Cain tapped the guitar neck, narrowing his eyes. "You're a bully. I've lived with bullies for the last ten years, and I've already taken all the bullying I can stand. If you ever try to torture me again—or if I catch you torturing Izzy—I swear I'll put a curse on you so nasty that you'll wish you'd never been born. Do we understand each other?"

"Yurgg..." Vince convulsed and spat out a clutch of shiny steelies. "Yes."

"Good." Cain stepped around him dismissively. "I'd get a big bowl to hold in your lap if I were you. You'll bring up a lot more marbles before the spell wears off in twenty-four hours."

"A whole...urp...day?" Four smoky little glass orbs trickled from Vince's lips as his mouth fell open in disbelief.

"That's right." Cain stalked out of the room, leaving Vince to regurgitate dozens of blue-and-green marbles onto the carpet.

"That was pretty awesome." Sammi followed him. "I was afraid you'd never stand up to Vince. For a demon, you're awfully polite and gentle."

"Well, this time he went too far." Cain scratched at his collar. "I hate being reminded of this thing. It's so humiliating."

"I don't blame you. You know, when you first came here, I wondered why you never took that collar off and why you always got so antsy when anyone looked at it." He frowned. "It wasn't Mr. Arkin who...?"

"No, no. Of course not." Cain shook his head. "Mr. Arkin is one of the best humans I've ever met. I'm sure he would never dream of enslaving a demon, even if he could. He's my boss, but he's not my master."

"Who is your master, then?"

"You wouldn't know him. He lives in New York and does behind-the-scenes dirty work for the government and some big corporations. He calls himself a consultant, but he's really nothing more than a..." What did Mrs. Babbitt call him? "A glorified assassin."

The collar bit down, but this time, Cain didn't mind the pain. He had agreed with Mrs. Babbitt's assessment for a long time, and it felt so deliciously rebellious and daring to actually express his thoughts about Mr. Warwick out loud for once.

Michelle dropped by again after dinner that night, mercifully interrupting the beginnings of another, nastier argument between Sammi and Vince over the name of the band. They had been seconds away from coming to blows when Izzy burst into the living room to announce that Cain's pretty girlfriend had returned.

"What's with all the marbles?" Michelle raised an eyebrow while Izzy became a ferret and crawled up onto the coffee table to frolic in a full-to-the-brim ornamental glass bowl.

Vince spewed two dozen cat's-eyes into one of Izzy's larger canisters, which he was holding on his lap.

"Vinnie got into a little wizard's duel with Cain this afternoon." Sammi smirked. "I think you can guess who won."

"Brilliant, Cain," said Michelle. "I should take you to school with me to deal with the stuck-up cheerleaders."

"I thought your dad was supposed to come back today. Has he decided to stay in Texas a little longer?" Cain asked hopefully.

"No. He's back, but he had to go out and give some speech or something tonight." Michelle's voice became serious. "I sneaked out because I wanted to make sure you knew."

"Knew what?"

"It's the Engineer." She drew in a deep, shaky breath.

"He took two more young men last night. I heard some guys talking about it at school."

A thick silence fell over the room.

"Who?" asked Sammi.

Michelle shook her head. "I don't know. I overheard the conversation at the end of the day, and I had to go right home from my last class so Daddy wouldn't be suspicious. I couldn't really stop and listen. I watched the news and read the papers afterwards, but they barely even mentioned it. The only thing the news covers nowadays is that stupid kindergarten case. All I know is that one guy was a guitarist and one was a bassist, and they both played for a band called Mad Chemistry."

"Maybe they'll mention it tonight." Sammi jumped up and fumbled with the controls on the television.

"I doubt it," said Michelle cynically. "I never see more than twenty words about it at a time in the newspapers."

"They *have* to." Tiny white sparks jumped and played about Sammi's fingernails as he searched for a news program. "He's taken ten people including us, for God's sake. No young musician is going to be safe in this city until he's behind bars."

Consequently, Michelle was right. A few programs made oblique references to "possible cult activity" in Los Angeles, and a local entertainment news channel briefly warned young male rock musicians not to walk alone at night, but the Engineer was not mentioned once.

"What the fuck?" Sammi fell back in despair as the last news program flashed over the screen. "Since when is a cult that the police aren't sure even exists more newsworthy than a real serial killer?"

Sammi jabbed his finger at the TV and zapped out an

angry blue jolt of electricity. The machine rocked on its perch and flipped spastically through several channels before coming to rest on something that seemed to be a Christian talk show.

"For those of you just joining us, we're talking about the role of so-called heavy metal music in modern American Satanic cult activity," the prim, elderly hostess was saying in a dull voice. "Our guest tonight is the Reverend Nathaniel Breen…"

Vince laughed, spraying a volley of yellow marbles across the room. "Hey, turn it up. My favorite comedian is on."

"Oh, Christ!" Michelle threw up her arms in exasperation. "Why does he *do* this to me? It's so embarrassing. Other girls think their daddies are embarrassing, but they don't know what embarrassment means. *Their* daddies aren't going on national TV and babbling away about how there's a huge Satanic conspiracy against the country's traditional values, and the rock stars are somehow leading it—"

"Wait a minute!" Sammi stared at her. "Breen is your—"

"Shh!" said Cain.

"Yes, he's my dad, but I try not to make it known." Michelle grimaced. "I get some strange looks from people when they find out about him."

Sammi turned to Cain. "Hey, man, did you know your girlfriend was Breen's daughter?"

"Yes, yes I did." Cain waved him to silence. "I want to watch this."

"…but that's where they're wrong, Diane," the Reverend Breen said in his deep, resounding voice. "All my fellow crusaders who theorize that this devil music is nothing more than a gateway tool to draw young people into the cult are gravely mistaken. This music is much more dangerous than any mere gateway tool. These twisted, degenerate heavy metal anthems are the hymns sacred to Satan himself, and the men who write and perform them are his highest priests. All the human forces of evil in this country answer to them and to them alone."

Izzy leapt out of the bowl of marbles in dismay, and Vince guffawed, spraying him with more hard glass projectiles. "Damn, it's hysterical! Where does he come up with these ideas?" said Vince.

"There are those who dismiss my theories as mere superstition," the minister continued. "To them, I offer the example of Cain Pseudomantis."

The hostess asked a question, but Cain didn't register it. Three black marbles dropped from Vince's mouth as he stopped laughing. Sammi leaned forward. Michelle groaned and slapped a hand to her forehead.

Izzy materialized beside Cain in his original shape. "Someone said your name on TV, Cain," he said with unusual gravity.

"Cain Pseudomantis is a man—an ordinary man, just like myself," the minister was saying. "An ordinary man with a gift for music. Now, a good man would use such a talent to glorify the God who gave it to him. But he does not. Instead, he plays at being a demon—and not simply by wearing false horns and a tail as he performs either. Everyone I have spoken to who has seen Cain Pseudomantis perform has told me that he does spectacular tricks to create the illusion that he has command of real demonic magic. Even his name is infused with evil: Cain, for the first murderer, and Pseudomantis, which translates from Greek as *false prophet*. Our children are listening to this filth on the radio and going to see this Satanist in concert halls."

"Is it possible, Reverend Breen," the hostess asked in her starchy voice, "that his posturing isn't sincere? Are his antics simply those of an up-and-coming young musician wanting to set himself apart from all the others?"

"I had considered that possibility," the minister admitted. "But then a friend of mine in the police department gave me a copy of something from the evidence locker."

An enlarged image of a photocopied sheet of notebook paper appeared across the screen. Cain stared at it.

The black pencil drawing was of a crudely rendered man with an electric guitar—no, not a man, a demon. The figure had curved horns and a slender, whip-like tail that curled around his muscular legs. Perhaps it was Cain's overwrought imagination, but that thick, teased mane of black hair did look very much like his own, and the figure's features bore a vague but unmistakable resemblance to his. A dark, indistinct press of slavish fans crowded around the demon rock star's feet. He was pointing the neck of his swallow-tailed guitar down at a girl in the crowd like a sword or a sorcerer's wand. The long-haired girl seemed to be rising, as if she were drawn helplessly out of the crowd by the sheer force of his charisma.

"This sketch was found in the home of Michael Anderson!" the Reverend Breen boomed. "Michael Anderson, the self-avowed devil-worshipper who sacrificed his own mother in a black magic ritual. It was in one of his school notebooks, and he admitted to drawing it. This is Michael Anderson's god—the dark, lecherous, corrupting god of heavy metal music—the irresistible false prophet known as Cain Pseudomantis!"

Izzy and Sammi fell to the floor laughing. Vince gagged as he snorted marbles through his nose. They all agreed it was the most ridiculous thing they had heard in a long time, but Cain had a slightly different reaction. The minister's words gave him a deep sense of foreboding. He was so nervous and upset that Michelle had to quietly lead him upstairs to calm him down.

CHAPTER NINE

ALBUM

CAIN KNEW EXACTLY WHAT time Sammi got up the next morning. He heard thumping and muffled grunts of pain from the loft—probably Sammi slipping on the marbles that Vince had thrown up in his sleep. He glanced up at the clock, thinking that eight-thirty was a bit early for Sammi to be up. Cain had grown accustomed to waking up at seven or eight, but it was not unusual for his band mates to stay in bed until noon.

Sammi trotted into the kitchen, nursing his right elbow, which seemed to be bruised. He looked relieved to find Cain at the counter.

"Morning, Cain." Sammi positioned himself across the counter. Cain noticed that he was holding his head at an odd angle, seemingly trying to keep eye contact without looking at the generous spoonful of raw hamburger in Cain's hand. "Where's Michelle?"

"She sneaked home last night." Cain ate his bite of hamburger and put down his spoon. "She had to get there before her dad came back and realized she was gone."

"Oh. Right." Sammi nodded, and then cleared his throat.

"So...um...we had a little talk last night after you went upstairs."

"About what?"

"About what to call the band. Izzy got the idea from watching that dumb talk show; he thinks we should name the band after you."

Cain picked up his spoon and stared at it. He felt the muscles around his jaw tighten, and his tail begin to twitch.

"Izzy thinks we should call ourselves Pseudomantis," Sammi continued. "I think it's a good idea. You're really the reason this band exists at all, and you've gotta admit it's pretty damn distinctive. Even Vince likes it—at least he didn't bitch too much about it. We just thought we should run it by you first since it's your name and all...What do you think?"

"Fine," muttered Cain. "I'm glad that's settled," he added in a bleak tone.

"Cain, look." Sammi leaned over the counter, concerned. "You're not the only rocker Breen has singled out. He's gone after every musician who's ever worn leather and spandex on stage in this city, even the bubblegum acts. You can't let him get to you, man. Don't think of it as an insult or a threat; think of it as free publicity."

Cain mashed the remaining hamburger in his bowl with his spoon, frowning glumly. "But not every musician who's ever worn leather and spandex on stage in this city is seeing Breen's daughter. I am."

Sammi shifted awkwardly. "Well, that complicates things, doesn't it? But even if he finds out about you and Michelle, what can he do about—"

"But that's not what I'm worried about." Cain swept the bowl aside. "I'm worried about that drawing, the one that

Michael Anderson person made of *me*. Is that how all humans see me, Sammi?"

"Oh, that?" Sammi blinked. "I actually thought it was awesome."

Cain shook his head. "I looked like I was about to attack a human woman for no reason, and I looked like I was *enjoying* it. I've never killed anything bigger than a raccoon, and that kill was only for food. But people still keep treating me like some kind of monster that kills things for no reason, and I don't like it."

Sammi seemed taken aback. "Cain, I don't think you're a monster. I doubt anyone who's ever met you thinks you're a monster. Even Vince doesn't—never mind all the crap he says about you. Trust me, nobody out there actually thinks you're out to hurt them. It's all just a gimmick to sell records, and it's a pretty good one too."

Cain made a noncommittal noise. He suspected that his "gimmick" was an effective attention-grabber because it touched on the real fear and distrust harbored by too many people.

"Oh, and you know what else?" Sammi tried again. "That drawing wasn't of you, no matter how much Breen wanted it to be. It couldn't have been."

"No?" said Cain doubtfully.

"No, man. That Michael Anderson kid drew the thing long before you had your big break." He frowned. "He must've because I think he killed his mom before you even started playing outside the Bayou Jewel. Yeah, I remember because Breen tried to make a secret Satanist plot out of that case too. I mean, this poor kid had no friends and had a crazy mom who beat him, and Breen and his posse turn him into a Satanist because he was a loner who drew weird doodles in his notebook. Anyway, he couldn't have drawn you because he didn't know you existed."

"But it looked just like—"

"Coincidence, man. He probably drew it because he thought a demon rock star would be cool. The drawing falls into Breen's hands somehow, and by then there's an *actual* demon rock star for him to pick on...you know, it didn't even look much like you," he added charitably.

"Maybe." Cain nodded, feeling somewhat reassured—of course the drawing didn't really depict him. Michael Anderson had to have made it long before he obtained his guitar, and Breen was deluding himself if he thought a doodle from Michael's school notebook had anything to do with Cain.

Yet one thing still bothered him. No matter what Sammi said, the demon rock star in the drawing really did look remarkably like him, down to his hairstyle and the curl of his tail. Cain had been struck by the resemblance right away, and he couldn't help but wonder how many of Breen's followers—and his own fans—felt the same way.

A boy—tall, lean, and rag-clad—sifting his hands eagerly through a big green dumpster. He brings out a glistening yellow bone. His horns become visible as he sits carefully down on the dented rim of the dumpster, the bone already in his mouth. His hair is thick and matted like a mane. His blue eyes are as deep and inscrutable as the depths of the ocean.

Michael sat bolt upright on his cot.

The Dark Lion.

This was Michael's name for the boy, for the creature he had seen in vision after vision through a series of recurring childhood nightmares. He didn't know where the name came from. One day, he had simply thought the words, and the words had stuck with the image. He also had no idea who the feral-looking horned boy was or if he was even a real person. Yet Michael felt as if he ought to know him. Sometimes he felt, disconcertingly, as if there was a part of him that did know the boy, and the memory was buried far down in a corner of his brain that remained stubbornly inaccessible—except during the blackouts. And he swore he would never have another one of those as long as he lived.

"Daddy?" Michelle shook her father gently by the shoulder. "Did you hear me? I have to get this form signed for school."

The Reverend Breen looked up from his toast, his eyes distant.

"Hmm?" he said. "What form is this?"

"It's for Career Day, Daddy," she repeated. "The school is going to have us job shadow someone."

"I'm not sure I like the sound of that."

"Don't worry, Daddy." Michelle sighed. "They've assigned me to follow a secretary."

The minister took the permission slip from her and held it gingerly between his thumb and forefinger as if it were poisonous. He squinted at it for a moment and then handed it back to her.

"I don't know if I want to sign this," he said.

"This project *is* going to be graded, Daddy. I can't just skip it."

"I don't like encouraging this sort of thing; young women ought to be finding husbands and settling down."

"I see." Sometimes Michelle wondered if this silly

202

outdated notion of her father's should offend her. She was a little irked that he thought even the most menial jobs were too much for his daughter to handle, but many of his other antiquated views bothered her far more. Still, the point was worth arguing. "Should I be more like your friend Senator Babbitt's wife, then? I hear she's a good old-fashioned stay-at-home mom who runs her very own foundation."

The minister's head snapped up indignantly.

"That's enough, Michelle," he said in a sharp voice. "My decision is final."

"Daddy?" Michelle was taken aback; usually, she and her father went back and forth for at least five rounds before he pronounced the discussion over. "Are you all right?"

Breen shook himself and stared up at her without saying anything for a moment.

"Sorry, sweetheart," he said. "I didn't mean to be harsh; I've just had a lot on my mind lately."

"Like what, Daddy?"

"Nothing you need to worry about." The minister picked up his coffee cup with a frown. "Just some work things; you'd find it boring."

"Daddy." Michelle sat down beside him. "I'd be happy to listen if you need someone to talk to even if the subject is boring."

The minister turned the cup in his hands as if he were conflicted. Michelle had almost given up on waiting for him to speak when he sat back and heaved a deep sigh.

"Oh, my dear," he said sadly. "Sometimes, I feel as if the world is falling apart around me, and I'm the only one who cares."

"Daddy?"

"Things were better when I was young." He drummed

his fingers on the table, speaking more to himself than to Michelle. "The world was...well...*safer*. Deviants and criminals were kept in their places. Then *he* came along and made a mess of things."

"Who?"

The minister started. A guilty expression flickered across his face, and Michelle got the impression that he had revealed more than he intended. "You were too young to know him," he said stiffly, "but when you were small, there was a rock star who called himself Eddie Morningstar."

"I've heard people mention him," admitted Michelle. She also had a small hidden collection of flyers and torn-out magazine pages with his picture on them, which had inspired fantasies that would probably make her father faint from horror. "Was he very famous?"

"Entirely *too* famous," said her father. "He would come into a town, and suddenly, all the young men there were growing their hair long and popping pills."

"*Just* because of him, Daddy?" said Michelle incredulously. She was a bit surprised by her father's conviction; if he was going to choose a member of Lion of Judah to blame for all the ills of modern society, she would have guessed that he would settle on JoJo Thorpe, who had done more drugs and seduced more women than any rock star during that time period.

"When he died, I thought that was the end of his bad influence." The minister was talking to himself again; his fists clenched and his eyes became distant and angry. "But today I still hear young people playing his music and see them copying his style. Even that upstart Cain boy looks entirely too much like him for comfort; I noticed the resemblance the minute I saw that flier."

"Really?" Michelle stifled an annoyed cough. Cain and Eddie did have the same glossy black hair and the same pale blue eyes. Actually, now that she thought about it, she realized that the two had extremely similar looks. She was a bit embarrassed that her father was the one to point out the similarity to her.

"Absolutely. The man was too powerful."

"Powerful?" Michelle looked at him askance. "Um…it sounds more like he was just popular, Daddy."

"Popular, yes." The minister shook his head. "But his popularity wasn't of the ordinary kind, my dear. Eddie was…a very dark man. He had knowledge of certain…secrets…that the human race would be better off forgetting, and he had precious little grasp on morality and sanity to hold him back from using this knowledge."

"Really?" This assertion was an interesting development; from all she had heard, Eddie Morningstar's "precious little grasp on morality and sanity" came from nothing more exciting or interesting than intermittent bouts of drug abuse. "What kind of—"

"You don't need to know," said her father abruptly.

"Come on, Daddy!" Michelle stared at him, a little hurt. "I'm curious now. What secrets did he know?"

The minister shook his head again and sighed deeply.

"Sometimes it's safest not to ask too many questions," he said. "I'll just say that Eddie Morningstar was a very dangerous man. You should stay well away from those who follow in his path."

"But Daddy—"

"Now, about this form," said the minister in an unmistakable this-conversation-is-over tone. He took the permission slip from her. "I'm sorry, sweetheart. I can't sign this in good conscience. There are far more constructive activities and lessons you could be doing. I don't know what on earth your school is thinking between this assignment and that sex-education class. They *will* be hearing from me."

"Fine," Michelle muttered under her breath. Part of her had been hoping her father wouldn't sign the form; she had been dreading the six hours of pure boredom that Career Day usually induced in students. But the story he had refused to finish haunted her. She wanted to know what bizarre myth he had built up around Eddie Morningstar. It was the first of his ideas that she found intriguing, albeit highly implausible. Her imagination could fill in the specifics until her father was ready to give them up, and she could satisfy any new fantasies that arose from her imaginings by spending time with Cain.

"I can't believe I agreed to Sammi and Izzy's crazy idea for a band name." Vince glared at Cain, spitting up a clutch of green marbles. "How the hell are our fans supposed to know how to pronounce *Pseudomantis*, let alone remember it?"

Cain tapped his guitar impatiently, his concentration broken for the fourth time. They were supposed to start recording today, but Vince's twenty-four hours weren't quite up. The sound engineers in the studio had put up with two clattering showers of glass and steel before they unanimously demanded that the problem be fixed. So Cain stood out in the hallway with his band mates clustered around him, trying to reverse the spell. Of course, Vince wasn't helping himself. Every time Cain thought he had found the perfect combination of notes, Vince broke in with another sarcastic remark.

"Then again, we might not have anything to worry about." Vince sneered at Izzy. "Izzy can pronounce it and that probably means the average four-year-old or any brain-damaged person could too."

"I'm *not* stupid, Vince." Izzy looked hurt.

"What did I tell you about tormenting Izzy?" Cain jabbed the neck of his guitar at Vince, making him flinch. "He's a lot smarter than you think he is. One of these days, he'll get you back."

Izzy beamed and turned bright purple.

"That'll be the day," muttered Vince, spitting out a big oxblood. "Well, I guess I'll just have to hope like hell that a shitty band name isn't enough to ruin all our careers. We might be able to save the name if we add a few umlauts or something."

Izzy scratched his head. "What are…oom-louts, Vince?"

"They're tiny worms that live in the tap water in California," said Vince in a perfectly solemn voice. "People drink them, and the worms crawl up into the people's heads and eat their brains until they can't remember who they are anymore. Umlauts will eat any brains they can find, but they especially like the brains of twenty-year-olds who play drums for rock bands."

Izzy began wailing that he had taken a drink from the tap that morning. Sammi lost his temper and blasted Vince with a jolt of lightning.

"Just shut up and let Cain take the fucking spell off you already, Sweetums." He threw up his hands in exasperation, scattering sparks in the air. "God, do you want to make this record or not?"

Vince slumped to the floor, moaning and clutching his burned chest. Cain took advantage of his silence to play the counter spell. Vince brought up one last handful of marbles on the final note.

"Done," said Cain wearily.

"I thought we'd never get started," Sammi grumbled. "Next time Vince starts acting like this, Cain, you have my permission to turn him into a cockroach."

Once they did get started, Cain was amazed to find how agonizingly slow the recording process was. He was repeatedly ordered to play the same riff more times than he could count to correct mistakes so minor his ears couldn't detect them. Meanwhile, Vince ruined plenty of perfectly good attempts by shrieking at his band mates or the sound engineers for a variety of imaginary errors and slights.

"What does it matter what Izzy looks like?" snapped Sammi after Vince swore at Izzy for changing color while he played. "It's a *recording*, for fuck's sake. No one can see him."

"What about when we're on stage, huh?" Vince punched the wall. "We can't have our drummer turning fucking *purple*. People will think he's gay."

"So what?" Izzy's lip jutted dangerously. "How can I help it if I turn purple when I'm happy? I don't care what people think about me anyway. I just want to play."

"We'll deal with that problem when we come to it," Cain growled, tapping his guitar. "If it even *is* a problem."

The bespectacled producer behind the soundboard— Cain couldn't recall his name—stood up and cleared his throat. "Boys, I think it's time you took a break."

"I don't need one," Vince half-lunged at the producer, making him flinch and duck down behind the soundboard. "I need these morons to get their damn act together."

Sammi jabbed a finger at him. "Shut up, Vinnie! You're

going to take a break, and you're going to come back from it ready to act like a human being, got it?"

The producer relaxed. "Good, good. Back in ten?"

Sammi nodded stiffly and stomped out the door, herding Vince with him. Izzy turned into a dog and bounded off. Cain stayed where he was. The more time he spent in the studio, the fewer strange looks he would receive. He was tired of people finding excuses to walk quickly in the opposite direction whenever he came near them. The producer and engineers had been giving him wary glances all morning, and now that Cain was the only band member in the room, they all seemed to be grasping for a good reason to leave for ten minutes. He tried to ignore them while he ran through some exercises Ty had taught him.

Sammi dragged an angrily protesting Vince into the studio by his wrist a full twenty minutes later.

"What the fuck is your problem, Sammi?" shouted Vince. "The receptionist was totally hot for me. If you'd kept your big nose out of it, I'd have gotten her into that empty office in no time."

"Oh yeah?" Sammi rolled his eyes. "I don't know much about women, but I'm pretty sure that when a woman looks at you like you tried to feed her a dead rat and says 'I wouldn't do you if my life depended on it,' she isn't just being coy. Leave her alone, okay?" He took a deep breath to compose himself. "Well, we're back and ready to record."

"Where's Izzy?" said Cain.

"He's not back yet?" Sammi's face fell. "Dammit, he was hanging out in the hallway when we left. Well, I'd better go look…"

A heavyset, red-faced security guard stepped through the open door. He carried a piece of thick poster board with a coffee cup upturned on it in his hands. A scrap of paper rested on top of the coffee cup. He squinted at it for a moment before addressing them.

"Are you guys"—he consulted the paper one more time—"Pseüdomäntis?"

He pronounced it as if the P weren't silent. Vince snorted and made an I-told-you-so face at Cain.

"Yeah," said Sammi.

"Are you missing a band mate?"

"Maybe."

"Maybe, huh? Well, is this *maybe* him?"

The guard tipped over the coffee mug, revealing a large goldfinch. The bird leapt off the poster board and flew around the room several times before turning into Izzy, who immediately ducked behind Cain.

"That's him," said Sammi. "Where was—"

"I caught him trying to jimmy the door to one of the studios." The guard leaned heavily against the wall, wiping sweat from his brow. "I went to stop him, and the minute he saw me coming, he turned into a damn kangaroo and bounced off, and I had to chase him—"

"Huh, I thought I saw a fat guy running around," sneered Vince. Sammi elbowed him.

The guard gave Vince a sour look. "I finally got him cornered in a supply closet, grabbed him and—poof!—he was a snake. He slipped out of my hands, and I had to tear the room apart to find him, and then...well, thank God someone left a coffee cup in there. If he'd gotten off the ground after he'd turned into that little bird, I'd never have caught him."

The producer sighed. "I'm sorry, Tom. I swear it won't happen again."

The guard nodded as if satisfied, but as he turned to leave, Cain heard him muttering, "It'd better not happen again. Next time I'm throwing him out on his ass. I don't care that he has a contract or that Mr. Arkin thinks he'll be the next big thing. It's not natural..."

"Damn, Izzy, you tried to break into a studio?" Vince grinned. "That's some serious criminal shit right there. Next thing we know, you'll be robbing banks."

"I was going to fly back here anyway." Izzy brushed himself off. "He didn't have to trap me like that."

"So why were you trying to get into another studio anyway?" said Cain. "Don't you like this one?"

"I like this one fine," said Izzy. "I didn't want to record in another studio. I wanted to get into the broken one."

"Studio 4B?" said Cain, remembering the sign on the door.

"That's the one."

Sammi scratched his head. "Why do you want to get into a broken studio?"

"To see if there's anything valuable in there," said Izzy.

"You idiot," said Vince. "Why the fuck would there be anything valuable in there?"

"Why not?" Izzy tossed a drumstick into the air and caught it. "If I had valuable things, I'd keep them in a place where no one would think to look for them. I bet Daggerspoint has lots of rare stuff that nobody knows about. I mean, they had the Morningstar demos, and everybody thought those were long gone."

"Mr. Unger," said the producer, who looked rather peeved by now. "Can you save the treasure hunting for your own time? I'd like to put your album out sometime this decade."

The tedious recording sessions stretched on for a week and then began to eat up another week. Cain began to hate the sight of the painfully white industrial interior of the studio and the long, empty hall. Also, to Cain's annoyance, Izzy's inexplicable fascination with studio 4B persisted and intensified. He kept trying to engage the others in speculation over what wonders might be hidden behind its sealed door, and he would sometimes stop playing in the middle of a take to daydream about unreleased albums and rare guitars.

Cain got home late in the evening on most days, and he was usually too tired to do anything except flop down in bed. So he was very glad that he never needed to seek out Michelle when he wanted companionship; she always came to him, and she was always willing to listen to him vent.

"Sometimes, I wonder whether the hassle is really worth it," he told her one night as they lay together on his bed. "It's been almost three weeks now, and we're still not done. In fact, I don't think we're even *close* to being done. Is it going to be like this with every album?"

"Hmm…probably." Michelle stroked his neck. "Albums are pretty complicated to put together. I've heard they can take months."

"Months?" Cain groaned. "I don't know if I can keep myself from killing Vince for that long or from putting a muting curse on Izzy. He keeps going on about studio 4B."

Michelle nodded thoughtfully. "You know, I can't help admiring his creativity. That's not where my mind would have gone at all." She gave him a sly grin. "So is there any part of you that hopes he's right? I mean, if he were right, you might find some stuff in there that would interest you."

"Like what?"

"Like, oh, a few of Eddie Morningstar's guitars." She ran a finger along his cheek. "So has anybody ever told you that you look a lot like him? Eddie Morningstar, I mean."

"I do?" Cain had never seen a picture of Eddie Morningstar; all he knew about him was that he played guitar for Lion of Judah and that Sammi revered him. In his mind, Eddie Morningstar was more like an unseen force of nature than a real person. He gave Michelle a wary look.

"Don't worry." Michelle chuckled. "It's a compliment. Eddie was really handsome. When I was, oh, twelve or thirteen, I had a huge crush on him. It pretty much broke my heart when someone told me that he died when I was eight."

"No one has ever told me that." Cain shrugged. "I didn't even know who he was until we got those tapes and Sammi started raving about him."

"Seriously?" Michelle looked at him askance, and then she cuddled up to him with a little laugh. "Oh, Cain, you're *such* an innocent. God, who hasn't heard of Eddie Morningstar by now? The funny thing is, I would've bet money that he was a huge inspiration to you. Your performance style is, like, half Eddie and half JoJo Thorpe. It's uncanny."

"But I don't sing, and I don't think I could sing like that if I tried." Cain could produce a greater range of vocalizations than the average human, but JoJo's range was far beyond his scope.

"That's not why, silly," said Michelle. "JoJo was multitalented. Someone in his family—his dad, I think, but I could be wrong—was a vaudeville magician in the twenties, and JoJo picked up a few tricks from him and worked them into the band's act. He was good at it too. I think you're pretty much what JoJo would be if he had Eddie's looks and guitar skills and, you know, some *real* magic to work with."

Cain raised an eyebrow at her. While living in the Warwick household, he had not noticed how fascinated non-magical people generally were with magic. The launch of his career made him aware of people's awe. He used to view his magic as a useful and practical tool, as a means of saving himself the work of cleaning the bathroom or rinsing all the dishes by hand. Now, he was treated as if he were some sort of rare creature with an extraordinary gift. The transition felt odd to him.

"Now, I know it sounds pretty hokey," Michelle continued, misinterpreting his expression. "But JoJo could pull it off because he was just that smooth." She pressed closer to him. "I mean, heck, there's some stuff you do on stage that would be hokey as all get-out if some human tried to do it, but you make it look sexy because you've got the scary-growly-monster thing down so well."

Cain nuzzled her hair, breathing in her peculiar strawberry-musk scent.

"You think so?" he said.

"Oh yeah."

"Good." He lay back nonchalantly, trying to draw power without looking like he was expending any effort. "Then you won't think it's hokey when I do *this*."

He released a burst of magical energy. Michelle yelped in surprise as it lifted her almost to the ceiling.

"Oh my god!" She flailed in the air like an inexperienced swimmer trying to get a feel for the water, gasping in amazement. The expression on her face veered between bliss and fear. "I...I'm flying...this is so awesome!" She looked down and blanched when she saw just how far away the floor was from the ceiling. "*Shit*. Put me down!"

Surprised by the sharpness in her voice, Cain willed the energy cloud back into himself too quickly. Michelle yelped again while she plummeted from the air and landed on the bed beside him, causing a great *thump* and a chorus of creaking springs. As she sat up slowly, dazed and shaking, a dull banging noise emanated from the ceiling.

"Hey, asshole!" Vince's muffled voice filtered down from the loft above them. "I know you're proud of your hot girlfriend and all, but could you keep the noises from your fucking down to a dull roar? I'm trying to get some goddamned sleep up here!"

"I'm sorry," said Cain, stroking her shoulder anxiously. "I thought you would like it."

Michelle shook herself and took a deep breath. "Oh, I did. It's just that…well, that's why I won't ever be a pilot. I love the idea of flying, but the act of flying scares the crap out of me." She gave him a curious look. "So, how did you do that? You didn't have your guitar."

Cain shrugged. "Oh, well, I don't really need the guitar to work magic. It does help me focus a lot, though; I should have gotten it before I tried lifting you. If I'd had it, I probably wouldn't have dropped you. Sorry about that."

Michelle put a hand over his mouth with a gentle laugh.

"You apologize too much—you know that?" she said. "Don't worry; I loved it. That's part of what makes you so sexy, you know."

Cain gave her an incredulous look.

"What? You don't believe me?" Michelle's arms worked their way around his waist, and her hands snaked into his pants. Her voice took on a breathy, eager tone. "Well, I guess I'll just have to show you, then."

Cain made a faltering guttural noise deep in his throat—the closest human approximation to the continuous growling purr that he would be emitting if he were in his true form. He still found it odd that humans were so fascinated with him, but he wasn't inclined to question their interest. After all, his demonic traits made Michelle happy.

Michelle was used to dressing in the dark. She wrestled herself into her clothes two feet from the bed where Cain lay sleeping contentedly. Her elbow nudged the bedside table and made the lamp rattle, but he didn't stir.

Poor baby, she thought with a happy sigh as she slipped out the door. *I really wore you out tonight, didn't I?*

She felt her way along the walls of the darkened hall. A small pool of light spilled out of the living room at the bottom of the stairs. Michelle followed it gratefully down the steps and paused for a moment in the doorway, peering in.

Izzy lay sprawled on the couch, cradling an empty vodka bottle in one arm as if it were a teddy bear. A few streaks of purple were frozen in his hair, and he grinned broadly as he snored. Michelle's eyes wandered to the coffee table, where four unmarked cassette tapes and a faded old notebook balanced precariously on one edge, crowded out by Izzy's forest of canisters and tins.

Her heart leaped into her mouth. When Cain had mentioned to her a few weeks ago that Mr. Arkin had given him the lost Morningstar demos and JoJo's notes, she had half-wondered if he was repeating some outrageous lie that Skeeter Judd had told about him. Yet she couldn't quite suppress the hope that he was telling the truth, and the

mysterious-looking black tapes lying on the notebook's frayed cover five feet away from her reawakened that hope.

She began to edge toward the table as quietly as she could. She reached to pick up the nearest tape, froze for a moment when Izzy twitched and muttered, and then continued. She could smell the alcohol rolling off of Izzy; he wasn't waking up anytime soon.

The stereo's cassette slot clicked softly when Michelle slipped in the tape and pressed it shut. She turned the volume knob to the lowest setting and pressed the "play" button.

Music filtered through the speakers. Michelle knelt beside the stereo and listened intently. The sound quality was not very good, and it was so fragmented that she was surprised Cain had managed to work whole songs out of the meandering notes, but she thought she could hear flashes of Eddie's style in some parts. A shiver of excitement ran through her.

The music faded out abruptly. The tape crackled on in silence for a moment, and then someone began to speak in the background. Michelle leaned in with interest. It occurred to her that she had never heard a recording of Eddie Morningstar's voice.

Eddie talked for several minutes in a steady rhythmic pattern; however, Michelle was having difficulty understanding the exact words. She thought she heard the words *knife*, *blind*, *pour*, and, curiously, *amen*. It sounded as if Eddie was reminding himself of the rhythm needed for the song's lyrics.

Were they the lyrics to an unreleased Lion of Judah song?

Michelle glanced over to make sure Izzy was still asleep.

She had an unreasonable fear that Cain and his band mates would be angry with her if they knew she had listened to these tapes without asking. She experimented with the tracking until the sound became clearer. She rewound the last section and listened to it again. Some of the words were still unintelligible, but now she could make out the gist of what the voice was saying in a grim monotone: "*Kkkkhh*...a thousand knives in his throat...pluck out his eyes and *ssshhh* him blind...pour poison into his ears and *kkkssshh fttt ftttt* into depths of madness and swiftly *krkttt* death upon him. So be it, so be it. Amen."

A soft electronic *pop* issued from the speakers when Michelle hit the "stop" button. She opened the slot, slipped the tape out, and turned it over in her hands, trying to get her breathing back under control. After a minute or two, the chill passed, and she stared at the tape in disbelief. How silly of her to be so spooked by an old collection of studio demos! Those words were only the lyrics to the song Eddie was working on; most of Lion of Judah's later works had dark and disturbing lyrics. Yet she couldn't bring herself to put the tape back in the stereo. She replaced it on the top of the stack without looking at it again, unable to banish Eddie Morningstar's voice from her mind.

The making of the album dragged on into a fourth week, and the rest of the people in the city began to think about Christmas. Cain sat on the porch late one cool night, watching the strings of red-and-green lights blink on and off in the windows of their neighbor's house across the street. They were much closer to being done now, but they were also working longer and more exhausting days in the hope of finishing sooner.

"Hey, Cain." Izzy dropped from the sky and landed on the porch beside him with a loud, startling thud. "Can't sleep?"

"I was just about to go to bed." Cain's heart raced. He had forgotten about Izzy's habit of sitting on the windowsill in the form of a crow on cool, breezy winter nights. "You should probably warn people before you just appear like that, you know."

"Sorry." Izzy shrugged. "*I* can't sleep. I keep thinking about that studio. Why do you think it's closed all the time?"

"They're probably doing something with the soundproofing." Cain sighed. Izzy had been talking incessantly about studio 4B for the last few days, and his band mates had all his theories on the subject completely memorized.

"I asked Mr. Arkin about it the other day," Izzy continued. "He said that there wasn't any cool stuff in there. He said that someone just made a mess and that they had to get it cleaned up before it could be used again. He didn't say what kind of mess it was, though. It must have been a pretty big mess to keep the studio closed so long."

"It probably has something to do with the soundproofing," Cain repeated patiently. "You know that if some of that stuff gets pulled out of the walls, they have to be really careful about replacing it properly."

"Yeah, it's probably something boring like that." Izzy looked glum.

"Probably." Cain surveyed the quiet street. The lights were still blinking in the windows of the house across the way, but most of the neighbors had turned off their Christmas displays for the night. The street was lined with softly lit trees that stood at regular intervals. The multicolored bulbs glowed eerily, illuminating a man walking up the street, a man with silver hair.

Cain gripped the stone railing. A sudden sinking feeling had made his legs unstable.

"Master…"

"Huh?" Izzy had not noticed the man walking up the street.

Cain didn't hear him. He could only stand helplessly and watch as Mr. Warwick's familiar, regal gait. He was drawing closer every second. His face turned in their direction; there was no doubt that he had seen them. He stopped at the bottom of the stairs, his glinting gray eyes locked on Cain.

"Cain," said Mr. Warwick in a firm, quiet voice. "Come here."

The collar jerked. Cain followed its prodding down the stairs with heavy steps. He was about to be dragged back to New York just like an uncomplaining dog would be dragged. He would probably not be allowed to take his guitar, and he would certainly never see Izzy, Sammi, or Vince again. The idea was more than he could stand. He would rather go back to the hated recording studio or to the alley behind the butcher's shop; he did not want to go back to New York with Mr. Warwick.

"Don't dawdle now." Mr. Warwick raised his hand in a beckoning gesture, and the collar's squeezing became more insistent. Cain had no choice but to go to him and stand still. He struggled to suppress the tears threatening to spill from his eyes while the old man inspected him.

Mr. Warwick walked around him in a slow circle, taking in his appearance with an air of cool impartiality.

"My, but you've changed," he said in a bemused tone, as

if he were talking more to himself than to Cain. "I never would have guessed it, but the rock star style becomes you. Bruce Arkin really does have a talent for bringing out the best in his performers."

"Please, Master, I need more time in the city." Speaking out of turn was always risky, but he was desperate. "Michelle has been holding out, but with a little more time, I might be able to change her mind." The collar bit him for lying, and he carefully concealed the pain. "Please, Master. I promise it won't be much longer."

Mr. Warwick paused for a moment, looking at Cain with raised eyebrows. He opened his mouth to say something, but he was unexpectedly interrupted because a Labrador-sized golden baboon charged down the steps and positioned itself between him and Cain.

"I know who you are," the baboon barked in Izzy's voice. "You're the one who put that collar on Cain! Well, listen to me, Mister…Mister…I don't remember what Cain said your name was, but you can't take Cain back to New York! He's the best guitarist in the city!"

"Izzy, get back on the porch," hissed Cain frantically. "He's a fully trained sorcerer; your magic is nowhere near as powerful as his."

Izzy didn't listen, and Cain and Mr. Warwick were both forced to leap back while the baboon expanded into a monstrous flame-red lion that was twice as large as a normal member of its species.

"I'll fight you if you try to take him," cried Izzy in a roar that sounded more like the yowl of an annoyed Siamese cat. "We *need* him here."

Cain craned his neck anxiously around Izzy's huge bulk, trying to catch a glimpse of the expression on Mr. Warwick's face. If the old man was annoyed...but he wasn't annoyed, thank goodness; he was smiling.

"Calm down, son," he chuckled. "No one is going to take Cain away."

The lion's hide slowly faded to tawny gold as the lion shrank to a more realistic size.

"Really?" Izzy mewed suspiciously.

"Absolutely." Mr. Warwick smiled at Cain over the lion's back. "I came here to give him my blessing, and my permission; he can make music for as long as he likes."

A fierce rush of joy shot through Cain. For a moment, he could not speak.

"You...you mean you..." he stammered.

"Approve?" said Mr. Warwick calmly. "I approve wholeheartedly. I admit I was a bit upset when I found out that someone else had commandeered my servant. But Mr. Arkin was very eloquent in your defense, Cain. He said that you were easily the best guitarist he had seen in his whole career, and he was fully prepared to surrender his very soul to me if I would lend you to him for a while."

"Master, you didn't..."

"Of course I didn't!" Mr. Warwick sounded disappointed. "How could you think such things of me, Cain? I let him borrow you free of charge."

Cain stared at him suspiciously. Mr. Warwick never did anything free of charge, even something so piddling as a simple good luck charm.

"Well...maybe I *did* make it clear to him that I might expect the odd favor now and again," he conceded. "But this arrangement just seemed so...appropriate. The whole time Bruce Arkin was praising you to me, I kept thinking of all those nights I spent in my study trying to concentrate, and your damned music would come filtering through the wall to distract me. Believe it or not, I sort of miss those days. Still, I couldn't deny that this was a singularly excellent chance for you to get some of that restlessness and hunger for music out of your system. And I really do want to see you succeed, Cain. In your ten years of loyal service, you really have become something much more than a slave to me—something not unlike a third son."

Cain's mind went blank. He had no idea how to process this information, and he only barely heard what Mr. Warwick said next.

"Go out into the world and make music, Cain. I release you from my service until you see fit to return." He turned to Izzy. "And what's your name?"

"Uh…" Izzy had cautiously edged back into his own shape, but his hair went a little red at the roots when Mr. Warwick addressed him. "I'm Izzy Unger."

"And do you always take the form of a baboon or a lion, Izzy?"

Izzy responded by becoming a wolf, a crocodile, a hippopotamus, a bison, and a dragon-like mythological hybrid of snake and bird in a series of transformations so rapid they hurt Cain's eyes.

"Well!" Mr. Warwick turned to Cain. "I'm afraid you gave your friend inaccurate information. It is true that I am much more versatile in my powers. In the narrow area where his talents lie, though, his magic may well be more powerful than mine. I am impressed; shape-shifters as talented as he is are extremely rare."

Izzy elbowed Cain in the side, whispering, "Did he just compliment me, or is he calling me a freak?"

"Oh…" Cain finally managed to snap back into focus.

"He was complimenting you, I think. He admires people with rare magical talents."

"Goodbye for now, Cain." Mr. Warwick was walking back up the street. "Goodbye, and good luck. I hope you appreciate all that Mr. Arkin has done for you, by the way. Very few record company executives would provide down-on-their-luck young artists with living quarters out of their own pockets, let alone personally oversee every step of their artistic development. You think about what you owe him, and be good for him."

"I will, Master, but wait a minute," called Cain. This talk of owing people things reminded him of something he had owed Steve for a long time. "I was just wondering if you might let Steve come visit me in the city. It must be getting close to his Christmas break, and I know he would like to—"

"Steve is here right now," said Mr. Warwick matter-of-factly. "Nathaniel Breen insisted that I give him a progress report in person, and because the old fool wanted me here over Christmas for some reason, I thought I might as well bring the boys. If you want to see Steve, however, you'll have to come visit us at the hotel. I'm never letting my boys out into this godforsaken jungle of a city ever again. The last time I was here on business, Lance went out on his own and woke up on the floor of some old church hours later with no memory of how he had gotten there. I don't know if it was drink or drugs, and frankly, I don't care to find out."

CHAPTER TEN

CHRISTMAS

FOR A FEW DAYS afterward, Cain wondered if he had imagined the events of that night. Mr. Warwick's allowance was too generous, too wonderful to be real. Surely Mr. Warwick would never simply let him walk free for as long as he chose; Cain's services were far too valuable to him.

But the collar was proof. It had gone quiet around Cain's neck the moment Mr. Warwick announced Cain's respite. It remained quiet all the next day. Even when Cain deliberately provoked it by saying aloud with all the conviction he could muster that his master was nothing but a hypocritical, money-grubbing, petty tyrant, it still hung loose, no more animated than a normal dog collar.

He began to further test his freedom, doing little things that Mr. Warwick had never allowed: walking barefoot on the wooden kitchen floor while in demon form, or lounging on the porch without a shirt. When he found himself singing a half-remembered song in Malakhu in the shower one morning, the full realization of his newfound freedom rushed over him. For the first time in ten years, he didn't have to run questionable errands or endure insults and condescension. Better still, he could lie beside Michelle and hold her without the sharp bite at his neck reminding him that he was merely putting off the inevitable surrender of the girl he loved to repulsive Lance. He practically flew down the stairs, eager to begin celebrating in earnest.

"Whoa, man!" Sammi blinked in astonishment as he walked through the kitchen door and caught Cain wolfing down an entire block of cheese. "What are you doing? I thought you only ate meat."

Cain swallowed a large mouthful of cheese. "I do. I mean, I usually do. Cheese is special." He bit off a large chunk and talked around it. "Mmm…See, my master used to give me cheese when I did a really good job on something."

"I thought you hated your master."

"Yeah, a little. But that's not the point." Cain stopped eating for a moment and frowned at the memory. "The way he would give it to me was pretty awful. He'd hold a pitiful little scrap of cheese over my head, and smile this fake-looking smile that I always wanted to smack right off his face, and tell me that I did so unusually well that he *supposed* I deserved a treat. I always got the feeling that he just wanted to show me he was the master." He tore off another chunk and swallowed it down half-chewed. "I always took the cheese, though. I like it too much to pass it up."

Sammi's expression changed to one of concern when Cain swallowed too fast and took another big bite before he was done coughing and gasping. "Say, man, are you going to eat that whole thing?"

"Oh, yeah."

"Okay then. You might want to slow down a little. You're gonna make yourself sick at this rate."

Cain gave Sammi a skeptical look. He couldn't imagine how something so delicious could make anyone sick.

As it turned out, Sammi was right. Half an hour after Cain devoured the last scrap of the cheese brick, his stomach protested violently, and he had to run to the bathroom. Yet, even while he was retching into the toilet, he wasn't sorry that he had eaten it.

Somewhere at the back of his mind lurked an uncomfortable suspicion that the whole arrangement was too good to be true, that Mr. Warwick had given him up far too easily. However, the heady mix of jubilation and misery from having eaten too much cheese quickly buried his doubts, and a few days later, Cain's relief at having lived through the last of the torturous recording sessions silenced the unease entirely.

It was Christmas Eve, and Cain was alone. His band mates had all gone off to various parties without him. Cain didn't really mind the oversight—large gatherings of humans still made him nervous—but he was starting to feel lonely. He had been hoping to visit the Warwicks this evening. It would be nice to see Steve again, even if he had to see Lance as well. He had realized too late that Mr. Warwick forgot to tell him where they were staying.

The night was unseasonably warm. Cain pushed a window open before turning his attention back to the new riff he was trying to compose.

"Cain!" cried a frantic voice from the open window. "Let me in. Hurry!"

The voice was higher in pitch than it normally was, but Cain recognized it immediately. His head snapped up in disbelief. "Steve?"

The open window seemed empty, but Steve's voice came again: "Damn, Cain, none of your band mates are here, are they? I'd die of embarrassment if they saw me like this."

"Like what?" Cain squinted into the darkness beyond the screen. "I can't see you at all."

"Just open the screen!" shrieked Steve.

Still perplexed, Cain popped the screen out of the window frame. A blur of toffee-colored hair vaulted through the gap and landed on the living room floor, and a sound of tiny claws scrabbling for purchase filled the room. Cain stared in wordless surprise at the squirrel for a moment before he guessed the truth.

"Steve!" He dropped to his knees beside the twitching animal. "What happened? Did your dad do this to you?"

It was unlike Mr. Warwick to use magic to discipline his sons, but Cain had always imagined he would step over the line someday.

"No." Steve's entire body drooped miserably, as if he wished Mr. Warwick had been the one to enchant him. "I did this to myself, and now I can't remember how to undo it."

"Steve!" Cain gave him a reproachful look. "You know you never—"

"You never cast a spell before you know how to reverse it." Steve groaned. "I thought I did know how. But I forgot I'd never memorized the spell to change *back* until I'd already changed."

"Oh, well." Cain sighed. "Just…try not to do it again, all right?" Steve was notorious for trying spells slightly too advanced for him; this was definitely not the first sticky situation Cain had been called upon to rescue him from.

"Yeah, yeah, yeah. Just change me back!" Steve's tail

puffed impatiently. "If your band mates came back and saw me like this, I'd have to kill myself."

Cain fumbled with his guitar, taken aback by Steve's excessive mortification. "They won't think any less of you if they know you can turn yourself into a squirrel, you know. Sammi and Izzy won't, anyway. Especially Izzy."

"Dammit, Cain, I can't be seen in the form of a *squirrel* by *a rock band!*"

Steve sounded as if he were on the verge of tears, and Cain got the definite impression that he somehow considered being seen in the form of a squirrel by a rock band the single most humiliating experience on the face of the planet.

Removing the spell was difficult. Cain tried to be gentle, but most human bodies simply weren't made to change as Izzy's could—swiftly and freely, without pain or effort. At least five times, he set his teeth and scaled back his efforts because Steve's bones began to warp and crack, or his skin showed signs of tearing, but at last, Cain completed the reversal, and Steve stood before him, sore and sheepish, but fully human.

"That's better," said Cain. "What were you doing running around as a squirrel, anyway?"

Steve stretched his aching muscles. "I had to get out of that hotel somehow. Dad was keeping us cooped up in there because Lance went out and did something stupid the last time he was here."

"You could have gotten run over by a car or killed by a stray cat." Cain knew he probably sounded like a scolding old grandmother, but he also knew that city streets were dangerous places. "You know your dad was keeping you in the hotel because he wants you to be safe."

"He wants Lance to be safe," said Steve sourly. "He wouldn't care if a street gang killed me and cut up my body to sell as dog food. He only bothers with me because he hopes Lance won't be as grumpy about not being allowed to go out and enjoy LA if I'm not allowed to either. Screw Lance. It's his fault dad is keeping us locked up in the first place."

"Still, you can't just go running off without telling him."

"Oh, yes I can. He won't notice I'm gone. I bet he won't even come to pick me up until right before it's time to fly back home."

"Pick you up?" Cain wasn't sure he liked the way Steve worded that declaration. It sounded like he planned to run away from home. "Pick you up where?"

"Here, of course." Steve plopped down on the couch. "I didn't run halfway across the city to drop in for a few minutes and leave right away."

Cain sighed. "You can't stay here, Steve. I don't think Mr. Arkin would mind, but you don't have your dad's—"

"I'll never *get* dad's permission." Steve buried himself in the cushions. "I had to run away. It was self-defense; Lance has been beating me up every day." He rolled up his sleeves so Cain could see the bruises on his arms. "Even becoming invisible doesn't help anymore. He's learned to see through that spell too."

"Well…" Cain softened. "I guess you could spend the night. But I'll have to take you back to the hotel tomorrow. You don't even have your things here."

Steve lifted his arm, snapped his hand through the air, and barked a command. Cain spun around when something crashed to the floor behind him. Steve's red suitcase lay on the carpet where no suitcase had been a moment before. It was compressed, as if it had fallen from a great height.

"I do now." Steve crossed his arms defiantly.

Cain looked from the suitcase to Steve.

"Fine." He sighed again. "You can stay for a while. Vince isn't going to like this."

When Vince returned at two in the morning, drunk and glowing with the stolen life forces of three or four unfortunate fellow partygoers, he upended a chair and lectured Cain about how annoying it was when one's roommate took in guests without one's permission. Cain finally gave up trying to calm him down and resorted to brandishing his guitar. Subdued, Vince slunk off to the loft, but not before hissing a "friendly" warning to Steve.

"It's tough being an energy-eating vampire, kid," he whispered in Steve's ear. "Usually, I'm pretty good at controlling myself, but sometimes I get hungry and lose control. Anyway, if you wake up and find me sucking the life out of you, just lie there and let me. If you struggle, I might get angry and melt your brains like cheese."

"What the hell?" Steve stared after Vince. "Is he really that crazy, Cain?"

"Always. He was just trying to scare you, you know. He can't really melt your brain." Cain thought for a moment. "But don't let him touch you, for any reason. Trust me."

Sammi stumbled home dazed and red-eyed ten minutes later. He accepted Steve's presence without question and shuffled up to bed before Cain could ask him what was wrong. Izzy was so drunk when he finally came in that he collapsed onto the couch, pinning Steve down for a moment before turning into a blotchy electric blue iguana and sinking into a deep sleep. Steve looked unnerved by this turn of events, but he carried the lizard to the armchair across the room without comment before settling back down and drifting off to sleep himself.

Steve was in high spirits when Cain wandered downstairs for breakfast the next morning. He sat at the kitchen table with Izzy, who looked remarkably alert and refreshed.

"Cain, this kid friend of yours is awesome!" said Izzy as Cain walked into the room. "I had a really bad hangover when I woke up, and he made it go away."

"Oh, it's just a spell I've been working on ever since Lance started hanging out with Kevin and Brett." Steve shrugged. "Those morons drink like there is no tomorrow, and I figured that an instant hangover cure might be worth some money to them. Or at least it might convince them to stop clotheslining me in the hall and dunking my head in the toilet. Too bad they're cheap as well as mean. Anyway, the spell is pretty primitive right now; it was really nice of Izzy to let me try it on him."

Steve spoke in a modest tone, but he was grinning proudly.

Sammi wandered downstairs a few minutes later. He stared at Steve with a confused expression on his face until Cain reminded him that they had met last night.

"Oh, yeah. I remember now," he said, not sounding as if he remembered the meeting at all.

"Are you all right, Sammi?" said Cain.

"Sure. I stayed up a little too late last night, is all."

Cain gave him a doubtful look, but he didn't press the issue. Whatever had been ailing Sammi last night had passed, and aside from the lapse in memory, he seemed his old energetic self.

Michelle sneaked over two days later. She seemed surprised to learn that Steve was Lance Warwick's brother, and Steve seemed delighted to find out that she was the object of Lance's desire.

"So you've been making it with Lance's crush since November, Cain?" he asked with a gleeful snicker after she had gone home. "Too bad Lance up and forgot all about her around that time. I would have loved to have seen the look on his face if he'd found out."

"Mmm hmm," said Cain noncommittally. He gathered that Vampire Vince had removed all of Lance's memories of Michelle in the church that day. That arrangement suited him just fine. He had seen the look on Lance's face when he'd found out, and he certainly didn't care to see it again.

The story of the Engineer seemed to hold a particular fascination for Steve. Sammi told him all he could remember of the night Vince was taken and the night he and Izzy were taken, and he rolled up his sleeves so Steve could see his scars.

"That's pretty intense." Steve's eyes wandered over Sammi's mutilated forearms. "I can't believe I hadn't heard anything about this guy till I got here."

"Yeah." Sammi flexed his right hand contemplatively. "You'd think a serial killer taking out rockers would be sensational enough to make national headlines—What?"

Steve was staring at Sammi's palm.

"That sign—do you have one on your other hand too?"

"Well—sort of." Sammi flipped over his left hand. "It's different from the other one."

"Huh." Steve frowned. "Does Izzy have the same marks?"

Izzy leapt up from the couch and thrust his hands in

Steve's face like a young child demonstrating to his mother that he really had washed his hands.

"And Vince…?"

"No, asshole." Vince glared at Steve from the armchair. "I wasn't taken by the Engineer. I just hit my head and lost my memory for a while."

"Vince has exactly the same marks," Cain whispered to Steve.

"I recognize them; they're Icelandic runes. This one"—Steve pointed to Izzy's left palm—"means 'danger' or 'harm.' The other one means 'to make harmless.'"

Cain scratched his head. "But that doesn't make any sense. You use those runes on things, not people."

Izzy glanced quizzically at Cain, as if to imply that Steve had lost him at the mention of Icelandic runes.

Sammi ran a finger over his palm in an apprehensive little circle. "Are these rune things supposed to actually do something?"

Steve fished around in his pocket. "Yeah. During Medieval times, warriors used to use them as a sneaky way to murder rivals by sending them into battle with weapons that didn't work." He pulled out a pocket knife and pointed to the symbols scratched into the blade. "I've tried them myself on this knife…Here, watch."

He stabbed the knife into his left palm with all the force he could muster. Sammi flinched, and Izzy squealed; even Vince went pale.

Steve calmly pulled out the knife and held up his hand. There was no sign of a wound, even though a good two inches of the blade had been sunk there a moment before.

"Shit," said Sammi reverently.

Vince coughed. Cain knew he was trying not to show

how impressed he was.

"That...was...fucking...*awesome!*" Izzy became a dog and leapt up and down at Steve's feet, tail thumping with excitement. "Do it again!"

"I'm glad *you* think it's cool." Steve blushed and beamed. "I made it to impress this girl I liked at school. During study hall, I told her to hold out her hand because I had a neat magic trick to show her, and when she did, I made like I was chopping off her fingers. She was fine afterwards, but she wasn't impressed." He ran his hands through his dark hair, blowing out his breath wearily. "Neither was dad when I got a week of detention for it."

"I think you tried to impress the wrong kind of girl," said Cain. Michelle would probably be delighted if he passed a knife blade harmlessly through her hand.

"So why would anyone put these marks on *us?*" said Izzy. "We're not gonna stab anyone."

"That's a good question." Cain frowned. "Those runes don't have any effect on anything alive, do they? A halfway-competent magician ought to know that."

"I bet we're not dealing with someone halfway-competent," said Steve. "I bet we're dealing with a dabbler who knows just enough to be dangerous. Harmful and make harmless...I think someone thinks you guys are dangerous, and he...or she...tried to neutralize the threat."

"Huh. Makes sense." Sammi bit his lip thoughtfully and contemplated his hands. "Breen would be my first suspect, but I don't think he'd touch any magic stuff."

"Breen the TV preacher?" Steve raised an eyebrow. "I wouldn't be so sure. He hired my dad to help him get rid of an imaginary devil-worshipping cult. Dad isn't actually doing anything about it, but Breen is still paying him."

"*Seriously*? Does he know what your dad does?"

"Oh, yeah." Cain nodded. "He didn't like the idea, but he didn't seem to think he had any choice. You're probably right, though; Breen wouldn't try any sorcery himself, especially since he thinks someone is doing it for him."

"It kinda worries me that he'd think of it at all," said Sammi.

Two days after Christmas, Steve mentioned that he had never seen the inside of a recording studio. Izzy insisted on taking him to Daggerspoint to show him one. The building was closed for the holidays, but locks and alarms had never obstructed Cain. They quickly and quietly gave Steve a full tour, leaving out only the janitor's closet and studio 4B.

"You know, Izzy, I wouldn't be so eager to get in there if I were you," said Vince when Izzy started explaining his latest theory on the studio's closure to Steve. "Sure, it *might* have cool stuff in it. But it might have some things that you'd be really sorry you found."

"Like what, Vince?" Izzy scratched his head.

"Well…" Vince made a point of glancing all around as if he feared someone might be eavesdropping. "I heard Mr. Arkin talking to some suit—somebody's lawyer, probably—about some kind of evidence that could get someone or other in trouble if the cops found it. Arkin told the guy not to worry; he'd just hide it in the vault until the whole thing blew over."

Izzy's hair turned bright purple, and he let out a squeak of delight. "You mean there really is a—"

"No, there isn't," Sammi broke in. "That's an urban legend, Izzy. I mean, even if there was a vault—and trust me, there isn't—do you really think Bruce Arkin would be

236

dumb enough to talk about it in front of a motor-mouthed asshat like Vince?"

"Vault?" said Cain.

"Oh, it's just some silly story that's been floating around," said Sammi. "Something about a magic secret room where rockers can put stuff they don't want anyone to find."

"Like the Morningstar demos!" Izzy danced with excitement, ignoring Sammi's impatient cough.

"Or the knife," Vince broke in. "But I don't think that's coming out anytime soon."

"What knife?" said Izzy.

Vince raised an eyebrow at Izzy. "What do you mean, what knife? *Everybody* knows about the knife."

"He's shitting you again, Izzy," said Sammi when Izzy looked to him for clarification.

"No, I'm not!" said Vince indignantly. "Don't pay any attention to Sammi, Iz. He's a blind Lion fan, and he doesn't want you to know the truth about Ty Thorpe."

Cain had been on the verge of ordering Vince to stop toying with Izzy, but now that his guitar teacher's name had come up, he couldn't help feeling a bit intrigued.

"What are you talking about, Vinnie?" said Sammi. "You sound like Skeeter Judd. There's no 'truth' about Ty that I don't—"

"Did you know he stabbed his big brother to death?" Vince smirked triumphantly.

Izzy's eyes bulged with horror. "But the papers all said JoJo had a bad trip and killed himself."

"Really, Vinnie, even coming from you, that's a pretty shitty thing to say." Sammi glared at Vince and gave Izzy a reassuring pat on the shoulder. "Don't worry, Iz. The papers were right; JoJo really did commit suicide. Ty didn't kill him."

"Oh, really?" Vince rolled his eyes. "High on acid or not, what kind of sick fuck offs himself by stabbing himself in the stomach? And why couldn't the cops find the knife? And don't you think it's just a little too convenient that Ty was the one who found the body? You mark my words, Izzy, Ty murdered JoJo and hid the bloody knife in the vault, and I bet you'd find it if you got into that studio. And once you've found it, well, I wouldn't like to be in your shoes. If Ty could cut down his own brother in cold blood, do you think he'd have any problem at all making you disappear to keep his secret?"

Izzy turned into a rabbit and hid behind Cain, his eyes darting nervously around the hallway as if he feared that Ty Thorpe might materialize at any moment and go on a murderous rampage. Sammi lost his temper.

"That's enough, Vinnie!" he shouted. "I don't want to hear another word about it. Ty loved JoJo. He was devastated by his death."

"Loved him?" said Vince, ducking behind Steve to put a barrier between himself and Sammi's electrified fingers. "He was jealous of him, more likely. I mean, JoJo was the big-shot frontman who got all the girls and attention, while Ty was just the quiet one who got stuck playing *bass*." He sneered at Sammi from behind Steve, who was clearly not happy about being used as a human shield. "I'm surprised he didn't kill JoJo sooner."

Izzy looked ready to cry. Sammi was so enraged that sparks were literally flying off him, and Cain guessed that he wouldn't be able to hold himself back from blasting Vince much longer. Steve tried to wriggle out of Vince's grasp, but

Vince held him fast. Cain was glad he had brought his guitar. Sammi couldn't put a stop to this nonsense without hurting Steve, but he could.

"Come to think of it, all the other members of Lion of Judah died in ways that were too damn convenient," Vince went on, too absorbed in his tale to notice Cain brandishing his guitar. "I mean, hell, JoJo gets stabbed, the drummer guy drives his car off a cliff, *and* a house Eddie's staying in burns down for no reason? Hell, now that Ty's wormed his way into Candiryde, I wouldn't be surprised if Jazz Brixton and Candi Jayne and Yuri Ustinov all have 'accidents' in a few years. The man is a goddamned serial killer. In fact," he grinned evilly at Izzy, "has anyone asked where he was on the nights the Engineer took his victims? 'Cause I wouldn't be at all surprised if—"

"Vince," said Cain in his most threatening voice. "Shut up. We've got to finish giving Steve his tour and get out of here before security catches us."

"Screw you, Cain," said Vince peevishly. "I'm just having a little fun."

"Then I might as well have a little fun too." Cain fixed his eyes on Vince and plucked the A-string.

There was no real magic in the resulting note; but there might as well have been. Vince immediately released Steve with a yelp of fear and flattened himself against the wall. He said nothing for the remainder of the tour, and he actually seemed to be taking pains to behave himself.

Once the tour was finished and they had successfully slipped out of the building without being seen, Cain peeled away from the others.

"Hey, I have a stop to make on the way home." He glanced back over his shoulder at his friends. "Now that

Steve is here, I've been thinking about someone else I owe a visit to. You don't have to come."

"Don't have to come?" Sammi did a sharp about-face. "You're not thinking of walking alone while the Engineer is still on the loose, are you? They found one of the last two guys who disappeared a few days ago, you know, dead, cut up, and crammed in a dumpster. It was the guitarist," he added grimly.

Izzy ran to catch up with him. "I'm not letting anyone put Cain in a dumpster," he said fiercely.

"I'll go too," said Steve.

"It's a long walk." Cain looked at them doubtfully.

"We don't mind!" said Steve gleefully.

They set off together. Vince followed them with an exaggerated air of indifference. Cain suspected that he was trying to hide his fear of being left alone in the deepening twilight.

The walk to the Hispanic neighborhood was shorter than Cain had thought it would be. The house was a little southeast of the Bayou Jewel, but he hadn't realized its location until now because the hectic car ride from the club had turned his sense of direction on its head. His plan had been to make his way to the club and backtrack to the Hispanic neighborhood from there; but he recognized a certain graffiti-scarred wall on the way. From there, his leading became more confident and instinctual, despite the growing unease of his band mates.

"God, Cain, they're worse than Lance and me," whispered Steve as Izzy began whimpering with fear after Vince whispered something to him. Sammi lost his temper again and shrieked at Vince that he would fry him like a marshmallow if he even thought of fucking with Izzy again.

"How did you manage to record a whole album together?"

"It's not that hard once we actually get down to business—if we can." Cain sighed. "Honestly, the real problem is Vince. Sammi and I keep him under control most of the time, but sometimes he just—"

Someone coughed loudly next to him. Cain turned around, expecting to see one of his band mates.

"Hey, *coñito*," said a hoarse voice. "I was hoping I'd find you again."

It was the crooked-backed man from the Hispanic neighborhood. Cain stared at him in surprise; he had not heard the man coming up behind him, and judging from the startled expression on Steve's face, neither had he.

"So I hear you've made a name for yourself." The man hobbled along beside Cain, chatting as if he'd been there the whole time. "I bet you'll have a good chunk of cash to blow when that album of yours comes out."

"I suppose." Cain glanced at the man, trying to recall his name; he could only remember Mrs. Delgado calling him Jodido.

"Come on," said Jodido, his sunken eyes lighting up strangely. "Any kid with a guitar and a pretty face can make himself a star in this town, especially with a big shot like Bruce Arkin backing him. Trust me, you're gonna have a lot of money to your name real soon, and I've…" He paused and glared at Steve, who was gaping at him. "Hey, kid, you got a problem?"

"Wha…?" Steve jumped and shook his head vigorously. "Um…no. No problem at all."

"How about you keep your eyes on the road?"

Cain couldn't blame Steve for staring. Jodido's thin hair was crusted with so much gel that it looked as if it had been painted on with India ink, and he was wearing a bulky leather jacket that might have been stylish if it weren't several sizes too big for him. Actually, Cain didn't mind the jacket because it partially covered up the shirt beneath it, which was bright green with a blinding fuchsia paisley pattern.

"*Anyway*," said Jodido with a last haughty glance at Steve. "You'll be rich in a year's time, boy. You take my word for it."

Sammi, Vince, and Izzy were trailing along ten feet behind them, too deeply engaged in a revived argument over Ty Thorpe's guilt or innocence to notice Jodido's appearance. Cain cast a longing glance at them over his shoulder and slowed his pace, hoping they would catch up and scare off Jodido. There was something about the little man that gave him an odd, unsettled feeling in the pit of his stomach.

"You think so?" He narrowed his eyes warily.

"Yes I do. And I've got something for you to spend your money on."

He fished around in the folds of his jacket and brought out a small plastic baggie full of brown powder.

"Dark Venezuelan." He held the baggie out with a grin. "One hundred percent pure and uncut. There's enough here to get you buzzed at least twenty times—thirty, if you're a lightweight. And you don't need to worry about the cops finding it. They don't care if you have it on you 'cause humans can't get high off it, only devils can."

Cain looked to Steve for help, but Steve was carefully staring directly ahead. His obvious discomfort increased Cain's uneasiness.

"Who says I'm a devil?" Jodido's comment had made

him even more uncomfortable. Mr. Arkin had given Cain the impression that only his band mates and a few people who worked for the label knew that he truly was a demon. The general public would be led to believe that he was a human in a clever costume.

Jodido chuckled indulgently and pointed to Cain's tail. "Nobody had to say it; the evidence is right there. Look, kid, you're lucky I found you. This town is crawling with dealers, but I'm the only one of them who'll sell to non-humans. Except Waheela." His eyes darkened, and he gave Cain a suspicious look. "You don't know any of those filthy dogs, do you?"

Cain toyed with the idea of saying that he did have a few Waheela friends in the hope that it would make Jodido lose interest, but he quickly decided against it. He had heard awestruck tales of the fierce white wolves of the north that could talk like humans from Steve, but the creatures were so rare and secretive that even Mr. Warwick knew very little about them. Cain doubted he could lie convincingly if Jodido started asking questions. He shook his head.

"Good." Jodido frowned. "Cheap, cagey bastards— Waheela. They're always trying to bargain everything down." He blinked and suddenly seemed to realize that the conversation had gotten off track. "They're not like you devils at all. You're always a pleasure to do business with." He shook the mysterious baggie with an inviting grin. "So, what do you say?"

Cain could hear Sammi, Vince, and Izzy arguing obliviously behind him. He was going to have to get out of this one on his own.

"I…I don't know," he stammered. "I'll have…to think about it…" He fumbled for a moment, and then a stroke of inspiration hit him. "I'd like to ask a friend of mine what she thinks. I'm just on my way to see her now."

"Oh yeah?"

"Yeah. You might know her—Mrs. Delgado, from that butcher shop…?"

The information had the desired effect. Jodido swallowed nervously and fell back a bit.

"You're going to see Delfina?"

"Mmm hmm."

"Oh. Okay. So…you'll think about it then?"

Cain nodded and picked up his pace a bit. Jodido spun around and hop-skipped off in the opposite direction.

"You really don't need to mention me to Delfina, by the way," he called over his shoulder. "Nothing personal; she just doesn't like me much for some reason. I really can't imagine why."

Steve craned his neck cautiously for a last glimpse of Jodido. He turned to Cain with an odd look on his face and seemed on the verge of saying something, but then, he shook his head and blew out a low whistle instead.

"Wow," he muttered to himself.

Jodido scurried back up the street as Sammi, Izzy, and Vince rounded the corner. Vince and Izzy were too deep in conversation to notice, but Sammi stopped him. They talked for a moment in voices too low for Cain to hear what they were saying. Then Jodido disappeared around the corner while Sammi continued walking.

"I'm telling you, Izzy, it doesn't matter," Vince said as they drew closer. "LA is only about five hours from Big Sur. Plus, Ty could've been in fucking Timbuktu when Eddie's cabin caught fire—he wouldn't have been any less guilty."

"But Vince, didn't, like, lots of people see him at the

Bayou Jewel right around the time the fire started?" Izzy trotted after Vince, playing agitatedly with his hands. "How could he have set fire to Eddie's cabin in Big Sur if he was in LA?"

Vince smirked. "No one has figured that out yet. See, if there's anything Ty Thorpe learned from his big brother before he put a knife in his gut, it was how to make people see what he wanted them to see. If Ty wanted everyone to think that he wasn't in the right place to burn Eddie's cabin down, then everyone's damn well going to think that…"

He brushed past Cain and Steve, too caught up in his theorizing to catch the half-hearted warning glance Cain threw at him. Izzy followed him, torn between horror and fascination.

"I give up." Sammi popped up beside Cain with a sigh of frustration. "Vinnie won't leave that crazy theory of his alone, and Izzy is totally eating it up. I swear to God, it's Vinnie's turn to wash the sheets if Izzy has nightmares tonight and pisses the bed." He thought for a moment. "Say, Cain, I know you've been taking guitar lessons from Ty, so…don't let this put you off him, okay? I don't know what Vince has against the poor guy, but Ty is *not* a homicidal maniac with a basement full of bodies."

"I'm sure he isn't." Cain found it impossible to imagine the soft-spoken Ty slaughtering his own brother in cold blood.

The sun had set by the time they reached the Hispanic neighborhood. All the stores along the main street were closed for the holidays. The butcher's shop was dark except for the string of green Christmas lights that twined through bright red paper chains adorning the windows. Cain sighed in disappointment. He had hoped Mrs. Delgado would be here; she had a habit of staying after closing time to clean up.

"Brilliant, Cain," grumbled Vince. "You drag us halfway across the stinking city to say hello to an empty street in some shithole ethnic neighborhood. I've got blisters on my feet now."

The front door banged open unexpectedly, and Mrs. Delgado bustled out, carrying an armful of bloody aprons.

"*Ay de mi*, why don't men ever keep their things clean?" she muttered to herself. "These are more blood than cloth. I don't know how Arturo can stand to wear them."

She stopped when she saw Cain standing across the street with his companions. Her eyes widened as they had the first time she had seen him, but with joy and relief now instead of fear.

"Arturo!" she called loudly while she scurried up the street toward her house. She didn't seem to care if she woke anyone. "Our *animal* is back!"

A few neighbors stuck their heads out their windows and doors, awakened by her cries. As soon as they saw what the commotion was about, they ran to waken others. Soon, about a quarter of the neighborhood's population was crowded into and around the butcher's shop, chattering excitedly.

"They want him to *kill rats*?" Sammi whispered to Steve while they watched Cain patiently sit and accept chicken scraps from a contingent of old ladies vying to be the first to lure him off to their infested houses or gardens. "Like a damn cat?"

Steve shrugged. "It stands to reason. I know dad had to teach Cain that the guinea pigs he used sometimes for

246

experiments weren't snacks."

"That's weird. And...kind of creepy, to tell you the truth. Cain did tell us that the people in this neighborhood fed him and helped him survive, but he never told us they thought he was like their living mousetrap or something. Freaky."

Cain munched on a gizzard and glanced gratefully at Izzy, who had drawn the attention of the few wound-up children in the room by taking his golden retriever form. They crawled all over him as they used to do to Cain, and Izzy submitted to their stepping and punching and tail-pulling with a doggy grin of contentment.

"Stop squirming, bitch." Vince had backed a young woman against the counter. He dug his searching fingers into her glossy black hair, pushing harder as she struggled. "I wanna see if you really do have a boyfriend or if you're just blowing me off. You'll regret it if you blow me off, you know. I'm gonna be famous soon...What the fuck? All your thoughts are in Spanish! Dammit, Sammi, come here and help me translate this slut's thoughts, will you?"

"Keep your hands to yourself, Vinnie," Sammi snapped. "And what makes you think I speak Spanish? Yeah, my granddad was Bolivian, but I never lived in Bolivia."

Steve gave Sammi a quizzical look. He wouldn't have known that the old ladies from the neighborhood wanted Cain to kill rats if Sammi hadn't translated for him. Sammi quickly turned to stare out the window and tossed some sparks at a flickering bulb on the string of Christmas lights.

The people in the shop set up a murmur of alarm at Vince's behavior. Cain noticed their discomfort and quickly reached for his guitar, glowering meaningfully at Vince.

Vince pushed the girl away and retreated into a corner of

the shop with a sullen grunt. The people of the neighborhood first let out a collective sigh of relief and then began muttering darkly about the ill-mannered, dangerous stranger who had come in with their *animal*.

"You okay?" Steve whispered to Sammi.

"Hmm?" Sammi flicked another, bigger spark at the bulb. It popped loudly and began emitting a steady glow. "Oh, yeah, I'm fine. I just…a lot of the older guys here remind me of my granddad. He hated me."

Mr. and Mrs. Delgado observed the action from behind the counter.

"So *el animal* is back at last!" Mrs. Delgado was glad to see him again, even if he had brought along those bizarre friends. Ever since her *animal* had vanished without explanation one night nearly two months ago, she could hardly go a day without thinking about that killer. Rosa from the bodega had assured her that a horned guitarist had started to play the club circuit around the same time *animal* disappeared, but she hadn't dared to believe the musician was her *animal* until now. "And he's become a big star too. Isn't it wonderful, Arturo?"

"Yes, it is," said Mr. Delgado. "But haven't you noticed that those four young men our *animal* brought with him…" He glanced apprehensively at Cain and his band mates. "I think they're *brujos*, Delfina."

"What a superstitious thing to say, Arturo." Mrs. Delgado had suspected the same thing from the moment she saw what they could do, but she had been making an effort not to show her anxiety. At least they hadn't done any real harm, and her *animal* seemed able and willing to keep them under control. "Since when have you been so ready to see witchcraft around every corner?"

"I think they're *brujos*," Mr. Delgado insisted. "Or at least three of them are. The blond one turned himself into a dog to amuse the children. The dark one just fixed the blinking bulb in the window that you've been complaining about..."

"Yes, he did." Mrs. Delgado avoided her husband's eye. "It was nice of him."

Mr. Delgado cleared his throat. "...by making electricity with his hands. If that isn't witchcraft, I don't know what is."

Mrs. Delgado glared at her husband. "Well, at least they're helpful *brujos*."

"What about the red-haired one? He was reading Teresita's mind until *el animal* made him stop."

"Arturo, they're just the other members of our *animal's* band. Why else would they follow him here?"

The priest had been roused with the others. He stood by the counter, feeling neglected while his flock lavished attention on the devil-boy.

"It may be that they're not really a rock band at all," he said loudly. "It may be that they're a coven, and your devil-boy is their master."

Mrs. Delgado laughed. "Now, *Padre*, you were the first to say that our *animal* wasn't dangerous."

The priest frowned. The devil-boy sat slumped on a stool that was too small for him in the middle of the room, looking like some horrible, hairy prehistoric beast. The old women of the neighborhood clustered around him, handing him food and patting his head as if he were a dog, talking to him in affectionate tones. It wasn't fair; that creature hadn't spent weeks learning another language and researching another culture to better minister to the people of this neighborhood. He hadn't labored over sermons for them, or officiated at their weddings and funerals, or comforted them during sickness. Yet the devil-boy got more attention from the priest's flock in a single evening than the priest garnered in a week.

A little girl darted toward the priest, shrieking with laughter. The priest sighed and bent down to tell her that she shouldn't dash around because running indoors wasn't safe or ladylike. To his surprise and terror, the crowd leapt back with yelps and shrieks of fright. An enormous gorilla was barreling toward him. He screamed and stumbled back against the counter.

"Whoa!" The gorilla stood up and became Izzy, who grinned winsomely at the gaping priest. "Sorry about that, dude. We're just playing."

The priest was too shaken to answer. He did manage a disapproving glare at the sinuous half dragon, half full-breasted woman tattooed on Izzy's right bicep.

None of the people who had seen Izzy in gorilla form were terribly eager to stand near him. Unfazed, Izzy swept the girl up on his back and changed into a stocky pony to give her a ride in the open space they left around him. The effortless rippling of his transformation made the priest's flesh crawl. His gaze turned to the other young thugs *el animal* had brought with him. Their talents were every bit as unnatural and as wicked as the shape-shifter's, if not worse. And they seemed to be aware of their deviance. The lightning-maker shifted and fidgeted, avoiding eye contact with everyone around him. The redhead stood sullenly in a corner, poised to lash out with those awful soul-invading hands. The younger one hadn't shown off his particular brand of sorcery yet, but the priest was certain he had one. Surely, they would have been run out of the neighborhood the moment they started showing off their disgusting black magic if they hadn't come in with hideous, deformed, and unreasonably popular *el animal*.

Jealousy is a sin, the priest reminded himself. Still, he thought he was beginning to understand why that blustering idiot Nathaniel Breen hated rock musicians so much.

"Mrs. Delgado," he muttered, "those young men definitely have some dark power at their disposal, and I'd bet anything it comes from the devil-boy. I mean, Jesus, Mary, and Joseph, he has a *tail* as well as horns. How could I have missed that before?"

Mr. Delgado ducked quietly into the stockroom, as if he wanted no further contact with *el animal's* band of sorcerers and no part in any argument with the priest.

Mrs. Delgado was silent for a while. The priest observed her watching her *animal* guzzle down meat scraps while their neighbors jockeyed for his attentions. The strained expression on the devil-boy's face suggested that he was no longer hungry and was eating to be polite—if one could call a devil polite.

"Maybe they do," she said.

"And doesn't that frighten you?" The priest's voice rose a bit.

"Not as much as some things." Mrs. Delgado turned away from him. "Excuse me, *Padre*. I have to take out the trash."

She hustled off. The priest called after her, but she didn't seem to hear him.

There were no trash bags by the back door. Mrs. Delgado stepped out into the alley empty-handed, her arms crossed tightly over her chest. She stared up at the gray sky, rocking on the balls of her feet. *El animal* was safe after all, and for that, she was grateful. But the priest was right; there was a great deal more to him than anyone had originally suspected, and that fact made her very uncomfortable. Her concept of the Devil was vague and ill-defined, a patchwork of old Indian trickster tales and various half-remembered Sunday school lectures. She had never put much stock in these stories, and the weirdly sweet, obedient horned boy who cowered in submission before broom-wielding old women and who defended little children from rats had come close to driving them from her mind entirely. However, *animal's* gang of unsavory disciples and the scaly blue tail that snaked down from the seat of *animal's* pants brought the stories rushing back.

The faint outline of a faded mural was visible on the wall beside the dumpster. Mrs. Delgado traced the remaining patches of color with her hands. She had to tell him to leave. It pained her to admit it to herself, but it couldn't be helped. She had unwittingly agreed to harbor the Devil in her own backyard. It would be cruel to her neighbors and friends to let him stay on, promise or no promise.

"Having second thoughts, Delfina?"

Mrs. Delgado didn't turn around.

"You didn't tell me, Lotus Blossom," she said.

"Tell you what?" A hint of amusement crept into the familiar soft, smooth voice. "That he is the Devil, and he has come with his coven to steal your soul? Of course I didn't tell you that, honey; it isn't true."

252

"He has a *tail*, Lotus Blossom."

"I don't see why that should matter. He was lost and alone and needed a friend."

Mrs. Delgado drummed her fingers against the wall, agitated. "Well, I can't let him stay anymore. I'm sorry. Maybe he's not *the* Devil, but he's still *a* devil."

A dark figure stepped into her peripheral vision. Almost against her will, Mrs. Delgado looked up and met the dark eyes staring into hers.

"Don't you worry, Delfina," said Crazy Loti. "He doesn't need to stay here. He's not in the business of catching rats anymore. But you shouldn't write him off just yet. Remember: you did promise."

"I didn't know what I was promising."

"I never give one of mine a job too big to handle. Trust me, Delfina, like you always have trusted me, and you'll both be rewarded."

The ragged old woman turned and walked off toward the street at an unhurried pace. Mrs. Delgado stared after her with growing exasperation, knowing from experience that it was useless to call her back. Yes, she had sworn, foolishly, to give the devil-boy food and shelter on the assurance that he wasn't dangerous. Now, that promise bound her. She should have pumped Lotus Blossom for more information about what she was getting herself into, or she should have flat-out refused to agree to anything until such information was offered. But it probably wouldn't have made any difference; Lotus Blossom was a Patron, a member of an ancient order of city guardians. Their origins were unknown, and their intentions were obscure. And they were certainly not known for their straightforwardness.

"Fine. *El animal* is welcome here whenever he wants to

come." Mrs. Delgado sighed. The *Padre* wasn't going to like this arrangement.

Loti glanced back over her shoulder. Her eyes glinted in the faint light from the open door.

"You won't regret it," she said.

Then she was gone, swallowed up in the darkness beyond the alley.

Chapter Eleven

The Show

THREE MORE DAYS PASSED, and Mr. Warwick showed no sign of coming to pick up Steve.

"We're supposed to go home on New Year's Day." Steve tried to smile sarcastically as he curled up on the couch. "I always did suspect that dad wouldn't care if I fell off the face of the planet."

"Maybe he guessed that you would come right to me." Cain didn't really feel inclined to defend Mr. Warwick, but he knew these words would comfort Steve. And perhaps, Cain felt as if he owed Mr. Warwick something for his temporary freedom. "I bet he trusts me to keep you safe. Or he's cooling down before giving you a good talking-to for running off like that."

Steve rolled his eyes. "Whatever he's doing, it looks like I'm spending New Year's Eve with you."

"Well, *that's* just fine." Vince popped his head out of the kitchen. "You got a babysitter for Junior tomorrow, Cain? He's sure as hell not coming with us."

"Why not?" said Steve defiantly. "I want to see Cain play."

"You and everyone else in LA. We're not pulling any strings to get you in."

"Well, not in the audience, anyway," said Cain, holding up a hand when Steve began to protest. "But I don't see anything wrong with letting him sit backstage while we—"

Steve cut him off with a yelp of joy. "You'd take me backstage?"

Vince groaned. "No, he wouldn't. That's the last thing we need: having some clueless kid underfoot the whole time on the biggest night of our careers."

"I'll stay out of the way," said Steve solemnly. "I'll be so quiet you won't even know I'm there. I promise."

"Oh, you'll be quiet, all right." Vince's eyes glinted dangerously. "If you even think of following us backstage, kid, I might get…hungry."

He took a slow, menacing step into the room, curling his fingers like claws. Steve hopped up and scurried around the couch, putting it between himself and Vince.

Cain reached for his guitar with a deliberate sweeping motion. "Don't even think about it, Vince. What's your problem anyway? Steve has been nothing but nice to you, and you have his word that he won't be any trouble."

Vince squinted apprehensively at the guitar. "Hey, Izzy," he shouted.

Izzy was standing in the kitchen. A box of cereal and a carton of milk sat on the counter in front of him. He dug a handful of cereal from the box and crammed it into his mouth as Vince, Cain, and Steve walked through the door. He then picked up the carton, took a swig of milk, and sloshed it several times before swallowing it.

"What the fuck are you doing?" said Vince.

"Eating breakfast." Izzy reached into the box of cereal

again.

"Whatever." Vince shook his head. "Look, Iz, I need you to help me talk Cain out of a bad idea, okay?"

"Really? What bad idea?"

"He wants to let that kid hang out backstage at our show tonight."

"You mean Steve?" said Izzy. "Oh, good. I like Steve. Now what's the bad idea?"

"Goddammit, Izzy!" Vince snorted in disgust. "What the hell do you know? You can't even pretend you're not half-animal!"

He rounded on Cain. "Mr. Arkin won't like it, you know."

"I'm sure Mr. Arkin will understand," said Cain.

Vince growled something unintelligible and stalked off. Cain sighed and turned to Izzy to make sure he was all right.

"I'm not half-animal." Izzy's lip trembled while he gathered up a few flakes of cereal that had spilled on the counter. "What is Vince so mad about? Did I say something wrong?"

"Of course not, Izzy," Cain assured him. "It wasn't your fault. Vince is mad at me right now, and he took it out on you."

"He doesn't like me, does he?" Steve made a face.

"I'm afraid not," said Cain. "But he doesn't seem to like anyone else either. Don't let it bother you too much."

"He used to beat up the mean kids at school when they called me a retard, you know." Izzy plodded into the living room and plopped down wearily on the couch. The others followed him. "He was a lot nicer before *it* happened."

He pulled out a battered old shoebox from underneath the coffee table, pried off the frayed lid, and sprinkled the leftover cereal flakes into it. Cain watched apprehensively. Izzy had no idea how close his habit of storing food in odd places had brought him to receiving a pummeling on several occasions. Yesterday, when Vince stepped into the shower and put his foot in a bowl of half-congealed chocolate pudding, Cain had to brandish his guitar to prevent a fistfight.

"Hey, don't you think you ought to throw that cereal away?" said Cain.

"Throw it away?" Izzy raised an eyebrow. "Why would I want to do that? It's still good."

"Then why not put it back in the box?"

"Because Bonzo needs breakfast too."

"Who?"

"Oh, Bonzo is just a little guy I found hanging around in front of the house last night," said Izzy, fiddling with something inside the shoebox.

"You didn't bring him inside, did you?"

"Bring who inside?" Sammi popped into the room with a worried expression on his face. "Izzy, you didn't let some hobo into the house, did you?"

Cain stared at him in amazement. He was beginning to suspect that Sammi had a sixth sense that let him instantly know when one of his band mates was doing something boneheaded.

"What? No!" Izzy shook his head vigorously. "I know better than that. I didn't let a person in—just Bonzo."

"Bonzo?" Sammi raised an eyebrow at Cain. Cain shrugged.

"*This* is Bonzo." Izzy pulled something small and fuzzy out of the box. "I found him eating out of the garbage."

Cain recognized the brown-furred creature in an instant.

The rat's presence in their home didn't bother him much; he had killed, been bitten by, and scurried over by so many rats in the Hispanic neighborhood that he hardly noticed them anymore. Even when Sammi gasped and stumbled back with a look of utter disgust, he wasn't bothered.

However, Steve's scream shook him. Sammi jumped and Izzy turned bright red while Steve leapt up as if he had been stung, looking around wildly. Cain saw the shift in Steve's expression when he realized that there were no suitable rat-killing weapons within his reach. Steve's hand flew up purposefully, and his eyes narrowed with the focus needed to cast a spell.

Almost without thinking, Cain pointed his guitar at the rat, which was regarding him with an air of haughty indifference. He played a single clear note, quickly distorting it into an unearthly howl, before releasing his own spell. Casting a spell was risky when someone was holding the target, but it was far less risky than whatever Steve was about to do in his panicked state.

The rat shrieked and writhed in alarm. Black feathers erupted from its body, poking out between Izzy's fingers, and its sharp little face sharpened further into a beak. Izzy dropped it into his lap with a surprised yelp. It was no longer a rat, but an unusually small crow.

"It's all right, Steve." Cain hurried around the couch, putting himself between Steve and the transformed rat. "No rats here, see?"

The crow shivered and picked itself up—or tried to. It leaned on its wings as if they were front paws and promptly toppled over again. Steve's eyes followed its movements in horrified fascination, and his hand slowly dropped back to his side.

"Sorry." Cain leaned over and whispered to Izzy. "Steve hates rats, and turning your rat into something he *isn't* afraid of was the first thing I could think of to do. I can put him back the way he was—"

"Sorry?" Izzy was beaming. "Why? That was the coolest thing I've ever seen. We should totally get a bunch of rats for the show."

"Maybe we should," said Sammi, wrinkling his nose in disgust. "But that isn't gonna be one of them."

"Sammi!" Izzy gave him a pleading look.

"Come on, Izzy—that's a wild rat. It's probably crawling with fleas and worms. It might have rabies too."

Izzy picked up the rat-turned-crow and clutched it protectively. Sammi tried a different tactic.

"You know what?" he said. "If you really want to keep that thing, go ahead. Just watch out for Vince. Once he finds out that there is a rat living in this house, I bet the first thing he'll do is run out and buy a shit-ton of rat poison."

"You think so?"

"I bet he will," Steve jumped in, staring at the crow. "I...I mean, *he'll* probably buy a million traps too."

Izzy's face fell. "Yeah, that's probably what he'd do." He contemplated the crow for a moment, sighing. "Oh, okay. I'll put him back outside."

"All right then." Sammi nodded, satisfied. "Do your stuff, Cain."

"Hmm? Oh, right." Cain pointed his guitar at the crow again, glancing meaningfully at Steve. "Steve, you might want to..."

Steve nodded and scurried out of the room as fast as he could. Cain watched him go with some perplexity. Steve's visceral loathing of rats was one of the most intense fears he had ever seen, and honestly, Steve's reaction seemed an odd response to a creature so frail that it could be dispatched with a single bite. He suspected that the fear originated from the day Lance had locked Steve in the attic.

Once Steve was gone, Cain made short work of the spell. Izzy sighed longingly while the black feathers receded into fur.

"I could get, like, a cage or something for him." There was a faint note of hope in his voice. "Vince would never know he was here."

"Put him outside, Iz," said Sammi firmly. "He'll be a lot happier out there."

"Yeah. I guess so." Izzy heaved himself up from the couch and shuffled out the door, rat in hand. His shoulders drooped sadly, and he had such a crushed expression on his face that Cain felt a momentary stab of guilt for not defending his right to keep pet rats.

"Don't worry, man," said Sammi. "He'll be fine. I doubt he'll even remember that rat tomorrow, what with the show and all. Still, you've got to admit he got a pretty good idea out of it. We should get a bunch of rats for you to turn into crows onstage. I bet it would make a pretty awesome visual—all of them sprouting wings and flying away at the same time."

"It would," said Cain doubtfully. "Except...Well, I don't know if I could get them to fly. I can change them so they look like crows, but I can't make them *think* they're crows. They'd probably just try to keep crawling around on the stage like rats."

"Oh. That's a good point." Sammi frowned. "Well, shit. I guess that's the end of that idea...unless you can, I don't know, train them somehow? Could you get some rats and turn them into crows a few times to get them used to it and then slowly teach them to fly?"

"That might work." Now that Cain thought about it, he sort of liked the idea. The vision of dozens of black wings billowing around him was strangely comforting. It resonated in the depths of his mind, speaking to an old memory he couldn't fully access, even now that the collar was out of commission.

"Great!" Sammi's voice interrupted his thoughts. "By the way, I came down here to ask you something…What was it? Oh yeah. Do have any idea what's gotten into Vince? He just stormed into the loft and started screaming at me that everybody was against him."

"Vince?" said Cain. "Well, the last I saw him he was having a fit because I didn't want to leave Steve alone on the night of the concert, and Izzy agreed with me. It is all right to bring Steve backstage, isn't it?" he added quickly.

"What? Sure." Sammi raised an eyebrow. "Is that all it was? I mean, Vince was so mad I couldn't understand half of what he was saying. I thought he'd, like, stolen memories from some paranoid homeless guy and then forgotten that they weren't his."

"But it is okay to bring Steve backstage?" said Cain. "I probably should have asked you first."

Sammi chuckled. "Hey, you don't need my permission. It's your party. Invite anyone you like. Vince will get over it." He paused for a moment. "I hope."

Vince was quiet on the way to the show. He sat in the back row of the bus, splayed across both seats, and glared fiercely at Steve. Cain paid little attention to him; he was too busy worrying that his hair wouldn't stay in place.

"Hey, are you okay?" said Steve after the bus went over a bump and Cain gasped and reached up to poke at his sloppily feathered bangs.

"I'm fine," he said. "I don't like the way people look at me when they see my horns—that's all. My tail either," he added, shifting uncomfortably. He had jammed his tail into his pants before they left. They had only been out of the house for ten minutes, and it was already throbbing with pain.

"No offense, but…won't you have to get used to that?" said Steve. "I mean, if you're gonna be out there performing, the horns and tail will be the first things fans notice. They'll probably want you to walk around with them hanging out."

Cain wasn't sure he liked the idea of showing off his horns and tail on purpose. He could handle people gawking at him while he walked down the street, but when he was trapped on a bus with nowhere to run to or hide…The sour, icy expression on the face of the sleek-haired, pinstripe-wearing businesswoman in the row across from them was enough to make him nervous, even though Cain was fairly certain that she wasn't looking down her nose at him, but at Izzy, who was loudly singing a particularly ribald verse of Candiryde's "Cherry-Popper" in the row behind them. He was relieved when Sammi finally signaled that they had reached their stop.

At the concert hall, Cain was whisked away for a sound check. Much to the annoyance of the engineers, he spent most of it staring in awe at the four big stacks of amplifiers, the snarl of cords, and the dozens of stage lights. He thought he had known someone, long ago, who would have loved this paradise of complex-looking machinery; but he couldn't for the life of him remember of whom he was thinking.

Someone knocked on Cain's dressing room door an hour before the show. He opened it and found Mr. Arkin standing in the hallway.

"So the big night is here!" He grinned and clapped Cain on the shoulder. "Excited?"

"A little," said Cain. He was also a little frightened, but he didn't say anything for fear that Mr. Arkin might launch into his terrifying anti-stage-fright lecture again.

"Good. Don't worry, kid. You'll do great." His smile faded a bit. "Say, why aren't you in costume yet?"

"Well…" Cain glanced back at the jumble of leather, spandex, and sequins hanging on the bar behind him. "I couldn't figure out how to put it on."

"That's right." Mr. Arkin snapped his fingers in frustration. "You didn't get it fitted beforehand, did you? I'm sorry; I meant to step in and twist the designer's arm until she scheduled a fitting for you. I don't know what her problem was; she acted like she was afraid you'd eat her or something once she figured out your horns and tail were real. But I've been so busy that I forgot. Well, since I'm here, I might be able to help—"

"Hey, Mr. Arkin!" Vince's voice interrupted him. "This kid I've never seen before got into the building somehow, and he's been stalking me. I think he's dangerous. Can I kick him out?"

"You jerk!" Steve's shrill, angry voice rang down the hall. "You told me Cain wanted to ask me something!"

Mr. Arkin raised his eyebrows at Cain.

Cain squeezed past Mr. Arkin and planted himself in the middle of the hallway with crossed arms. Vince stopped in his tracks and looked guilty. Steve heaved a sigh of relief.

"Mr. Arkin, this is my friend Steve Warwick," said Cain

calmly, scowling at Vince. "I've been asked to keep an eye on him while his father is in the city on business."

"That doesn't mean he has to take the brat everywhere," snapped Vince. "Look, I can toss him out the door right now. Just give the word, and I'd be happy to do it."

"Steve Warwick?" Mr. Arkin spoke up before Cain could start arguing. "You must be Jesse Warwick's son."

"Oh…" Steve seemed a bit taken aback. "Yeah. I am."

"I should have known. You look a lot like him." Mr. Arkin chuckled and held out his hand to Steve. "But you must get tired of hearing that. Steve, I'm Bruce Arkin. Your dad has done a little work for me over the years. He's a great guy. It was nice of him to let me borrow Cain."

Vince looked from Mr. Arkin to Steve and back again, his cheeks bright with indignation. Cain grinned in amusement, and Vince went even redder.

"So we all know each other now," he grumbled. "That's just great. But don't you think that kid will be in the way backstage?"

"Eh, I wouldn't worry about it." Mr. Arkin shrugged. "I'm sure Cain can keep him out of trouble; he's had plenty of practice with you from what I've heard."

Vince gritted his teeth and flexed his fingers as if he wanted more than anything to dig them into the deepest and most tender part of Mr. Arkin's psyche.

"This is the most important night of my career," he said, taking an ominous step toward Mr. Arkin. "I don't want some fucking snot-nosed teenager underfoot the whole time."

Mr. Arkin didn't budge. Cain couldn't help but admire him because he stood his ground so calmly, showing no fear of those dangerous hands. Cain had flinched, even though he knew that Vince was too afraid of him to attempt another assault on his mind.

"What about Cain?" said Mr. Arkin in a firm voice. "It's the most important night of his career too. So he has unexpected responsibilities to take care of. We'll all just have to do the best we can. The show must go on. By the way, did you really just call Steve a 'snot-nosed teenager'? That's pretty rich coming from someone who celebrated his eighteenth birthday not so long ago."

"Yeah, well, I'm mature for my age and shit," Vince snapped. "And what are these responsibilities you're talking about? Cain just wanted to bring his stupid friend along."

"Cain is keeping an eye on Steve during his time in the city, Vince. Steve's father told me so himself when I met with him the other day. That sounds like responsibility to me."

"But…"

"The matter is closed, Vince. Now go get into costume already."

Vince glared at Mr. Arkin. "Fine."

"He's a bit temperamental, isn't he?" Mr. Arkin shook his head as Vince turned on his heel and stormed off. "Sorry about that, Steve. Of course you can hang out here tonight. But be sure not to let Cain keep you too late. Your dad wants you back at the hotel by eight sharp tomorrow."

"Oh. Okay." Steve did a poor job of hiding the disappointment in his voice.

"Don't worry, kid," said Mr. Arkin. "You'll have some great memories to take home from your LA vacation. Say, do you want to help Cain with his costume? I bet you'll figure out how to fix it faster than I could."

Steve nodded and dashed into Cain's dressing room, as

if he were extraordinarily glad to have a place to hide from Vince. Cain followed silently. Something was bothering him. Mr. Arkin must have known about Steve's visit long before he had, and Mr. Warwick hadn't even bothered to discuss it with Cain. Maybe he was reading too much into it, but the circumvention almost seemed like a deliberate, subtle reminder from Mr. Warwick that he was still a demon and that he had to have a master.

"But Vince," Izzy's voice filtered through the dressing room door. "I don't know if I *can* keep from turning purple on stage. Half the time, I don't realize I've turned purple."

Vince snapped something in reply, and Izzy whimpered a feeble protest. Cain drummed his fingers impatiently against the counter. Unless Sammi stepped in to rescue Izzy soon, he would have to do it himself. That would mean he'd have to leave the safety of the dressing room.

Steve pressed his ear to the door. "So, aren't you going to help Izzy? It's starting to sound pretty nasty out there, and I'm not hearing Sammi's voice."

"Oh, I want to help," said Cain. "But if I go out there…" He poked regretfully at his costume.

"Your clothes look fine," said Steve. "Come on, Cain, Izzy is dying out there. Everyone is gonna see you dressed like that anyway, you know."

Cain squirmed and made an uncomfortable noise in the back of his throat. Steve was right; dozens of people (hundreds if he was unlucky) would see him in these clothes before the night was up. The thought made him blush and squirm. He wanted to put off the reveal as long as he could, but Izzy's whimpering had risen to a scream, and Sammi still hadn't shown up.

"Ow, ow, ow—not those memories, Vince," Izzy howled. "Please, that was the happiest night of my life! I promise I won't turn purple on stage tonight. I *promise*."

"Not good enough," growled Vince. "I want you to promise that you won't turn purple on stage ever. Swear your life on it. Now!"

Steve made an impatient hurrying motion. Cain took a deep breath, snatched up his guitar, and banged the door open.

"Vince, leave Izzy alone," he shouted, hoping the guitar gave him some semblance of authority despite his ridiculous appearance.

Vince leapt back, snatching his fingers out of Izzy's mind like a child who had been caught stealing from someone else's lunchbox. Izzy reeled against the closed door of Sammi's dressing room with a moan of relief. Cain was comforted to see that they were attired as outlandishly as he was; Izzy's muscles strained against his sparkly flame-patterned jumpsuit, and Vince seemed to be wearing nothing on his upper torso but a tangle of artfully tied chains and torn red handkerchiefs.

"Fine. Let Izzy fucking turn purple on stage whenever he wants." Vince glared at them. The imitation tribal tattoos painted on his cheeks trembled with indignation. "Never mind what it does to our image."

Cain's eyes wandered over Vince's chains and scarves and his tight red-and-orange tiger print pants. "Why would Izzy turning purple hurt our image when we're all wearing thick makeup and silly clothes? I doubt anyone will notice."

Vince gave him a lofty look and stalked off.

"See, Cain?" Steve stepped out of the dressing room, where he had been watching the confrontation from the doorway. "It's not so bad—everyone else is dressed the same way. I don't know what you're so worried about anyway. You look great."

"But I might as well be naked." It was not that the outfit revealed a vast expanse of bare chest; that feature by itself would have been bearable. It was that the outfit was incredibly tight. The black spandex pants, the high boots, and—most embarrassing of all—the red flame-detailed leather codpiece might as well not have been there at all because they concealed absolutely nothing. As if to drive home the insult, the costume was also uncomfortable. His feet were already throbbing with dull pain from the tight boots, and the codpiece was chafing a bit.

"I'm not joking." Steve actually sounded jealous. "You'll get all the girls now. Of course, they'd just laugh at me if *I* dressed like that. But you can get away with it."

"Get away with it?" Cain involuntarily covered his groin with his guitar. "How? Izzy had to nearly get his brain turned inside out before I was able to leave the dressing room. I don't think I can force myself to go out looking like this in front of all those people."

When show time came, Cain lingered nervously in the wings until an impatient stage hand herded him into position. Then the lights came up, and his breath caught in his throat.

Mr. Arkin had been running an aggressive advertising campaign throughout the city all month. Cain had been peripherally aware of it before tonight, but he knew that he had been its primary focus. Now, as he stood alone on the stage staring out at the packed auditorium, he was amazed at the sheer number of people in the audience. He hoped that his complete mortification at having all those eyes fixed on his near-nudity was not showing on his face. A soft murmur—were people chanting his name?—rose from the crowd. Cain took a step toward them, leaning forward slightly to regain his balance. Those ridiculous boots had heels that added several more inches to his height, and he hadn't gotten used to walking in them yet.

He raised his guitar and played a single note. The crowd was silent for a moment and then erupted in the single loudest cheer he had ever received.

Their enthusiasm threw him for a moment. *Don't sweat it*, he forced himself to remember Mr. Arkin saying. *Just do what you always do. They'll love it.*

There was a microphone set up at the front of the stage. Cain made his way to it with the swagger he had worked for weeks to perfect, all the while keeping the audience fixed with a steady, hungry gaze—*like you're going to steal all their souls*, Mr. Arkin had advised him. But Cain truly couldn't imagine what he would do with all those souls even if he wanted to steal them.

Cain leaned down to the microphone—it was set for Vince—and leered at the crowd. A sigh of anticipation filled the auditorium.

"Hey," he growled in his most fearsome stage voice. "I haven't even started yet."

More cheers and laughter erupted from the crowd.

Cain drew power from inside himself as he played a short riff. He didn't need Mr. Arkin to tell him that most humans expected certain things of demons, and now he did all he could to satisfy those expectations. While lashing his tail furiously, he conjured up a cloud of cold blue fire and let it lick over his hands and hair for a moment before blasting it into the crowd. The flames fragmented into the shapes of bats and tormented ghosts, writhing and clawing themselves out of existence as they dropped into the massively styled hair of the first five rows.

"That's what you came to see, huh?" He thrust his head forward aggressively as their hoots of joy and amazement died down. "Well, guess what? I've got something even better to rot your nasty-ass little human souls with tonight."

Dry ice fog began to flow over the stage. Cain raised his arms as if he were summoning it—the only artificial effect the band would use for the rest of the show.

"You've probably been wondering what I've been doing for the last month," he continued, his black-lined eyes still riveted on the crowd. "I'll tell you what I've been doing. I've been getting my fucking band together."

Cheers.

"You wanna meet them?"

Louder cheers.

"Good." Sammi and Vince materialized out of the fog behind him and took their places as planned; a large purple bird of an indeterminate species shot up from the stage, wheeled out over the audience, swooped down behind the drums, and became Izzy. "Because you're going to meet them whether you want to or not, and they're gonna help me tear your happy little world apart. This is Pseüdomäntis, motherfuckers—Izzy Unger on drums, Sammi Amp on bass, Vampire Vince on vocals, and Your Worst Nightmare on guitar." Cain threw his head back and let out his best maniacal laugh as he fell away from the microphone. "Welcome to Hell!"

The show went better than any of them expected. There was only one near-disaster: about halfway into the set—just before they launched into "Bite Me (Like the Bitch You

Are)"—Vince unexpectedly lunged down into the audience and wrapped his free hand around the head of a young blonde woman in the front row.

"So what're you talking to your friend about while I'm trying to sing?" he snarled at her while she moaned and struggled and her lanky boyfriend tentatively put his fists up. "Let's take a look at your thoughts and find out. Ha!" Vince smirked up at the rest of the crowd. "She's a virgin, and she wants to lose it with her boyfriend, Tim O'Malley here, tonight. That's what's more interesting to her than a fucking rock concert. By the way, her name is Cynthia Baker, she lives in Pasadena, and the most embarrassing moment of her life was that time in middle school when she dropped her towel in the girl's locker room." He released her just as Sammi began to flex his hand. "I'm right, aren't I?"

Cynthia Baker shrank away from the stage, mortified.

"Of course I am." Vince grinned evilly at the audience. "I can read minds—that's my special superpower that Sammi didn't want me to show you assholes tonight. One of them, anyway. I can also suck out people's souls by touching them." He lunged at Cynthia, who cowered down even further and screamed. "Wanna see, bitch?"

"Vinnie!" Electricity crackled through Sammi's hair as he raised his finger. "No stealing souls. You know Cain likes to keep our fans' souls all to himself."

The crowd roared with delight.

It was past midnight, and Cain was exhausted. He had hoped Sammi would keep an eye on Izzy and Vince so he could run Steve back to the hotel; but Sammi disappeared somewhere almost as soon as the after-show party started, and Steve had fallen in with a group of girls. Izzy didn't really need much supervising; he was lolling happily in the arms of three blonde admirers. But Vince was always a wild card. Right now, he looked almost peaceful, drinking a beer as he eyed another shapely girl, but Cain knew that it would take only one mention of the Engineer to set him off.

A young man in a leather jacket pushed his way through the crowd, laughing and proudly brandishing two glasses full of clear liquid. He caught sight of Cain, went quiet, and immediately turned around to scurry back the way he came. Cain leaned sadly against the wall. He had noticed that some of the people at this party seemed all right with his presence, but none of them were going out of their way to talk to him.

Skeeter Judd was seated at the small wooden table in the middle of the green room. Cain remembered the story Skeeter had started telling backstage after the Hellhound concert. Right now, he looked like the most promising source of entertainment in the room. After one last glance to make sure Vince and Izzy were behaving themselves, he stepped out of the corner and made his way to Skeeter, keeping a respectable distance so as not to spook him again. Then he waited for another story.

Skeeter didn't seem interested in telling stories at the moment. A small rectangular mirror and a single razor blade lay on the table in front of him. As Cain approached, he took a baggie full of something white and powdery out of his pocket and poured its contents onto the mirror. Then he picked up the razor blade and began to scrape the substance around the surface of the mirror with painstaking strokes, eventually separating it into three neat lines. Cain watched him curiously.

Skeeter admired his handiwork for a moment, grinning in anticipation. He rummaged in his pocket for his wallet, pulled out a bill, and rolled it into a tube. Then, as if it were the most normal thing in the world, he stuck one end of the makeshift straw up his right nostril and bent over the mirror to noisily suck the first line of powder into his nose. Cain could no longer contain his curiosity.

"Skeeter," he blurted. "What on earth are you doing?"

Skeeter rolled his head languidly around. He sat for a moment, grinning. When he noticed that it was Cain who had addressed him, he leapt up from his chair in panic.

"It's not mine!" he yelped, swaying in place, unable to decide whether to flee or fight. "It...uh...my drummer, Dog, asked me to hold it for him. He'll be back...soon..." He snorted wetly and lifted a hand to wipe his nose. A chagrined expression passed over his face. "I mean, sure, it's mine. But it's just a little coke, man. You wouldn't drag me off to Hell just because I did a little coke, would you?"

"Coke?" Cain looked at the two remaining lines of powder. Coke was the name of the fizzy brown drink that Steve and Lance liked. Skeeter's explanation only served to increase his confusion.

"It's not fair!" A whining tone crept into Skeeter's voice. "*Everybody* in this town does coke. You can practically buy it at the drugstores here. Why should I be the one to go to Hell for it? Why can't you take Johnny Revolver from Big Bertha instead? The dude is crazy; I've seen him inject whiskey right into his veins so it'll make him more drunk. Better yet, how about you take that little Mexican guy with the gimpy back...what's his name...Jodido? He sold this shit to me. I'd never have done coke if it wasn't for him. It's all his fault."

Cain perked up at Jodido's name. Apparently he sold to humans as well; this white substance of Skeeter's was

274

probably something similar to the brown powder he had tried to sell to Cain. But Cain still needed more information. He had been under the impression that humans swallowed their drugs, or injected them with a needle.

"But why are you sucking it into your nose?" he said.

Skeeter opened his mouth to protest again, and then he shut it.

"Why am I...?" he blinked suspiciously at Cain. "You mean you don't know? You've never seen anyone do coke before?"

Cain shook his head.

Skeeter squinted at him for a moment. Then he laughed loudly.

"Well, now you have," he said. "Man, look at your face! Don't worry, it doesn't hurt or anything."

"Really?" Cain cast a doubtful eye over the steady flow of snot dripping from Skeeter's reddened nostrils. "It looks like it should hurt."

"It does sting a little," Skeeter conceded. "But once it kicks in...God, you feel like you can do anything." He gave Cain a sideways look. "So are you sure you're not gonna take me to Hell?"

"Pretty sure."

"That's good." Skeeter's demeanor was changing. His fingers had begun to twitch, and he was talking noticeably faster. "You know what, kid? For a devil, you're all right. Just like your drummer over there." He jerked his head in the general direction of Izzy, who had shifted into his cuddliest dog form to attract more girls. "Nicest guy you'll ever meet. He used to do coke with me sometimes, but he won't anymore. He says it made him do some stupid things. Know what?" He leaned toward Cain and spoke in what he must have thought was a whisper, but anyone could have heard him from ten feet away. "Izzy won't talk about it, but when he was taken, the Engineer did some kind of sick experiment on him and gave him coke to dull the pain. That's the real reason he won't do coke anymore—it reminds him of all the hurt he went through. It's sad. Somebody ought to get him to a shrink."

Skeeter turned his attention back to his lines. Cain glanced over at Vince. The mention of the Engineer made him uneasy. He was wondering if Skeeter would be able to understand in his current state that he shouldn't talk about the Engineer in front of Vince when Steve burst through the crowd, two girls stumbling along in his wake.

"This is the most awesome night of my life, Cain!" Steve held up his enchanted knife triumphantly. "I've shown this to about twenty people now, and they think it's the most mind-blowing thing anyone has ever made. This one girl said she wanted to have my baby when she saw it."

"You do realize they're drunk, don't you?" said Cain. He also thought that both the teetering, senselessly giggling girls looked at least three years older than Steve.

"Of course I do!" Steve grinned wickedly. "That's the only good thing about drunk people—everything entertains them. Remember that time Lance, Kevin, and Brett broke into Kevin's dad's liquor cabinet, and when Lance came home, I showed him a potion and told him it would make everything taste like cotton candy if he drank it? He believed me because the potion was pink like cotton candy. If he hadn't been so plastered, he wouldn't have ended up with nasty oozing sores all over his body."

"I do remember that—now that you mention it. Didn't you get in pretty serious trouble?"

Steve winced at the memory. "Hooyeah! But it was worth it."

"I'm glad you enjoyed yourself, but we should get you back to the hotel now." Cain yawned. "You have an early start tomorrow."

"In a minute, in a minute. There are still some drunk girls I haven't impressed yet." Steve slipped back into the crowd before Cain could catch him.

"There can't be *that* many more," he called after Steve, even though he had a sinking feeling that this was not the case. A disproportionate percentage of the party's population was female. Steve could probably spend all night finding new girls to impress.

"Oh, let him have fun a little longer," laughed a familiar voice when he prepared to chase after Steve. "I don't think he'll have many opportunities in New York to get hit on by drunken Sunset Strip bottle blondes who are four or five years older than he is."

"Michelle!" Cain turned happily to her. "When did you get here?"

"Oh, I've been here the whole time. It took me a while to talk my way backstage," she said coolly. "Daddy was easier to get past, thank God. He totally bought my story that I was going to a New Year's sleepover at a friend's house. I think it probably helped that he had the miracle to distract him."

"Miracle?" repeated Cain. "What miracle?"

Michelle rolled her eyes. "Oh, just some water stain on a wall somewhere. Somebody thought it looked like an angel, so they sent pictures to daddy—along with a hefty donation to his ministry, of course."

"That doesn't sound like much of a miracle."

"Well, the money was enough to convince daddy. He was on Cloud Nine all afternoon. He didn't even bother to ask me the name of my friend as I walked out the door." Michelle giggled. "If I'd known he was going to be that out of it, I wouldn't have gone to the trouble of paying Jessica Baxter fifty bucks to pretend I was staying at her house. Anyway, let's do something special to welcome in 1983."

Cain took stock of the rest of the party while Michelle's arms slipped around his waist. The three girls were still cooing over Izzy the dog. His tail thumped against their bare thighs, and the girl on the far right didn't seem to mind that he had buried his nose in her crotch. Vince was in the corner, wrapped in a vigorous, but apparently amicable, embrace with the girl he had been eyeing. And another girl screamed in horrified delight while Steve sawed harmlessly through her wrist. They should be fine if he left them alone for a few minutes.

"That sounds like a great idea." He began to lead her along the fringes of the crowd of revelers. "Let's find an empty dressing room."

This task was easier said than done. Other couples already occupied three of the six dressing rooms, and a fourth room was packed with seven young women who were sharing an odd-smelling white cigarette and giggling raucously.

"Here, Cain. This one is empty..." Michelle pushed open the door to the room in which Cain had gotten ready and stopped mid-step in the threshold. "Oh, sorry!"

Cain peered over her shoulder. Ty Thorpe was in the dim room, seated in front of the makeup mirror. He turned slowly around to face them when the beam of light from the open door fell on him. He was holding something in his left hand, which he deftly stuffed into his jacket pocket before Cain got a good look at it.

"I'm sorry," Michelle repeated, backing up a step as Ty climbed to his feet. "We didn't know you were in here. We'll try another room."

Ty watched her without blinking until she stopped protesting and stared back in awed silence.

"No need," he said calmly. "I should be going anyway." He glanced at Cain. "Great job tonight, by the way."

Michelle and Cain stepped back to let Ty pass. He ambled off in the opposite direction of the party, toward the stage access door.

"Strange guy, isn't he?" Michelle shook her head. "I mean, who sits in a dark little closet all by himself while there's a party going on outside? Still, I guess I can't fault him too much. He did a damn fine job as your guitar teacher. Plus, he used to work with Eddie Morningstar."

Cain nodded, wondering if it meant anything that Ty had specifically chosen to sit in the dark in his dressing room and stare into his mirror. "Did you see what he was holding?"

"He was holding something? I didn't notice."

"Yeah." Cain raised an eyebrow at her. He knew that most humans couldn't see in the dark as well as he could, but it wasn't that dark in the dressing room. "Something small. He put it in his pocket when we opened the door."

"Oh. Well, it was probably a lighter or something." Michelle picked up his hands and tugged him playfully through the doorway. "Come on, let's celebrate."

When they emerged half an hour later, everything had gone forbiddingly quiet. Cain hurried into the green room and found most of the partygoers gathered in an anxious little knot. Izzy, now half-man, half-generic-animal and visibly drunk, stumbled out of the crowd.

"Cain, Cain, you gotta help us!" He waved his massive fur-covered arms frantically, almost hitting Michelle in the face. "I think Vince killed some chick!"

Cain pushed his way through the densely packed gawkers and found Vince staring down at the limp, pale body of the same girl whose lips had been locked with his when Cain and Michelle left. He was rubbing his mouth in slow, rueful strokes, and he looked up sheepishly as Cain entered the circle.

"I didn't mean to do it this time," he muttered. "Instinct took over once I got aroused, that's all. Her energy didn't even taste good. It was all thick and artificial—like drinking plastic. Anyway, she'll be fine again in an hour or two. I don't know what everybody has their fucking panties in a bunch about."

"Shut up, Vince," Cain hissed at him as he felt for a pulse.

He found one. It was faint, but it was definitely there. He turned to reassure the worried onlookers. "He's right, she's still alive, and that means she'll revive in a couple hours. I think there are spells that could make her wake up faster, but someone else here knows how to do those better than I do…Izzy, where's Steve?"

"Over there." Izzy pointed vaguely over the heads of the crowd.

Cain stood and followed Izzy's gesture. Steve was pinned to the wall on the other side of the room by a busty, drunken blonde, who was a head taller than he was and nearly twice his weight and age. His arms flailed ineffectually around her back as she bit and sucked at his face, cutting off his air supply and leaving lurid crimson lipstick stains all over his mouth.

Cain heaved a deep sigh. "All right, I think we've had enough partying for one night."

It took them some time to find Sammi. He had apparently spent most of the party sprawled unconscious on the floor of the one dressing room Cain and Michelle hadn't tried.

"He wasn't drinking," Izzy poked the used syringe lying on the carpet with his toe. "He was shooting up. Vince says he's been shooting up since Christmas."

Cain trudged off to find his guitar. He was certain now that a lot of effort and drama could be saved in the future if he made sure to never leave his band mates unsupervised among large groups of ordinary people.

Chapter Twelve

The Center

THE HOTEL WAS ONLY ten minutes away, but Izzy and Vince refused to let Cain escort Steve there on his own. Izzy was quick to point out that this arrangement would mean that Cain would have to walk back to the bus stop all by himself in the dark, and the Engineer's happiest fantasy was probably to stumble upon Cain walking all by himself in the dark.

"I'll bet that guy would love to kill someone famous," he speculated grimly.

"Yeah," Vince agreed. "And if the Engineer killed you, we'd have to pay someone to do pyrotechnics for us."

They followed Cain to the hotel, dragging a half-conscious Sammi with them, and waited outside while he said goodbye to Steve in the nearly deserted lobby.

"Well, back to New York tomorrow." Steve stared balefully at the elevators as if they were gallows and he had been sentenced to hang on them. "Back to New York; back to dad; and back to Lance. Doesn't *that* sound like one big barrel of fun?" He glanced over his shoulder, wiping away a few smudges of transferred lipstick. "I wonder if dad would let you adopt me."

"I'm sure he'll let you visit me now and then." Cain fished around in the pocket of his jeans; he had just gotten an idea. "Or maybe you could come on your own. Steve, do you know how to use a traveler's arrow?"

Steve stopped and turned around with a look of powerful interest in his eyes. "Sure. I mean, I do in theory. I know the incantation from one of dad's books, but I've never been able to find an actual traveler's arrow to use it with. Why?"

Cain showed him the turquoise-studded amulet. "Your dad gave me one; that's how I got here. I've been keeping it close, just in case, but seeing as I probably won't need it anytime soon…well…I might as well let you borrow it for a while."

"No way!" Steve reached hungrily for the silver arrowhead. "Dad had one of these all along? I *begged* him to get me one when I was a kid, but he said they were too rare. God, I used to daydream about having one whenever I was hiding from Lance."

"Wait!" Cain held the amulet just out of his reach. "Are you sure you really know the incantation?"

"Of course I'm sure."

"You were sure you knew the transformation spell too. I don't want you to end up lost in the middle of Australia or something."

"What are you, my mom?" Steve made a grab for the amulet. "Of course I know the incantation. I still recite it in my head every day while I think of all the places in the world I'd rather be than New York."

Cain let him take the amulet. "All right, then. But I would like you to promise that you won't skip school to visit and that you won't spirit Lance to a desert island somewhere and leave him there, even if he deserves it. Fair enough?"

"Sure, sure!" Steve hurried to the elevator, so excited that he only managed to pick up about half of what Cain said. "I promise. This is so cool. This is fucking awesome. Thank you, Cain! See you soon."

The elevator door closed behind him. Cain noticed that the clerk behind the reception desk was alternately staring at his horns and rubbing her eyes as if she thought she must be seeing things. He hastily rearranged his hair to cover them.

A patch of pearlescent, inky silver sky was visible from a window set high up in the wall of the dim holding cell. Soft ethereal light trickled down from the narrow opening, bathing Michael Anderson's pocked face in an eerie glow. He stared up into the clouds, his face turned deliberately away from his visitor.

"Michael," said Dr. Brown in her most authoritative tone. "You don't want to talk to me. I completely understand. But you have to; time is running out. Listen, in two days you'll be brought before a judge who'll decide if you're well enough to stand trial. You're not. You should be in a hospital instead of jail, and I can prove it, but you need to help me." She took a deep breath. "We need to talk some more. About your school, your drawings, your mother, anything…"

Michael did not speak, but he inclined his head, ever so slightly, in her direction. He immediately had to turn away again; her anxiety hit him like a blast of cold air, pummeling his temples and heart.

"Last time we talked," she continued, "you seemed like you wanted to tell me more."

Michael lifted his left hand and studied the scars on his

palm. There was so much he wanted to tell the kind doctor. He wanted to tell her about the horned boy who haunted his dreams. He wanted to tell her about Jim Kellerman's voice, about the terrifying unpredictability of the visions and blackouts, about loneliness, about pain and fear. He even wanted to tell her about mama—how she had been sick in her own way. Voices had whispered in her head that the Devil was after her, commanding her to scrub her young son's hand until the skin was raw and bleeding, until the mark the Devil had left on him was finally gone.

Michael's jaw clenched.

He remembered what the Devil's mark had looked like.

It banged against his mind in a flash of green light: the near-perfect circle and the five-pointed star within it. He also remembered that each of the star's points held its own peculiar little squiggle that looked like a letter of some unknown language. He could see once again how dark and striking the ruddy-colored mark had been against the smooth, white baby-skin of his palm.

Michael went rigid while another vision rolled through his body.

The Center. The roiling core of searing, pulsing, permutable energy. The beating heart of existence. It calls, it beckons. Its multitude of whispers and hums and trills coalesce into one great Voice, multi-toned and terrible.

Awaken, it says.

I feel it shiver in the atoms of the tabletop and floor. I feel it battering the cells of my body.

Awaken and manifest, it says to me.

Michael wrenched himself into the waking world.

"I won't have it," he said in an angry tone.

"Won't have what, Michael?"

Michael did not answer. He knew that the kind doctor was following his gaze as he glared defiantly through the single high window at the spot where he knew the Great Entity lay hidden behind the thin veil of reality, watching him. He also knew that she could see nothing there but an unremarkable swath of night sky.

Cain's band mates were waiting for him on the sidewalk. Izzy and Vince looked around when Cain emerged from the hotel, but Sammi kept staring straight ahead.

"Hey," he called to them. "Is Sammi any better yet?"

Cain had made an attempt at the party to magically bring Sammi out of his stupor, but he had been at a loss over how to counteract the drug. The best he could manage was getting Sammi into a zombie-like state of half-awareness. Now, Sammi could walk and vaguely perceive the world around him, but his coordination and sense of direction were still very impaired, so someone had to help him along. Unfortunately, Izzy insisted on being the one to do the helping, and Izzy was still drunk. Sammi's shins were likely bruised black and scraped raw by now from all the fire hydrants and railings Izzy had accidentally led him into.

Vince shrugged. "Still stoned out of his gourd."

"Oh, well, there's not much more we can do about that." Cain sidled up to Izzy, casually extending a hand to grab Sammi's free wrist. "Say, Izzy, why don't you let me walk him the rest of the way?"

"I can do it." Izzy swung Sammi around to face homeward, scraping his shoulder against the wall. "It's not far, and there aren't *that* many fire hydrants."

Sammi moaned and flexed his shoulder weakly, but he did not protest.

"All right," Cain conceded. "You can walk Sammi to the bus stop. But please try not to knock Sammi into any more garbage cans. You'll wake the whole neighborhood."

Vince kept pace with Cain, walking with unusual jauntiness. He actually seemed to be in a charitable mood for once.

"You know, I was afraid tonight would be a disaster," he grunted in what passed as a cheerful voice for him. "But they loved it. I guess it doesn't matter to them that we're some corporate suit's pet project and not a real band."

"Oops. Sorry, Sammi," said Izzy from somewhere behind them.

"I think they especially liked my mind-reading bit," Vince said. "Can you believe the nerve of Sammi, telling me not to show off my powers on stage? That was the best damn part of the show. I think I'll read someone's mind every night."

Cain coughed politely. He would have been direct, but his guitar was not within easy reach. "Oh...ah...yes. About that, Vince, I don't think—"

Vince didn't seem to hear him. "I'll admit that you got some of the bigger cheers of the night, though. Who'd have thought your black-magic-bullshit routine would be so popular? You're onto something, Cain. We should take full advantage of your powers."

"I thought we already were taking advantage of them," said Cain. Whatever Vince meant by taking "full advantage" of his supernatural abilities, he was sure it couldn't be pleasant. He probably wanted him to summon an earthquake or a hurricane in the middle of a set.

Vince's eyes narrowed shrewdly. "See, sucking the life out of that girl tonight got me thinking. Johnny Revolver and

AK Andrew from Big Bertha pretend to kill a girl on stage as part of their act. So I was thinking, well, why not do them one better?"

"Sorry, Sammi," said Izzy again.

"Do them one better how?" asked Cain cautiously.

"I think we should kill a girl on stage too." Vince's eyes shone with bloodthirsty excitement. "Not for pretend, though. For real."

"Kill a girl on stage?" Izzy loped to catch up with them, Sammi shuffling along helplessly in his wake. "Who's going to kill a girl on stage?"

Vince grinned. "We are. I say we cut off her head. That would be the most dramatic way."

"I think it would be crazier if we cut her stomach open and pulled—" Izzy shook himself and blinked. "Say, Vince, *why* in the world would we kill a girl on stage at all?"

Vince grunted in annoyance and kicked over a nearby trash can. Several mice scurried out of the strewn bags, along with a cat-sized gray dybbuk. The dybbuk chased after Vince, swiping at his calves with its bony little paws and chattering angrily. Vince didn't react, which didn't surprise Cain. Dybbukim were spirit-creatures—hunched, scurrying, monkey-like things that skulked in shadowy places and collected food scraps from human trash heaps. Steve had told him once that some humans believed they were the souls of the wicked dead. Cain was amazed that any humans knew of their existence at all. Dybbukim were invisible to most people, and even he usually had a hard time picking them out of the darkness in which they wallowed.

"Hee hee, monkey," muttered Sammi, squinting down at the sidewalk.

Vince rolled his eyes. "She won't stay dead, dumbass."

Izzy frowned. "But you said—"

"Don't you see? We kill the girl, and Cain brings her back to life."

"Oh, no." Cain shook his head. "I can't do that. It's impossible."

"What do you mean, impossible?" Vince's brow clouded, and he shook his leg in the general direction of the dybbuk that was still chasing him, catching it in the side by sheer luck. "Are you telling me you can make me puke marbles all day and turn a rat into a crow, but you can't cut a girl's head off and put her back together?"

"I could probably make her head stick back on, if that's what you mean by 'put her back together,'" said Cain. "But she'd still be dead, and there's nothing I could do about that."

"You can't bring dead people back to life, then?" Izzy seemed disappointed. Cain suspected that the minute Vince suggested he could revive the dead, Izzy had started to envision Cain resurrecting a long-deceased favorite uncle or a favorite pet.

"It's impossible for *me*," said Cain. "I'm not capable of that kind of high-level magic."

The dybbuk let out a throaty grunt of frustration and attacked Vince's leg, sinking its jagged little teeth into his calf. Vince bent down and slapped it so hard that Cain could hear its bones cracking from five feet away. It fell to the pavement with a muffled shriek. Sammi began to say something in a scolding tone, but he was cut off sharply when Izzy dragged him through a row of manicured bushes.

"Fucking bugs," muttered Vince. "I thought I wouldn't have to worry about them in the city. So, Cain, if nobody can bring people back to life, then why have we heard so many stories about it happening?"

The dybbuk picked itself up and wheezed at Vince. Cain's eyes followed it as it slunk into a nearby alley, nursing a broken nose that healed completely before it was out of his sight. He wondered how to explain resurrection to Vince when he did not fully understand it himself.

"I wouldn't say that *nobody* can bring people back to life," he admitted. "I think—I *think*—I've heard of people doing it before. But it's really, really rare—"

"So why can't you just find out what the hell they did and do it yourself?" Vince interrupted.

Cain raised his voice. "Because bringing someone back from the dead requires extremely strong magic, and my powers are not that strong. As far as I can tell, some people don't even consider resurrection magic; they put it the miracle category."

"Wait." A hint of irritation crept into Vince's voice. "Miracles are different from magic now? Since when?"

"Since forever. Magic is everywhere, and so easy to channel that anybody can use it—as long as they have the Gift like we do, that is. But the power you need to pull off a miracle—creating life from nothing, raising the dead, healing a wound instantly without causing pain—comes from a totally different place than regular magic does."

Vince gave Cain a nasty look. "Okay, now you're just fucking with me. Magic is everywhere, and everyone can use it, except no one can use this one kind of magic that comes from outer space or something…What the fucking fuck? Where is this 'totally different place' it comes from anyway?"

Izzy brightened. "Ooh, I hope it really does come from outer space. That would be so cool."

"Nobody knows," said Cain, maneuvering himself between Vince and Izzy as Vince moved to drive his elbow into Izzy's stomach.

"Yeah, you mean *you* don't know," Vince scoffed. "Or else, you're being an asshole and not telling me. There's no way this awesome and useful stuff has been around so long—so long that it's worked its way into that Bible story about what's-his-face—and nobody has ever studied it."

"Resurrection doesn't happen often enough to be studied," said Cain, clenching his fists impatiently. "No one can predict when it happens either, and we really can't predict who it happens to—even Steve's dad can't do any of that. The only people in the world who *might* have the power to do miracles at will would be the greater gods, and good luck getting them to answer any questions."

"Gods? You mean there's more than one god?" Izzy raised an eyebrow, confused.

Vince still couldn't reach around Cain to elbow Izzy's side, so he contented himself with spitting in his general direction. "No, moron. Cain's officially making shit up as he goes along. I mean, gods? Come on! That's the only damn thing he could have come up with that's less believable than mystery magic from outer space." He rolled his eyes. "Course, it was pretty smart of him to add them to his story. Hell, no one ever sees them, and they just hang out in the sky not talking to anyone—if they exist at all. No one is gonna get in touch with one to prove him wrong."

"Oh, you'd be surprised," said a voice from the darkness ahead of them. "More gods walk in the world of mortals than you know. Chances are you've met a few, or you know someone who has."

Vince, Izzy, and Cain stopped in their tracks as Crazy

Loti wheeled her cart out of an alley a few feet ahead of them, her white dog trotting beside her. Sammi stopped too. His dilated, half-closed eyes focused on her with great effort, and a flash of intense childlike interest lit up his blank face.

"Ooh," he murmured. "A shiny lady."

"Shiny?" Izzy inspected the ragtag old woman with the shopping cart dubiously. Cain understood Izzy's bewilderment; he would not have described Crazy Loti as *shiny* either. "No, Sammi, that's just the smack making you see things," said Vince scornfully. "That's not a shiny lady; that's a dirty old homeless woman."

Sammi shook his head. "No, man, she's shiny."

"Whatever." Vince waved his arms in Crazy Loti's direction. "Go on. Go away. We don't have any change."

"Always with the change." Crazy Loti leaned on the handle of her shopping cart, chuckling softly. "I wonder why everyone thinks I want change. I've certainly never asked for any."

"She doesn't want any change, Vince," said Cain. "Trust me. I know her from my old neighborhood."

Vince began to advance upon Crazy Loti, raising his hand menacingly. "Didn't you learn anything living on the streets, Cain? Money is all the bums in this city ever want. Hell, I'll be *so* glad when we're all rich enough to be chauffeured around this stinking city, and then we won't have to fight our way through the filthy riffraff to get to the bus stop—ow!"

Crazy Loti raised her arm in a swift, startling flash of movement and caught Vince's hand in midair. She squeezed him with little effort, and with a pretty firm grip too if the sounds of creaking bones and the pain in Vince's eyes were any indication.

"You'd best mind your manners, young Vincent Sweet," she said calmly. "I've been around this world ages before you were born, and I've seen things your mean little brain couldn't conceive."

"Oh man, she's fucking shiny," slurred Sammi.

Vince snatched his hand away as soon as she released him. "Fine, you don't want any change. What *do* you want?"

Crazy Loti turned her deep, steady eyes on him, making him fidget uncomfortably. "Well, Mr. Sweet, I thought you might like an answer to your question. Your outer space theory wasn't that far off, actually."

"Really?" Izzy brightened. "Cool!"

Vince raised his arm to jab at Izzy, but a glare from Loti must have made him think better of it because he quickly lowered his arm again.

"The thing you should know about magic," she continued, "is that it flows from the Center into all that exists, all that was, and all that will be. It drives the planets in their orbits and the flow of blood in your veins, and it pulses in the fiery cores of the stars. Without it, the universe would collapse and die. But the further magic gets from the Center and the longer it exists in the world, the less potent it gets, and after a while, it fades away and is replaced by more. On some very rare occasions, an emanation from the Center will keep its full power much longer than other emanations. The gods can perceive these outflows and harness them to do great acts of creation, destruction, or wonder—or to work such acts through another being, if they so choose." She gave Cain a strange look but continued with her explanation before he could ask her what was up. "That's how miracles happen. Like I said, they're very rare.

But even the most degraded magic is powerful and dangerous. I hope you boys realize how privileged you are to have it—and what huge responsibilities rest on your shoulders because of it."

Izzy was listening to her explanation with shining eyes. Cain could tell that any distrust Izzy might have had of the old woman was gone.

"Did you hear that?" He gave Sammi's arm a tug. "Our powers come from space!"

Sammi made a feeble attempt to pull his wrist out of Izzy's grasp, muttering something about light and about people being blind.

"How do you know all this?" said Cain. He was a bit taken aback by the certainty in her voice. Even Mr. Warwick wasn't able to give a clear answer about the nature of magic.

Loti shrugged. "I've been around long enough to figure things out. Anyway, that's the difference between miracles and magic—as best as I can explain it. Do you understand now, Mr. Sweet?"

"No I don't," grumbled Vince. "I have no idea what the two of you have been smoking, but you both sound more fucked up than Sammi."

Loti let out a patient sigh. "Then you should mull it over until it's a little clearer to you. You ought to have some idea of how your own powers work. Oh, by the way,"—her tone became more upbeat—"I hear congratulations are in order for your first show."

"Thanks," said Cain. "Were you...?"

"Goodness no." She chuckled. "I'm a bit old to be going to concerts. But I certainly knew it was going on—just like Nathaniel Breen did."

Vince snickered. "Isn't that great? I hope the old fart

294

goes on TV and throws a huge fit about us."

Cain shifted apprehensively.

"I'd be careful what I wished for if I were in your place, Mr. Sweet," said Loti softly. "At any rate, I think your band mate Cain is wishing for the exact opposite reaction, and I don't blame him. Now, if you boys will excuse me, I have a city to protect."

She swung her cart around without another word and wheeled off down the street. The dog stood staring up at Cain for a moment, its head cocked to one side. Then it loped away on its slender legs. The sound of its paws padding on the pavement receded into the distance.

"Well, what the fuck was that all about?" muttered Vince. "You say you know that old bat from your neighborhood, Cain?"

"Sort of," said Cain.

"Well, she talks like some kind of psychotic fortune cookie." Vince flexed his hand sulkily. "Don't tell her where we live, okay?"

"I won't," said Cain. Something told him that Loti already knew where they lived, but he didn't tell Vince about his hunch.

"I dunno," said Izzy. "I kind of liked her. She sounds pretty smart. Right, Sammi?"

"She was shiny," muttered Sammi. "Dude, she was actually *glowing*. How am I the only one who noticed that?"

Dad could have sent us home. The thought bounced around Steve's head for the sixth time that day. *We sure as hell didn't need to come along on this stupid errand.*

He tried to show his annoyance as little as possible, knowing from experience that getting visibly frustrated wouldn't do him any good. If Jesse Warwick got it into his head to drag his sons along on a last-minute detour to El Paso on their way home from Los Angeles, then he was going to do it. The obvious solution would have been for Mr. Warwick to send Steve and Lance on to New York while he took care of whatever sordid business he had in El Paso by himself. That would have been the considerate thing to do. It wouldn't have forced Steve to endure an extra night cooped up in a dingy hotel room at the mercy of his brother.

Steve slouched sulkily in his uncomfortable little seat. To top it all off, their flight was delayed. He had burned through his last bit of reading material an hour ago, and Lance, who was trying unsuccessfully to put the moves on a girl sitting by a nearly empty gate, was his last source of entertainment.

Lance seemed to be telling the girl a story. Her expression grew steadily more disgusted as he yammered on, and before he was halfway through the tale, she scooted to the empty seat on the other side of her and put her bag firmly down between them on the one she had vacated. Lance's eyes darkened, and he leaned deliberately over the bag like a cat about to pounce on a mouse.

Mr. Warwick was taking the snag in his travel plans quite well. He was fully absorbed in his ancient copy of Hiram Levi's *The Sacred Art of Spellcraft*, glancing away from the yellowed pages only to jot something on one of the many sheets of notes spread out on the seat beside him.

"Really, Hiram, do you have to be so obtuse?" he muttered, addressing the book's long-dead author. "I like symbolism as much as the next person, but not when I have to spend *days* just trying to decipher one line of instruction for a spell…"

Steve turned his attention back to Lance and the girl, who now appeared to be using the unoccupied row of seats across the gate for a lively game of musical chairs. He was deeply tempted to make the game more interesting. After a final furtive glance to make sure his father still wasn't paying attention, Steve prepared a simple curse in his head. Cast correctly, it would break down the last of Lance's weak inhibitions for a few minutes and then wear off without leaving any trace of its existence, hopefully after Lance got slapped or kneed in the groin.

"Stephen Gideon Warwick," said Mr. Warwick without looking up from his book. "Curse your brother, and quite a bit of time will pass before you are allowed to visit Cain, or set foot anywhere near Los Angeles for that matter."

Steve flinched and suppressed a yelp of surprise.

"How did you know?" he grumbled.

"Your shoulders tense when you're about to cast," his father answered shortly. "You should stop doing that; it's bad form."

Steve tipped his head back with a groan, stretching for patience. He didn't even have the small amusement of watching his brother's failing seduction attempt anymore. Lance's would-be new girlfriend had fled to the ladies' room to escape him.

"Dad," he said. "When can I visit Cain again?"

Mr. Warwick glanced up at Steve. He had a pinched look on his face, as if he considered it a terrible inconvenience to have to tear his attention away from his research to answer the question.

"I don't know," he said. "I don't have business in Los Angeles anytime soon."

"But I can...uh...make my own arrangements." The

traveler's arrow sat heavily in Steve's pocket. He longed to whip it out right then and there and transport himself to the Sunset Strip faster than Lance could get himself rejected by a girl, but he thought it probably wasn't a good idea to let his father know he had it. "You wouldn't have to do anything but tell me when—"

"I don't think so, Steve."

"Come on, dad!" Steve clenched his fists. "I didn't curse Lance."

"That has nothing to do with it," said Mr. Warwick. "I don't want you spending too much time around those tattooed louts Bruce Arkin chose to be Cain's band mates, Steve. I won't have my son tagging along with them on their forays to bars and whorehouses, picking up their lower-class ways."

"Dad, Cain wouldn't let them take me to a whorehouse," said Steve indignantly. He was deeply irked that his father was so convinced that Cain would tear off his clothes and run amok in the streets if he didn't have a respectable adult human to dictate his behavior.

"Oh, he would." Mr. Warwick shuffled his notes moodily. "He wouldn't know any better. It took me the longest time just to teach that damned devil not to relieve himself in the yard, let alone wear clothes. I have no doubt he'll forget a significant portion of what I've taught him during his stay in the city, and I'll have to start all over again when his career is over. Demons are inveterate savages, Steve, and keeping them even slightly civilized is a constant and uphill struggle. You'll understand one day when you have a servant of your own."

"I'll never have a servant of my own."

Mr. Warwick looked up from his notes again. His eyes

narrowed.

Steve met his gaze with an air of quiet defiance. He had heard his father's argument dozens of times, and he refused to be swayed by it.

"You will," said his father.

"I don't need one."

"You'll think differently someday."

"No, I won't. Dad, it just wouldn't feel right. I've told you that before—"

"Stephen, I will not get into this argument with you again. Regardless of what you feel, it is your right and responsibility to keep a servant. It will be Lance's responsibility too, once he...er...blooms." He cast a pained eye in the direction of his older son, who was making an aggressive play for another girl at the far corner of the gate. "So few men have the power and inner strength to bend a demon to their will, and every demon needs a master."

"I don't think Cain needed one," muttered Steve under his breath. He had not intended for his father to hear him.

Unfortunately, Mr. Warwick had impeccable hearing. A frown appeared on his brow, and his fingers rapped impatiently against the pages of his book. "Oh, really?" he said. "Have you ever met a fallen angel, Steve? You'd think it would be awe-inspiring, but it isn't. Most of them aren't much more intellectually curious than dogs. They have no drive or ambition, no flexibility of thinking, and they have unfortunately infected their half-human offspring—Cain included—with their utter lack of the ability to progress as a species. I'll get out the scrying mirror when we get home and show you the valley in the Inner World where Cain lived before he came to us—it's like a preserved Stone Age settlement. His tribe lives in a series of *caves* that they carved into the cliffs. Can you imagine that? We humans build thirty-story skyscrapers, and these nearly divine beings still dig holes for themselves like rats do. I doubt they'd even have fire if most of them hadn't married human wives in the old days."

"Dad, you've shown me the Inner World," said Steve. "It looked to me like Cain's tribe got along just fine without humans bossing them around."

Mr. Warwick drummed his fingers on his armrest impatiently. "Stephen, the impulse toward servitude is woven deeply into the very fiber of every angel's being. Fallen angels and demons can't function without someone constantly telling them what to do. If I hadn't taken Cain in, he'd be living in a squalid little rock cave and eating raw meat with his bare hands like the other unmastered demons. We humans are always continuing to advance our culture and technology. Without intervention, demons would be left so far behind that they'd never be able to catch up. Does that sound 'fine' to you?"

Steve shook his head sullenly. He knew that nothing would change his father's mind on this matter. Mr. Warwick would stubbornly maintain his obsession with civilizing the demon race, even though his obsession didn't make any sense. From Steve's few fleeting glimpses of Cain's people in the scrying mirror, he had deduced that they had the power of flight and invisibility, and they could bend lesser elemental spirits to their will. Plus, the elders of the tribe— the ones who were pure angel with no human blood in them—didn't seem to need to eat. He couldn't imagine what "civilized" things like cars and telephones could offer these creatures that their considerable magical talents didn't already provide.

"I'm glad you agree." Mr. Warwick's voice took on a final tone. "It is absolutely our right and duty to be good shepherds…"

He trailed off as the girl Lance was trying to seduce stood up and began to move toward the restrooms. Upset that his quarry was escaping for a second time, Lance scrambled after her, not-so-subtly smacking a hand across her backside as he did so. The girl let out a sharp little gasp and slapped him. He reeled back while she fled, his mouth working indignantly.

Mr. Warwick seemed to forget what he had been talking about. His jawline stiffened, and his eyes went cold.

"Bah!" he muttered. "Little hussy. My son isn't good enough for you, eh? I'd cover your face and hands with warts if I thought you were worth the trouble."

He picked up his book and started reading again, still grumbling under his breath about fickle sluts. The girl disappeared into the restroom unharmed. She was lucky. Steve had noticed that a healthy percentage of the girls who rejected Lance found themselves suffering from mysterious dermatological ailments until Lance fixated on another girl and Mr. Warwick decided that he wasn't angry with them anymore.

Izzy woke up the next morning with a vicious headache. Cain offered to soothe it for him, but Izzy flinched and went sickly green at the thought of guitar music. So he abandoned the idea and left Izzy sprawled across the couch in the darkened living room. Izzy listlessly switched on the television, and he turned the volume down almost to nothing.

"Did he have more than was good for him last night?"

asked Sammi when he finally came down, poking his head through the living room door before he trotted into the kitchen at his peculiar quick, jerky pace.

"I think so." Cain looked up from his pork chop lunch. "I tried to make him more comfortable, but he wouldn't let me. Are *you* all right?"

"Sure I am." Sammi seemed completely surprised at the question. "Why wouldn't I be?"

"We found you passed out in your dressing room last night."

"Oh yeah. I'm fine, man. It was just a little heroin."

Cain raised an eyebrow dubiously. "You looked dead. We practically had to carry you home."

"Yeah, I guess you must have. Thanks." Sammi sounded a bit embarrassed, but otherwise, he seemed unconcerned. "Really, I'm fine. I probably just did a little more than I should have. So did you really have to carry me home?"

"Pretty much." Cain thought it was better that Sammi didn't remember the manhandling he had received from Izzy.

"Huh. Well, I guess I should be more careful about how much I shoot up next time."

"Next time?" Cain remembered the syringe on the dressing room floor, and his stomach churned. "You're going to do it again?"

"Well, sure." Sammi chuckled. "It's no big deal. Say, are you all right? You don't look too good."

"I'm fine." Cain shuddered. "It's just...I really hate needles."

"Oh. Well, some people do. I'm not crazy about them either. But I guess they just don't bother me enough to avoid them, you know?"

"Are you sure that heroin stuff is safe to put in your body?" Cain thought of the splitting headaches Izzy tended to get from a night of too much drinking and of Skeeter's reddened nose and fevered movements after inhaling his powder. All the human drugs he had encountered so far seemed to cause fairly uncomfortable side effects, but Sammi's faint had seemed more dangerous than the other unwanted reactions.

"Oh, I'm sure it's fine." Sammi shrugged. "The worst thing it ever did to me was make me have this really weird dream last night. You were in it, actually."

"I was?"

"Yeah. I dreamed that I was in this dark street, and I could hear you and Vince talking ahead of me, and I kept trying to catch up to you, but this huge yellow blob was dragging me around and knocking me against walls and streetlights and fire hydrants. It hurt, and I was starting to get really mad." He frowned and rubbed his shin reflectively. "In fact, that part of the dream felt so real that I still ached when I woke up. There was something about a little gray monkey and a shiny chick too...I don't remember that part as well. Isn't that weird?"

"Er...yes, that is weird. Very weird." Cain had been planning to encourage the belief that it was all a dream, but now he wanted to know how much Sammi actually remembered about the walk home. "A gray monkey, you say?"

"Of course," said Sammi. "It was part of the dream. I think Vince was being mean to it for some reason, and I was mad at him for it. Come to think of it, I was mad at you guys too at that point—maybe because of the shiny chick. I could see her, and you couldn't. Or was it that we all could see her, but I was the only one who could tell she was shiny? I can't remember. Anyway, it was a really weird dream."

Cain wanted to ask more questions, but Vince barged into the kitchen, bleary-eyed and rumpled yet in high spirits.

"Twelve noon, on the dot." He gave the clock on the far wall a satisfied glance before he lurched past them. "Good. I didn't sleep through it."

"Didn't sleep through what?" Sammi called after him.

Vince took a bowl out of the cupboard and hastily tossed some cereal into it. "Only the best comedy show in town. I heard from some girl at the party last night—not the one whose energy I ate—that Breen had a spy in the audience. Today he's supposed to go on some daytime talk show and warn the whole country about how dangerous we are. Come on, you're going to miss it."

He swept up his cereal and vanished into the living room. Cain and Sammi glanced at each other and followed him.

Vince found the correct channel as they came in. Izzy covered his head with a pillow and moaned in protest when Vince cranked the volume up before perching expectantly on the sturdy coffee table.

The Reverend Breen's imposing, craggy face seemed to fill the whole screen. His jowls trembled like a bloodhound's and his eyes shone with intensity as he spoke.

"…worst sign of the moral degradation of America I've seen yet," he boomed in his deepest, most commanding voice. "Believe me, brothers and sisters, that's saying quite a lot. After all, I've seen a fourteen-year-old boy sacrifice his own mother in a dark cult ritual. I've seen child-molesting devil-worshippers infest our schools and churches and neighborhoods, despite our fine police force's best efforts to keep them out. I've seen the rock musicians of this city shamelessly use the lie of the so-called Engineer to draw police attention away from very real Satanist criminals, hiding their own insidious agendas—a tactic that continues to be frighteningly effective despite my best efforts to make police investigators aware of the hoax…"

"What?" Sammi snapped at the TV, livid red sparks leaping from his body. "You think we've been *lying* about the Engineer? Well, guess what, asshole? We've got actual fucking bodies to back up our lie. Hell, we've got real scars and real witnesses too. You've only got your own crazy delusions."

"Calm down, Sammi," said Vince. "It's just Breen. What the fuck do you expect?"

His tone was relaxed and jovial, but Cain noticed that his eyes had gone dark.

Four of Izzy's tins clattered to the floor when Sammi snatched a newspaper off the coffee table. He hunkered down in the armchair and opened the paper with an abrupt jerk of his arms, as if trying hard to ignore the TV. The Reverend Breen's ramblings seemed to be quickly losing their charm for him.

The minister continued. "In light of these travesties, you may think it near-sighted of me to devote so much attention to the antics of a single new and—for now, at least—rather obscure heavy metal band. Am I right?"

Some upstaged, overpowered talk-show host made an unintelligible reply off-camera.

"Well, you're wrong." His eyes narrowed. "Remember, this band deals in the darkest and most evil form of music under the sun—if, in its horribly perverted state, it can even be called music. And surely I don't need to remind you that

Cain Pseudomantis is its lead guitarist and focal point.

"I was fortunate to get a very reliable informant into the audience at the first public appearance of this abominable new band, this Pseüdomäntis. Let me tell you what he witnessed. First and foremost, Cain was up to his old trick of posing as one of the dark princes of Hell. This trickery is diabolical enough, but now he's gathered together an equally disreputable gang of fellow musicians and illusionists. In the show, they took the role of a coven of warlocks who served their demonic master. They were bowing and doing homage to Cain while they infected the ears of our young people with their devil music. In his evil name, they—"

Cain switched off the TV and stalked angrily to the window. The others stood in silence for a moment. None of them seemed inclined to turn the TV back on.

Sammi stared at the blank screen. His hands clenched the edges of his newspaper, sparks floated from his fingers, and dozens of brown scorch marks began to appear on the page.

"So that's why the cops don't give a rat's ass about the Engineer's victims," he said darkly. "Breen has been feeding them some bullshit idea that the whole thing is a big lie we evil rockers made up. I knew he was putting lots of pressure on them to focus on his cult crap, but...damn. He's pure evil, man. Pure fucking evil."

Cain nodded stiffly. Out of the corner of his eye, he saw an odd expression flit across Vince's face.

The expression was not an easily identifiable one. It wasn't sorrow or anger, but it had elements of both of those emotions. It was not pain either; though there was pain in every line of his body. It could have been a look of defeat, of disgust with the world, but that assessment still didn't seem quite right. Although Vince's shoulders were slumped and his eyes were fixed miserably on the floor, he seemed on the verge of saying something important.

Then the moment passed, and Vince let out a somewhat forced laugh.

"Come on, guys," he sneered. "You're not going to let this dumb shit get to you, are you? I mean, who really takes that guy seriously? It's like a tabloid ate a bad comic book and puked into Breen's Bible, man."

Izzy sighed sadly.

Sammi clenched his fists. "The police seem to be taking him seriously."

Cain turned to the window and glared into the street. He was irked that Breen and his followers found the idea of humans serving a demon so repulsive. He seriously doubted that any of them would be at all moved if someone went on a talk show to preach about the injustice of Cain being forced to serve Mr. Warwick against his will.

CHAPTER THIRTEEN

THE MISSION

"GO ON, CAIN." IZZY beamed with pride. "Sign your name on the paper."

Cain eyed the three long-haired teenage boys warily. They had him backed up against the wall and surrounded. One of them had thrust a pen into his hand, and all of them waved scribbled-on flyers at him.

"Do I have to write anything other than my name?" he asked Sammi over his admirers' heads. He remembered Mr. Arkin telling him that he would probably encounter fans who would ask for autographs, but these boys had simply charged up to him and Sammi and Izzy, waving flyers and bellowing demands for their signatures. He had not expected the fans to be quite so assertive in their autograph seeking.

"If you want to, I guess." Sammi raised an eyebrow. "But you don't have to write anything else. Me and Izzy only signed our names, and most fans are perfectly happy with that."

Cain's writing wasn't much faster than his reading, but he took the papers one by one and signed his name as quickly and as neatly as he could between the bold, blocky, lopsided letters of Izzy's signature and the spidery scrawl of

Sammi's. He was painfully aware of the young fans' eyes on him the whole time, and a flood of relief shot through him when the boys took their papers back in a chorus of ecstatic thank-yous and bounded off.

"What was all that about?" he asked Izzy. "Those boys were so loud and pushy. I'd still have given them autographs if they'd just asked quietly."

"That means we're real rock stars now!" Izzy turned into a goat and gamboled around Cain's legs.

"It does?" Cain tried to puzzle out Izzy's explanation, but he was not at all clear on why being accosted in the street by rude strangers who aggressively demanded their signatures made them real rock stars.

"Don't worry about it," said Sammi. "They just got excited to see their favorite rock stars. We'll probably run into lots of fans like them. Come on, let's get to the store."

Izzy was still in a happy haze. "Just think, guys—soon we'll have *hundreds* of people lining up for that!"

Cain still felt nervous, fidgety, and inexplicably stupid from the strange encounter. He wasn't sure he liked the thought of hundreds of people lining up to ask for his signature. He wasn't sure he liked the idea of *ten* people lining up. Three people had been more than enough.

While Sammi deliberated over which brand of beer to buy and Izzy loaded up on chocolate bars and sugary cereal at the store, Cain spent most of his time crouched behind a display, standing very still and hoping no one would notice him. The grocery store already made him nervous with its painfully bright fluorescent lights and maze-like aisles; a mob of autograph-demanding fans would make the experience even more daunting.

To his great relief, none of their fellow store patrons

seemed particularly interested in anything except the contents of their carts. The walk home was uneventful as well, until Sammi suddenly halted mid-step and motioned for Cain and Izzy to stop.

"What's up?" said Izzy.

"Johnny Revolver at twelve 'o clock," said Sammi.

Cain brushed his horn-concealing bangs out of his face and saw a tall man emerging through the wrought iron gates of what appeared to be some sort of park.

"Who's Johnny Revolver again?" he said to Sammi. The name sounded familiar.

"Big Bertha's guitarist," said Sammi.

"Oh, that's right. Skeeter Judd mentioned him."

Sammi had shrunk against the stone wall that surrounded the park, and he motioned for Cain and Izzy to do the same. "Come on, get against the wall and shut up. We can't let him see us."

"Why not?" whispered Cain.

"Johnny will kick in your teeth for no reason. Ever since Jim died, he's been really edgy," whispered Sammi. "And he's always in the worst mood right after he visits Jim's grave."

"Jim Kellerman was the first guy the Engineer took," said Izzy to Cain. "The cops thought that crazy Michael Anderson kid killed him at first."

"How did the cops figure out that the Engineer killed him?" asked Cain.

Sammi frowned. "You know, I don't think they ever really did. From what I heard, the cops just let the case go cold once they found out that Michael didn't have Jim's blood on his clothes. But Johnny was convinced right from the beginning that someone else killed Jim, and he was right.

He was Jim's best friend."

"You know what?" said Izzy. "Johnny may be crazy, but he was really good to Jim. Still is. He goes and puts a bottle of Night Train Express on his grave, like, twice a month."

Johnny stood outside the gate for a minute or two. He brushed back his jet-black hair and exhaled a long shuddery sigh. Cain caught a glimpse of his face and saw that his eyes were red and moist. Then he spun on his heel and stalked off down the street.

"Okay, he's gone," said Sammi. "We can go now—"

"Hey!" An unfamiliar voice cut him off. "Izzy Unger, right? We're all *huge* fans…"

Cain's heart sank. He looked up and saw Izzy enthusiastically chatting with not three, but *four* young men who had apparently materialized from nowhere. He tried to reassure himself that these people meant him no harm, that they only wanted him to write his name on their papers. Groups of strange humans made him slightly anxious. He could keep the anxiety under control when the humans shouted and cheered at him from a distance, and he could handle humans who quietly tossed him scraps of meat. He was even learning to tolerate being jostled by noisy drunken revelers at parties. But he couldn't stop his breath from quickening with fear when humans were pushy and demanding, when they cornered him and shoved papers in his face and loudly ordered him to sign his name and wouldn't leave him alone until he gave in.

Sammi had joined Izzy's conversation with the four fans. Cain noticed that they did not seem to be aware of his presence yet, but he knew that a nearly seven-foot-tall man with a tail would not be able to lurk unnoticed in the background for long. He started inching toward the gates.

Maybe he could hide behind the wall until the fans lost interest and wandered away.

Cain scurried through the gates and closed them behind him. His sigh of relief died in his throat when he turned and remembered that he had stepped into a graveyard. He hovered by the closed gates for a moment, surveying the quiet sea of white headstones that stretched out before him. Everything appeared peaceful, but an unsettling air hung over the grass and the headstones and the flowering dogwood trees. He was beginning to contemplate going back out and taking a chance with the fans when everything changed.

The change happened quickly and without warning. As Cain watched, the world around him seemed to cease to be real. The bright green of the manicured grass faded, and the headstones became two-dimensional. The trees darkened and formed indistinct outlines against a faded sky. Izzy's chatter cut out behind him like a radio being switched off. He let out a startled yelp, but his voice was muffled.

In the frightening silence that followed, Cain heard every footfall of the boy approaching him.

The boy was pale and thin. His hair was the color of dirty straw, and he had sad brown eyes. He flitted aimlessly among the headstones, walking in Cain's direction as if purely by chance. His arms were crossed, his shoulders drawn in, and he shivered as he walked. Cain had never seen anybody look so lost as this boy did.

"Hey," he called to the boy, his voice distorting oddly in the bizarre half-reality into which he had stumbled. "Are you all right?"

The boy started and fixed his eyes on Cain with sudden intensity.

"I...where am I?" he whispered.

Cain stepped forward eagerly, relieved that the boy could see him. Then the boy got a proper look at his face and stumbled back in sudden terror.

"I know you..."

"Sorry." Cain stepped back again, trying to appear as non-threatening as possible. "You probably do know me. I have a band...It's okay; I'm not going to hurt you. What's your name?"

The boy flinched and threw up his hands as if to protect his face. His left hand opened to reveal a sprawling, livid scar. Cain's breath caught in his throat at the sight of it. Then the boy seemed to partially overcome his fear. He walked toward Cain with timorous steps, reaching out with both hands.

"What's your name?" Cain tried again, fighting against the sense of dread that had begun to prickle at the back of his neck. "Look, if you need help, I can—"

The boy lunged forward and seized Cain's wrists. His grip was terrifyingly warm and real.

"Beware the zeal of the Righteous Man," he said.

His voice boomed through the frozen air of the cemetery, and an unpleasant heat radiated from the spot where his scarred palm touched Cain's skin. He was saying something else now, but Cain was too unnerved to listen. He stumbled back with closed eyes, trying to break the boy's grip, and his foot struck something hard.

The resulting loud *clink* jarred the world back into normalcy. When Cain opened his eyes again, the world was three-dimensional and in motion once more. There was no sign of the boy.

Cain blinked and stared at the ground, trying to clear his

head. He saw the thing he had kicked—a glass bottle with a stylized locomotive engine on the label. The red liquid inside it sloshed when he poked it curiously with his toe. It was lying against a gray headstone. Cain squinted at the letters carved into the headstone, painstakingly separating them into words:

JAMES ALLEN KELLERMAN
1960-1982

A shiver of horror ran through Cain as he realized that he found the grave Johnny Revolver had just visited. He also thought he knew why the boy had visited him here.

Izzy and Sammi found him kneeling by the headstone a few minutes later. Izzy relaxed and breathed a sigh of relief, but Sammi sprang forward and grabbed his wayward band mate roughly by the shoulder.

"Dammit, Cain," he shouted. "Were you back here the whole time? You scared the crap out of both of us, running off like that! For all we know, you could've been snatched by the Engineer."

Cain looked up, his eyes wide.

"It's Breen," he said.

"What are you talking about, man?"

"It's *Breen*," he repeated. "Breen is the Engineer."

Sammi and Izzy exchanged a puzzled glance.

"How do you know?" said Izzy.

Cain looked at the humble little headstone and the offering of fortified wine that lay beside it.

"I know," he said, "because Jim Kellerman told me."

Michael Anderson sat up with a start. He was shivering,

and his thin blankets were soaked with sweat.

He had seen the Dark Lion.

It had happened so quickly: one moment he had been lying in his cot, and the next moment he had been in an open space, among rows and rows of graves. A strange and frightening sky had been overhead, and a personage from his nightmares loomed before him. Nothing like it had ever happened to him before. He had been terrified, desperate to believe that the scene before him was a dream.

Yet now that the dim safety of his cell surrounded him again, he was anxious. Not from fear, but from the thought that he had not fully conveyed his message. He had no idea what the message meant, but deep down inside, he knew that every word of it was of dire importance.

"It can't be." Michelle paced through the living room, stepping carefully around Izzy's piles of trinkets and rumpled clothing. Cain wrapped his tail around his legs, not knowing if he should comfort her.

"It can't be daddy," she said. "I don't care what this Jim Kellerman says."

"You should." Vince snorted sarcastically. "It's pretty impressive he can talk at all, considering his mouth is probably rotted off by now."

"Say *what*, now?" Michelle stopped her pacing and stared at Vince.

"Jim Kellerman is dead," Sammi explained. "He was the Engineer's first victim."

Michelle blinked. Cain couldn't blame her for being confused. She had walked into the room halfway through his description of what he had seen in the graveyard, well after he and his band mates had discussed that particular little detail.

"Oh. I guess that makes…" She stopped herself and shook her head to clear it. "Wait, no, that makes *less* sense! How could you talk to him if he was dead? Did you call him up or something?"

"No!" Cain shook his head vehemently. "I'd never do that! I don't think it's even possible. I'm telling you, Jim Kellerman was just *there*…"

"Hanging out by his own grave and hoping you'd wander by?" Izzy scratched his head. "I dunno. It seems like that would get boring fast, even for a ghost."

"Are you sure he even *was* Jim, Cain?" said Sammi. "I mean, you've never met the guy."

"He had to be," said Cain. "He looked exactly like how you described Jim—skinny, blond hair, brown eyes. His left palm was ripped up too, like the Engineer tried to carve a rune there and made a mess of it. He *had* to be Jim."

"No, he didn't," said Vince. "You said this kid looked about fourteen, dumbass. Jim was twenty-something when he died."

"That doesn't mean his soul has to look like a twenty-year old," snapped Cain. "Disembodied souls can look any age they want. Guys, this is serious—souls usually go right to…to…" He struggled to recall the truth, but his freedom had not restored his memory. His mind pulled up a few fuzzy images of a glowing, silvery haze before giving up. "…to…wherever they go after they stop being alive. This soul had something important enough to say that he stuck around for months to tell someone. We can't just ignore him."

"Well, he was wrong!" Michelle had picked up one of Izzy's tins from the coffee table. She turned it over and over in her hands. "I know my daddy. He's a snob, a narrow-minded prude, an attention whore, and as greedy as they come. But he's not a killer. He doesn't have it in him."

She shrieked and leapt back when Steve materialized from somewhere near the light fixture and fell to the floor with a heavy, painful-sounding bang. Izzy's tins rattled like they were in a miniature earthquake, and everyone present jumped back with a startled yelp.

Steve twitched and climbed weakly to his feet, clutching his head. Vince grunted in disgust.

"You again, kid?" he grumbled. "I thought Cain sent you home to your daddy."

"I'm allowed to visit." Steve thrust out the traveler's arrow dangling from his hand in an anemic display of defiance before he teetered and staggered toward the couch. "Cain says so."

Vince glared at Cain. "Since when?"

"Since that night at the hotel." Cain pushed his way to Steve's side when he started to look as if he might fall again. He eased him onto the couch. "Maybe it wasn't the brightest idea I've ever had, but I gave him a charm so he could travel here whenever he wanted to visit. I'd like to stress, though, that I gave it to him under certain conditions. It's not my fault that he didn't listen."

"What are you talking about?" said Steve irritably. "Lance is safe at home."

"It's Wednesday, Steve."

"Yeah. So?"

"You promised not to skip school, remember?"

"Did I?" Steve shrugged and avoided Cain's gaze. "Well, I'm not really breaking my promise. I got suspended for disruptive behavior."

"Again?" Cain asked wearily. He had lost count of all the suspensions, detentions, and reprimands Steve had gotten for what his schools all euphemistically called "disruptive behavior." Mr. Warwick's deep pockets and native talent for intimidating people had probably saved him from being expelled outright dozens of times. "What for *this* time?"

"Well..." Steve scratched his head. "Remember Brett Johansson? You know, Lance's big football player friend?"

"The one who looks like a black-haired, slightly smarter copy of Lance? Or the big blond one?"

"The big blond one."

"What did you do to him, Steve?"

Steve crossed his arms. "Before I answer that, I'd like to remind you that Brett Johansson is the one who thinks it's the funniest thing in the world to corner me in the boys' room and stuff my head in the toilet. He's also the one who always calls me 'Voodoo Boy.'" He rounded on Vince, who was snickering. "It's not funny! I hate being called Voodoo Boy!"

"All right, I understand." Cain held up his hands in a placating gesture. "What did you do?"

A little smirk crept across Steve's lips. "Remember my knife? Well, I pulled it on him this morning when he grabbed me. I told him it was a spirit knife that doesn't hurt the body at all, but it cuts away little pieces of souls. He's a superstitious idiot, see, and I hoped it would be enough to keep him off my back for a while. But he just kept dragging me to the toilet, so I had no choice but to stab him as hard as I could." He shook his head. "You know, I knew it would freak him out, but I didn't think it would scare him as much as it did. I mean, it's not like I turned him into a mink like I did to Amanda Maxwell—"

"Steve, you *turned someone into a mink?*" Cain couldn't decide whether to be horrified or proud. Transformation spells were difficult to perform, even for experienced casters like Mr. Warwick, and they had never been Steve's strong suit. "When did that happen?"

"Oh...um...a while ago. I told her I liked her, and she laughed in my face. I got so mad it just...kind of...happened." Steve played with his hands for a moment and quickly changed the subject. "Anyway, I didn't think the whole knife thing was that scary. But Brett fainted like a little girl. That's why I'm suspended for two weeks."

"Two weeks?" said Cain incredulously. Steve had gotten much shorter suspensions for much worse offenses in the past.

"Actually, that wasn't all I did," said Steve. "See, Brett was lying there helpless at my feet and...well...I guess I must've thought it would be a shame if I didn't work some magic on him, just to show him who's boss. I don't see what everyone got so worked up about anyway. Dad swooped in to get rid of the pimples before his parents even found out."

"Steve!" said Cain reproachfully.

"I know, I know." Steve rolled his eyes. "I already got the whole routine from the principal: blah blah blah antisocial behavior blah blah blah persistent discipline problems. Young Stephen may be better served by alternative schooling options if he cannot learn to control his *disability* among normal students, Mr. Warwick. Huh, you should've seen the look on dad's face when she said that. My point is I was provoked."

"I believe you." Cain sighed. Steve usually was provoked, but somehow he was almost always the one who ended up getting in trouble for the disasters that resulted. "Actually, I'm glad you're here. You could help us do a little spying."

Steve brightened up. "Ooh, sounds like fun! What do you want me to do?"

"Well, that depends. Have you been practicing your invisibility spells?"

"Not much." Steve shrugged. "They just don't fool Lance anymore."

"That's all right. Lance isn't the one you need to fool."

"I'm your guy, then." Steve gave Cain a quizzical look. "So…um…if you don't mind my asking, *why* do we need to do some spying?"

Cain glanced back at his band mates and at Michelle, who all stood in a confused little knot behind him.

"We have to clear something up," he said.

Cain paid a visit to the butcher's shop early the next morning. He took care to be noticed along the way, strutting down the sidewalk and waving his tail to make himself more conspicuous. By the end of his journey, he had attracted a sizable knot of curious fans and small-time tabloid photographers. Cain was embarrassed by the attention, especially when Mrs. Delgado burst out of the shop and loudly scolded him about what a naughty devil he was, going around to all those fancy nightclubs like he was a king while rats overran the shop, and did he want her and her poor husband to lose their business and starve? Yet Cain managed to control his anxiety, and he took Mrs. Delgado's rants in good humor, even when she dealt him a stinging thwack across the calves with her broom when he failed to start clearing rats out of the dumpster quickly enough. He wanted to have a solid alibi in case Breen discovered the plan.

While Cain killed rats in the alley under Mrs. Delgado's watchful eye, an elderly maid walked to her employer's house in Beverly Hills, grumbling under her breath about the damned buses that only got her halfway to work. After rounding a bend, she heard three or four people walking on the other side of the street, and she looked in the direction of the sound. No one was there. The footsteps came closer until they seemed to be passing her, a mere ten feet away, but she couldn't see anyone.

Then the sound stopped directly across the street from her, in front of a house enclosed by a stone wall with a heavy iron gate. Before she could dismiss the noise as the workings of over-stressed nerves and move on, the keypad that locked the gate spontaneously exploded in a flash of bright blue electric light, and a fierce crackling noise jolted through the air.

She jumped and yelped. Brown smoke and the thick, choking smell of burnt plastic drifted toward her. To her great bafflement, the keypad remained whole, but a few small scorch marks tinged its edges. Lights winked on and off under the transparent skin of the keypad's buttons, which beeped and blipped as if unseen fingers were frantically punching them. Then, with a grating, mechanical click, the gate swung open.

The maid swallowed hard and hurried down the sidewalk, keeping her eyes forward. Someone—or something—had just entered through that gate. If she lingered too long, it might come after her.

Besides, if her memory served correctly, that house belonged to Nathaniel Breen. Surely he could deal with whatever demons had invited themselves in; he seemed to think he was holy enough to identify and eradicate them.

The gate shut of its own accord after she moved on. The sound of gravel crunching moved across the driveway. A cluster of foot-shaped dimples appeared, vanished, and reappeared in the neatly manicured grass, moving across the lawn in a steady line until they arrived at a place where three enormous trees with droopy, flowering branches formed an enclosed bower against the wall. Once Steve was sure that Sammi, Izzy, and Vince were all safely inside it, he raised his arms in a symbolic shedding gesture to throw off the cover of invisibility.

"Okay, people can see us again," he whispered. "That was some great work with the keypad, Sammi. I wish I knew enough about electronic stuff to control it with spells. Maybe I'd actually get to watch what I want to watch on TV for once."

Sammi shrugged modestly. "Hell, I wish I could become invisible."

"I wish you could've picked the lock after the old bat wasn't watching anymore," grumbled Vince. "What's the use of being invisible if we broadcast our presence across the whole damn neighborhood anyway?"

"I didn't see her," growled Sammi. "If you did, you should have warned me. So, why don't we get on with the plan?"

Steve clambered up one of the trees and ensconced himself in the fork of two branches to keep watch. He squinted across the empty lawn. Michelle stood silhouetted in the large kitchen window, staring expectantly into the yard, and the Reverend Breen was nowhere to be seen.

"All clear," he murmured.

Sammi nodded. "Great. Do your stuff, Izzy."

Izzy became a big yellow rabbit and waddled out into the yard.

Michelle saw the rabbit from the kitchen window and sighed with relief. It was about time the boys showed up; she didn't know how much longer she could have kept up the pretense of washing her now-spotless breakfast dishes.

"Michelle," said her father from the living room, where he was reading the paper. "Shouldn't you be leaving for school now? You'll be late."

The rabbit sat up and twitched an ear. Michelle nodded knowingly; that gesture was the signal.

"I'm just headed out the door, daddy," she called.

A series of sharp, high-pitched barks rose suddenly from the floor near her feet. Abednego, her father's fat, spoiled old dachshund, had seen the rabbit as intended. She moved toward the kitchen door where that smelly, overweight excuse for a dog liked to lie and gaze mindlessly out into the yard.

"Michelle?" called the Reverend Breen.

She froze in mid-step.

"Yes, daddy?"

"What's gotten into Abednego?"

Michelle looked down at the dog, which was smashing its bulk violently and repeatedly against the door.

"I think he needs to go," she said.

"Ah. Please do let him out when you leave, then."

"Yes, daddy."

Michelle pushed the door open to release the dog, thanking her lucky stars that Cain had opted not to come along on this mission. On the night she sneaked Cain into her home, Abednego had immediately lunged at him and snapped at his ankles. She tried to calm the dog, but nothing worked, and she ended up shutting it away in the basement until Cain left. The dog's reaction had puzzled her. Abednego wasn't the friendliest dog in the world, but she had never seen it take such an intense dislike to anyone so quickly.

As Michelle slipped through the gate and shut it behind her, Abednego tore as fast as its stunted little legs would carry its bloated body toward the rabbit. The rabbit watched the dog calmly until it was quite close. Then, when the dog's teeth were inches away from sinking into its neck, it whisked around and plunged through the curtain of branches. The dog barreled in after it, sweeping leaves and blossoms aside with furious jerks of its head. The rabbit sat right in front of him, cornered against the wall, as if waiting to be captured and torn to pieces…then, with no warning at all, it stood up on its hind legs and swelled rapidly into a towering human man.

The dog skidded to an awkward halt, its simple little brain jammed and overtaxed by the impossible transformation. It failed to notice the other strange humans until one of them clamped his hands around its shoulders. Then, before Abednego could bark an alarm, a horrible wrenching sensation convulsed through it and it lost consciousness.

"Yuck!" Vince pushed the dog's limp body away with a revolted grimace. "That was the worst energy I've ever tasted, hands down. It was like rotten meat and dirty socks and old newspapers and…damn, I don't even want to *think* about it."

"He'll be okay, right?" Izzy poked the dog anxiously. "You didn't take *all* his energy, did you, Vince?"

"Of course I didn't, you idiot." Vince wiped his mouth distastefully. "Do you think I'd eat any more of that disgusting dog's energy than I absolutely had to? Now start making yourself look like it already."

Izzy nodded, reassured. He knelt down beside the enervated dog. He rolled Abednego over several times, noting any distinguishing marks. Then, just when Vince began to cough impatiently, his body rippled and compressed itself into the shape of a fat dachshund identical to Abednego.

"Finished," he yipped.

"Do you remember what to look for?" said Sammi.

"Um...yup." Izzy's muzzle twitched. "Knives, bloody clothes, books about runecraft..."

"Hurry up!" Vince shooed Izzy off with menacing sweeps of his hands. "We don't have all day, you know."

"Right, right." Izzy skittered off across the yard and squeezed through the kitchen door, which Michelle had deliberately left ajar.

Inside the house, Izzy sat up on his hind paws and glanced furtively around. The kitchen was empty; he was free to begin his search. The well-stocked knife block on the kitchen counter caught his eye. There were definitely knives in the house.

But the kitchen could come later. *Start from the top, and work your way down*, he remembered Michelle saying.

Izzy trotted out of the kitchen, tiptoeing past the living room where the Reverend Breen still sat reading his paper. Climbing the stairs was exhausting work in the dog's squat

325

little body. Izzy was panting and sweating by the time he reached the top. He reverted to his natural form for convenience.

The upstairs portion of the Breen household was bigger than it had looked from the outside. Izzy stood staring down the cavernous hallway for a moment, unable to remember what Michelle had told him was behind each of the five doors. He eventually picked one at random.

The first door led to a den with a wraparound couch, a television, and a bar. Izzy stared into the sumptuous red-carpeted room, enraptured. He had never seen a TV so big before. The fully stocked bar surprised him too; he had no idea that Nathaniel Breen drank.

Even though the den was fascinating, there seemed to be no sign of the Engineer's crimes in there. Izzy ducked out and tried the next door.

It led to a smaller room that seemed to be an office. Izzy brightened at the sight of the books crowded onto the shelves and the papers piled on the big cherry wood desk. He thought he might find something useful there.

He was quickly disappointed. The books were all Bible commentaries, collections of sermons, and anthologies of inspirational essays. The piles of papers were donation records. Izzy opened drawers and cabinets and rummaged through them, thinking that the evidence he needed could be hidden, but he only uncovered office supplies and dust. He didn't find the binder until he peeked into the desk's bottom drawer.

He almost disregarded that too. It was old and battered and unassuming, stuffed with what looked to be more boring financial papers. He was about to close the drawer again when a bit of glossy paper sticking out of the rim of the binder caught his eye.

Funny, he thought. *That looks just like the helmet the fat lady wears on that one Big Bertha album cover.*

Izzy cracked open the binder. He was shocked to see a comic-book-style illustration of a fierce-looking obese woman who was wearing a spiked German helmet and straddling a machine gun—the cover art for Big Bertha's debut album. At last, he found something that warranted a closer look. He worked his hands under the binder and pulled it out of the drawer.

The contents of the binder formed a five-inch stack. Izzy thumbed through it, his amazement growing. He found flyers, articles, and promotional photos from every band he knew and from a number of bands that had already faded into obscurity: Rotten Jack, Piranha Tank, Femme Fatale, and so on. All of them were neatly organized by labeled dividers into devoted sections. He also saw the faces of some of the Engineer's victims. Jo and Andi Cochran posed with their band mates on a Piranha Tank flyer, and Foxy Fred wrapped seductively around a microphone stand at a Rotten Jack concert in a grainy newspaper photo. Izzy swallowed hard and closed the binder.

As he was putting it back, he noticed a thick manila envelope in the spot where the binder had been. It was labeled EDDIE MORNINGSTAR.

Izzy frowned as he pulled out the envelope. For someone who hated rock musicians so much, Nathaniel Breen had an awfully big collection of rock music memorabilia.

The envelope held no papers. The only thing in it was a book with yellowed pages and a peeling leather cover. Izzy slid it out of the envelope and turned it over in his hands, wondering what on earth this book could have to do with Eddie Morningstar when it looked like it was printed decades before the legendary guitarist was even born. Then he noticed the gilded letters of the title:

The Sacred Art of Spellcraft
A Treatise

By
Hiram Levi

Izzy's grip tightened around the book's spine. This book could be important. Maybe spellcraft wasn't quite the same thing as runecraft, but the two crafts couldn't be that different. At any rate, it didn't look like the kind of book Breen ought to have lying around—

Footsteps rang in the hall.

"Crap," muttered Izzy. He might have to assume Abednego's form any minute now, and he had already forgotten Abednego's distinctive marks. He held his breath and prayed that the Reverend Breen would not come into the study.

The door handle turned.

He didn't have a choice. The contents of the binder scattered on the floor as Izzy turned into a generic fat dachshund. He seized the book in his teeth and braced himself to run.

Sammi stood under the trees, anxiously looking up into the branches at Steve's leaf-obscured figure. He should have signaled Izzy's return by now.

Vince slouched against the wall nearby. He kicked at an

exposed root, scowling.

"This isn't gonna work," he muttered.

"You don't know that," said Sammi. "Be quiet. Someone might hear us."

"Oh, I know I'm right," growled Vince. "I don't know what possessed you to go along with this stupid idea in the first place. Izzy is gonna get distracted by the first shiny thing he sees—"

"Guys?" Steve whispered down from the treetop. "Izzy is coming back, and he doesn't look too happy."

Izzy burst through the branches, shedding his last traces of canine features. His normally placid blue eyes were round with panic.

"We've gotta get out of here," he whispered before anyone could ask him what was wrong. "I messed up big-time in the house."

"What the hell did you do?" snapped Vince.

"Breen caught me taking—" The kitchen door banged open, and Izzy flinched. "I'll tell you later."

"Shit!" Steve half-shimmied, half-fell out of the tree. "Breen is coming, fast—and he's headed right for the trees. I don't think I can make us all invisible again before he gets here."

Izzy started to push back through the branches. "I'll distract him. You guys go meet Cain, and I'll catch up with you." He paused for a moment and turned back to his band mates, who were standing in silent surprise at his uncharacteristic decisiveness. "Go!"

The Reverend Breen strode resolutely in the direction of the trees where he had seen his afflicted dog take shelter. He had not been prepared for this scenario. He couldn't have been prepared; no one could possibly be prepared to come away from a relaxing, civilized, pleasantly normal morning of reading the paper over a cup of coffee, only to be suddenly bowled over by one's own possessed dog. The stab of horror that had come over him when he found Eddie Morningstar's manila envelope lying empty on the floor had been so intense that he almost mistook it for a heart attack.

Yet he knew that he mustn't show how shaken he was. Whatever evil spirit had taken possession of Abednego, he could not let it leave his property with the thing it had stolen.

Branches rustled, and a small furry body popped abruptly into sight. It was not a pudgy lapdog, but a bright golden monkey with a fluffy tail. The minister stopped for a moment, staring at the creature with his mouth open. Then he saw the stolen book in the monkey's hands and pulled himself together.

The monkey turned and shuffled toward the wall. Halfway there, it turned around and hopped up and down, chattering and waving the book at the Reverend Breen as if it wanted him to follow it. Breen glared at it and planted his feet firmly in the grass.

"Give that book back," he ordered.

The monkey hop-skipped closer to the wall and shrieked mockingly.

"I said give it back," he boomed in a voice full of authority. "I command you to give it back, by the power the Lord has given me to cast out evil spirits…"

He paused for dramatic emphasis before ordering the vile little creature to depart to the depths of Hell from whence it came, and then he froze. Over the monkey's obnoxious yelps, he thought he had heard another sound. He listened, and found he could just make it out: a perfectly human voice talking in a whisper near the gate.

"Dammit, Sammi, I told you this shit wouldn't work," it said. Then it was gone.

The minister stared out into the deserted garden, looking for the source of the voice. Had he imagined it? He strained his ears, squinting in concentration, but he heard nothing except the monkey's incessant shrieking.

Yes, that must be what happened, thought Breen as he steeled himself to confront the demon monkey again. *I imagined that voice. How strange that I would, though! The only Sammi I know of is that squirrely little Mexican from the devil-boy's band.*

But he had a much more pressing problem to worry about right now. The monkey had sidled over to the foot of the wall, book still in hand, and seemed to be thinking of climbing over.

"Don't you dare!" Breen lunged forward with his arm outstretched. "I command you not to leave my property with that book!"

He must have looked much more intimidating than he felt. The monkey saw him coming and puffed up in fear. The minister froze again when he saw that it was *actually* growing larger, effortlessly shifting to the form of a different monkey with a longer tail and a stockier body.

Something clicked in Breen's mind. The devil-boy had other bandmates besides Sammi. One was the vicious vocalist who did humiliating mind-reading tricks with unsuspecting audience members; Vince, he was called. Then there was the drummer who seemed to mold his own body like clay, imitating both animals and people perfectly—what was his name again? Breen glared at the monkey in sudden recognition. "Izzy," he rumbled.

The monkey lashed its tail with surprise and fright. It tucked the book under its arm and pelted for the wall. Breen saw what it was doing and lunged desperately to grab the book, but it was too late. The monkey scrambled up the uneven whitewashed stones, easily avoiding its pursuer's grasping hands. It sat on top of the wall, staring back at the house for a moment while clutching the book to its chest; and then it plunged over the wall and was gone.

The Reverend Nathaniel Breen stood in the empty lawn, shaking from shock. Abednego staggered out of the trees and nuzzled miserably at his feet, but he took no notice. They were gone. The devil-boy's acolytes had had made off with the one item in the whole world he absolutely did not want to see fall into their wicked hands.

Yet in a way, he was glad that those filthy lowlifes had trespassed so boldly on his property. Now that they had revealed the full extent of their evil, he saw his duty more clearly than ever.

Chapter Fourteen

Caught

THE BOOK'S PAGES WERE fragile. Cain carefully flipped through them, and his shock and disbelief grew stronger. He didn't bother trying to read the intimidating walls of text that crowded each brittle, yellowed leaf, but most of the symbols were familiar; he had seen Mr. Warwick use them. He couldn't imagine how this book had come into Breen's possession, but it looked like a legitimate primer on sorcery.

"And you're *sure* you found this in Breen's desk?" Steve asked Izzy for the third time. "Like, actually in a drawer with other stuff like it was meant to be there? It wasn't in a secret compartment or anything...?"

"Nope." Izzy shook his head. Cain could feel him staring over his shoulder at the intricate glyphs on the page. "Like I said," Izzy continued, "it was right under the binder. Breen *had* to know it was there."

Cain took a quick peek at Michelle, who was standing a few feet away from the couch where Cain and his band mates sat. She shifted nervously while she watched them study the book, inspecting the scene like an inexperienced swimmer eyeing a wild stretch of ocean. Her face was pale.

"It doesn't make any sense," she muttered. "Why would daddy keep a book like that in the house?"

"Why?" Vince piped up before Cain and Sammi could shush him. "Because he's a fucking hypocrite, that's why. He goes on TV to bitch about us witchcraft-practicing rock stars, and then he goes home to cast spells behind closed doors. That's what he does."

Michelle timidly leaned in for a peek. Cain turned the page again to reveal a crude illustration of a man with a knife standing over a black dog. The dog was howling in pain, and the man seemed to be slitting its throat. Cain swore he could hear her stomach churn before she looked away, and Vince leaned in with renewed interest.

"A spell to cause your enemy's death, huh?" he said. "Hell, why don't we just use that to take care of the Engineer? It seems like it'd be worth a dog."

Izzy gasped and gaped at him in horror.

Steve shook his head. "No, it wouldn't be worth it. Blood magic makes you scary powerful, but it'll also turn you into a screaming, ranting, and seeing-imaginary-monsters-around-every-corner lunatic."

Michelle swallowed hard. She turned and walked slowly out of the room without a word, hugging her arms to her chest. Cain noticed her leaving and got up to follow her.

"Michelle, wait!" he called. "Steve didn't mean it like that. I'm sure your dad doesn't—"

Sammi caught his wrist and pulled him back. "Let her go, man. She needs some time to herself. I would too if I'd just found out my dad might be the Engineer."

"He might not be the Engineer," said Steve. "I mean, this book seems to have everything *but* runes. I haven't seen one so far."

"Well, we haven't even made it halfway through the book yet," said Izzy.

"And even if Breen isn't the Engineer," Sammi added, "he has documented every move every rocker on the Strip has made for the last five years in that binder. I don't care if it's for his ministry or whatever, it's still pretty damn creepy if you ask me."

Michelle sauntered up the driveway, backpack hanging off her shoulder. She forced her face to settle into an expression of detached boredom. Maybe if she acted casually enough, her father might ignore the fact that she was almost two hours late getting home from school, or at least he might simply ground her without trying to wring a reason out of her. It was her only hope. With all the conflicting emotions roiling in her, she doubted she could handle one of his protracted reprimands without letting them bubble explosively to the surface.

The front door was locked, which was a good sign. It meant that her father was not home to notice that she was late. Michelle sighed with relief as she dug for her keys. She would have plenty of time to calm down, think things over, and get that horrible image of the man and the dog out of her head—

The front door swung open with a creak. The Reverend Breen stood in the doorway, his face grave.

"Um…hi, daddy," squeaked Michelle.

"I've been waiting for you to get home," said her father. "Come into the living room with me. We need to talk."

She followed him silently, trying not to wobble on her feet as she walked. Something in her father's expression filled her with hot, roiling dread.

The minister lowered himself into his blue chair with a weary grunt. Michelle sat down on the couch across from him.

"I'm sorry I'm late, daddy," she said preemptively. "Some classmates invited me to go out for pizza and ice cream after school, and I didn't—"

Her father held up a hand for silence. When he finally spoke, his voice had a strange evasive stiffness to it. He sounded very much like he had when she had asked him, as a very young child, where babies came from.

"Sweetheart," he said. "Remember how I've always told you that your grandparents—my mama and daddy—were good Christians?"

"Of course." Michelle didn't see how she could possibly forget; her father couldn't resist hammering that story into her head. He would proclaim his parents' Christian virtues whenever he had the chance. "Why?"

"Well, it's God's own truth." The Reverend Breen sighed. "But...even as good as they were, they weren't perfect. No Christian is perfect. They wanted to make their children strong in their faith, and if we faltered...they would set us straight with a heavy hand."

"How so?" said Michelle awkwardly, caught off guard. She couldn't imagine why her father was suddenly so anxious to talk about his long-dead parents.

"If they saw a stumbling block on our road to salvation, they would simply remove it. I was never allowed to listen to secular music or read books they hadn't approved. My sister wasn't allowed to date. They considered art and leisure frivolities. If we'd had a television, I suppose we wouldn't have been allowed to watch anything except the news. And if we rebelled against the rules—and you can bet your Aunt Janice and I both did—then there would be discipline meted out…sometimes with a belt or coat hanger. I know it sounds harsh, but it worked. I wouldn't be the man I am today if they hadn't been so firm with me."

Michelle shifted nervously. She fervently hoped he wasn't considering using his parents' disciplinary methods. Her father had never laid a hand on her in her life, but if something—like suspecting that his daughter somehow aided and abetted Izzy's break-in, for example—made him angry enough, then maybe…

"Yet I am aware that their methods," his voice became strained, as if it pained him to admit it, "well, that they might not be one-size-fits-all. That in fact, they might lead some to turn away from the Word altogether, like my sister did. That's why I swore when you were born that I would never try to raise you as my mama and daddy raised me. I hoped to guide you to the Lord along a gentler path. With God's help, I've stuck to that plan…but it's hard sometimes. Harder than you can imagine. And there are times—like now—when I have to step in."

"Why? What happened, daddy?" Michelle was alarmed now, and her father was sweating and seemed profoundly uncomfortable.

The minister sighed deeply and rubbed his temples.

"You're nursing an obsession, my dear," he said. "A dangerous infatuation with a dangerous man—"

Michelle avoided his eye. "Daddy, I have no idea what you're talking—"

"Michelle, I've seen the albums and the pictures you've tried to keep hidden from me. I also saw the look in your eyes that morning when I spoke of him…I think you knew about Eddie Morningstar long before I ever mentioned him to you."

Michelle's mouth dropped open. Her relief that her father wasn't talking about Cain clashed strongly with her anger that he had dared to go snooping in her room. She tried to speak, but nothing came out except a little gasp.

"It's all right, sweetheart," said her father quickly, mistaking her indignation for shame. "I'm only upset that you tried to hide things from me—not that you have a simple schoolgirl crush, even if that...man...is the object. You can't help who you're attracted to. Lord knows I've learned that truth the hard way. But you absolutely *can* choose not to act on such attractions. I'd hoped that you would come to that decision through your own discernment, but it seems you need a bit more help in this case."

"Help with what?" Michelle's voice rose. "Not acting on my attraction? I don't see how I'm in any danger of that—"

"You need to break the hold he has over your mind. In light of...recent circumstances...I believe your infatuation could put you in spiritual and physical danger—"

"But Eddie Morningstar is *dead*, daddy! How can he put me in danger when he's been nothing but a pile of ashes stuck in an urn somewhere for eight years?"

The minister picked up a newspaper from the coffee table. He didn't speak, and for a moment, Michelle thought he was going to ignore her by pretending to read it in a fit of childish pique. But he did not open it.

"The matter isn't that simple," he said at last. "Eddie was a rare breed. He had certain...talents...that only come around once a lifetime, or so I'm told."

"What talents?" Michelle leaned forward with new interest. She hadn't forgiven her father for the snooping yet, but at least she might finally get the details of his anti-Eddie

Morningstar paranoia.

Her father set the newspaper down on the coffee table. Again he said nothing for a long time.

"As I've told you before, sweetheart," he muttered, "the heavy metal lifestyle caused an explosion of witchcraft in our fair city. The irony, though, is that most of the young men and women who practice witchcraft have no real power. The danger they pose to decent folk like us comes from their reckless pursuit of the hedonist's lifestyle, not from anything their confused little chalk-circle-and-candle rituals could achieve."

"But what does that have to do with Eddie?" asked Michelle, wondering where on earth her father had witnessed these "chalk-circle-and-candle rituals." The musicians at the clubs were always far too busy with the serious business of pounding back drinks and having sex with everything that moved to bother with bogus witchcraft rituals.

The Reverend Breen took a deep breath.

"Eddie was different," he said. "He had real power, a real ability to inflict harm."

Michelle nodded. She thought she had identified the source of her father's paranoia.

"Daddy…" She paused for a moment, carefully editing anything her father could mistake for "sass" out of her phrasing. "I'm no expert, but…I think all the crazy magic stuff at Lion of Judah concerts were just tricks, and JoJo did most of them anyway."

"Well, Eddie's most dangerous work was done offstage," her father said. "He meddled in the dark arts, and unfortunately, he had quite a talent for harnessing dark powers. Toward the end of his life, when the final madness came over him, he could kill with a single word."

"I...had no idea." She nodded incredulously. "So...um...how do you know all this information, daddy? I've never seen anything about Eddie in the Black Book."

"I don't keep anything of Eddie's in the Black Book," said the minister. "He has a separate file...Anyway, that's what I need to talk to you about." He leaned forward, concern in his eyes. "Sweetheart, while you were at school, there was a break-in."

He spoke in the same forced tone of calm reassurance that he had used whenever she skinned her knees as a child. Michelle was annoyed, but she knew what he expected of her. She dutifully feigned a surge of girlish fear complete with widened eyes, fluttering hands, and a genteel gasp.

"Goodness, daddy, why didn't you tell me sooner?" she cried. "What did they take? My jewelry is still there, isn't it?"

"Oh, yes, yes, of course!" He made a placating gesture. "None of your things were touched; I promise. Everything in the house is accounted for, save for one item."

"What was that, daddy?" she asked innocently.

The Reverend Breen rubbed his eyes. Michelle could hear his breathing speed up slightly. She could tell that he was stressed and afraid even though he was trying hard not to show it.

"Something of Eddie's," he said. "Something that I foolishly thought I could keep hidden away in an upstairs drawer, where it would never hurt anyone again."

Something clicked in Michelle's mind.

"That book," she said. "It wasn't yours, was it? It was Eddie's."

"Yes." Her father shuddered. "And that, Michelle, is

what I wanted to warn you about. This powerful artifact of sorcery has fallen into unknown hands, and whoever has it…" He gave her a pained look. "Whoever has it may target you as well as me."

Michelle let out a theatrical gasp of horror and silently prayed that her father had not called the police. She strongly suspected that these "unknown hands" were not as unknown to her father as he would have her believe.

"Now, I don't want to alarm you," he continued. "Whatever evils might be in store for my flock and family, I'll put on the armor of God and fight tooth and nail to protect you. But there's only so much I can do. You must take some steps to protect yourself as well—by keeping your thoughts pure. If those pictures are in your room, he has an opening into your mind and heart."

"Who has an opening, daddy? The thief?"

"The devil."

Michelle nodded cautiously, watching his face. She was sure now that he knew who was behind the theft. He spoke of the thief, of Cain, as if he were speaking of the true, literal Devil. Was it possible that her father had realized Cain's elaborate stage performance and horns and tail weren't ruses? She wouldn't put it past him to discover Cain's abilities and origins now—not after finding out that he had been hiding a genuine spell book that had once belonged to Eddie Morningstar in his desk drawer.

"I understand, daddy," she said. "I'll get rid of that stuff. I promise."

"Good girl." The minister picked up his newspaper again, turning it over in his hands nervously. Michelle nodded and got up to leave.

"One more thing, my dear."

Michelle had been moving toward the door. She turned around after he uttered these words and found him staring at her with a knitted brow.

"I don't believe I told you that the stolen item was a book," he said. "How *did* you know it was a book?"

Oops. He didn't tell me, did he? Michelle thought. She scrambled for a plausible answer. Fortunately, she had gotten quite good at spinning lies at a moment's notice. She barely missed a beat before the bogus explanation came together and rolled off her tongue.

"Well, daddy, I took a peek inside that folder once," she said faux-shamefacedly. "When you asked me to put something in the Black Book for you, I saw the folder with Eddie's name on it, and I got curious."

"You didn't read it, did you?" The minister's face went pale.

"Goodness no!" Michelle shook her head. "I didn't even take it out of the envelope. I was hoping to see Eddie Morningstar stuff, not a dusty old book."

She had not had any earthly idea that there had been a book or anything else in that folder until Izzy's ill-fated raid. Michelle had *almost* stolen a look inside that envelope several times. When her father had sent her to fetch various documents and supplies from the study, she was drawn to the folder by the lure of Eddie Morningstar's name. But she had wisely resisted the temptation. Despite the apparent disorder of her father's papers, she knew that he had an almost supernatural ability to tell when someone had rifled through them. She half-expected him to narrow his eyes and inform her that he knew she hadn't touched Eddie's file; but to her relief, he actually seemed to buy her story.

"I see." He relaxed and sat back on the couch. "Well,

I'm glad that you didn't read it. Now, please do get rid of those Eddie Morningstar things, sooner rather than later."

"Yes, daddy," Michelle lied. As happy and relieved as she was that her father was probably not the Engineer, she would be damned before she threw away a stack of vintage posters, a collection of magazine articles, and three of her favorite records for his sake. Maybe Cain would hold onto them for her. Maybe he could also shed some light on how a drugged-up rock star like Eddie had managed to get his hands on—and use—a book of powerful black magic spells.

Mr. Arkin had shed his friendly and informal manner. He leaned over his desk, drumming his fingers in a steady rhythm as he eyed Cain's band mates. Sammi and Vince met his gaze, but Izzy stared at the floor. Cain stood in the corner, watching the scene unfold.

"Congratulations, guys." Mr. Arkin's hands came down flat on his desk with an exasperated slap. "You've achieved something that most musicians spend their entire career slaving for but never get. The whole city is talking about you, especially Nathaniel Breen."

Vince let out a little humorless grunt of laughter. The others were silent.

"In fact, the good minister can't say enough about you—you in particular, Cain." His eyes wandered to the corner where Cain huddled as unobtrusively as possible. "He seems to think that you sent Izzy, Sammi, and Vince to his house to *steal* something. You wouldn't happen to know anything about that, would you?"

"Breen is full of shit," Sammi piped up indignantly before Cain could answer. "We didn't steal anything. It was just a stupid prank, and Cain wasn't even there."

"I see," said Mr. Arkin in a strained voice. "Tell me…this prank…are you sure it didn't involve taking anything of his? Because the Reverend Breen is adamant that you did take something."

Cain's gaze flicked over Vince's and Sammi's faces. Vince was the very model of stubborn stoniness, and Sammi was full of fiery indignation. Izzy, on the other hand, looked extremely guilty and squirmed in his chair as Mr. Arkin's eyes came to rest on him. Sammi spoke again before Izzy could, rubbing his bruised forearm wearily.

"What did we supposedly steal?" he asked.

Mr. Arkin opened his mouth and then closed it again. "Does it matter?" he said at last. "Look, guys, just give me a straight answer. It's important."

"You want a straight answer?" Sammi raised his voice. "Like I told you before, we—Izzy, Vince, and I—got a little drunk and climbed over Breen's garden wall, just to see if we could, and then we climbed right back out again. We were only in his yard for, like, two minutes, and we didn't take anything."

Cain admired Sammi's ability to take charge of the situation, but he wasn't sure Mr. Arkin was buying Sammi's assertions.

"Is there anything you'd like to add to that, son?" Mr. Arkin turned to Izzy again.

Izzy flinched and looked like he wanted to melt into the floor, but he mumbled no.

"Are you sure?"

"Mr. Arkin," said Sammi firmly. "You know what Breen is doing here. He can't get us dropped from the label for being Satanists, so he's trying his damnedest to make us out to be ordinary criminals. It's just another move to drive us off the airwaves. Don't you see that?"

Mr. Arkin narrowed his eyes at them, scrutinizing each of their faces in turn like a police interrogator searching for weaknesses that might get a suspect talking. Cain doubted he would find any; they had all solemnly sworn before they came into the office to keep the results of yesterday's raid a secret for fear that Mr. Arkin would order them to return their spoils. Even Izzy was more terrified of letting that book fall back into Breen's hands than he was of any punishments Mr. Arkin could dole out.

"Of course I do," said Mr. Arkin. "It's just…Look, guys, I want you all to stay away from Breen from now on— especially you, Cain."

Cain's eyes narrowed.

"*Especially* me?" he said. "Why?"

"Yeah. Sure." Mr. Arkin didn't seem to hear him. "Now let's see…no scandal short of murder usually has much shelf life in this town, as far as the press is concerned, but this prank of yours has serious sensationalist potential. If we're lucky, the worst should blow over in a week or so—"

"But I wasn't even there." Cain raised his voice. "Why should I be more careful than everyone else?"

Mr. Arkin coughed impatiently.

"You've heard Breen's rants against you," he said. "I think you know why. Anyway, about the press—I'm a little surprised they haven't come sniffing around already. But they're bound to start soon, and when they do, you answer any question about Breen or weird rituals with an automatic *no comment*—understand? I'm afraid that goes double for you, Cain."

Cain stared at him, clenching his fists in sudden anger. He felt as if Mr. Arkin was bent on scolding him alone for

the incident despite the fact that Mr. Arkin knew they all had
had a hand in it.

"Can't you tell Breen to leave me alone?" he said.

Mr. Arkin shook his head. "No, I can't. As I was saying,
this incident might blow over. But if Breen is persistent, and
the camera-jackals are bored enough to allow the rumor to
stick around, I'll be the one to decide when and how it needs
to be dealt with, okay? I don't want to open the paper
tomorrow—or in a week or a month from now—and find
out that you guys have been keeping this alive by blabbing
about it. And I *really* don't want to find out that any one of
you has decided to confront Breen."

He looked directly at Cain as he said this last statement.
Cain met his gaze with a rebellious glare.

"So what if I do?" he snapped. He crossed the room and
stood beside his band mates, directly in front of Mr. Arkin.
"Why should I take Breen's abuse?"

"Hey, chill the fuck out, man," hissed Vince, punching
Cain in the side.

Cain shook him off. "Breen is telling lies about us. We
shouldn't have to sit back and let that happen; we ought to
be able to defend ourselves. But he's free to go on lying
about us all he wants, and you won't let us do anything to
stop him. That's not fair. It's just *wrong*, Mr. Arkin."

"You think I don't know that?" said Mr. Arkin sharply.
Anger flashed in his eyes for a moment. Then he deflated in
his chair and heaved a tired sigh.

"Look," he said. "I'm sorry. I know you don't deserve
the crap Breen has been saying about you. But he's got as
much money and as many powerful friends as I do. He's not
stupid, and he's not above fighting dirty. Plus he puts
himself out there as a good Christian preacher out to save

abused children from the Devil, and your whole career is based on looking like the Devil. If you make an enemy of Breen, he won't rest until he finds a way to prove to the whole country that there's a reason those 'special effects' you use are a little *too* realistic. I can tell you right now which side of the argument most humans' sympathies will fall on once that shoe drops. I know it's not fair. But this is a fight you can't win."

Cain groaned. Mr. Arkin was probably right, but it sickened him to admit it. Still, Mr. Arkin's cautiousness was a bit of a surprise to him. Bruce Arkin's career had taken off when he put out a bondage-themed Candiryde video that no other label would touch, and he had happily shrugged off the controversy it generated. His sudden squeamishness seemed out of character. Cain's band mates seemed to share this sentiment; they exchanged puzzled looks.

The phone on Mr. Arkin's desk rang loudly. Sammi flinched, and Izzy leapt into the air with a yelp of fright and turned into a ferret.

Mr. Arkin answered the phone with a slow, listless sweep of his arm, pausing for a moment to cast a long-suffering glance at the dark spot of urine Izzy had left on the chair cushion.

"Hello?" He answered the phone, keeping his voice low. "What? Yes, he's here," he said, glancing at Cain. "I...really? I'm afraid I don't know anything about that." There was an odd note of apprehension in his voice. He listened for a minute. "Yes, yes, of course I will, but with all due respect, I don't see how it was *my* responsibility to...to..." He stammered for a minute, and then he sighed. "I'm sorry. Of course you're right. I'll tell him right now."

Mr. Arkin set the receiver back in its cradle and turned

347

to Cain with his eyebrows slightly raised.

"It was Mr. Warwick," he said. "Is his son visiting you again?"

Sammi and Vince stared at Mr. Arkin in amazement; they probably had never heard him speak so deferentially to anyone before. Cain wasn't surprised at all; he had seen Mr. Warwick's uncanny ability to gain the upper hand in business relationships in action many times before.

"Ah…yes. Yes, he is," said Cain.

"Well, he wants me to tell you that he'll be arriving in the city on business, and he expects you to have his boy— Steve, was it?—ready to go home in two days' time. He also says…" He glanced ruefully at the phone. "He wants me to tell you that you should have known Steve was being punished, and he's very disappointed in you."

Cain scratched at his collar, which he hadn't been able to remove even after he had gained his temporary freedom. A surge of ill temper shot through him.

"You know what?" he snapped. "You can tell Mr. Warwick that if he wants Steve back, he can come and tell me to my face."

He turned and stalked out of the room.

"Cain, wait!" Sammi scrambled up and ran after him. "Where are you going? Come back. Man, what's gotten *into* you?"

Izzy and Vince sat for a moment, shifting uncomfortably. Then Vince lurched to his feet and stomped out the door with a sullen farewell grunt. Izzy shot Mr. Arkin an apologetic look and scampered off. As he started down the hall, he overheard Mr. Arkin muttering to himself.

"I would've expected this kind of outburst from someone like Vince," he said in an incredulous voice. "But from Cain? Damn, I *knew* his docile and well-behaved nature was too good to be true. Then again, what do you expect from a goddamned demon?"

It was a cloudy morning. Cain lay on the couch, a shabby old medical textbook open on his knee. He had pulled it out of one of Izzy's many piles of tattered books and magazines two weeks ago, hoping to figure out the exact mechanism by which heroin made Sammi pass out. It had not disappointed him; after laboriously sounding out hundreds of unfamiliar words, he had come across a chapter that had several large sections of text devoted to heroin. In four days, he'd only managed to slog through a third of the chapter.

He finished a particularly long paragraph with a groan of relief and cast a longing glance at his guitar. He had no idea why this book was in Izzy's possession. He couldn't imagine Izzy poring over mind-numbing, dense, and boring treatises on arcane concepts like deacetylation and opioid receptors. Then again, Izzy rarely made any use at all of the random bits of junk he brought home.

Cain turned his attention back to the page. He had to get through this chapter; Vince had found Sammi sprawled in the bathtub that morning. This time he hadn't even pulled the needle out of his skin before the stupor overtook him. Someone needed to know how to wake him next time.

There was a brisk knock at the door. Cain gladly pushed the book aside and got up to answer it.

It was Mr. Warwick.

"Hello, Cain," he said softly.

"Master." Cain had forgotten that he was supposed to have Steve ready to go. He felt his tail wrapping around his knees in a submissive little curl even as he tried to straighten up defiantly.

"I've come to pick up Steve," said Mr. Warwick in a short but not unfriendly tone. "Is he ready to go as I asked?"

"No." Cain resisted the urge to call Mr. Warwick "Master" again. Now that he had the freedom to act as he wished, he planned to show the old man how much he hated being scolded and ordered about. "I told him he could do some sightseeing today since his visit was so short."

"Did you, now?" Mr. Warwick's calm, bland expression did not change. "Well, there's no harm in that. I suppose I can find him myself." A small, dry smile played at the corners of his lips. "But I'm forgetting my manners. Since I'm here, I ought to ask how you're doing. Are you enjoying yourself in the city?"

"I am," Cain replied in a cold voice. He volunteered no further information; if information was what his master wanted, he would have to work for it.

"Your band is doing well?"

"Yes. Yes, we are," he said resentfully. He knew what Mr. Warwick was doing. He adopted that maddening false air of friendliness whenever he knew he had the upper hand and wanted to remind someone of his or her place. It had always been mildly amusing to watch him use it on powerful politicians and businessmen, but Cain didn't find it funny at all now that the duplicity was turned on him.

"I'm very glad to hear that." Mr. Warwick's smile widened. "It's good to know that you've been using your time off in a productive manner. But there's something I need to tell you before I run off to rescue Steve from whatever boneheaded mess he's almost certainly got himself into wandering around the city alone."

With a quick, snake-like movement, he reached out and touched Cain's collar. The leather rippled and a spasm of searing-cold pain shot viciously down Cain's spine. His knees gave way, and he crumpled on the stoop, gasping and staring at Mr. Warwick's feet through a throbbing red mist.

"I'd like to remind you," he continued in the sickeningly friendly voice, "that your freedom is a privilege, not a right. One more insubordinate, ill-behaved outburst like the one in Mr. Arkin's office, and you're coming right back to New York."

Cain tried to struggle to his feet, but an aftershock of nausea and vertigo made him drop again.

"I'm still your master." The faintest hint of coldness crept into Mr. Warwick's voice. "I'll be your master until the day I die, no matter how many screaming fans you have and how many surgically enhanced sluts throw themselves at you. Remember that, and behave yourself."

He turned smartly on his heel and walked off, leaving Cain doubled up on the stoop.

Cain had no idea how long it took for the pain to subside, but it felt like hours. He finally managed, by groping blindly, to grab the banister. While he slowly pulled himself up, pausing frequently to dissipate the star-shaped flashes of light that flickered in his field of vision, he caught a glimpse of a tall woman walking down the street with hurried steps. She paused in front of the stoop and looked up at Cain, awkwardly juggling three glass bottles of milky blue liquid. She wore a large pair of wraparound sunglasses and had a red scarf wrapped, babushka-style, around her head.

"Hey!" An angry voice rang down the street behind her. "You're not gonna get feverwort extract cheaper anywhere else, you know! Come to me bitching about how much I'm soaking you for again, and you can go right back to paying those rip-off prices your guy in New York charges. Just a friendly warning."

The woman took one last furtive glance at Cain and fled. A familiar figure in a bright lime-green suit came hobbling along in her wake. He leaned on the bottom of the banister, out of breath, shaking his head incredulously.

"*Fifty dollars* for two and a half liters?" muttered Jodido, spitting on the sidewalk in contempt. "Maybe—*maybe*—you could get half a liter of low-quality stuff for fifty, on a good day, but for two and a half liters of the good shit? Damn! Spoiled little twat. Does she think I brew the stuff out the goodness of my heart? I swear, one of these days…" He finished the statement with a mimed strangling motion. Then he noticed Cain watching him and quickly pasted a forced smile over his face.

"Oh, hi there, *coñito*," he said. "I didn't know you lived here."

Cain backed up against the door. He didn't like the idea of Jodido knowing where he lived. There was something about the little man that gave him a queasy feeling in the pit of his stomach.

"Hey, sorry you had to see that," Jodido said, not noticing—or perhaps ignoring—Cain's discomfort. "Every time that silly bitch comes to make a buy, she gives me shit over the price. I guess she must have it in her head that feverwort is like a bottle of vanilla from the fucking supermarket." He took a flask out of his jacket and took a long swig from it, scowling. "She could care less that I nearly broke my back picking that stuff under grubby overpasses and then spent a week making sure it steeped just right so it wouldn't poison anyone. That's Waheela stinginess for you."

"You mean she was…" Cain arched his eyebrows and gaped at Jodido.

Jodido rolled his eyes. "Yup."

"But she didn't look like one." The woman had borne no wolf-like features that he could see, though maybe that was why she was wearing the scarf. He supposed there could have been a pair of fluffy canine ears tucked beneath it.

"Well, you don't look much like a devil either, when you turn yourself into a human." The scrawny drug dealer chuckled meanly. "That's exactly what that backwoods bitch did, by the way, to land herself one of the richest men in the city. Personally, I think she just got him good and afraid she'd hunt him down and bite off his dick if he ever tried to leave her—and now she spends all her time squeezing me for feverwort to keep her little half-breed pup in the dark about the dog side of its nature. Humph, if I'd been in her place I would've saved myself a lot of money and trouble and just drowned the little freak at birth."

Jodido took another sucking gulp from the flask. Cain watched him, curious in spite of his apprehension.

"But why would a Waheela want to be with a human in that way?" he mused. He and Michelle at least shared roughly similar anatomy, no matter which form he took.

"Beats me. I'm not a goddamned sex therapist." A trickle of thick brown liquid dribbled from the corner of Jodido's mouth. "Man, fuck that conniving Waheela whore. Fuck all the rich people in this fucking city. They don't want product for a good price; they want miracles for chump change. Fifty dollars for two and a half liters of feverwort extract! Maybe I won't watch the pot so closely next time. I take care not to poison her precious puppy with a dose of bad feverwort, but its safety obviously isn't worth an extra two hundred bucks to her."

Whatever was in the flask was beginning to affect him. His voice rose and fell in volume at random intervals, and his hands twitched furiously. He lifted the flask again but missed his face entirely, dumping a big splotch of brown on his shoulder. Cain stood uncertainly on the doorstep; he knew that he should probably slip inside while Jodido was absorbed in his rant, but he found himself unable to stop staring at him. There was something uncomfortably amusing about the scene the little man was making. He was posturing like a monkey that had been taught to throw obscene gestures.

"Know what, *coñito*?" Jodido took another drink from his flask and belched loudly. "Your buddies are loud and annoying, and they only buy the mundane stuff, but at least they're halfway decent customers. They don't try to screw me."

"My buddies?" Cain remembered what Skeeter had said about getting his coke from Jodido. "Like Sammi, you mean?"

"Sammi Amp?" Jodido lurched forward and struggled up the steps, clinging to the banister. "Sure. I've sold to him a couple times. Strange guy—nervous as a cat—but he always pays up, and he never complains. Same with Johnny Revolver, Joey Gatling, and the Judd brothers. Though that Skeeter boy could talk the ear off a deaf dog." He wobbled and grabbed the banister with both hands to save himself from pitching backwards. "So yeah, you rockers are the best to do business with. But you know..." His eyes gleamed hopefully. "I could do with more customers like you."

Cain didn't like this sentiment one bit, nor was he comfortable with the greedy expression that had overtaken Jodido's features. Yet he fought the urge to flee; an idea was forming at the back of his mind. If Sammi had gotten his heroin from Jodido, Cain could also get heroin from him. If he had an actual sample of heroin to experiment on, he could learn how to magically counteract its effects more easily than he could by studying a tome of incomprehensible jargon.

"Well," he said in a casual voice, "I have been meaning to try something new."

"Oh yeah?" The greed on the dealer's face grew more pronounced. "What's your pleasure?"

"Maybe a little heroin…"

Jodido pulled up short.

"Heroin!" The oil in his hair gleamed as he shook his head in disbelief. "Nah, you don't want to try *that*, kid. It'll make you sick."

"Really?" Cain put on his best look of bewilderment. "My friend Sammi hasn't gotten sick from it," he said, even though Sammi had gotten sick from it, in a way. "He says it's great—that it makes him have good dreams. I've wanted to try some for a while."

"Yeah, well, your friend Sammi is a human. Smack doesn't work the same for devils. It'd just give you a really nasty rash." Jodido put the flask back and stuck his hand in his back pocket. "You'll want something different, something that you can actually get high off of…ah, here!"

He pulled out a small brown object and lunged forward, clumsily tossing it in Cain's general direction. Cain caught it.

"What's this?" He inspected the object in his hand; it

was a small plastic bag full of brown powder, similar to the one Jodido had shown him on the way to the Hispanic neighborhood, but this mixture had little flecks of a red substance mixed in with the brown.

"My own personal mix." Jodido patted the pocket where he kept his flask conspiratorially. "Cocoa for soothing the nerves, with just enough nutmeg and red chili to…um…expand your mind. And like I said before, you can't get in trouble for carrying it either 'cause humans can't get high off it like we can. Heh, their loss…"

"We?" said Cain suspiciously. He had assumed that the scrawny drug dealer was another human, albeit a rather odd-looking one.

Jodido responded with a loud, grating laugh. "Ha, it's kicking in—here come the colors again. Oh yeah, I needed this fix. Yup, kid, I said 'we.' I may not be a devil like you, but I'm no monkey either."

"What are you, then?"

Jodido dragged himself up the last few steps. He was so unsteady on his feet now that he almost didn't make it, and he leaned in to Cain too closely.

"Someone who doesn't like this shithole world any more than you do, boy," he whispered.

His breath smelled sickly and rotten. Cain stifled a cough and backed as far away as he could.

"I knew what you were the minute I saw you in that alley," muttered Jodido, his happy mood dissipating rapidly. "As soon as I saw that collar…heh, we're in the same boat, *coñito*. You know what it's like to be sent away from your own home and made to take orders from stupid humans who think they're better than you." He spat on the stoop, narrowly missing Cain's shoe. "Fucking monkeys. I'd *love* to show them who's boss, but my superiors would kill me if I ruined their little racket."

Cain shifted uncomfortably. He had no idea what Jodido was talking about or how to calm him down.

"Hey, kid," Jodido waved his arm vaguely at Cain. "You keep that stuff, okay? It's not heroin, but if you mix it in some hot water and drink it down, it'll do some of the same things for you. If you like it, I've got more you can buy. Oh, and don't try to make your own mix with chocolate from the grocery store. Their shit is so old and stale that you'll barely get a buzz from it, and monkeys like to load it up with white sugar besides. Heroin might give you a rash, *coñito*, but white sugar could kill you."

Cain had more questions, but Jodido was already stumbling down the steps. He landed unsteadily on the sidewalk, swept his skinny hand through the air in an awkward solute, and staggered down the street. A neatly groomed young couple walking their dogs swerved to let him pass.

"Don't tell Delfina I gave you that, *coñito!*" Cain heard him yell over his shoulder while the young man glowered at Jodido and grumbled about people not looking where they were going. "She'll try to take it from you. She doesn't get folks like us. She can't understand our *needs*, you know?"

Cain noticed the young woman staring at him with a prim, sour-faced expression of disapproval. He ducked his head and hastily retreated into the house.

The old textbook lay open on the couch. Cain plopped down next to it, but he did not pick it up. He was more interested in the brown and red powder Jodido had given him. He sheepishly weighed the baggie in his hand. His hasty plan to obtain a heroin sample on which to experiment hadn't gone as planned. He doubted his experiment would work now. At a loss, Cain tentatively opened the bag and sniffed its contents. A familiar scent hit his nostrils, pungent, earthy, and sweet. It was a scent he had smelled many times from Steve's and Lance's candy bars.

The mysterious brown powder seemed to be nothing more than ground chocolate. His annoyance mingled with a desire to laugh. Surely Jodido didn't actually think ordinary chocolate would work on him the same way heroin worked on Sammi, regardless of the fact that Cain was not human. Mr. Warwick wouldn't have allowed the stuff in his house if he thought Cain might regularly be using it to put himself in a stupor.

Cain dabbed some of the mixture onto his fingertip and stared at it dubiously. He didn't trust Jodido enough to put it in his mouth, whether or not it was chocolate. Instead, he brought it close to his nose and sniffed it again, deeply, to confirm his suspicions. The substance was drier and looser than he expected. A plume of powder flew into his nose. He coughed and sputtered, and the chocolate smell became overwhelming.

The spreading sensation of pleasure took him by surprise. It radiated down from his face and coursed through his limbs, wrapping his mind in a strange, velvety fog. Without a second thought, he brought his chocolate-stained fingers to his mouth. A jarring bitterness and a burning sensation erupted on his tongue, which was quite unpleasant until a heady rush of euphoria overpowered the acrid taste.

Cain fell more deeply into the couch, unable to move. The rush and the foggy calmness mingled and intensified. All his fears and cares melted away. He no longer gave a damn about the Reverend Breen's sermons, or about boring books on human medicine, or about making sure Vince didn't attack anyone. He didn't even blink when a ghostly, distorted image of Mr. Warwick materialized by the armchair and began to scold him in nonsense words. And he wasn't startled when Izzy's canister collection bubbled and overflowed with evil-looking black tar.

Slowly, for the floor was heaving like a waterbed, he got up and sauntered into the kitchen through a gasping mouth of a door that contracted and expanded in a broken rhythm. He took great pleasure in throwing Vince's favorite gesture—a one-finger salute—at Mr. Warwick as he went.

The kitchen was full of cheese. Great blocks and wheels of cheese poured in a yellow-orange avalanche from the refrigerator and cupboards, and the table groaned under its weight. Cain pounced on the pile, ripping into it with bare hands and teeth. For every chunk of cheese he ate, three more materialized, and he devoured them all, laughing with fierce joy. He was beyond the reach of the world; even Mr. Warwick couldn't touch him.

Then it was no longer cheese he was holding, but a book. The book from the Reverend Breen's house. Its pages flipped of their own accord, blurring like hummingbird wings. Cain's stomach began to churn while he watched them. He reached out to close the book, but the cover felt heavier than lead, and the pages eluded his grasping fingers.

Then it fell open.

Cain staggered back in fear at the sight of the star-and-circle symbol, the one that had plagued the corners of his mind for ten years. It sprawled across the yellow page like a malignant cancer. The symbol was scrawled in a black ink that seemed to be glowing somehow, as if backlit by an evil light. As he watched, the light intensified, radiating out from the glyphs within the star's points.

The glyphs flashed bright green.

Cain jerked back with a yelp of pain, clutching his eyes. When he dropped his hands, the world was normal again. An empty cheese wrapper lay crumpled on the table beside the book open before him.

Because he was still groggy from the chocolate, he didn't notice Sammi watching him through the kitchen door. Cain bent feverishly over the book. His head still throbbed with pain, but he had to figure out what that symbol meant. He somehow felt as if his very life depended on it.

The world was a thick, warm mass of soft, cream-colored cotton.

Michael Anderson sank into the chair like a rag doll. The pills were kicking in. He had been reluctant to take them at first, but now he looked forward to his twice-daily dose. The medication quieted the thoughts of those around him, and it kept his own mind and sight firmly in the present.

"Michael, can you hear me?" The kind doctor's voice echoed hollowly in his ears. "I said, how are you doing?"

"Good," he said slowly. The pills did make speech more difficult, but that was his only complaint about them. "Feel better."

The doctor's voice came creeping through the fog again, distorted and patchy. "That's...good to hear. I...They've been good to you?"

"Mm hmm." Michael's head felt heavy. He let it loll gently on his shoulder while he spoke. "I..."

He trailed off and stiffened.

The cotton lifted.

The five-pointed star with its indecipherable glyphs—I see it. I feel it. Long ago, when mama scrubbed it away, she thought it was gone. But it's never gone. It's a part of me. It looms over me, around me, within me. It is my crime, my prison, and my shame.

With great effort, Michael smothered the vision beneath the protective veil of the pills. The world was thick and hazy again, and he was at peace. Almost.

Another vision wormed its way past the barrier.

He lifted his head. The kind doctor was still there. He could see the fuzzy black outline of her against the soft pink background. Slowly, painfully, he forced his hand to extend. He vaguely felt her flinch when he grabbed her wrist.

"I want things to draw with," he said.

"They…offer art classes, Michael…"

"No, I want things to draw with." The pills made it hard to be expressive, but Michael's voice gained intensity from frustration. "Whenever I feel like it, in my room."

There was a sickening pause. When the kind doctor spoke again, he thought she sounded unsure of herself, but the words themselves were exactly what he wanted to hear.

"I'll see what I can do."

Michael slumped back down in his chair, satisfied. Drawing would help him gain control. When he put the visions down on paper, they went away. Drawing didn't keep them away for long, certainly not as long as the pills did, but it helped, and every bit of help he could get was a blessing.

Chapter Fifteen

Publicity

THE DULL HEADACHE BROUGHT on by the chocolate mix stayed with Cain for hours. He spent most of the day lying in bed, plunking out a steady and monotonous tune on his guitar while he squinted at the open book, slowly deciphering the florid text beside the star-and-circle symbol. Looking at the hated thing pained him even more than the headache, but he persisted.

Izzy pushed open the door to his dim room without warning, letting in a stream of brilliant light from the hallway. Cain flinched and covered his face.

"Oops. Sorry." Izzy snagged the door with his foot and pulled it back so the light was no longer falling in Cain's eyes. "Hungover, huh? I didn't know you drank."

"What's up?" said Cain.

"I'm going out tonight," said Izzy. "I was hoping you'd feed my rat this evening since I won't be here."

"Um...okay." Cain rubbed his eyes. "Since when do you have a rat, though? I thought you got rid of your rat."

"I did. I got another one from...uh...a pet store." Izzy's eyes shifted nervously. "Yeah, a pet store. So...um...will you feed him for me? It isn't hard. You just take a handful of food from the jar beside his cage and drop it in."

"No problem," said Cain doubtfully. He was fairly certain that the rat in question was not from a pet store.

Izzy grinned. "Awesome! I'll owe you one." He paused in the doorway. "Oh, by the way, there's no need to say anything to Sammi or Vince. About my rat, I mean. They're totally fine with him being here. Plus they're not even home right now, so why bother them, right?"

He turned into a monkey and scurried away before Cain could question him further. Cain shrugged and turned his attention back to the book. He made it through two more sentences before taking a much-needed break to feed Izzy's rat.

The rat's cage was made from two discarded water cooler tanks. Izzy had cut off the tops and stapled them together into a large hollow cylinder. Despite its size, Cain had trouble finding it; it had been strategically placed behind a broken crate and a stack of magazines so as not to be visible from the doorway. A plastic pickle tub that had a new, hand-written label bearing the words "Rat Food" sat beside it.

Cain eyed the dark brown rat that lounged in the shredded paper and wood chips inside the cage. As he suspected, it did look suspiciously like a fatter version of the rat Izzy had "rescued" from the trash can. He wondered how and when Izzy had smuggled the rat back into the house.

The rat food jar was half-full of a mix of dry oatmeal, bread crumbs, various cereals, and other scraps that Izzy had apparently swiped from the kitchen when no one was looking. Cain shook what he thought was an acceptable amount of food into his hand and sprinkled it into the cage through a hole cut in one of the jugs. The rat ignored the offering, glaring malevolently up at him.

"You're welcome, Bonzo," Cain muttered.

The doorbell rang while he was walking back to his room. He hurried down the stairs to answer it and found Michelle at the door. She was holding a bundle of records and rolled-up posters that seemed ready to spill out of her arms at any moment.

"Michelle!" Cain was relieved to see her. He had not heard from her since she walked out of the house without a word three days ago, and he had been afraid that she was angry with him for exposing her father's crimes. "Look, about that book...I..."

"It's okay, Cain," she interrupted. "I'm not mad at you. We've got a lot to talk about, but could I unload this stuff first?"

"Sure." Cain's eyes wandered down to the papers in her arms. He could see part of an album cover in the mess. It featured a man's face staring mysteriously from a sea of kaleidoscopic colors. The man had black hair, pale blue eyes, and features that bore a vague but unmistakable resemblance to his own. "Hey, is that...?"

"Eddie Morningstar?" Michelle glanced down at the album as she stepped into the house. "Yeah. Look, Cain, I know this is going to sound weird, but I'd like to leave this stuff with you for a while. I've kept it hidden in my room for years, but daddy found it. He told me to get rid of it, and I'm kind of afraid he'll get rid of it himself if I don't. I need a new hiding place so that daddy can't rifle through my things like a damn thief while I'm at school."

"That's fine," said Cain. "I can stick them somewhere in my room if you like."

Michelle made a beeline for the stairs, shifting her arms to keep a sheaf of magazines from slipping out of the bundle. "Thank you so much. It took me a long time to collect this stuff, and some of it would be pretty hard to replace."

Cain trotted eagerly after her. He was always glad to have an excuse to get Michelle into his room.

"I think one of the dresser drawers would be best," he suggested as she looked around the room for a suitable hiding spot. "Or the closet, maybe. If you leave that stuff in plain sight, Sammi might steal it."

Michelle selected a drawer and nudged aside the shirts in it to make room. "Really? Sammi doesn't strike me as the stealing type."

"Maybe not, but he practically worships Eddie Morningstar. You should have seen him the morning we got the demo tapes—he almost ran me over to grab them."

"He's got good taste in music." Michelle began to stack the albums and papers in the drawer. "Speaking of Eddie, I have something really important to tell you. You know that book Izzy found in daddy's office the other day?"

"What about it?" said Cain apprehensively.

"It wasn't actually daddy's."

"How do you know?"

"He told me."

Cain gave her an incredulous look.

Michelle arranged the shirts over her pile of memorabilia with a sigh. "I know what you're going to say, Cain—of course your daddy would lie about that; he's gotta cover his ass, right? Well, you didn't see the way he talked about that book. He was terrified of it—talked about it like it could poison you if you touched it, even for a second."

Cain glanced back at the book. "But he had it in his study."

Michelle turned around. "Yeah—stuck away in an envelope and buried under a huge, heavy binder in a bottom drawer. He's never used that book; I'm sure of it. I got the feeling he only kept it at all because he was afraid someone else would find it and use it if he tossed it. He says it belonged to someone else."

"Who?" said Cain.

"That's the weird part. He says..." She hesitated and raised an eyebrow. "You're not gonna believe this, but daddy says it was Eddie Morningstar's book."

If she had told him that Izzy was secretly the Engineer, Cain could not have been more surprised. He stared at her with his mouth open.

"I know." Michelle made a face. "That's pretty much how I reacted too. But he was totally serious. And...it makes sense, in a weird way. Now I understand why he's so creeped out by anyone who reminds him of Eddie...What?"

Cain had whipped around to grab the book off his bed. He put his index finger in between the pages he had been reading so he wouldn't lose his place, and then he closed the book and showed her the front cover.

"Look at this," he said.

"Look at what?"

"The letters." He held out the book to her. "I didn't pay much attention to them because they don't look like they should be there, but... I think they spell *Eddie*."

Michelle squinted at the title page.

Cain pointed to the name *Eddie,* which was written in bold black letters next to a simple, yet expressive, hand-drawn goat skull.

"Wow," she said reverently. "That's Eddie Morningstar's signature, all right—I'd recognize it anywhere. Daddy was telling the truth; this book really did belong to Eddie."

Cain's face fell. "Are you sure? That signature couldn't have been copied by...someone else?"

She frowned. "If you mean my daddy, I'm pretty sure the answer is no. He wouldn't be caught dead writing in that book, even to frame Eddie. If you don't believe me—"

"I'm sorry," he said hastily. "Of course I believe you. But...none of this makes sense. If this was Eddie's book, how did it end up in your dad's desk? And Jim Kellerman told me—"

"Look." Michelle's tone softened. "I don't know how daddy got hold of that book. He could have sneaked backstage at a Lion concert and swiped it, bought it in a used bookstore, whatever. All I know is...well, even if he *was* using it to do evil things, he can't use it anymore. Jim only told you to beware of the 'Righteous Man'—who I still think could easily be someone *other* than my daddy, by the way. He didn't tell you to stage a raid on his house and disarm him. I think you did more than enough to lay poor Jim's ghost to rest."

"I suppose so," said Cain glumly. Something about the situation still didn't feel right to him, but he didn't argue because he didn't want to upset Michelle and because he didn't know how to explain his vague sense of unease.

"You know what, though?" Michelle gave the book a suspicious glance. "I bet Jim would rest a lot easier if you burned that thing—or chucked it in the ocean. I don't care if it belonged to Eddie. It's bad news."

"I can't," said Cain. "Not yet anyway. I think..."

"What is it?" Michelle seemed alarmed.

Cain tried to soften the stricken look that he knew had come over his face. He opened the book to the page he had saved and showed her the five-pointed star within its perfect circle. Michelle silently read the florid caption: "A Most Ancient Spell to Bind All the Demons of the Earth, Male and Female."

"This is the shape I see," he said quietly. "Whenever I don't obey my master...whenever I try to remember my past life...I think Mr. Warwick somehow uses it to keep me here, Michelle."

Michelle's eyes wandered apprehensively over the page. The symbol must have seemed simple and innocent-looking to her; yet as she studied it, she shivered and frowned. Then she looked confused. Cain followed her gaze and saw that she was studying the glyph in the star's topmost point. This particular glyph was illegible. In fact, it had been obliterated. The part of the page where it had been was scuffed and scorched, as if someone had scratched it out with a penknife and then passed a lit match over it. A faint smell of smoke still lingered on the paper around the erased symbol.

"Weird, isn't it?" said Cain. "I don't know why that one glyph got scratched out. I guess Eddie must have done it for some reason. Maybe he was high."

Michelle pushed the book away. "I wish he had scratched out all five," she said darkly.

Half an hour before his show the next night, Cain had the worst bout of stage fright he had ever experienced. A sudden wave of acute fear hit him while he sat in his dressing room applying eyeliner, leaving him feeling as if his stomach had crumpled like a paper bag. He had to put down the eyeliner pencil because his hands were trembling. Staring at his wide-eyed, half-made-up face in the mirror didn't help ease his anxiety. He tore his gaze away from the mirror and stood up. Maybe a quick walk would settle his nerves.

The dressing rooms at this club, the Rubber Room, were situated along a narrow L-shaped hallway. Cain dodged a gang of black-clad stage hands and ducked under several light fixtures as he rounded the bend and wandered down the hall. The bare corridor was as claustrophobic as the dressing room. His stage fright did not subside; in fact, it grew steadily worse.

Raised voices met his ears as he approached the end of the hallway. They echoed in the emptiness, so Cain couldn't tell where they were coming from. He ducked into a cramped little lounge to avoid the fight, only to walk in on Sammi and Vince in the middle of an argument.

"Dammit, Vince, why did you have to say that anyway?" said Sammi angrily. "Izzy is messy sometimes, but it's not like he's hurting anything."

"Not hurting anything, huh?" Vince pointed at the small wooden table in the center of the room. "You call that not hurting anything? He was hardly in here for ten minutes, and it's already a dump. What happens when the Rubber Room gets infested with roaches, and they find out that moron's food caused the infestation? They'll ban us!"

Cain blinked at the table. It was covered with a bag of chips that had toppled over and spilled on the floor, an open can of salsa that had several streaks of red goo running down its sides, a large chocolate bar that had a single bite taken out of it, a sandwich crust that had a bit a cheese stuck to it, and a crumpled snack cake wrapper that had a few fluffy crumbs next to it. As far as Izzy's messes went, this one wasn't that bad.

Sammi rolled his eyes. "You think they'll ban us because a few chips got spilled on the floor? I know you don't really believe that, Vinnie. You just wanted an excuse to be a jerk to someone. Now go find Izzy, and say you're sorry for calling him a drooling, shit-for-brains pig."

"Fuck no." Vince watched Sammi's hands warily, but he stood his ground.

"Do it now, Sweet." Sammi jabbed a finger at Vince. "We need Izzy to be in a fit state to go on with us in half an hour. You've got ten minutes to find him, apologize, and calm him down. Oh, and don't try to get away with some bullshit fake apology like 'sorry you can't handle the truth' this time, or I'll sic Cain on you."

"Fine." Vince spun on his heel and stalked toward the door, knocking over the jar of salsa with a petulant swat on his way out. A big glob of salsa splattered over the snack cake wrapper and the chocolate bar. He pushed past Cain without even a small grunt of acknowledgement and disappeared down the hall.

"I swear, Vinnie, one of these days..." Sammi made a jerky strangling motion with his hands. Then he met Cain's gaze and straightened up.

"Hi, Cain," he said. "Sorry you had to see that. I was just dealing with a little spat."

"Need any backup?" Cain groaned inside at the thought of forcing Vince to apologize to Izzy again. He was not in the mood for drama right now.

"Nah, I think I've scared him into behaving himself. If Izzy starts wailing again, I'll just poke my head out of the dressing room and give Vinnie a good jolt to keep him in line."

Sammi hurried out of the room. Cain noticed that Sammi's makeup had been applied sloppily, and he was scratching his arm when he left.

Once he was gone, Cain sat down in one of the canvas chairs at the table and rested his head in his hands. He felt as if he might throw up at any minute, and the sharp, vinegary smell of spilled salsa wasn't helping his nausea at all. He wished he could overcome the malaise. If it weren't for the growing nausea, he would be happy to clean up this mess. Izzy wouldn't mind, and the gesture would keep Vince pacified for a while.

He raised his head and tried to find something to focus on other than the fact that he had to go on stage in twenty-five minutes. The chocolate bar caught his eye. He thought it strange that he had watched Steve and Lance consume hundreds of those thoroughly unpalatable-looking brown bricks over the last ten years, and he never knew that a sprinkle of chocolate powder could send him into a rush of carefree euphoria.

Cain's stomach heaved, and he wiped sweat from his brow with a shaking hand. He found himself regretting that he had shoved the baggie of chocolate powder into the pantry and had vowed never to touch it again. He would have given anything for the tiniest pinch of the stuff—just enough to calm his frayed nerves and steady his breathing. He gave the chocolate bar a tentative poke. It was too bad Jodido said that store-bought chocolate could kill him...

But Jodido *would* say that, wouldn't he? The dealer had been awfully eager to part Cain from his money. Most likely, the ordinary chocolate in the grocery store was just as good, and Jodido had been trying to scare him into buying his substantially pricier product instead.

Cain picked up the chocolate and shook the salsa off it. A little bite wouldn't hurt him, and he doubted Izzy would care. He sniffed the smooth bar cautiously—it had the same scent as Jodido's powder, but it was less strong—and bit a tiny piece off the corner. He began to chew, and he soon wished he hadn't shaken off the salsa. This chocolate had the most overpowering, cloyingly sweet flavor he had ever tasted. To make matters worse, it melted into a thick slime that adhered to his tongue and teeth, coating his whole mouth with the awful taste.

His anxiety and nausea intensified. Desperate for relief, he choked down a few more bites before the lingering sweetness started to make his teeth hurt. The bar tasted nothing like the bitter powder, and he wasn't feeling any effects from it. Soon, he gave up in despair and stumbled back to his dressing room.

Strangely, once he had washed the repulsive taste out of his mouth and sat down to finish getting ready, he felt a little better. By the time Sammi banged on his door and shouted that it was time to go on, his fear had receded to a vague uneasiness that he was able to ignore. He grabbed his guitar and headed out.

The crowd seemed bigger and rowdier than usual that night. Cain had to dodge several flying cups and beer bottles over the course of the opening song, and the fans' constant shrieking was audible above the music. As the last note died down and Cain stepped forward to introduce the band, they let out a cheer so loud that he feared he wouldn't be able to make himself heard over their noise.

"Hurry it up, Cain," Vince mouthed at him from across the stage.

Cain leaned into the microphone, fighting off the strange

fuzzy feeling that buzzed in his head. He was having trouble remembering the words he was supposed to say.

"Say something already," snapped Vince as the shouts began to go down. "We don't have all fucking night."

Cain gripped the microphone furiously. He suspected that Vince wanted to do his mind-reading act as soon as possible. His signature routine consisted of dragging an attractive woman out of the audience at random to poke around in her brain and make rude comments about her thoughts. *But the women don't seem to have a problem with it*, thought Cain with a mixture of pity and amazement as the fuzzy feeling began to creep back. A little knot of them pressed in beneath Vince, levering themselves up on their toes as if offering up their brains to him. Maybe they didn't realize how much the intrusion would hurt or how cruel Vince could be. Or maybe they thought the act was just a trick. They were in for a rude awakening when Vince buried his fingers in their skulls.

Still, it was better they find out the truth about the band's abilities from Vince's routine than from, say, Sammi's lightning-juggling act. An image flashed through his mind of concertgoers staggering out of the club with twitching limbs and electrified hair. The thought struck him as hilarious, and he began to laugh.

"What the fuck is so funny, asshole?" Vince's voice sounded far away. "God damn it—get away from the mic. Maybe you can't handle talking for thirty seconds, but I can."

Cain allowed himself to be pushed aside. He couldn't remember for the life of him what he was supposed to say or what song they were supposed to play next. The increasingly angry and impatient shouts from the crowd faded until he no longer noticed them. The room filled with a soft, oppressive fog that steadily pressed in around him, darkening everything in spite of the glaring stage lights, making him sleepy and unsteady on his feet.

"Whoa. Careful!" Sammi stepped up and caught Cain as he almost fell forward. Sammi's thin form rippled and distorted as he moved, as if Cain were watching him from under deep water. "What's wrong, man? Do you need to go sit backstage for a few minutes?"

Something was definitely wrong. Cain stared at Sammi, trying desperately to dig through the cottony white haze clogging his brain to find words for the problem. He didn't see the bottle flying toward him until it hit him in the chest.

The sting of the glass against his skin cut through the fog for a moment. He clearly remembered leaping up with a snarl and seeing the people in the front row stagger back in fright. Hands grabbed him, pulling him down, and agitated voices squealed in his ears. Then everything whirled and became indistinct. Colors swirled around him, flowing into unrecognizable shapes that dissipated as soon as he tried to focus on them. He experienced a brief sensation of spinning through the air, and then the colors settled into place.

Cain opened his eyes and found himself in front of the Delgados' butcher shop. The sun hung directly above him, even though the show had started at night. He had no memory at all of how he had gotten there. Dazed and unsteady, he took a step toward the shop.

The pavement under his feet tilted as he moved forward. Houses and shops rushed by him like cars, and he was on the flat gray cement rooftop of a skyscraper when he regained his footing. The sky overhead was dark, and lights flickered in the windows of the high-rises surrounding him. A man stood a few feet away from him, looking down on the street below from the ledge. They had to be at least twenty stories high. Cain edged toward him cautiously. The cement felt oddly insubstantial beneath him. When he was close enough to make out the man's familiar craggy features and luxuriant, curly, ink-black hair, he straightened in surprise.

"Ty?"

Ty didn't look around. He shuffled slowly across the ledge, cradling something Cain couldn't quite see in his left hand.

"Ty?" Cain tried again. "Hello? Can you hear me?"

Ty still didn't respond. Puzzled, Cain stepped up onto the ledge next to his guitar teacher. The effort made the buildings around him undulate and the bricks beneath his feet wobble, but everything fell into place again after he stood perfectly still for a few seconds.

Ty was so close to the edge that the toes of his boots were hanging off of it. He had an unsettling blank expression on his face, which was broken only by lines of tension in his cheeks where his jaw clenched. He teetered, a hairsbreadth away from plunging into the street below. For one sickening moment, Cain thought he was going to fall. Then Ty raised his left hand.

He was holding a knife. The faint light from the windows of the high-rise across the street glinted off its glossy black hilt. The blade itself didn't reflect any light; it was covered completely with a matted-looking, reddish-brown stain. Cain felt his stomach sink. He hoped the substance was rust.

Ty shifted his toes even further over the edge. His fist tightened around the knife, and he stared at it with shining eyes. His body rocked forward, and for a moment, he looked like he was going to jump.

Then a little shudder of resolution ran through him, and he backed away from the ledge. Cain saw him run his fingers lovingly over the blade after he stepped down onto the rooftop.

"Hey!" Without thinking, Cain started to run after him. "Wait! Ty, can't you see—"

The roof fell away beneath him. The whirling sensation returned and did not subside this time. Cain was being spun helplessly and aimlessly around the city. Sometimes, he was dropped within two feet of a rooftop or a street, and sometimes he was shot up so high he could see rough, brown-and-green hills beyond the sea of lights. The city itself was moving too, flowing and rolling like a vast living thing. Houses and high-rises glided beneath him in a sinuous river of light and blue glass. Sometimes when he swooped down toward the street and scrambled in vain for a foothold on the bucking pavement, the walls of the buildings became transparent, and he could see people moving around in them: eating meals from white plastic trays in front of the TV, standing in a slow-moving line in front of a small barred window, or nursing drinks around a long wooden counter.

Then he flew upward and did not drop again. The city receded into a pinpoint beneath him, and he shot straight up into the gray clouds. A tiny glimmer of light—was it a star?—shone directly ahead of him. Cain focused on it in a futile attempt to calm his nausea. Still, he barreled on. The clouds thinned and disappeared around him, and night rolled across the blue morning sky.

The little light continued to gleam in the distance. It was slightly bigger now, but it wasn't noticeably closer. Cain slowly realized that the light was not a star. The glow it gave off was different, less cold, and it was a different color entirely from the many blazing ice-white stars that now surrounded him. The light was a pale, shifting, and diaphanous gold, with flashes of blue and purple and green in its heart.

Gradually Cain stopped flailing, his urge to stop growing steadily weaker. The light pulsed in the distance, and every drop of blood in his body pulsed in response to it. He had to reach it, even if he had to cross the whole universe to get to it. A massive red planet shot by on his left, but he hardly noticed. The light was all that mattered. He rushed toward it, faster and faster, and the stars faded away behind him—

Without warning, he stopped dead. The light was gone, extinguished like a match. He felt a strange, steady tugging at the back of his head, and then he plummeted, heard a loud rushing sound, and plunged forward to empty the contents of his heaving stomach.

"Hey, take it easy," said a familiar voice from somewhere close.

With great effort, Cain stopped gagging. He was kneeling on something cool and solid. He sat up slowly, aided by someone who was pulling his head upright by the hair.

"Sammi?" he croaked. "Is that you?"

The effort of talking made him gag again. Acting on instinct, he threw himself forward. Thankfully, he could now make out the blurry form of a white toilet bowl in front of him. The hand grasping his hair loosened a bit.

"Sorry," he muttered when the fit had passed.

"That's okay," said Sammi. "Take your time. I don't think you'll be bringing up much more anyway; you got most of it out on the way home."

"Home?" Cain sat up shakily and looked around as much as his throbbing head would allow. He was indeed home, sprawled on the cracked turquoise tile of the bathroom floor. Sammi stood over him, holding the hair out of his face with one hand. Cain stared up at him in confusion. "How did we get here? We were at the club...I thought..."

"Yeah, we were." Sammi seemed uncomfortable. "But we had to stop the show and get you out of there after...what happened."

Cain frowned. He had no idea what had happened after they took the stage. The few memories his mind had retained of the evening were fragmented and dreamlike.

A little line of worry appeared on Sammi's brow; he seemed to be regarding the incomprehension on Cain's face. "Don't you remember any of it?"

"I remember the lights going up, and I remember Vince being impatient."

"You don't remember freaking out?"

Cain blinked. Now that he thought about it, he did have a scattered recollection of jumping up and roaring.

"I freaked out?" He rubbed his throbbing temples, trying to clear up his memory. "How?"

"Well...um..." Sammi shifted nervously. "You kind of...just take a look at your hands, man."

"Huh?" Cain reluctantly peeled his hands away from his face and squinted at them. For a moment, he had no idea what Sammi was talking about. They were the same hands they had always been, with their curved black talons and neat rows of smooth blue scales.

Then it hit him. He scrambled up with a loud, awkward

clattering of hooves on tile and stared at his reflection in the little square mirror over the sink. His wild-eyed face was framed by a mane of black "hairs" that were actually quill-like feathers, and blue scales had replaced every inch of his skin. He was in full demon form.

"See what I mean?" Sammi's anxious face popped into the corner of the mirror. "You were about to take us into the next song when some dumbass in the audience threw a...a beer bottle, I think, and it hit you, and the next thing anyone knew you'd turned into...that."

"You mean I changed right in front of the audience?" Cain's mouth fell open in shock.

"Yep," said Sammi. His eye twitched. "By the way, that's not, like, permanent, is it? You can change back into what you were before, right?"

"What? Oh, yeah, of course." Cain glanced at his reflection. "This is how I really look. I just go around in human form so people won't be as afraid of me."

Sammi grimaced. "I don't think your disguise is gonna fool anyone who was at the Rubber Room last night anymore."

"That's for sure. I can't believe you changed right in front of them, you stupid dirtball."

Cain turned and found Vince leaning against the open bathroom door, scowling, with his arms crossed in disapproval.

"Go away, Vinnie," said Sammi curtly.

"I...I can't remember changing," Cain stammered. He couldn't imagine how he could be so foolish as to change in front of a whole club full of people. "I'm so sorry I lost—"

"Well, you did." Vince rolled his eyes. "And after you fucked up, you jumped ten feet into the air and fucking *roared* like a goddamn lion. Then you *started to float* over the stage. If Izzy hadn't jumped up and pulled you down by the ankles, you'd have flown right over the crowd and—I don't know—rained brimstone down on them or something. You fucking idiot, why didn't you get a tattoo on your face that said 'I am totally a real demon with real demon powers' while you were at it?"

"Vinnie!" Sammi wagged a finger at him. "I thought we agreed not to give Cain a hard time about this!"

"*You* agreed to that," muttered Vince. "By the way, asshole, Mr. Arkin wants to talk to you tomorrow morning. In his office. Alone. Have fun getting dropped like a bad date."

He scurried off. Sammi made an exasperated face and turned back to Cain.

"Sorry about that," he said. "I tried to make Vinnie promise not to be such a jerk."

"That's all right." Cain had one last wave of nausea and heaved into the sink; but nothing came up. "Does Mr. Arkin really want to talk to me in his office tomorrow?"

"Yeah," said Sammi. "I wouldn't worry about it too much, though. About a year ago, he called Johnny Revolver into his office for throwing some guy through a window, and Johnny is still here."

Cain tried to take a step back and wobbled; he was used to walking on human feet instead of hooves.

Sammi held out a hand. "Hey, are you gonna be all right?"

"Sure. I feel a lot better now." The sensation of being unsettled was gone, and he felt fine aside from a little residual fuzziness in his mind.

Sammi let out a sigh of relief. "Good. I'm gonna go get Izzy now. The poor guy was a hot mess by the time we got you home. I think he was scared you were going to die. We had to feed him half a bottle of whiskey to calm him down."

He lingered in the doorway for a moment.

"Hey, man," he said without turning around. "I've gotta ask."

"Ask what?"

"Were you high on something?"

Cain's tail twitched. He gave Sammi a wary look. For no reason he could discern, he suddenly felt ashamed and unwilling to tell the whole truth.

"I might have eaten something that didn't agree with me before the show," he muttered.

"Oh?" Sammi's tone didn't change. "Like what?"

"Dunno. I just got a little sick."

"Okay." Sammi glanced over his shoulder. He sounded disappointed. "Feel better, then."

He left without another word. Cain stayed where he was, staring into the sink, his tail wrapped guiltily around his leg. He swore to himself that he would never touch chocolate again, and he would stick to his vow this time. Eating chocolate wasn't worth the humiliation or the violent vomiting.

Mr. Arkin sent Chelsea to drive Cain to his meeting. She hadn't warmed up to him at all since that first day she dropped off his breakfast. He could actually sense the tension in her body while she drove; her frame was rigid, and her knuckles were white on the wheel. He wished she would relax. Her anxiety was beginning to exacerbate his own nervousness, and he was already jittery because he laid awake half the night worrying that Mr. Warwick would be waiting at the Daggerspoint headquarters to punish him for making a scene.

"So," she said while they waited at a long stoplight. "I…um…hear the Engineer struck again."

"He did?" Cain looked at her eagerly. He hadn't heard anything about another kidnapping.

He caught a glimpse of Chelsea's face. An odd expectant expression formed in her eyes, as if she were anxious to see how he would react to the news. He sensed that he was being tested in some way.

"That's awful," he said in as sad a voice as he could muster. "Was it someone I know?"

"Oh, I doubt it." Chelsea suddenly became very focused on adjusting her side-view mirror. Her hand trembled while she fiddled with the controls on the door. "The poor kid was fresh off the bus. He hadn't even found a day job yet."

"I hope they find him alive." Cain squirmed in discomfort. Nothing he said seemed to lessen the infectious fear that radiated from every inch of her body.

Chelsea stole a quick glance at him.

"They might," she said in her tiny, squeaky voice. "He's only been gone for about five days—"

"Five whole days?" Cain stared at her, nearly forgetting to sound gentle. When the other victims were taken, the news had spread in half the time. "Shouldn't people know about the kidnapping by now?"

"Er…" Chelsea flinched. "They…uh…yeah, they probably should. It's a shame, isn't it?"

The light turned green, and Chelsea started driving again. They rode in silence the rest of the way, but every now and then, Cain caught her furtively studying him. He got the feeling that he had said something she had not expected. Perhaps she thought that the city's resident demon would be happy to hear another victim had been taken, so he would have another soul on which to prey. Maybe that assumption was the reason she always kept her face tilted away from his—because she thought he could get at her soul through her eyes. Cain had heard about these silly rumors.

Or maybe she just thinks I'm ugly, he thought as he stared out the window, trying not to let her discomfort affect him any more than it already was. This thought wasn't the happiest notion, but he still found it less distressing than the alternative.

The atmosphere in the car was so tense by the time they pulled up in front of the Daggerspoint headquarters that Cain was almost relieved to escape into Mr. Arkin's office. Within five minutes, he wished he could be back in the car again. Mr. Arkin was tense and moody, his usual easygoing manner gone.

"Well, Cain, I honestly don't know what to make of your little outburst last night," he said. "On the one hand, it could be the smartest career move you've ever made. Your stunt certainly got everybody talking. We've been deluged with requests for interviews. On the other hand—"

"Interviews?" Cain stiffened. He didn't like the idea of being repeatedly grilled by complete strangers on the intimate details about his life.

Mr. Arkin seemed surprised by his apprehension. "Yes, interviews—that's the good news. I would've had you do some before, but no one was interested for some reason. I guess they thought you'd be a flash-in-the-pan. Now they all want a piece of you—and that brings us to the bad news."

"Bad news?" said Cain glumly. He had thought the interviews *were* the bad news.

Mr. Arkin sighed. "You'll really have to watch yourself

from now on, Cain. *Everyone* will be waiting for you to slip up, not just the Reverend Breen and his posse of crackpots. So you'll have to be very careful what you say on *About Town* this evening—"

"This evening?" He couldn't help interrupting a second time. He had been under the impression that Mr. Arkin was at least going to give him a few days to prepare and to resign himself to the idea of being interviewed.

"Of course." Mr. Arkin drummed his fingers on the desk. "People saw what you did last night, and they want answers. The problem is...well, I wouldn't exactly call them closed-minded, but they've got some very definite expectations of what demons are like. We've got some damage control to do, right away. Now pay attention: there are things you should and shouldn't say in an interview, and you need to remember them all. Oh, and before I forget, whatever you were high on last night...lay off it for a while, okay?"

Mr. Arkin gave him an hour for lunch after the meeting, warning him to be back in time to make it to the studio at two.

"Two?" Cain was puzzled. "I thought you said *About Town* came on in the evening."

Mr. Arkin chuckled. "It does. They just film it at two. Then they edit the hell out of the footage and pump it up with fluff before it goes on the air at eight: profanities are bleeped over; weird little cartoons are added; and background music is inserted—that kind of thing. That's why I'm starting you out on *About Town*. It's a pretty forgiving show for rookie mistakes. Just watch out for Lana Willis. Sometimes I think she only agreed to host that show so she could flirt with all her guests."

Lunch brought a few minutes of relief. Cain managed to catch several pigeons on the sidewalk. Mrs. Delgado had chased away most pigeons that landed near the butcher's shop before they wandered within his reach, and he avoided eating them at the house for fear of upsetting Izzy, but the dark sweet meat of a freshly killed pigeon was satisfying enough that he was willing to furtively enjoy one in the darkest corner of an alley every now and then. He was sure to run to the restroom and wash his face afterward.

"So, Cain, it must be really hard." Lana Willis leaned toward him, her breasts straining against her low-cut pink dress. "Being the only demon in the city, I mean. There must be so much *temptation* for you!"

Cain shifted forward in his uncomfortable little shell-shaped plastic chair to give his cramped tail some relief. He kept his eyes firmly fixed on Lana. Despite Mr. Arkin's instructions to connect with audience members through eye contact, he had quickly decided it wasn't a good idea. Most of the studio audience had been regarding him with wary fascination since he had emerged, blinking and disoriented, onto the light-bathed set. A few of them were even wide-eyed and shivering with fear, like Izzy was sometimes when he knew a particularly gruesome scene was coming in a scary movie, and he wanted to leave the room, but he also didn't want to miss the excitement. He worried that if he locked eyes with some of these people, they would head for the door, screaming.

"Well…" He thought for a moment. "You do have really good cheese here. I eat more of it than I should."

Apparently, his answer was a good one. A little ripple of tense laughter ran through the audience, and out of the corner of his eye, Cain noticed some of the less-spooked people in the front row relaxing a little.

Lana laughed too. "Cheese?" she said, casually crossing

her legs in such a way that the slit in her skirt opened up to her mid-thigh. "You mean you don't have any cheese in Hell, so you had to come all the way up here for your cheese fix? That's adorable! But what about...you know...the *other* temptations?"

"Other temptations?"

"Come on." Lana's eyelashes fluttered. "You know there's a reason crazy old Nathaniel Breen keeps calling this city the Sodom of the twentieth century. We've got drug dealers and junkies and streetwalkers and brown-nosing parasites galore here—and we're darn proud of it! You must meet dozens of them every day."

"I have met a couple," he admitted.

"All those naughty, naughty sinners." Lana's voice took on a sultry note. "Everywhere you turn, you must see them doing those 'wicked and depraved acts' Breen is always whining about."

"I...guess so?"

"Don't you just want to...*punish* them all?" A happy little shudder ran through her, and her already heavily rouged cheeks flushed with pleasure. Her hand fluttered up and landed, not so casually, on his knee for the fourth time since he took the stage. "I mean, you're a big strong guy. I bet you could beat the sin right out of the baddest bad girl in seconds."

Cain gave her an apprehensive look. He considered Mr. Arkin's advice: tell people what they want to hear whenever possible. The gruesome tales Lana probably wanted to hear weren't likely to win him many human friends. He decided to try for a compromise.

"I don't know about girls," he said slowly, shifting his legs in a polite-but-futile attempt to dislodge Lana's hand.

"But I did kind of punish our lead singer for being a bully once. Bullying is a kind of sin, I think."

"Oh?" Lana's hand began a slow migration from his knee to his thigh. "Do tell!"

"I made him vomit marbles. Just for a day, and I even stopped the vomiting a little early, but Vince definitely doesn't try to bully me anymore—"

"Wait." The hand stopped moving up his thigh. "You...say you made him vomit marbles? Did I hear that right?"

"You did."

"So you...force-fed him marbles until he hurled?" Lana's brow knitted in confusion.

"No!" said Cain quickly, cutting off a few horrified whispers from the audience. "That sort of thing could've killed him. I put a spell on him."

"A spell?"

"Yeah. It didn't hurt him; it just made him spew marbles all over the place for a while. I had no choice. Izzy had locked himself in his room to get away from Vince because he was being so awful, and on top of that, he insulted my girlfriend..."

He trailed off. The few audience members who had started to relax were getting tense again, and he feared that anything he could say would make it worse. Even Lana seemed put off. She pulled her hand away and uncrossed her legs with a nervous little cough.

"Oh yeah...I guess you can do stuff like that, can't you? For a minute there I forgot you were—you know—for real." She glanced meaningfully at his tail. "So...um...you...say you have a girlfriend?"

Cain nodded, grateful for the change of subject. "I met

her when I moved to the city. She's not a demon like me," he added quickly, half-remembering something Mr. Arkin had said about people liking him better if they could identify with his experiences. "She's a human—a perfectly ordinary one too—with no magical powers."

"And she's okay with what you are?" The salacious light began to return to Lana's eyes, but she made no move to touch him.

"She thinks the whole demon thing is sexy, actually."

"Really? Wow." Lana blinked. "I thought I knew about every weird peccadillo in existence. It just goes to show you learn something new every day, right?"

A few people in the audience laughed. The sound was a relief to Cain, but he still couldn't help feeling a bit stung.

"Tell us a little more about this girl who's so perfect for you, Cain," Lana continued. "How did you meet her?"

Cain opened his mouth and shut it again. He realized too late that Michelle probably wouldn't appreciate him blathering about their relationship on a television show that her father could easily be watching.

"I'd rather not say," he muttered.

"You don't want to embarrass her, huh? Okay, then. What's she like? Does she come to your shows and stuff?"

"I'd rather not say that, either."

"Why not?" Lana chuckled. "Are you ashamed of her or something?"

"Of course not," said Cain. "It's just…if I say too much about her, her family might find out about us, and we don't want that to happen. They wouldn't be happy if they knew we were dating. They're very religious."

"Religious, you say? I assume you mean they're Christian?"

"Yes…"

"Nathaniel Breen's type of Christian?"

Cain started to nod, but the sly look on Lana's face made him pause.

"I don't know. Maybe, I guess," he said. "I don't really know a lot about Christians. Why do you ask?"

Lana's smug grin grew wider, and she gave his knee a quick, indulgent pat.

"He's an interesting guy, Breen," she said in a conspiratorial tone. "He's totally crazy, of course, but that voice of his…Sometimes I listen to the Christian radio stations to hear his gorgeous voice—so deep and smooth and velvety—it just turns me on. You know, I hear he has a daughter."

"I'd heard that too." Cain tried to sound disinterested. "But he's so nasty to me I've pretty much stopped paying attention to—"

"She's a pretty little thing, Breen's daughter." Lana shivered and let out a wistful sigh. "I don't remember her name at the moment, but God, I saw her picture in the society pages once, and she's got the thickest, most *sensual* brown hair. I'd say she's about eighteen maybe. Like, oh, that pretty brown-haired girl in that tabloid photo of you a while back."

The audience muttered and buzzed behind him. Cain swallowed hard.

"Oh, her?" He shrugged. "Yeah, she was nice. I don't really remember her, though."

"You don't?" She sounded incredulous. "Really? Who could forget a sweet little thing like that?"

The muttering from the audience grew louder. Cain began to wish he had said that his girlfriend's family wouldn't approve of him because they were vegetarians, or even because they thought him too ugly for their daughter.

"I guess I remember some things about her," he said desperately. "But not much."

"I hope you at least remember her name. Michelle, maybe? She looked like a Michelle."

"Yes. That could be right." With great effort, he managed to keep the rising panic out of his voice. "It was a long time ago, and there are always so many girls chasing us around."

"So there are." Lana grinned. "How does your girlfriend feel about that?"

"Well…" Cain hastily pulled up one of Vince's lines. "A rock star's girlfriend has gotta like sharing, right?"

To his relief, Lana seemed to like this answer. She laughed and returned her hand to its former place on his knee.

"Oh, honey, don't I know it," she said sympathetically. "See, that's what I told all my boyfriends—and girlfriends— when we started going out. 'Sugar,' I always said, 'if you want to be with me, you've got to learn to like sharing; there's no two ways around it.' I mean, I really have no time to deal with jealousy. Who does?"

She launched into a long story about a time she had dated two brothers at once without either of them knowing about the other. Cain nodded and smiled, so grateful for the subject change that he gladly kept his legs still when her hand found its slow, inevitable way back to his thigh.

Chapter Sixteen

Escape

CAIN COULD TELL THAT Vince was in a foul mood. He slumped in the armchair, glowering silently at Cain who was making a determined effort to ignore him. A solid weeklong roll of interviews and talk show appearances had left Cain exhausted and frustrated. A tussle with Vince was the last thing he wanted to deal with right now. He deliberately buried his nose in a book, keeping his guitar close in case Vince tried anything.

Vince lifted his foot and gave the coffee table a violent shove. Izzy's tins rattled loudly.

Cain flinched, his concentration broken. "What's your problem?" he snapped. "Look, I already told you that I'd let you do all these interviews in my place if Mr. Arkin would let me. It's not like they're much fun for me."

"I don't care about stupid interviews," grumbled Vince. "If I wanted to have some perky jackass ask me what my favorite color was—or some shit like that—I'd go back to kindergarten."

Cain rolled his eyes. Just two days ago, Vince had thrown a spectacular tantrum when he found out he wasn't invited to appear on *Metal Edge* with Cain.

"What *is* the problem, then?" he said.

Vince made a guttural noise of disgust. "I haven't been laid once this week."

"Oh." This news was hardly surprising; Vince could be charming when he was trying to get a girl to sleep with him, but he couldn't keep up the charm for more than an hour or so, and word of the dangers of a date with Vince had spread rapidly among female club regulars. "I'm...sorry?"

Vince's frown deepened.

"Like hell you are, asshole," he growled. "It's your damn fault."

"What?"

"You heard me. I can't get tail to save my life all of a sudden, and it's because of your ugly ass."

Cain stared at him in confusion. He couldn't recall doing anything that even vaguely resembled interfering with Vince's love life.

"I don't...What are you talking about?" he stammered.

"You know exactly what I'm talking about! I used to score ten times a night, with all the best-looking chicks at the party. Now I'm lucky if I can get into an ugly girl's panties."

Cain rubbed his eyes wearily. "Are you sure that's because of me and not because you call your girlfriends bitches and sluts to their faces and suck out their energies when you get too excited?"

"Hah!" Vince smacked one of Izzy's tins off the table contemptuously. "That never mattered before—I had chicks rubbing up against me and begging me to read their minds at every party. It didn't matter if I treated them like crap, as long as they could score with me. Do you wanna know what changed?"

"Not really," said Cain, deliberately reaching for his guitar. Vince was too worked up to notice the pointed gesture.

"*You* did!" he shouted. "Your freakishness scared the girls away from me!"

"Vince…"

"You fucking dumbass! If you'd just gone on letting everyone think you were human, this wouldn't be a problem, but *no*. You had to go and let the whole damn world know that your demon routine wasn't an act, that you actually are an ugly, scaly, snaggle-toothed—"

"*Vince…*"

"Grunting, savage, roadkill-eating *monster*. You just had to go and ruin everything for me. I fucking hate you."

Cain had given all the warning he had the patience to give. He focused on Vince's mouth and plucked out a few jangly, off-key notes in rapid succession.

"Do you wanna know something else, asshole?" Vince powered on. "It's good you have that collar. It's for the safety of us *real* people. You're too stuprrr wharrgarbl glll blub. Reepeepnini ud…"

His expression shifted when he noticed that the sounds coming out of his mouth were not the words he intended to say. To Cain's immense relief, he fell silent for a moment, pawing at his throat.

"Urrgh…hut oo oob?" he said accusingly.

Cain set down his guitar and turned his attention back to the book. "Don't worry; it'll wear off in an hour."

Vince's mouth dropped open, and his hands curled into white-knuckled fists. His air of utterly shocked outrage puzzled Cain; he should have expected something like this to happen.

"Ooo…" he shouted. "Ooo ppp ppplll plfffuugimg pfuggging afftard—ram!" His face flushed bright red, and his chest puffed up as if it were in danger of exploding from the pressure of all the bottled-up invectives he desperately wanted to hurl at Cain. For a moment, he looked as if he might try to speak again. Instead, he flung up both hands with middle fingers held rigid.

"Yeah, I love you too, Vince," muttered Cain.

Defeated, Vince spun around and stormed out of the living room. Even without the ability to talk clearly, he managed to make a statement of his exit; his footsteps reverberated through the front hall as he stomped up the stairs, and Cain heard a series of sharp bangs once he'd reached the top. It sounded as if he was slamming all the doors on the second floor as hard as he could.

The noise of Vince's tantrum died down, and Cain put aside his guitar with a sigh. He had been in the mood to study, and now his concentration was ruined.

He wasn't likely to make any breakthroughs anyway. He had read the instructions for the demon-binding spell a dozen times over, and it seemed frustratingly foolproof: usable only by humans, fully effective until the caster's death, unbreakable by will or force. Cain scowled at the all-too-familiar star symbol. The text called it *Solomon's Seal*, which was such a mundane-sounding name for something so hateful.

Disgusted, he dumped the book onto the couch. He was in desperate need of a break, and he thought he knew where to find one.

The lock on the front door stuck, and he had to fumble with it. When he finally looked up, a searing white flash exploded across his field of vision.

Then another. Then another.

Cain stumbled back, throwing a protective hand over his face. His eyes absorbed starlight and candlelight easily, but they had a hard time adjusting to the glaring floods of electric light that modern humans preferred. Spotlights made his temples throb even when he went out of his way to avoid looking into them, and camera flashes could cause full-blown headaches. When he finally managed to force his eyes open again, he was surrounded by fifteen men and women, all waving cameras and black-tipped microphones at him, all shouting questions.

"Cain...Mr. Pseudomantis!" Their voices erupted in a garbled chorus. They were competing with each other to be heard. "How does it feel—Is it true you—Nathaniel Breen has said—About the trial of suspected cultist Michael Anderson—Off the record, can you say—Any involvement in cult activity?"

The cameras flashed again. Cain flinched and pressed himself against the door. The voices were growing louder and more aggressive. A few of the bolder reporters began to edge up the stairs. Mr. Arkin had advised him to calmly push through such crowds without saying a word, but he couldn't bring himself to do that. His first impulse was to duck back into the house, but the greedy expressions on the reporters' faces made him fear that they weren't above forcing their way in after him.

The change started in his hands. He felt his skin hardening into scales and his claws lengthening. He didn't need the intense concentration normally required to shed human form. This transformation was a reflex, his body's natural response to being cornered.

The reporters noticed it too. They scattered with noises

of alarm, clacking cameras together in their hurry to get away, but to Cain's dismay, only two or three of them fled the scene. Those who remained prowled around in tight knots like a pack of hungry dogs, never taking their eyes off him, working their courage up for another salvo.

Cain took a deep breath and launched himself into the air with a push of his legs. They couldn't follow him into the sky.

The ground along with the flurry of flashing cameras rushed away beneath him. He was flying for the first time in months, and it was exhilarating. Yet it was tiring too. He was out of practice, and the focus needed to keep himself aloft made his skull feel ready to crack open.

A tall brick building loomed to his right. He touched down on top of it and rested for a few minutes, listening to the rumble of traffic below him.

A cool breeze sprung up, flowing westerly and slightly southerly. Cain climbed back into the air and followed it, bouncing from rooftop to rooftop to save his energy. He trembled with happy anticipation, for his jerky, erratic flight carried him steadily closer to Beverly Hills and to Michelle.

Candi Jayne woke up to the sound of someone rummaging through her bathroom.

A soft growling sound rose from her throat as she rolled out of bed. She hated being roused in the middle of the night, especially when she was attempting to sleep off the loopy effects of her allergy medicine. If another crazy fan was in there rummaging through her things in search of the perfect souvenir to take home and jerk off to, she would make sure he paid for his fun.

Her bare feet made no noise while she padded across the

carpet. The bathroom door hung slightly open. She crept up to it, caught a glimpse of a shadow moving along the floor on the other side, and shoved it with all her strength.

The wood creaked as it banged into the trespasser's shoulder. He grunted in pain and fell sideways into the tub, pulling the shower curtain down with him.

"Gotcha, pervert!" Candi charged into the room with her lips peeled back in bloodthirsty triumph. She pounced on the wriggling lump under the curtain, raining blows on it with her fists. "You want a trophy from Candi Jayne's apartment to take with you, huh? Well, how about some motherfucking scars?"

The person under the fallen curtain giggled and rolled over. Candi stepped back with an indignant gasp when his face emerged from the tangle of fabric.

"Yuri!" she cried angrily. "How the hell did you get in here?"

Yuri Ustinov sat up in the tub, dangling his legs carelessly over the rim. He brushed his downy auburn hair out of his eyes and stared up at her with a boyish grin.

"Dammit, Yuri, you almost gave me a heart attack!" She snatched the shower curtain from him and started putting it back on the rail. "I thought you were another stalker trying to steal my underwear."

"Nah," said Yuri. "You're not getting any more stalkers, not after you beat the stuffing out of that last one. Skeeter says the word got around."

He heaved himself upright with fluid grace and leapt out of the tub. While Candi struggled to put the curtain back up, he hopped from foot to foot and regarded her with his peculiar wide-eyed gaze.

"You shouldn't use so much hairspray," he said

earnestly. "They test it on animals, you know."

Candi stepped away from the shower with an exasperated sigh. "You broke into my apartment to lecture me on the evils of AquaNet? Are you serious?"

Yuri whooped and bounded out of the bathroom like an overly excited puppy. Candi hurried after him, shaking her head. She found him sitting on the edge of her bed, his green eyes alive with excitement.

"Well?" she said patiently. "What is it?"

He drummed his fists excitedly against the mattress. "I was right! I tried to tell Jazz—but did he listen? Of course he didn't! But I was right, and Jazz was wrong!"

"Wrong about what?" said Candi. Jazz was wrong about a lot of things, in her opinion.

Yuri launched himself from the bed without warning, almost knocking into her. He stared into her eyes with an expression so exuberant and joyful that he looked mildly unhinged.

"The devil-boy is a real devil!" he crowed. "I saw him!"

"Cain Pseudomantis?" Candi blinked.

Yuri nodded proudly.

"And how exactly did you figure this out?"

"Well," he said. "It all started yesterday after practice. Jazz wouldn't believe me when I told him that devils are real. I told him that Skeeter said they were real, and I told him how my dad saw some once, but he just rolled his eyes and said that Skeeter was a moron and my dad was just a nutso old commie Russian hermit. So I set out to prove him wrong."

"How? You didn't go and pester poor Cain, did you?" Candi squeezed the bridge of her nose wearily. Yuri could be incredibly persistent when he fixated on an idea, and he was impervious to social cues even at the best of times. An apology to Cain might be in order.

"I tried. I mean, I couldn't let Jazz insult my dad or Skeeter like that, could I?" He shrugged. "But I never got the chance. Cain flew away before I could get to him."

Candi stared at him.

"Flew away?"

"I was walking down his street." He picked up a stray hair tie from her bedside table and played with it, stretching it out and folding it in on itself. "He stepped out of his house when I was about halfway to him, and a bunch of vultures ambushed him. I was going to run and help him out, but he flew away before I got there."

"You keep saying he flew away. What do you mean? He doesn't have any wings. Did he happen to be carrying a broomstick or a magic carpet, or do all devils just keep helicopters folded up in their wallets?" She couldn't resist injecting a little sarcasm into her response; she was still annoyed about being woken up in the dead of night.

Yuri snorted contemptuously. "Of course not! Devils just float up into the air like Superman when they want to fly. Honestly, Candi, I don't know why I bother having serious discussions with you if you're just going to be silly."

"My apologies—I'll try to be more serious in the future." Candi watched Yuri twist the hair tie into an elaborate braid and wondered what it was like to live in his weird little head. She made a mental note to start gently encouraging him to spend less time around Skeeter Judd. The planet might collapse someday under the weight of the massive loads of complete and utter horseshit those two could bounce off each other.

Something terrible was going to happen soon.

Michael Anderson awoke from a deep sleep. He knew this truth the moment he opened his eyes. He stared at the spotless white wall of his new living quarters. He had been sent to live in this place after his trial. They were talking around him—all of them at once—and he couldn't shut out their voices.

Did you hear? said one incessant, high-pitched voice from inside the walls—the voice of electricity pulsing in the wires. *Tomorrow at dawn—fast, fast, fast they'll move, with anger and vengeance. Did you hear?*

Another voice replied from the pipes in the ceiling—the silky, flowing hiss of water. *The closed door won't hold— the floods build against it. They'll build and batter and push until they break their way through.*

Michael covered his head with his lumpy gray pillow. The doctors and their pills had not been able to rid him of the voices after all. To be fair, they were not entirely unsuccessful. His mind was quieter now, and the minds of those around him were closed and inscrutable.

But the pills didn't drown out *these* voices, which did not come from his mind, but from elemental spirits that were as old as the universe itself. They were not subject to humans or their medicines. There was nothing the doctors could do about their chatter. He had no idea how he knew this information, but he did. He had woken up knowing it that morning even though no one told him.

The mattress was hard and uncomfortable. Michael climbed out of his narrow bed and paced the linoleum floor, his bare feet tracing the muddled beam of light spilling from the room's single, high-set window. The elementals in the walls and ceiling prattled on, their voices mixing into a never-ending buzz. He began to feel desperate.

The least amount of noise seemed to be coming from the wall that faced the foot of the bed—the wall on which the white paint was marred by rust-colored streaks where water had seeped through. The streaks twined together, forming a crude image of a man with wings. Michael wandered over to the wall and sat down on the floor at the feet of the image. It wasn't a comfortable place to sit, but looking up at the stain pacified him. It awakened a memory so ancient that he wondered if the reminiscence came from a time before he was born. The recollection was more like a formless impression of deep love and contentment than a real, concrete memory.

You.

A new voice. It came from beyond the walls, beyond the gardens outside, beyond the road. Beyond the sky.

Awaken.

Michael sat up stiffly.

Rise again.

His heart pounded, and his temples began to throb. He somehow knew the voice was called the Center, the Great Entity, and the Maker-of-Itself, among many other names he didn't care to acknowledge.

"No."

Michael curled into an obstinate little ball at the feet of the angel, straining to shut out the Center's call. Drawing would quiet the voice. Where were his pencils and paper? He needed them. Desperation burned in his gut as the pill-haze began to evaporate.

He began having a vision. The kind doctor was in the vision, sitting in her office, holding papers on her lap. He reached into the vision and touched her mind. He had not known he could touch the minds of other people before this moment.

The realization terrified him. He curled further into himself, pressing his eyelids shut and jamming his fingers in his ears. Gorge rose in his throat. It was wrong of him to do that to the doctor. It was *evil*.

Dr. Brown was going through paperwork before her next appointment a mile and a half away from Michael Anderson's cell. She felt a chill and a prickling at the back of her skull.

For no apparent reason, she thought of Michael.

"Damn," she muttered to herself. "I need to get that boy his pencils."

Michelle hurried upstairs to change clothes immediately upon arriving home from school. Nights like tonight had become an increasingly rare opportunity for her. Her daddy was away at a meeting for one of his many charitable projects, leaving him unable to keep constant watch on her as he had for the last few days.

She struggled into her pink miniskirt, resolving to try Cain first. Of all the boys she had been with recently, Cain was the most pleasant to be around. He was one of the few whose company was as enjoyable as his body. But Cain's days were pretty full now, and she had her needs. If he wasn't available, there were always plenty of willing candidates at the clubs. She and Cain were not officially an item, after all.

But he seems to think we are, she thought. Michelle pushed the notion from her mind. There was no reason for her to be ashamed about hooking up with another man occasionally; that stab of guilt was a useless, irritating fragment of the silly old-fashioned values her daddy had unsuccessfully tried to hammer into her mind. She was sure that Cain had bedded at least one groupie behind her back, and that was fine with her.

The doorbell rang. Michelle groaned in exasperation. The only person who rang the doorbell at this house was her father's secretary who came to drop things off occasionally. If she didn't let him in, her daddy would probably find out and want to know why she didn't answer the door.

"Coming!" she shouted.

The doorbell rang again. Michelle hurried down the stairs and into the front hall where she nearly tripped over an irritable and apprehensive Abednego. She told the dog to stop pacing and flung the front door open. When she saw what was standing on the stoop, she stumbled back with a shriek of fright.

The thing took an eager step over the threshold. It was huge and looming, man-shaped but taller and more powerfully built than any human, and it had a sweeping crest of coarse glistening black quills instead of hair. Thick, electric blue scales covered every inch of skin exposed under its too-tight clothes. Its hands were armed at the fingertips with wicked hook-like talons. It extended its arms as if to embrace her. She dodged back to put the snarling dog between her and the monster, searching for a weapon out of the corners of her eyes.

"Michelle!" To her great surprise, she recognized the voice that came from the creature's fanged mouth. "Are you all right? I didn't *scare* you, did I?"

"*Cain?*" Michelle stopped looking for weapons and stared at him in shock.

"Yeah." He took another step forward. Now she could see hints of him in this frightening new form: the peculiar blend of shyness and curiosity in those cat-like blue eyes, the cautious way he moved when approaching people, and the tail that twitched or wrapped around his leg when he was anxious. "I wanted to see you. Your dad's car wasn't in the driveway, so I thought I'd—ouch!"

Abednego had dashed forward with a howl of rage and locked jaws around his ankle. *That must be Cain*, Michelle decided.

"Get off me!" Cain danced around in a tight circle, shaking his leg. "Ow! What did I ever do to you, you little monster? Get *off*!"

He dislodged the dog with a powerful kick; Abednego went sailing into the dining room, hit the floor with a loud thud, and immediately scrambled to its feet for a second attack. Cain thrust out his hands, palms forward, and Abednego came to a jerky halt mid-charge. Before the dog could gather its wits for another attack, Cain flicked his fingers, making an odd shooing gesture. The dog's fat body began to slide steadily backwards, as if it were being dragged by invisible hands. Abednego yelped and scratched at the floor, trying to gain a footing, but to no avail. It vanished into the kitchen, and a final sweep of Cain's arm made the door close after him.

"That really hurt." Cain knelt down and rubbed his ankle. "I think he even broke the scales a little. What in the world did I do to make that dog hate me so much, Michelle?"

"Sorry about Abednego," said Michelle. "He doesn't really like anyone except daddy; he doesn't even like me. If I'd known you were coming, I'd have shut him up in the kitchen myself."

"I'll try to warn you next time, then."

"I wish you'd warned me this time," said Michelle irritably. "Jesus, Cain, what if daddy had answered the door?"

"I was pretty sure he wouldn't," said Cain. "I watched you walk up the driveway from the roof, and—"

"From the roof?" Michelle interrupted him. "What do you mean?"

"I flew there," said Cain casually. "Anyway, you looked like you were in a good mood. You never look like that when you're going home and you know he'll be there."

Michelle squinted up at him, wondering if he was pulling her leg about being able to fly. It was surprisingly hard to tell. Those scales added new contours to his face, and his voice was deep and strange.

"Fair point," she said. "Look, Cain, don't take this the wrong way, but I've gotta ask."

"Ask what?"

"What...um...what *happened* to you?"

Confusion flickered across his face.

"You mean today?" he said. "Well, I got into a fight with Vince—sort of—and some people with cameras tried to corner me. Other than that, nothing much happened."

"No, no." Michelle shook her head. "I mean, what happened to your body? You look...so...different."

"Oh. This is how I look normally, when I'm not in human form."

"So you just...decided to look like that today or something?"

"I changed form to get away from the camera people." His tail twitched anxiously. "You don't like it?"

405

"No, of course I like it." She wasn't quite sure she did like his new appearance, but she didn't want to hurt him or make him angry. "I just wasn't expecting it."

To her relief, Cain seemed satisfied. She drew in her breath sharply as his hands closed around hers, half-expecting those dagger-sharp claws to leave some nasty cuts. They did not; in fact, they rested so lightly against her skin that she could hardly feel them when he started leading her up the stairs. Even when a low, ragged growling sound rose from his chest and she pulled away in dismay, she felt nothing except a very faint and brief poke.

The growling faded, and he turned to her with concern in his eyes. "Are you all right?"

"Yeah." She forced herself to smile. "I tripped."

They went into her room. Michelle expected Cain to shapeshift back to human form once the door shut behind them, but he was still blue and scaly when she turned around. Maybe he couldn't shapeshift as easily as Izzy could. He bounded over to the bed and curled up on it, waving his tail expectantly.

"I'm so glad to see you," he said. "I've wanted to see you all week, but Mr. Arkin has been keeping me so busy."

The growling started up again, and Michelle belatedly realized where she had heard it before. It was a deeper, more resonant version of the guttural noises he sometimes made during sex. Perhaps that terrifying sound was simply the demon's version of a cat's happy purr. The thought relaxed her a little, but she was still tense.

"Um…" She took a reluctant step toward him. "Aren't you going to change now?"

He stopped purring.

"I wasn't planning on it."

"It's just…I'm a little worried about…your new hardware."

She lifted her hands and flexed her fingers meaningfully. Cain blinked at her for a moment.

"You mean my claws?" he said at last. "Oh, you don't need to worry about them. I won't hurt you."

"I know you would never *mean* to hurt me." Michelle flinched as one of his hands casually stroked her beloved— and expensive—old pink satin bedspread. "But if you put your hand in the wrong place at the wrong time…"

"I never put my hand in the wrong place at the wrong time." He shrugged. "Not when I'm in my real shape, anyway."

"Uh huh." She studied his claws dubiously.

"Really, I don't!" he insisted. "Here, watch."

He lunged forward and slapped both hands palms-down on the bedspread. Michelle gasped in horror as he kneaded and swiped at it like a cat sharpening its claws on a chair.

"Damn it, Cain!" She darted forward angrily. "That was my favorite…"

Her voice trailed off, and she stared at the bedspread in amazement. It was as perfectly intact as it had been before Cain touched it—no rips or gashes, no snag marks.

"See?" Cain grinned. "I've got plenty of control over my hands. I won't hurt you. Steve thinks I have more nerves in my fingers than a human does—or something like that."

Michelle stepped back, scrambling for another reason for Cain to change back to human form before she could touch him. His fingers may have been nimble enough to make JoJo Thorpe jealous, but those claws still looked like they could rip through solid metal with one swipe, and his deftness might deteriorate once he became overexcited. Yet while she gazed at his powerful blue body, working up the courage to order him to stop stalling and change already, a stray thought flitted through her mind. *Daddy would have a heart attack if he could see Cain right now.* A real, live demon, complete with claws and fangs, was lolling in his innocent daughter's bed.

She made up her mind.

"I believe you," she said, mentally scolding herself for being seven flavors of crazy. "But could you promise me one thing before we start?"

"What's that?"

"I'd like you to…you know…not use your hands this time."

Cain glanced at his hands, then at her.

"Fair enough," he sighed.

While still fighting a lingering shred of fear that she was gambling with her life, Michelle slid into bed beside him. The vibrations of his purr rippled against her skin. Her breath caught in her throat for a moment when his hands shifted, but she relaxed when she realized he was simply undressing. She followed suit. Now that her apprehension had subsided a bit, her curiosity was building. Even though his new form was alarming, she thought it possessed a strange, exotic beauty.

Cain rubbed against her, nuzzling her neck. Michelle reached up, tentatively, to stroke his bare chest. The scales were glassy, smooth, and warm. She felt his tongue moving lazily along her collarbone and then down over her breasts. A deep shudder of pleasure ran through her, and she didn't notice one of his hands brushing her when he rolled over on his back. She straddled him, rocking her hips against his. The bedsprings squealed and the headboard rattled against the wall. Neither of them heard the car pulling into the driveway.

Then the front door slammed. They both froze, and Michelle went pale.

"Shit," she whispered. "Daddy is not supposed to be home tonight."

Footsteps sounded from the entryway, and they were soon mingled with the dog's barking. Both noises began to move steadily up the stairs. Cain scrambled up and gathered his clothes.

"Into the closet—hurry!" Michelle leapt up after him, tucking her miniskirt behind a pillow and struggling into her jeans. "He won't find you if you huddle down in the back right corner."

"He won't, but that dog will." Cain hurried to the window.

"But you can't go out the window—the trellis won't hold your weight. It barely holds mine." Michelle shuddered at the memory of her many struggles down the rickety trellis. It was a terrifying way to escape, but sadly, it was the only route that let her avoid her father's bedroom *and* her father's office.

"That's okay. I won't need it."

He launched himself through the open window with a push of his legs. Michelle stifled a scream, expecting him to plummet two stories. Instead, he zoomed straight up like a rocket, and a moment later, she heard a muffled thud when he landed on the roof.

"Holy shit." She stared after him in astonishment. "I guess you weren't joking."

Abednego's barking jarred her back to reality. The dog was right outside her door now, scratching to be let in. She hastily unzipped her backpack, pulled out a textbook and some papers, and spread them out on her bed.

"Michelle?" Her father knocked on the door. "Are you in here?"

Michelle hopped onto the bed and pulled the textbook into her lap.

"Come in, daddy," she said sweetly.

Abednego barreled in with astonishing speed for such a fat, bow-legged little dog. The dog's head swiveled around for a moment, scanning the room. It waddled up to the bed, sniffing and growling, and heaved awkwardly upward onto its hind legs. The Reverend Breen stood in the open doorway with crossed arms and a furrowed brow.

"Hi, daddy," she said. "Did your meeting end early tonight?"

"It did," said the minister, looking at the dog instead of his daughter.

"That's nice." Michelle shuffled through her notes. "What's wrong with Abednego? He never wants to be in my room."

"I imagine he'd want to be in any room other than the kitchen for a while." The Reverend Breen's frown grew deeper. "I found him shut in there. The poor thing was half-crazy by the time I let him out."

"Really?" Michelle put on her best expression of false regret. "I'm afraid that's my fault. I made myself a snack after school, and I'm pretty sure I shut the door behind me afterwards. He must have come into the kitchen while I was eating, and I didn't notice."

"You didn't hear him barking up a storm down there?"

"I was pretty deep in my homework. I've gotta catch up in..." She glanced down at the textbook and caught a glimpse of a colorful periodic table. "Chemistry. If I did hear him, I probably assumed he'd seen a squirrel in the yard."

"Ah." His face softened a bit. "Well, no harm done. Still...it is a bit strange."

"What's strange, daddy?"

"I've never seen him this worked up before. And he made a beeline for this room, where he never goes...and he hates climbing stairs...It's almost as if..."

He took a step into the room, squinting suspiciously at the closet. Michelle silently thanked God that Cain hadn't taken her advice as her father's hand came to rest on the door handle.

"As if he thought there was someone else here," he said.

"I don't know why he would think that." Michelle pretended to turn her attention back to the textbook.

Her father opened the door and stared into the closet, nudging the jumble of clothing inside with his fingers. Satisfied that the closet was empty of unauthorized boyfriends, he turned and squatted down slowly, peering under the bed. When that search proved futile as well, he heaved himself up with a grunt and moved on to the small attached bathroom. Michelle's uneasiness gave way to irritation.

"There's no one in this room but me, daddy," she said.

"Oh, I know, sweetheart. I just worry about you; that's all." The Reverend Breen wandered out of the bathroom and started opening all the drawers in her dresser, even though most of them were too small for the most talented of contortionists to fit in. Then he seemed to notice the open window for the first time and reached out to close it.

"This house does have air conditioning, you know." A

hint of gentle annoyance crept into his voice. "You're free to turn it on when you get too hot. I'd prefer you use it, in fact. I don't want bugs getting into the house."

The dog seemed to lose interest in the bed while the Reverend Breen spoke. It turned and sniffed its way to the window, where it immediately reared up and started growling again.

"Odd," murmured the minister. The dog scratched at the wall and made a weak attempt at a leap to the windowsill. "This is the most energy I've seen out of him in a while. I wonder if there's someone in the yard." He stuck his head out the window.

"I doubt it, daddy." Michelle scrambled for a way to distract him, but not for Cain's sake. Unless Cain was foolish enough to hang from the gutter by his toes and blow a raspberry in her father's face, she was sure the old man wouldn't see him on his rooftop perch. She had simply had enough of her father's prying. "The gate is pretty secure."

"Not as secure as one might hope." The Reverend Breen leaned farther out, squinting down into the garden.

"So how was the meeting tonight, daddy?" The question seemed a pretty safe way to divert his attention, even if she did have to listen to a boring soliloquy on her father's fundraising work.

"Ah, it went well enough." The Reverend Breen squatted down to pat the dog, which had given up trying to scratch its way up to the windowsill and had stopped growling, though it remained alert with nose and ears pointed to the ceiling. "We've very nearly met our goal, and dear Mrs. Thackeray will definitely be coming to the banquet. I was so worried she wouldn't make it; she doesn't get out much anymore."

"That's wonderful, daddy."

"Isn't it?" Her father sighed. "I just wish we'd brought in a bit more money. Voice in the Wilderness does so much good for abused children, and we could do so much more with better funding. It's too bad charity seems to be the last thing on people's minds nowadays."

"Yup, too bad." Michelle shifted impatiently.

"I suppose it would help some," he continued, "if the current crop of movie stars and musicians running around this town weren't such a shiftless lot. Rhoda Thackeray is a lovely lady, but she hasn't been in a movie since 1948. If we had someone a bit more...current...associated with the foundation—someone the young people today would recognize and respect—well, that would do more to drive up donations than I ever could."

Abednego's ears perked up, catching the rustle of Cain shifting his weight on the roof, and it immediately started barking again. Michelle took advantage of her father's distraction to roll her eyes at him.

"What on earth is the matter, Abednego?" The Reverend Breen stopped scratching the dog's head and stood up. "I hope you aren't possessed again."

He leaned out the window and scanned the garden for intruders once more. Michelle knew that the lawn and the fringe of trees beyond it were still empty. The minister stole one last uneasy glance outside and closed the window, unaware that Michelle's lover Cain Pseudomantis sat on the roof four feet above him.

It was nearly three in the morning by the time Cain got home. He waddled slowly up the stairs, very sore from lying on the hard tiles of the Breen house for what seemed an eternity while he and Michelle waited for her father to go to bed. Still, he was glad he had waited. Michelle had allowed him to fly her down into the garden, where they finished their tryst on the soft mossy ground under the trees. He shuddered with pleasure at the memory as he fumbled with the lock.

The key stuck again, and he had some trouble unsticking it. When the front door finally swung open, it missed hitting Sammi in the face by two inches.

"Oh!" Cain started. "Sorry about that—I didn't know you were still up."

Sammi didn't seem to care that he had narrowly escaped a bloody nose. He stared blankly at Cain, playing with his hands.

"There you are," he muttered. "I've been waiting for you."

"You have?" Cain glanced up at the unlit light fixture directly above Sammi's head, puzzled. Why wait in the dark hallway instead of on the nice comfortable couch in the living room, with the lamp on?

"Yeah. We've gotta talk."

"About what?"

"You've gotta stop Vince." A hint of urgency crept into the odd flat tone Sammi was using. "I tried to stop him, but he just kept going. He's going to ruin everything, Cain."

Cain groaned. "What did he do this time?"

"He ate the glass. I told him not to."

"Vince ate *glass*?" Lance had thrown enough kitchenware at Steve during tantrums for Cain to know that broken glass could easily cut human skin. Cain's scales offered him a little more protection from sharp objects, but he shuddered to think what sort of damage glass would do to a person if it were swallowed. He gaped at Sammi in horror. "Why on earth did he do that? Is he all right? How much did he eat?"

"All of it!" Sammi's arms floated up in vague exasperation. "The bottles from the beer, the jars from the jam and peanut butter, the bathroom mirror, and every last window in the house. He even ate the TV screen."

Cain raised an eyebrow. He could see three windows from where he was standing, and they were all perfectly intact.

"All the glass in the house." Sammi's voice took on a singsong quality. "He took it, smashed it into pretty little shining pieces, and swallowed them, one by one, to find the piece that would fill the hole in his eyes. He hasn't found it yet. He won't stop till he does. They've hid all the windows in the city from him, but he'll keep eating till the hole is filled."

He lurched forward and seized his confused band mate by the arms. Cain glanced into his glazed, unfocused eyes and solved the mystery: Sammi was either sleepwalking, or he was so full of heroin that he had no real idea what he was saying.

"We've gotta stop him!" There was definite panic in Sammi's voice now, and he had begun to sweat. "He's going up the ladder—up and up and up—and when he gets to the top he'll smash the sky into a billion pieces! We've gotta stop him before he kills us all, man!"

"Sammi, I think it's time for you to go to bed now," said Cain, shaking his arms in an attempt to free himself. "Say, do you think you could loosen up your grip a little? You're hurting me—"

Sammi's eyes bulged in frustration. "Dammit, man, we can't sleep now—there's no time. Vince wants to *eat the sky*! He'll swallow it down, every last scrap, and then there'll be nothing between us and *them*. I've seen them up there, lurking in outer space. The sky is the only thing keeping them away; once it's gone, they'll come shooting down and take us out one by one."

"Sammi!" Cain managed to pull his arms free. "I meant it's time for *you* to go to bed. I'll deal with Vince."

Sammi tried to wander out the front door. "I'll come with you—"

"No." Cain held him back. "You need your sleep. Don't worry about Vince. I can deal with him on my own."

It took some arguing, but he was finally able to convince Sammi to go to bed. Even then, he didn't go quietly, muttering all the way about a cold fire churning and the seas boiling. The journey took a long time. Sammi could barely set one foot in front of the other without pitching forward, and Cain had to half-carry him most of the way. The ladder to the loft gave him a few anxious moments. He ended up hefting Sammi over his shoulder like a sack of flour, and they both ascended the ladder without injury and without waking Vince, who was fast asleep on his air mattress and was definitely not snacking on the sky.

"You go stop Vince right now—do ya hear?" mumbled Sammi as he crawled onto his rumpled futon. "The whole world is counting on you."

"Don't worry; I will. I promise."

Sammi nodded, satisfied, and collapsed onto his tangled blankets. He was snoring within minutes.

Cain climbed down from the loft and trudged off to his own room, looking forward to a rapid fall into slumber. Yet as tired as he was, he couldn't sleep. After fifteen minutes of fruitless tossing and turning, he wandered downstairs to the living room, guitar in hand.

A single beam of golden electric light filtered into the room through the street-side window. Cain sprawled on the couch, well out of the light, and fingered the guitar's strings—not practicing exactly, but trying to take his mind off his struggle to get to sleep. It worked. The guitar slid out of his hands as he rolled over and began snoring.

When he woke, the warm glow that shone through the window was mingled with the cold blue light of early morning. Someone was moving around in the front hall. Cain heard heavy footsteps and sat up to investigate, tail twitching. He caught a glimpse of Vince shuffling past the entrance to the living room with a pack of cigarettes in hand. The front door opened and then slammed shut.

Cain flopped back down onto the warm, soft couch. There were no interviews or shows scheduled for today; he could sleep as long as he liked. Contentment rolled over him like a thick blanket as he began to drift off again, and he didn't notice the commotion on the doorstep until a series of loud thuds and bangs from upstairs startled him awake. He sat bolt upright in time to see Sammi stumble toward the front door as fast as his groggy body would allow.

"Fuck it all," Cain heard him mutter. "Six in the morning, and Vince is already stealing memories? God, why can't I be in a band with normal guys?"

Cain snapped into full wakefulness when he finally registered the muffled shouts and scuffling coming from the front door. He scrambled up from the couch and followed Sammi.

A terrifying sight met their eyes on the stoop. Vince's victim was a young woman in neat business clothes. His hands were locked around her neck, and he was shaking her, battering her against the iron railing. She clawed desperately at his arms; her long nails drew blood, but Vince showed no pain. Izzy stood at the foot of the steps, having just arrived home from a party. He stared up at the scene with his mouth open in shock, and his forgotten keychain slid out of his hand.

"Why did you do it, bitch?" Vince shrieked.

"Vince, stop!" Cain's eyes widened with horror as he recognized the woman. "I know her—she's Mr. Arkin's assistant Chelsea. She's here to bring me food."

Vince ignored him. "Didn't you hear me?" He yanked Chelsea toward him until his nose was an inch from hers, spraying her with flecks of spittle as he screamed. "I fucking asked you a question! I want to know why you did it!" His right hand released her neck and burrowed into her hair. "Now talk, or I'll stick my fingers in your head and dig around until I find what I want! I will squeeze your brains to pulp until I get that memory, you evil little whore, and then I'll suck every last trace of life out of you so you can't warn him."

"Sammi, do something," said Cain. "I forgot to grab my guitar!"

Sammi didn't respond. He was standing blank-eyed and slack-jawed in the doorway.

Chelsea let out a strangled little squeal and went limp when Vince's fingers pushed into her brain. Cain couldn't wait to act any longer. He gritted his teeth and stepped forward, drawing his arm back. He brought his fist down on Vince's temple, not with his full strength, but hard enough that Vince crumpled in an unconscious heap at his feet when the blow connected. Cain stared down at him for a moment, shivering.

"I'm so sorry," he said to Chelsea in a shaky voice. "I have no idea what got into him. We'll make sure he never does it again, I promise."

"Oh, that's all right." Chelsea kept her eyes down, and she knelt on the stoop, gathering up her scattered packages with trembling hands. "I...I've heard of Vince and his...temper, kind of expected...expected to be attacked someday. I'll just give you the meat and go."

"You're shaken. Come in and sit down for a while."

"No!" Chelsea cast a quick terrified glance at Sammi. "I really have to go. I'm running late."

She dumped the squashy bundles of meat into Cain's arms and ran down the steps. But even though she was fast, Izzy was faster. He changed into an enormous red wolf and blocked her path with his body, snarling—the first truly menacing sound that Cain had heard him produce.

"Izzy, what are you doing?" Cain juggled his packets helplessly. "Let her go! She just came to drop off some food! Look, I have it right here. Sammi, I really could use some help right now."

He turned to give Sammi a pleading look. Sammi didn't notice; he was staring down at Chelsea. His back was stiff, and his jaw was clenched. He scratched his arm so hard that his sleeve bunched up to reveal a livid black bruise below the crook of his elbow.

"Son of a bitch," he muttered furiously. "Son of a *bitch*. It's *her*."

"What do you mean, 'it's her?'"

"She's the one." Little glints of electricity crackled along Sammi's skin while he raised a finger to point at Chelsea. "She led us to the Engineer."

Chapter Seventeen

Partners in Crime

"*CHELSEA* LED YOU TO the Engineer? That can't be right." Cain looked wildly down at Chelsea and then back up at Sammi. "She works for Mr. Arkin. She's been bringing my groceries since October."

"Seriously?" Sammi looked utterly aghast. "Fuck, man. That's really, really creepy. All this time, you've been eating food the Engineer's accomplice touched, and you didn't even know it!"

Chelsea seemed to brace herself for a mad dash to her car. A loud growl from Izzy made her think better of it.

"Please, I don't know what they're talking about." She shrank against the railing, appealing to Cain. "Your band mates must have me confused with someone else."

"Like who?" Sammi elbowed Cain aside and advanced on her. "The bitch who promised to help us find our lost friend and then drugged us for the Engineer to take away, maybe?"

Chelsea rocked experimentally on the balls of her feet, as if she were trying to determine whether she could leap over Izzy without hurting herself.

"Sammi, what are you talking about?" Cain wrung his

hands, wishing he had thought to grab his guitar.

Sammi rounded on Cain, scattering sparks over the stoop. "I'll tell you what I'm talking about! You know how we went to look for Vince that night? Well, when morning rolled around and we still hadn't made any progress, Izzy suggested we try asking around at Vince's work to see if anyone there had noticed anything weird. One of the mechanics there said that on the day Vince disappeared, he'd been really excited because he had some sort of meeting at Daggerspoint Records. We thought either Vince or this other mechanic had had a pipe dream. Do you know how many bands in this city never make it past the front door of any record company, let alone Daggerspoint? Still, we thought the tip was at least worth checking out. So we made our way to the Daggerspoint headquarters, and guess who we ran into?"

He shot a glare at Chelsea, who seemed to be wishing she could melt into the concrete.

"That's right." Sammi turned back to Cain. "We explained the situation to this Chelsea and asked her if she knew anything about Vince's meeting. She got the *weirdest* look on her face. God, we should have known. Anyway, she invited us to her apartment for breakfast while we figured things out. She invited us—two scruffy, strung-out-looking guys she'd never met—into her home without so much as a blink. Yup, we definitely should have been suspicious." He smiled ruefully. "But we were so tired and hungry that we weren't thinking straight, and we sure as hell didn't want to be *rude* to Bruce Arkin's secretary. Anyway, we followed her to her apartment. We ate the eggs and bacon she made for us, started feeling all woozy and lightheaded, and then...hospital."

A flash of horrified guilt passed over Chelsea's features.

"Christ, that day was so fuzzy before," said Sammi. "I tried to remember what led up to...but it was all a haze...when I remembered anything at all...I thought what I *did* remember must have been a bad dream caused by the drugs. But now that I've seen her again, it's like it all happened yesterday."

"Look, you don't understand," she whispered in a flat, defeated voice. "I didn't know what I was getting myself involved in. If I had...God, I never would have—"

"We don't understand?" Sammi poked her sharply in the arm. She convulsed and shrieked, and Cain heard the pop of electricity. "Well, tell us what we don't understand, then!"

Chelsea backed as far away from Sammi as Izzy would allow. She rubbed her arm, shook her head slightly, and looked up at Cain with pleading eyes. Cain couldn't meet her gaze.

"Suit yourself." Sammi advanced on her. Webs of electricity danced between his fingers while he extended his arm to touch her again. Izzy snapped at her when she tried to squeeze past him.

"Of course, you could be right. Maybe we don't understand the whole story." Sammi's eyes narrowed ominously. "Maybe we are mistaking you for someone else. Maybe we think you're just the Engineer's accomplice, but the truth is that you *are* the Engineer."

Chelsea shivered in abject fear. Sammi brushed his hand so close to her forehead that her bangs rose and swayed like seaweed.

"I understand now," he continued, his voice growing louder and angrier. "You thought you'd never get caught, didn't you? I mean, you're a nice, respectable businesswoman—who'd ever believe you were a serial killer?" The latticework of neon-blue current between his fingers grew brighter, and his hand inched ever closer to Chelsea's face. "You didn't count on three of your victims getting rescued, did you, bitch?"

"I'm not the Engineer!" shrieked Chelsea. "I find an index card with the name of the…chosen young man on my desk. I get him into the building with as few people seeing him as possible, and I slip him the drug to make him sleep. Then I leave him to be…picked up." She shuddered. "That's all I've ever done; I swear!"

"The building?" Cain found his voice at last, and it was full of horror and disgust. "What building? You mean your apartment building?"

She shook her head miserably.

"Then where?"

"The Daggerspoint headquarters."

She spoke the words in a tiny, guilty whimper. Cain gasped; Sammi clenched his jaw; and Izzy's ears flattened against his skull.

"But Izzy and I didn't…" began Sammi.

"That was different," said Chelsea. "You had already barged in through the front door. God only knows how many people saw you. I panicked. I called him afterwards, and he said he'd take care of it."

Sammi wagged his fingers impatiently. "Where does he take the victims after you drug them?"

"I don't know."

"Okay…who is he, then?"

"I don't know," she repeated, her voice hoarse.

"You said you called—"

"Yeah, but I don't know his name." Chelsea's hands

fluttered frantically. "I only met him once, and even that guy might not have, you know, *been* him. The guy I talked to in person looked like a college student, and there was something about the way he said things...It was almost as if he'd been given a script to read. The voice on the phone wasn't his voice, either. I don't even know what exactly the drug is—it just sort of shows up on my doorstep. I can't point you to the Engineer."

"Fuck." Sammi clutched his head feverishly. "That's a problem...but you said you had his number? We could use it to find him...Look, you need to call him right now. Tell him—"

"I CAN'T!" She screamed the words with such force that Izzy and Sammi both jumped back in surprise.

Chelsea took advantage of their confusion: she broke away and scrambled into her car. Izzy became a cheetah and started to speed after her, but he wisely veered onto the sidewalk when the reverse lights blinked on and the car backed up to the stoop. She tore off down the street, leaving a long swipe of melted rubber on the asphalt.

"Fuck." Sammi stared after her for a moment. "Fucking *hell*. Every one of the Engineer's victims passed through the Daggerspoint headquarters, and we had no idea."

Izzy trotted up the stairs, wide-eyed. "That's horrible. We might have been in the building at the same time as some of them."

"Dammit, we shouldn't have let her get away!" Sammi kicked the railing in frustration. "She knows more about the Engineer than she told us—I'm sure of it. She's probably running off to tell him what happened right now."

"What's wrong?" said Izzy to Cain.

Cain rubbed his arm, thinking of his first day at

Daggerspoint when the nurse pulled out her long bright needle.

"I just remembered something," he said. "I've been meaning to ask you guys—did Mr. Arkin make any of you get tested for AIDS too? You know, by taking blood samples?"

"*Blood samples?*" Sammi gaped at him. "No, man. I remember Mr. Arkin encouraging me to get tested before I signed, but I don't think it's required or anything."

Cain frowned. "So he didn't have your blood drawn right there in the office."

"Yuck." Izzy made a face. "Maybe in a horror flick. Why?"

"Mr. Arkin had a nurse draw blood from me." Cain winced at the memory. "He said it was an AIDS test."

They all stared at each other.

"Chelsea works for Mr. Arkin," said Sammi darkly. "You don't think…"

"We'd better wake up Vince and tell him," said Izzy.

"He won't want to listen, you know," grumbled Sammi. But they carried Vince inside and waited for him to regain consciousness before discussing the matter further.

Once awake, Vince seemed to have forgotten all about his outburst, and if he *had* attacked Chelsea, he vehemently denied that the attack could have had anything to do with the Engineer. Even so, he listened intently to the bits of information they had gleaned from Chelsea. Once they finished, he did not hesitate to offer his opinion.

"What a big, steaming pile of bullshit," he sneered. "The Engineer has a whole bunch of people helping him, *and* he's taking his victims right out of the Daggerspoint headquarters? Hah! I bet if Chelsea had told you he killed

Kennedy, you would have believed her."

"I don't care how far-fetched Chelsea's story sounds, Vinnie." Sammi's eyes flashed angrily. "It's the best information we've gotten so far—the *only* information, in fact. The question now is how could a mass murderer be operating under all our noses?"

"I'll say." Vince tossed his hair over his shoulder with a contemptuous snort. "The story has got more holes in it than a pair of Izzy's socks. Even if this Chelsea chick *did* manage to get a whole bunch of guys into the building without anyone seeing them, how did the Engineer get them out again?"

"I don't know." Sammi deflated.

"Maybe he used the janitor's cart?" Cain thought an invisibility spell would be an easier way to dupe everyone, but he doubted that the Engineer, who tried to use runes intended for objects on people, had the skill or talent to use one. "It's big enough."

"It sure is." Vince rolled his eyes. "But why the fuck would anybody roll the janitor's cart outside? If I saw someone doing something that weird, I'd get real suspicious."

"Hmm," said Sammi moodily. A discouraging silence fell over the room.

Izzy perked up suddenly. "What if he never took them out of the building?"

Sammi and Cain started and looked at him with new interest. Vince's face darkened.

"What if he did use the janitor's cart like Cain said?" Izzy continued. "Only, instead of taking it outside, he took it to some closet or empty office where he knew no one would bother him..." His eyes widened. "You know, Mr. Arkin never did tell me who made the mess in studio 4B."

They all stared at each other.

"What do we do now?" said Cain.

"We've gotta get into that studio," said Izzy. "I heard people at the bar saying there's still one guy missing. Maybe he's alive!"

Sammi shook his head. "I think we should call the police."

"What if they don't believe us?" Izzy hopped up from the couch and walked resolutely toward the door. "What if the guy dies while we're wasting time with them? We've gotta get him out now, before Chelsea can tell the Engineer we're onto him."

"Whoa, whoa, whoa, Iz!" Sammi scrambled around the couch and stood in his path. "You can't go running off on a one-man rescue mission. Remember how that worked out for you last time?"

Izzy tried to edge around Sammi, with no success. "It won't be a one-man rescue mission if you guys help me. See you in front of Daggerspoint in an hour."

He turned into a weasel and scurried between Sammi's legs. Sammi threw up his arms in exasperation.

"What are you going to do, huh?" he called into the hallway. "Kick the damn studio door down?"

"Of course not." Izzy's voice replied. "I'm gonna go around to everyone I know from the clubs and get as many of them to come with me as I can. We'll all go and ask the security guys to open it up for us, really polite and nice-like. If they won't, *then* we'll kick the door down."

Twenty minutes later, Sammi squinted up at the words on the unlit neon sign above the door of Cherry Blossom

427

Sushi Bar. They were closed. Of course they were closed; it wasn't yet ten in the morning. He leaned against the door frame with a weary sigh. Vince was tracking down Dog and the Judd brothers, and Cain was catching up to Izzy. Sammi should have put a stop to this half-assed plan before Izzy made it out the front door. But he had been caught off-guard, wakened from uneasy dreams of glinting glass fragments and luminous dead-eyed monsters lurking in the dark and cold of outer space only to come face-to-face with the Engineer's accomplice.

Sammi peered into the darkened restaurant one more time, and halfheartedly jiggled the locked door. When he turned to leave, satisfied that he could at least tell Izzy he had tried, a thin, black-haired woman materialized from the darkness inside the building. She saw him before he could escape and cracked the door open, studying him with an air of disapproval.

"Harold's friend?" she said.

Sammi blinked stupidly at her for a moment. Then he remembered that Johnny Revolver's real name was Harold Yamamoto.

"Um...yes," he said. "I'm a friend of Harold's."

The woman—Johnny's mom, he assumed—yanked the door fully open.

"Back room," she grunted, gesturing with the blue rag in her hand.

Sammi stepped reluctantly over the threshold. Johnny's mom resumed washing the windows with a resigned shake of her head.

The inside of the restaurant was dark, except for one pool of yellow light that spilled through a doorway in the far left corner. Sammi made his way to the light, knocking into several tables while he walked.

The "back room" was a small private banquet hall with a long, narrow table. The table was scattered with empty beer bottles and an overflowing ashtray. The three members of Big Bertha—Johnny Revolver, AK Andrew, and Joey Gatling—sat together there, along with a very tiny, very pretty blonde woman who had Johnny's big arm draped over her shoulders. The men were in the middle of a card game.

"So, anyway, this drunk I was telling you about," said Johnny, studying the cards in his huge rough hands. "There we were, minding our own business at the bar, when he started groping on Viv. Right in front of me, man. I told him to back off. He took a swing at me. I dropped him. That's why our manager is pissed at me now."

"You must've dropped him pretty hard." AK Andrew looked up from his own hand, puffing on his cigar. "I haven't seen old Stick-In-The-Mud this pissed at you since you chucked Viv's shrink out the window."

Johnny glared at Andrew. "I didn't chuck him out the window, dumbass. I had a frank talk with him. I had to do something; the bastard was filling her head with lies."

Joey chuckled. "I guess you must have talked him right through the window, then. You're lucky that awning was there for him to land on."

"No, I would have been lucky if there had been an open sewer down there for him to drown in," grumbled Johnny.

"Come on, Johnny." The blonde woman—Viv, apparently—spoke up. "Give Dr. Wakefield a break. He was trying to help me."

Johnny's voice softened. "Yeah, I know, baby. But he was doing a shitty job. Giving people screaming nightmares about weird stuff that never really happened isn't helping them."

"But it did happen, Johnny." Viv looked hurt. "It must have happened. I remember it."

Sammi hovered in the doorway, waiting for an opportunity to announce himself. He cast a doubtful eye over Andrew and Johnny. They were both built like gorillas, though Johnny was a bit thinner. Andrew's massive biceps were slathered with tattooed images of guns and knives, and Johnny's olive-colored skin was pocked with dozens of scars from fights. Joey Gatling was somewhat more approachable with his slight frame and soft baby face. Sammi regarded him curiously. A rumor was going around the clubs that Joey had been a woman named Joanna before he started taking testosterone pills. Maybe Vince had gotten the idea for his stupid used-to-be-a-girl story from that rumor.

Joey must have sensed that someone was staring at him. He looked up, met Sammi's gaze, and grinned.

"Hey, dudes," he said. "We've got company."

Johnny and Viv stopped their argument. The steady stream of smoke trickling from Andrew's mouth faded. They all stared at Sammi.

"You that guy from the devil-boy's band?" said Andrew, without much enthusiasm.

Sammi gulped and nodded.

"What do you want?" growled Johnny. "Have you come to show us a magic trick?"

"Johnny, be nice," whispered Viv, casting a fearful glance at Sammi. "What if he, you know, *does* something?"

Johnny pulled her closer, and his tone became gentle again. "Babe, he's not gonna turn us into toads. I keep telling you, all that devil stuff isn't real; it's just hype to sell more records." He glared suspiciously at Sammi. "Why are you here? Our manager didn't send you to lure us out, did he?"

"No," squeaked Sammi. In the back of his mind, he knew that he could blast Johnny across the room with a lightning bolt before Johnny could throw a single punch, but he couldn't fight back his fear. Johnny Revolver simply exuded the air of someone people crossed the street to avoid. It was a wonder that timid, delicate little Viv could cuddle up to him so comfortably. With her glossy, perfect platinum-colored curls and fluttering sky-blue painted eyelids, she reminded Sammi of a porcelain doll.

"Oh yeah?" Johnny stood up and made his way around the table, squinting at Sammi. "This place isn't even open yet. Why else would you come here? Come on, you're helping Stick-In-The-Mud to bust us, aren't you?"

"No!" Sammi shook his head vigorously. "I swear I'm not! I've never even met your manager. Look, I didn't come here to start anything. I came to ask for your help."

"Is that a fact?"

Johnny crossed his arms over his chest and glowered, silently daring Sammi to convince him. Sammi took a deep breath.

"Look, this is going to sound really weird," he began. "But my band mates want to get into this one recording studio at Daggerspoint that's been closed for repairs forever, and they need some muscle to help convince the security guys to open it. They think there's...uh...something hidden in there."

"I'll bite," said Andrew, taking a drag on his cigar. "What do they think is in that studio?"

"They think the Engineer might keep his victims—"

Hands were suddenly around his throat, cutting him off. Johnny had practically flown the rest of the way around the table and grabbed him, pinning him to the wall.

"Are you shitting me right now?" he snarled.

"Urrrg…No!" Sammi gasped. "No…I promise…"

Johnny gave him a skeptical scowl, and his grip tightened. Sammi began to writhe in panic.

"Really!" he croaked. "Vince saw…her…woman who…took us…to Engineer."

Johnny let go.

"What's that?" he said gruffly.

Sammi slumped to the floor, shielding his face with his hands. "Her name is Chelsea, and she works for Mr. Arkin. Vince met her this morning and made her admit she lures people to Daggerspoint for the Engineer like she did to us, and I swear to God I'm telling the truth!"

Johnny stared at the wall, chewing his lip. Then he jerked his head at his band mates.

"Boys," he said, "get your crap together. We're going to Daggerspoint." He poked Sammi with his toe. "This better not be a joke. If we get into that studio and don't find anything, I'll kick your ass so hard your grandchildren will be sore."

Andrew and Joey tossed their cards down eagerly. Viv hung back, giving Sammi cockeyed glances until Johnny slipped back around the table and put his arms around her, whispering in her ear. She eventually followed him at a reluctant crawl, clinging to his hand.

Joey paused in the doorway as they all trooped out. He glanced down at Sammi, who was rubbing his neck and thanking his lucky stars that he only had to deal with Vince.

"Sorry about that," he said. "This Engineer stuff is kind

of a sore spot for Johnny. He was good friends with Jim Kellerman. Do you remember him?"

Sammi struggled to his feet. "Sure, I remember Jim. He was a hell of a bass player. Losing him was a shame."

"Yeah. Johnny took the news of his death pretty hard." Joey sighed. "Don't worry, we won't let him kick your ass if it turns out you guys were wrong about that studio. Just try to stay out of his way."

"Oh, I will," Sammi assured him.

"Good." Joey nodded in approval. "Oh, and I don't think you should do any of your weird magic stuff either. Viv has been going through some crap lately, and that kind of thing freaks her out. When people scare Johnny's girlfriend, they tend to make their way through second-story windows at a high rate of speed, if you know what I mean."

"Come on, Yuri," said Candi, glancing at her watch. "Jazz will bite our heads off if we walk in the door twenty minutes late again."

Yuri looked up from the stray dog he was petting. "Jazz survived two car wrecks, five drunken spills off the stage, and a cocaine overdose—waiting twenty minutes to start rehearsal one more time won't kill him."

Candi grinned wickedly. Neither she nor Yuri was particularly eager to get to rehearsal. Dawdling until Jazz was beside himself with frustration was the only enjoyable part of their band's interminable practices. They had gotten quite good at timing their entrance such that they often managed to saunter through the door at the exact moment he blew his top. Sometimes Candi did feel a twinge of guilt for leaving Ty alone to deal with their lead guitarist's bad temper, but Ty could take care of himself. Besides, even if she and Yuri were knocking themselves out to be on time, they would still be late most days because of the animals.

Today was no exception. Candi watched Yuri move among the tangle of cats, dogs, rats, and mice that pressed around his feet and climbed his pant legs. He believed that his father was some kind of Russian forest spirit, and sometimes she was halfway convinced that this idea was the only one of his weird Skeeter Judd-inspired notions that could have a grain of truth to it. Animals adored him. Mean old alley cats rubbed against him and cried for his attention. Mangy street dogs frisked around his ankles like puppies.

"Yeah, I agree," she said, bending down to pet the least nasty-looking dog in the group. "What will kill Jazz is that stick stuck so far up his ass you couldn't pull it out with fireplace tongs. That can't be good for his organs."

A pigeon flew down from a nearby roof and landed on Yuri's shoulder as he chuckled. The dog Candi was trying to pet saw her hand inching stealthily toward its head. It shrank away from her with a snarl, and she flinched.

"They might like you more if you loosened up a little." Yuri glanced at her, stroking the pigeon's back. "Animals know when you're tense."

"Or maybe they just don't like me."

A big yellow cat appeared around the corner and walked purposefully toward them. Candi ignored it at first, assuming that it would join the mob of flea-bitten fur at her band mate's feet. She was very surprised when it trotted up to her without so much as a glance at Yuri. It looked at her with pleading eyes.

Yuri chuckled. "That guy seems to like you."

Candi regarded the cat doubtfully. Her attempts to pet friends' cats usually ended with a hiss and a swipe. She had never had a cat come near her voluntarily, let alone gaze up at her with big, adoring eyes.

The cat mewed and stroked her calf with its paw. She looked to Yuri for guidance.

"Put your hand down, nice and slow," he suggested. "Let him sniff it."

Candi gave him a sideways glance. That tactic had never ended well for her in the past. Whatever scent or vibration Yuri gave off that attracted animals to him, she exuded the opposite one.

"What if that cat still has claws?" she said. "Jazz will kill me if I get my hand shredded and can't play bass."

"Please?" Yuri turned his most charming smile on her. "Come on, there's gotta be an animal that likes you out there. Just try. If you get hurt and Jazz gives you a hard time about it, I'll train a pigeon to crap in his hair."

"Will you make Jazz pay for my shots too?" Candi retorted. Still, it was hard to resist Yuri's smile. She bent down reluctantly to offer her hand.

The cat launched itself at her chest with a squeal of joy. She yelped and toppled backwards, involuntarily catching the animal in her flailing arms. Yuri ran to catch her, scattering startled dogs and cats around the alleyway.

"Oh, wow." Candi climbed to her feet, staring at the loudly purring cat in her arms. It squirmed in closer to her body and buried its face in her cleavage. "I guess you were right, Yuri. He definitely likes me. I don't think he'll let me put him down."

A big, dark shape rounded the corner before Yuri could reply. Most of the animals scattered with yelps of dismay when it stepped into the alley and advanced toward them. Candi's eyes narrowed warily when she caught sight of the figure's face and horns. She hadn't been present to witness the devil-boy's so-called transformation. And she had been certain that whatever Yuri had seen yesterday was a fantasy brought on by overexposure to Skeeter Judd's fibs. But now that Cain Pseudomantis was walking toward her, with his long tail swaying all-too-convincingly behind him, Skeeter's gothic stories about demon magic didn't seem as far-fetched.

Cain took a few more slow steps into the alley, scanning the area uncertainly, as if he had lost something. Then his eyes fell on Candi, and he stopped dead in his tracks.

"Izzy!" he cried. "What the…What are you *doing*? Stop that!"

Candi raised an eyebrow. She knew Izzy Unger by sight only, but he was hard to miss with his unruly lion's mane of golden hair and elaborate dragon-woman tattoo. If he was somewhere in this narrow little alley with her and Yuri, she certainly would have noticed him.

"Um…Candi?" said Yuri, pointing to her chest. "I think that cat really, *really* likes you."

Candi frowned. She had just begun to notice that the cat was steadily growing heavier in her arms. She looked down in time to see the last few patches of striped yellow fur recede into the skin of a very red-faced and sheepish Izzy.

"What the fuck?" She leapt back, pushing him away from her. "Get off me, creep!"

Izzy lurched backwards, overcorrecting his imbalance, and turned into a small bear. He rolled over with a grunt and then stood up again, slowly edging back into human form.

"I'm so sorry!" Cain scurried between Izzy and a very angry Candi. "He didn't mean any harm; really, he didn't. Sometimes he gets carried away."

"I'll say he does." Candi brushed herself off, giving both

of them a withering look. "What do you want?"

Cain swallowed and backed away from her, as if her fury unnerved him. Was Cain afraid of her? Candi found this idea amusing. She was barely five feet tall, but maybe her fire-engine red hair, long and cruelly sharp poison-green nails, and flashing dark blue eyes gave her an air of fierceness and unpredictability.

"Um...Izzy, why don't you tell her why we came?" he said.

"Huh? Oh, sure." Izzy stared at Candi with a big dreamy grin spread across his face, oblivious to the icy glower she was giving him in return. "We wanted to...um...we thought...hmm...I can't quite remember. It'll come to me in a second."

Yuri and Candi exchanged a suspicious glance.

"Come on, Izzy," Cain whispered. "Don't you remember? Chelsea? The Engineer?"

"What?" Izzy kept giving Candi puppy eyes. "Who's Chelsea and what does she have to do with...oh, *shit*!" He tensed, and his hair flushed a brighter shade of red than Candi's. "The Engineer! That's what we came to tell you— we know where the Engineer takes his victims!"

Yuri blinked like a startled owl. Candi's mouth fell open.

"What was that?" said Yuri.

"That Chelsea chick told us," Izzy babbled on, waving his arms in agitation. "Vince recognized her because she took him. She told all the guys who were killed that they were going to have meetings at Daggerspoint, and she took them there for the Engineer to get, except she took me and Sammi to her apartment instead, and the Engineer took us to Daggerspoint. He keeps them in a studio there that's been broken for a long time. There's still one guy missing. We've gotta get into that studio and save him. Come on, they're all waiting for us to get there!"

"What?" said Candi irritably. Izzy had talked so fast that she only picked up about a third of what he said. "Who will be waiting for us?"

"People from the clubs on the Strip, the ones who know that the Engineer is real. We're all gonna make them let us into the studio and save that poor guy."

Yuri frowned. "How will we make them let us in there?"

"Any way we can." Izzy turned into a greyhound and sprinted out of the alley. "Come on! That guy has been missing forever; he might be dying right now for all we know. Hurry!"

He disappeared around the corner. Cain groaned in exasperation and followed him at a run.

"Sorry," he called back to Candi and Yuri. "I've gotta keep an eye on him. He doesn't look where he's going when he's excited. We'll see you at Daggerspoint, I guess."

Candi and Yuri stared after him for a moment. Then they turned to stare at each other.

"What the flying fuck was that?" said Candi at last. "A cat jumps on me and turns into a horny dude; Cain Pseudomantis shows up; and we get some crazy-ass story about the studio. Fuck! I didn't take a double dose of my medicine again, did I?"

"Nope." Yuri knelt down to stroke a cat that had ventured out now that Cain and Izzy were gone. He glanced up at Candi, chuckling softly. "See, I told you those guys were for real."

Candi rolled her eyes.

"Maybe they're for real, and maybe they're not," she

growled. "All I know is I'm knocking that Izzy guy flat on his ass if he touches my boobs again. Come on, we should get to rehearsal. Jazz is probably ripping his hair out by now."

Yuri seemed to have the same idea. He was walking resolutely down the alley, the cat scampering along at his heels.

"Come on," he called back over his shoulder. "Let's catch up."

"Catch up to who?"

Yuri grinned at her. "To Cain and Izzy, of course."

"Wait." Candi scrambled after him. "You want to blow off practice for some sort of wild goose chase at Daggerspoint?"

"It might not be a wild goose chase," said Yuri. "They say the devil-boy's band mates are the only guys who were taken by the Engineer and lived to tell about it."

Candi made a face. "Yeah, but they also say that the devil-boy's band mates are all a few bricks short of a load. You saw that guy jumping around and blabbering on. There might not even be a Chelsea or a closed studio at Daggerspoint."

"Oh, there's a closed studio, all right. I saw it the last time I was there." Yuri threw an arm around her shoulders. "Honestly, Candi, where's your sense of adventure? You've been talking my ear off for months about how you'd like to take care of the Engineer, once and for all."

"Yuri, I'm *not* getting myself arrested for breaking into a studio at Daggerspoint because a magical pervert hallucinated the boogeyman in there."

Yuri's green eyes gleamed with mischief.

"Jazz will hate it, you know."

Candi's eyes narrowed suspiciously. She knew what he was doing.

"Yup," he continued. "Jazz will be so pissed about it. Not only will we miss rehearsal, but if everyone is there like Izzy said, and Jazz misses all the excitement, he'll flip out. And he *will* miss the excitement, you know. He won't let anyone drag him out of his precious practice for *any* reason. And when he finds out afterward that we were there—oh, he'll shit a brick! Won't that be worth seeing?"

"Dammit, Yuri. I hate you sometimes." Candi sighed. "Well, let's catch up with the devil-boy. We've got a wild goose chase to join."

There was no sign of the promised multitude when they got to the Daggerspoint headquarters. Cain finally got Izzy to stop mooning over Candi, and they stood on the cement steps in front of the building, scanning the stream of pedestrians on the sidewalk for familiar faces.

"Well?" Candi rapped her long fingernails against the iron banister. "Where is everyone?"

"I'm not sure," said Cain anxiously. Sammi and Vince weren't usually late.

"I think there's some kind of loading area around back," said Izzy. "Maybe they went to wait there."

As if on cue, a very agitated Sammi burst out of the narrow alley that led to the area behind the building. He flew up the stairs, completely ignoring Candi and Yuri, and began yelling at his own band mates.

"God damn it!" he shouted. "I've been waiting here with the Big Bertha guys for a good half-hour. Where the hell have you been?"

"Johnny and Andrew and Joey are here?" Izzy squinted

into the street. "I don't see them."

"They're hiding behind the building. They didn't want their manager to know they were here." Sammi coughed impatiently. "Do you have any idea how many times Joey had to talk Johnny and Andrew out of beating my ass for dragging them out here while you guys were dawdling? Now where the fuck is Vince? And why do those fucking cars keep honking? You didn't let Izzy run into the street and cause an accident, did you?"

Cain looked up. An unusual number of car horns were indeed honking, and most of the noise was coming from a nearby side street. He saw the problem right away: a huge group was crossing the street. They formed a line so long that he couldn't see where it ended. Big gangs of oblivious tourists in this area were nothing new to Cain. He had seen several of them filing up to look at the building on his way to recording sessions. He paid little attention to this one until the red-headed young man at the front of the column broke away and pelted across the street, narrowly avoiding several cars on the way.

"Thank God!" Vince heaved a huge sigh of relief when he reached the sidewalk. "I thought I'd never get away from that blowhard. I swear he didn't shut his mouth once all the way here."

Cain followed Vince's annoyed glare across the street and saw Skeeter Judd's trademark sequin-encrusted cowboy hat bobbing along at the front of the enormous crowd.

"Vince, what the fuck?" Sammi stared at the crowd making its way across the street, which was causing more stopped traffic and shrieking horns. "I thought you were just going to get the boys from Hellhound. Who are all those other people?"

Vince threw up his arms in resignation. "Hey, it's not my fault. That moron Skeeter had to drag along everyone he knows."

Cain scanned the crowd one more time. There were about twenty familiar faces at the front of the line, but the sixty or seventy bodies shuffling along behind them might have been aliens from Mars for all he knew.

Sammi seemed to agree. "I doubt Skeeter personally knows all those people, Vinnie," he said.

"I'm sorry." Vince rolled his eyes. "Did I say everyone he knows? I meant everyone he met on the street who would stand still long enough for him to talk at them. I told you he couldn't keep his mouth shut! He must have dragged about a million Hellhound fans with us, *plus* those tabloid reporters, a few hookers, a couple tourists, and a bum or two. He even insisted on tracking down some guys who roadied for him."

Skeeter had found his way across the street. He sauntered up to Vince and clapped him on the shoulder as if they were old friends.

"Hey, there's strength in numbers, right?" he said. "If we're gonna beat the Engineer today, we've gotta have superior firepower. Besides, I don't know why everyone is always so down on roadies. I *like* roadies. They listen to my stories."

Vince curled his fingers and clenched his teeth so hard that Cain was surprised they didn't shatter. Sammi wagged a warning finger at him.

The crowd began to break apart. The regular club-goers, along with a few curious teenage fans, wandered up and stood in a little half-circle around the stairs. The others milled around in the street, talking among themselves, snapping pictures of the building, and further clogging the already congested flow of traffic.

The group around the bottom of the stairs tightened. Someone in the crowd coughed, and Izzy began to fidget impatiently. Cain became aware that they were all looking at him.

"Hey, devil-boy!" A man in a pink-and-blue leopard print t-shirt and acid-washed jeans spoke up. Cain recognized him as Keenan MacFarlane, the guitarist for Warning Signs. "Do you mind telling me what the fuck is going on? Skeeter Judd just barged into my apartment babbling about some kind of weird-ass conspiracy. I thought for sure he was drunk, but your thug of a lead singer wouldn't let me give him some coffee and toss him out. He said he'd eat my energy if I didn't follow them to Daggerspoint."

Cain swallowed nervously, casting around for words. Keenan's face wasn't the only grouchy, suspicious one in the gaggle of long-haired men and denim-clad women gathered at the foot of the stairs. He was tempted to tell them that this whole affair was Izzy's idea, not his.

"Well," he began. "See…um…I know it sounds strange, but we think the Engineer has been keeping his victims here, in an empty recording studio."

The suspicion in the faces staring up at him didn't subside. Keenan said something nasty-sounding under his breath.

"Look, I know it sounds hard to believe," Sammi broke in. "But we have evidence."

"Oh yeah?" said a man in a leather jacket whose face Cain didn't recognize. "What evidence?"

"The Engineer's accomplice—the woman who led the Engineer's victims to him—works here. Vince recognized her this morning. Now he remembers how she lured him off to Daggerspoint by promising him a meeting with someone high-up and then drugged him—just like it happened yesterday."

Vince glowered, but Sammi subtly pointed a finger at his chest, and he said nothing.

"She brought all of the victims here for the Engineer to pick up," Sammi continued. "We heard that fact right from her lips. I swear to God. She couldn't say where he took them afterward, but we have a theory."

"Yeah, that he keeps 'em in that one studio that's been closed for so long," Skeeter piped up. "That sure does explain a few things. Why, I was walking down that hall just last night, and I was sure I heard screams coming from—"

"You know what, Skeet?" Goober interrupted him. "I bet it would come in handy to have someone guard the back door. If the Engineer is here right now, he might try to escape."

"Ooh! I bet you're right!" Skeeter dashed up the stairs past Cain and Sammi, seemingly unaware of the simultaneous sigh of relief that Goober and Dog let out while he vanished into the building. Yuri broke away from the crowd and followed him.

"Hey, a guy has gotta have backup," he yelled over his shoulder when Candi protested. Cain wondered if Yuri offered backup just so he could listen to Skeeter's stories.

The rest of the crowd did not move. They hung back and whispered among themselves until Keenan appointed himself their spokesperson and moved closer to the stairs, crossing his arms.

"So what if you're wrong?" he said. "What if that broken studio is just a broken studio, and the missing guy isn't there?"

The doors banged open behind them before Cain or Sammi could answer. Johnny, Viv, Andrew, and Joey filed out, followed by an irate security guard who stood in the doorway, glaring after Johnny and Andrew.

"Don't come back here till you've learned to keep those tempers under control!" he shouted after them. "If I had my way, you wouldn't be back at all!"

He shot one last glower at the knot of young men at the foot of the stairs, muttered something about young hooligans loitering in the street, and then vanished into the building. Johnny didn't seem at all concerned that he had just been thrown out in disgrace in front of everyone; he swaggered up to Sammi, threw an arm over his shoulder, and grinned down at the crowd.

"What if the missing guy is not there, you ask?" he said to Keenan. "Easy—we decide what to do after we find out the truth."

There was a slight edge to his voice as he made this assertion. Cain noticed Sammi shifting uncomfortably beneath Johnny's arm. Cain gave him a sideways glance, but Sammi just shrugged.

"I know what you're saying," Johnny continued. "The whole thing sounds fishy to me too, honestly. But I think it's at least worth checking out."

Keenan's expression became more sullen. He had dark circles under his eyes, and he blinked and squinted as though the sunlight hurt him. Cain wondered if Skeeter and Vince hadn't roused him from an attempt to sleep off a bad hangover.

"Yeah, well, maybe it is worth *someone* checking out," he muttered. "But why the fuck should we do it? We're not cops."

Johnny's arm fell away from Sammi's shoulder. He stalked down the stairs and advanced on Keenan, his face stormy.

"Why shouldn't we do it?" he said in a quiet, eerily calm voice that Cain found ten times more frightening than Vince's most out-of-control tantrum. "You think the cops gave a damn about Ted Hanson? Foxy Fred? The Cochran brothers? Huh? Hell, I tried to call the cops when Jim Kellerman was taken. Do you know what they said? They said that my friend was probably just passed out drunk somewhere, and they told me to stop wasting their time. I could've told 'em Jimmy never drank without a friend who would make sure he got home safely, if they hadn't *hung up* on me."

Cain watched the crowd while Johnny made his speech. A few people still looked skeptical, but sorrow and cold anger were steadily overriding any lingering signs of doubt on most of their faces. He wondered how many of them had been through similar ordeals with missing friends.

"Fucking useless pigs." Johnny's voice rose and broke a bit. "You'd think they'd have started taking us seriously when they found Jimmy dead, right? Well, they didn't. If you want to make a cop toss you into the drunk tank when you ain't drunk, all you have to do is mention the Engineer. They think we made him up. And the bodies keep piling up; eight are dead for sure, last I heard. It would've been eleven if the devil-boy's band mates hadn't been found through sheer dumb luck. So no, we're not cops, but it's on us to take care of our own. Come on, let's go. If that last missing guy is anywhere in this building, I'm not leaving till we get him out!"

He turned and stormed back into the building. Viv scurried after him, as if she didn't want to be left outside on the doorstep with Cain and Sammi. The others stayed put for a moment. Then Goober and Dog broke away and dashed up the stairs. Candi plodded reluctantly after them. Everyone else followed, gradually, in twos and threes, until only Keenan and one confused teenage boy in a threadbare Hellhound shirt stood on the sidewalk. The boy glanced at Keenan, shrugged, and started up the stairs. Keenan lagged after him, grumbling all the way.

Sammi and Cain went in last. Joey popped up between them when they stepped over the threshold.

"Huh, Johnny is crazy, but he sure knows how to work a crowd," he said to Sammi. "So is this the devil-boy we've all been hearing so much about?"

Sammi nodded. "Cain, this is Joey Gatling. He's the drummer for Big Bertha."

"Drummer and Johnny-wrangler." Joey shrugged. "So, what's your plan for getting into that studio?"

"Izzy thinks we should ask one of the security guards nicely to open it for us," said Cain.

"You think that'll work?"

Sammi winced. "God, I hope so. His plan B involves kicking the door down."

Joey pulled something shiny out of his jeans pocket and tossed it to Sammi. "Eh, I don't think it'll come to that. Here, you might need these."

"Keys?" Sammi blinked in surprise after he caught the object. "How did you get…?"

"Easy," said Joey. "Skeeter Judd and Yuri Ustinov let us in through the back door, we all went to the lobby, and Johnny and Andrew faked having a fistfight. Viv got in on it too, made like she was scared and started screaming. Anyway, while that security guy was busy yelling at Johnny and Andrew to knock it off and at Viv to calm down, I took his keys off him. We thought you'd need them."

"Damn." Sammi stared reverently at the keys. "That was brilliant."

Joey chuckled. "It was Viv's idea, actually. She can be pretty damn smart when she feels like it." A hint of anxiety crept into his tone. "By the way, I'd stay out of Johnny's way for at least a week if I were you guys. Now our manager is gonna be pissed at him even more. Not only did he beat up that drunk at the bar, but now he also made a big scene at Daggerspoint."

Some of the tourists from Skeeter's gang had wandered in with the rescue team. They meandered through the halls, stopping to look at things or to take pictures at random intervals, without regard for anyone trying to get past them. They held up the group directly as well. Cain noticed Dog and Andrew being pulled out of line to sign autographs and a hapless Keenan fleeing a gang of girls who were aggressively flirting with him. At one point, he felt something grip his tail and turned around to find a tiny boy staring up at him with a look of utter bewilderment in his eyes.

"Snake?" he said to Cain.

"Henry!" The boy's mother descended on him and pried his pudgy hands off Cain's tail. "You get away from that man right now! What have I told you about talking to strangers?"

"Snake, mommy!" The boy pointed wildly at Cain, his eyes wide.

The woman snatched him up and hurried away. "It's just

a silly costume, sweetie. Come on, we'll have daddy take us away from this nasty place, and we'll go get ice cream."

Cain scurried off to rejoin the group with his tail held as high as it would go to discourage any more tail-grabbing. He was glad that his ability to stay patient with acquisitive human children had strengthened since the day he bit Lance.

Finally, they reached the hall with the studios. It was very tightly packed once they had all squeezed into the corridor. Sammi and Cain almost had to climb over several people to get to studio 4B. Sammi pushed the first key on the ring into the lock and attempted to turn it; it didn't work.

"Crap—there are enough keys on this ring to lock up the entire city of Pasadena," he muttered while he tried the next one. "This could take a while."

"Why don't I save you some time, then?"

Mr. Arkin was standing in the doorway to his office with his arms crossed. Everyone turned to look at him, and the tense buzz of their talk died down.

"Sammi," he continued. "What are you doing? You know that studio is out of order—and how on earth did you get those keys?"

Izzy had been standing on the other side of Sammi, eagerly awaiting the opening of the door. Now that Mr. Arkin had appeared on the scene, he turned into a cat and tried to slink guiltily off into the crowd. Sammi bent down and caught him by the ear before he could escape.

"Oh, no you don't," he hissed. "This was your idea. You get to tell the boss what we're doing."

Izzy changed back and stood staring at Mr. Arkin, as if frozen in terror, until Sammi elbowed him in the side and mouthed the words *tell him now*.

"We had to!" he blurted. "Please, oh please, don't drop

us from the label or get us arrested! The police don't care, so we had to—"

"Had to what?" Mr. Arkin raised an eyebrow.

"The last guy the Engineer took is in that studio!" Izzy remembered the urgency of his mission again. He snatched the keys from Sammi and started jamming them into the lock at random. "We've gotta get in there right now. He's been gone for weeks!"

"*What*? You really think…of all the hare-brained…" Mr. Arkin took a deep breath, as if forcing himself to speak calmly. "Look, I don't know where you got that idea, but it's simply not true. There's nothing behind that door except four walls that a drunk sound engineer kicked in afterhours one night—certainly nothing worth staging an angry brawl in the lobby over."

Johnny and Joey kept their expressions neutral, but Andrew looked a tiny bit guilty. "We didn't—"

Mr. Arkin sighed. "Don't bother, Andrew. I know my artists. When Tom from security told me that he'd just broken up a fight between AK Andrew and Johnny Revolver in the lobby, I knew something was fishy. Johnny is a mean SOB, but he's also loyal enough that he'd never lay a hand on his own band mate. The brawl was a diversion, wasn't it?"

Andrew nodded. Mr. Arkin shook his head.

"I am impressed by your ability to organize, anyway," he said in a weary voice. "Say, Izzy, would you mind not jamming any more keys into that lock? I don't want it to break too."

"I'm almost done," said Izzy, wrenching the ill-fitted key violently from the hole. "It's gotta be one of these three. I've tried all the others."

"It isn't. The key to studio 4B isn't on that ring."

Candi pushed her way through the crowd and walked up to Mr. Arkin.

"So where is it?" she asked.

Cain watched her face curiously. She didn't seem abashed by Mr. Arkin's presence like the others, and Mr. Arkin's expression became cautious and guarded when she approached him.

"Only a few higher-ups here have keys to that studio," he said reluctantly. "We don't have anyone booked to fix it yet, and not many people need to get into it."

"I assume you've got a key," said Candi. "Would you let us in?" Her tone made it clear that this was not a request.

"I'd really rather not."

"We just want a quick look inside."

"Candi, I'm telling you, there's nothing in there to see."

"Then what's the harm?" She gave him a disarming smile. "You open the door for a second; we all take a peek and see for ourselves that there's nothing there; and then we never bother you about it again. Come on, I promise you nobody is going to mess up that studio any more than it already is. Ten minutes to clear up a creepy rumor—that's all we ask."

Mr. Arkin stared over Candi's shoulder at the locked door to studio 4B, chewing his lip.

"All right," he said at last. "But don't get into the habit of thinking you can rule this place by mob. This here is a strictly one-time event."

He trudged into his office. Candi watched him go and then turned to the others with a triumphant grin on her face. Cain and Sammi stared at her in frank admiration, and Izzy began to look lovelorn again.

Mr. Arkin was in his office for nearly fifteen minutes. Cain had started to wonder whether he really had any intention of coming back when he finally emerged and walked over to them with a disgruntled air, carrying a small silver key.

"I had to rip up every drawer in my desk to find this damn thing," he grumbled. "Remember, just one quick look, and then I don't want to hear any of you so much as mention the word *Engineer* to me again. Got it?"

He turned the key in the lock and threw the door open.

CHAPTER EIGHTEEN

SECRETS

THE FIRST THING CAIN noticed was the smell. It rolled out into the hallway as soon as the door opened. The others near the front of the line seemed to notice it as well. Candi staggered back with a disgusted grunt, Sammi and Izzy covered their noses, and Johnny made a face.

"Satisfied now?" Mr. Arkin gestured impatiently into the empty control room, oblivious to the stench. "There's no one in—"

"Hell no! I'm not satisfied." Candi stepped over the threshold. "Where's that awful smell coming from?"

"Candi, wait." Mr. Arkin made a halfhearted grab for her wrist, but she shook him off. Joey Gatling broke away from Johnny's side and followed her, giving Mr. Arkin a jaunty what-can-you-do shrug. They stood in the control room for a moment, looking around uneasily.

"It seems clean enough." Candi ran a finger along the mixing console and inspected the thick layer of dust she had picked up. "Well...if you can call this clean, that is."

"Dust shouldn't reek like that." Joey opened the door to the machine room and peered inside. "It smells like a rat got in here and died somewhere—at least I hope it's a rat."

Candi bent over the console, levering herself up on her toes to gain some height, and squinted through the rectangular window above it. A puzzled line appeared on her brow.

Mr. Arkin coughed and stepped closer to the open door, making an impatient beckoning motion with his hand. Cain could tell that he was nearly bursting with eagerness to get Candi and Joey out of the studio, but he also seemed reluctant to go inside himself.

"*Now* are you satisfied?" he said.

"Nope." Candi turned and gave him a wary look. "Those walls you said got kicked in look fine to me. And why is there a bed in the live room?"

"A...what?"

"A bed. There's a bed in the live room. What's it doing there?"

Mr. Arkin fell back a step.

"A bed?" he muttered. "That can't be. That's ridiculous. Why on earth would there be...?"

"Oh, for fuck's sake!" Candi strode resolutely to the door and grabbed his hand. "Here, come see for yourself."

Mr. Arkin allowed himself to be dragged inside. Cain followed him, almost involuntarily; something was drawing him into the studio despite the sense of foreboding building inside him. The others hung back in the hallway, except Johnny, who took a deep breath and trudged after Cain.

"Stay with Andrew, babe," he said when Viv started to follow him.

"See?" Candi had Mr. Arkin by the window now. She pointed at the smudged glass. "Like I told you, there's a bed in there."

"What the hell?" Mr. Arkin opened the door to the

studio proper and stepped in.

The smell was stronger inside the inner studio. Cain tried to breathe slowly and shallowly when he stepped through the door after Mr. Arkin, but the stench still crept into his nostrils, making his eyes water and his gorge rise. It was an acrid smell, with an undertone of sickly sweetness, and it reminded him of something unpleasant he knew he had once seen. He had a garbled recollection of an unidentifiable, enormous animal collapsing to the ground, dark red fluid gushing from its neck.

Then Johnny shoved his way past Cain, and the memory was lost.

"Shit," said Johnny. "That little twitchy dude was right. There was something going on in here."

Cain held his breath and took stock of his surroundings. This studio was bigger than the one where they had recorded their album. A hospital gurney sat in the middle of its polished floor. He edged closer to the gurney, inspecting the sprinkling of rust on its dented metal frame. The sleek, unblemished walls and recording equipment surrounding it gave it a jarring and out-of-place look.

"How strange," said Mr. Arkin. "I have no idea what that's doing here—I'm sure there's a logical explanation, though."

Candi began rummaging through one of the little isolation booths at the far end of the studio. She quickly emerged from the room, carrying something long, thin, and brown.

"I think this is your logical explanation," she said quietly.

Cain stared at the object in her hand. It was a leather bandolier with the black hilts of about a dozen knives poking from its pouches. One pouch near the bottom was empty. Mr. Arkin went pale.

"There are other nasty things in that room," she continued, shaking the bandolier accusingly at Mr. Arkin. "There are needles and tubes and bottles of oozy green stuff—pretty much anything you could think of to use as props in a gory horror movie. Even if we're wrong and nothing in this place has anything to do with the Engineer, *somebody* was definitely up to no good in here."

Joey had quietly crept into the main studio. He yanked off the stiff and grimy gray army blanket that covered the gurney. The lumpy mattress beneath it was stained with ominous brown spatters. Three flat wooden protrusions with long leather straps jutted from the gurney's frame. They did not look as if they had originally been part of the structure; the wood and leather seemed much newer. Someone had bolted them there: two were at the sides about ten inches below the headrest, and the third was at the foot of the bed. The straps hung open as if waiting to receive the next young man's wrists and ankles.

"Amen to that." Joey reached down with a shudder and picked up the end of another leather strap that looped under the gurney. It was long enough to clamp around the waist of a thrashing victim. "I think it's time you called the police, Mr. Arkin. They won't listen to us, but they might actually listen to you now."

Mr. Arkin gave no reply. He leaned heavily against the wall, staring at the gurney, his face ashen.

A loud crash made Cain's head snap up in surprise. Johnny had punched the glass out of the door to the other isolation booth. He leaned forward and pushed his arm into the small rectangular hole where the window used to be, reaching for something on the other side.

"Hang in there, kid," he said in a strange fevered voice to someone none of them could see. "We're gonna get you out of here. I just need to get this damn door open."

"Johnny!" Mr. Arkin snapped out of his shock. "What on earth are you doing? You promised not to mess up the studio any further!"

He shot Candi an accusing look. Candi shrugged.

"You should've unlocked the door then," growled Johnny, pulling his arm back and punching the frame in frustration. "Fuck. I can't quite reach—"

"Unlocked the door? How could...the isolation booth doors don't lock, Johnny."

Johnny ignored them. He braced his foot against the wall, clamped his hands around the handle, and gave the door a vicious yank. The door ripped off its hinges in an explosion of creaking wood and squealing steel. Mr. Arkin winced, and Joey dodged a bit of flying debris.

"Deadbolt," Joey said, bending down to pick up the bulky square of dark metal that had almost hit him.

Mr. Arkin said something that Cain didn't hear. He could no longer shut out the foul smell or the unpleasant spinning sensation behind his temples. His knees threatened to give way under him. He sat down on the edge of the gurney, rubbing his eyes, unable to stand being in the studio for another minute yet somehow unable to walk out.

"Oh my god." Candi stumbled back against the gurney, shaking him out of his half-faint. He looked up, and he immediately wanted to vomit.

The isolation room lay open before him. Inside it, Cain could see a bundle of rags and old pillows arranged into a crude bed. On the bed, huddled in the corner, was a scrawny boy who looked to be about sixteen. Long, tangled, greasy hair partially covered his face, and he was so pale that the line of stitched cuts peppering his arms stood out like slashes of ink on paper. One of the more recent cuts was swollen and festering with yellow pus. The boy's bones stood out in sharp relief under his sunken skin. He stared at his rescuers with glassy, listless eyes, too weak to raise his head.

Cain made a sound of anguish deep within his throat. He used to imagine the act of a soul leaving its body to be an easy, peaceful process, like shucking off an uncomfortable wool coat. But it wasn't easy or peaceful; it was agonizing and cruel and sordid. The soft rasps and gurgles of the dying boy fighting for his last few breaths distressed Cain beyond measure.

"*Now* do you believe us?" Johnny's voice sounded distorted and far away. "Go call an ambulance, for fuck's sake. We've gotta get him out of here *now*."

Something shifted in Cain's mind. A dark shape that might have been Mr. Arkin moved past him, exiting the room. His friends and acquaintances exchanged more words, but he couldn't make out any of them. The world was spinning around him as it had that night after he ate the chocolate bar. The walls wobbled and undulated like wheat on a windy plain. Candi's, Joey's, and Johnny's faceless forms flitted vaguely in front of him, chattering in nonsensical whispers. Nothing in the room looked real.

Except the soul.

Cain noticed it gradually—a tiny speck of light bobbing among the shadow puppets. It made its way in his direction, becoming more solid and distinct. He could pick out its features by the time it floated past the gurney, leaving a luminous string of bluish mist in its wake. It had the face of the boy in the isolation booth.

The soul made its way slowly to the open door. The odd vapor trail it was giving off grew thinner as it went and was soon on the verge of disappearing altogether. Cain had never seen anything like the vapor before. He forced his eyes to follow its path. It snaked back to the body in the isolation room, like a diver's air hose, or a vein.

"I'm afraid it's no good." Candi's voice became clear for a moment, filtering through the impenetrable buzz of white noise that rang in Cain's ears. "He's too far gone."

No.

Cain struggled to his feet. The floor rippled beneath him. He had to steady himself against the gurney for a moment before staggering to the isolation booth. That boy wouldn't die, not if he could do anything about it. He followed the faded ribbon of mist that seemed to connect soul to body, struggling to stay upright on the heaving floor. The boy's features finally became clear. Not knowing what else to do, he knelt down, concentrated, and released as much healing energy as his fogged mind could muster. The effort left him winded and gasping. The ruined body absorbed his spell like a dry sponge, showing little visible improvement. Cain almost gave up.

Then the boy's blank eyes snapped into focus, and the misty trail briefly flashed with an electric glow.

Blood rushed in Cain's ears while he mustered the force for one last try. When he released the amassed energy, he felt as if his life was being torn out of him. He crumpled to the floor, unable to move or talk or even lift his head. A tremor of satisfaction ran through him when he caught a glimpse of the wayward soul drifting slowly but steadily in the direction of its body.

Michael Anderson found an artist's pad and a pack of colored pencils lying on his bedside table that morning. He pounced on them like a starving man on food. His brain was roiling, and his next pill would not arrive until lunch.

A voice hissed in the background of his mind while he sketched. This noise wasn't the clamor of the elementals; they had quieted down hours ago. This voice, a steady and persistent whisper, was something far more insidious. It came from somewhere within himself, from a long-ago blocked-off corner of his brain. He supposed the doctors here would call the voice his subconscious. He had never told anyone about the whisper, not even the kind doctor. He didn't want her to get curious about it. Studying the voice would mean dragging it out into the open and giving it free reign.

The last time he had allowed the voice free reign, he had awakened to find a stranger's mangled corpse at his feet and his mother dead.

Michael swiped the pencils eagerly over the page, thickening lines, adding color, brushing in shadows. Not being allowed to draw whenever the mood struck him had been agony. Drawing was the only thing that quieted the voice down. He could feel it dying away to a soft hum in the back of his mind, just like it did after he took the pills. As long as he drew, the voice couldn't make him know things.

On the other hand, he could only draw what the voice wanted him to know. It was a vicious cycle, really.

Michael sketched a man hesitating by the threshold of a door. The door stayed vague and ill-defined while he filled in the other details. He knew that it wasn't important.

Instead, he focused on the man, giving special care to his face. He had seen that face many times before, in dreams and in fits and in the momentary darkness his blinking eyelids created. That face was one of the things the voice made him know. It frightened him, yet there was something about it that drew him in—some memory, some long-ago, half-formed glimpse into the distant past.

The voice grew unquiet.

Michael scribbled harder. He mustn't think about it. He must simply draw. The voice went quiet again.

Yet the presence behind the voice was still there.

It was there when he filled in a touch of shadow on the man's cheek. It was there when he wondered which of the three blue pencils would best capture the blue of the man's eyes. It was there when he sharpened the points of the horns and when he went back to add a slight correction to the curve of the tail.

It was there.

It was always there.

Go in, it said to the man on the paper as he drew. *Don't fear. Go through the door.*

Michael paused in his drawing to fiercely smudge the already ill-defined door.

Dark Lion in the wild heart of the city, said the voice, *open the door and behold the horror of the Righteous Man's works.*

Michael tried to turn the page—he could come back to this drawing later—but he couldn't. The man who had the horns and tail of a demon held his attention. The voice continued speaking, gaining strength.

I know you, Dark Lion. I remember you well. Do you remember me?

Michael clamped his hands over his mouth. He had, without intending to, said these words out loud. Thankfully no doctor was there to hear.

The next few hours were a blur. Cain had muddled memories of people flooding into the studio. Then someone's arms were around his waist, hefting him out of the way. He had no idea how he got back to the house and up to his room, but he clearly remembered collapsing into bed with a groan of relief. He was asleep before his head hit the pillow.

The room was dark when he awoke. He was about to roll over and go back to sleep when noises from downstairs roused him—bangs and thuds, unfamiliar voices, and a high-pitched scream. The events of the day rushed into his mind, causing a torrent of fear. Then the door flew open behind him, and he leapt up with a strangled growl, fully expecting to confront the Engineer coming for revenge.

The people at the door staggered back with shrieks of fright. To his surprise and relief, Cain recognized Keenan MacFarlane's leopard print shirt. The two miniskirt-clad girls on either side of Keenan were also familiar; he had seen them at various after-show parties at the clubs.

"Hey, man, what's your problem?" said Keenan. "No need to snarl at us like that—the ladies wanted to meet you."

"Oh, come on, Kee." The taller of the two girls squeezed his bicep playfully. "Try not to be such a grump for once. I mean, how often do you get to talk to a guy who can perform real miracles?"

Cain stared at her in utter bafflement. Before he could open his mouth to ask her what in the world she was talking about, Sammi muscled his way into the room and planted himself firmly between Cain and the three interlopers.

"The show is over," he said. "Let's all go back downstairs and enjoy the party, okay?"

"Well, who died and made you the king of Hollywood?" Keenan glared at Sammi. "We wanted to meet the guy who kicked the Engineer's ass—hell, everyone does. When is he coming down?"

Sammi made an imperious shooing motion with his arms. "Like I've been saying, he'll come down when he's ready. He's shy. You've just gotta be patient with him; give him some space."

"But we've already been patient!" The other girl made a pouty face. "We've been waiting for, like, a whole hour!"

"Then waiting a little longer won't kill you."

Sammi crossed his arms and squared his shoulders. Keenan balled his hands into fists, but the taller girl tugged his arm.

"I wouldn't start with him, Kee," she whispered. "Remember what he did to that redheaded guy who almost hit Skeeter?"

Keenan tried to stare Sammi down a little longer. Then he turned on his heel and stalked off, muttering something about pushy little piss-ants. The two girls hurried along in his wake. Sammi swung the door closed behind them with a sigh of relief.

"Sorry about that," he said to Cain. "The whole damn world wants to see you, and they couldn't get it into their heads that you were sleeping. I've been trying to keep them out of your room, but I've got a lot on my plate. Vince keeps picking fights with people downstairs."

"What are they doing here?" The townhouse had not seen many visitors. It was only a ten-minute bus ride from the clubs, but it was also in what Mr. Arkin called a "recovering neighborhood." Cain was not clear on what the neighborhood was recovering from, but as far as he could glean from Vince's gripes, this statement somehow meant that the people who lived around them all expected each other to be impeccably quiet and never have any fun whatsoever.

"Partying." Sammi shook his head. "It started out on the Strip, but folks started trickling over here when you didn't show. Speaking of which, do you think you might possibly be ready to come down soon? I know you're tired, but I've got a mini-riot on my hands."

"They want to see *me*?" Cain gaped at Sammi. People never sought him out at parties. In fact, a lot of the regular partygoers at the clubs still went out of their way to avoid him.

"Hey, you heard Keenan: they want to meet the guy who kicked the Engineer's ass."

"But I didn't kick the Engineer's ass. The Engineer wasn't even in the studio."

"The last victim was, though."

Cain sat down heavily on the bed. A vivid memory of the ravaged boy in the isolation booth flashed into his mind.

"Is he all right now?" he asked, gripping the bedspread anxiously.

"Dunno. I heard he made it to the hospital alive. One of the paramedics said that he'd probably make it. They got him out of the studio just in time." Sammi gave him a sideways glance. "So...um...if you don't mind my asking, what exactly happened in there?"

Cain's tail twitched while he tried to think. His recollection of the last few hours was still hazy.

"What are people saying happened in there?" he said at last.

"Depends on who you ask," said Sammi. "Johnny and Candi are pretty well convinced that the kid died and you brought him back to life somehow. Skeeter thinks you brought him back to life *and* mauled the crap out of the Engineer, and he's got way more people listening to his side of the story than usual this time."

"I didn't bring him back to life," said Cain weakly. "He was still alive."

"Joey thinks he was still alive too," said Sammi. "He says it looked more like the kid was about to die and you sacrificed your own energy to keep him alive till the ambulance got there—like what Vince does, except in reverse. I believe *him*, personally."

"But weren't you there?" Cain clutched his head. That muddled image in his mind of a big crowd rushing into the studio, talking all at once around him...When exactly had that happened? "You must have seen—"

"I didn't," said Sammi. "I never set foot in that studio, Cain. Izzy didn't either. We were about to follow you when you went in, but we both just...froze. Some of the others followed the paramedics in when they showed up, but not us. We stayed in the hallway freaking out." He shuddered. "Vince couldn't take it. He sneaked out of the building to have a smoke the second we turned our backs on him. I'm sorry we wimped out on you, man, but it was just way too much—"

Another scream from downstairs interrupted him. Sammi threw up his hands in disgust and bolted for the door.

"God damn it!" he shouted. "Can't Vince keep his hands to himself for five fucking minutes? Hang on. I'll be right back."

Cain climbed out of bed. He paced slowly around the room, agitated. What had happened in that studio? His last clear memory was of slipping into an odd chaotic dream state that reminded him uncomfortably of his chocolate-induced hallucinations. He also vaguely remembered the blurred image of a disembodied soul teetering on the brink of escape and the rush of energy he expended to bring it back.

A brief wave of dizziness rolled through him, and he put his hand on the wall for support. His mind wandered to an old image of Steve sitting on the floor of his father's study with a big book open in his lap. Maybe Steve could help clear up the mystery. He started toward the phone, but after two steps, he remembered the phone was in the kitchen, and now there was a mob of drunken partygoers between him and the kitchen. He wasn't ready to talk to all those people just yet. Besides, it occurred to him that Mr. Warwick—or, if he was very unlucky, Lance—might answer. And he needed to talk to Steve discreetly.

His eyes fell on the worn cover of *The Sacred Art of Spellcraft*, which Sammi had left on his bedside table, and he realized that there was more than one way to send a message.

He searched the book for a simple awakening spell, but he didn't have much hope of finding a straightforward one. Human magic had always seemed needlessly complicated to him. Fortunately, he found a spell that was relatively brief. All the necessary items were readily available or easily improvised: his house key would work as "bait," a sock that Steve had forgotten would work as "scent," and a fragment of old newspaper that had drifted in from Izzy's room could convey the message itself. He groaned inside when he realized that his guitar was still lying on the couch downstairs, but he could get by without it.

Cain frowned at the newspaper scrap. He tore out the words *come, to, now,* and *help,* as well as the necessary letters to form *LA* and *need.* He also signed his name on a blank area. Tearing everything out neatly took more time than he liked. He arranged the paper scraps in the proper order on top of the dresser and set the sock down beside them. Everything was ready.

The only electrical outlet in the room was behind the bedside table. Cain nudged the table aside and unplugged the ancient clock radio. A twinge of apprehension ran through him as he sat cross-legged in front of the outlet with the book open on his lap, dangling the metal house key from the key ring in his fingers. Awakening an elemental was dangerous even for an experienced practitioner like Mr. Warwick.

He focused on the outlet and released a steady stream of energy into it. But when he opened his mouth to begin, what came out was not the florid diction of the human spell. A steady high-pitched hum broke from him—the sound of electricity buzzing through wires. Cain stopped focusing on the socket, cursing his ineptitude. Where on earth had that outburst come from? The spell hadn't called for it—

Then the key shifted and tingled against his skin, and he looked down to find himself staring into the glowing pink eyes of an electricity elemental.

The little creature stopped nosing at the key to stare back at Cain. It was the size of a small iguana, lithe-bodied and long-tailed, with two ethereal blue whiskers that trailed from its elongated muzzle like the barbels of a catfish. A spectral luminescence emanated from its semi-transparent form, bathing the floor around it in soft light.

The elemental abruptly lost interest in him and dashed away to sniff at a hanging corner of the fuzzy blue bedspread. White sparks floated from the tips of its whiskers as it buried its face in the fabric, leaving dozens of pinpoint-sized scorch marks. Cain watched smoke rise from the bedspread in shock. Awakening it had been so easy. That thing he had done—the strange humming—where had it come from? How had he known to do it?

The sound of the door opening interrupted his thoughts. Cain peered over the top of the bed, expecting to see Sammi. His heart sank when Skeeter barged into the room, red-nosed and snorting like a dog.

"See there?" Skeeter turned to the sour-faced blond man who he had dragged in with him, pointing at Cain. "I told ya the horns weren't fake. If they were fake, why would he be wearing them in his room where no one can see them?"

The other man yanked his arm out of Skeeter's grasp. He hung back in the doorway, glowering at Cain with an unmistakable glint of deep hostility in his eyes.

"Yeah, whatever," he snapped. "That doesn't prove anything. If thousands of dumb kids were throwing money I didn't deserve at me just for wearing rubber horns, I'd never take 'em off either."

Cain took a deep breath to calm himself and stood up slowly. By some stroke of luck, the elemental hadn't noticed the interlopers yet, but the static electricity in one blanket couldn't hold its attention forever.

"Hi, Skeeter," he said nervously. "I didn't know you were here. Say, I don't mean to be rude, but would you mind—"

"Cain, you gotta show Jazz here what's what," said Skeeter in a loud, indignant voice, raising a hand to wipe his dripping nose. "He won't listen to plain sense."

Jazz muttered something unintelligible and rolled his eyes at Skeeter.

Cain cast an anxious glance at the elemental. It was floating several inches off the floor with its head craned in the direction of Skeeter's voice; it was definitely curious. He scuffed his foot several times over a nearby patch of carpet. It pounced to absorb the new static charge, and Cain redoubled his effort to get rid of the visitors.

"Look, Skeeter, I really can't talk right now," he said. "I'll be downstairs in a couple minutes, I promise. I just need to—"

Skeeter didn't seem to hear him. He pushed farther into the room, staring expectantly at Cain. "Go on, show Jazz that you're a real devil! Do some of that freaky stuff you do on stage. He can't say it's all cheap smoke and mirrors if you set his hair on fire with your mind right here and now, can he?"

Jazz snorted. "Oh, please. I toured with Lion back in '71. I promise you that JoJo Thorpe didn't have to be on stage to make a guitar pick disappear and then reappear from beneath your nose. Even offstage, it was just a silly trick."

Skeeter opened his mouth to reply, but no words came out. His head snapped forward, and he stared at something over Cain's shoulder.

"Whoa!" he shouted. "What the holy hell *is* that thing?"

Jazz gaped in amazement as well. The elemental had popped up from the other side of the bed. It hovered there, its pink eyes fixed on Skeeter. Cain took in the scene and forced himself to appear calm.

"Oh, that?" he said in a nonchalant tone. "That's just...uh..." The elemental inadvertently brushed a trailing whisker against his cheek when it floated by him, giving him a small shock. Inspiration struck. "That's Zap. He's a pet."

"Well, I'll be damned!" Skeeter's eyes followed the curious elemental as it flitted around his head, sniffing his curly brown hair. "See, Jazz, you've gotta believe he's a real devil now! Who else would have a magical lizard-thing made out of lightning for a pet?"

"Don't be stupid, Skeeter." Jazz seemed to have gotten over his amazement, or at least, he seemed to have collected himself enough to hide it. "I'm telling you, it's just a trick. Hell, I could do it if you gave me the right stuff."

Skeeter laughed and fidgeted as the newly-christened Zap noticed the silver chain around his neck and started mouthing it. "Crap, it tickles! So, Jazz, how is he doing this trick?"

Jazz worked his mouth for several seconds. The carefully suppressed bafflement in his eyes became more apparent.

"Holograms, I guess," he snapped.

"You guess?" It was Skeeter's turn to look baffled. "I thought you said you could do it."

Jazz tossed his sculpted mountain of hair and glared at Skeeter. "Well, if you don't know the trick, I'm sure as hell not gonna give it away. You kids play nice now. I'm off to join the grown-ups downstairs."

He stomped away in a huff. Skeeter stared after him in bemusement.

"Can you believe that guy?" he chuckled. "Seriously, *holograms*? Why in the world is it so hard for him to believe that you're a real, live devil with a pet lightning-lizard?"

"Maybe he doesn't want to believe." Cain hurried over to the dresser to grab the sock. "Here, let me get Zap off you. He's not supposed to bother people like that."

"He ain't bothering me," said Skeeter, squinting at the elemental. "Say, are you sure he's a he? Those pink eyes and pretty little whiskers look kinda girly to me."

"Did I say he? I meant she," said Cain distractedly. It didn't matter which pronoun he used; elementals had no gender. His main concern was getting it away from Skeeter. He was surprised at how well-behaved the creature had been so far. It had probably been awakened before, by someone with much more experience at wrangling elementals than he. But there was no guarantee that it would stay well-behaved.

Zap found the sock far less interesting than the felt underside of Skeeter's hat brim. The elemental wouldn't even look at it until Cain rubbed it so vigorously against the bedspread that holding it made the hair on the back of his hands stand on end.

He tossed the sock down on the dresser, ignoring Skeeter's further insistence that he wasn't bothered. Zap streaked after it. While it scurried around the rumpled sock on its spidery little legs and stroked the fabric with its whiskers, Cain set to work on the scraps of newsprint. Tiny spots of light appeared on the yellowed paper and gravitated toward the ink while he concentrated. The letters soon lit up like neon. He dragged a hand gently over the paper, peeling the light away. A ghostly, glowing facsimile of the words hung in the air before him. He drew in a deep breath, preparing for the final and most important part of the spell.

"Cool!" Skeeter's voice exploded in his ear. "What's that for?"

Cain jumped, and the glowing letters faltered. He

managed to regain control long enough to blast the message in Zap's direction. The letters cut through the air in tight formation, zeroing in on the unsuspecting elemental. Its head snapped out of the folds of the sock when they sank in, and its eyes darkened to bright red. It launched off the dresser and pinwheeled through the air, hissing and throwing off sparks. Then it streaked across the room and vanished into the outlet with a pop and a whiff of scorched plastic.

"It's all right," said Cain hastily as Skeeter stumbled back in vague horror. "She's just carrying a message to my friend in New York."

"Oh!" Recognition dawned in Skeeter's eyes. "That was what the glowing, floating words were for. How's she gonna find your friend?"

"She is...specially trained," Cain lied. The so-called special training consisted entirely of implanting those words, which would ping around relentlessly in Zap's tiny brain, driving the elemental crazy until Zap offloaded the information onto the owner of the sock. But Skeeter didn't need to know that.

"Boy, you are the eighth goddamned wonder of the world," Skeeter chuckled, throwing a friendly arm around Cain's shoulders. "Come on, let's get you down to the party. Everybody wants to see you."

Cain reluctantly allowed himself to be led out of the room. He didn't want to go to a party, but now he felt as if he no longer had an excuse to stay in his room. Dread built within him as the buzz of talk and clinking beer cans hit his ears. He remembered Sammi saying that *everyone* had come to the house, and he pictured the entire first floor packed solid with a sweaty horde of people ready to jostle, prod, and yammer at him.

To his surprise, the front hall was empty. About ten people were drinking and chatting in the living room—the biggest crowd he had seen in the house at one time—but the group was nowhere near as large as he had expected it to be.

"So where is everybody?" he asked Skeeter.

"Oh, most of 'em went outside."

"Outside?"

"Yeah. It was getting kinda stuffy in here, so lots of folks stepped out to get some air."

"Hey!" Yuri Ustinov bounded out of the living room like an excited lapdog, shouting a greeting at Skeeter. "You finally got him to come down!"

"That I did," said Skeeter with a triumphant grin. "And I got him to show Jazz some of his demon powers too."

"Cool," said Yuri. "It's about time someone gave Jazz a good hard dose of reality. I bet he still doesn't believe, though. That dude is just impossible."

"Isn't he though?" said Skeeter sadly. "Oh, that reminds me: you owe me ten bucks."

Yuri snapped his fingers. "That's right! I forgot. Dang it, Skeeter, you're so smart. My dad didn't even know that devils could bring back the dead. How do you *know* all these things?"

"Lucky guesses, mostly," said Skeeter with a modest shrug. "But I've gotta give the devil-boy some credit; he's the one who actually did the miracle, after all."

Cain squirmed awkwardly when it dawned on him that Skeeter and Yuri were talking about his supposed exploits. He opened his mouth to give them the real story, but Candi Jayne swooped out of nowhere to intercept Yuri before he could say anything.

"God, I'm so sorry about him," she said to Cain.

473

"Sometimes he acts a little...off...around other people. He doesn't mean anything by it." She herded Yuri into the kitchen, whispering to him as she went: "Dammit, Yuri, didn't we have a chat about this? You can't talk about a guy like he's not there when he's standing right in front of you. That kind of thing makes people uncomfortable."

Skeeter stared after them for a moment, shaking his head. "I don't know what her problem is. I think Yuri is a great guy. Anyway, we should be getting outside."

Sammi burst through the front door, dragging Vince with him. He stopped when he saw Cain and Skeeter.

"It's about time," he said gruffly. "Here, take a turn babysitting Vinnie, will you? I'm exhausted. I gotta take a breather. Oh, and go say hi to your fans already, for God's sake."

He dropped Vince's arm and scurried up the stairs. Vince stayed where Sammi left him, staring at Cain and Skeeter with a dull, dazed expression. Cain guessed that he was either drunk or recovering from multiple shock treatments.

"You heard the man," Skeeter chuckled, propelling Cain toward the door. "Off to the party with you."

Cain had been to plenty of crowded parties before, but no party he had experienced during his time in the city had prepared him for the mob outside the door. He couldn't see the sidewalk, street, or even the cars parked on the curb because hundreds of people were milling around, climbing streetlights, taking turns trying to balance on a nearby fire hydrant, tossing empty beer bottles around, and—in the case of one couple he glimpsed from the corner of his eye—having sex against the railing of the neighbors' house. Their whoops and screams were so loud that the frustrated honking of three drivers trying to maneuver cars through them was barely audible.

"Where did they all *come* from?" He shouted to Skeeter.

"You mean these folks?" Skeeter chuckled. "From the clubs on Sunset. Where else?"

"*All* of them came from the clubs?" Cain stared out at the packed street incredulously. "I didn't know there were this many people around there."

"Are you kidding?" Skeeter clapped him on the back. "The whole Strip used to be like this every single night— one big party. The whole Engineer business put a huge damper on the scene by the time you showed up. Everyone was either too scared to go out at night or too sad about their dead friends to have much fun. But now that you've taken care of the Engineer for us, the party is on again."

"I didn't…" Cain began, but Skeeter had already melted into the sea of bodies.

One of Keenan's girlfriends stumbled toward him. The plastic cup she was carrying slipped out of her hand when she caught sight of his face. Some of her cheap wine splashed on his shoes.

"Oh my god!" Her piercing shriek carried over the noise of the party. "He's finally here!"

Another girl, whom he thought he recognized from some of the parties at the clubs, dashed over and reached out to grab his hand. "What the hell took you so long? We've been waiting for you *forever*. Come on, I've got a friend who wants to meet you."

In a split second, Cain was surrounded. The crowd shifted like an amoeba, instantly enclosing him in a solid wall of excited faces and waving arms. Several people were talking to him, but he had no idea what they were saying.

They all chattered at once, each trying to be louder than the other. Their voices blended together and were lost in the general uproar. He smiled and nodded in reply, knowing he would never be able to make himself heard over them unless he shifted to demon form and let out a full-blown roar.

Several hands shot toward him, waving various booklets, scraps of paper, pencils, and pens in his face. He dutifully dashed out as many autographs as he could, squirming with embarrassment while dozens of eyes watched his slow and clumsy writing. To make matters worse, several cameras started flashing after he handed back his fifth or sixth autograph. Cain set his teeth, resisting with all his might the urge to flee for dear life into the sky.

Eventually his admirers' attention drifted. They stopped shouting at him and demanding autographs, but more people pressed in to take their places. After what seemed like hours, the novelty wore off, and fewer people noticed him in the crowd. Cain gladly pushed his way out of the gang of revelers and fled to the safety of the house.

He closed the front door behind him with an exhausted groan, longing to drop back into bed. His relief shattered when Vince staggered out of the living room with a defeated air, nursing his arm. Cain winced. He had forgotten that Sammi had asked him to keep an eye on Vince.

"So what did you do this time?" he asked in resignation.

Vince poked sullenly at the beginning of a black eye. "I didn't do a damned thing. That fucking barbarian Johnny Revolver started it. I was minding my own business, talking to Joey Gatling, and he just pounced on me. He practically wrenched my arm out of the goddamn socket, and he punched me to boot."

"I'm sure he did." Cain tried not to let a derisive grunt

escape. This was not the first time Vince had used the I-was-just-talking-to-the-guy defense. "Are you all right?"

"I'll be fine once I've slept it off," growled Vince. "I'm off to bed."

"Okay. Good night." Cain dashed into the living room to make sure Joey wasn't hurt.

Joey was sitting in the armchair. Viv hovered over him, feeling his forehead and looking into his eyes like a nurse. Johnny sat across from them on the couch, watching them impassively. He nursed a beer in his left hand, while his right gripped the neck of Cain's guitar.

"Really, Viv, I'm fine," said Joey while Cain watched the scene from the doorway. "He just startled me a little."

"You didn't look like you were startled." Viv leaned in to get a closer look at his eyes. "You went all stiff, like you couldn't move at all. It was scary."

"Well, it was kind of scary while it was happening," Joey admitted. "I don't know how he did it, but it really felt like he was poking around inside my brain."

Cain took a deep breath and stepped into the room. It was just his luck that Vince attacked a friend of the one man in the city who had a reputation for being more violent, more quick-tempered, and scarier than Vince himself.

"Are you sure you're all right?" he said to Joey. "I know what a shock it can be the first time Vince reads your mind—"

He was cut off by a sharp shriek from Viv, who dived behind the chair and peered at him around the armrest. Her eyes shone with terror, and the tiny portion of her forehead and right cheek that he could see had gone chalk-white. Johnny immediately leapt up from the couch and placed himself between Cain and Viv, brandishing the guitar like a sword.

"You," he snapped. "You're coming to the kitchen with me. Now."

"I'm sorry," said Cain meekly. He was a full head taller than Johnny, but Johnny still managed to loom over him. "Was it something I said?"

Johnny's scowl deepened.

"Now, I said."

Cain marched off to the kitchen. He scanned the room and decided to place himself behind the counter, conveniently close to the knife block. He was so exhausted that he might not be able to get a spell out if Johnny attacked him.

"Johnny." Viv cautiously murmured from behind the chair while her boyfriend stalked out of the room. "Don't—"

"Don't worry about me, babe," said Johnny over his shoulder. "I've got this under control."

Cain took an involuntary step closer to the knives when Johnny strode toward the counter and raised his right arm as though he intended to use the guitar as a bludgeon. To Cain's relief, he simply plopped the instrument down on the counter.

"You should put your stuff away when people come over," he said. "I took this off Jazz Brixton. I caught him hiding in the bathroom with it, yanking the hell out of the strings and mumbling to himself that he'd find out what 'the gimmick' was. Whatever that means."

His tone was not quite friendly, but it was no longer threatening either. Cain began to relax.

"Thanks," he said. "Listen, back there in the living room with your girlfriend—I didn't mean to—"

"Don't worry about it." Johnny sighed. "That wasn't

your fault. She saw some therapist guy last year 'cause she wanted to stop being anxious all the time. I thought therapy was a great idea at first, but he only made her worse. Now she sees cults and devil worshippers everywhere, and she thinks they're all out to get her."

"Well, *I'm* certainly not out to get her," Cain assured him, reaching for his guitar. "I promise I don't have anything to do with any cults, no matter what Nathaniel Breen says."

Johnny's hand shot out, pinning Cain's to the counter.

"I know that most of Breen's rants are bullshit." Some of the sharpness had returned to his voice. "But sometimes, there's some truth to what he says, isn't there?"

Cain tried to pull his hand away. Johnny gripped him tighter.

"What are you talking about?" he said, unable to keep his voice from squeaking with fear.

Johnny leaned over the counter, staring at him with terrifying intensity.

"You did something in that studio." His eyes narrowed. "That kid rolled over and died, and you brought him back."

"I don't really think that's what happened."

"Oh yeah?" Johnny released his hand, but his expression didn't become any less suspicious or angry. "I know what I saw. He stopped breathing and was glassy-eyed. Candi said she couldn't find a pulse. Then you put your hands on him, went into this weird trance, and passed out, and he woke right up."

Cain began inching toward the knife block again. Why was Johnny so upset with him for saving someone's life?

"I honestly don't know what happened any more than you do," he said in the tone he used to use to pacify Lance.

"I can't bring people back to life. It's impossible."

Johnny maneuvered around the counter, forcing Cain to back up against the cabinets. "It didn't look too impossible. Don't lie to me. Breen is right about you in one way: whether or not you're a demon, you're definitely something more than human. I just want to know why you were using those powers of yours for a fucking stage show while guys like Jim suffered and died."

Cain's first impulse was to reach for his guitar. He began to do so, but a fierce scowl from Johnny made him think better of it.

"Is everything all right in here?"

Johnny started and backed away. A mildly sheepish look passed over his face.

"We're fine, Ty," he said without turning around.

Ty Thorpe advanced into the kitchen with his slow, deliberate stride. He rested his elbows on the counter, folded his right arm deftly over his left, and turned his heavy-lidded gaze on Johnny.

"Good," he said. "I'd hate to catch you not playing nice—especially since I went to the trouble of talking that guy at the bar out of pressing charges, *and* I put in a good word for you with Mr. Arkin."

"You did?" Johnny stared at him in surprise. "But you weren't even at the bar."

"Stuff gets around," said Ty mysteriously. "Don't worry, it wasn't any trouble. Say, speaking of Mr. Arkin, have either of you seen him? I need to talk to him."

Johnny raised an eyebrow. "I thought you said you'd already talked to him."

"Yeah, I talked to him last night. Something else came up today that he should know about, but I can't find him anywhere. He's not at his office or his home."

"Huh." Johnny frowned. "The last time I saw him, he was heading into his office with a couple policemen after the ambulance picked up that poor kid. I guess he must have left."

Ty turned to Cain. Cain shook his head.

"So you have no idea, then?" Ty's expression did not change, but his right hand fluttered anxiously. "Well, that's okay. I'll just have to keep looking. So, Johnny, how's that girlfriend of yours?"

Johnny started. "Crap! She's probably freaking out, thinking devil-boy here killed me with fire and brimstone or something. Excuse me."

He hurried out of the room. Ty turned to watch him go, drumming his fingers on the counter.

"Strange guy, Johnny," he said. "Good heart. Worst temper in the world. Mr. Arkin keeps telling me to stay out of his problems and let his manager deal with him, but I help him out when I can anyway. I know his manager won't. He'll just sit Johnny and his band mates down and yell at them like they're schoolchildren." He sighed. "You've got some experience dealing with difficult band mates yourself; I'm sure you can guess how that approach goes over."

"Yes. I know what you're talking about." Cain regarded Ty curiously. His guitar lessons had grown more infrequent as his performance schedule filled out. He hadn't seen his teacher for about a month; he also didn't remember seeing him at Daggerspoint that morning. "So you say you have to talk to Mr. Arkin? I'll tell him the next time I see him."

"Don't worry about it," said Ty. "It's not that important. I'll just try him again tomorrow. Thanks anyway, though. Oh, by the way…"

He paused for a moment, rubbing his arm thoughtfully. Cain couldn't read his expression.

"About what you and your friends did today," he continued. "It was very brave and very noble of you. But you haven't taken down the Engineer."

"I know." Cain made a face. "Johnny wouldn't let me forget."

Ty nodded. "Yeah, I figured neither one of you would be in much danger of joining in with those screaming drunks outside and forgetting that the Engineer was still out there. You're both smarter than that. Still, there's one thing every newcomer to this city should learn, Cain: nothing is as it seems here. You saved someone's life today, and everyone is in love with you for it, but it might have gotten you into more trouble than you know."

"What kind of trouble?" Cain gave him a wary look, fighting back the unsettled feeling that churned in his stomach. "Do you think the Engineer might come after me now?"

Ty was already on his way out. He paused in the doorway and gave what might have been a stiff nod. Cain studied his profile. There was something odd about his left hand. It seemed to be twisted into a vaguely unnatural position, as if he were trying to hold something while simultaneously making his hand look empty, but Cain couldn't be quite sure. The contortion was subtle enough that a human eye would have missed it entirely, and he himself might not have noticed it if Ty hadn't lingered for a second or two before vanishing into the hallway.

Chapter Nineteen

Damage Control

CAIN WAS ROUSED EARLY the next morning by sounds of scuffling. He sat up groggily, annoyed at the prospect of having to deal with Vince before he was even properly awake. But he soon realized that the commotion was coming from inside his room. Alarmed, he opened his eyes completely and found Izzy trying to push someone through the window.

He seemed to be having difficulty completing the task. His victim's wiry brown arms flailed at him, and a bare foot aimed a kick in the general direction of his shin.

"Look, it's not hard," he said in a pleading tone. "Just grab the gutter and pull yourself up. I won't let you fall."

"I can't go out there!" wailed the other man in a high, cracked voice. "They'll see me through the hole in the sky, and they'll come down and kill me!"

Cain recognized the voice as Sammi's and leapt up in dismay.

"Izzy!" he shouted. "What are you—"

"Shhh!" Izzy craned his head toward Cain. "If we get much louder, he might hear us. Come on, I need help getting Sammi onto the roof."

"The roof?" Cain stared at him. "Why?"

Sammi broke free. He ran for the door at full speed, but Izzy caught up to him, turned into a walrus, and plopped down on top of him. He clapped a flipper over Sammi's face to stifle his shrieks and looked up at Cain with desperation in his eyes.

"There's a cop on the doorstep," he whispered. "Didn't you hear the doorbell ring? I bet he wants to ask us some questions about the Engineer."

"Oh. Okay." Cain couldn't imagine what a cop having questions about the Engineer had to do with Sammi needing to climb onto the roof. "Shouldn't we let him in?"

"We can't," said Izzy. "Not until we get Sammi out of here. He's high. That cop would take one look at him and haul him off. There's a crooked piece of gutter that hangs down right over your window. I think he could make it onto the roof if he grabbed it. But he's too freaked."

The doorbell rang again. Izzy flinched.

"I gotta go let in that cop," he said. "He'll think something is fishy if I keep him waiting any longer. Would you do me a huge favor and hide Sammi? He'll listen to you."

Cain could see Sammi's eyes over Izzy's flipper. They were fiery and fear-crazed, and sparks floated out of his hair while he struggled. Sammi didn't look particularly inclined to listen to anyone.

Izzy took Cain's doubtful silence for assent. He rolled off Sammi and bounded out the door, changing shape as he went.

"Thanks a bunch, Cain," he called over his shoulder. "I owe you one. Hell, we both do."

Sammi sprawled on the floor for a few seconds,

breathing heavily and staring at the ceiling. When Cain took a cautious step toward him, he scrambled up and backed against the wall.

"Get away from me!" His eyes flashed with anger, and more sparks exploded from his hair and fingertips. "I don't care what you say; I'm not going outside, especially not on the damn roof where they could pick me off like a fish in a barrel. I already almost died once."

"But you have to get on the roof," said Cain in what he hoped was a soothing tone. If the cops realized Sammi was high, they might arrest him, and the rumors and gossip generated by such an arrest might discredit their recent discoveries about the Engineer, leaving more young musicians vulnerable. "Don't worry, it won't be long. I'll even go up with you and keep...uh...*them* away. Whoever they are."

"You can't keep them away," said Sammi. "No one can. If they want to get at you, they'll get at you, and they'll burn right through anything standing in the way to do it."

The front door slammed shut downstairs. Sammi jumped, and the panicky light came back into his eyes.

"Oh shit. They're in the house!" he moaned. "I knew I wasn't safe anywhere. I might as well lie down and die right now."

"You should try hiding on the roof," said Cain.

"What!" Sammi gave him a scornful look. "Go sit under the open sky so they can see me even easier?"

Cain could hear Izzy talking to someone in the foyer downstairs. They were too far away for him to make out words, but the other voice sounded brusque and unfriendly.

"Well...they *might* be able to see you easier," he conceded. "But you might be safer up there too. They live in the sky, right? And they came into the house to look for you?"

Sammi nodded suspiciously.

"So if they came all the way down here to find you, they won't expect you to go up and hide so close to their home, will they?"

It was the best idea he could come up with on the spot. He hoped that Sammi was addled enough to accept it.

He was. Footsteps started up the stairs, and Sammi cowered beside the dresser with a wide-eyed glance at the door.

"They're coming, aren't they?" he whispered. "Well, fuck. I guess the roof is worth a try."

Getting Sammi onto the roof was not easy. Cain didn't trust Sammi's ability to climb the gutter in his current state, and he tried to boost him up instead. The tactic might have worked if Sammi had not suddenly seemed to forget what he was doing halfway up. His body went slack and slid off the roof. Cain lunged out the window and caught him with a stifled gasp.

The footsteps were right outside his room now, coming nearer and nearer to the threshold. Cain leapt up to grab the hanging gutter. It creaked and trembled under his weight while he swung out the window and half-climbed, half-flew to the roof with Sammi hanging limply from the crook of his other arm.

He had to do some more climbing to find a spot where they could sit. The roof was more sloped than it appeared from a distance, and though he could keep his balance on the rough shingles, he doubted that Sammi could. They scrabbled their way to the partially crumbling brick chimney-pot and used it to stabilize themselves. Soon after they settled down, Cain heard Izzy's voice floating up from his open window.

"Like I told you, he's not here right now," he was saying.

"Isn't he?" The cop's voice resonated. "Why do I get the feeling you're lying to me, son?"

"I'm not," said Izzy frantically. "I swear you didn't hear him talking, and you didn't see his tail going out the window. You couldn't have. No one could jump out that window without breaking his legs."

"Yeah, well, if anybody in this town could jump out that window without breaking a leg or disappear into thin air when it suited him, it'd be him, wouldn't it?" The other voice sounded unimpressed.

Cain let go of the chimney and started cautiously down the roof. The cop seemed to want to talk to him, not to Izzy. He made it halfway before Sammi rolled past him. Cain caught him a mere second before he plunged over the edge.

"Sammi!" he whispered. "Are you all right?"

Sammi regarded him with calm, half-focused eyes, his panicky fear of "them" apparently forgotten.

"Izzy said something about a cop," he mumbled. "If there's a cop, I should tell him…" he trailed off.

"Tell him what?"

"Tell who?"

"The cop."

"Oh yeah." Sammi blinked and frowned intently. "The cop. I guess I was gonna tell him…uh…something or other…"

He trailed off again. Cain gave him an indulgent nod.

"That's okay," he said. "Maybe you can tell him later."

"I need to tell him what I remember about the Engineer."

Cain stared at him. "But you don't remember anything about the Engineer."

Sammi flinched. A strange guarded look passed over his face. "I remember some things," he muttered.

"Like what?" Something in Sammi's tone made Cain doubt he was lying. He wondered if he could manage a spell to force Sammi into sobriety without the use of his guitar.

"Not much," said Sammi. "White light. Burning. Fear and pain and tears and the smell of blood." He whimpered and curled into a ball. "No...no...I don't wanna talk about it. I don't wanna."

"Sammi..." Cain felt an unpleasant crawling sensation in his stomach. "Do you really remember those things? Why didn't you tell me?"

Sammi moaned and shook his head. "I couldn't...I can't...It hurts too much. Smack makes it go away sometimes. Look, I wish you wouldn't sit so close to me, man. It's dangerous."

"But you could help them catch—"

"I'm serious." Sammi tried to shuffle away from Cain. "You've got a bomb in your guts, man. It could go off at any minute," he said in a doggedly sincere tone.

"It's all right," said Cain patiently. "You don't have to tell them anything. They want to talk to me anyway. Let's get you comfortable."

After some extensive coaxing, Sammi eventually allowed himself to be herded back up the roof. Cain helped him brace his back against the chimney-pot. He mumbled something inaudible and promptly fell so deeply asleep that a rough shake of his shoulders failed to wake him.

Sammi was a restless sleeper; he might toss and turn away from the chimney and off the roof if left alone. Cain groaned and sat down to watch him. He crouched there for a few minutes, following Sammi's arm spasms with his eyes and thinking how strange it was that the house had a chimney when it had no fireplace. Nothing untoward happened, and he had almost made up his mind to risk a quick visit downstairs when a familiar voice rang out.

"Cain!" it shouted. "Come down off that roof, and bring Sammi with you!"

Cain jumped.

"Yes, Mr. Arkin," he said.

Mr. Arkin was waiting in Cain's room. At another time, he might have sat casually on the edge of the bed, but now he stood with his arms crossed and his jawline stiffened. Izzy hovered behind him, playing nervously with his hands.

"Can't you wake him?" he said to Cain, who was setting Sammi's still-unconscious form down on his bed.

Cain looked up in surprise. He had never heard Mr. Arkin speak so curtly before.

"Um...Mr. Arkin?" Izzy piped up. "I'm...uh...afraid we can't. Sometimes when he's coming down, he just conks out and sleeps like he's dead for an hour or two. Waking him up when he's like that doesn't really work, even when Cain does it with magic. Sorry."

"Hmm." Mr. Arkin rubbed his eyes wearily. Cain could see that they were dark-ringed and puffy beneath his fingertips, as if he had stayed up all night. "I would have liked to talk to all of you at once. Well, I guess you can always fill him in later."

"On what?" said Cain.

Mr. Arkin jerked his head toward the door.

"Vince," he shouted. "Get in here!"

Vince staggered into the room, nursing a cup of coffee

in one hand. He was missing some skin along his knuckles, and the black eye that Johnny Revolver had given him last night was now accompanied by another, newer-looking shiner. He clutched his head and glared at Mr. Arkin.

"No need to fucking scream in my ear like that, old man," he snapped. "Jesus Christ. I'm right here."

Cain shifted guiltily when he remembered that he had promised Sammi he would watch Vince last night. "Vince, you look awful. What happened?"

Vince opened his mouth to talk, but a pointed look from Mr. Arkin made him close it.

"Your band mate put his fist through your neighbor's door last night," said Mr. Arkin. "*After* participating in at least one fistfight and leaving an impressive number of unconscious bodies in his wake, I might add."

"Well, they all had it coming," muttered Vince. Cain growled at him to shut him up again.

"This is bad," Mr. Arkin continued. "This is very bad. We'll need to do some serious damage control—and soon."

"Why?" Izzy scratched the back of his neck. "Vince eats people's energy all the time. It's not like it's a new thing."

"Well, this time he picked a very unfortunate night to act out. Folks are already on edge from the whole—unpleasantness—back at Daggerspoint. Your powers are just freaking them out more, especially since you were the ones who oh-so-conveniently found the victim."

Vince's eyes darkened. Izzy looked horrified.

"But nobody thinks *we* had anything to do with that guy being kidnapped!" he cried. "How could they? We saved that kid! You should have seen the party last night—everyone was treating us like heroes."

"I know, I know," said Mr. Arkin. "But a kidnapped

teenager was just found cut up and half-dead in a crowded building where someone—anyone—should have noticed him a long time ago, and people who *aren't* your fellow partygoers—people who weren't there to see the rescue, people who see you guys as rock n' roll thugs—want answers too. And when people want answers, someone is always going to step up and give them some—whether they're the right ones or not. You should have heard what the good Reverend Breen had to say about you on the Millennium Coalition this morning."

Cain could imagine. He involuntarily bared his teeth.

"You're all going to stay out of trouble for a while." Mr. Arkin's tone was final. "That's an order. We're going to get you as much good press as we can too: community service, charity work, volunteer work."

"Fuck," muttered Vince. Cain made no move to shush him this time. He was beginning to get the definite impression that they were being punished for whatever Breen was saying about them, and this thought rankled him.

"And you can count on a percentage of your album sales going to support a worthy cause," he said. "I'll let you choose the cause, but there will be no getting out of it. I'm also handing you over to a manager. I should have done that a long time ago, actually. I'm too old to run Daggerspoint *and* chase you all over the city. Any questions?"

Cain had plenty of questions, and Izzy's expression suggested that he did too, but neither of them dared to speak up. They shook their heads. Vince grunted.

"Good," grumbled Mr. Arkin. "Now think about what cause you'd like to give to; I'll need to know soon. And don't go too far. You boys have a PSA to shoot tomorrow morning."

He turned on his heel and hurried out the door before any of them could speak, grinding his jaw as he went.

"PSA?" said Cain to Izzy as soon as he was gone. "What's—"

"It's a lame preachy commercial where we tell people not to do crap," snapped Vince before Izzy could answer. "This is bullshit. Charity is for washed-up has-beens and perky starlets too airheaded to know that they're not really making any difference."

"Maybe it won't be so bad," said Izzy hopefully. "I mean, we just have to give some money and do a commercial, and maybe we *will* make a difference."

Vince rolled his eyes. "We won't. And you're crazy if you think it'll just be one commercial. Arkin is pissed 'cause he didn't know that there was a fucking torture chamber in his own studio until we showed him, and he's out to punish us by giving us crap jobs and throwing away our money. Ugh, I knew that whole nice-guy shtick of his was a big crock of shit. If you strip away the smiles and handshakes and ass-kissing, all music execs are the same."

"Well, we might at least decide who we want to give money to, since we can," said Izzy. "Does anybody have a favorite charity?"

Cain shrugged. He knew little about charities, except that Mr. Warwick hated them but gave money to some anyway to keep up appearances. "The only charity I can think of is Breen's project. What is it called? Voice in the Wilderness, I think."

"That foundation for kids he's always flogging on his shows?" Izzy guffawed. "Hah! Can you imagine how pissed Breen would be if he had to invite us to one of their fancy banquets?"

Vince smirked. "Yeah, that would serve the old fart right—except then I'd have to wear a damn tuxedo, and I wouldn't be caught dead in one of those."

Cain thought back on the bit of conversation he had overheard from the Breens' roof. The Reverend Breen probably would pitch a massive fit if he got his longed-for celebrity support from the one rock star he hated most of all the rock stars in the city. Cain was half-tempted to do it, but he was sure that Mr. Arkin's admonition to stay out of trouble included *not* provoking fights with horrible televangelists.

After Mr. Arkin left, Izzy dutifully carried Sammi up to the loft and then disappeared into his room. Vince slunk off somewhere. Cain didn't follow him, but he had a sneaking suspicion that his unruly band mate was dead-set on causing trouble to spite Mr. Arkin. What he wanted to do was see Michelle, but he didn't dare chance a visit while her father was on high alert. Instead, he wandered down to the living room with his guitar.

A ring of the doorbell roused him from his practice. He heaved himself up from the couch with a weary groan, half-expecting it to be some policeman or other hauling Vince home. His heart sank further when he opened the door to find Mr. Warwick standing on the stoop.

"Hello, Cain," he said. "I trust you wouldn't mind watching Steve for a few days while I take care of some business in the city?"

Cain peered around Mr. Warwick and saw Steve smiling eagerly, shifting his red suitcase from hand to hand.

"Not really," he muttered. "But I—"

"Good, good." Mr. Warwick's tone told him that this

request was not optional. "Now, if you'll excuse me, Nathaniel Breen demands my immediate attention—thanks mostly to you."

"Thanks to me, Master?" Cain writhed inside at using the hated word again, but he sensed that he needed to be cautious.

"Yes indeed." Mr. Warwick's expression became stormy. "I heard about your little escapade at the record company. Shame on you, Cain. I thought I taught you better than to go prying in places you have no business being."

"Dad..." Steve stepped forward.

"This doesn't concern you, Steve," snapped Mr. Warwick. "What were you thinking, Cain? You made Nathaniel Breen look like a fool for not believing in the so-called Engineer murders, and now he wants *my* hide for it. As if it were my fault he made an ass of himself."

"I'm sorry, Master," said Cain meekly. He wasn't sorry for saving that boy, but he also didn't want his collar activated again.

"I should hope you are. I had to drop everything and fly across the whole damn country because of you. If Bruce Arkin hadn't practically begged me on bended knee to give you a second chance, I would be sending you on your way to the room behind my study—*without* your guitar—this very moment. Do you understand?"

"Yes, Master. It won't happen again." The effort of sounding sincere left him exhausted.

"It had better not," grumbled Mr. Warwick. "You've used up all your second chances. Remember that I have been very gracious, and behave yourself. Oh, by the way..."

He opened his briefcase, pulled out a small green container with a heavy rubber lid, and handed it to Cain.

"Steve tells me that this thing belongs to you," he said. "Kindly don't send it to my house again. I'll be back in a few days. Make sure Steve behaves himself."

He turned on his heel and strode off, leaving Cain and Steve on the doorstep. Cain inspected the container that Mr. Warwick had handed him. He couldn't see what was inside through the opaque plastic.

"Wait!" Steve put up a hand in alarm as he began to peel off the lid. "Be careful."

It was too late. Cain dropped the container with a yelp when a hissing mass of electrical energy shot out of it. The freed elemental pinged off the floor, leaving a jagged scorch mark on the front hall carpet, and shot up the stairs.

"Geez, Cain!" Steve rushed over to stomp on the smoldering patch of carpet. "If you wanted me to come over, why didn't you just call instead of sending a damn blue salamander to zap the words right into my brain? I know I've showed you how to use a phone."

"I know. I'm sorry. There were lots of people in the house, and I couldn't get to it."

"Well, I've gotta hand it to you—that was a pretty impressive piece of magic. I didn't know you could make an elemental carry messages."

"Is that why I really got yelled at?" Cain glanced at the scorch mark on the carpet. "I've never worked with elementals before—not that I remember, anyway. Did it set your house on fire or something?"

"The outlet it came out of got some black marks," Steve admitted. "Mostly, dad was just being dad, though. He's been in a pissy mood all day."

"I wonder why he isn't trying to get more money out of Breen." Cain frowned. Dissatisfied clients didn't usually put

Mr. Warwick in a foul temper; they made him eager to quick-talk them into believing that they were somehow to blame for the failure of the spell, and they should therefore pay more fees for improved results.

"Part of his bad mood might be my fault, honestly." Steve dropped his suitcase by the front door. "The school called the other day."

"Suspended again?"

"I was asked not to come back, actually."

"Oh." Cain was not surprised. "That's too bad. What happened?"

"Nothing serious. Lance's stupid friend Kevin smeared worm guts from the biology lab in my hair, so I messed with his science project a little."

"How much is a little?"

"Uh..." Steve stared at the floor. "Okay, maybe more than a little. His class was dissecting frogs, see, so I found his frog, smeared some of dad's flying ointment on it, and put it back in the bag. Then I hid in the corner until third-period biology so I could see the look on his ugly face when his frog flew away from him."

"That was all?" Now Cain was surprised. If Steve was going to get kicked out of school, he had always assumed it would be for something much less tame.

Steve winced. "Well, the problem was I forgot that Amanda Maxwell was in third-period biology too, and she's kind of been freaked out by anything to do with magic since I...well...you know. When Kevin's frog shot out of the bag and floated up to the ceiling, she had some kind of breakdown. She had to be sent to the nurse's office and everything. Oh well. At least I get to start over at another school next year." He sighed. "So...um...you say you need help with something?"

"Yeah," said Cain slowly, wondering where to begin. "I need help with a couple of things, actually. See, what happened was—"

He was cut off by a series of loud thumps and screams. Sammi appeared at the top of the stairs, his eyes wide with fright. He did a wild acrobatic dance, swatting at a streak of blue light that zipped around his head like a hummingbird eyeing a particularly juicy flower. Steve and Cain watched him in silent awe.

"Help!" he shrieked. "Get it off, get it off, get it off! It's trying to kill me!"

The blue light dive-bombed him. Sammi lurched forward, overbalanced, and tumbled down the stairs. He sprawled at Cain's feet in a trembling heap. The light shot after him and solidified into its salamander-like form when it landed on his chest in a little explosion of sparks. He yelped again and put out sparks of his own.

"Sammi, it's okay," said Cain quickly. "That's just Zap, and I don't think it's going to hurt you. It senses the electricity in you—that's all."

"Zap?" Sammi stared at the elemental in a daze. "You gave it a name? Why? What is...? Where did it even *come* from?"

He crab-walked a few feet, attempting to escape the fascinated elemental. Zap skittered effortlessly after him and landed on his shoulder. Its long, many-forked tongue shot out to lick his face. Cain couldn't help smiling. Skeeter was right; Zap's graceful body and long, wispy whiskers did have a rather feminine appearance.

"I called it...her here," said Cain. Maybe if he spoke of the elemental as if it were a common household pet, with a gender and a personality, Sammi might find its attentions less threatening. He glanced at Steve. "Look, I have some stuff to tell Sammi that's pretty important. I'll have to finish explaining why I need your help later. Sorry."

"That's fine." Steve chuckled. "There is never a dull moment in this house, is there?"

They all retired to Cain's bedroom. Sammi sat patiently on Cain's bed while Cain tried to send Zap home. But Zap refused to be banished back into the wiring. Cain and Steve lobbed every spell they could think of at her for half an hour, but she clung adamantly to Sammi's shoulder, seemingly immune to their magic. Eventually Cain gave up and relayed Mr. Arkin's message to Sammi as best he could while the happy elemental buzzed around the room. Steve stared at them both in growing amazement while Cain relayed the tale.

"Mr. Arkin is *punishing* us for saving that kid's life?" said Sammi in disbelief. "That doesn't sound like him. Are you sure that wasn't just the spin Vince put on it 'cause he was in a bad mood?"

Cain shook his head. "No. I was there too, and he definitely sounded mad at us. I've never seen him like that before."

"Maybe he just thinks we made him look bad." Sammi tried, without success, to pluck Zap out of his hair. "He'll cool down soon."

"Damn!" Steve piped up. "You mean you not only found the Engineer's last victim, but you saved his life too? Why the hell haven't I heard about this yet?"

"It only happened yesterday," said Cain. "See, what happened was—"

"Daggerspoint employees dropped a tip to the police."

Cain looked up in surprise at the unfamiliar voice. A tall, dark-skinned woman stood in the doorway, leaning against the door frame. She had a head of curly chestnut-dyed hair that was even more voluminous and imposing than Jazz Brixton's, and she wore a pair of sharp, angular lime-green wire earrings that swung from her ears.

"That's the company's official statement," she continued. "Several concerned, *anonymous* Daggerspoint employees dropped a tip, and police discovered that poor young man during the course of a routine follow-up. You'd do well to remember it; Mr. Arkin would like all his artists to keep their stories straight."

Cain raised an eyebrow. Mr. Arkin had assured him plenty of times that it was all right to stretch the truth in interviews, but he had never gotten the impression that Mr. Arkin condoned flat-out lying.

"We'd do well to remember it?" said Sammi indignantly. "Excuse me, but who the hell are you, anyway?"

The woman gave Sammi a haughty look. "Cheryl Bancroft. Your new manager. Now let's go. We have…"

She trailed off in mild surprise when Zap emerged from Sammi's hair and floated toward her. The elemental flitted around Cheryl for a moment, nosing at her blouse and long silver-beaded necklace. Then she abruptly decided that Sammi was more interesting and zipped back to him. Cheryl blinked, shook her head, and resumed talking as though nothing had happened.

"We have a PSA to shoot. Come on, everybody into the car."

She had such an air of command in her voice that they began to obey without thinking. Sammi hauled himself up

499

from the bed and shuffled along after her, grumbling. Cain started to follow without commenting, but he paused in the doorway when something occurred to him.

"What PSA?" he said. "I thought that we were doing the commercial tomorrow."

Cheryl stopped and glanced over her shoulder at him. She seemed affronted that he had dared to question her.

"Yes, you do have a shoot tomorrow," she said. "And now you have one today as well. Mr. Arkin called in some favors. He thinks you need all the good PR you can get."

She strode over to Izzy's closed door, gave one sharp knock, and then flung it open without further ceremony. Cain caught a glimpse of Izzy lying shirtless on his rumpled bed, playing with something small and brown—his pet rat, Bonzo. He scrambled up with a startled shriek and hastily stuffed the squeaking rat out of sight somewhere in one of his mounds of trash.

"Now come on," she barked. "Your frontman is waiting in my car, and I'm pretty sure he's the type who'd slash my tires just because he was bored and couldn't think of anything better to do...Hey, you!"

Steve had been tagging after Cain. He stopped in his tracks when Cheryl addressed him.

"You part of the band, kid?"

"Uh...no," he mumbled.

"Wait here, then. You're not invited."

Steve slunk back into Cain's bedroom, muttering and casting offended looks at Cheryl. Cain, Sammi, and Izzy plodded after her with a gloomy sense of inevitability.

"Damn," Sammi muttered to Cain. "She got Vince into her car without help? She must have been an even bigger bitch to him than she was to us!"

"I can hear you, Mr. Guerrero." Cheryl's voice floated up from the bottom of the stairs. "Not everybody is deaf like you rockers are, you know. And you're right, I was a bitch to him. Bitchiness gets the job done."

Izzy was up to his waist in a sea of small children. They swarmed around his legs, tugged at the fringe on his jacket, and shouted out their favorite animals. Every now and then, he obliged them with a transformation. As Cain watched from the corner of the room, Izzy abruptly shrank out of sight beneath the children's bobbing heads. A moment later, he shot up in the form of a purple monkey. He grabbed onto the rings of the gaudy plastic model of Saturn that hung over his head and swung there, making exaggerated monkey-chatter noises while the children giggled and jumped up and down with excitement.

The children's willowy teacher stood a few feet away, watching the scene with an increasingly uncomfortable expression on her face. It was clear to Cain that she had no idea what she was in for when she ushered the four of them into her classroom to meet the fifteen children hand-picked by the school to be in their PSA. He couldn't help but feel a bit sorry for her, even though she was inadvertently responsible for his current pain and exasperation. She had insisted that they "get the kids used to them" before shooting the PSA on the playground.

Unfortunately for Cain, a good number of them got used to him by grabbing at his tail. They hadn't tormented him long—most of them gravitated toward Izzy after a few minutes, while the rest wandered away to watch Sammi make sparks—but their curious squeezes and yanks had worn his patience down to a ragged stub and left him feeling as if someone had filled his spine with boiling oil.

The door banged open, making Cain and the teacher jump. Cheryl stuck her head into the room.

"The film crew is almost set up," she said. "You're on in ten, boys, so wrap it up in here. Vince, wipe that nasty look off your face. You're here to tell folks that child abuse is a bad thing, not advocate for it."

Vince turned his sullen glower on her. He stood by himself in the same far corner of the classroom he had retreated to upon walking through the door. None of the children had approached him in the whole half-hour of their visit, and Cain didn't blame them. He could practically feel the waves of hostility that radiated from every line of Vince's body.

Cheryl's eyes narrowed. "Wipe that look off your face, I said."

Vince scowled harder.

"Vince, dear." Her tone grew sweet, even as her eyes blazed and her sharp green earrings waved like battle standards. "Surely you aren't going to make me...you know...again in front of your band mates?"

Vince flinched and immediately pasted a false grin on his face.

"That's better. Now, like I said, you're on in ten. Be ready."

She shut the door behind her. As she did, a little girl wandered away from the group surrounding Izzy and toddled over to Cain. He set his teeth when she reached for his tail, but the yank he was expecting never came. Instead, she held it lightly, running her fingers over the scales. A little shiver of revulsion ran through him at the touch, but he suppressed it and focused instead on silently reciting the lines that Cheryl had parceled out to him in the car. She had grudgingly assured him and his band mates that there would be cue cards on the set if they got stuck, but Cain had his lines memorized. The sheer horror of the words had cemented them in his mind.

Each year, more than one million children are the victims of abuse and neglect in America, many at the hands of members of their own families.

One million human children, every year, in one country alone, were being hurt and terrorized by people who were supposed to love them. Cain had not realized the gravity of the issue until Sammi assured him on the way over that such things did indeed happen in the real world, outside of the Reverend Breen's disturbing fantasy life.

The little girl took a break from studying the patterns of light reflecting off his scales to stare up at him. He stared back. One million was such a high number that he had trouble picturing that many children. He wondered if any of the children in this classroom were among the million. He wondered if this little girl was one of the unlucky ones. A dull leaden sensation settled in his stomach when this thought crossed his mind.

The door opened again. Izzy and Sammi looked up from their interactions. Vince's forced smile faded. Cain assumed that Cheryl had come back to usher them to the set, but then he noticed that the shell shock on the teacher's face had given way to horror.

"I'm so sorry, sir," she babbled. "This wasn't my idea, I promise. All I knew was that someone famous was coming to do the commercial, and I was to make sure the kids were here and ready to go by one. When these four showed up, everyone else was already here. I had to make the best of it."

The Reverend Breen stepped calmly into the room, holding up a hand to shush the terrified teacher.

"It's all right, Lesley Ann," he said. "You're a bright girl. I know that you would never suffer such a"—he shot a withering look at Cain—"dismal lapse in judgment."

"No, sir," she whispered, sitting down at her desk with a sigh of relief. The children had gone respectfully silent as well, and the little girl dropped Cain's tail and scurried away to join the others. Sammi, Izzy, and Cain shifted and swallowed nervously while Breen raked them with a baleful gaze.

Vince did not. He sauntered out of the corner, staring the minister directly in the eye.

"Have you come to pick up your kid, Rev?" he said in a tone that carried a not-so-subtle hint of mockery. "That's weird. I thought your daughter was a little older."

He gave Cain a sly grin. Cain desperately shook his head and mouthed the words *please don't*, silently vowing to turn Vince into a potted cactus and give him to Mrs. Delgado for Christmas next year if he breathed another word to Breen.

"My daughter is indeed older." The minister drew himself up to his full height. "Not that it's any of your business, Mr....Sweet, is it? I'm here to check up on the school."

"So you're moonlighting as a teacher." Vince's mocking tone was even less subtle now. "The old folks who watch the Millennium Coalition have finally started buying food for themselves instead of forking their whole pensions over to you, huh? Tough luck."

"Shut the hell up, Vinnie," hissed Sammi.

Breen's eyes narrowed, and his face flushed red with anger. "You shouldn't go talking about things you don't understand, Mr. Sweet. For your information, I'm here on business. A good portion of my—according to you—ill-gotten funds go to support this place. But you already knew that, didn't you?"

He rounded on Cain when he spoke these last words. Cain leapt back, startled.

"Uh…no…no, actually, I didn't know," he stammered. He didn't even know the school's name. He hadn't seen a sign out front. Cheryl had herded them into the building rather quickly.

His bewilderment angered Breen further. The minister advanced on him with squared shoulders and a set jaw.

"Don't lie to me," he said icily. "You boys can feed me all the falsehoods you want, but you'll never hide the truth from me. Those cameras and lights on the playground are just a ruse, aren't they?"

The Reverend Breen advanced further, glowering at Cain as if to penetrate the depths of his soul. Cain shook his head, hoping his expression adequately conveyed his deep confusion.

"You're here to recruit," snarled Breen. "The teens aren't quite pliable enough for your tastes anymore, are they? But these young ones are so impressionable, so easy to mold…Well, I'll have you know I won't sit idly by while you corrupt and destroy innocents so you can gain more power and control. I won't have you turn these children into devil-worshippers."

The unhappy leaden feeling in Cain's chest flared up again, but this time it was mixed with fiery anger. A single furious thought burned in his mind: how dare this self-righteous old man accuse him of these horrible, sickening deeds? The minister had no evidence to suggest that Cain was capable of such crimes, and he probably wouldn't even recognize Cain on the street if were not for his horns and guitar. How dare he say this garbage—and to Cain's face, no less! Cain's tail lashed with rage, and his lips peeled back in an instinctual display of challenge.

Breen seemed to take this reaction as an admission of guilt. Triumph flashed in his eyes, and his chest puffed out a bit more.

"So the Beast bares his fangs at last!" he cried. "I knew you would. Oh yes, you may have this whole city fooled with your rather suspicious sudden interest in charity work, but I know that you're just as filthy—or filthier—than your followers. If given the chance, the vicious, blood-lusting devil in each and every one of you will come out every time. I guarantee it!"

Izzy stepped timidly forward and said something Cain didn't hear. His anger was almost suffocating him now; he was seconds away from pouncing on Breen when the door banged open.

"Well, well, well." Cheryl strode briskly up and placed herself between Cain and Breen. "What a pleasant surprise. You're the last person I expected to see today, Reverend Breen. Sorry, I'm Cheryl Bancroft, Cain's manager. What can I do for you?"

"You can call off that travesty of a PSA you're about to shoot, for one." A sulky note crept into Breen's voice, and he scowled at Cheryl as if to silently chastise her for ruining his fun.

"Hmm, I'm afraid that won't be possible," said Cheryl.

"Confound it all, I cannot allow these wicked men to put on a show of advocating for the very children they aim to inflict irreparable damage on, and at an institution my foundation supports, no less!"

Cain heard no more of their argument. He took advantage of Cheryl's turned back to slip out the open door and walk down the brightly painted hallway, past an elderly janitor who dropped his mop and stared at him with his mouth open. He ignored the old man and walked faster, desperate to escape the oppressive atmosphere of the school.

A tight jumble of swings and monkey bars stood to one side of the school. Cain could see cameras set up among the playground equipment when he emerged from the front entrance. Most of the camera crew milled about on the playground, making last-minute adjustments to their tripods and microphones and lights, but a few of them lounged in the grass, eating lunch and chatting.

"Hey, there's our star," said one of the black-shirted cameramen as Cain passed him. "I hope the rain holds off till we get the shooting done. I bet he don't like water much. Devils in stories never like water."

"Yeah, yeah, I bet not," said his grizzled companion, without much interest. "Anyway, this little blonde honey I was telling you about. Like I said, she's so jacked up she actually believes me when I tell her I can get her a bit part in this movie she was looking to try out for, and the next thing I know, her clothes are flying off, man, and I tell you..."

The man's voice faded into the distance as Cain walked on with his head down and his teeth clenched. A few raindrops fell around him. The houses near the school gave way to factories and warehouses, but still he kept moving, not caring where he would end up as long as there were no people there to accuse him of vile crimes or to talk about him as if he were invisible. More raindrops started falling. Pedestrians scurried past him, occasionally looking up with flashes of recognition in their eyes. A few fans made moves to approach him, but they wisely stopped themselves when they saw the expression on his face. The buildings to his right were replaced with a body of water.

Something brushed against his leg. Cain looked down and was surprised to see a skinny brown dybbuk loping purposefully along the sidewalk. He hesitated for a moment, and then began to follow it. Dybbukim rarely ventured into the daylight. When a dybbuk came out during the day, it usually did so because its hiding place had been disturbed. This one would be in search of a new hole to curl up in; some shadowy, remote alley or abandoned building away from people and their tromping feet. It might lead Cain to someplace where he could be alone.

The dybbuk abruptly turned down a narrow, chained-off service road half-hidden behind a gaudy sign. He squinted at the sign; the words "Redondo Beach Marina" were painted on it in bright aqua letters. Cain had never heard of Redondo Beach, but the fact that no one else on the sidewalk seemed inclined to use the road was encouraging. He stepped over the yellow-painted chain and continued on his way.

The dybbuk scampered down the road, leading Cain past a parking lot that was surrounded by a high fence topped with barbed wire. A tin-roofed building stood behind the fence. Through the building's windows, Cain could see a forest of pulleys and steel racks. Two men were tinkering with a disembodied boat engine in front of the building. They stopped and followed Cain with their eyes while he hurried past them.

A sickle-shaped breakwater extended into the ocean at the end of the road. The dybbuk hopped onto it, sniffing the air eagerly. Cain climbed onto the breakwater as well and followed its curve, treading carefully over the slippery and uneven rocks. He stopped halfway out and stood staring over the green, roiling expanse of the ocean. Raindrops slashed against his face, and he kicked moodily at a beer bottle that had gotten wedged in a crevice near his foot. The steady lapping of the waves made him slightly queasy—he distrusted big bodies of water for reasons he had long ago forgotten—but he didn't mind the ocean's company now that the school and Breen were far behind him. Waves didn't spit out insults or give nasty looks.

"Cain!" Sammi's voice rang out behind him, cutting through his thoughts. "Jesus, what were you thinking, walking out like that?"

His band mates were making their way toward him, struggling over the rocks. Sammi and Vince looked annoyed, but Izzy hopped happily along and kept stopping to watch crabs scurry by or to examine bits of flotsam caught at the base of the breakwater. Cain hadn't realized that they were following him.

"Fuck!" Vince lurched and threw out his arms for balance when his foot skidded on a wet patch. "Yeah, asshole—what were you thinking? Now Queen Bitch is gonna be pissed at us for bailing, and Bruce Arkin is gonna be pissed 'cause she's pissed. Nice going, dumbass."

Sammi made a jerky beckoning movement. "Come on, if we really haul ass, we might have a chance of getting back before Cheryl stops arguing with Breen and notices we're gone."

"You know what?" Vince's voice took on a wistful tone. "I wish I could've stayed to watch the fight. Two snotty motherfuckers like that—one of 'em is sure to cold-cock the other before it's over."

"Oh, for Christ's sake, Vinnie," said Sammi with a sigh of resignation. "Come on, let's go. We really don't need to get Mr. Arkin any madder at us than he already is."

Cain didn't budge. A wave lapped against the breakwater, soaking the tips of his shoes. He kicked the beer bottle into the ocean.

"I want an apology from Breen," he said.

"Yeah, well, I want an army of strippers," sneered Vince.

"I'm serious," said Cain fiercely. "He had no right to say that I…" He couldn't bring himself to finish the sentence. "I want him to look me in the eye and tell me that he was wrong."

"He's not going to, you know," said Sammi. "He wouldn't apologize to you if you gave his stupid foundation a million dollars. I think it would kill the guy if he even had to stoop to shaking your hand at the fundraising banquet."

"If that's what it takes to get a little respect, I'll give him all the money he wants."

"Come on, Cain." Sammi gave him a pained look. "Breen is an asshole, yeah, and I'm really sorry he treated you that way. But we can't afford to get into a pissing match with him. I'm pretty sure Mr. Arkin is *this close*"—he held up his hand, making a nearly microscopic space between his thumb and forefinger for emphasis—"to deciding we're more trouble than we're worth as it is. Just come back with us and shoot the stupid commercial, okay? Please? I know *I* don't want Cheryl chewing my face off for flaking out."

Cain glanced at his band mate. Sammi's face was sickly pale, and the bags under his eyes were visible beneath his sunglasses. More rain was falling now, but not enough to be responsible for the thick sheen of moisture on his forehead.

"All right," he sighed. "I'll go back and do the commercial. But I still want an apology from Breen."

Sammi nodded unhappily.

Vince threw back his head with an exaggerated groan of relief. "Thank God," he said. "For a minute there, I was scared we'd be stuck here all day. Come on, Izzy, we're leaving. Cain is done with his sulk."

Izzy had wandered a fair way down the breakwater. He squatted near the edge, sifting through the seaweed as if he had lost something.

"In a minute," he shouted.

"Damn it all to hell, Izzy!" Vince threw up his arms in exasperation and lumbered his way to his drummer's side. "What did you drop in the water, moron? Your keys or your wallet?"

"Neither." Izzy didn't look up from his search, not even to show any sign of hurt at being called a moron. "I didn't drop anything. I thought I saw something shiny."

Cain caught a small flash of movement near Izzy. He was surprised to see the dybbuk pacing nervously near Izzy's kneeling form. He had stopped watching it once he got onto the breakwater, assuming that it would crawl into the first crevice it found. How strange that it was still out in broad daylight, and that it was lingering so near to a human.

"It's probably a dead fish or some garbage," said Sammi while he and Cain hurried after Vince. "Come on, Iz, we've got a job to finish. We can go to the beach this weekend if you want."

I bet it's a dead fish, thought Cain, noting the hungry look in the dybbuk's eyes and the way it licked its lips while it paced.

Izzy stuck his hand deeper into the undulating seaweed,

frowning with concentration. "No, I'm pretty sure it wasn't garbage. It looked like gold. Dang, where *is* that thing? I'm positive I saw it around here somewhere."

"Gold?" Vince snorted. "We're on a shitty pile of rocks in the middle of the damn ocean, dumbass. Why would there be any gold out here? Besides, gold doesn't float."

"Got it," said Izzy triumphantly. "It's definitely gold— or some kind of metal anyway. It feels like a bracelet or a necklace."

"Well, grab it and let's go already," said Vince.

"Hold on; it's caught on something."

Izzy groped under the slick of dead vegetation, muttering to himself while he tried to dislodge the mystery object. A line appeared on his brow, and he suddenly went quiet. Cain was about to ask him what was wrong when Izzy turned to his band mates with an expression of dread on his face.

"Oh my god," he whispered. "This...this isn't what I think it is, is it?"

He slowly lifted a narrow, branch-like thing out of the water. It was so covered in seaweed that Cain didn't realize what it was until Sammi and Vince stumbled back with gasps of horror.

It was an arm. An arm clad in sodden cloth and attached to a limp, waxy hand. The bracelet Izzy had found was still fastened around the wrist of a corpse. Against the paper-white flesh, the bracelet's faceted red stones looked like drops of condensed sun-fire.

"Shit," muttered Vince. Cain and Sammi stared in terrified silence. Izzy sat transfixed, as if unable to drop the arm despite his growing revulsion. None of them spoke.

Izzy gave the arm a tentative tug. More of the arm and

part of the shoulder rose dripping from the water. The hand fell open to reveal two intersecting gashes on the palm, both deep enough to expose bone. He gagged and turned green, but he kept pulling.

"What the fuck are you doing, Izzy?" said Vince.

"Getting her out of the water," said Izzy with a shudder.

Sammi shook his head. "I don't think you should. If that's a crime scene—and it sure as hell looks like one—the cops won't be happy with you for messing with it."

"Well, we can't leave her floating like trash." Izzy closed his eyes tightly when the lolling head began to emerge from beneath the waves. "That's just not right."

The rest of the body came up slowly, trailing seaweed. Izzy laid it as carefully as he could against the rocks, keeping his eyes shut the whole time.

"Poor thing," he said to the air in front of him. "I wonder who she was."

"A hooker, probably," said Vince in a strained voice, angling his head so he wouldn't have to look at her. "Let's get out of here."

Cain took a reluctant step closer. He slowly knelt down beside the bedraggled form of the dead woman. There was something oddly familiar about her. He squinted intently down at her broken nails with their remnants of pink polish and investigated the many deep stab wounds that peered through rips in the tattered remains of her clothing. He was unable to shake the feeling that he had seen her before. From the corner of his eye he noticed the dybbuk sidling closer to the corpse. It lunged forward suddenly, saliva flying from its open mouth. Cain threw out an arm to block it from leaping on the dead woman; it bounced off his outstretched hand and crumpled on the rocks, momentarily bleeding. He saw

Sammi and Vince frowning at him in confusion and tried to disguise the gesture as an attempt to brush the hair from her face.

"Cain, I really don't think that's a good idea," said Sammi in an agitated tone.

"Hold on. I think I know who she is." A shudder of deep revulsion ran through Cain as he felt the woman's dank hair shifting beneath his fingers, but he carried on. A cheekbone with a deep cut running over it came into view, then two clouded blue eyes and a broken nose, then a livid crater where the other cheekbone had been smashed in. The face was familiar too, even though it was bruised and mangled. There was something about the eyes especially, the way they appeared frozen in a fearful, pleading gape...A realization hit him, and he fell back with a sharp cry. Izzy whipped around to see what was wrong, got a good look at the body, and promptly vomited off the side of the breakwater.

Cain curled up with his tail looped around his knees, shivering in horror, while Sammi and Vince stared silently down at the battered corpse of Mr. Arkin's assistant Chelsea. The dybbuk picked itself up and crept toward the body. Its long black tongue wormed its way into the wound on Chelsea's cheek. Cain heard it swallow, but he was too numb to drive it away again. The sky darkened and the rain began to fall in earnest.

Chapter Twenty

Wounds

CAIN HAD ONLY BEEN asleep for a few hours when the memory jarred him awake.

Her name was Onoskelis.

I remember her scrawling humans' letters on the rocks. I remember the way her eyes shone when she explained their meanings to me—A,S,R,C,P,N,Z. Oni adored humans. The Makers, she called them. She collected broken tools from their trash heaps and dreamt of their machines.

"One day," she said to me, "I'm going to live in the Outside. I'll have a real house with electric lights and fresh water whenever I want some. I'll never have to waste energy on casting spells or on wrangling up a bunch of grumpy old elementals. The Makers live the best lives in the world!"

Then one day, she was gone. The tribe sang mourning hymns for her as if she were dead, yet there was no body laid out and painted with rust pigment, no offerings of dried meat or polished lake stones. No one would tell me why this ritual was different. My father and the other Elders would only say that she'd "gone away." But I remembered Oni's endless talk about the Outside, and I suspected she had gone up.

I had torch-lighting duty the next day. As I scurried through the valley with my taper, someone called my name. When I saw no one behind me except old Ashmedai, I almost continued on.

Then he said he had something to tell me.

I froze. Ashmedai was gaunt and stooped, barely taller than a human man. Only his threadbare wings, which he kept wrapped tightly around his body like a cloak, marked him as an Elder. I had never heard him speak before.

But he spoke to me then. In his whispery voice, he told me of the lost children, the ones who went to the Outside and were taken by humans. Many of them died, he said. Some had lived, but it would have been better for them if they had died too. He told me of the beatings, starvation, and rape in store for all captured Malakim and warned me that if Oni ever came back, she would not be the same. I was shaking by the time he finished, my tail wrapped around my knees in a frightened little curl, and I could only ask how he knew about these things.

Slowly, painfully, Ashmedai unfolded his wings. The body underneath them was twisted like a broken doll's, crisscrossed with luminous silver scars.

"Because," he whispered. "It happened to me."

Cain bolted upright in bed. The familiar green light flashed, wiping away the memory and replacing it with an image of Chelsea's battered body and clouded eyes. His heart raced, and he was covered in clammy sweat.

Muffled voices came from somewhere downstairs. Cain rolled out of bed. Maybe if he sat up and listened to his friends' chatter for a while, it would drive that horrible picture from his mind. He followed the voices to the living room, where he found Steve and Izzy sitting on the couch.

"See, Izzy, the shape is what makes it so effective," said Steve, pointing at an open book on the coffee table. "The problem with magic is that it gets weaker as it gets older, until it wears off completely. That's why my dad has so many returning clients. But if you cast your spell on something like this circle here"—he tapped the page with his index finger—"then the magic can't escape. It just keeps going round and round in its own little closed circuit."

"Uh huh." Izzy nodded, but Cain guessed from his tone that he had no real idea what Steve was talking about.

Steve continued his explanation. "You've still got to be careful, though, because magic doesn't work quite like the rest of the world does. If it's trapped, it builds up *more* energy as time goes on. So you've got to, you know, release some of the pressure somehow, so your enchanted ring or whatever doesn't suddenly explode in your face one day. That's what the star is for—those lines pull extra energy out of the circle and let it dissipate without making the spell weaker."

Izzy yawned and gestured to the book. "So what are the little squiggles inside the star for, and why is one of them scratched out?"

"You mean the Five Holy Bonds?" said Steve. "Well, see, this one is Geburah, for strength; this one is Netzach, for victory. Hod here means divine glory; Malkuth means earthly power. Then there's the fifth one, the one that's always scratched out. Yesod, it's called. I think it means something like beginning or foundation. And…That's pretty much all I know. Dad didn't tell me much about them when he was teaching me about Solomon's Seal. He wouldn't even tell me why Yesod is scratched out. I've got this theory, though, that the Holy Bonds don't actually do anything. I think some evil little asswipe of a Gifted person added them to make himself feel like he was some big hero for kidnapping and enslaving innocent demons."

Cain noticed Izzy squirming with boredom. He coughed loudly, causing both Steve and Izzy to turn around.

"Hey, Izzy, what's up?" he asked. "I thought you were going to the Rainbow with Vince."

"I was," said Izzy. "But I just didn't feel like going out. Steve was nice enough to keep me company. He's been trying to help me take my mind off…"

A visible shift came over Izzy's demeanor. His jaw stiffened, and he stared at the coffee table with misted eyes.

"I keep seeing her, Cain," he whispered.

"You mean Chelsea?" Cain's tail twitched uneasily.

Izzy nodded. "It's weird. She might as well have killed those guys herself, the way she led them to the Engineer. I know I wouldn't have these scars if it weren't for her, and Vince wouldn't be angry and unhappy, and Sammi wouldn't be hooked on smack. I kind of hate her for all of those things, to tell you the truth. But seeing her beat the hell up and thrown away and left to rot…nobody deserves that. Nobody. I hope the police found her."

"I'm sure they did," said Cain. His memory of most of the previous day was a blur of numb shock, but he did have a scattered recollection of Sammi placing a quick anonymous call from a payphone on the way back to the school. They had also managed to complete the commercial in a mechanical fashion. Cheryl scolded them afterwards for their unenthusiastic line readings. The Reverend Breen glared at them the whole time, but Cain had been too shaken up to let it bother him.

"Yeah," Steve chimed in. "Redondo Beach is a pretty

nice place. I hear that a lot of famous people keep their boats in the marina there. The cops probably got there really fast."

Cain nodded. They were all silent for a moment.

"He's still out there, though," said Izzy. "The Engineer, I mean. That's what scares me."

"Maybe they'll finally catch him this time," muttered Cain, without much hope.

"Yeah," said Izzy listlessly. "Maybe they'll—"

A loud, splintering crash sounded through the house. Cain and Izzy jumped, and Steve scrambled to his feet.

"What's Vince up to now?" groaned Cain.

"Vince isn't here," said Izzy. "He went to the bar. And I'm pretty sure Sammi is asleep."

Several smaller crashes interrupted him. Then, after a few seconds of tinkling glass, Cain heard the dull thuds and shuffles of someone rummaging through a room upstairs. Izzy's eyes widened, and his hair went bright red.

"Crap," he whispered. "We've got a burglar."

"A burglar?" Steve whispered fearfully. "Damn. We should call the cops...Hey, where are you going, Cain?"

"To try and scare him off," said Cain, transforming quickly into his demon form. He glanced down sadly at his taloned fingers. "Humans think I'm scary anyway; I might as well put their prejudices to good use."

He crept up the stairs with Izzy and Steve following quietly at his heels. Izzy stepped on a creaky floorboard, flinched, and turned into a bat.

The upstairs hallway was dark. Cain's door stood slightly open, and neither light nor sound was coming through it. Izzy's room was similarly lifeless. The noises were closer now, and they seemed to be coming from the bathroom. Cain noticed another noise as well, a high-pitched electric whine.

"Cain." Steve tugged at his arm. "What if he's got a gun?"

"He might not know a gun can hurt me," Cain whispered back. Many humans seemed to harbor odd ideas about what was harmful for demons. A few days ago, he had overheard Skeeter Judd telling an enraptured Yuri Ustinov and an exasperated Candi Jayne that Cain Pseudomantis could only be killed by a magic bullet that had been forged by melting down Eddie Morningstar's old guitar strings and then blessed in a certain church in Memphis. He drew himself up to his full height, put on a fearsome expression, and threw open the door.

Sammi sat huddled by the bathtub with Zap clinging to his arm. His fingers sifted through piles of glass fragments with quick and fevered movements. He did not look up when Cain stepped over the threshold. Zap tugged at Sammi's hand and whined louder when he grabbed up an especially sharp piece and blood began to flow.

"Damn," he muttered. "Damn, damn, damn. It doesn't fit."

"Sammi?" Cain took another cautious step into the bathroom, attempting to avoid the broken glass that littered the tiles. He saw right away where the fragments had come from: the mirror on the medicine cabinet was smashed, and only a few slivers remained in place against the wood backing. The rest sat in prismatic heaps on the floor, and Sammi seemed intent on examining every last piece.

"That's not it either!" Sammi tossed away the glass chunk with growing frustration and snatched up another. "Well, is it this one? It's gotta be...gotta be..."

He held it up to his eye like a monocle and squinted into

it, heedless of the blood trickling steadily down his arm. Zap flitted around him, throwing off small agitated explosions of red sparks. Cain was disturbed to see dozens of tiny dark splatters scattered among the glass on the floor.

"What are you doing?" he said, keeping his voice even so as not to upset Sammi further. "Do you know you're bleeding? I think you should put that glass down."

"I already got that piece," said Sammi irritably, pressing the mirror fragment closer to his eye. "Bleeding, pain, tears, white light, fear—those are the pieces I have. It's the face I need, *his* face—the one hole in my eyes. I can't be like Vince anymore, man. I can't let that thing sit and fester. I gotta fill it or he's won; he's won and gone to…"

Sammi abruptly hurled the glass against the floor. A strangled sob tore from his throat, and he brought both fists down on the pile of broken glass with a sickening crunch.

"Fuck!" he shrieked. "Fuck all you cocksucking sons of bitches! You're not what I need. No, no, the hole is still wide open, and all I remember is the pain and not the face that caused it, and I *need* to remember, I need, I need…"

He punched the glass again, harder this time, leaving a smear of blood on the tile. Cain could see dozens of mirror shards sticking out of his flesh like a tiny mountain range; they must have been hurting him immensely, but he showed no sign that he felt the pain. Zap let out a shrill, crackling wail of distress.

"Oh my god!" Izzy pushed his way past Cain and rushed to Sammi's side. "Sammi, stop it! You could kill yourself doing that."

He grabbed Sammi's wrist and tried to haul him upright. Zap's eyes went red. She streaked toward Izzy like a miniature comet, her whiskers throwing off a trail of angry sparks. Izzy stiffened when she latched onto his wrist. A jerky convulsion ran through his body, propelling him backwards against the wall and dislodging Zap. She flew into the bathtub, bounced, and came at him again. Izzy had the presence of mind to turn into a small, swift bird of prey and fly out of the bathroom before she reached him. The enraged elemental charged after him.

Sammi leapt to his feet. He looked around wildly, shivering and sweating, and his arms chopped through the air in an erratic windmill motion. Blood droplets showered from his hands as he flailed, speckling the sink and walls. His fevered eyes fixed on Cain.

"No!" he hissed. "Don't come any closer! I don't know your face, but I know you, and I won't go. I won't go back, do you hear? No more cuts. No more restraints. No more fire. Whoever you are, you bastard, you've tortured me enough!"

"It's all right, Sammi." Cain took another slow step closer, putting his hand out in a placating gesture. "You're safe at home. Nobody is going to hurt you. If you'll just let me—"

The lightning bolt took him by surprise. It hit him so fast that he didn't feel it at all until he had staggered out the door, hit the wall, and slid to the hallway floor. Even when Steve screamed in horror and the sensation of a heavy sledgehammer striking his heart and lungs exploded in his chest, he didn't fully grasp what had happened until Sammi charged after him with both index fingers extended and smoldering.

"I won't take any more of it," he screamed. Jagged tongues of electricity rippled under the thick layer of sweat on his skin. He began to shudder violently. "Poison dripping on me, mixing into my blood, flowing through my veins, burning, burning till I want to die. Something ripping up inside me. No…can't move…can't…hardly…breathe!"

His arms jerked, and he pivoted around with a sharp gasp. He spun on his heels several more times, staring at the open bathroom door, at Cain, and at Steve, who sat huddled with fright in the doorway to Cain's room. Panic shone in Sammi's eyes, and the electricity licking through him intensified until the air around him crackled and the carpet beneath his feet began to smoke.

Cain watched through a gray haze while Sammi fixed both fingers on him. He was in shock and couldn't bring his limbs to move until he caught a flash of movement to his left.

"Steve!" he shouted. "Be careful!"

It was too late. Steve rammed into Sammi's midsection, setting off a small blast of sparks. A thin tongue of half-formed lightning bounced harmlessly off the wall above Cain's head. Sammi hurtled backward and tumbled down the stairs, dragging Steve with him. Cain staggered upright and lurched after them, wincing at the loud thumps that marked their downward journey. He found them sprawled side-by-side on the front hall carpet. Steve leapt up, rubbing a bruised elbow and gaping at Sammi's outstretched form. Sammi's hands were still bleeding heavily, and he was stunned, but he seemed otherwise unhurt.

Izzy materialized from the kitchen. His eyes went round with fright when he saw Sammi. "Holy crap! What happened?"

"Sammi freaked out," murmured Cain, rubbing his chest. "He was about to zap me, and Steve tackled him. They went down the stairs together."

"Really?" Izzy turned to Steve with an admiring gasp. "You tackled Sammi when he was just about to let loose? Wow. You're a lot braver than I am."

"I don't feel very brave," muttered Steve, who looked a bit stunned himself. "I feel like I'm lucky to be alive, actually."

"Izzy, where's Zap?" said Cain. He wanted to calm down Sammi and heal his wounds, but he feared to think how the blue salamander would react.

"You mean that little flying lizard thing?" Izzy shuddered at the memory. "In the kitchen. It wouldn't let me alone, so I shut it up in the breadbox."

Cain crept to Sammi's side and tried to pick up his hand. Sammi flinched and twisted away.

"No," he muttered. "It hurts. Don't touch…Don't want…"

"Come on, Sammi." Cain reached for his hands again, only to have him pull them farther out of reach. "I can heal those cuts, but I really need you to hold still."

"If you need him to hold still, why don't you put him in front of the TV?" said Izzy. "I caught him watching TV while he was high a couple times; it totally zoned him out. I think I could've cut off his arm, and he wouldn't have felt it."

It took some coaxing, but they finally lured Sammi into the living room and sat him down on the couch. Izzy picked up the remote, but he did not turn on the TV right away. He looked troubled.

"Are you all right?" Cain asked him.

"Sure." Izzy frowned at the remote. "It's just…this might be my fault, Cain."

Cain shook his head. "Sammi hurting himself might be

your fault? That's not right, Izzy. You didn't get him high."

"No, but it may still be my fault." Izzy massaged the bridge of his nose wearily, and Cain thought his eyes looked moist. "See, after that run-in with the cops, I found Sammi's stash and flushed it. He must have gone out and bought some more."

"You got rid of Sammi's stash?" said Cain. This was encouraging news. He had thought that he was the only one who was uncomfortable with Sammi's heroin consumption; his band mates rarely mentioned the issue, and their fellow club regulars always talked about their own drug use so flippantly.

"Smack isn't good for him," said Izzy. "Haven't you noticed that big bruise on his arm, or the way he always looks tired and sick nowadays? Vince is worried about him too, even though he'd never admit that he is. I thought I was doing the right thing by flushing that crap—I didn't mean for him to buy a whole new stash! God, what if his dealer cut the new stuff with, like, drain cleaner or something, and that's why it made him freak? He'd never have bought it if I hadn't—"

"Izzy, it's okay," said Cain gently. He was relieved to hear that his band mates felt the same way he did, but Sammi's wounds needed tending immediately. "It wasn't your fault at all. I'm sure I would have done the same thing myself if I'd thought of it. Do you think you could find a channel Sammi likes while I start healing him?"

Even after the TV was turned on, Sammi squirmed restlessly for a few minutes. Then he noticed the TV and began to relax. Soon he was so absorbed in the flickering screen that he did not wince when Cain quietly picked up his left hand and began to pull out the embedded glass shards.

525

Extracting the glass took longer than the healing itself, and Cain was relieved when Steve plucked up the courage to help. They both shivered every time they dug out another sharp chunk, but Sammi didn't seem to care. He stared at the screen with unblinking eyes and a big foolish grin plastered on his face, chuckling at random intervals. Izzy stood to the side, flipping the channel whenever Sammi showed signs of boredom. Soon the glass sat in a small bloody pile on the coffee table, and Cain was ready to begin the healing spell. He cupped Sammi's hands in his and let the power flow, swathing the wounds in a shimmering, golden blue haze that became gradually brighter as the bleeding slowed. Pink scar tissue appeared and began to creep over the lacerations; they were almost closed when Sammi suddenly went rigid.

"It's okay, it's okay," Cain heard Izzy saying. "Don't worry. I'll just change the channel so you don't have to listen to him."

"No!" Sammi snatched his hands away from Cain. Glowing motes of magical energy scattered over the couch when he leapt up to grab the remote from Izzy. "I wanna hear what he's saying!"

Cain rolled sideways to escape Sammi's flailing legs. Sammi wrested the remote from Izzy and clutched it to his chest, glaring at the TV. Izzy muttered fearfully and made a half-hearted attempt to grab it back, but Sammi clutched it harder and growled and threw off sparks until Izzy backed off. Steve had been inching away since he had finished helping with the glass removal. He took this new development as a good cue to leave the room entirely, half-muttering an excuse about unfinished homework on his way out. Cain decided not to resume the spell; the injuries would easily finish healing by themselves now. Instead, he turned around to see what had made his bassist so upset. He wasn't surprised when he saw the Reverend Breen's face on the TV screen.

"Some people think there is no devil-worshipping cult, simply because they haven't seen anything about it in the news lately," he was saying. "Well, let me tell you right now: as Christ warned his followers of the dangers of complacency, so I must warn you of the real danger we continue to face in this city and in this great country of ours. Your children are still in grave danger of being recruited by the Satanists, brothers and sisters. I know this truth because I have seen the cultists at work with my own eyes."

He paused to take a sip from the crystal water glass balanced on the corner of his podium. Sammi kept his eyes fixed on the screen, breathing heavily.

"Believe me," Breen continued. "I know how far this cult will go to get innocent little ones in thrall to them. Just yesterday, I witnessed the disheartening spectacle of Cain Pseudomantis himself swaggering into a school full of children, in broad daylight, bold as a lion after his prey, acting under the guise of charity. Charity! As if that creature had a soul capable of caring for the welfare of others!"

Cain felt an unpleasant tightness in his chest, and he couldn't help baring his teeth at the TV. Mr. Warwick had more than once refrained from punishing him when he did something wrong in favor of grumbling out loud that no punishment he could devise would sink in because, after all, demons like Cain had no souls and thus were incapable of fully living up to human standards of decency. The slander was utter nonsense, of course—how could he be alive without a soul?—but for some reason, it had always stung him deeply.

"I can't tell you how disheartening this act of moral perversion is," thundered Breen, striking the podium with his fist. "And to add insult to injury, the rock musicians of this city continue to keep the lie of the Engineer alive to provide a smokescreen for the crimes of their lackeys. Just yesterday, an anonymous tip led police to the battered body of a woman, who was identified as a suspected accomplice of the so-called Engineer. This news hasn't spread widely yet, but it will…and I fear the consequences when it does. I fear that people will jump to the conclusion that a dangerous killer is still on the loose, preparing to attack the poor, pitiful rock musicians who so bravely exposed him. There's no doubt in my mind that many gullible young people will believe this pernicious falsehood. After all, they weren't there to see Cain and his disciples sneak away from the school and their own manager a convenient hour or two before the call was placed and the body found. Our young people look at these men and see the pleasure that their music provides, but they don't see the men's cold-blooded willingness to choke the life out of an innocent woman to advance their evil agenda."

Cain's mouth dropped open. He turned to stare at Izzy, who looked every bit as horrified. Did Breen just say what Cain thought he said? No, he couldn't have—surely not even he would go that far.

Sammi jabbed his finger at the TV with a strangled cry of rage and fired off a massive lightning bolt. The sound of Breen's sermon was cut off abruptly with a violent, white flash, and acrid smoke filled the room. Cain leapt up to open a window. When the smoke cleared, he saw Sammi hunched over, shaking in a fit of ragged sobs in front of the smoldering ruins of the TV. Izzy hovered nearby, trying ineffectually to comfort him.

"Fuck you, old man," gasped Sammi. "How can you say we're lying? How *dare* you say I'm lying when I remember...I remember..." More sobs burst out of him.

A small flicker of movement near the door caught Cain's eye. He instinctively turned in its direction, assuming that Steve had heard the commotion and had come down to see what was wrong.

But Vince was watching them. He looked down at Sammi with a baleful expression on his face. His jaw was clenched, and his teeth appeared to be grinding. He took a deep breath and moved as if to join the others; but after a moment of indecision, he turned on his heel and stalked off into the kitchen, closing the door behind him with an angry thud.

Michael Anderson woke that morning to find that the walls of his room had become transparent. He could still see the outlines of them, hanging before his bed like slabs of solid air, and a single blank rectangle that had once been the window towered high above him. Beyond them, stood the garden, where a man walked side-by-side with a nurse and where a disheveled woman in a bulky gray shirt sat sobbing under a flowering tree.

He tore his eyes away from them. He didn't want to know their stories. Their stories would be too much for him. Too many stories already pounded at his mind in a steady tide of fear and confusion and sadness the moment the pills wore off. If he knew them all, he would implode under the weight of them. He focused on the brick wall that enclosed the garden instead, taking comfort in its solidness.

Then, without warning, it became as transparent as the

walls of his room.

Not again.

Michael's arms flew out in dismay. He felt himself being sucked into the void, just like he had been sucked into it on the day he met the Dark Lion in the graveyard. People and cars and storefronts and street signs rushed by him in a dizzying whirl. Then they all stopped.

He was still in bed in his room at the hospital; he knew he was there because he could feel the rough covers under his clenched hands.

Yet he was also standing on pink-and-cream tiles in a bathroom. A young brown-haired girl in a gauzy blue nightgown was there, kneeling with her back to him. While he watched, she bent convulsively forward and vomited into the toilet.

She finished and sat halfway up, breathing hard. After a few minutes, she vomited again. Michael stared at her. There was something familiar about this girl. He had never seen her before, but he instantly recognized a part of her, something small and easy to miss, a tiny, living spark buried deep beneath her pale sweat-frosted skin.

The pull started again. This time, he let it carry him away. If he stood there any longer, he would start to know things about the girl. And he didn't want to know things about her. He was already crammed to bursting with stories.

While Michael Anderson woke miles away, Michelle Breen stood up shakily to brush her teeth yet again. She stared at the toilet with a perplexed air. This morning was the fourth morning in a row she had vomited. She had assumed she had food poisoning or the stomach flu the first few times, but her symptoms had persisted so long that she doubted either of those conditions was causing them.

The toothpaste tube was empty. She rummaged around under the sink for a spare, dislodging a box of tampons. A little shudder ran through her when she stuck the toothbrush in her mouth. Given a choice between the nasty bitter flavor of coffee and the taste of toothpaste mingled with vomit residue, Michelle thought she would rather have the coffee any day.

The toothbrush clattered in the glass when she put it away, and she bent down with a grunt to pick up the scattered tampons. Her hands froze, hovering over the white tubes. A wave of horror shot through her. When had she last used one? Her mind scrambled, and she came up with a scattered memory of being annoyed at finding a few drops of blood on her new white panties over two months ago.

Cain disliked riding in cars. He disliked the unnerving hum of the engine's vibrations beneath him, and he disliked how the low ceilings and the nearly nonexistent legroom made him feel claustrophobic. But more than anything, he disliked how the seats offered him nowhere to put his tail. He had to choose between sitting on it or draping it awkwardly off to one side in a position that tended to give him cramps. He chose the sideways position for the ride to the show that night because it hurt him slightly less than the other position when they went over bumps or around sharp curves, and Izzy was driving.

A twinge of apprehension ran through him as he climbed into the front seat. Izzy's car was a huge, dented old lime-green Cadillac that was so big and boxy that it reminded Cain of the tanks in the old war movies that Lance liked to watch. The car had simply appeared at the curb one night a few weeks ago. When asked about it, Izzy said he had "bought it off a guy" for a couple hundred dollars. Vince and Sammi had been skeptical that Izzy paid so little, but Cain soon suspected that the price had actually been a bit high. He had never heard any car make such a horrible, jarring, gravel-rasping-against-steel noise as this one did when Izzy turned the key in the ignition.

The engine's angry grating grew louder as the car lurched forward. Izzy's driving was impulsive and dramatic: he accelerated with a heavy foot, came to jerky stops, and took broad, sweeping turns. Cain let out a sharp yelp when an enormous bump shook his seat. Some nearby pedestrians scattered with waving arms and screams of fear when the car whipped past them.

"Sorry about that," said Izzy calmly while he steered the car back onto the road with another tail-rattling bump. "I think I went up on the curb a little there."

"A *little?*" snapped Vince from the back seat. "You were practically driving on the sidewalk. Didn't you see those people running for their lives? One of these days you're gonna kill someone with your shitty driving, dumbass!"

"Shut up, Vince," grumbled Sammi. "Do you want to go back to riding the stupid bus to every show?"

His voice sounded strained, and Cain suspected that he was defending Izzy's driving only to prevent a doubly dangerous in-driver's-seat crying fit.

Vince looked like he was about to shoot back another nasty comment when a violent shudder ran through the car. A few tendrils of smoke escaped from under the hood, and Cain coughed when an acrid whiff of burning chemicals assailed his nostrils. Izzy hastily pulled to the side of the road.

"Crap," he groaned. "Not again."

He scrambled out of the car, and the others followed him. Vince was the first at his side.

"Not again?" he shouted. "What do you mean, *not again*? Does this sort of thing happen often?"

"Not really." Izzy reached to lift the hood. "Just once a week or so."

"Once a…!" Vince shoved him aside. "Get out of the way, moron! I swear to God, if this pile of junk makes us late to the gig, I'm setting it on fire. Why the hell did you buy it anyway? We're not playing at dives anymore; you've got enough money now that you don't have to drive a pile of junk around."

Izzy pouted. "My car isn't a pile of junk, Vince. She's only got about forty thousand miles on her, and she's a really cool color too."

Vince didn't reply. He was too busy waving away the small explosion of smoke that had mushroomed into his face as soon as he opened the hood. Cain watched him in amusement as he danced in place, blasting out a steady string of profanities.

Vince's tantrum died down into sullen muttering as he tinkered with the engine. Then Cain heard voices and looked up to see a crowd of girls pointing at Izzy and chattering. They did not seem to have noticed him. He slipped into a nearby alley and hid behind a pile of empty crates, determined to keep out of their line of sight. He could only handle so many interactions with strange humans in a day, and he had heard that the show tonight was sold out.

He took stock of his surroundings while he waited for them to leave. The alley was cluttered with boxes and piles of discarded brick, but its walls were clean except for a bit of bright green graffiti. Cain squinted at it for a moment and was amused to discover that it read "Pseudomantis Rulz!"

"You look a little out of it, honey," said a voice to his right. "I hope you haven't been raiding your drummer's chocolate stash again."

Cain spun around in surprise and discovered that Crazy Loti was standing right beside him.

"You know about that too?" he said glumly.

"Of course I know about it," she said. "It's my job to know what happens in the city, remember? Anyway, I really do hope you haven't touched any more chocolate since that night; it's bad for you. I suppose Nicanor put that idea in your head?"

"Nicanor?"

"Most of his customers call him Jodido," she explained.

"Oh yeah." He nodded. "He did tell me about chocolate."

"Ah, I should have known." Loti shook her head in disgust. "He was trying to turn you into another loyal customer, no doubt. Nicanor has never been able to resist making an extra dollar. I should have known something was up when he started following you around Delfina's neighborhood."

"That was him?" Cain sighed. He knew he found Jodido creepy for a reason. "Why didn't he just show himself, then?"

"I imagine he was afraid Delfina would notice. Strange, isn't it, the way a full-blooded god can be scared off by a mostly ordinary human with a broom and a fighting streak?"

"Jodido is a *god*?" Cain stared at her. He had never met a god to his knowledge; but even if he had, he couldn't imagine one willingly taking the form of a man who couldn't walk without shuffling. He also couldn't imagine that a god would believe that wearing a green-and-fuchsia blazer over red pants was a tasteful fashion choice.

Loti frowned. "I wish folks wouldn't call him Jodido—that's not a nice thing to call anyone, even a drug dealer. And he is a god...just not a particularly powerful one. I imagine that's why he's been reduced to pushing cocaine and heroin on the streets of a human city."

Cain wondered why a god would need a job at all. Maybe it was better not to know.

"But that's not what I came to talk to you about." Her voice dropped to a whisper. "I also know what happened in that studio. Do you?"

"No, actually," he said hopefully. "I called in my friend Steve to help me puzzle it out, but we haven't really had a chance to talk about it much."

"I'm sure he'll tell you that you were very, very lucky," she said gravely. "You started healing that young man at the exact right moment. The link between body and soul hadn't quite broken yet, and your spell made it strong enough to hold. If it had been completely gone, well, he still would've lived again, if you'd put enough energy into it."

The look in her eyes told Cain that she was serious, but he could only shake his head.

"But that's impossible," he said.

"No," Loti said. "Not impossible. That's the one secret Gift granted to your whole race, the strangest leftover from your half-divine parentage: you can raise the dead if you choose. But you can only do it *once* in your lifetime. If you'd gotten to work on that boy after he'd properly died, he would've lived again, but at the cost of another life. Your life. His second chance would've meant your death."

A prickly chill played across Cain's skin. No, Loti had to be mistaken. The world didn't work that way. Yet he remembered the wrenching sensation, and the darkness closing in on him. Had he really come so close to death in that studio? An uncontrollable shaking took hold of his hands, and he closed his eyes to quiet the sudden whirling in his brain.

"But how...?" he whispered with his eyes still squeezed shut.

"Steve can tell you more about it—if you convince him that you won't try it again, that is. He'll hold back, I think, because he's terrified of losing you. Now go catch up with your friends. And for heaven's sake, don't buy anything from Nicanor. I've got far too many drug-addled young men running around my city as it is. I don't want that for you, child. You're far too sweet."

Cain took a deep breath and opened his eyes, wanting to ask many more questions, but he was alone. The alley was empty except for him and, a few seconds later, Vince, who stomped up to him to snarl that the car was running again.

"Well, let's go, dumbass!" Vince waved his arms impatiently. "Izzy's shitheap could break down again at any second. What the fuck are you doing in this crappy place, anyway? Looking for someone?"

Cain glanced around the alley, still shaken. "I...don't know."

They all piled into the car. Cain spent the rest of the ride staring out the window, oblivious to the bumps and jerks and Vince's loud complaints from the back seat. Then his door opened, and Sammi stood over him.

"Hey, man," he said. "Aren't you coming? We're here."

Cain blinked. They had indeed arrived at the venue; the

car was crookedly parked. Vince and Izzy were headed for the stage door, still locked in an argument over whether or not Izzy's car was a shitty pile of tin barely worthy of the scrap heap.

"Yeah." He slowly disentangled himself from his frayed seat belt.

"Cain?"

He paused and glanced up at Sammi.

"Are you all right? You look like something is bothering you."

There were heavy bags under Sammi's eyes, and his face was a sickly pale color. He looked like he had quite a few things of his own bothering him. Cain decided that he didn't need another thing to worry about.

"I'm fine," he said. "Let's get inside."

They walked to the stage door in silence. When Cain opened it, he was surprised to see Mr. Arkin in the hallway, leaning against the wall with his arms crossed as if he had been waiting for them. Vince and Izzy stood behind him. Izzy was chewing nervously on his lip, but Vince did not look worried at all. Cain couldn't quite read Vince's expression, but he almost seemed smug.

"Into that dressing room." Mr. Arkin jerked his head toward a nearby door. "Now."

His tone was so short and angry that they obeyed without a word. Cain scurried into the dressing room with his band mates at his heels and immediately ensconced himself in the far corner; he thought it best to let Mr. Arkin have the one chair in the room.

Vince had a different idea. He plopped down in the chair and casually splayed his legs. Cain saw him flash a brief, insolent grin when Mr. Arkin stepped into the room and found himself without a place to sit.

Mr. Arkin wasted no time. He tapped his foot impatiently, raking the boys with a disapproving scowl that eventually came to rest on Vince.

"So which one of you called Nathaniel Breen this morning?" he asked.

Izzy mumbled something unintelligible. Vince smirked. Cain and Sammi exchanged a puzzled glance.

"Called Nathaniel Breen?" said Sammi cautiously. "Why would we—"

"I'll tell you why." Mr. Arkin's glare deepened. "Because *someone* went and pledged a hundred grand to the Voice in the Wilderness campaign for abused children in the band's name—that's why. Then that same someone went out and bragged about it to every reporter he could find. That someone is one of you, and I want to know which one. Any ideas, Mr. Sweet?"

He had not taken his eyes off Vince for the duration of the whole speech. Cain suspected that he already knew who did it.

"Hmm…dunno," said Vince innocently. "Maybe Cain did it."

"Oh, really?" Mr. Arkin raised an eyebrow. "*Cain* dug up Breen's home phone number, calculated the minimum amount of money he'd need to give to get onto the foundation's gold donor list, and made a pledge? Cain barely knows how to use a phone, Vince."

Cain gave Mr. Arkin an indignant look. His knowledge of human technology certainly had a few holes and weak spots, but he knew how to use a phone. He had come a long way from the early days of his captivity when he had thought that Mr. Warwick's gas stove was a box of trapped fire elementals and the television was some sort of scrying mirror.

"I'll ask one more time." Mr. Arkin's eyes narrowed. "One of you called Breen this morning. Did you call him, Vince?"

Cain regarded Vince with amazement. After all Vince's laments and rants about the injustice of compulsory charity, this donation sounded far out of character for him. Yet he had been inexplicably missing in action for most of the morning.

"Maybe," said Vince with a shrug. "Why do you care, anyway? You said we could give our money to any charity we wanted."

"I didn't think you'd do it in a way that would motivate Breen to call my office and give me hell for a whole hour." Mr. Arkin threw up his arms in exasperation. "Honestly, Vince, only you could give money to help abused children and do it *spitefully*. I hope you can at least pretend to behave yourself at the donor's banquet in two weeks."

Sammi raised an eyebrow. "Why would we go to the donor's banquet? I mean, Breen didn't actually *accept* our money, right? There's no way he's that desperate for cash."

"Well, he doesn't have much of a choice now that the news has spread all over the media. He won't be happy about it, but he'll probably take the money and invite you to save face."

"But we don't have to go, right?" said Izzy. "I mean, he won't want us there anyway, and I don't wanna get dressed up for—"

"If he invites you, you're going. End of story."

"But—"

"No buts," said Mr. Arkin tartly. "You're all going to

that banquet, and you're going to get dressed up and make clean, polite small talk and eat the boring rubbery chicken entrée just like all the other donors. If that doesn't sound like much fun to you, well then, maybe next time you're tempted to pull a stunt like this, you'll stop and consider that actions have consequences, even for rock stars. Do you understand?"

Cain, Sammi, and Izzy nodded miserably. Vince tried and failed to look properly chastened.

"Good. Now get ready for your show."

He stalked out of the dressing room, shaking his head. Before he rounded the corner, he pressed his fingers to his temples with a deep sigh. Cain heard him muttering about something that he "really didn't need right now."

"Damn you, Vince," said Sammi as soon as Mr. Arkin was gone. "You gave money to Breen just to piss him off? What's wrong with you? Hell, how did you even get his number?"

Vince shrugged. "I went through Cain's hot little girlfriend's backpack one day while she was upstairs fucking him."

"You did *what?*" Cain stared at him, appalled. "When was this?"

"Dunno—a month or two ago," said Vince. "Don't get your codpiece in a wad. I just wanted to see if she had an address book or something in there; she might've had a few girlfriends who'd be up for some screwing. Anyway, she had a card with all her daddy's different phone numbers on it, for emergencies, I guess. I copied his home number and put the card back. I thought I'd prank the old man, but I couldn't think of any good pranks until this morning."

"Good prank?" Izzy blinked. "Uh...Vince? I think this

thing is more serious than a prank. I mean, it'll be all over the news. And won't we have to shake Breen's hand and stuff?"

Vince cackled wickedly. "That's the point, moron. It'll kill that fat fuck to have to shake our hands and thank us for our generosity and caring and shit and to talk about how awesome we are in front of a whole roomful of his little yes-men. He'll be beyond pissed, man. It'll be great. Heh, if I have to give away my hard-earned money, I might as well get a show out of it."

Anger flashed in his eyes, and his tone suddenly became threatening. Besides," he added. "He deserves it. I've had it with the low-down, lying shit he's been saying about us. Hell, he made one of my band mates cry this morning. God damn it, nobody makes *my* band mates cry except me."

CHAPTER TWENTY-ONE

FINE DINING

THE REVEREND BREEN WAS ominously silent in the days leading up to the Voice in the Wilderness donor banquet. The closest the band came to hearing from him was on the day an exhausted-looking Mr. Arkin showed up at the house bearing a neat little beige envelope.

"Boys," he said as he handed the card inside to Cain, "you've got a banquet to go to."

"Ooh…fancy!" Izzy took the card from Cain and tilted it, making the gold lettering flash in the light. "I bet there'll be candles and silver and waiters holding those trays of little appetizer things." His face fell. "And that probably means I'll have to get *really* dressed up—like in a tux. Crap."

"Shit." Vince's face fell too. "We probably will have to wear tuxes, won't we? Well, fuck it. I didn't even think about that."

"Maybe next time, you will think," growled Mr. Arkin, rubbing his bloodshot eyes.

Shortly after he left, Cheryl stalked into the house without a word to anyone and started rummaging through the kitchen cupboards. Cain couldn't imagine what she was up to until she called everyone into the kitchen for something she called a "remedial table manners lesson."

"Now let's try this one more time." Cheryl massaged her temples wearily. "They've just brought your salad out. Which fork do you use?"

Izzy's hand hovered tentatively over the two forks to the left of the plate. He had a harried expression on his face, and his gaze flicked desperately from fork to fork.

"Hey!" Cheryl rounded on Sammi, who was making subtle gestures toward the fork farthest from the plate. "Quit helping him! You might not be able to help each other at the banquet, you know."

Cain studied Cheryl's curious makeshift place setting. Despite Mr. Warwick's best efforts to educate him, he had never understood why humans insisted on following an elaborate code of proper tableware usage. He found that if he needed a fork but couldn't find one, a spoon would usually do. None of Cheryl's rules made sense to him, and since they did not have proper dishes or tableware to practice with, her directions were even more confusing. The dummy place setting had been cobbled together from a motley assortment of junk, and each item represented something else: Sammi's cheap, mismatched flatware was "tableware;" a couple chipped plates were "china;" two beer steins were "wine glasses;" and an out-of-date road map of Nebraska was a "placemat."

"Uh…" Izzy plaintively pointed to the inside fork. "That one, I guess?"

"No!" Cheryl threw up her arms in exasperation. "Why is this so hard for you? Okay, look, a formal place setting is like an apple. You've got to eat the skin on the outside before you can get to the inside part, right? The silverware on the *outside*, farthest from the plate, has to be used before the silverware on the *inside*. Outside first, inside last—that's the rule to remember."

"But…but…" Izzy pointed to the single spoon above the plate. "That spoon is not on the inside *or* the outside. It's just sorta floating there."

"That's the dessert spoon, Izzy," said Cheryl impatiently. "Don't worry about that one; it's the last piece of silverware you'll use."

"But Cheryl," Vince interjected, shooting a sly grin at Cain, "if a place setting is an apple, that would make the dessert spoon the stem, and you don't eat the stem. Besides, you didn't say the dessert spoon was last. You said the inside silverware was last. Does that make the dessert spoon inside-inside, or just last-last?"

Izzy's face fell further, and he clutched his head as if it hurt. Cheryl ground her teeth in frustration.

"Stop confusing him!" she snarled. "Look, Izzy, forget what I said about the apple, okay? When they bring you your salad, use the outside fork. When they bring you your soup, use the outside spoon. When they bring you your main course, use the inside silverware. Then when dessert comes out, the dessert spoon will be the only thing that's left. Got it?"

"Sort of," said Izzy, wringing his hands. "But…what if they serve salad and no soup? Then there'll still be a spoon on the outside when the main course comes."

"Well, sometimes it's okay if your salad fork or soup spoon doesn't get used before—"

"But you said it wasn't okay!" Izzy looked like he was genuinely beginning to panic.

"You know what?" said Cheryl. "I think it's time for you to take a break. Vince, you're up next. Come here and show me how to hold a fork properly."

"Hey, are you okay?" whispered Cain after Izzy hastily backed away from the table, red-faced and sweating.

"Yeah," sighed Izzy. "It's just...I hate taking tests in front of other people. I freak out and forget all the answers, and I always feel like everybody is watching me. It brings back some bad memories of school."

"I don't see why *we* had to get sucked into this mess," grumbled Sammi, glaring at Vince, who was embroiled in a lively argument with Cheryl over whether the death-grip-like way he held his fork was good enough for polite company. "Vinnie was the one who went and kicked the beehive like a dumbass. Mr. Arkin should make him go by himself."

Izzy nodded. "I'm kinda worried about Mr. Arkin. He's been acting really weird and creepy ever since...you know. Did you see the bags under his eyes?"

"I don't like it," muttered Sammi. "I don't believe for a minute that story he's been spreading around that the Engineer set up shop, and he had no idea. He knows something that he's not telling us; I'm sure of it."

Vince threw the fork down on the table with a resounding bang and stormed out of the room. Cheryl made a half-hearted attempt to call him back and then rounded vengefully on the remaining band members.

"Cain, you're up," she snapped. "Which one is your salad fork?"

Cain ran over to the table. He studied the odd arrangement for a moment before managing, through a combination of remembered snippets of Cheryl's lectures and sheer luck, to point out the correct fork.

"Huh." Cheryl's prickly demeanor softened a little.

"That's right. At least one member of the band will pick up the right fork when the salad comes out."

"Uh…Cheryl?" Cain swallowed nervously. "At the banquet…what if…what if they give me something that I…don't really like?"

"Take a couple of bites to be polite and push the rest around your plate," said Cheryl. "Now which one is the soup spoon?"

"But…um…what if I *can't* eat it?" Cain had tried to eat a head of lettuce once, out of curiosity. The experiment had resulted in him emptying the contents of his stomach all over the expensive new living room carpet, and it had earned him a solid thump in the small of his back with the fireplace poker when Mr. Warwick saw the mess he made.

"Couple of bites to be polite; push the rest around your plate," repeated Cheryl.

"But I…"

Cheryl narrowed her eyes at him.

"Never mind," said Cain, wondering how much food he could hide in his napkin before someone noticed.

A thin man who Cain had never seen before stood behind Mr. Arkin's desk. He held a clipboard and a long measuring tape in his hands. Mr. Arkin was leaning against the front of the desk, making a big show of dusting off a framed picture. Neither he nor the thin man spoke. Cain shifted nervously in his chair, glancing over at Izzy and Sammi for guidance. Neither of them seemed to know the purpose of the meeting either. They were both standing, hanging back from the desk, and they looked confused and anxious.

"So what did you drag us in here for at ten in the

morning?" said Vince.

"I was afraid you wouldn't show up if you knew why I wanted you here." Mr. Arkin kept his attention on the picture. "It's time to get your measurements."

Izzy scratched his head. "But the nice costume lady already took our measurements."

"He means for tuxes, Iz," whispered Sammi.

"What the hell do we need tuxes for?" Vince gave Mr. Arkin a pained look. "Can't we just wear our stage gear?"

"Absolutely not," said Mr. Arkin. "You don't wear leather pants and a codpiece to a black-tie dinner, especially not when most of the guests attending will be conservative Christians. Which reminds me—Vince, since you started this kerfuffle, you get first measuring. Go on, and don't give Frank here any trouble."

Vince followed Frank out of the office, grumbling all the way. Cain saw Sammi and Izzy exchange an uneasy glance.

"Uh…Mr. Arkin?" said Izzy.

"I'm not changing my mind. Your RSVP cards have already been sent."

Izzy flinched and looked hurt at his sharp tone.

Sammi cleared his throat. "It's not that," he said. "It's just that we'd rather…um…wait our turn outside. You know…"

He jerked his head toward studio 4B.

"Oh!" said Mr. Arkin in a much kinder voice. "I see. Sure, do whatever you need, as long as you don't go farther than the front steps."

Sammi and Izzy leapt up and hurried out the door almost in unison. Cain started to follow them, but something made him hang back. He stayed in his chair, watching Mr. Arkin turn the picture over in his hands as if inspecting it for residual dust. How much did he know? Cain had seen his face that day in the studio, and he had appeared every bit as shocked and horrified as everyone else. Yet there was something in his demeanor that made Cain wonder if Sammi was right.

Mr. Arkin finished dusting the picture and set it down directly in front of Cain. Then he wandered over to a nearby filing cabinet and started rummaging aimlessly through a drawer. Cain leaned forward to study the picture. A pudgy little blonde girl with dark blue eyes grinned mischievously back at him.

"I'd like to open up that studio again," said Mr. Arkin, without turning around. "But it's probably not worth the trouble. Nobody wants to do any recording in it, and I honestly can't say I blame them."

Cain quickly sat back and pretended he hadn't been looking at the photo. If he had been caught poking around Mr. Warwick's desk, he would have gotten a scolding for not minding his own business, or worse.

"Look," Mr. Arkin continued. "I know there's been a lot of talk going around after...what happened. People are saying that I (or another higher-up in the company) must have been involved somehow, that I must have known what was going on. And because of the way the boy was discovered, I don't blame them. But as long as you're listening, I'd like to set the record straight."

"About what?" said Cain warily.

Mr. Arkin strode over to the desk and picked up the picture frame again.

"Look," he said. "I know I haven't been easy to get along with these past few weeks. I'm sorry. It's just...I needed some time to regroup."

"Oh." Cain shifted uncomfortably. He had no idea what else to say, or why Mr. Arkin was telling him this information in the first place.

"I'm so disappointed with myself right now." Mr. Arkin stared at the photo. "I went into this line of work because I hated how cruel and impersonal the music industry was. I thought I could be the last good guy in the business. But then I started to move up the food chain, and things piled up. So I let some of the smaller stuff go and trusted other people to take care of it...then more stuff piled up, and I found more people to trust...and after all those years of telling myself I was the most hands-on and with-it boss in Hollywood, one of those people I trusted was running a murder ring in one of my own studios. That's what stepping up to be the good guy gets you in this town." He sighed and shook his head. "I don't even remember when or how the key to that studio ended up in my desk. Chelsea—may she rest in peace, poor thing—probably put it there and fed me the drunk-sound-engineer explanation. And I swallowed it whole, because I was *too busy* to check."

Cain frowned. Would it have been so hard to unlock one studio and take a quick look inside, just for a minute? The studio was barely ten feet from Mr. Arkin's office; he couldn't leave the building without walking past it!

Mr. Arkin kept his eyes fixed on the photo.

"Can I ask you something?" he said.

Cain nodded.

"Is there someone in your life, someone you love?"

"Um...I...suppose so?" He was caught off-guard. He knew that he loved Michelle, Steve, and his band mates. But the question seemed to have sprung up from nowhere, and it had nothing to do with studio 4B or the Engineer.

"How much do you love this person, Cain?"

"Er..." He shifted and lashed his tail unhappily. He didn't like when humans talked of love that way, as if it were a plank of wood to be measured and weighed. "Enough, I think."

Mr. Arkin's hands tightened around the picture frame. Cain could see the muscles in his jaw quivering.

"Enough that you'd do anything to protect them?" he whispered.

He rounded on Cain. His eyes had a haunted look to them, and a muscle in his cheek twitched. "Enough that no matter what you saw, no matter what you heard or suspected, no matter what you felt in your bones, you'd look the other way?"

Cain swallowed hard. "I don't know..."

"Look," Mr. Arkin pleaded. "You need to promise that this conversation will stay between us. You deserved an explanation, but giving it to you was a huge risk. If *he* finds out...he'll go after my daughter, Cain. He'll hurt my Candace."

The Engineer had threatened Mr. Arkin's daughter—that was why Mr. Arkin had left him to his own devices in that studio and why Mr. Arkin had been so jumpy when Candi asked him for the key. The pieces clicked into place in Cain's mind, while at the same time, a surge of rage bubbled up in him at the revelation that the Engineer was willing to harm a child to make Mr. Arkin cooperate.

Mr. Arkin's voice interrupted his thoughts. "Please understand, though, that I'm not telling you this information so you can try to save the day again. You can't go after him; it's too dangerous. He could—"

A timid knock on the door interrupted him, and the tailor

poked his head into the room.

"Ah." Mr. Arkin forced a smile. "It looks like Frank is ready for the next customer. Why don't you go, since you're here?"

Cain stood up reluctantly. "Shouldn't Izzy or Sammi go next? I'm…uh…not ready yet."

"Don't worry. You'll do fine," chuckled Mr. Arkin. He sounded cheerful and relaxed again, but he looked as if his stomach hurt.

Michelle turned the hanger slowly, inspecting the blue satin dress. She wasn't sure about this one; the skirt was a respectable length and it hid most of her cleavage, but it had off-the-shoulder straps. Her daddy gave her pinched looks whenever she wore something that left her shoulders bare.

After a few minutes of deliberation, she tossed the dress onto the bed next to the ridiculous pink fantasy with puffed sleeves that she wore sometimes to keep daddy from whining. She had also decided against the green sheath with the slit in the side that she kept "forgetting" to sew shut. Her daddy could purse his lips and shake his head and carp about modesty all he wanted; seeing as his method of helping her shop was to hand her money for clothes and then grumble about her choices once they were already purchased and worn, he was damn lucky she bought dresses that had straps at all. Then again, it would probably be wise of her to wear something her father approved of tonight. She had struggled to convince him to let her go to the banquet at all.

Michelle shook her head as she recalled the argument. It staggered her that her father had thought she wouldn't see through his transparent ham-handedness. He ended up agreeing to let her go only on the condition that she stay near him all night so he could make sure she "didn't run into any trouble"—which meant that there would be someone at the party whom he didn't want near her.

Too bad that someone was the only reason she was willingly giving up a Saturday night for a boring charity ball.

She ran her fingers over the smooth, iridescent fabric of the blue dress, lost in thought. Her promise to her daddy complicated things. With his watchful eyes on her, she would have more difficulty slipping away and getting Cain alone to tell him about the pregnancy. Then again, the banquet was probably a bad time to drop that news on him. He would be overwhelmed and out of his depth as it was. Really, she was going to keep a friendly eye on him and to make sure her daddy didn't give him too hard a time. Of course, he needed to know as soon as possible, but the news could wait until after the banquet.

The dress rustled softly when Michelle touched it. She sighed and admired the way it reflected back the dim light of her bedside lamp and emitted a soft blue sheen. *I might as well enjoy it now while it still fits,* she thought. Soon, she wouldn't be able to wear it anymore.

Cain's tuxedo came with a long strip of glossy sky-blue fabric for him to wrap around his neck, concealing his collar. It looked soft, but once it was actually pinned in place, Cain found it to be stiff, hot, and uncomfortable. By the time Cheryl herded them all out the door, he felt like he was being slowly strangled to death. His band mates didn't seem to be faring any better. Izzy fussed with his sleeves and tie. Sammi already looked exhausted. And Vince tugged at his hair, which had been pulled back into a sleek ponytail

552

despite his protests. "Aren't you coming with us?" Cain called over his shoulder to Cheryl as the limousine pulled up to the curb.

"Nope." Cheryl did not budge from the safety of the front stoop. "I'm not invited. I just came to get your asses out the door on time."

Cain nodded in response and then sat down gingerly in one of the leather seats. Mr. Arkin had opted not to pay for a pair of tuxedo pants customized with a tail hole. Instead, he had insisted that Cain hide his tail down a pant leg, and Cheryl in turn had ordered him to tape it down so there would be no danger of a "creepy moving lump." He and Sammi had done the taping as loosely as possible, but there was only so much they could do to make electrical tape comfortable.

Vince pulled down his ponytail with a rebellious grunt the second the car door was shut. Sammi coughed in vague disapproval but said nothing, probably because his own carefully combed hair was already beginning to frizz and puff up.

"Dang, this thing is itchy." Izzy dug his fingers into his armpit. "Still, the limo is cool. I like limos. Maybe this party won't be so bad after all."

"Don't be a moron, Izzy." Vince fiddled with his tie, making a sour face. "It is going to be a big fat fucking drag, and you know it."

"And whose fault is that, Vinnie?" snapped Sammi. "I swear, you and your damn big mouth—Oh crap! Hey, driver, pull over a minute!"

Cain followed his horrified gaze and saw a little streak of blazing blue-white light keeping up with the car, bobbing up and down outside the window.

"Is that Zap?" he asked. "I thought you left Zap in the loft."

"I tried." Sammi stood up and scrambled for the door, even though the car had not fully stopped moving yet. "I gave her a static balloon to play with, but she must've gotten bored and followed me. Hold on, I'll send her home."

Zap stopped with the car and hovered expectantly beside it while Sammi climbed out. He gave her a stern look, cleared his throat, and pointed up the street.

"Go home," he said.

Zap responded by flying over to him. She floated down onto his shoulder and nuzzled his neck and ear with a happy buzzing purr. Sammi glanced at the staring, slack-jawed crowd of pedestrians surrounding him and turned very red.

"No, Zap." He injected more firmness into his voice. "No cuddles now. Go home."

The elemental stayed put on his shoulder. He tried to brush her off with his hand, but she took this gesture as an invitation to coil around his wrist like a snake. More pedestrians stopped to gawk as he shook his arm, telling Zap to go home several more times with increasing frustration.

"Fine," he said at last. "If you won't go home, I'm damn well turning around and taking you home!"

"Do we have time to take Zap home?" said Izzy after Sammi climbed back into the car. "I thought we had to be there in, like, five minutes."

Sammi let out a long, exasperated sigh. "I only said that for the benefit of all those idiots watching me. Okay, driver, we're ready again. Sorry about that."

The driver was also staring openmouthed at Sammi and Zap through the little window in the front. For a few moments, he didn't move; he seemed to be collecting himself before driving again.

"But we can't take Zap to the banquet with us," said Cain. He couldn't imagine Breen taking kindly to her presence, especially if it was clear to him that she was a pet of one of Cain's band mates.

"I don't see what choice we have," said Sammi glumly. "If we make a trip home now, we'll be a good half-hour late for the banquet, and Mr. Arkin will have our asses. We'll just have to take our chances."

"Hmm, maybe Izzy is right that this shit won't be so bad after all." Vince grinned. "I can't wait to see the look on Breen's face when he gets a load of that freaky little dragon thing."

"He might not see her," said Sammi. "Zap will probably hang out in my hair the whole time."

He was right. Zap happily burrowed into Sammi's hair, instantly defeating the last tenuous traces of the artificial neatness that Cheryl had imposed on it before they left. Vince seemed inspired; he ruffled his hands through his own hair several times to make it as messy as he could. Izzy kept his ponytail, but his tuxedo was rumpled and crooked from his constant scratching. Cain felt stiff, sweaty, painfully awkward, and overdressed. He was sure that he and his band mates made for a sorry-looking bunch when they arrived at the stately old hotel where the banquet was being held.

Cameras flashed as they climbed out of the car. Cain groaned inside and soldiered on in spite of them. He wondered why the photographers were bothering at all; they couldn't have been getting very good pictures with his blinded, scrunched up eyes, Vince's constant scowl, and Sammi's wild hair and shell-shocked expression. Then again, Izzy was waving, grinning, and striking poses to make up for them all.

Finally, the flashes died down. Cain's eyes took a few minutes to adjust. When they did, he found himself standing in a red-velvet-lined foyer that had tall, glass-paned doors at one end. The doors stood open, revealing a massive open room full of people in bright clothes.

"Oh my god, Cain!" Izzy popped up beside him, pointing enthusiastically at some female guests. "Look! It's Rhoda Thackeray!"

Cain squinted at the group of silk-and-jewel-clad older women. He couldn't tell at which one Izzy was pointing, and they all looked the same to him anyway. "Who's Rhoda Thackeray?"

"She was in lots of the old movies my mom used to make me watch," said Izzy. "The movies were pretty boring, but she was awesome. She had gorgeous boobs. Say, you know what? As long as I'm here, I might as well go meet her."

"What's the point?" said Vince peevishly. "She's like eighty now, moron. Those gorgeous boobs must be sagging to the floor."

"I'm not a moron." Izzy looked hurt. "Sure, she's old, but…it's still cool that she made all those movies, you know? And I bet I won't get another chance to say hi to her; she probably doesn't get out much anymore."

"Just let him go, Vince," snapped Sammi before Vince could reply. "It's none of your damn business which movie stars Izzy likes."

Izzy plunged into the crowd, seemingly intent on intercepting Rhoda Thackeray. Vince began to follow him.

"Oh, for God's sake, Sweetums." Sammi rubbed his temples wearily. "Don't try to stop him. You dragged us all into this bullshit—the least you can do is let Izzy get something nice from it."

"I'm not gonna stop him." Vince smirked evilly. "Why would I? I wanna see the fireworks happen when Izzy tells one of Breen's biggest supporters that he used to think of her tits and jerk off when he was twelve."

"Shit!" Sammi looked horrified. "She is a pretty hardcore holy roller nowadays, isn't she? Hey, Izzy! Wait! Come back!"

Izzy was already well out of hearing range. Sammi groaned and hurried after him.

"Come on." He gestured frantically at Cain. "We've got to stop him before he gives Mr. Arkin a reason to drop us from the label and blacklist us."

Vince trotted after him, rubbing his hands with glee. "I bet the hag throws her drink on him. She probably thinks she's too high-class to slap anyone. Then again, even dried-up, ugly old actresses have that flair for drama."

Cain started to follow them, but he found it difficult to make his way through the crowd. People stood in tight little knots all around him, too engrossed in their conversations to notice him trying to slip by. Something about them made him nervous; they were too perfect and crisp, and their bland smiles had an unnerving forced quality to them. He squeezed through whatever tiny openings he could find, reluctant to draw attention to himself by asking these people to let him through. Sammi's puff of hair bobbed through the sea of neatly slicked heads ahead of him as he wove his way to the center of the room.

"Ahem."

The pointed cough carried over the noise of the crowd. Cain looked down in surprise. A thin woman with straw-colored hair and sharp gray eyes blocked his path. A short, balding man stood behind her, peering over her shoulder. He made a nervous little snuffling sound when she took a step forward.

"So," said the woman. "You must be Cain Pseudomantis."

Cain nodded slowly. The woman's hair was pinned up on the sides of her head as smoothly as fresh ice and then exploded into a jungle of extravagant curls along the ridge of her scalp. Cain barely managed to refrain from laughing. Perhaps, she intended it to resemble the crest of a rare bird of paradise, but the effect instead reminded Cain of frayed foam rubber that had burst through a rip in an overstuffed couch.

"Ah!" The woman's voice took on an almost greedy tone, and her chest puffed out with triumph. "I never thought I'd come face-to-face with you of all people at this lovely event. I've been wanting...no...*needing* to speak to you for a long time."

"You...have?" Cain involuntarily backed up a step, wondering who this woman was and why she was eyeing him as if he were a delicious and unguarded chocolate cake.

Her male companion gasped in horror when she advanced. Cain studied his face, but he could not place him either. He was a tiny man, nearly six inches shorter than the odd-haired woman, and rather round. *Round* was definitely the first word that popped into Cain's mind as he regarded the man. His face, belly, hairless scalp, and even his hands with their short and pudgy fingers made a strange collection of soft circles and ovals.

"Cora," whispered the man. His voice was deep and smooth and soothing, despite being tense with fear. "I'm sorry, but have you gone mad? Drawing his attention to you is not—"

"Oh, stop worrying, Nigel," laughed Cora, cutting him off and advancing farther into Cain's personal space. "Think what an opportunity we have here: we might learn something vital to our research."

Cain tried to back up again, only to bump against another guest's back. The man he had bumped coughed huffily at him and went back to his conversation without moving.

"What research?" he said. "Who are you? Do you work for Breen?"

The woman stiffened. Cain got the impression that she was offended he hadn't recognized her.

"No, I don't work for Nathaniel," she said. "Though I suppose you could say I work with him, in a manner of speaking. I am Dr. Cora Hammond. Perhaps you've heard of my work: I specialize in recovered memory therapy."

"Oh." Cain nodded again, although he had no idea what she was talking about. He'd never heard of recovered memory therapy. The only people he could think of who might need lost memories recovered for them were the victims of some of Vince's shenanigans. Maybe this Dr. Hammond was a professional mind-stroker who pieced together minds fractured by less-than-responsible practitioners of the Gift.

"Cora," began Nigel, speaking through clenched teeth. He reached out tentatively as if to pull her back, but she seemed to sense his hand moving, and she flicked her arm out of his reach.

"I have to hand it to you," she said to Cain. "You're getting better at what you do. My most recent patients' minds are practically swiss cheese, the blocks are so strong, and I'm having a devil of a time—no offense, of course—getting them patched up to the point where they even remember that they were abused at all."

Cain gaped at her in horror. Vince couldn't be attacking enough people to keep a doctor who specialized in reversing memory theft in business. But if enough people started believing he was, Cain didn't care to imagine the trouble their suspicions could cause.

"I'm sorry, but I don't know what you're talking about," he said firmly. "Vince isn't ripping up all your patients' minds. We always keep a close eye on him, and if he messes with anyone's mind, we make him fix it."

"Vince?" Dr. Hammond blinked. "You mean to say your red-headed henchman inserts the blocks? My goodness! No wonder my interviews were going nowhere: I was trying to draw out the poor dears' recollections of the wrong person!" She turned to her companion, who was frozen and gaping at Cain like a cornered mouse hoping a snake would fail to see it. "Did you hear that, Nigel? I suspect you'll have to change the way you dig up buried memories too."

Nigel made a very tiny squeaking noise and tried again to pull Dr. Hammond away. She sidestepped him and continued her interrogation. "I never would have guessed in a hundred years that the redhead was your go-to guy for brainwashing." She frowned thoughtfully. "It's such a delicate and sophisticated bit of mental programming. My best guess was that he was the muscle, the one you'd go to if you needed an errant follower punished, and you..." Her voice trailed off and her frown lines deepened.

Cain could feel his taped tail wanting to twitch anxiously. This bizarre talk about blocks and mental programming—terms which he had never heard even Breen use—made him suspect that Dr. Hammond was a little more unhinged than Breen's average follower, and he really didn't like the way she was looking at him. Unfortunately the crowd behind him was still impenetrable, and he doubted Mr. Arkin would be happy if he made any sort of scene, even to protect himself from a delusional stalker.

"So…um…what exactly is Vince doing to these people?" he asked, playing for time while he searched for an escape route.

Something made the little round man push aside his fear. He stepped up beside Dr. Hammond and looked at Cain with an odd pout that he probably meant to be a fierce glare.

"What is he doing?" His voice took on a fierce, booming tone that mismatched his body drastically. "You know perfectly well what he's doing, sir—you and those vile, cruel worshippers of yours!"

Cain was so taken aback that he nearly stumbled into the man behind him again. He opened his mouth to tell this Nigel that no, he didn't know perfectly well, and he certainly didn't have any worshippers (cruel or otherwise), but Nigel motored on.

"When I opened my practice here six years ago, there wasn't a single ritual abuse victim to be found in the city." His pasty cheeks flushed pink with anger. "Nowadays hardly a patient crosses my threshold who hasn't got repressed memories of cult activity—women, children, all young and vulnerable and fragile, all subjected to the foulest torments imaginable by those who hail you as the god of this world. I've treated children who were raped with curling irons and knife handles, women who were forced to impale their own newly born babies on metal spikes, men who…"

Nigel continued his rant but Cain could no longer hear

him. A sadly familiar sick feeling churned in Cain's stomach. He had run into two more humans who inexplicably believed that he tortured men, women, and children. He quickly abandoned his plan to argue with them, for fear that it would only get Nigel more worked up; Nigel seemed to be more out of touch with reality than Cora. His eyes darted around the room, searching more urgently for a way to melt into the crowd, but Nigel's steadily rising voice had attracted the attention of everyone who happened to be standing nearby. They pressed around in a tight, impenetrable circle, watching the spectacle unfold. Despite all of Mr. Arkin's and Cheryl's grave warnings that high-class charity balls and magic didn't mix, he began to consider flying or shrinking to escape.

Dr. Hammond kept Cain fixed with an eager gaze, seemingly oblivious to the scene her friend was making. "It is quite impressive: the sheer range of horrors your people can make an impressionable young mind forget," she said. "Now tell me, how do the mechanics of this drug or spell work? Are they similar to the methods of mind control you use on your fans? Or does that scheme require an entirely different technique? Whatever it is, it's diabolically brilliant; the complete control it gives you—"

"Ah yes, complete control," Nigel broke in again. "The same complete control you use to leave them sapped and broken—and then you turn them out into the world for us to sort out!" He had worked himself up into such a fit of fury that he actually did look slightly fearsome now. "All I can say is that it took a damned lot of cheek for you to show your face here, of all places, and I—"

"Dr. Wakefield." A third voice cut through the room, coldly, from behind him. "Is everything all right?"

The crowd parted slightly, admitting the Reverend Breen into the circle. Cain tried to back casually away, but there were still too many people behind him.

"No, I'm afraid everything is *not* all right." Nigel drew himself up indignantly. "Reverend Breen, did you know that *he* was here?"

Breen's eyes followed the stubby finger Dr. Wakefield jabbed in Cain's direction.

"Why, of course I knew," he said with a chuckle. "I invited him. Bless me, Doctor; I hope you don't think I'm old enough to be going senile!"

Dr. Wakefield would not be put off. "But surely you know who he is!"

"Of course I do," said Breen. Cain listened for traces of malice or distrust in his tone, but he didn't find any. "Dr. Wakefield, this is Cain Pseudomantis, one of my newest donors...But it seems you've already met. Now, if you and Dr. Hammond will excuse me, I'm afraid I must borrow young Cain for a moment."

He walked away, leaving the two dumbfounded doctors in his wake. Cain followed him with a sense of impending doom. Breen led him to a table piled with several platters of shrimp and cheese cubes. Michelle stood to one side of the table, shifting her weight impatiently. As soon as his gaze fell on her, his eyes lit up with recognition. Michelle gave Cain a warning look. He turned reluctantly away and pretended he hadn't seen her.

The table was in a relatively sparsely populated corner. Cain shivered in anxious anticipation; now that they had a bit more space and fewer witnesses, he expected Breen to drop his polite mask and blast him with yet another vicious accusation.

The blast never came. Breen turned to him with the same mild expression, cleared his throat, and spoke in a respectful tone.

"I'm terribly sorry if Dr. Wakefield and Dr. Hammond upset you," he said. "Dr. Wakefield recently had an unfortunate run-in with a certain rock star far less couth than you, and I'm afraid he's decided to hold it against your entire profession. As for her, she's an excellent therapist, but she gets a bit too wrapped up in her research sometimes. I trust you're all right?"

Cain was too startled to do anything but nod. He regarded Breen suspiciously, half-wondering if Izzy was making up for the boredom of the evening by using his shape-shifting to play jokes on his band mates. He doubted that Izzy knew words like *couth* and *senile*, but it seemed much likelier that Izzy was playing a trick on him. The Breen he knew would not actually treat him with kindness.

"Good, good." The minister extended his hand. "I just wanted to take a moment to welcome you. Your generous gift to the foundation was…rather unexpected, but very much appreciated."

Cain chanced a quick glance at Michelle before taking the proffered hand. She looked as mystified as he was.

"I'm sure it'll be a pleasure doing business with you," said Breen with a final disarming smile. "Please, enjoy yourself tonight. The bar has a fine selection of French wines—oh, excuse me. I do believe Mrs. Babbitt is trying to get my attention. Come on, Michelle."

He swept off into the crowd with Michelle following at his heels. He reached out to clasp his daughter's wrist as she passed Cain, and Cain thought he saw a brief hostile glint in the minister's eyes, but he was too shocked to be certain.

The room was uncomfortably warm, and the constant low drone of chattering voices was making Cain nervous. He shuffled along the wall, looking for his band mates. Several minutes passed, and he saw no sign of them, but his search took him to an open door through which a cool breeze blew. He peered through the door and saw that it led to a small tiled courtyard with a fountain in the middle.

No one was in the courtyard. He slipped through the door with a sigh of relief, hoping to cool down a bit before resuming his search. The strange collar-covering scarf around his neck had started to bunch up. He straightened it as best he could, knowing full well that it looked every bit as ridiculous on him as a pair of skin-tight leather pants.

"You'd do better taking it off and putting it back on again, I think," said a familiar quiet voice behind him. Cain jumped and turned around.

"Ty?" he said in surprise.

Ty Thorpe stood with his foot up on the rim of the fountain's basin, leaning on his knee. His jeans and simple black T-shirt contrasted oddly with the elegance of the setting. He reached down and trailed his finger through the water.

"I'd have left it off altogether if I'd been in your place," he said. "Then again, Bruce Arkin probably didn't give you a choice, did he?"

Cain shook his head. "I don't think he wanted my collar showing."

"Figures." Ty gave him a glance that might have been anxious, but with his heavy-lidded eyes, Cain couldn't be sure. "Say, I've got to ask, have you ever been to a high-society to-do like this before?"

"This is my first one," said Cain. He hoped there would

never be a second one, but nothing worked the way he expected in LA.

"Yeah, I figured that too. How are the folks in there treating you?"

Cain looked at the ground. "Fine, I guess."

"You guess?"

"Well...one woman asked me some really disturbing questions, and a man yelled at me. It was creepy. They both seemed off."

"Breen yelled at you?" Ty's eyes narrowed.

"No, somebody different." Cain shifted uncomfortably under Ty's probing gaze. Why was he so interested in how his evening was going? "I think his name was Dr. Wakefield."

"Oh, him." Ty let out a dry laugh. "Good old Nigel Wakefield, patron saint of the brainwashed cult survivors. I should've known he'd be here. I'm surprised he had the nerve to yell at you, though. You mean he was actually yelling? Like, real, top-of-his-lungs, in-your-face yelling?"

"Well, I'd say he was talking pretty loudly," said Cain. "And he was saying...He seems to think I did horrible things to all his patients."

"Does he now?" said Ty. "Well, I wouldn't worry too much about it. Wakefield's patients have a bad habit of walking out of his office in worse shape than they were going in; he sure did a number on Johnny Revolver's poor girlfriend, for example. Nah, it's Nate—sorry, Nathaniel Breen—I'm worried about."

Cain shrugged. The encounter with Dr. Hammond and Dr. Wakefield had left him rattled enough that Breen seemed the least of his worries. "He shook my hand and said he was sorry that Dr. Wakefield upset me, and he welcomed me to the banquet. He was even smiling. It was weird."

Ty looked back at the open door. A shade of suspicion passed over his face. "Well," he said slowly. "I'm glad to hear he's behaving himself. Hey, I think people are starting to find their tables in there. You'd better get back to the party."

"Aren't you coming too?" Cain regarded Ty curiously. Probably not, considering the way he was dressed; but why would he be here at all if he wasn't a guest at the banquet?

"Nah." Ty chuckled. "I'm not invited. I was just headed to Redondo. This place was on my way, so I stopped in to make sure old Nate was treating you right. Hey, Cain?"

"Yeah?"

"Try to keep your head low tonight, okay? I've got a feeling."

He turned and strode off into the shadows of the flowering bushes before Cain could ask him what he was talking about. From the far right corner of the garden came the sound of creaking hinges; he must have found an unlocked service gate to slip through. Cain stared after him for a moment, enjoyed a last breath of cool night air, and ducked back into the room.

People were indeed finding their seats at the round dinner tables in the middle of the room when he returned, but a few guests were still milling around. As he hovered among the tables, wondering how to figure out where they wanted him to sit, he nearly collided with Izzy.

"Whoa, careful!" Izzy steadied the dainty high-stemmed glass in his hand. "I don't want to spill."

"*That's* what you're drinking?" Cain eyed the clear liquid in the glass dubiously. He had thought it was water at first, but the strong alcohol fumes told him otherwise. Izzy preferred to heavily dilute his hard liquor with sugar or fruit juice. Cain had once witnessed him emptying an entire can of whipped cream into a half-full bottle of vodka. Izzy also hated olives, and this drink had a fat green olive floating in it.

"Nah," said Izzy. "This is Mrs. Thackeray's drink. I'm just bringing it to her. You know, Cain, I know you don't drink and all, but you really should check out the bar. It has, like, everything, and it's all free. Breen told me I could have as much as I wanted."

"You mean he told you that too?" Cain raised an eyebrow.

"Yeah, I guess," said Izzy in a distracted tone, peering over Cain's shoulder. Cain guessed that he was too busy keeping Mrs. Thackeray happy to focus on anything else. "It was really weird. He must have had me mixed up with someone else. Well, I gotta go. I'll see you in a minute, though. We're all at the same table!"

He hurried off as fast as he could without spilling the drink. As Cain stared after him in bewilderment, he felt an urgent tap on his shoulder. He turned and found himself face-to-face with Sammi.

Sammi stared up at him, swaying on his feet. A nearly empty glass was in his hand. He looked haggard and had sparks floating out of his hair, though Cain could not tell whether they were coming from him or from Zap.

"Hey," he said in a weary voice. "Could you come here for a minute? We've got a problem."

"What's up?" said Cain.

"Vince flat-out refuses to leave the bar." Sammi shook his head in exasperation. "And you know what? Even if he wanted to find his seat, he couldn't because he's too damn drunk to walk a straight line. Breen told him he could have all the alcohol he wanted, and now he's hell-bent on pounding back as much as he can before he passes out."

"Breen told him that?" Cain frowned. "Izzy says Breen told him he could have all the alcohol he wanted too. And he told me—"

"Yeah, he said the same thing to me too." Sammi rubbed his eyes with his free hand. "Hosts are supposed to do that. Guests aren't supposed to take it as a challenge."

Cain shifted uneasily. Something about the whole situation felt wrong. He wanted to tell Sammi about his suspicions, but Sammi looked so tired and sick and preoccupied that Cain couldn't bring himself to worry him further.

Cain followed Sammi to the bar, where they found Vince leaning precariously against a nearby high-topped table. He was in the process of raising a glass to his lips. Sammi dashed over and grabbed his wrist.

"Give it a rest, Sweet," he said. "You've had more than enough."

Vince wrenched his arm away, spilling the rest of his drink on the floor. "Fuck you, Sammi."

"Everybody is finding their tables, asshat. Come on, let's go."

"Hey!" Vince thrust his empty glass into the air. "Nother vodka 'n tonic here!"

"You wanna play hardball?" Sammi's eyes narrowed. "Fine. Cain, do your stuff."

Cain sauntered up to the table and bent down to Vince's eye level. "Vince, you can get your ass to the table right now, or you can vomit marbles for a week straight. Which will it be?"

Vince gave Cain a look of pure hatred and lurched upright.

"Good choice," said Cain. "Okay, Sammi, we can find our table now…Sammi?"

Sammi stomped up to them from the direction of the bar, holding a full glass. "I thought I might as well take advantage of Breen's generosity and have one more Coke and rum. It's a party, right?" he added in a joyless tone.

His hands trembled as he raised the glass. Cain was alarmed by the anger in his voice.

"Sammi, what's wrong?"

"Nothing." Sammi shook his head moodily. "It's just…that woman and what she said…God, it pissed me off so much."

"What woman?" said Cain. "You mean Rhoda Thackeray?"

"Nah, she barely even looked at me." Sammi shrugged. "She was giving Izzy all her attention by the time I got there. Then they wandered off together, and I lost track of them when some crazy bitch cornered me and asked a shit-ton of prying questions about my life. I was dumb enough to answer some too. That's what I'm mad about."

"The questions?"

"No." Sammi's knuckles whitened as he gripped the glass. "What she said afterward—she told me my dad must have abused me when I was little. I tried to tell her that my dad died when I was two and I don't even remember him, but she said—get this—that my memory of…of…the Engineer is a fake 'patch memory' or some crap that was implanted in my brain so I wouldn't remember the real abuse from my dad. Then she treated me like an idiot when I said it wasn't a fake memory, and she kept telling me she could fix me somehow—help me 'become integrated' again—whatever the hell that means. Who does that twat think she is, telling me what I remember and what I don't? I know it happened; I sure as fuck wish it hadn't, but it did, and I'll never get it out of my mind no matter how hard I try."

Cain nodded in sympathy. "Yeah, I think I know who you're talking about; she cornered me too. She didn't try to tell you *I* put that memory in your mind, did she?"

"Nope. She didn't say who she thought put it in, just that it was fake."

"What memory of the Engineer did you tell her about?" Cain asked out of curiosity. He was surprised Sammi had volunteered any information at all to that woman.

Sammi looked away. His jaw muscles tightened, and more sparks floated out of his hair.

"I'd rather not say."

"Oh." Cain sensed that it was time to back off. "So…um…I guess we should find our table. Where's Izzy?"

"Probably with Rhoda Thackeray." Sammi shook his head in amazement. "It was the damndest thing. She was looking at him like he was something she'd scraped off her shoe, but then he said he liked this movie of hers, and her face just lit right up, and now she thinks he's the best guy on earth. I bet it helps that he's been running drinks to her all night too."

Nearly everyone was seated now. They set off together in the direction of the tables. Vince was weaving and leaning against Cain for support. Sammi walked behind them, leaving a steady trail of angry red sparks in his wake.

CHAPTER TWENTY-TWO

CRASHING DOWN

CAIN CRANED HIS NECK to watch Michelle push salad around her plate at the head table. He wished that she could join him at the little table he was sharing with his band mates. Her presence might alleviate his crushing boredom.

White-coated waiters made their slow way through the forest of seated guests; they had finished serving the head table, and were moving on to the round tables in the center of the room. Those who had been served raised forkfuls of lettuce and tomato to their mouths in quiet contentment. Soon Cain too would be presented with a plate of inedible greens, and some nebulous rule of human hospitality demanded that he eat them.

"Hey, Izzy," he whispered. "When our salads come out, would you take a few bites of mine?"

"Hmm?" Izzy blinked. "Uh…sure, I guess. Why?"

"Because I can't. Cheryl says I have to eat a few bites to be polite, but vegetables make me sick."

"Oh. I just wouldn't eat any then. How is Cheryl gonna know?"

"What if she asks me?" said Cain. "If I say I ate some, she'll know I'm lying."

Izzy frowned thoughtfully. "Hmm. I guess you could take a couple of bites and then spit them out in your napkin. That way, you wouldn't really be lying."

Cain poked glumly at his filled wineglass. He didn't particularly want to pretend to eat the salad either. After his failed attempt to eat lettuce, even the smell of it made him feel ill.

Izzy picked up his wineglass and took a tiny sip. He grimaced, swallowed with some difficulty, and smacked his lips. "The wine's good, I guess," he said.

"It is?" said Cain doubtfully.

"Mrs. Thackeray says it is," said Izzy. "She knows a lot about wine. She told me that this wine has notes of oak, coffee, and chocolate."

Cain picked up his wineglass and sniffed the dark red liquid. He thought he detected a faint whiff of a scent somewhat like chocolate, but the wine mostly just smelled like rotten fruit.

"I don't think *I* can taste any of those flavors, though." Izzy took another sip and sloshed it around in his mouth before swallowing it. "Except maybe oak; I don't really know what oak tastes like. I guess I don't drink enough wine to know how to—oops!" He leapt up so fast that his chair toppled over. "Mrs. Thackeray wants her martini topped off. I'll be right back."

He dashed over to Mrs. Thackeray's table, leaving Cain alone with Sammi and Vince. Sammi scratched his arm between tense swigs of wine; he was clearly not in the mood to talk. Cain contented himself with watching Izzy fawn over Mrs. Thackeray. She was a large, sharp-nosed woman, swathed in layers upon layers of flowing gold and aquamarine silk. Too much lipstick and sky-blue eye-shadow glared from her face, and a sparkling bib of faceted white stones swung from her neck. Her table companions were mostly women her age, all clad in similar gowns in shades of forest green, purple, royal blue, and vivid orange. They wore chunky ostentatious jewelry, and sequins sparkled along their arms as they sipped their drinks and ate their salads. Cain regarded them curiously, wondering why the men were restricted to plain and identical black tuxes while the women were encouraged to wear a wide variety of gowns in wild splashes of color.

Vince grumbled and swatted at the air while a waiter tried to gently nudge a salad plate in front of him. Sammi had already gotten his salad, and Cain could smell the sour vinegar scent of the dressing from Izzy's plate. He waited for the waiter to place an equally vile salad in front of him, but the waiter abruptly left, leaving Cain's place setting empty.

"Um…okay," he muttered. "I guess I don't get a salad, then?"

"You're lucky." Sammi poked listlessly at his plate. "God damn it—I hate salads. I hate all the dry, boring-ass food they serve at these things." He took a big swallow of wine. "I wish this stuff was stronger. I could use something to calm my nerves."

Cain was about to reply when a flash of movement caught his eye. He looked up in time to see a waiter setting a plate down in front of him. To his surprise and relief, it was piled high, not with salad, but with raw sardines.

"Huh." Izzy popped up beside him. "Guess that solves the salad problem."

Vince made no move to touch his salad or to sit up at all. Sammi picked at his, but he seemed not to have much of an appetite. Izzy set his chair upright, plopped down in it, and happily started shoveling up his salad—with the correct fork, Cain noticed. Now that no one was testing him, he had picked it up on his own.

"You know," said Izzy through a mouthful of salad. "I've never seen you eat fish before. I didn't think you could."

Cain swallowed a whole sardine, wondering why humans didn't think that he could eat fish. Mr. Arkin had never sent Chelsea to the house bearing a packet of fish filets, and Mr. Warwick rarely fed him anything that wasn't beef, chicken, or pork. Maybe humans thought there was no water where he came from, in so-called hell.

He ate another sardine, and another, and another. The saltiness of the fish made him thirsty. He reached for his water glass, found that it had not been refilled, and looked around for a waiter. A few waiters still bustled around the edges of the room, topping off drinks and taking away empty plates, but the others had disappeared. Cain raised his hand and tried to flag one down, but they were too far away to notice.

Cain stopped eating his sardines. If he kept eating them, he would eventually have to drink something, and he wasn't sure he trusted the wine.

"Are you okay?" said Izzy. "You're making a funny face."

"I'm fine." He smacked his lips. "I'm just a little thirsty, and I don't have any water. I drank all of mine before the salads came out."

"I'm sure the waiters will give us all refills when they bring the next course," Izzy assured him. "I'd give you mine, but I drank it. If you really can't wait, I guess you

575

could sip some wine."

"I'd rather not," said Cain. "It might make me sick. Besides, I don't want to drink anything from the bar tonight."

"Why not?"

Cain played with his napkin. "Because something is up. I don't like the way Breen told us all to help ourselves to the bar—almost like he wanted us to get drunk."

Izzy frowned. "Like he wanted us to get drunk? I'm not sure what would be in that for him."

"I don't know," said Cain. "Maybe he wants us to ruin his party so he can go on TV and tell everyone what awful guests we were, or something like that."

"Maybe," said Izzy. "But that sounds like a bad plan. I mean, wouldn't it make all his rich friends mad at him for giving us drinks?" He suddenly sprang to his feet, responding to Mrs. Thackeray's fluttering hand. "Excuse me. I'll be right back."

Cain glanced at Vince, who was awkwardly slumped over the table. Maybe Izzy was right, but he still didn't particularly want to try the wine. Even if it didn't make him embarrassingly drunk and hungover, he was certain that it would taste disgusting.

The main course was emerging from the kitchen. A waiter whisked away Cain's sardine plate and put another plate in its place. Vince raised his head from the table with great effort and glared at Cain.

"The fuck?" he slurred. "How come we get pussy little bits of chicken and you get steaks? What'd you do to make everybody suck your dick all of a sudden?"

Cain inspected the pile of raw steaks on his plate. To his relief, he heard the sound of liquid pouring, and his water glass was full when he looked up. He took a grateful swig of the water and turned his attention to the pile of steaks. He wasn't hungry enough to eat all of them, but he could probably manage a few bites to please Cheryl.

Izzy reappeared and plopped down next to Cain, digging into his chicken and potatoes and green beans with gusto. Vince tried to sit up and take a bite, apparently decided that eating took too much effort, and slumped down again. Sammi didn't touch his food. He was sweating, and looked pale.

"Are you all right?" Cain whispered to him.

"No I'm not," said Sammi. "My stomach hurts, and I have a bitch of a headache, and being in this place isn't helping. All these people are so super polite and fake, they just creep me out. Excuse me; I'm going to the can."

He stood up unsteadily. Zap poked her head out of his hair, and he gently pushed her back in. Cain thought of following him, but he decided against it. Cheryl had searched Sammi for drugs before they left the house, and Cain could sympathize with his wanting some time alone.

The steak was tasty. Cain nibbled on it, taking care to eat the way Cheryl had shown him even though the silverware felt awkward in his hands. Soon he realized that he was hungrier than he thought he was. One whole steak vanished, then another. Cain thought that it was the best beef he had ever tasted, and he began to fee lightheaded and oddly cheerful.

"Hey, are you all right?" said Izzy. "You're starting to sway a little."

"I'll be fine," said Cain. He felt better than fine; the deep, soothing warmth radiating through him was unexpected but very relaxing.

"Oh. Well, I guess you can take care of yourself." Izzy stood up. "Hey, I'll be right back. Mrs. Thackeray wants me again."

Cain pounced on his remaining steaks, forgetting silverware in favor of his hands and teeth, his good mood increasing. Peripherally, he noticed Michelle watching him with worried eyes. He swept up his glass with an unsteady hand and shot her a big grin, chuckling to himself at the thought of the wonderful times they had shared without her stuffy old father having any idea. Then he turned to Dr. Wakefield, who had been glaring at him since the meal started, and waved. Soon the steaks were gone, and Cain leaned back with a sigh of contentment.

"Hey, Cain." Izzy tugged at his shoulder. He had apparently finished helping Rhoda Thackeray, but Cain had not seen him return. "I think Breen wants you to stand up."

Cain climbed to his feet unsteadily. The floor seemed to be rippling beneath him.

"And I would like to welcome the newest face in this illustrious fellowship," the minister was saying. "Ladies and gentlemen, I give you Cain Pseudomantis."

A flurry of polite applause ran through the crowd. Cain became briefly flustered because he wasn't sure what was expected of him next. He half-recalled Mr. Arkin saying something about people lifting their glasses during this part of the evening; but no one in his range of vision had lifted their glass.

"Nothing makes my heart quite so glad," the minister continued, "as a young person who cares about changing the world for the better. I would like to thank Mr. Pseudomantis for his generous gift, but I'm afraid I must preface my thanks with an apology."

A low murmur ran through the room. Cain swayed on his feet, staring through the growing fog. His strange evening was relentlessly getting stranger. After greeting him as an honored guest and apparently going out of the way to research and accommodate his diet, Nathaniel Breen was now about to apologize to him. He wondered if the good Reverend Breen had lost a bet with Mr. Arkin.

"As you all know," said Breen. "I've made a few…accusations…against Mr. Pseudomantis in the past. In fact, I encountered a bit of backlash for inviting him to join us tonight."

The minister shot a glance in the direction of Dr. Wakefield's table. Cain thought his expression was probably meant to be reproachful, but it looked more like a conspiratorial smirk. A little shudder of foreboding flickered in the back of his mind, but he ignored it. After all, maybe Breen's facial muscles had simply gotten so used to holding their usual positions that he always looked smug, whether he meant to or not.

"I must confess I was rather opposed to extending the invitation myself." Breen sauntered around the head table and began to make his way across the room, still holding his glass aloft. "Nothing I've encountered in my life has left me quite so stricken and dumbfounded as that one fateful little phone call. I tell you it left my head reeling—how could this creature, this literal demon from Hell, be so concerned about the welfare of the very children he ought to be trying to corrupt and destroy? So, as I always do in a tight spot, I prayed for guidance. I soon received an answer."

Cain shivered and fidgeted while Breen drew steadily closer. He had begun to notice that everyone in the room was staring at him.

Michelle leaned over the tabletop, wringing her napkin. Cain gave her a pleading look, but she shook her head helplessly.

"Consider this creature." There was a definite smug note in the minister's voice now. "Bound to this earth by the black magic charm that he wears around his neck, living among humans, sleeping and eating among humans, utterly unable to escape the presence of humans anywhere he goes, day after day, year after year. Surely such constant familiarity would make its mark even on the most twisted of minds after a while. He would see the nobler qualities of our race—compassion, charity, and the rest—and strive to emulate them. Perhaps he's even developed some dim, primitive semblance of a conscience to tell him that he *must* do these things, for they are good and right."

He had reached the middle of the room where Cain was seated. Cain wished he was allowed to make himself invisible.

Breen stepped around the table and stood face-to-face with him, placing his hands on his hips. "Yet he is still a demon," he said. "If the veneer of humanity should wear thin on occasion, if he should revert temporarily to the natural drives that motivate him to lie, to cheat, to spoil the purity of our young people—the very same drives that have just now pushed him to overindulge at the bar and tear his dinner apart like a wild animal, as you can plainly see from the blood on his face—if he should from time to time display such shocking, vicious relapses to his normal diabolic state, can we blame him? Why, of course we cannot. We cannot blame him any more than I can blame my dog for soiling the carpet."

He had blood on his face? Cain raised a trembling hand

to check; it came away wet and pink. He squirmed with embarrassment as hundreds of disapproving eyes bored into him. Perhaps he had eaten the last couple steaks a bit messily, but he couldn't be drunk, could he? He hadn't had any wine. Yet the room was starting to blur and spin around him, and a persistent, thick fog clouded his brain.

"No, no." Breen caught his arm when he tried to sit down and make himself scarce. "We must make a toast."

Cain's eyes darted around the room as his panic grew. Sammi was still gone and Izzy was staring blankly at the scene unfolding before him; Vince had barely bothered to open his eyes for Breen's speech. Michelle sat trembling with silent disgust and anger behind her father's back.

The minister raised his glass. He no longer made the slightest attempt to hide the triumph in his expression or the venom in his voice.

"To Cain Pseudomantis," he said. "Tonight we commend his valiant attempt to simulate the inherent goodness of the human spirit, despite his soulless state, which will inevitably draw him back to his old evil ways once the night is over. And for that, my friends, I am truly sorry."

He took the obligatory sip from his glass, smirking as he did so. Cain stared at the ground. He felt a belch wanting to escape his lips, and his attempt to stifle it filled his mouth with the flavor of the beef he had eaten. But there was another taste there too, a sweeter, earthier one.

Chocolate.

The fog in his mind cleared for a moment. The beef—it must have been rubbed with cocoa powder. Cain swayed in place, unable to tell whether his unsteadiness came from intoxication or shock. How had Breen known about chocolate's effects on him? How could he possibly have known? Cain's own band mates didn't know that Izzy's candy bar had gotten him high on the night he accidentally disclosed his true nature.

"Now you may sit down," Breen whispered to Cain. "I think I've made my point, eh?"

A white-hot spark of rage cut through Cain's dulled senses. No, he would *not* sit down. Why should he do anything at Breen's say-so? The old man had set him up, humiliated him, and insulted him to his face. He lurched toward the minister, his eyes blazing.

"You've made your point?" he snapped. "What point? That you're really good at pretending to be nice to your guests and then treating them like shit when they least expect it? Is that your fucking point? Well, if it is, good job, asshole!"

The words poured out before Cain could stop them, and a fierce wave of satisfaction rushed through him once they had. He would almost certainly be in serious trouble with Mr. Arkin later, but the chastising would be worth seeing Breen explode.

The minister grinned and gave his shoulder an indulgent pat.

"Well, son, it looks like you've been hitting the bar too hard," he said in a loud voice. "I knew you would. I probably shouldn't have served alcohol at all, but the forfeiture wouldn't have been fair to some of my more responsible supporters." He turned to wink at someone, probably Rhoda Thackeray.

"You said I could drink!" shrieked Cain, further angered by his enemy's lack of anger. "You practically ordered me to—and all my band mates too! And I didn't even have a drink—you put drugs in my food! Was that your plan all along? Were you hoping we'd make a big scene so you could throw us out?"

Breen remained unruffled. "Now, now, don't go blaming others for your bad judgment, Mr. Pseudomantis. Please, sit down, have some black coffee, and relax. Nobody likes a mean drunk."

He turned to the crowd once more and sadly shook his head, as if to say, "Do you see what I put up with in the name of Christian charity?" Then he regarded Cain with the same falsely benign expression he had put on when he began his toast.

Cain ground his teeth. It had been so easy to make Breen furiously angry when he wasn't trying, but now that he actually wanted to make the old man angry, his efforts were as futile and frustrating as trying to rip holes in water.

"Please, Mr. Pseudomantis, sit down," Breen repeated. "For the sake of the children and young people you've so briefly decided to care about."

Cain's fury was nearly suffocating him now. Fortunately, his ability to work up magical energy was stymied by the fog in his mind. If he'd had access to his full capabilities, he doubted he could hold himself back from changing into his true form, baring his teeth and claws, and showing the minister just how mean a drunk he could be.

"At least I care about them at all!" he shouted. "If you really cared about young people, you would have done something to help the rockers on the Strip when the Engineer started picking them off. You didn't give a shit about them! But it wasn't just that you didn't care, was it? You *hated* the boys who were taken. You were glad when they were tortured and killed, weren't you? You're just like my master: you don't care about anyone unless they're worth money to you. You don't even care about your own daughter!"

Breen's neck and jaw muscles stiffened. For a moment, his cheeks went red.

"I beg your pardon?"

Cain pounced on the subject with fierce enthusiasm as the horrified murmurs of onlookers reached a crescendo around him. "You heard me. You don't care about her. She doesn't see you for weeks at a time because you're off attending some conference or taping some stupid TV show. You don't know what she likes or wants because you never spend time with her." He lunged forward and stared into the Reverend Breen's beet-red, quivering face, savoring his anger. "I know more about what's going on in her life than you do because she—"

Michelle turned dead white. She shot up out of her chair, slicing her hand across her throat in a frantic shut-up motion, but her father's enraged bellow saved her the trouble of stopping Cain's speech.

"That's enough!" Breen brought his fist down on the table with so much force that Vince yelped and sat bolt upright. "How dare you say such things to me? My daughter is none of your concern!"

"She made herself my concern," said Cain, the words rushing out before he could register Michelle's rapidly blanching complexion. "Haven't you ever asked her what she does when you're out of town? Because I can tell you exactly what she does."

The minister stumbled back, and his face went from bright red to sickly, papery white. "I won't be talked to like this by a foul-mouthed, drunken devil," he snarled. "I'll

584

have to ask you to leave now. You and your worthless associates may show yourselves out or be escorted out, your choice."

Cain looked directly into Breen's eyes, reveling in his moment of triumph. After all the indignities he had suffered due to the old man's malicious lies and trap-setting, Cain felt oddly exhilarated by driving Breen into this towering rage. The fierce hatred radiating from every line of the minister's body invigorated him and made him want to be more outrageously rude.

"Leave," repeated Breen. "And don't you dare think about coming back."

"Don't worry, I won't. Maybe, though, I'll tell Michelle to say hi next time she hops into bed with me."

The minister lunged forward with startling speed. In slow motion, Cain saw his hand shoot out. Then he felt a vicious tug when Breen grabbed him by the layers of cloth around his neck, collar and all. The horrified murmurs that had been running through the room intensified to a collective gasp, and several men at the next table leapt up to intervene. The minister waved them off and pulled Cain's head down to human eye level.

"How dare you," he snarled. "You filthy, lecherous animal, how *dare* you talk about my daughter that way?"

His grip tightened. Cain tried to wriggle away, but Breen held him fast. The minister's eyes were blazing. Other guests joined the two men who hovered nervously on the sidelines, but none of them made a move to help.

"Listen, Hell-beast." Breen pulled him closer, shaking him. "You can go after the souls of other young people all you want. But Michelle is my daughter. If you touch her— her body or her soul—I will hunt you down and kill you."

Cain shrank away. He had no doubt that Breen was enraged enough to fulfill that promise. The growing-but-silent crowd of spectators surely would not stop him.

"Daddy!" Michelle elbowed her way through the crowd. "Daddy, stop!"

Breen went a bit paler at the sound of her voice, but his grip did not loosen. "Go back to the table, sweetheart. I've got this under control."

"No, you don't!" Michelle pressed on defiantly to her father's side and started to pry his fingers loose. "Let him go, daddy! Do you have any idea how crazy you look right now?"

Cain felt the pressure slack off his collar as Breen rounded on his daughter. He stared at her with a mixture of anger, indignation, and utter bafflement engrained on his face. Michelle finished wresting Cain from his grasp and placed herself between them, glaring at her father. The murmurs from the crowd became louder.

"If you didn't want him here, why didn't you just ask him to leave?" Michelle spoke quickly, her voice rising in volume and pitch. Cain could see her shoulders trembling. "He would have left if you had asked. There was no need to get him drunk and then needle him into making a scene."

The minister twitched and sputtered. His eyes darted from Michelle to his horrified guests and back again.

"Go back to your seat," he whispered furiously. "I'll deal with you later."

"No." Michelle crossed her arms.

"This isn't your business, Michelle."

"But it is, daddy. I can't sit quietly while you insult a guest to his face and threaten him with violence, especially..." She glanced back at Cain, took a deep, shuddery breath, and turned to face her father again. "Especially not when the guest...is someone I care about very much."

Breen's face crumbled in horror. He staggered back against the table, staring at his daughter with fevered eyes. Michelle did not move from her position in front of Cain, but her shoulders drooped. She seemed exhausted by her outburst.

"I'm sorry, daddy," she sighed. "I was going to tell you as soon as—"

A loud pop cut her off. As the guests collectively turned in the direction of the sound, several bulbs in the chandelier above them exploded loudly like gunfire. Cain lunged to shield Michelle from the rain of sparks and broken glass, but her father pulled her away. When he looked up again, the lights were flickering madly and panicked guests rushed around him, shielding their heads and screaming. Something small and blazing streaked around the room, bouncing off the walls, ceiling, and floor. Spurts of blue fire erupted on every surface it touched. Cain followed the blue thing's movement with his eyes, fascinated. When a fleeing guest knocked into him and jarred him back to reality, he noticed that Izzy was no longer at the table, and Vince was gone as well.

A tall man pushed his way through the crowd, dragging another man and a terrified woman with him. The woman screamed when the blue light touched down near her. Cain recognized Izzy, Vince, and Rhoda Thackeray as intermittent flashes of light illuminated their faces.

"Cain!" Izzy ran up to Cain as fast as he could with an old lady clinging to him and a half-conscious man draped over his shoulder. "You've gotta do something!"

The blue light leapt into the chandelier above their heads, causing more bulbs to explode.

Mrs. Thackeray threw up her hands with a dramatic shriek and then angrily addressed Breen. "My stars!" she cried. "If this isn't the most outrageous thing I've ever seen! I told you no good would come of inviting that filthy devil, Nathaniel. I told you."

"Heh." Vince stared up at the sparks floating down from the chandelier, quite unfazed. "I didn't know the party was gonna get this exciting. If I had, I wouldn't have drunk as much."

"What's going on?" shouted Cain over the din.

"It's Zap," Izzy shouted back. "She's freaking out, and I can't find Sammi to stop her!"

Mrs. Thackeray's heavily painted eyelids fluttered impatiently. "Goodness me, but I'm flustered," she said in a loud voice, tugging at Izzy's sleeve. "Isaiah, dear, be a good boy and get me a drink, why don't you?"

"In a minute," said Izzy. "Something is wrong, Cain. You've gotta get Zap to calm down."

"How?" Cain squinted up at the chandelier, where the elemental clung to the sputtering remains of one of the bulbs. She was red-eyed and shivering so hard that her entire body appeared to be a solid cloud of sparks.

The Reverend Breen seized Cain's arm and pulled him close. Cain caught a glimpse of his pale, rage-filled face when the lights flickered again.

"I don't care how," he snarled. "Just stop it from frightening my guests and doing more damage to the room than it's already done—whatever it is. If you get it handled quickly, *maybe* you won't hear from my lawyer."

He released Cain with a final, venomous warning glare

and pushed himself between Mrs. Thackeray and Izzy.

"Come now, Mrs. Thackeray," he said calmly. "We should get you to safety outside."

"Outside!" Mrs. Thackeray stomped her foot and tossed her neat white curls as if offended. "You expect me to stand out in the elements at my age?"

"I'm terribly sorry." The minister's tone was conciliatory, but a pained expression briefly passed over his face. "You only have to be outside until Mr. Pseudomantis gets that pet of his under control, which I'm certain he'll do most speedily."

Mrs. Thackeray muttered under her breath for a while longer, but she allowed herself to be led away. Most of the guests had already fled for the door. The Reverend Breen followed the last few stragglers, jerking his head at Michelle as he did so.

"Come along, sweetheart," he shouted over his shoulder.

Michelle did no such thing. "So," she said to Cain. "How are you going to get that thing down?"

Cain stared up at the panicking elemental with an unhappy shrug. "I don't know. She doesn't really listen to anyone but Sammi, and usually she doesn't even do what he says."

"I'll go and try to find him again." Izzy dashed off with Vince in tow.

Zap leapt off the chandelier and landed near Cain's feet with a splash of sparks. She scurried up to him and ran in tight circles around his legs, buzzing and crackling frantically. Several times she stopped with her nose pointing to a curtain at the far end of the room.

"Ow!" Michelle clapped her hands over her ears as Zap's high-pitched whine rose to a screech. "If that's not an unhappy noise, I don't know what is. I think she wants you to follow her, Cain."

Dread built within Cain's chest. He lifted a heavy foot to go wherever Zap led him, even as a little voice in his mind told him that he would not like what he'd find. A glimpse of the Reverend Breen storming toward him with a face bubbling like a volcano preparing to erupt motivated him to walk faster, but he still had a sudden impulse to run in the opposite direction.

Zap shot across the floor and headed directly for the curtain. Cain blinked for a moment when Zap seemed to vanish into the wall, but then he noticed a door half-hidden behind the folds of burgundy velvet and realized that the elemental must have slipped under it.

"Hey, that's a good idea." Izzy popped up beside him. "Why didn't I think of that? I bet Zap will lead us right to Sammi."

"Or she'll go and hide in a closet 'cause she's just a dumb ball of energy," muttered Vince, rubbing his eyes irritably. "Don't waste your time. The door probably won't even open."

Cain tried the handle, hoping that Vince was right. A dull pain throbbed in his stomach when it turned easily. The door creaked open, revealing a murky little room. Izzy plunged into the darkness beyond the threshold immediately. Vince went with him. Cain hung back, squinting into the gloom. The room seemed to be some kind of storage space. A bulky pile of nondescript cloth sat directly in front of him, and two rows of dusty music stands stood to his right, jutting up crookedly from the floor like the parched ribs of a beached deep sea creature. He thought he saw something else too: a shifting light bobbing above the pile of cloth. He thought it was Zap at first, but its glow wasn't bright and fierce like the elemental's. It was soft and muted, almost filmy.

A strangled shriek snapped him back to awareness. He turned and saw Izzy tugging desperately at a dark mass that was sprawled on the cloth bundle.

"Wake up!" he shouted. "Come on, wake up! Open your eyes!"

Cain rushed to his side and discovered that the dark mass was Sammi's limp form. Sammi's jacket was gone, and his sleeves were bunched up. An empty syringe still dangled from the crook of one elbow, and a thin crust of yellow foam had congealed around his mouth. Zap lay curled on his shoulder, licking his cheek. Sammi did not respond to her touch or to Izzy's pleadings.

"Don't do this!" Izzy shook Sammi harder. "Come on, wake up! You've gotta be asleep. You're just passed out. I know it. You'll wake up any minute now...any...minute..."

His voice trailed off with a whimper. Cain looked down at Vince, who had slid into a sitting position against the wall without Izzy to support him. He had a dull expression on his face.

"Give it up, Izzy," he said in a hopeless tone. "It won't do any good. He's gone."

The heaviness in Cain's chest was mingled with a cold piercing sensation, as if thousands of ice crystals were crawling through his veins. Sammi's head lolled around as Izzy continued to shake him. Cain stared at his band mate's gray skin and flat, unfocused eyes. He knew that Vince was right; Sammi was not going to wake up.

"Dammit, where did you even get that stuff?" Izzy whipped the syringe out of Sammi's arm and threw it against the floor in a sudden burst of anger. "How did you get it out of the house? Cheryl should've took it off you. Hell, *I* should've took it off you. I should've stood in front of the door and not let you out until you turned out your pockets! Why didn't I? God, it's all my fault. This is all my fucking fault."

He broke down into racking sobs. Michelle maneuvered her way around Cain and raced toward Izzy.

"No," she whispered while she tried to pry his hands from Sammi's wrists. "This isn't your fault. This isn't your fault at all. You couldn't have known."

Zap gave a quivering wail of anguish. Cain could feel his voice wanting to join the elemental's, but a sharp cough at the doorway interrupted him. He spun around to find the Reverend Breen standing there, tapping his foot impatiently.

"Well?" said the minister in a tone of weary disapproval. "What on earth is going on now?"

Cain was too stunned to reply, but Michelle piped up for him, in a cold voice. "They just found their friend dead, daddy. It looks like he overdosed."

The minister fell back against the door frame. An expression of sadness passed over his face, and the anger left his eyes. For a moment, Cain thought he might actually say something kind. Then he heaved a deep sigh and rubbed his temples.

"Dear me," he muttered. "Dear, oh, dear me. As if you boys hadn't already made this night quite memorable enough. Well, anyway, I suppose the deceased deserves a prayer, regardless of who he was. Excuse me, Mr. Pseudomantis."

Cain allowed himself to be shouldered aside. A heavy numbness set in as he hovered uselessly in the doorway. He found himself wondering, in a detached way, if perhaps Izzy was half-right. They had all seen the way Sammi behaved when he was high—his fits and fevered hallucinations and coma-like sleep—so maybe he and Izzy and Vince should have seen the danger more clearly. But what could they have done to stop it? His mind struggled to come up with a solution. Should they have searched him for drugs three times a day? Should they have locked him in his room and only let him out for shows? Cain's mind raced, but each idea was more implausible than the last. Yet he could not shake the sickening feeling that if only he had done something, somehow, Nathaniel Breen would not be kneeling down right now to send off Sammi's soul with a reluctant blessing.

"Our God and our Father," droned the minister while Izzy sobbed and Vince huddled against the wall with his eyes fixed on some distant point. "It is true that Mr—Guererro, was it?—was a sinner of the worst kind. He lived in sin and died in sin, and he is no doubt worthy in your eyes of eternal suffering in the pits of Hell. Yet we beseech you to be merciful, to withhold from him a greater measure of the torments reserved for him."

Anger cut through Cain's numbness. Sammi did not deserve this demise. He thought of all the times Sammi had stepped in to break up fights, or to save Izzy from being bullied, or to encourage his band mates, and the whole time Sammi was helping others, he was struggling with his own muddled memories of the Engineer, memories that constantly gnawed at his mind. He must have wanted desperately to shoot up and forget them. If there was anything Sammi certainly did not deserve, it was a cruel and early death.

The gauzy blue light still shifted in the air above

Sammi's body. Vince, Izzy, and Michelle gave no indication that they could see it, nor did Breen, who was kneeling almost directly in front of it. He guessed that it was an artifact of the broken bond between Sammi's body and soul. The soul itself was nowhere to be seen; he supposed it must have passed into the strange twilight realm where he had met the soul of the Engineer's last victim. A deep wave of regret washed over him as he thought of that day. If only he had found Sammi before that vital connection had broken, he might have been able to call him back.

Cain turned and left the room. He had noticed a silver tray loaded with bonbons sitting discreetly on a small table in a corner of the ballroom when the banquet began. He hurried over to it, hoping that some of the chocolates were still there. The buzz from his drugged steak was already beginning to wear off.

A few remained on the tray. Cain picked up three and wolfed them down, trying not to notice the sickly sweet taste or to think too hard about what he was planning to do. He swallowed the last bit of chocolate and walked resolutely back to the closet.

Breen was still praying over Sammi when he returned. He barely noticed him there; the chocolate and sugar had combined in his system, forming a swirling haze in his brain that slowly blocked out everything but the blue light.

"Cain?" He heard Michelle's voice echoing through the mist. "What's wrong? What are you grabbing at? There's nothing there."

The floating shred of light wrapped around his hand like seaweed around driftwood, neither warm nor cold but ever-so-faintly soft against his skin. He had to find Sammi's soul before the chocolate wore off and his own fear of death set in.

Cain clutched the little spark of life to his chest, took a deep breath, and stepped beyond the veil.

Michael's fork slipped from his fingers. It clattered forgotten onto his plate as his back stiffened and his nostrils flared.

He saw.

He couldn't avoid it. The image slipped across his field of vision as the moon inevitably eclipses the sun. He closed his eyes, but it remained clear.

The Dark Lion stood before him. He wore stiff, formal clothing, and his tail was hidden, but Michael knew him on instinct, from the set of his back and from the glint in his eyes. The image expanded, blotting out the long beige table and his little platter of watery mashed potatoes and dry beef.

"Hey, kid," said the old man seated next to Michael. "You gonna finish that steak?"

The words echoed distantly in Michael's ears. He was no longer in the dining hall. He was in an unknown dark room, unseen by the people surrounding the dead man who lay cradled on a bed of filthy cloth on the floor. He saw their grim, sorrowful faces, and he knew what was about to happen.

The Dark Lion took a determined step forward, as if he were walking into a doorway that only he could see. His blue eyes glazed over and lost their focus as he slipped into the space between worlds. He held a tiny weak light protectively in his hands. It pulsed when he passed through the door. Soon the dead man would wake and draw breath, even as his savior breathed his last.

You.

Michael stiffened.

The Voice was speaking to him again. His hands instinctively flew to his ears to blot it out, but it seeped through the barrier.

Awaken and manifest. The command reverberated painfully in his skull. *You must not allow him to die. The Righteous Man still goes unchallenged; he must be stopped, and the Dark Lion must stand against him. You must awaken and save them both.*

Desperate protests flooded Michael's mind and leaked out of his mouth in an incomprehensible whimper of gibberish. A long-stifled part of him was unfolding in the depths of his brain. Each raw, hesitant spurt of its blossoming hurt him like a hot needle in his flesh. The Great Entity had called him out. He had to obey It; yet even now, with so much at stake, he was determined to resist.

I can't, he screamed in his thoughts. *I've been in this world too long. I don't know how to save them.*

You know quite well.

Michael clenched his teeth fiercely. A sob ripped through his chest. He didn't want this burden. He had had enough of voices and knowing and wild, fevered visions. He would give them all up, along with every drop of blood in his body, just to be Michael Anderson, an ordinary boy living his ordinary life.

Think back. The Voice took on a rumbling tone of impatience. *Think back to the time before you were Michael Anderson, before you knew the confines of any human body. Go back to the beginning of all things, when you held the spark of creation in your hands. You still hold that spark. It stirs within you even now. Call upon it. Send it forth.*

The Dark Lion's eyelids flickered, and his mouth moved

vaguely. He had found his friend's soul. There was very little time. Michael could feel the Great Entity becoming angry. Sharp stabs of heat prickled the back of his neck, and the ground beneath his feet began to tremble.

I will not allow this defiance. Are you truly so fearful and broken that you will not awaken, even to save him?

The prickling spread and mellowed. It was no longer painful; in fact, it was quite pleasant and relaxing, but Michael was not enjoying it. He knew what the Great Entity was doing. He had refused to awaken, and now It was going to force his awakening.

I will not be denied. The Voice rattled his bones and buffeted the inside of his skull. *Awaken, my stubborn child. Awaken and manifest. I command it.*

The warmth intensified. Michael stiffened as a pure tide of searing, atom-shivering energy rushed into him. It carried more power than anything his current body had ever channeled. Yet he remembered it vividly. This energy was the same force that had drawn the continents from the bed of the ancient sea and brought forth the first tiny living creatures from the mud of their shores. There had been a time, thousands of eons ago, when he had wielded it with ease. Now he flailed his arms like a drowning man while it ripped through him.

Against his will, he reached out and touched the Dark Lion's mind.

Then it was over. Dizzy and drained, he staggered backwards and lost his footing. His head struck something hard, and, mercifully, he knew no more.

Cain opened his eyes. The walls, floor, and clutter had melted into a single indistinct mass that undulated gently around him, fluctuating between shades of silvery gray and soft blue. The people in the room had become outlines, standing stark and black against the hazy background, but he paid no attention to them. All that mattered now was the glowing figure before him.

"Sammi!" he shouted, his voice echoing strangely in the shimmery emptiness of the between-space realm. "Sammi, can you hear me?"

The soul turned its head slowly. Its face was not quite as mobile or expressive as the face of a living human, but Cain recognized Sammi's features, and he thought he saw a faint gleam of understanding in its eyes.

"I think I can save you," said Cain. "All you need to do is follow me. Come on."

The soul stayed put. It stared at Cain blankly when he gestured towards the dark room.

"Save me?" it said. "From what?"

Its voice was hollow and expressionless, but it was definitely Sammi's voice. Cain took a step closer.

"We need to get you back into your body," he said.

Puzzlement flitted over the soul's features.

"My body?" it said. "Aren't I already in my body?"

Cain shook his head. He was a bit taken aback by Sammi's dazed air. Hopefully it was only a temporary, fleeting side effect of the shock of dying.

"No." He tried to inject as much urgency as possible into his tone. "You're dead, Sammi. I can bring you back, but I need you to help me."

"Oh." The soul calmly raised its luminescent hands and stared at them. It did not seem at all upset or frightened. "I'm dead, am I? So this is what it's like."

A dark spot appeared at the left corner of Cain's field of

vision. He could clearly see the rows of music stands through it.

"You need to follow me, Sammi," he said in desperation. "I can't stay in this place for much longer. If you'll just let me pull you back into the world with me, I can help you live again."

The soul gave him a doubtful look, but it began to float toward him. It moved with a graceful, serene—and, just now, maddening—slowness. The dark swath of reality expanded raggedly in Cain's vision like fire burning through a sheet of paper. Sammi would not make it to his side soon enough. In a few more seconds, he would wake up in the dusty storeroom, and his chance to save Sammi would be gone forever.

Gathering all his strength about him, he lunged forward. Maybe if he could grab hold of the soul before the vision faded, he could pull it through into the mundane world. The effort nearly winded him. Every fiber of his being was trying to withdraw into the storeroom now, and his desperate push in the opposite direction felt like a swim through tar.

Then a deep calm came over him.

With the calmness came a shift in perception. Suddenly, it seemed strange that he had thought he needed chocolate to push beyond the world's thin veil. He could see the veil clearly, right in front of him, behind him, above and below him. And he knew he could now easily and casually reach out and draw it back like a curtain.

"Sammi," he said. "Come to me."

The soul obeyed, slipping into the room through the bright white slit in the fabric of things. Cain allowed the portal he had created to ripple shut and started leading the soul to the center of the room.

Michelle and Vince gasped. Izzy stopped sobbing. The Reverend Breen, who had finished his prayer and had stood up to leave, froze in his tracks when the translucent shape of the soul lit up the room. Cain didn't dwell on their reactions; he was too busy being *aware* of other things. Sounds and sights and smells flooded into his mind in a chaotic torrent. He heard the rhythmic crunches of a mouse's teeth chewing through plaster. His vision bored through the wall, allowing him a brief glimpse of the mouse's black fur before coming to rest on a janitor who had crept into a broom closet in the building next door and fallen asleep. A silvery ribbon of drool crept out of the corner of the old man's mouth as he snored. Cain tore his gaze away and tried to shut out the vibrations of water flowing far under the earth and the pulses of ancient stars throbbing millions of miles above his head. He had to concentrate; there was still work to be done.

He stepped around the gaping minister. The soul followed him, moving even more slowly now, but its sluggishness no longer mattered. Cain felt as if he had all the time in the world to finish this task.

"Cain?" said the soul.

Izzy let out a little shriek and jumped back as it spoke. Michelle's eyes went round with fear and amazement.

"What is it?" said Cain. He took it as a good sign that Sammi still knew his name.

"I don't remember the world being like this." The soul waved a hand in front of its face, as if clearing away a spider web. "Was it always so…I don't know…heavy?"

"You know, I think it was," said Cain in surprise. Now that he thought about it, the atmosphere in this world felt much heavier than the light, ethereal atmosphere of the realm from which he had rescued Sammi's soul. If the mouse's burrowing and the janitor's snoring and the whoosh of water in the pipes and the soft cosmic hum of the stars and the steady pneumatic hiss of air in the lungs of the people in the room were anything to go by, this world was also a noisy and cluttered one. Yet Cain was beginning to realize that he liked the busyness of this world. It was lively and vibrant and comforting. It made him feel less alone.

"Oh." The soul's face fell as much as a soul's untroubled face could. "Yeah, I think I remember now. Oh well. I guess I'll get used to it once I'm alive again."

They had nearly reached the center of the room now. The Reverend Breen scuttled back in holy terror when they approached and stood over Sammi's body.

"Go ahead and get back in," said Cain to the soul. "I'll take care of the rest."

He was still not quite sure how he was going to rejoin the soul with the body, but his certainty that he *could* do it grew with every second that passed.

"I'm not sure that I want to go back," it muttered. "I remember being shut up alone somewhere, shivering, and my whole body was burning with pain that wouldn't go away. I remember wanting to go to sleep and never wake up...and then...after a quick, sharp little poke to my arm, the pain was all gone."

Vince had been staring in utter astonishment at the scene unfolding before him. Bracing his hand against the wall, he climbed unsteadily to his feet.

"Come on, Sammi," said Cain. "The pain won't be that bad once you're awake again."

"No. The pain is gone now. The darkness is gone. I don't want them back."

"Wait!" A spark of horror rose in Cain's chest when the

soul began to float away. He had more power flowing through him now than he had ever held in his life. Every atom of his being hummed with raw, achingly pure magical energy that cried to be released. He could easily force Sammi back into his body if necessary. Yet he could not bring himself to do it, not against Sammi's will. Maybe it was wrong to let his band mate die when he could save him, but it seemed even more wrong to drag him screaming and fighting back into a life he no longer wished to live.

"Life isn't always like that, you know," Vince said.

The soul started and looked sharply at Vince, as if it had just noticed him. Cain did the same. He had never heard Vince speak so gently before.

Vince flushed bright red and clamped his mouth shut. Cain sensed that he had surprised himself by speaking up. He staggered back against the wall as if he might fall again, but he stayed upright. After a few seconds of shocked silence, he took a deep breath and started again.

"You do feel that way sometimes, don't you?" He spoke quickly, his voice rising as his speech progressed. "Like you'll never be able to forget the pain, the terror. You worry that the memory will keep repeating itself in your head, over and over, until the day you die. No, listen!" He held up a hand for silence when the soul tried to speak. "Sometimes the pain goes away for a while. On some days, you even feel pretty good. But then, something happens to remind you about it—or sometimes nothing happens; the memory just comes on out of the blue, with no warning at all, to haunt you. You start thinking, hell, what's the point? I'll never be the same again. That's when you start trying to forget."

The soul's filmy hands shifted nervously. Cain began to see some of Sammi's twitchiness in its movements.

"The needle," it said softly. "I remember the pain fading away when I used it."

"Yeah, I bet you do." Vince clenched and unclenched his fists with poorly concealed impatience, and his tone began to regain its familiar snappishness. "You shoot up to make it go away. I know. I drink and fight for the same reason. But the pain comes back. It always does."

Breen finally managed to shake off some of his fear. He raised his hand in a warding off gesture and began to babble something about ghosts. Vince rounded on him with a fearsome glare.

"Would you mind shutting up, old man?" he snarled. "This is really fucking important."

Breen's mouth snapped closed. His face reddened with indignation, but he did not speak again. Cain did not intervene. As strange as it seemed, he was glad to see Vince acting like himself again.

The soul did not seem to notice the interruption. It was edging back toward the center of the room. Little wisps of the smoky substance of which it was composed rose from its shoulders in agitated curls.

"Then why would I want to live again?" it said. "If that's what it's like."

"Haven't you been listening, dumbass?" said Vince. "I said life was like that *sometimes*. Sure, there'll be the times you feel like you can't go on. But you know what? The good days—the ones where you feel like you could play ten gigs in a row and still plow twenty chicks afterward—make it all worth it. There'll be plenty of days like that too, and we'll have even more of them as time goes on. The story doesn't end here, man. It can't. I haven't even finished living through the first chapter, and neither have you."

A flicker of recognition rose in the soul's eyes.

"I think I remember good days," it said.

"Yeah!" Izzy spoke up, his voice still husky from crying. "You remember when our album came out, don't you?"

A faint smile played on the soul's lips. "I was so relieved. Being in that studio for hours every day was tough, but then the album was done, and I remember thinking, you know, look what I made." It sighed happily. "I didn't shoot up that night. I didn't even want to."

"Vince is right," said Izzy. "You'll have more days like that one. Maybe you'll have some bad days too, but we'll be there to help you through them—me and Cain and Michelle and Vince. If you need help, all you gotta do is ask. There's nothing we wouldn't do for you. Nothing. Besides," he added. "If you stay dead, Zap won't ever forgive you."

As if on cue, the elemental reluctantly peeled herself away from Sammi's body and floated toward his soul. Her beady eyes darted from body to soul and back again, flickering in confusion. Then she darted back to her perch on the body and gave the soul an expectant look. Eager sparks beaded from her whiskers, leaving tiny scorch marks on Sammi's white shirt. Cain noticed the soul watching the elemental fondly.

"Will you let me bring you back?" said Cain in a shorter tone than he intended. The power building relentlessly within him was becoming painful.

The soul turned to him with a smile.

"I think I'm ready now," it said.

CHAPTER TWENTY-THREE

THE ENGINEER

THE SOUL MOVED IN extreme slow motion, gliding without sound over the bare floor. Breen stepped into its path with his arms raised, but he stumbled back with a strangled gasp as it passed effortlessly through his body. Then the soul folded in on itself, like a billowing strip of tulle, and was gone, absorbed into the mound of flesh and bone. Cain knew that it was time for him to do his part. He stepped forward and knelt beside Sammi, laying a hand on his cold forehead.

The painful throbbing in his skull steadily dissipated as he released the mysterious energy into Sammi. His piercing visions of the world around him faded to ordinary sight, even as every organ, artery, and nerve in the body before him sharpened and stood out in relief.

"Beat," he said to the heart. Its slack purple ventricles shivered and pulsed. Stagnant blood in the tiny veins beneath his fingertips began to stir, then to creep, then to rush.

"Breathe," he said to the lungs. They expanded, soft and cloudlike, and Cain heard the slow hiss of air trickling into them.

The pressure in his head was gone now, but the power continued to flow. It barreled through him in a reckless, unstoppable torrent, like water through a burst dam, and he had a frightening feeling that he was not controlling it. Rather, the power conformed to his commands because it *chose* to do so.

Another wave of energy rushed from him. Sammi's muscles spasmed and his eyelids fluttered. The thin slimy-looking film that had formed over his eyes dissolved. Michelle's gasp of awed fear and Izzy's steady chant of *"oh my god, oh my god, oh my god"* floated on the edges of his hearing. He wished ruefully that they could see what he was seeing. He had no idea that humans possessed such a beautiful, intricate lacework of veins and nerves or so many perfectly interlocked organs. He was absolutely mesmerized, watching them all awaken, one by one, stirring and undulating and throbbing in a coordinated living jigsaw puzzle.

He had only one step left: he had to give up his life force and transfer the energy to Sammi. He reflected on this sacrifice for a moment, and his fear returned.

Do it.

Whether the voice came from his own thoughts, or from something outside himself, Cain could never be sure. He felt hobbled, weakened, and wrested from his body. A last cloud of burning energy built in his chest unprompted, and he heard his voice give the final command.

"Wake up. Live again."

He expelled the pent-up force with a silent scream of pain. The energy exploded from him in a relentless blast of raw heat. He felt as if all of his skin had suddenly been torn off. Before the pain overwhelmed him, he caught a brief-but-satisfying glimpse of Sammi lifting his head and raising an unsteady hand to wipe his mouth. Starbursts spattered across his vision in a riot of searing green and neon blue. Then the colors solidified, inexplicably, into a huge bare-looking room where the boy from the graveyard sat at a long table with a dozen people seated around him.

Jim? he cried. *Jim Kellerman? Is that you?*

The boy did not seem to hear Cain. The boy's eyes glazed over; his mouth moved without sound; and jerky little shudders ran through him. Then his entire body convulsed, and he was flung violently into another table behind him. He crumpled to the floor, a pool of dark blood forming lazily under his head. The pool grew and spread and deepened and reached out to Cain. Cain sank into the boy's blood, struggling for air, and then, the blood turned to cold rushing water. Big hands clenched tightly around his waist, pulling him toward the light that sparkled far away on the water's surface, but he was being dragged so unbearably slowly that he feared he would drown anyway.

Then the drowning sensation was gone. The world faded to peaceful, static white light. Something soft and warm pressed against his back. He rolled over with a deep sigh, drifting off into a welcome sleep.

Something tugged at his arm.

Cain was so tired that he shrugged it off. He dozed for a while, ignoring the steady, insistent pulling. Then he shifted in his sleep, and a prickle of sharp pain in the crook of his elbow woke him. Cain grumbled and poked at the affected spot, which felt as if it were covered by an uneven layer of bumpy gauze. Puzzled, he cracked his eyes open and squinted at his arm.

The gauzy substance was a big square of porous white

tape. A curl of tubing protruded beneath it. The tubing looped up to a mysterious bag of clear fluid that hung from a metal pole. Cain's eyes followed the tube from his arm to the bag and back again, and his finger reached to poke the tape.

"Dammit, Cain, what the *hell* were you thinking?"

Cain whirled around and found himself face-to-face with a very upset Steve.

"Don't ever do that again!" Steve's hands trembled indignantly. "You scared the crap out of me!"

"I...I did?" Cain glanced around him. The walls of the room he was in were such a painfully bright white that he could not focus on them for long. He could make out a curtained window and a plain aqua-colored chair in the far corner behind Steve. "What did I do?"

Steve was too worked up to register the question. "Your little stunt landed you in the hospital, for God's sake! Do you have any idea how bad this could have turned out? Someone upstairs must really, really like you, because if any other demon tried to pull that off, they'd be wearing a toe tag."

Cain heard a door open to his left. He perked up at the sound of a familiar voice cutting through Steve's rant.

"It's a good thing Cain is so lucky, huh?" Michelle swept into the room with a paper bag in her arms, and Sammi trailed along in her wake. "Thanks so much for waiting with him while we got ourselves situated, Steve. Now, why don't you get yourself some breakfast at the café across the street?"

"I'm not hungry." Steve gave Cain a dark look.

"Sure you are." Michelle dropped her bag at the foot of Cain's bed and took Steve's arm. "Even if you weren't, you've been up all night; you'll need coffee to wake you up. Come on, I've been to this place before, and there's a pretty girl working behind the counter there. I think she'd like you a lot. Come on."

"Well…" Steve reluctantly allowed himself to be led out the door. "I guess I should probably eat something. But I'm still pissed at you, Cain."

Sammi walked over and sat on the edge of the bed as soon as they were gone. He swung his legs and drummed his fingers against the mattress. Cain regarded him curiously; Sammi mostly seemed his usual self, but there was something different about him, something difficult to identify. He seemed to have an inner glow, similar to the one Vince got from eating someone's energy.

"I'm sorry Steve went crazy on you," he said. "We called him to tell him what happened after the ambulance took you away, and he freaked. Hell, he got to the hospital before Michelle did, and she rode along with you."

"Why did I have to go to the hospital?" Cain peered around the little room again. Its spotless glaring whiteness made him nervous. "I just passed out. I'm fine now."

Sammi craned his head to look at Cain. The strange luminosity that hung about him was much more evident in his eyes.

"It's ten in the morning," he said. "You went down at about nine last night, I think. We couldn't wake you up, and then you started thrashing and gasping like you couldn't breathe, and we didn't know what else to do."

"What?" Cain heaved himself out of bed and lumbered over to the window. He pushed the faded beige curtains aside and blinked in disbelief at the bright morning sunlight that poured through the thick panes.

"I guess it took a lot out of you, huh?" said Sammi.

"I guess." Cain reached out to touch the glass. It was solid and warm under his fingertips, but he was not entirely convinced that he wasn't still hallucinating.

Sammi got up from the bed and walked over to him.

"So did you know it could have killed you?"

Cain stared at him. "Who told you that?"

"Steve did," said Sammi. "About a million times, in fact—that's why he was so freaked. He said that if you even thought about trying to bring someone back to life again, he'd kill you himself. But you didn't know you might die, did you? I mean, if you did…"

Cain clenched his jaw, wondering how to answer. Sammi had enough to worry about without knowing that he came perilously close to getting a second chance at life by virtue of a friend's untimely death.

"I didn't really think about it," he said at last. "I must have figured that if I could bring back the guy in the studio, then maybe I could bring you back also. Then something strange happened."

"What?"

Cain frowned. "This weird surge of magic just appeared from nowhere. It wasn't mine, but I knew exactly how to use it, like I'd used it every day of my life…and I could see the mice in the walls and the organs in your body and…everything." He shook his head. "It was almost like…well…what I think humans would call a miracle. I know that sounds crazy."

"Oh, I believe you," said Sammi. "I remember going back into my body. It felt so…I don't know, heavy and useless, like it wasn't part of me anymore. I was about to give up and leave it behind for good when the warmth hit

me. I could feel everything in me coming back to life again."
A haunted expression passed over his face. "God, it hurt so much—like a million lasers burning through me, only worse. But I didn't want it to stop."

"I was hurting you?" Cain cried in alarm. Despite the searing agony the mysterious power had caused him, he had not even considered that it might have caused Sammi pain as well. "Was it really that bad? Why didn't you tell me?" he added, not realizing how foolish he sounded until the words left his mouth.

Sammi laughed—the clearest and most genuinely happy-sounding laugh that Cain had heard from him in a long time.

"You know, I tried," he said. "But it turns out it's kind of hard to make your mouth move when you're still partway dead. Nah, don't worry about me, man. I'm better than I've been in a long time. I'd be more worried about Izzy if I were you."

"Why? What's wrong with Izzy?"

The door opened behind them and Michelle walked in, sans Steve.

"He was even more freaked out by the whole thing than Steve was," she said. "Look, don't take this the wrong way, but...he took one look at your face after you told Sammi to wake up and started hyperventilating like crazy. He kept saying that God was in you, and I could kind of see why he'd think that. The whole thing was a little scary. Even my daddy was speechless."

"Scary?" Cain turned back to the window and studied his reflection in dismay. "What do you mean? I don't look any different, do I?"

"No, no," said Michelle in a reassuring tone. "Not

anymore, you don't. But while you were working on Sammi—hmm, how can I describe it?—a *light* was shining out from inside you, a weird radioactive light that made you too dangerous to touch. You looked a little like Sammi does now, only way more intense."

It was Sammi's turn to be dismayed. He spun around and joined Cain at the window.

"So where's Steve?" said Cain, hoping to change the subject. The more he thought and talked about last night's events, the more disturbed he became. When the power overtook him, he had felt even more utterly powerless and manipulated than he had felt during the first few days of his captivity.

"He's still at the coffee shop." Michelle chuckled. "I figured you could both use a break, so I introduced him to the girl who works there. I think they'll get along famously."

"Oh, good," said Cain, trying to hide his anxiety. Steve wasn't nearly as bad as his brother at interacting with girls he wanted to date, but Cain could not deny that Steve had some spectacular flubs on his record. "We should go join him and…um…watch from a distance."

"We can't go anywhere until you're checked out of the hospital."

"But I feel fine."

Michelle shook her head. "It's not quite that simple. The doctor still has to see you and tell you you're good to go, and there'll be papers to sign and stuff. You don't even have real clothes on right now; we had to bring you some from home."

Cain glanced down at the shapeless blue smock in which he had been dressed and wondered why it was not considered "real clothes." Maybe it was a bit flimsy and not terribly flattering, but it covered everything that humans preferred to see covered.

Michelle picked up the bag and helped him rummage through it. "Here—we can get some pants on you, at least. You'll have to wait until they take the IV out to put on a shirt."

"IV?" said Cain.

"That tube in your arm." She pointed. "Didn't you notice it?"

Cain glanced down at the forgotten plastic piping. He was a bit surprised to see that the metal pole was now behind him instead of beside the bed, but then he noticed the four little black castor wheels at the pole's base.

"Oh yeah." He poked the pole with his foot, unable to imagine what use the contraption served. "Well, that should be easy enough."

"Cain, wait!" Michelle grabbed his hand when he began to pick at the tape. "You can't get it out just by pulling off the bandage. The nurse actually has to take it out."

"Take it out of where?" Cain pinched the tube curiously. "It doesn't seem like it's actually *in* anywhere—just sort of stuck on."

Sammi started making a frantic shushing gesture, but Michelle was already answering Cain's question.

"No, the tape just helps to hold it in place. It's actually stuck in by a needle and—"

A shriek from Cain cut her off. Sammi rushed to help calm him down, but Cain was already panicking. He swiped wildly at his arm. The freshly ripped-out IV tube whipped Sammi across the chest, and he fell back with a gasp. Cain somersaulted backwards onto the bed and landed mid-transformation. His claws plucked the remaining scraps of tape off his bicep while his skin hardened into scales. He hunched on the bed, staring wide-eyed at the puddle of liquid spreading sluggishly from the disconnected needle.

"They were putting that stuff inside me?" he gasped in horror. "*Why*? It isn't poison, is it?"

"Of course not!" said Michelle. "Cain, this is a hospital. They're not going to poison anyone here. They just want to help you."

Cain looked around the little room again and shuddered. If shutting him up in a stark white cell and pumping his veins full of an unknown potion from a sinister hanging bag was the hospital's idea of helping him, he would have preferred not to be helped at all.

"Well, I feel fine now." He snatched up his pants and struggled into them. "Let's get out of here."

Michelle threw up her hands in exasperation and started to protest, but she was interrupted when the door opened again and a nurse popped her head into the room.

"Is everything all right in here?" said the nurse. "I thought I heard…"

Her voice died in her throat when Cain turned to face her. She went rigid with fear. Cain tried to see himself through her eyes: an enormous, scaly blue *thing* that crouched on the bed, twitching its tail like a cat about to pounce and staring at her with eyes that had a spark of strange bright fire in them.

"Wait!" Sammi hastily thrust out an arm to reassure her. "He's not gonna eat you or anything."

But his reassurances came too late. The nurse leapt back and slammed the door. The clatter of her running feet and her repeated high-pitched screams for security faded down the hall.

"Crap," muttered Michelle. "That changes things a bit. Hmm, we'd probably save ourselves some trouble if we could get you out of the building without being seen."

"Oh, I think I can manage that," said Cain as he transformed back into human form, his voice muffled by the shirt he was trying to pull over his head as fast as he could without snagging it on his horns.

Steve was still chatting with the girl in the coffee shop. Cain tried to get his attention, but Sammi stopped him.

"Come on, man, let's get you home," he said. "Izzy is worried sick about you, and Steve's happy where he is right now. He can catch up later."

Against his better judgment, Cain agreed to leave Steve at the café. He pressed his tail close to his body and put his head down, letting his hair fall over his horns as he hurried after Michelle and Sammi. He was not in the mood to be recognized and stopped right now.

Sammi threaded his way through the people on the sidewalk with admirable speed and grace. Coming back from the dead seemed to have given him renewed energy; he soon left Cain and Michelle far behind, but Michelle did not seem to mind. As soon as the crowd thinned a bit, she took Cain's hand and looked up at him expectantly.

"Hey," she said. "I'm glad you're okay."

"Thanks," said Cain, giving her a gentle squeeze.

"I hope you don't mind that Izzy and Vince weren't there when you woke up. Izzy was too much of a wreck to go to the hospital, and Vince…Well, he was actually being really quiet, but he's still Vince."

"I understand," said Cain. "I hope Izzy isn't still a wreck?"

"Hmm?" Michelle shook herself and blinked. "Oh, he's calmed down some since last night. I'm sure seeing you will help him, though."

"Are you all right?" Cain regarded Michelle curiously. She had a strange distant expression on her face.

"I'm fine. I...have something important I'll have to tell you later."

"What?" His face fell. "Did I do something wrong?"

"No, no," said Michelle quickly. "It's nothing like that. It's a good thing. But we should really wait until we have some privacy to talk about it."

He was about to press her for more information, but Sammi suddenly popped up in front of them.

"Hey," he said. "I'm sorry I got so far ahead. I forgot that one of you just got out of the hospital. I'll slow down a little."

Sammi's idea of "slowing down" had them following him at a half-run the rest of the way. By the time they reached the front steps, Cain was so winded he could hardly climb them. Izzy charged down the inside stairs as they entered the house. Cain stepped through the door in time to see him run up to Sammi.

"What did they say at the hospital?" he demanded. "He's still okay, right?"

"Whoa, Izzy, keep it down a little!" Sammi chuckled. "You'll wake Zap. It took me forever to get the little monster into her outlet. Don't worry about Cain; he's fine. You can ask him how he's feeling yourself if you'd like."

Izzy blinked and whipped his head around like a confused owl. He had dark livid bags under his eyes, and his hands were trembling. Cain suspected that he had stayed up all night and choked down a great deal of coffee to keep himself awake. Then he caught sight of Cain and Michelle standing in the door. His entire demeanor changed, and he flushed bright purple.

"You're back!" He dashed headlong toward them, forcing Sammi to leap aside. "You're back, and you're alive!"

Cain felt the breath rush from his lungs as Izzy caught him in a crushing hug. Then Izzy abruptly released him. The purple tinge in Izzy's skin and hair suddenly shifted to a red one, and his normally serene blue eyes blazed.

"You scared the crap out of me, you know that?" he yelled. "First you had that weird light coming from you, and then your eyes went all glassy, and then you fell on the floor and started shaking—God, I thought you were gonna die! Don't ever do that again, you hear?"

"Yeah, Cain." Sammi grinned and winked. "Don't you dare save my life ever again. What the hell were you thinking?"

Izzy looked embarrassed. "Sorry, Sammi. I didn't mean it like that."

"It's okay, Iz," said Sammi. "I'm just yanking your chain. It was a pretty scary thing, wasn't it? I'm glad Cain came through it all right." He took a deep breath and glanced around. "So…where's Vince?"

"He's still up in the loft," said Izzy. "He hasn't come down since we got home last night. I guess he must've fallen asleep."

"Well, let's go wake him up. He wasn't showing it much, but he was definitely worried. Come on, Cain."

"Actually, could you guys go on ahead?" said Michelle. "I have something to tell Cain."

"Oh yeah?" Izzy perked up curiously. "What's that?"

"Well…" Michelle glanced at Cain. "It's private."

Sammi gave her an understanding nod and tugged at Izzy's sleeve. "Come on, Iz, let's let Michelle and Cain talk."

Izzy followed Sammi up the stairs at a reluctant pace, staring back at Cain and Michelle all the way. As soon as they were gone, Michelle turned to Cain with a strange pinched expression on her face. She did not speak right away, and Cain's apprehension began to flare up again.

"What's up?" he asked cautiously.

"Um…" Michelle opened her mouth and shut it again. "I…Well, to tell the truth, I have no idea how to say this."

"Just say it," said Cain, trying to sound calm in spite of the panic slowly rising in him. He wracked his brain to remember what awful deed he could possibly have done to make her look so profoundly uncomfortable.

"Okay." She sucked in a deep, shuddery breath. "Sorry—it's just that I never really thought I'd ever have to have a talk like this, you know? I was always so careful about protection; living with daddy, I had to be. But when I was with you…" She shook her head in annoyance. "It was stupid of me, I see that now, but you have a tail and eat raw pigeons. You can *fly*, for God's sake! We obviously aren't the same species. I didn't think I needed to use protection with you. Look, it could turn out to be nothing, but you should know…" She turned a deep shade of red and lowered her voice. "I missed my period, Cain. I've missed it for the last three months."

"Oh." Cain blinked. Long ago, Mr. Warwick had given him a brief and vague description of a certain biological function specific to human women. At the time he had thought that this particular function sounded too grisly, too undignified, and too much of a waste of perfectly good blood to be real. Then he had listened to Vince bitterly accusing various women who had offended him of being "on the rag," and had started to notice a regular pattern in the nights Michelle declined sex because of a "headache." But he had never completely confirmed his suspicions because he couldn't imagine a polite and non-embarrassing way to ask any woman—even Michelle—if it was true that she bled from her private parts once a month. This moment seemed like the best opportunity he would get. "So...um...you mean you didn't—?"

"That's right: I didn't bleed this month," said Michelle, rubbing her eyes. "And that might mean—"

"YOU'RE GONNA HAVE A BABY!"

Cain stumbled back with a yelp of surprise when Izzy mysteriously sprung up out of the floor and appeared beside him. Michelle started too, but she regained her composure much faster than Cain did.

"Izzy, where the hell did you come from?" she gasped. "You went upstairs with Sammi! I *saw* you leave!"

"Yeah, but you didn't see me come back down!" Izzy clapped his hands gleefully. "I turned into a mouse as soon as Sammi got busy trying to wake up Vince. I'm glad I did too. Man, I'm so excited! Kids are so much fun. Especially other people's kids."

"We'd have told you anyway once we were ready," grumbled Michelle. "I mean, geez, is a little patience too much to ask for? You don't see Sammi or Vince eavesdropping like school kids."

"Eavesdropping?" Sammi popped up at the top of the stairs. "Izzy, did I hear you yelling that somebody was gonna have a baby a second ago? You didn't mean Michelle, did you?"

"Well, so much for keeping it secret till we decided what to tell daddy." Michelle turned back to Cain. "Look, Izzy is right. I wanted to let you know that I think I'm pregnant, and if I am…then you'll be a dad soon."

Cain stared at her while the impact of the words finally sank in. He had no idea what to say. A whirlwind of conflicting joy and fear began to churn within him, and he could not decide which emotion was dominant.

"Isn't this great?" Izzy danced in place and flushed a shade of purple bright enough to put the tackiest neon signs on the Strip to shame. "I can't wait until this kid is born. I'll practically be an uncle!"

Sammi cast an apologetic glance at Michelle. "Come on, Izzy. We should give Cain and Michelle a few minutes by themselves to talk."

His curiosity satisfied, Izzy followed Sammi back upstairs. Cain felt Michelle tugging his hand. He followed her to the couch in the living room, still somewhat in a haze.

"Look," she said to him as soon as they had sat down. "I know if you've been talking to someone like…oh, Keenan McFarlane or AK Andrew, you may have heard…certain stories. But I swear I'm not a gold digger. I didn't get pregnant on purpose to make you marry me or give me money or some stupid crap like that. You're not mad at me, are you?"

"Of course not!" Cain looked at her askance.

"Good." Michelle gave a sigh of relief. "We still have to decide what to do about it, though. If I'm really pregnant, I mean."

"What is there to decide?"

"Well, for example, we need to decide how we'll take

care of the baby, and whether we'll raise it together. Also…" She faltered, and her voice took on a pained tone. "Sooner or later, I'll have to tell daddy. Don't worry: I won't make you take part in that conversation. I think that'd only make things worse."

"He doesn't know yet?" said Cain.

"Nope," said Michelle. "I sure as hell wasn't going to tell him last night in front of all his guests, and I didn't think that telling him before I sneaked out this morning was such a good idea either. I'm really not looking forward to telling him, but he's got a right to know. Plus, I kind of feel like he suspects we've got something big going on anyway. Maybe not *this big*, but definitely something."

"Is he very angry?" said Cain.

"I'm not really sure. He wouldn't say a word to me the whole ride home, and I'm pretty sure he stayed up all night. He's really acting weird. But if he is angry, He may…" She winced and lowered her voice. "Look, don't freak out, but he might try to talk me into stopping the pregnancy. I'm not saying he'll definitely go that route—he's been dead-set against abortion his whole life—but I could see how he'd think that this was a special case. If that happens, I'll—"

A firm knock at the door interrupted her.

"I bet that's Steve," said Cain.

"Oops." Michelle scrambled to her feet. "We did kind of abandon him at the café, didn't we? I hope he's not mad at us."

Two more knocks sounded as Cain and Michelle walked into the front hall. As Cain started to open the door, Izzy appeared and barreled down the stairs.

"I'm coming! I'm coming!" he shouted. "Hold your horses." He pulled up short at the bottom of the stairs when he saw Cain and Michelle. "Oh...you've got it. Never mind."

"It's probably just Steve coming back from breakfast," Cain called up at him. "You can stick around if you want."

"That's okay." Izzy turned and started back upstairs. "We've almost got Vince awake. Sammi made him sit up for thirty-two whole seconds."

Cain nodded understandingly. Then he turned his attention back to the door and opened it, expecting to see Steve. When he saw the person who actually was standing on the doorstep, his stomach squeezed into a tiny, quivering knot.

Mr. Warwick tapped his fingers rhythmically against the porch railing. His black eyes glinted with strange intensity, although his smile was perfectly bland and calm.

"Hello, Cain," he said.

As if by instinct, Michelle moved closer to Cain's side. And Izzy stopped climbing the stairs. "Master," said Cain in a weak voice.

Mr. Warwick reached out and grabbed his hand. He turned it up and ran his fingertips over Cain's palm like a fairground fortuneteller, knitting his brow with concentration. Cain stood still, letting his master poke and prod him. He was sure that Mr. Warwick would have something to say about his behavior toward the Reverend Breen last night. Perhaps his compliance would put the old man in a good mood and soften the blow.

"Well, well, well." Mr. Warwick finally looked up, and to Cain's surprise, he was smiling. "This may well be one of the most extraordinary things I've seen in my entire career."

Michelle made an impatient noise deep in her throat. Cain knew she deeply disliked Mr. Warwick because he was the "cruel bastard" who had imprisoned him in a magical shock collar. Cain guessed that Mr. Warwick's failure to acknowledge or even glance at her—even though he must have seen her standing beside him—did absolutely nothing to endear Mr. Warwick to her.

"Excuse me," she said loudly. "I don't believe we've met. I'm Cain's girlfriend, Michelle."

Izzy flinched when she spoke up and stepped cautiously down a few steps. Cain flinched too; he could hear the challenge beneath Michelle's polite tone, and he was sure Mr. Warwick had picked up on it as well.

"A lovely name for a lovely girl," said Mr. Warwick, sweeping up Michelle's hand with a single quick movement and raising it to his lips. "I've been eager to meet you, especially in light of recent circumstances."

"Recent circumstances?" Michelle allowed her hand to be kissed, but Cain sensed that she would have strongly preferred to yank it away and give Mr. Warwick a good solid kick in the shins. "You don't mean the baby, do you? How did you...?"

"Baby?" Mr. Warwick blinked. "You don't mean to tell me that you're...expecting, do you?"

Cain squeezed Michelle's other hand as she blushed bright red and involuntarily glanced down at her stomach. He hoped with clenched teeth and stilted breath that Mr. Warwick would not realize that this Michelle was the same Michelle he had sent Cain to retrieve as a girlfriend for Lance.

"Ah," said Mr. Warwick with a chuckle, seeing her reaction. "Goodness me, you young people don't waste any time, do you? No, that was not what I meant. I'm talking about something much more recent...and much more unusual. Now, I must borrow Cain for a while. Could you give us a minute, my dear?"

Michelle clutched Cain tighter and gave Mr. Warwick a forced smile. "Oh, you can say whatever you have to tell him in front of me. I don't mind."

"Come now." Mr. Warwick chuckled. "I can't imagine you would find our conversation very interesting. Besides, it wouldn't be proper of me to discuss the more...*esoteric* secrets of my trade with an outsider, particularly a young lady."

Cain could feel Michelle tense beside him. He knew she hated when people spoke to her in a patronizing tone. She took a deep breath, as if to prevent her anger from bubbling over. Her father had probably given her plenty of practice for situations like this one. Her muscles shuddered, and she let them relax. She gazed up at Mr. Warwick with wide eyes, tilting her head subtly to one side.

"You're right: I'm afraid I wouldn't find it very interesting," she said with a passable giggle. "Cain tried to explain to me how some of that spell stuff worked once, and I didn't understand one bit of it—all those symbols and funny words. I don't know how you keep them straight. Your secrets will be totally safe with me."

Cain had never heard her speak in that way before. He started and stared at her with raised eyebrows. She shot back a look warning him to play along.

Mr. Warwick thought for a moment. Then he cleared his throat and spoke. "I won't keep Cain long." He flashed an indulgent smile at Michelle. "You have no need to waste your time listening to us talk business. I'll return him to you in time for lunch, and as a sign of goodwill," he pointed at Cain's neck, "before he comes back, I'll remove that collar.

I'm permanently relieving him of his duties as my servant."

A fierce wave of joy surged through Cain even as doubt seethed in the back of his mind. Could he really have heard Mr. Warwick correctly? The goodwill gesture didn't seem right somehow. The Mr. Warwick he knew would never just show up on his doorstep and set him free purely out of the kindness of his heart, would he?

Michelle was not ready to give up. She planted herself firmly in Cain's path and fixed Mr. Warwick with pleading eyes.

"Look, I'd really rather not leave his side right now," she said. "He just got out of the hospital, and he's still kind of weak."

She gave Cain a subtle jab with her elbow while she spoke. He quickly slumped his shoulders and let out a pathetic rasping cough.

"Please, please let me tag along," Michelle said. "I promise I won't tell anyone what you say to him. I probably won't even remember most of it."

Mr. Warwick's gaze flicked from Cain to Michelle and back again. Cain could not quite read his expression, but there was a calculating glint in his eyes.

"Bless you, child," he murmured. "You really are persistent in your devotion, aren't you? Ah, very well; you may come with us. I'll try to make this quick. Come along, Cain."

He turned on his heel and strode down the front steps. Cain glanced at Izzy, who was still on his perch at the top of the stairs, and nodded. Izzy visibly relaxed. He seemed satisfied that Cain was not about to be snatched away to New York. He trotted back upstairs. Cain and Michelle turned to follow Mr. Warwick.

Mr. Warwick led them along at a brisk pace, first through the neighborhood surrounding the townhouse, then onto a main road with lots of shops. Cain noticed that Michelle fell back to look at a window display at the same time that Mr. Warwick paused to conjure a road map from thin air. He unfolded it and squinted at the elaborate network of lines on the paper, shaking his head.

"Damn these streets," he grumbled. "No matter how many times I make my way through this wretched city I can never remember...left or right? Let's see, if Vine is here..."

"Master?" Cain spoke up shyly. "Where are we going?"

"To my hotel," he said shortly. "I'll need some things from my room to properly free you."

"There are a lot of hotels to the left and down one of those bigger streets, Master," said Cain, hoping that Mr. Warwick would free him faster if he was good and helpful. "My friends go to parties there sometimes."

"Ah!" Mr. Warwick snapped his fingers. "I remember now—it is left we want. Good boy, Cain."

He started off again. Cain followed, scurrying to keep up. Michelle dawdled along a few feet behind, pretending to be engrossed in the colorful clothing and sparkling jewels that peeped out of every window; but Cain suspected that she was straining her ears for any sign of conversation. He watched her over his shoulder, admiring her ability to walk sideways without tripping herself up or knocking into anyone.

"Cain." Mr. Warwick's voice startled him out of his reverie. "Do you know why I'm freeing you?"

"No, Master," Cain answered truthfully. He had wracked his brain and simply could not think of any reason for Mr. Warwick to free him.

Mr. Warwick was silent for a few minutes. Then he heaved a deep sigh and spoke. "Last night," he said, "I was returning to the hotel after a meeting. As I walked through the lobby, the floor began to tremble beneath my feet. The tremor became stronger until several potted plants and a cup of pens on the front desk toppled over. Then everything was still."

"Earthquake, Master?" said Cain incredulously. He had not noticed an earthquake last night, and his band mates had not mentioned one.

"I thought so at first," admitted Mr. Warwick. "But then I felt the energy that crackled through the air around me, and I knew it was no ordinary earthquake. More magic than I've ever felt in one place at one time played on my skin and shivered in my bones and shook every atom in my body. I'm not a religious man, Cain, but I suppose you could say it was a spiritual experience for me. I stood in abject awe of the one who was channeling that great power. I felt I would willingly give every last cent I have for the privilege of throwing myself at his feet and begging him to teach me his secrets."

Cain swallowed hard. Had his bizarre blast of energy really been powerful enough to cause shockwaves that were felt by Gifted people throughout the city? He shuddered at the memory of the overwhelming power, unable to imagine how he had wielded it without being blasted to bloody fragments.

"Imagine my surprise this morning," Mr. Warwick continued, "when the rumors already spreading throughout the city all named you as the miracle worker—my own demon servant who barely knows how to read or write or use his silverware at the dinner table. But now that I've examined you in the aftermath...I doubt you can see it, but wisps of that same great power still hang about you, and you have a certain air of...well...sanctity. If you were human and a Christian, I suppose Nathaniel Breen might say you have the Spirit of the Lord upon you."

"Is that why you're letting me go?" said Cain meekly. He wanted to angrily mutter that he could read and write just fine, but he doubted that correcting his master would do him any good.

"It is. I see now that I must. You've had the privilege of performing a true miracle, and a miracle worker is not fit for the life of a slave, even if he is just a demon."

Cain vaguely registered Michelle popping up beside him to clutch his arm, but he was still too numb with utter amazement to catch what she said to him in an intense whisper.

"Before I release you," Mr. Warwick continued, "I was hoping that you would do me the honor of helping with one last experiment, for old times' sake."

Cain started to nod, but a twinge of suspicion—or was it Michelle's nails digging into his skin?—held him back. "What kind of experiment?"

Mr. Warwick glanced back at them. A strange little smile played about his lips.

"One I've been working on for a while now. I think you may just help me perfect it. What do you say?"

Cain scratched at his collar, trying to work out a good response. He had no desire to put up with Mr. Warwick's all-too-familiar steady rain of snide verbal abuse and rapid-fire orders even one more time, but he had a deep sickening fear that refusing the request would make the old man change his mind about freeing him.

"Well..." he said slowly. "I *guess* I could...just one more time...but...Master?" He tugged once more at the studded leather band around his neck. "Couldn't you take this off first? I promise I won't run away."

"*Cain.*" Michelle's sharp whisper and the sudden pain of her nails gouging his arm snapped him to attention. "Where the hell did he take us?"

Cain turned to ask her what on earth her problem was. The words died on his lips when he took his eyes off Mr. Warwick and took a good look at his surroundings. The salmon-colored house in front of them was big, impressive, and it was definitely not a hotel. In fact, it did not look as if anybody had lived in it for years: massive cracks zigzagged through the stucco walls; the roof was a shabby patchwork of missing and broken tiles; and most of the windows were covered with graffiti-slathered plywood sheets.

"Do you think I'm stupid, boy?" Mr. Warwick was climbing the half-crumbled staircase that led to the front door. He glanced back at Cain with a scornful smirk, his friendly demeanor suddenly gone. "If I release you now, you'll bound off like a spooked rabbit, and I'll have missed the opportunity of a lifetime. Now come along. The faster we finish up, the faster you can go home with your little woman, eh?"

Cain let out a low nervous growl. He did not want to go anywhere near that house; it had a deep-set air of foreboding and despair that sent his hackles up. His eyes scanned the shadows for lurking shapes. He shuffled back a step, but the collar shuddered back to life as soon as he did. It bit down so viciously that his knees buckled, and he fell to the sidewalk with a groan.

"Cain!" Michelle dropped down beside him. "Cain, are

you all right?"

Mr. Warwick had turned around on his perch by the house's grand, old wooden front doors to look down at them.

"Hurry up," he said in a sickeningly cheerful voice. "I haven't got all day, you know." He nodded imperiously at Michelle. "You will wait outside until we're done. I'm sorry I can't offer you more comfortable accommodations."

"No!" Michelle sprang up to follow Cain as he jerked to his feet like a badly manipulated puppet and lurched up the stairs, yanking at his collar and gasping all the way. "I'm not leaving him! Cain, what's wrong? You bastard, what are you *doing* to him? Stop it, stop it right now!"

A livid expression crossed Mr. Warwick's face. He lifted a hand and smacked at the air. Michelle immediately staggered backward, as if she had been slapped, and toppled to the pavement below. Cain lunged against the force dragging him up the stairs in an attempt to catch her, but the effort was a futile one. He bared his teeth at Mr. Warwick and snarled as loudly as the choking collar would allow, heedless of the extra stab of pain that resulted. Mr. Warwick scowled at Cain, glanced down at Michelle, and suddenly seemed to change his mind.

"Very well," he said stiffly. "You may come in if you like. I still don't think it's proper, but I suppose you might be useful for securing his cooperation."

Michelle climbed shakily to her feet and ran up the stairs, shooting Mr. Warwick a look of pure hatred as she did so. Cain felt the warmth of her hand when she slipped it back into his, and he squeezed it for comfort.

The doors creaked when Mr. Warwick opened them—a long, drawn-out, rasping noise that sounded uncannily like a moan of pain. He strode confidently into the blackness beyond them. Cain staggered after him, clinging to Michelle, unable to suppress his shudders of cold fear or his whimpers while his feet passed unwillingly over the threshold.

"Hey, Vince," said Sammi gently. "Don't you think you ought to...you know...actually *eat* something with breakfast?"

Vince looked up from his third beer. His hair was a greasy web of snarls, and his eyes were red and puffy, but he could still manage a white-hot, glass-shattering glower.

"Or not." Sammi sighed and backed out of the kitchen, unwilling to pick a fight over something so trivial. "Never mind."

He closed the door behind him and trotted across the hall. Izzy leapt up from the couch when he came into the living room.

"Well?" he said eagerly. "How did it go?"

"Not much better for me, Iz." Sammi shook his head. "Good thing we don't have much beer in the house right now. At the rate he's going, he'd drink the whole state of California dry by noon if he could."

"Last night sure did a number on him." Izzy plopped back down on the couch and rubbed his temples wearily. "God, I'm so sorry I tried to get him to speak up about the Engineer all those times. If I'd known he'd have such a rough time talking about his pain...I didn't know he'd take it so bad—"

"Who says I took it bad?"

Sammi and Izzy jumped, and Vince swaggered into the room, beer still in hand. He plunked down next to Izzy with a grunt.

"I'll have you know I took last night just fine," he muttered around another swig of beer. "Just fine."

Sammi and Izzy exchanged a worried glance, but they said nothing. Vince was silent as well, sloshing the remaining liquid around in his nearly empty bottle. Then he let out a soft belch.

"I know exactly what I gotta do now," he said.

"Are you…" Izzy coughed nervously. "Are you going to…you know…tell the police about…about that night?"

Vince reached behind his head, drawing out a glowing ball of memories. He held it up with a contemptuous grunt.

"Hell no," he muttered. "I'm gonna do what I should've done months ago—put this shit in a box and drive to Monterey and bury it in the forest somewhere so I'll be rid of it forever. Then I'll finally have some peace."

"Vince…" Sammi began, casting about for the right words.

"But you can't!" Izzy leapt up again, his eyes round with horror. "You can't do that, Vince! You're the only person in the whole world who knows who the Engineer is. You've got to go to the police!"

"A fat lot of good that would do." Vince's eye twitched. "You think the cops will listen to me? They don't listen to anyone. And they'll think I had something to hide 'cause I waited so long to come forward."

"Well, you've got to try."

"No I don't." Vince shoved the memories back into his head and climbed unsteadily to his feet. "My mind is made up. Izzy, I need to borrow your car."

"No, you don't." Sammi grabbed his shoulders and tried to encourage him to sit down again. "You're drunk, Vince. Look, just wait until Cain comes back, okay?"

"And let him join your little let's-all-cock-block-Vince party?" Vince shook him off with a scornful snort. "Fuck you. Izzy, where are your damn keys? Hand them over or I'll pound your face in."

Izzy shuffled over to Vince with a defeated air. He started to fish around in his pockets, and for a moment, Sammi thought he would give in; but then he squared his shoulders and looked Vince in the eye.

"No," he said. "I can't let you get rid of those memories, not yet. I know holding onto them is hard on you, but you've got to tell *someone* what you saw, or make some drawings, or…or something."

Vince shuddered. "Stop, Izzy. You don't know what you're talking about, you stupid moron."

"I'm not stupid!" Izzy deflated a little, but he continued his argument. "Look, just tell one person who the Engineer is. Just one person, that's all we're asking. Then you can dump those memories any place you want. I'll even drive you there. Please?"

"I don't know who he is," said Vince through gritted teeth. "I don't know his name. God, why don't you all just leave me the fuck alone? All I want is to get rid of these memories."

"But you do remember his face, don't you?" shouted Izzy. "Why won't you just tell us what he looks like?"

"I can't!" shrieked Vince. "Can't you get that through your fucking thick skull? I can't talk about it, it hurts too much!"

"You were talking about it last night!" Izzy's voice rose and threatened to break. "Dammit, Vince, what's wrong with you? You'd have given the shirt off your back to help a guy out before you were taken. Now it takes a friend killing himself to make you pull your head out of your ass for five seconds and remember that it's not always about you!"

Vince's fist moved so fast that Sammi did not register it slamming into Izzy's stomach until Izzy groaned and doubled over. Then Vince descended on Izzy's prostrate, gasping form with arms flying and eyes blazing.

"Fuck you, Izzy!" he screamed. "You think I've been keeping this shit to myself just to screw everybody over? You think I don't like to talk about it because I'm being fucking *petty*? Go suck a dick, you mouth-breathing half-wit! Fuck your sourpuss daddy and your fat cow of a mama. Fuck all your grubby little brothers and sisters. Fuck your Aunt Helga and her shitty cooking, and fuck you and the shit-ass junk heap of a car you rode in on!"

His blows increased in frequency and intensity while he ranted. Izzy whimpered in fear and tried to slink away, but Vince stayed on top of him. In desperation, he changed into a dog, then an ape, then a large bird. Vince yanked at tails, arms, legs, and wings to keep him in place, seamlessly continuing his constant rain of abuse. Sammi hovered on the sidelines with ready bolts of electricity playing at his fingertips, waiting for a clear shot at Vince.

He thought he saw an opening, but then Izzy changed back to human form and slumped to the ground in exhaustion. Vince straddled him and grabbed his hand. Sammi flinched when he realized what Vince was about to do.

"No!" he shouted, raising an arm menacingly. "Let him go, or I'll…!"

He was too late. Vince buried Izzy's hand in his tangled red hair and set his own hand firmly over it, staring into Izzy's face with a deranged air. Sammi's mouth dropped open in horror and shock. He had not known that Vince could force other people to look into his mind. When had he learned to do that? Sammi had never noticed him practicing or experimenting with any such technique.

"You want to know how it feels?" Vince snarled. "You want to know what it's like to be me, every stinking second of every stinking day? Well, here you go, asshole!"

Izzy squirmed and whined while Vince pushed down. Then, suddenly, Izzy froze. He looked shocked for a moment. His eyes went round and his breathing became ragged; then a violent shudder ran through him. He stared at a spot on the ceiling and cringed, as if he saw a fist—or a knife—coming down on him. His jaws remained clenched shut, but a high-pitched wail of pain escaped from them—a horrible, drawn-out squeal that made Sammi clutch his arm in sympathy.

"Do you know who that is?" cried Vince. "That's the fucking Engineer, asshole! Is this what you wanted to see? Do you like having this picture in your head, huh? I hope you do 'cause I sure as hell don't!"

He relaxed his grip. Izzy's hand slid down and flopped on the floor like a dead fish, and Sammi took the opportunity to release his pent-up lightning blast. Vince shrieked and fell heavily to the floor beside Izzy. Sammi rushed over to check on them both. Vince was merely in shock, as he expected, but Izzy's condition gave him a few minutes of serious anxiety.

"It's okay, Izzy," he cooed while he tried to coax his drummer out of a shivering, sweaty fetal position at the foot of the coffee table. "Vince isn't gonna hurt you anymore. Do you think you can sit up for me?"

Izzy allowed himself to be unfolded and slowly set

upright. It was hard work. Izzy's torso was a solid mass of rock-hard muscle that felt as if it easily weighed several tons. Sammi strained his arms and back, and levered him into a sitting position with a final grunt, shaking his head at Vince's incredible luck that Izzy had chosen to flee rather than to fight. One well-aimed punch from one of those arms would have left Vince lying on the floor, concussed and toothless.

"It's all my fault," muttered Izzy. "All my fault. I should have known."

"No, Izzy," said Sammi in a soothing tone. "It wasn't your fault at all. Vince was way out of line."

Izzy did not seem to hear him. He sat staring at an invisible point in the distance with a dazed expression, moving his mouth soundlessly. His hands twitched and clenched in a staccato rhythm.

"Dammit, Vince!" Sammi descended on his lead singer, who was just beginning to groan and stretch his limbs. "What'd you do that for, you jerk? I think you broke Izzy's brain."

All three of them flinched when the front door slammed. Footsteps echoed in the hall, and Steve trotted into the room with a distant look in his eyes and a dreamy smile on his face.

"Hey, guys," he said, as if it were a daily occurrence to find Vince sprawled out, half-unconscious and Izzy slumped on the floor, covered in bruises and cuts. "Where's Cain? I have some good news for him."

"He's not here," said Sammi.

"Oh." Steve blinked. "That's right—he's still in the hospital, isn't he? Crap. I totally forgot."

"No, he's not in the hospital anymore; he's just not here.

Izzy said your dad showed up to borrow him for a few minutes." Sammi gave Steve an impatient glance. "I'd appreciate a little help here. You're the one who knows about this stuff."

"Um...sure. What's wrong?"

"Vince forced Izzy to look into his mind somehow. I don't know what exactly Izzy saw, but it really messed him up."

"Damn." Steve started to kneel down beside them. "I didn't know Vince could do that. Well, mind-stroking isn't my strong point, but I'll see what I can—"

Izzy started and scrambled to his feet. He ran to the window and stared out into the street, trembling.

"Fuck," he said in a low, intense voice. "Fuck. I was right there. Why did I let him go?"

"Let who go?" Vince climbed onto the couch and plopped into a half-sitting, half-sprawled position. He blinked peevishly at Izzy. "What the fuck is going on? Damn, I've got a mean hangover."

Sammi shot Vince an icy glare.

Izzy whipped around to face them. His eyes had a fevered look, and his face was very pale.

"We have to find Cain," he said. His hands began to tremble again. "Damn, if only I'd stuck my head out the door to see which way they went...Steve, do you still have that magic necklace thing you can use to get around?"

Steve frowned. "Necklace? Oh, you mean the traveler's arrow. Sure I do; I carry it with me all the time."

"Well, you have to use it!" Izzy lunged at Steve and grabbed him by the shoulders, shaking him like a rag doll. "We need you to get us to Cain right now, okay? Go on, do it!"

"Whoa, Izzy, calm down!" Sammi saw the terrified expression on Steve's face and leapt up to intervene. "You said Cain would be back in a minute. Can't you wait until—"

"We can't! Vince showed me the Engineer's face, and I know who he is, Sammi! I've met him before. We've got to warn Cain before it's too late!"

"Warn...him...about...what?" Steve shouted as best he could through Izzy's shaking. "I thought you said he was with my dad."

"Let him go, Iz." Sammi tried to pry Steve free once more. "We can tell Cain when he gets back."

Izzy stared at them with wild eyes, his chest heaving.

"Don't you get it?" he shouted. "That face I saw in Vince's memory...He showed up at the house this morning to take Cain somewhere, and...and I just stood there and let them walk away together. Cain is *with* the Engineer right now!"

Chapter Twenty-Four

Ritual

CAIN STUMBLED INTO THE dark interior of the old house step by agonizing step. The collar was a band of white-hot fire around his neck. An oppressive stench assailed his nostrils, and a distant whispering noise played in his ears. In his pain, he could not tell where it was coming from, but it sounded like someone sobbing in another room. He gathered what remained of his strength and made one last attempt to resist. A violent electric shiver ran through the collar, and it bit down so hard that he lost his footing.

"Stay where you are," said Mr. Warwick. The collar pulsed ominously, and Cain slumped to the floor rather than endure the torture again. Michelle dropped down beside him, throwing her arms around him like protective wings.

"Good boy." Mr. Warwick's voice was distorted eerily by the dull ache that throbbed in Cain's temples. "Now, if you'll excuse me, I must run out to pick up some supplies."

Mr. Warwick swept past them, his footsteps ringing hollowly against the dry floorboards. The doors banged shut behind him, and the whispery sobbing increased in volume and pitch. It was gradually joined by what sounded like more sobbing from different voices. The noise sent little

639

stabs of fear through Cain's bones. He pressed Michelle to him, hoping that her ragged breathing would drown it out. It did not.

"Cain." Michelle tugged his hand. "Come on, he's gone. Let's get out of this place."

"I can't." Cain huddled against the floor, fervently wishing he could. "He told me to stay. If I tried to leave—"

He shut his mouth like a trap because the sobbing suddenly rose to a shuddery piercing scream. His tail thrashed, his eyes widened, his nostrils flared, and his hands flew up to cover his ears.

"What's wrong?" cried Michelle in alarm. "The collar didn't hurt you because *I* was talking about leaving, did it? Oh God, I'm so sorry."

"It wasn't the collar." Cain scanned the grand sweeping staircase in front of them and the cavernous rooms to their left and right, searching for the source of the sound. "It's this place, this house. Something is wrong about it."

"What?"

"Can't you hear that?" said Cain incredulously. "Someone is whispering and sobbing off in the darkness, and I heard this horrible scream."

The screaming started up again, louder and clearer and seemingly much closer to them. Michelle gave him a dubious look and started to speak, but he held up a hand for silence.

"There it went again," he whispered once it died back into low sobbing. "I think I heard words that time— something like, 'Let me go, for the children's sake, please,' and then it stopped again. Didn't you hear it? It was so loud."

"No." Michelle shook her head. "I didn't hear anything.

640

But…"

"What is it?" Cain stopped peering into the shadows long enough to notice the thoughtful frown on her face.

"It's just…Are you sure that's what it said? The scream, I mean?"

"Pretty sure. Why?"

"Because," Michelle paused and looked around uneasily, "I think I might know what this place is."

"How? You haven't been here before, have you?" Cain shifted his legs, trying to find a slightly less uncomfortable sitting position. The boards beneath him were warped and uneven, and a dark rust-colored stain ran across them in a long, jagged slash from the threshold to the middle of the spacious front hall where they sat. Then the stain curved off into the room to their left like a railroad track veering into a gigantic yawning tunnel. The air was stale and stank of mold and dust. He couldn't imagine Michelle wanting anything to do with this house.

"Oh, no." Michelle shuddered. "I've never seen this place in my life, but I think I've heard of it before. Skeeter Judd used to talk about it all the time. He never told you about it?"

Cain shook his head.

"No?" said Michelle. "I'm surprised. See, when I first moved here, I…um…went on a few dates with Skeeter, and he kept talking about this old abandoned mansion he wanted to sneak into. He'd heard it had ghosts, and he wanted to see if it was true. I wouldn't let him take me—daddy would've found out what I was up to for sure if we'd gone and got collared for breaking and entering—but he wouldn't shut up about it. He said it was where the Lost Lambs Orphanage murders happened."

"You mean children were murdered here?" Cain shivered. That would explain the strange noises and the oppressive atmosphere; violent death had a way of leaving its mark even on the happiest of places.

"Oh, goodness no!" Michelle's voice interrupted his thoughts. "You poor thing; you look so horrified. Don't worry. Skeeter told me more about those murders than I ever, ever wanted to know. He says the rich lady who ran the orphanage out of her house and these four rich guys who were her biggest donors were murdered here."

Something skinny and cat-sized stirred in the darkness of the room to their left. It came closer, slinking low to the floor, and Cain started when he recognized the creature's floppy ears and flat round eyes. It was a feral dybbuk. Its presence corroborated Michelle's story; dybbukim made their homes in old death-haunted buildings. This one crept toward them, and as Cain watched, it was joined by another dybbuk that materialized from somewhere under the staircase.

"So none of the orphans were hurt?" said Cain. A third dybbuk scampered out of the room to their right and sat near the entrance with its head cocked curiously. The others circled Cain and Michelle, making suspicious little huffing sounds. The one from the room on their left was covered in sparse and mangy sallow fur; the mottled brown one from under the stairs had ragged ears that looked as if a dog had chewed on them; and both were so emaciated that he could see every single bone in their curved spines. The gray one from the room on the right seemed a bit better nourished, but it had an ugly latticework of thick sickly-pink scars across its face. Cain shuddered as he tried to imagine an injury horrific enough to leave permanent marks on a dybbuk's miraculously resilient hide.

"Skeeter says it happened while the kids were in bed," said Michelle, clearly unaware of the diseased dybbukim that prowled around her, although she shivered and her eyes darted nervously when the yellow one's dragging tail brushed against her knee. "The lady and her friends were all playing cards in her parlor, and somebody broke in, mowed them down with a gun, and then cut their throats with a knife. One of the men didn't die right away, but the killer must not have noticed. He managed to drag himself all the way to the front door before he finally croaked. Skeet told me the kids found their mangled bodies the next morning, but I hope to God he made that part up."

Cain glanced down at the ominous stain on the floor and noticed something slightly off to the side of it: a series of smaller stains of the same color, staggered at regular intervals. In the dim light, he could just make out that the smaller stains all shared an uncanny resemblance to a hand with splayed fingers. At the same time, he noticed that he was sitting on part of the bigger stain. He swallowed hard and risked the wrath of the collar to scoot away from it.

"So did they ever find out who did it?" he asked, not because he wanted to know who would do such awful things, but because he wanted to keep Michelle talking so she would make no sudden moves and the dybbukim would be less likely to attack her.

"No. The police were pretty stumped by the whole thing. Apparently—"

She flinched when the door banged open. The dybbukim scattered into the shadows with grunts and shrieks of dismay while Mr. Warwick strode up to them with another man in tow.

"I'm sorry I kept you so long," he said. "I had to go fetch Lance from a coffee shop the next street over. I didn't want to leave him alone too long in this place."

The other man stepped out from behind Mr. Warwick, and Cain suppressed a groan when he recognized Lance's features. If he absolutely had to assist Mr. Warwick with one more experiment, he would have preferred that Lance not be present for it.

"Now," Mr. Warwick said as he swept by them, continuing on to the enormous winding staircase. "Come along, Cain. The sooner we finish our business, the sooner we can all leave this wretched place."

Cain immediately scrambled upright and began to follow, but Michelle hung back.

"You're going upstairs?" She frowned suspiciously at the rickety steps and the cracked and rotting ceiling. "Far be it from me to tell you what to do, but I'm not sure this place is safe, to be honest."

Lance rolled his eyes at her and started to say something, but Mr. Warwick shushed him and turned to Michelle with a smug grin.

"You don't have to come along if you don't want to, my dear," he said placidly.

Cain could see Michelle clenching her teeth, and she jogged to catch up with him. She clutched his hand as they climbed onto the first step, and the entire staircase groaned like a dying animal. Cain heard the constant echo of sobs in the background intensify for a moment, and then it died away into a drawn-out wet gurgle.

The three dybbukim crept out of the dark room and chased after the intruders, their skinny claws scuffing against the rotted floorboards, creating a noise that sounded like mice scurrying in the walls. The gray one paused halfway up the stairs. It lifted its head and stared toward the ceiling, huffing and tasting the air with its tongue. Its nose caught a stray whiff of unfamiliar scent, and the darkness around it shifted in a way it did not recognize. The house's voices had gone silent. More were coming. They would arrive soon, very soon.

It slunk back downstairs and crouched in the doorway to the old parlor, waiting. A spider dangled down from the murk above it as it waited, and the dybbuk lunged and snatched the spider off its thread. A dim satisfaction flashed through its body as it chewed. Its mind was a dull and slow-moving little thing, but from some small forgotten corner, a half-formed memory arose, compelling it to wait for the strangers who were soon to arrive. They would need its help. And although it had no idea why or how they'd need its help, it would wholeheartedly give it to them.

Cain grew steadily more apprehensive with every step he took along the narrow upstairs hallway. The stale smell was stronger here, and the one time he dared to risk glancing over his shoulder, he had caught a glimpse of the two more feral-looking dybbukim stalking after them like jackals anticipating a fresh kill. He peered through an open door as he passed and caught a glimpse of a large room with tall windows. The room's walls were covered in grimy peeling wallpaper that had blurred and faded outlines of frolicking cartoon animals emblazoned on it. A teddy bear lay on the threadbare carpet in the gray light that filtered through the dirty windows, its limbs splayed and gutted.

Two more dybbukim scampered out of the room when

they passed. One had a scabrous olive-green hide and a stump where its tail should have been; the other was the same color as the rusty stain in the front hall and had only one eye. They joined the two from downstairs, licking their thin lips greedily.

Cain tore his gaze away from the dybbukim and noticed Lance leering at Michelle. He narrowed his eyes and pulled her closer.

"Hey Cain," said Lance. "Nice hot girlfriend. I haven't met her before, have I?"

"No," said Michelle coldly.

Mr. Warwick coughed with disapproval, and he opened a door at the far end of the hallway. "I've told you a thousand times, Lance, now is not the time to be thinking of girls. Today is a very important day for you."

Cain set his teeth and passed through the gaping black doorway, the promise of freedom pulling strongly at his mind.

The few windows in the room were entirely boarded up, and the room was almost perfectly dark. A single shaft of light filtered through a crack in the plywood. Cain could just make out a long row of ghostly white beds. He flinched in pain when Mr. Warwick conjured a blinding flash of blue light that illuminated everything in the room in brilliant detail.

Mr. Warwick lifted his hand. With a flick of his wrist, he sent the bright mote of light flying toward a little brass chandelier that was decorated with vines and roses. The light split into fragments as it flew, and each piece settled into one of the dead bulbs in the chandelier's leaf-shaped terminuses. They shone an intense white-blue, bathing the room in a harsh glow.

646

"Now, Lance," said Mr. Warwick with a commanding nod.

Lance slouched reluctantly over to one of the child-sized brass beds and sat down. The mattress gave off a thick cloud of rotten-smelling dust as he did so, and Cain couldn't help but feel a tiny thrill of satisfaction at the disgusted look on his face.

"You'll have to excuse the shabby venue," said Mr. Warwick pleasantly, turning to Cain and Michelle. "I hate doing these things in a hotel room because I constantly worry that some fool housekeeper will barge in. This building is one of the few places in the city where we are truly unlikely to suffer such interruptions. From what I've heard, even the local gangs avoid it."

Cain believed that most people, even gang members, would go out of their way to avoid this place. He could sense Michelle glancing around uneasily at the bare, peeling walls. He followed her gaze. The condemned building was miraculously graffiti-free.

"Now, Cain," Mr. Warwick said, gesturing in Lance's direction. "It's time."

"Time for what, Master?" said Cain, ignoring his mounting distaste for using the hated term. He told himself to be patient. Soon, the hated collar would be gone, and he would be free.

"It's time for you to heal my son of his affliction," said Mr. Warwick.

"Affliction, Master?" Cain squinted at Lance, who looked perfectly healthy and not at all in need of a healing spell.

Mr. Warwick didn't seem to hear him.

"It's strange, isn't it?" He shook his head thoughtfully.

"It's strange that all my power and knowledge, all my years of teaching and coaxing and experimenting did no good—none at all. Yet Lance's powers will be awakened. He will truly have the Gift before the sun sets tonight—all because of you."

Cain swallowed hard, and an icy little shiver ran through him. Was this request some sort of joke? He had no idea how he'd even begin to go about doing such a thing, let alone complete it with total success in the space of a day. It was impossible.

Maybe that was the point, Cain mused. Maybe Mr. Warwick didn't want him to succeed at all. Maybe his plan all along was to force Cain to carry out a task at which he was sure to fail miserably, and then he'd keep him bound in servitude.

"But Master," he cried, turning to Mr. Warwick in desperation. "I don't…How am I supposed to just give the Gift to Lance?"

Mr. Warwick smiled and showed them a small cylindrical object. Cain caught his breath in fear when he saw the light glinting off a long needle.

"The same way you gave it to your young rocker friends," he said.

An ancient flag hung above the fireplace in the room to the right of the house's entrance hall. It was thin and fragile and dangled from the nails that held it in place by a few crumbling threads, preserved by the still dry air. Now the air had become agitated. A draft stirred and swirled, creaking through the scattered wooden chairs and children's desks, picking up a few yellowed sheets of paper that had lain untouched on the floor for nearly fifty years. As the papers flitted around the room like moths and the threads that held the flag in place disintegrated, four dark figures materialized from the ceiling and came down among the small desks with a muffled bang.

Dust settled around them. The flag fluttered gently down and landed in a heap at Sammi's feet. Vince coughed and glared at Steve.

"So where the fuck are we?" he growled. "I thought you said you were taking us to Cain, kid."

"Yeah, well, he's somewhere close." Steve staggered to his feet, rubbing his head irritably. The last thing he remembered clearly was his conversation with the pretty girl in the coffee shop. Now he had a nasty lingering headache that he couldn't explain and three rock stars leading him on a wild goose chase, and he was in no mood for Vince's nonsense. "Like I told you, that's how a traveler's arrow works—unless you know *exactly* where the person or thing you want to go to is, it'll just set you down somewhere near your target. Sometimes you get lucky, and sometimes you don't. We'll have to look around until we find him."

Vince glanced around the dark room and grimaced with distaste. "What's the point? There's no way he's anywhere near this shithole you dumped us in. What the fuck is this place anyway? It looks like some kind of super-fancy old frontier school. I bet we aren't even in LA anymore."

Sammi carefully unfolded the flag and squinted at it. He could just make out the remains of the brown-bear-and-single-red-star design on the faded fabric.

"I think we're probably still in California, at least," he said. "This looks like our state flag."

Izzy shuffled nervously around the room, inspecting the desks and chairs and the smudged old chalkboard shoved away into a far corner. Suddenly, he froze, and his head snapped up.

"What's up, Iz?" said Sammi.

"That voice," said Izzy in a tense whisper. "Didn't you hear it?"

He turned into a cat and crept out of the room before anyone could reply. A moment later, he crept back. His eyes were round with fear when he reverted back to human form.

"We've gotta find Cain and get out of here, like, right now," he whispered. "There's something wrong about this place."

"Well, yeah." Vince swiped at a nearby desk and coughed disapprovingly at the cloud of dust he had stirred up. "It's a fucking wreck. I doubt anyone has set foot in here in years."

"That's not it." Izzy moved toward the door and made an impatient beckoning motion. "I heard this voice—not Cain's or anyone else's I knew, just this far off, raspy, kind of hollow voice—saying, 'help us' over and over again. But when I got to where it was coming from, no one was there. And when I was coming back, I noticed this huge...dark...smear...thing...on the floor. I think it might be...you know. Come on, we can't leave Cain here for a minute longer."

Sammi followed, resisting a strong urge to find the nearest door or open window and run screaming into the street.

"Hey, Iz," he whispered while they climbed the stairs with hesitant steps. "Do you think Steve will be all right? Vince hit him pretty hard."

"Yeah, I think so." Izzy stared a bit guiltily at the floor. "I'm sorry we had to let Vince take his memory, but...he wouldn't have helped us otherwise. I don't get it, Sammi. He keeps talking about how much he hates his dad, but the minute I tell him who the Engineer is…I thought the poor kid was going to die. 'It's not true, it's not true, he's my dad, it *can't* be true.' You'd think his dad meant the whole world to him."

Sammi stared off at a distant point in the shadows.

"Well, families are complicated, Izzy. You can love someone close to you and hate them more than anything at the same time." He sighed. "Still, I wish we'd gotten a chance to try to calm him down before Vince ripped out a chunk of his memory. When he goes upstairs and finds his dad here…"

"I think there's a good chance he won't go upstairs," whispered Izzy. "I bet he thinks there are rats up there. We might be able to get Cain out of here without him seeing his dad at all."

Sammi nodded, but he doubted their luck would be so good.

Steve finally plucked up his courage. He followed Izzy and Sammi, walking on his toes and scanning the shadows for rats. Vince hung back, glaring after the others.

"Great," he growled. "Just follow him blindly, why don't you? First he drags us all off to some flea-bag old ruin that might not even be in the same city, and now he's hearing voices. I'm telling you, there's nothing here! It's just a dusty, crappy, rat-infested, moldy old—ow!"

Something nipped his calf. He squinted at the floor, raising his foot to crush the offending pest. A lone piece of paper drifted lazily in the breeze his sudden movement had stirred, but nothing else was behind him.

"Right," he muttered. "I guess it has bugs too. Well, I'm

still not—ow!"

He felt another nip, then another, then another. A sudden brief blast of pressure slammed against his calf, as if a small warm body had thrown itself against him. He stumbled a few steps in the direction of the door, hopping and flailing in pain.

"All right, all right," he snapped at the empty room. "You win—whatever the hell you are!"

He stomped off in a huff, breaking into a run to catch up to Izzy, Sammi, and Steve once he reached the front hall. The gray dybbuk slunk after him unseen, chirruping with pride over a job well done.

Cain stared at the bright needle, trembling with horror. He wanted desperately to throw Mr. Warwick aside and run as hard as he could, down the stairs, through the crumbling front door, and blindly out into the street. "But Master," he gasped. "How could I have given the Gift to them? The Engineer took them, and then—"

"And then they escaped?" Mr. Warwick chuckled. "Surely it must have occurred to you, Cain, that their survival might not have been any mere accident? I had every reason to want them alive; they were my first successes and the beginning of my hope for Lance."

"So, it was you." Michelle's voice rang through the room, clear and angry. Cain could see her shoulders trembling, but from the set of her back, he guessed that she shook from hatred rather than fear. "You're the Engineer. You tortured all those kids to death, and—"

"I am not the Engineer." Mr. Warwick cut her off with an icy stare. "The Engineer is an urban legend, a caricature of a crazed serial murderer invented by a gang of inner city delinquents. I am simply a thorough and meticulous researcher in a very dangerous field. As for torturing kids to death, well, after the first experiments failed so miserably, I don't see what else I could have done but end what remained of the unfortunate subjects' lives."

"I don't understand." Cain jerked back involuntarily when Mr. Warwick took a step toward him. He was unable to tear his eyes from the needle. "How could they not have had the Gift at all, and then suddenly have it because of me? It's impossible."

"It's not impossible, boy. I did it, and with your help, I'll do it again. Now, hold out your arm."

Cain swallowed hard, and his tail clanged against the bedframes on either side of him as he swished it violently back and forth in sheer terror. He feared he knew exactly what Mr. Warwick wanted from him.

"I don't understand, Master," he whimpered in a pitiable attempt to put off the moment of horror as long as he could. "The studio at Daggerspoint…How did you keep it closed for so long, without Mr. Arkin…?"

"Oh, he knew," said Mr. Warwick. "Certainly not all the details, but he absolutely did know I was using it. But he never told anyone because Bruce Arkin knows what's good for him. I hope you won't hold it against him. He was doing it out of love for his daughter, you see. It's a bit of a long story. All you need to know is that she wasn't born fully human. When she was quite young, Bruce engaged my services to make her 'normal,' as he called it. Now he fears for her emotional well-being if…ahem…*someone* were to reveal the truth to her."

Cain blinked. He remembered Jodido's rant against the stingy Waheela-bitch who had become a woman and married an unnamed rich record company executive. And Mr. Arkin did mention to him once that Mr. Warwick had done some work for him in the past. Cain realized that on the day Jodido gave him the chocolate powder, he might have caught a glimpse of Mr. Arkin's wife.

"Now that's enough stalling." Mr. Warwick took a step toward him. "Give me your arm, Cain."

"Please, Master!" Cain shrank away from him. "I...I don't see why you need me for this...this...experiment."

Mr. Warwick made an impatient noise. "Even you can't be this dense. You know full well why: I used the last of the sample Bruce Arkin kindly collected for me on the last subject. I don't think it took, to be honest, but since your unruly friends snatched him away before I could make a final examination, we may never know."

Cain cowered against the wall. He felt sick to his stomach, and his lips peeled back in a ragged snarl even as the collar bit down to keep him quiet. His master would not take his blood. How could Cain live with the burden, knowing the pain all those young men had gone through, knowing that his blood would make horrible, repulsive Lance far more powerful than he deserved to be? The house's desolate voices wailed in his ears, and the dybbukim prowled hungrily around his ankles while he resisted. He would not allow it. He would die first.

"I'll have none of that!" Mr. Warwick grabbed him roughly by the wrist. "It is beyond absurd for a big strong demon to be so afraid of a silly little needle. Now hold out your arm, and take it like a man."

Cain recoiled and snapped at his master's hand. The bite did not connect, and the collar bit down so hard that his vision blurred, but a fierce thrill ran through him at the small act of disobedience.

"Stop it!" Michelle pushed her way in front of Cain and planted her feet squarely on the floor, glaring up at Mr. Warwick. "Leave him alone! Let him go right now, or I'll..."

"Or you'll do what, exactly?" said Mr. Warwick with a mocking sneer. "Now stand aside. Provided my servant stops bringing further well-deserved punishment down upon himself, this will only take a moment."

Cain saw what happened next through a red haze. Michelle's arm shot out, with her hand held stiffly palm-up, in excruciating slow motion toward Mr. Warwick's face. For a split second, he noticed the shift in Mr. Warwick's expression, and the ominous way his hands fluttered, and Cain's breath caught in his throat with fear for Michelle.

Then the heel of her hand connected with a wet crack. Mr. Warwick screamed and stumbled back, clutching his nose, his dignity lost for a moment. Michelle launched herself at him with a scream of rage, flailing her arms wildly. He was thrown off guard and dropped under her onslaught like a cut redwood. The syringe flew out of his hand and skittered off across the floor. The four skulking dybbukim squealed in savage excitement as Michelle bore down on Mr. Warwick with both fists, punching and scratching, her eyes blazing.

"Not so high and mighty now, are you!" she shrieked. "You nasty, scummy, miserable excuse for a human being! You think you're better than he is? You think you've got the right to hurt him and make him do stuff he doesn't want to do? Well, you can ride a rail right to Hell, you disgusting piece of trash—you and that knuckle-dragging throwback of a son of yours! Take that and that and *that*!"

She drove her knee viciously into his groin.

Cain crouched frozen on the sidelines while they grappled. Part of him felt an exhilarating rush of mean satisfaction at the scene unfolding before him, yet he also noticed that Mr. Warwick was rapidly getting over the initial shock of the assault.

"Michelle," he hissed, risking the collar's wrath. "Michelle, kick him again. Hurry! If you let him pull himself together, he'll—"

A sharp pinch from the collar cut him off just as Michelle was jerked back in the midst of a final shriek of rage, dragged off of Mr. Warwick by her hair. Cain looked up, and his heart sank.

Lance had come to his father's aid. He had Michelle's arms pinned to her sides, and even though she writhed like an angry snake and thrashed her ankles in the general direction of his shins and he looked legitimately terrified at the prospect of trying to keep her under control for much longer, his grip did not falter.

Mr. Warwick climbed to his feet, wiping blood from his face with wrathful strokes. Cain wilted at the sight of the cold fury in his eyes.

"Master, please—" he whimpered. Mr. Warwick thrust a silencing hand at him, and the collar cut off the rest of his plea.

Mr. Warwick stood over Michelle, trembling with barely contained anger. She stared unrepentantly back at him.

"Stupid girl," he said in a quiet and even voice that made Cain's skin crawl. "That was a very unwise thing to do."

Michelle said nothing, but from her narrowed eyes and the defiant thrust of her chin, Cain suspected that she would gladly and unhesitatingly do it again if given the chance.

"How dare you strike me!" Mr. Warwick's hand balled into a fist, and he drew it ominously back. "You're a disgrace to your father's good name, Miss Breen. It's high time someone taught you a thing or two about respect."

Cain lunged forward with a strangled growl. Mr. Warwick waved him off and rounded on Michelle again.

"But I suppose that can wait for another time," he said stiffly. "Right now, the most important order of business is making that idiot devil behave himself. Well, I hate to waste magic on the likes of you, but it can't be helped."

He raised his right arm toward Michelle and began to chant under his breath. The air around him crackled with energy, and a faint glow ran down his arm and into his hand. Three of the dybbukim chattered nervously and scurried away from him, but the tailless one was too busy lapping at a few small droplets of fresh blood on the floor to notice the magic generating. Cain realized what was about to happen and choked out one last desperate plea.

"No! Leave her out of this, Master, *please*."

It was too late. Mr. Warwick brought his hand down and rapped Michelle's forehead with his fingertips. Cain saw a brief flash of greenish light where his fingers touched her head, and he heard a sharp electric pop.

Michelle screamed and arched her back so violently that Lance finally lost his grip. She stumbled forward, thrashing at the air, and fixed her terrified eyes on Cain. To his horror, Cain saw that her eyes were changing. They grew rounder overall while the pupils compressed into slits, and the irises faded from brown to blue and spread until the whites disappeared completely. Fur sprouted on her hands and arms as she waved them in front of her, and her form rapidly shrank until there was no Michelle. In her place, a sleek

657

caramel-colored Siamese cat crouched trembling on the floor.

Mr. Warwick seized the squalling cat by the scruff, expertly avoiding a desperate swipe from her claws. He held the writhing animal in front of him with vague disgust.

"It's a strange thing, isn't it?" he said to Cain. "The police and society in general will kick up a big fuss if you kill a person—even if the person richly deserves to be killed. That sort of public commotion is such a nuisance, in fact, that I even regret losing my control with Bruce's nasty little minx of an assistant, even though she was about to turn me in—the treacherous bitch. Yet if you were to slit, say, a cat's throat, or bash in its skull, or wring its neck, or gut it alive—"

"No!" Cain crawled toward his master's feet, weakly raising his hand. He felt a burning desire to change to his real form and bury his claws in Mr. Warwick's throat, but his strength was so sapped that he could barely lift his head to look into the old man's eyes while he begged for Michelle's release. "Let her go, please, I'll do what you want, I swear."

"Good boy." Mr. Warwick smiled coldly down at him. "Humph, I suppose I could've saved myself a lot of grief if I had just changed the little slut over the moment we set foot in the house. Now stay where you are while I find the syringe."

He tossed the cat at Cain's feet with a contemptuous grunt. She landed upright in a movement that was somehow simultaneously graceful and awkward and gazed down at her tail and dainty paws and narrow little chest with a low wail of anguish. The dybbukim loped up to them with interested grunts. Michelle seemed to see them now. She stiffened and flung herself into Cain's lap with a terrified squeal. Cain hugged her close as the four scrawny dybbukim prowled around them, sniffing the air hungrily.

Mr. Warwick shuffled over to them, syringe in hand. The cat hissed at him, but Cain held out his arm with a shudder and swallowed a despairing whine while the needle pierced his skin.

"Will you please let us go now, Master?" he whispered once the syringe was withdrawn. "I gave you what you wanted, like I promised."

"Hmm?" Mr. Warwick held the blood sample up to the light with a triumphant smile. "Oh, all in good time. Be patient."

Cain stared at the floor with a defeated groan. The cat mewed sadly and stroked his chest with her paw. He laid his hand gently over it as he would have done with Michelle's human hand, taking small comfort in its warmth. He had never felt so helpless in his life.

Mr. Warwick brushed dust from a nearby table and set the syringe on it. He nodded to Lance, who returned to his place on the bed.

"Now, Lance," said Mr. Warwick. "Give me your right hand."

He drew something black and shiny out of his jacket pocket. Lance followed the object with nervous eyes.

"So...um...when am I gonna go to sleep?" he asked. "Aren't you going to—"

"No, Lance."

Mr. Warwick brandished the object. Cain caught a glimpse of the shimmering blue-green mosaic work on its handle, and a fragmented memory of a trip to Mexico came rushing back to him. He had seen that knife before. Had he picked it up for his master during one of his errands? The memory was just out of reach, but a wave of nausea washed over him when he realized that the scars on his band mates' hands and arms must have been the work of the same blade.

"What?" A glimmer of confusion and fear flashed in Lance's eyes. "But dad, you said—"

"Never mind what I said." Mr. Warwick made an impatient motion with the knife. "You must fully experience your awakening, in mind and in body and in spirit."

"The others didn't!" Lance pulled his hand back as if he had touched hot glass. "You said you kept them asleep for days. I don't see why I shouldn't—"

His father hushed him with a sharp gesture. "Full awareness is necessary for full transformation, Lance. You don't want to end up like Cain's shiftless friends, with only one piddling talent to your name. The redheaded one was lucky he got two; the sleeping draught didn't quite work on him. Humph, he was nearly unmanageable, especially in the later stages of his awakening. Now, hold out your hand."

Lance drew his arms close to his body and shook his head. He was shivering, and the flicker of fear in his eyes was quickly growing into full-blown horror. He looked uncharacteristically small and fragile, and Cain began to feel a tiny bit sorry for him.

"Very well." Mr. Warwick's lips moved silently, and his eyes narrowed in concentration. Lance realized too late what his father was doing. Mr. Warwick's fingertips brushed his forehead when he tried to dodge them. His shriek of rage and terror cut off abruptly, and he collapsed on the bed, his limbs dangling limp and useless off the edge. His eyes flitted and rolled in desperation while Mr. Warwick drew close, the knife glittering in his father's hand.

Cain watched in horrified fascination as Mr. Warwick

drew the knife's point over Lance's upturned palm. Lance shivered and whined through his locked jaws, and Cain found himself keening in sympathy. Through the blood that welled from the cuts, he could see the shape Mr. Warwick was forming: the sharp angles of the second rune Steve had identified from Sammi's hands, the one he had said meant "to make harmless." Mr. Warwick chanted under his breath, an eerie glow playing about his eyes and fingertips.

Then he laid his hand over Lance's palm, heedless of the blood that still flowed from the fresh wound. A muffled scream broke from deep within Lance's chest, and for a moment, Cain could detect a strange metallic taste permeating the air.

The glow coursed into Lance, backlighting every mole and blemish on his skin, storming along the paths of his veins and infusing his pain-fogged eyes with an unearthly luminescence. As the knife made more cuts, one after another on Lance's bare arm, Cain realized that the runes had another meaning, one that Steve had either not known about or not cared to talk about. By invoking the runes in reverse, Mr. Warwick meant to give power to his powerless son. The method seemed to be working, in a harrowing way. Lance's voice was already hoarse from wordless screaming. His eyes fluttered, and he appeared to be slipping out of consciousness.

Mr. Warwick paused to slap his son awake. Cain shuddered at the expression of calm satisfaction on his face.

He doesn't care about Lance's pain, Cain thought incredulously. *He's torturing his own son, maybe to death, and he still thinks that what he's doing is good and right.*

"I'm so sorry," he whispered to the cat as Mr. Warwick's hand wandered over to the table where the syringe lay. "You were right. Jim Kellerman was trying to warn me about my master, not your dad."

Mr. Warwick paused to give Cain a sour look. "Hush, boy, you'll break my concentration. I don't know any Jim Kellerman."

Of course he didn't. Jim Kellerman was a nameless failure to him, a botched experiment to be thrown away on the street. He must think of all his early victims that way. Cain shuddered with revulsion and hatred. He wanted to tear out Mr. Warwick's throat so badly that the longing hurt more than the bite of the collar.

As if in answer to his wish, a blinding blue flash lit the room. Cain heard the cat yowl, and the collar went completely slack around his neck. Once he had blinked away the searing motes of light imprinted across his vision, a curious sight met his eyes.

Mr. Warwick lay sprawled on the floor, gasping and clutching his chest. Sammi stood in the doorway with his finger still smoking. He looked terrified. Vince and Izzy advanced into the room at a run.

"Oh my god!" Izzy ran to the bed where Lance lay, his eyes wide with horror. "The bastard took another one. Come on, we've got to help him!"

"Leave him." Vince pulled Izzy away from the bed. "That one is not worth saving. We've gotta get Cain out of here."

Izzy cast a vaguely horrified glance at Vince, but he followed his band mate's lead. Cain felt the steady and reassuring pressure of their hands under his arms, pulling him upright. He shifted the cat in his arms to keep hold of her while they began to drag him toward the door.

Mr. Warwick lifted his dust-streaked face from the

floorboards. He fixed his eyes on Cain.

"Stop!" he shouted. "Don't you dare leave this room!"

The collar came back to life again. Cain's legs went limp from the searing pain, but Izzy and Vince held him fast and did not seem to notice that he was no longer pulling his weight. They pushed past Sammi, who still stood in the doorway with a shell-shocked expression on his face. As they left, Cain realized that the cat was no longer in his arms.

"Michelle…" he gasped.

"Michelle is here too?" Izzy's eyes widened. "Crap. We'll have to go look for her."

"Well, let's get him out of here first," grunted Vince, throwing Cain's arm over his shoulder. He then turned and jabbed Sammi in the side with his free elbow. "Hey, snap out of it already!"

Sammi shuddered and took a deep breath. He looked as if he were considering shooting another lightning bolt at Mr. Warwick, but the livid expression on the old man's face must have made him lose his nerve. He whipped around and joined the others, his footsteps echoing hollowly in the empty hall.

Cain struggled feebly all the way down the stairs. The collar was hurting him so badly that he could not explain Michelle's plight to the others. He tried to tell Izzy as best he could through gasps and grunts, but Izzy only seemed to pick up about a quarter of it.

Steve was waiting for them in the front hall. Cain was surprised to see him. Did he know about his father? Or had he stayed behind because of all the rats that surely lurked in the attic and upstairs rooms of the ancient house?

"Okay," he shouted up at them while they approached.

"You found him; that's great. Now will someone please tell me what the heck is going on?"

"Nothing," said Izzy evasively. "We've just gotta get Cain out of here, is all."

"Ow!" Vince flinched when Cain stumbled and accidentally kicked him in the heel. "How about a little gratefulness, asshole? I just saved you from the fucking Engineer!"

Steve stared at him with wide eyes. "The Engineer?" he said in a peculiar shriek-like whisper. "*That's* who we were rescuing Cain from? Holy shit, we've got to go to the police right now!"

"Later, okay?" Izzy glared at Vince before he addressed Steve. "Not now. It would...be too complicated."

"Getting out of here is our main worry." Sammi popped up beside them. "I bet you anything that monster is gonna start chasing after us any minute."

Cain experienced a startling moment of clarity through his unbearable agony. He heard no noise of pursuit. What he did hear were the faint sounds of scuffing claws somewhere upstairs, and above the scuffing, the high-pitched scream of a cat.

"Hey, what the fuck are you doing?" said Vince sharply as Cain wriggled out of his and Izzy's grasp and started crawling back up the stairs. "That's the wrong way, dumbass! We're trying to bust you out of—" His rant ended abruptly in an indignant shriek when Cain snapped at his hand.

"You know, he was trying to tell me something about Michelle," said Izzy. "Dammit, I bet she's still up there."

"Well, we sure as hell can't leave her." Sammi did a sharp about-face and charged after Cain, who was still tenaciously dragging himself upward. "Come on, let's go."

"No, not you." Izzy held up a hand to discourage Steve. "There are...um...rats up there. Big nasty ones."

In spite of his weakened state, Cain made it to the top of the stairs before his band mates did. The sounds were coming from the room with the big windows and faded wallpaper. He saw a flash of green light shine briefly through the door and staggered over to investigate.

A thick smell of burnt plaster hit him when he poked his head through the doorway. He froze in horror at the sight that met his eyes.

Michelle was still in cat form. She ran around the room as fast as her paws could carry her, swerving and rolling to avoid the five dybbukim that chased her like famished dogs, all snapping at her flanks and trying to grab her tail. She clutched something tightly between her teeth. As she swept past the door, Cain saw the light from the windows glinting off the needle and recognized the blood-filled syringe.

Mr. Warwick stood in the center of the ruined nursery, next to the discarded teddy bear. Cain could not tell whether he could see the dybbukim, but his attention was focused on Michelle, and he quaked with barely suppressed rage.

"For the last time, Miss Breen," he snapped, "you can't run forever. Now hand over the syringe, and I'll let you go without doing you further harm."

The cat pelted on, sliding to one side to avoid a snap from the mottled dybbuk's jaws. Cain shook as he began to realize the full extent of her plight. He doubted that she could stop running even if she wanted to; the hungry dybbukim would be on her in seconds if she did. His stomach sank when the sallow one broke away from the rest of the pack and bore down beside the terrified cat, blocking her path to the door.

Mr. Warwick extended his arm and blasted a neon-green bolt of pure energy in Michelle's direction. It just missed her and hit the tailless dybbuk instead. Cain bit back a shriek when the acrid smell of burnt flesh hit his nostrils. He ached to run in and save Michelle, but he didn't dare; Mr. Warwick would notice him if he did, and then he and Michelle would be in an even more desperate situation.

A long dark purple tentacle snaked over the floor. The cat let out a strangled yip as it wrapped around her waist and whipped her out the door. The pursuing dybbukim came to a scrambling, squealing halt, staring in stupid confusion at the spot where their intended prey had been a moment before.

"Wow." Izzy's voice came from somewhere behind Cain. "I thought I must have heard you wrong when you told me Michelle was a cat. I guess not."

"Come on!" Cain turned and caught Izzy by the arm. "*He's* in there. We've got to get out of here right now."

The collar bit down again. Hands grasped his arms as his legs buckled and threatened to send him tumbling to the floor. Cain heard Vince and Sammi talking in tense whispers while they dragged him toward the stairs. He glanced over his shoulder to make sure Izzy still carried Michelle before he fully allowed himself to be led.

The cat went limp with exhaustion in Izzy's arms. He caught the syringe as it fell from her mouth and brought it close to his eye, squinting with curiosity.

"What is this stuff?" he muttered. "It isn't blood, is it?"

"Yeah," gasped Cain. "It's mine...Master took it."

"Ew." Izzy grimaced and held the syringe at arm's length. "That's why he brought you here—because he wanted your blood? *Why*?"

"He can tell us later," said Sammi gruffly. "We've gotta get him out of this godforsaken cesspit first. Come on, we're almost to the door."

Cain looked up with great effort. He could see the dark stain on the floor, and the imposing oak doors with their curved brass handles loomed before them. Sammi was reaching to open them. He had no idea what they would do once they were safely outside—the collar was hurting him so badly he could no longer stand on his own—but a momentary shudder of relief went through him anyway at the promise of finally being free of the house and its screams.

Sammi stood motionless, his hands frozen over the doorknobs.

Vince coughed impatiently. "What the fuck are you waiting for, asshole?" he snapped.

Sammi rounded on him indignantly and pointed at the doors. "Well, I don't have much of a choice, do I? Hold on, maybe we can still get out one of the windows."

He scurried past them and vanished into the room on their left. Cain stared at the doors. The handles were gone, and in their place was a flat, bubbling slick of liquid metal that started spreading over the doors and the walls on either side of them. The doors were soon completely devoured, and he could see that the walls of the hallway would soon share the same fate. The house shivered as the liquid metal crept along, and the desolate screaming started up again. Cain covered his ears.

Steve popped up beside them and walked over to the gleaming slab of solid brass that stood where the doors had been. He ran his hands along the wall so that his fingertips hovered just above the metal, working his mouth in frustrated confusion.

"What is...? How did this even...? I've never seen any spell that works like..." He rounded on them in high dudgeon. "What is this? What the fuck is this, and who's doing it? Why won't anyone tell me what's going on?"

Sammi reappeared from the other room before anyone could answer. "It's no good. The windows are already covered. They must've had metal handles or something. So, Steve, you know lots of magic. Do you think you can maybe do something to fix this?"

"No!" Steve's voice cracked and squeaked out of pure indignation. "I'm not doing a damned thing until someone tells me exactly what's going on!"

The house's mind-shattering, desolate screams drowned out the rest of his rant in Cain's ears. Izzy rushed over to Steve, letting go of Cain in the process. He slumped helplessly to the floor, unable to support himself or to block out the terrible noise of the house. He tried in desperation to distract himself by wondering why it was still so bright in the front hall when the outside light from the doors and windows had been cut off.

An eerie glow undulated along the floor, reflecting light from the ceiling. Cain realized that six motes of blue light had settled onto the empty prongs of a big angular chandelier. In the otherworldly luminescence, he could see the dark outlines of four dybbukim loping down the stairs ahead of a darker human figure that walked with a purposeful stride.

"Dad?" Steve's voice cut through the house's howling. "Dad, what are you doing here?"

"Steve, wait."

Cain caught a flash of movement from the corner of his eye and looked up in time to see Izzy reaching out to grab

Steve's arm. "I'm sorry. I didn't want to tell you. It would've been so awful for you."

Steve shook him off and stumbled toward the staircase in a daze. He was shivering violently, and Cain could see the sickly expression on his face. He stood at the bottom of the stairs, gazing up at his father.

"You were the one up there the whole time?" he said in a distant voice. "You were the one they were running from?"

"Not now, Stephen." Mr. Warwick swept past his son and advanced on Cain and his band mates. The four dybbukim walked ahead of him, growling and sniffing the air. The remaining dybbuk limped along behind, still recovering from its burns.

Izzy whimpered as he approached. Sammi trembled and scratched his arm. Vince assumed a fighting stance.

"Cain," said Mr. Warwick in a tone of poisonous, false politeness. "Now that your little friends have had their fun, I would like my blood sample back now, please."

"No," croaked Cain. "I don't have it."

The collar bit down, but not very hard because he was technically telling the truth. Mr. Warwick tapped his foot impatiently.

"I'm not in the mood for games, Cain," he snapped. "I know one of you has that syringe. If you don't hand it over right now, I can and will take it from you by force. But," his voice became a bit gentler, "if you give it to me without any further trouble, you may go."

Izzy yelped as Vince snatched the syringe from him and held it up. "Is this what you're talking about, old man?" he shouted.

"Yes, yes it is." Mr. Warwick took a step forward and stretched out his hand. "Give it to me."

Vince twirled the syringe between his fingers, frowning thoughtfully. "This stupid thing is all you want from us? If we fork it over, you'll let us all go, just like that?"

"Vinnie, what the hell are you doing?" hissed Sammi.

"Shut up," Vince hissed back at him.

"I will indeed let you all go if you give me that syringe," said Mr. Warwick solemnly. "You have my word. You've no idea how important this experiment is to me and to my son."

Vince smiled. "In that case, we'd be happy to give it back. Wouldn't we, guys? Except...Do you promise you'll leave all the rockers in this city alone and never bother them again if we do? They're not your biggest fans right now, honestly."

"Ah, I'm glad to see that one of you has some plain good sense," said Mr. Warwick with an indulgent chuckle. "Very well; I promise on my honor as a businessman. Now, let's have that syringe, eh? I'd like to finish my ritual now."

Helpless anger surged through Cain as Vince stepped toward Mr. Warwick, holding out the syringe. In the back of his mind, he knew that Vince was doing the sensible thing. There was no other way out; Mr. Warwick had them trapped, and he would get his blood one way or another, but the admission sickened Cain.

Vince paused, tossing the syringe casually into the air and catching it again. A wicked smile flitted over his face.

"Here's that blood you wanted, you evil old bastard." He dashed the syringe as hard as he could against the floor at Mr. Warwick's feet, where it shattered in an explosion of red droplets. Cain felt a breathtaking jolt of pain from the collar as Mr. Warwick screamed in rage. For a split second, the spilled blood lay on the floor, glistening and velvety and a full shade darker than human blood; then the prowling dybbukim swarmed around it. The four unscathed ones reached it first. The tailless one limped along at their heels and pushed its way into the tight huddle of their bodies with some difficulty. Cain heard the soft moist sounds of their tongues lapping.

"Holy shit!" Izzy staggered back, staring at the blood, which seemed to be vanishing into the floor. "I *knew* there was something wrong about this house!"

Mr. Warwick glowered and thrust out his hand, holding his finger rigid. Vince had seen Sammi make the same gesture enough times that he knew what was coming, and he tried to dodge out of the way.

As fast as he was, Mr. Warwick was faster. The glaring white-blue bolt of electricity that erupted from his extended finger caught Vince in the shoulder. Izzy screamed in horror when Vince stumbled back with a shriek of pain.

Sammi half-caught him as he fell. Plumes of acrid smoke curled between Vince's fingers where he clutched the injured area, and the sleeve of his t-shirt was also blackened and curled at the edges. His face was sickly pale.

"I wouldn't bother with him if I were you," said Mr. Warwick to Sammi. "Hmm, you're the one who got the talent for electricity manipulation, aren't you? I'm afraid that's a trick you haven't learned yet. Unlike your rather primitive little lightning bolts, you see, mine stay with the victim. Your friend is sadly still burning, slowly and painfully, in the spot where my bolt hit him. And like any fire, this one will spread through his body as it consumes, which is rather unfortunate for him because it is quite unquenchable. In a few hours, he'll be dead. Unless…" He inclined his chin in a lordly manner, smirking at Cain. "Unless my servant finally sees fit to obey me."

Cain looked over at Vince's contorted, sweat-frosted face.

The dark patch of charred skin on his shoulder was visible between the fingers of the hand he still held protectively clamped over it, and Cain could see two or three veins of black creeping slowly down his bicep.

"Don't dawdle now, Cain." A slight singsong tone tinged Mr. Warwick's voice. "If you hurry, maybe your friend won't lose his arm."

"Dad!" Steve ran up and grabbed his father's wrist. He was paler than Vince, and he seemed about ready to throw up. "Stop! This is crazy! This is *evil*. Don't you see that? What's wrong with you? Why are you doing this? Why can't you just leave them—"

Mr. Warwick rounded on Steve and shoved him against the wall. Steve slid to the floor in a quivering, shocked ball, and his father shook himself off and turned back to Cain as if nothing had happened. Cain shuddered at the cold hatred in his eyes.

"My son will get what is rightfully his," growled his master, "with or without your willing cooperation, boy. Now hurry along, for your friend's sake."

The collar loosened and went slack when Cain stood up. He could not put off the evil moment any longer. If his obedience meant his friends had a chance of getting out of this place unscathed, he had to obey. His tail longed to curl around his knees in defeat, but he resisted the impulse and bit back the whimper trying to rise from his throat. He looked Mr. Warwick fully in the eyes, straightened his back, and took a resolute and bitter step forward.

CHAPTER TWENTY-FIVE

VICTORY

MR. WARWICK DREW THE knife from his jacket pocket, and he seemed to be smiling in anticipation. Cain moved toward him with slow and heavy steps. His collar had abruptly died, and the sudden absence of searing pain seemed to leave his body without sensation. He couldn't register Lance's wordless screams and groans floating down from the second story. He couldn't feel the floor pressing against the soles of his feet as he walked. He couldn't feel the bodies of the dybbukim brushing against his legs as he stumbled through their huddle and sent them scattering. The scuffing of their claws sounded distant and muffled to him, as if he were hearing it through a wad of wet cotton.

The blade glistened, reflecting the dead-white glow of the witch lights on the chandelier. As ravaged and numb as he was, a tiny shudder of fear ran through him when he looked at it. Another memory fragment flashed through his mind. He was on the outskirts of a remote desert town in Mexico. A tall dark-skinned man handed the leather-wrapped blade to Cain without a word, staring at him the whole time with green eyes as hard and as impassive as the glittering turquoise on the handle. Suddenly, the star symbol flashed before Cain's eyes as it always did, and he couldn't remember anything else about the knife. But something about it unsettled him every bit as badly as did the house with its disembodied voices and indelible stains; he suspected that many victims had left their blood in the grooves of the polished flint.

"What are you doing, boy?" Mr. Warwick's voice snapped in his ears like a firecracker, sending a brief shockwave through the collar. "Every second you waste moping is a second my son remains deprived of what's rightfully his."

Cain glanced back at his band mates. Vince lay stretched out on the floor, still pressing his hand to his burned shoulder. His face was so pale that every freckle along his cheekbones stood out in relief. Sammi paced helplessly nearby, away from Vince so that the sparks floating off him would cause no further burns, Cain guessed. Izzy knelt beside his friend and patted him gingerly, but he drew back when Vince moaned in agony at his touch. The cat hung half-forgotten from the crook of Izzy's arm, looking up at Cain with mournful eyes. He swallowed his anger and revulsion and turned back, trying not to think about what awaited him upstairs.

The cat twisted out of Izzy's grasp. He made a grab for her, but she dodged away from him and pelted down the hall, twisting and skittering to avoid the still-hungry dybbukim as they advanced on her with their tongues out. Cain gasped when her claws sank into his calf.

"Michelle!" Izzy pulled himself together and called after the cat, who was now climbing Cain's leg like a tree. "What are you doing? Come back!"

"Leave your girl downstairs, Cain," said Mr. Warwick

curtly, without turning around.

Cain's strength was so sapped that his arm began to obey the command of its own accord, reaching down to slap the cat off his leg. She grabbed it as it passed over her and began to clamber up his arm, staring up at him with grim determination.

"Now, Cain," said Mr. Warwick.

A ripple of heat formed around Cain's neck at the command. He braced himself for it to become a full-blown, burning torment as he made a half-hearted attempt to shake the cat off. She pulled herself up onto his shoulder undaunted. Yet the pain did not come. The heat vanished, and the collar went slack.

The cat had slipped her paws around it.

No one ever grabbed Cain's collar except Mr. Warwick. Steve and Lance had avoided it altogether. Cheryl and Sammi, who had helped him put on his makeshift collar-concealing ascot before the banquet, only touched its outer surface. And Michelle's hands and mouth always glided over it when they made love. Even the children in the Hispanic neighborhood had kept their grubby fingers well away from it when they climbed on him. His mind went completely blank with shock.

He rested his hand gently on the cat's soft back. She hooked her claws into the leather and tugged in a futile attempt to tear it. She let out an almost human wail, and Cain clutched her to him.

Mr. Warwick advanced on them, his face dark with anger. "I said, leave her here. If you won't remove her, I will."

Cain whimpered and involuntarily took a step back, shielding the cat as best he could. To his surprise, the collar did not hurt him, but he could feel a faint tingle from the portion that still touched his skin.

Mr. Warwick bit his lip. Cain saw a brief shift in his expression and a flash of something that might have been fear in his eyes. Then it passed, and he glared impatiently at Cain.

"Stupid, stubborn beast," he snarled. "You really aren't going to budge until she's taken care of, are you? Well, I suppose if I must, I must."

His hand shot out like a snake. The cat's wailing rose to a scream when his fingertips brushed her, and Cain staggered, overbalanced as the weight of the cat on his shoulder rapidly increased to Michelle's full human poundage. He had the presence of mind to roll in order to avoid landing directly on top of her, but he did so a half-second too late and pinned her legs under his body. He instinctively reached out to help her, stammering apologies.

"There—that's the last time I'll deign to humor you today," snapped Mr. Warwick. "Hurry along now."

Cain began to stand up, but a sudden sharp pressure on his neck jerked him down and away from his master. Michelle still had her hands hooked under the collar. It slid this way and that as she yanked at it, glaring defiantly up at Mr. Warwick.

"No, he won't hurry along!" she shouted. "You bastard, you said you were going to let him go! You're going to keep that promise, even if I have to rip this damn thing off him myself!"

She gave the collar a mighty tug. Cain gagged and squirmed in agony, not because the collar itself was hurting him, but because Michelle's hands were so much bigger than the cat's paws that they left almost no room for him to breathe. She pulled it tight, and what little breathing room he did have disappeared completely. The leather cut into his flesh and squeezed off his windpipe. He heard Mr. Warwick saying something in an angry voice, far above his head, but the words could not penetrate the cottony tingling sensation in his brain.

Dark shapes moved around him, shifting in and out of the light. Steve bent over him, shouting at him to let go—or was he shouting at Michelle to let go?—and he felt another hand grasp the collar. Then another dark shape from the periphery materialized as Sammi. Another hand settled at his neck.

"Just a few more steps, Vince." Izzy's voice floated into the huddle, and Cain felt two more hands join the cluster around his neck. One was warm and had a strong grip; one was cold and clammy and fluttered vaguely near his collarbone. For a moment, Cain's vision became clear, and he saw them—Michelle, Steve, Izzy, Vince, and Sammi—all standing in a protective phalanx around him, holding him by the collar.

"Hey!" Izzy turned to face Mr. Warwick, his voice squeaky with fear. "If you want Cain, you'll have to come through all of us first."

Then Cain's vision blurred again, and for a few seconds, the world went completely black. He began to panic. His collar was pulled so tight that his desperate, shallow gasps brought in almost no air at all. He worked his own fingers under the leather to create a tiny bit of breathing room. The collar shuddered violently when he touched it, and fireworks exploded in his brain.

He felt a change, a shivering in the Center of things.

Suddenly everything was clear. The pressure against his

neck rapidly grew lighter until the collar seemed to float away altogether, and a deep sense of calm and satisfaction came over him. The grim faces and outstretched arms of his friends stood out in bright relief, radiating an aura of strength and safety, and his calm increased when he looked at them. Something had fallen into place.

He had no time to wonder what that something might be. Mr. Warwick frowned and made a broad shooing motion with both arms. Cain felt his friends' hands leave the collar as they were jerked away, angrily shouting and screaming, tumbling back like dry rags picked up by the wind. He crouched against the floor, shivering and alone.

"*Now*, Cain." Mr. Warwick's arm descended on him, reaching for his collar. His arm was the color of a black night and looked miles long against the soft blue light from above. Cain cringed away from him and waited for the inevitable shock of pain.

It did not come.

Mr. Warwick was the one who screamed in agony the moment his fingers touched the leather.

Mr. Warwick snatched his hand away and staggered back, clutching the banister. The color slowly seeped away from his face. "Cain," he said in a trembling voice. "Stand up. I order you to stand up."

In a daze, Cain began to obey. Then he stopped abruptly and dropped back to the floor in utter astonishment. He felt nothing around his neck except the bulky press of ordinary leather.

Mr. Warwick's face crumbled like dry mud, and his hands trembled. For a moment, Cain thought he might faint.

Then he stiffened. A surge of fierce rage lit up his features, and he lunged forward with a hand that seemed to morph into a talon in Cain's slowed and distorted vision. Michelle had fallen closest to him. She was still huddled on the floor in shock and did not see him until he had her by the throat.

"What have you done?" he snarled in her face, shaking her like a ragdoll. "You little bitch! Do you have any idea how much effort it takes to properly bind a demon? Do you?"

He shook her harder, pulling her closer until his nose almost touched hers. She lurched forward like a puppet as he dragged her, too startled and frightened to fight back.

"You've ruined everything!" His face trembled with passion while he screamed at her. "All my hopes of finding a cure for my son's shameful condition, my countless hours of hard work and valuable research...I don't know how you did it, but you've stolen it all away, and I'm going to make damn sure you pay for it!"

Michelle pulled herself together enough to throw a punch at him, but she did not have the advantage of surprise this time; her fist glanced harmlessly off his cheek. He shoved her roughly down before she could lash out again, pinning her to the floor. Cain watched in frozen terror as Mr. Warwick squeezed Michelle's throat until she gagged, peeling his lips back in a savage, joyless grin. He had never seen Mr. Warwick lose complete control before; yet with the scene unfolding before him and the memory of Chelsea's battered corpse vivid in his mind, he could believe that it had happened out of his sight, many times.

The knife had fallen from Mr. Warwick's hand when he pounced. It lay on the floor a few feet from Michelle, glittering in the dust. She must have noticed it in her peripheral vision because she made a desperate grab for it, but Mr. Warwick beat her to it with a lunge. His eyes flashed with hatred as he drew it back for a vicious blow, aiming the blade directly at her throat.

Cain leapt up with a howl of distress. The next few seconds were muddled in his mind; he had a blurry impression of the knife skittering off into the shadows after he knocked it out of Mr. Warwick's hand and of Michelle shakily sitting up and gasping for air. Then everything became clear again, and he held his former master pinned to the floor, and claws he did not remember sprouting were pressed to his chest and neck.

The low, steady snarl that had been trickling from Cain's throat grew into a full-blown roar of triumph. The collar could no longer hurt him. After ten long years of degradation, he finally held his master at his mercy—his master who was also the Engineer. He could take whatever revenge he wanted, and the old man couldn't do a thing about it. Blood rushed into his eyes and his lips peeled back and his grip tightened around Mr. Warwick's throat.

"Wait!"

Cain looked up in surprise at the sound of Steve's voice.

"What are you doing?" Steve staggered up from the floor. "You're not going to...to..."

Someone grabbed Cain and tried to tug him back. The muscles in the hand grasping his shoulder were so tense with anxiety that his own heart began to race again.

"Look," said Steve in a pinched and miserable tone. "I bet you probably really, really want"—he closed his eyes and shuddered—"to rip out his throat right now. God knows he deserves it. But I can't..."

Cain relaxed his grip to give Mr. Warwick some breathing room. He shivered in horror as the full realization dawned on him that he had come perilously close to tearing Mr. Warwick to pieces in front of his own son.

"Don't worry," he whispered to Steve, watching his captive from the corner of his eye. "I promise you I won't do anything to him as long as he lets us all go, without taking any of my blood, and leaves us alone from now on."

He noticed a strange expression pass over Mr. Warwick's face. The old man's eyes flicked from Steve to Cain and back again, and they had a stricken look in them. Cain could feel his former master's chest trembling with impotent rage beneath his hand. Then the moment passed, and he was eerily calm.

"Ah, I feared this would happen someday," he said sadly. "Now you see what I've been trying to warn you about, Stephen. The great Hiram Levi went the same way, you know. He taught his demon servant to read and write, dressed her in fine clothes, loved her like a daughter—and died a gruesome death when she turned on him. Well, since you seem to think I deserve to follow in his footsteps, watch what Cain does to me and remember it. This knowledge may save your life the next time you're tempted to treat a savage, bloodthirsty devil like a trusted pet."

Another blinding surge of anger ran through Cain. His claws pressed in again, and he felt a nearly irresistible urge to bury them in Mr. Warwick's flesh. Yet something held him back. He thought of all the times he had been half-strangled for disobedience, and he thought of all the death and pain and ruin that the old man had inflicted on the lives of his friends, but he also thought of Steve, who was standing over them, breathing in short ragged bursts, his face the color of old oatmeal.

"Cain!" Footsteps rustled against the dry floorboards

behind him, and Sammi slipped into his field of vision. "Cain, you can't kill him, not yet anyway. If you do, Vince will die."

Cain cast a quick glance over his shoulder at his other two band mates. The livid black streaks had worked their way down Vince's arm, almost reaching his wrist. Sickly brown smoke still trickled from the originating wound, and he was curled into a quivering fetal huddle, no longer making any attempt to hide his sobs of pain. Quaking in horror at what he had almost done, Cain turned back to Mr. Warwick and tightened his grip once more.

"If I let you go, old man," he growled, "will you cure my friend?"

A cold smirk flitted across Mr. Warwick's lips.

"No."

Cain let his claws dig in farther, but Mr. Warwick did not flinch.

"I want what's mine and my son's," he said. "If you won't give it to me...Well, let me live or kill me, the outcome for that foolish crony of yours will be equally hopeless either way."

An icy sensation rippled under Cain's scales while he stared into his former master's perfectly calm face. A piercing scream from Lance echoed through the house, but Mr. Warwick didn't react.

"Dad!" Steve's voice was shrill. "What's wrong with you? You'd really rather *die* than let this go? It's not the end of the world that Lance sucks at magic. You have me, and—"

"Yes, I have you." Mr. Warwick's lip curled disdainfully. "Not that it's any comfort. You are a cringing, insecure child preoccupied with the good opinions of others while being utterly inept at winning them, and you're always ready to turn your back on your family at a moment's notice. You don't know the meaning of the word loyalty. You're entirely too much like your silly cow of a mother for comfort, boy! I would be ashamed to call you my heir."

His tone was quiet and devoid of anger or passion, but Cain still picked up on the venom dripping from his words. The sheer hate and rage behind them took his breath away. His claws involuntarily clenched tighter, but he resisted the impulse to use them. At this point, he would not put it past the old man to deliberately goad them into killing him out of sheer spite at having his will thwarted, leaving Vince to die a slow, horrible death and Steve traumatized.

Steve said nothing. Cain looked anxiously up at him and saw that his face was deadly pale. He stood as still and as rigid as a steel pylon, except for an almost imperceptible tremor in his hands.

Mr. Warwick seemed to take grim satisfaction in his son's hurt. He tilted his head as far as he could without being punctured by Cain's claws to watch Steve's reaction, and he opened his mouth for another salvo.

The words never came. Mr. Warwick looked shocked, and Cain could see the color leaving his face again.

"Vince, what are you doing?" Sammi's horrified voice rang through the hall.

Mr. Warwick let out a thin gasp and tried to push Cain's claws aside so he could sit up. His hands faltered and dropped to the floor. His head lolled weakly, and he stared up at the ceiling with eyes that were quickly clouding over and losing their focus. Cain turned around sharply at the sound of scuffling behind his back and saw Sammi making a valiant attempt to restrain Vince, who had latched onto Mr. Warwick's ankle with his good hand.

"Vinnie, stop!" Sammi tried to dislodge his fingers. "Look, I want to kill him as much as you do, but he can't fix you if he's dead, okay? Please, you've gotta let go!" He turned in desperation to Steve, who stood closest to him. "Hey Steve, how about a little help here?"

Steve crossed his arms tightly over his chest and backed away, shaking his head. The sick horror on his face had been replaced by cold, intense anger, and Cain guessed that at least for the moment, he would not be terribly broken up if Vince did kill his father.

Vince clung on like a leech. His burned arm still hung useless at his side, but his eyes were fiercely bright, and the rest of his body glowed with vitality as Mr. Warwick's energy flowed into him.

"He won't fix me anyway," growled Vince. "You heard what he said. Well, if I've got to die, I might as well take this asshole with me."

"Vince!" Sammi tore at his hair in desperation. "Come *on*! Killing him right now isn't going to help anything."

Izzy dashed out of the shadows. He leapt on Vince and grabbed his hand with an unusually businesslike air, slowly prying his fingers off of Mr. Warwick's ankle. Vince writhed and head-butted, but his injured arm and Izzy's strength put him at a definite disadvantage. Izzy easily wrested him away from his intended prey—just in time; Cain could barely feel Mr. Warwick breathing under his fingertips.

Sammi rushed to Cain's side and peered over his shoulder. "Is he dead?"

"Not quite."

"Too bad." Sammi sighed. "Vinnie has pretty much screwed himself over, I'm afraid. Unless you can do something to help him?"

Cain turned to look at Vince, who glared sulkily back from the headlock in which Izzy was holding him. He supposed he might be able to counter Mr. Warwick's spell somehow, but not without a great deal of potentially dangerous experimentation, and almost certainly not before the livid burn creeping down Vince's arm had consumed the entire limb. Still, he had to try.

"Oh my god!" Michelle ran toward him with a cry of relief that reverberated through the high-ceilinged hall. "Thank goodness you're all right! What happened? How on earth were you able to save me from him when you're still wearing the collar?"

"I…I don't know." Cain let her fall into his arms. "It just…stopped hurting me all of a sudden."

"Hey!" Vince used a burst of his stolen energy to squirm out of Izzy's grasp and lurched toward Cain, cradling his arm. "How about you talk to her after you help me, asshole? This fucking hurts!"

Glad for once to see that Vince was healthy enough to be cantankerous, Cain hurried to his side and inspected the injury. He was relieved to find that it was not quite as deep and appalling as it had looked from a distance. Cain thought that he could probably heal it completely in a few hours, as long as he could stop the fire. He spread his hands over the burn, but Vince pulled away before he could get a spell going.

"Don't touch it, dumbass!" Vince shielded his shoulder with his good hand. "What if I get some kind of infection from the weirdo demon germs on your hands? Besides, touching it makes it hurt worse."

"I have to touch it to heal it, Vince," said Cain through

clenched teeth, amazed at how quickly his relief had worn off. "Look, just let me work, okay? The pain will be bad, but it won't last long."

"Fine." Vince rolled his eyes and extended his arm stiffly, wincing as he did so. "But make it quick."

"I'll try." Cain inspected the wound again, estimating which parts of it would cause the least discomfort to Vince when he touched them. No areas looked particularly promising. He picked a spot at random and moved his hands cautiously toward it, hoping that Vince would have the decency not to make too much of a production out of his pain.

Then, unexpectedly, a lean brown hand appeared in Cain's peripheral vision. Before he could even figure out to whom the hand belonged, it upended the glass vial it was holding. A stream of clear liquid splashed over Vince's shoulder and upper arm. The burn sizzled when the liquid made contact, and a big puff of briny-smelling steam billowed up into Cain's face.

"Fucking fuck!" he heard Vince scream. "What the hell did you do, you dumb overgrown lizard? I thought you said you were going to heal me, not dump a gallon of acid on me! Shit!"

Cain waved away the last swirling tendrils of steam, looking around in confusion. He was amazed to find Crazy Loti standing beside him. She calmly put her empty vial in some hidden pocket among the jungle of multicolored rags that made up her clothing, smiling serenely up at Vince.

"That isn't a very nice thing to say, Vincent Sweet, to someone who was trying to help you," she said. "Besides, it wasn't acid, just pure, wholesome seawater. It's good for what ails you."

"Seawater?" Vince gaped indignantly at her. "Well, no wonder it hurt so much! Cain, why the hell did you let your crazy old bag-lady friend pour saltwater on—"

"Vince." Cain held up a hand to stop his band mate's rant, staring at his shoulder. "I think it really is doing you good."

"What are you talking about?" Vince craned his neck to look at his injury. His face was angled away, but Cain saw him do a double take when his eyes fell on a patch of blistered skin. It was lightening and smoothing out while they watched, and the spidery brown streaks on the arm were rapidly receding.

"Feeling a bit better now, Mr. Sweet?" said Loti.

Vince lifted his head and gave her a sulky scowl. "It still hurts."

"I suppose that's the closest to a thank-you I'll get." She chuckled and turned to Cain. "Are you all right, honey? You put up quite a fight—and against your own master too."

"I think so." Cain pawed at his neck. The collar was still inactive. "I ache a little...Wait...How did you know I was fighting my master? Were you here the whole time?"

"No, honey." Loti sighed apologetically. "I wanted to be, but I'm not supposed to work that way."

"How did you even get in here?" Izzy scratched his head. "The doors still have that shiny stuff over them."

"Doors or no doors, there's no place in this city that's not open to me, Mr. Unger."

Cain looked her up and down, his tail twitching with curiosity. He caught a flash of movement near her feet and saw the five dybbukim circling around her, nuzzling her stained green skirt like friendly cats.

"Come along now." She grabbed his arm with a

businesslike air. "We should be keeping an eye on your former master. He's not one to turn your back on, that one."

Cain allowed himself to be led to Mr. Warwick, who was still sprawled unconscious on the floor. Izzy trotted after him; Sammi followed Izzy; and Vince slunk after Sammi. Michelle raised an eyebrow when Cain and Loti swept by her.

"Who the heck is that?" she whispered a little too loudly to Steve. Cain hoped that Loti's hearing wasn't as good as his. "I wonder if she's the weird old homeless lady Cain told me about, the one who told him to buy his guitar?"

Cain could feel Steve looking in their direction. Cain squinted at Loti's face, trying to size her up as if he'd never met her. She suddenly made him uneasy. Something seemed to surround her, some invisible aura of greatness that made the room seem too small to contain her and the walls of the house too flimsy to hold her.

"I don't know," Steve muttered. "He never told me about any homeless woman. But whoever she is, I think we should stay out of her way. She obviously knows plenty about magic, and she has some sort of…something…surrounding her."

Michelle nodded. "I noticed. I don't think many people can cure burns with seawater."

Mr. Warwick groaned and stirred. He sat up slowly, clutching his head. His eyes cracked open and fixed on Cain, and his arm swept up in a leaden motion.

"You," he snarled. "Don't think for a moment that you can walk out of this house without my say-so. You're still my servant, damn it! I still own you."

Cain drew himself up proudly, luxuriating in the persistent slackness of the collar and his own rising righteous anger. He still had no idea how or why he had been freed, but it was clear to him that he was no longer bound to Mr. Warwick, and that monster of a man had no right to tell him he owned him. He was about to fire back an angry reply when Loti stepped in front of him.

"No, you do not," she said to Mr. Warwick. "Your power over him is gone. You will leave this city immediately, and you will do no harm to anyone on your way out."

Cain stared at her in astonishment. He did not remember her voice ever sounding quite the way it did now—deep and commanding and compelling, filled with immeasurable strength. Izzy and Vince were staring at her too, with their mouths wide open. Mr. Warwick scrambled to his feet and loomed over her, but even he looked a bit daunted.

"How dare you," he said in a furious-but-trembling voice. "You have no authority over me, and it's certainly none of your business what I do with my own servant."

Loti squared her shoulders and met his gaze without fear. A radiant sheen flickered in the air around her.

"It is now." The walls creaked as she spoke; dust rained from the ceiling; and a tremor rippled through the floorboards. "You made it my business the day you slunk into my city and murdered in cold blood. If the Conclave had allowed me to intervene, I'd have stopped you in a heartbeat. Well, I'm here to tell you that I don't give a damn what's allowed anymore!"

She raised her hand and thrust it, palm up, in Mr. Warwick's direction. He staggered back as if she had slapped him, and the indignation in his eyes gave way to fear.

"Leave and don't come back," she snarled while the ancient walls of the house groaned in protest and the five dybbukim chattered with excitement. "You will offer no further violence to the good people who live here, and you will take nothing more from them. Let the Princes of the Conclave do what they will to me, as long as you never harm anyone I'm sworn to protect again. Go. I declare you outcast."

Mr. Warwick's chest puffed out with a final burst of anger, and he stepped forward, raising his fist as if to strike her. Then he stopped mid-step. His shoulders drooped and a shade of deep weariness passed over his face. For a moment, he looked immeasurably older than the forty or fifty years that Cain guessed he had been alive.

"All right, then," he muttered. "I know when I've been outgunned. I'll go collect my son." His eyes wandered over to Cain, becoming dark and grim as they did. "Stupid, stubborn devil, you should have let me take your blood. You have so much raw power. If you had only given a small measure of it to Lance, he could have finally become a great man. You'll squander that immense potential of yours on silly stage tricks."

He slunk up the stairs with a defeated air. Cain was still staring after him in utter amazement when Steve tugged his arm.

"Holy shit, Cain," said Steve in an awed whisper, glancing at Loti. "Why didn't you tell us that you were friends with LA's Patron?"

"LA's what?" said Cain, taken aback by the awe and dawning recognition on Steve's face.

"You don't know what a Patron is?" Steve's voice squeaked with fear. "Cain, that woman is the guardian of the whole city!"

Loti smiled. "That's awfully flattering of you, Stephen.

I'm not the guardian of the *whole* city. Los Angeles is a big and populated place; we're up to seven Patrons now. I'm not even a terribly important one. But we can talk about that later. Are you still feeling all right, honey?"

"I guess," said Cain.

"Good. Let's all go outside, shall we? You must be dying for some fresh air."

She turned and strode purposefully toward the staircase. Cain and Izzy followed her, as did Vince, who was still rubbing his shoulder and grumbling. Steve and Michelle hesitated, and then they hurried to join the others.

"Hey, Cain, am I missing something?" Sammi ran to catch up to him. "Who's the old witch-lady, and why is she acting like she knows you?"

"She calls herself Crazy Loti," Cain whispered back. "I introduced her to you on the way to the bus stop after our first show."

"Oh." Sammi frowned. "I guess I must have been too out of it to remember. But now that you mention it, I think I do remember meeting someone..." He trailed off, looking thoughtful.

A small vestibule stood under the staircase. Its walls were obscured by a thin layer of metal, but the metal rippled back when Loti approached. A smudged glass door was revealed as it receded, and the metal molded itself into a handle as she reached for one. The door creaked open. Cain almost sobbed with relief at the sight of bright daylight. The house shuddered and sighed as they stepped out, and the five dybbukim scattered into the shadows and dust of the interior, as if glad to be in full possession of their territory once more.

The door led to a small courtyard surrounded by white

walls. A dry marble basin (the remains of a fountain) stood in the center of the courtyard, surrounded by broken and uneven cobblestones, two crumbling stone benches, and several Pampas-grass-choked flowerbeds. The high walls muffled sounds from the street, giving the area an atmosphere of preternatural silence.

Vince sat down on one of the benches with a weary grunt. Sammi and Izzy followed his example, and Steve perched on the rim of the fountain base.

Cain felt Michelle's hand slip into his. "Thank God," she said. "I thought I'd never get to breathe air that didn't smell like mold again."

"So are you all right?" Cain threw an arm around her shoulder and pulled her close, studying her face anxiously.

"I think so." Michelle rubbed her arm with a wince. "My muscles feel a little stiff in places, but not as much as I thought they'd be. Hey, Cain, I want you to promise me that you'll never, ever change me into a cat or anything else, okay?"

"Of course I promise. I'd never put you through that."

"Good. It hurt more than anything—like I was being split open and burned at the same time." She shuddered at the memory. "But it's over now, thank goodness. I'm more concerned about you, honestly. What in the world happened in there? With the collar, I mean?"

Cain rubbed his neck. "I don't know. I just remember all of you standing around me with your hands under it, pulling me back, and then...well...One minute the collar was burning me so much I could hardly stand it, and the next minute, the pain was totally gone."

"I think I can tell you why the pain stopped." Loti stepped around the fountain and walked toward Cain, holding out her hand. "Here, show me your collar."

"What?"

"Your collar, honey. I need to see it."

Cain frowned, wondering how to go about showing it to her politely. At last he leaned awkwardly forward to bring his neck to her eye level.

"No, no," she laughed. "Take it off."

"But I can't." His hands floated up to the collar even as he protested, and the buckle came undone easily.

"I'll be damned," said Steve in an awed voice. "Cain, you're free. Completely free."

Cain handed over the collar in a daze. His joyful astonishment quickly mingled with disgust when he noticed that he felt naked without it.

She took it with her fingertips, cautiously, as if she feared it might be electrified. Cain watched as she stretched out the leather, bending it at regular intervals.

"What's she doing with it?" said Izzy. Cain shrugged.

"Looking for something," said Loti. "Hmm, now where could it...? Ah, here!"

A fine slit appeared on the lining of the collar when she bent it near the buckle. She worked her fingers into the slit and pulled out something thin and yellow. She handed it to Cain.

"Have a good look at this, all of you," she said.

It was a folded slip of paper. Cain opened it slowly as his friends gathered around. He feared that his claws would shred it if he moved too fast. Then he noticed the tingling of magical energy in his fingertips, and he slowed down even more. Izzy did a double take when he unfurled it.

"I've seen that before!" he said. "It's that thing from the book."

"What book?" said Sammi.

Izzy scratched his head. "The one we stole from Breen's house. Steve showed it to me one night when you guys were out."

Cain turned the paper over in his hands, cautiously regarding the all-too-familiar symbol. An eerie purplish gleam coursed down one of the star's lines.

"Whoa," said Steve. "Be careful with that paper, Cain; there's still active magic on it. But...how can that be? Solomon's Seal binds for life, and dad isn't dead."

Izzy was squinting at the paper. He cleared his throat and pointed to it with a puzzled frown.

"Hey, Steve," he said. "Wasn't only one of the little squiggly things supposed to be smudged?"

Cain studied the fine lines of the five-pointed star, trying to pick out the glyphs. He saw the three-pronged shape, the spade, and the bird caught mid-flight, but when his eyes fell on the upper left point of the star, where the complex circle-and-triangle glyph should have been, he saw only a blurry smear, just like the one in the topmost point. He frowned, perplexed; it wasn't like Mr. Warwick to be so careless and smudge part of a spell.

"That's weird," said Steve. "Netzach was erased somehow."

"Oh, it didn't just get erased." Loti's eyes shone. "Very few remember this truth: Solomon's Seal was once a harmless tool for interaction between humans and gods. Then an ambitious king saw the potential it held and used the darkest blood magic to imprint it with the Five Holy Bonds, twisting it into a tool of enslavement and conquest. So it stayed until, oh, eleven years ago, when a good man gave his life and sanity to break the Foundation Bond. His sacrifice left it unstable enough for Cain to break the second—"

"Wait a minute!" Sammi interjected. "You're saying Cain freed himself from that collar somehow?"

Cain looked up sharply.

"Why are you so startled?" Loti said to him with a chuckle. "You did break the Bond of Victory. Don't you remember? That moment when all your friends reached out to protect you and when you laid your hands on the collar in defiance at the same time...?"

Cain blinked. He had felt something—a split second of perfect calm—yet his doubt grew stronger. After more than a decade of enslavement, he couldn't imagine how he could have altered the awful spell that bound him, especially not by a simple accident.

"Here, honey." Loti handed the collar back to Cain. "You should keep that in case your old master comes looking for revenge. Now that you've left your mark on it, it may give protection instead of pain. Oh, and you may notice that your memory hasn't returned yet—but it will. Just give it time."

She abruptly turned and made her way to the door. Cain made a noise of exasperation; yet again, she was about to leave him with many more questions than she had answered.

"But why me?" he called after her. "Why was I able to break the bond?"

"I honestly don't know," she said, without turning around. "But it may have something to do with the fact that the first bond was broken on the day of your capture— maybe even at the very same moment. Now, if you'll excuse me, I have a city to tend to."

She vanished into the darkness of the house. Cain and

his friends were not inclined to follow her right away. They sat in the ruined courtyard for a while, breathing the still air and feeling the warmth of the sun on their faces. They were too tired and overwhelmed to speak.

Steve took the collar from Cain and ran the worn leather through his fingers. His shoulders drooped wearily.

"My dad will want me to meet him at the airport," he muttered, breaking the silence. "I'm not going. I don't ever want to see him again, but...I don't know what else to do. I'm too young to get a good job, and I don't have any grandparents or anything."

"Stay with us," said Cain resolutely. He wasn't sure what Mr. Arkin would have to say about that solution, but he knew that he could never send Steve back to New York, not after what they had witnessed that day.

"Hell no," muttered Vince. "The house is way too crowded as it is."

"Shut up, Vince," said Izzy with uncharacteristic forcefulness. "You can stay as long as you like, Steve. We're not handing you over to the Engineer."

Steve smiled weakly and sighed with relief. Vince glowered indignantly at Izzy, opened his mouth, and quickly shut it again. He must have decided that he did not have the strength for another fight.

"Come on, everyone," said Sammi. "Let's take Cain home."

A wooden door was set in the wall of the garden. Izzy walked over to it and tried the handle. He looked pleasantly surprised when it swung open. They began to file out of the garden, glad to be spared a walk through the sad decay of the old mansion. Cain reached for Michelle's hand.

"Hey," he said. "Aren't you coming?"

Michelle hung back by the fountain, staring up at the looming house with a pensive expression on her face.

"Cain," she said. "You told me once that you got captured ten—more like eleven now—years ago."

Cain nodded as he steered her into the house.

"Do you remember what time of year it was?"

"No," said Cain, frowning. His memories of the day of his capture were as fuzzy as his memories of his previous life. He wasn't particularly hopeful that they would clear up with time, as Loti had promised. "I just remember it was cold and gray outside. Why?"

Michelle gave him a sideways glance. "Well, if you were captured in late November of '72—that's about when Eddie Morningstar died. I just thought that was an interesting coincidence."

Cain froze.

All the anecdotes that Sammi and Vince and Skeeter Judd had ever recounted about Eddie Morningstar popped into Cain's mind: his frequent illnesses and caginess with interviewers and reporters; the paranoia and obsessiveness that marked his last few months of life; and the mysterious cabin fire that had killed him in spite of the wet autumn weather. These things were all symptoms of a Gifted person who had ruined his mind and body by overextending his talents.

What if Eddie broke the first bond? Cain thought. The realization made him stop in his tracks.

If Eddie had given everything—his career, his reputation, his mind, and eventually his life—to create the initial weakness in Solomon's Seal, then Cain owed Eddie more than he could ever repay. For that very same weakness had allowed Cain some access to his memories and had eventually enabled him to break free from his master's clutches. Cain stumbled, and his eyes filled with tears. He owed Eddie his freedom.

"Hey!" Michelle's voice cut through his reverie. "Are you coming?"

He looked up and saw her standing in the mellow daylight that spilled through the door. As she beckoned to him, he realized something: he could repay Eddie. In fact, he had already begun to repay him by breaking the second bond and ensuring that he had not died in vain. If he could only find a way to break the other three bonds, if he could render that evil symbol useless forever, he'd not only be able to honor Eddie's memory, but also save others as Eddie had saved him.

Cain hurried through the open door and joined his band mates on the sidewalk. Even though he was relieved of the collar, he felt more tied to the human world than ever.

"Let's go home," he said to them.

Michael Anderson lay shivering on the ground between an unfinished pillar and a pile of cedar logs. His eyes stubbornly riveted themselves to the horror unfolding before him for the tenth or eleventh time even as he tried desperately to look away, to wake up. It was no use. The vision played out and reset itself and played again, skipping immediately from conclusion to beginning.

He was witnessing the execution of a slave. She knelt a few feet away from him, and her slender taloned hands were bound behind her back with heavy rope. The bright desert sun glinted off her tortoiseshell-colored horns as she glared up at the line of dark-skinned and bearded human men who stood facing her with long spears in their hands. Michael could see others like her from where he sat. They were all horned and scaled, and their long tails dragged in the dust. They huddled together in a tight half-circle around the condemned slave. More humans stood around them, brandishing spears and swords and whips, but Michael knew the humans had nothing to fear. A power greater than any human weapon held these creatures in place; they could only shiver and whine in anticipation of what was about to happen, although some did pick at the strips of oxhide tied around their necks in futile rage.

The line of men parted and another man, taller and more ornately dressed than the others, stepped through. He carried a gleaming sword. He stared down at the slave for a moment, his eyes alight with intense hatred. She stared back undaunted. He raised his sword, slowly and deliberately, as if he wanted to savor the moment.

A collective wail rose from the other slaves when he brought the blade down on her neck, but her defiant gaze did not falter. After seeing it happen so many times, Michael knew why.

The sword was a slender thing with a brightly polished bronze blade and a gold hilt—a ceremonial weapon—not nearly strong or sharp enough to pierce the bound slave's scaly hide.

Michael finally managed to wrench his eyes away as the tall man bore down on her in growing fury, ramming and slashing her with the increasingly blunted blade. He knew what would happen. The sword would finally break after leaving the shallowest of scratches on the prisoner's throat. Her executioner would snatch a spear from one of the guards and drive it into the tiny wound, as hard as he could.

Michael crouched by the pile of logs with his eyes shut and his ears plugged against the eerie howls of the other slaves. He mistimed the vision and looked up when he thought it had reached its conclusion once more. Instead he found that he had opened his eyes for the worst part: the few seconds near the end.

Four guards brushed past him, carrying the nearly lifeless body of the slave. He saw blood spilling out of the ragged wound on her neck, dripping down into the sand and staining the guards' tan linen tunics. The blood was darker than her bright red scales. He saw her chest rise and fall with gurgling labored breaths. He saw her golden eyes cloud over even as they rolled toward him in desperation and seemed, for one terrible second, to fix on him. Michael knew that she would be carried out of the city and hung from the main gate by her hair as a warning to other slaves of her race who tried to rebel. He felt the accusation in her gaze like a kick to the gut.

The scene whirled and started again. Michael recoiled in anger. The whole history of this universe lay in his mind. He should have been able to pull up any memory he wanted, from any point in time. So why did he keep returning to this one, this shameful and half-forgotten chapter that left him wracked with a deep guilt he couldn't explain?

He got up and ran, scrambling over the logs and through the great unfinished temple whose pillars stood dark against the bright sky like tombstones, the temple the poor dead slave had been helping to build before her rebellion. On and on he ran, through the dusty streets of the city and into the wild desert beyond while the blue sky above him darkened to a star-dusted night. He did not care in which direction he headed. It did not matter now. He was a prisoner in his own head, haunted by crimes committed lifetimes ago. He was already lost. His legs became heavy and his lungs burned. Cities sprang up from the wilderness, and nations rose and fell around him. He ran over mountains and plains, lakes and seas, not slowing his pace until he was surrounded by the skyscrapers of a city he knew very well. He collapsed in the street as people walked and drove by without seeing him. He sobbed in relief at the familiarity of it all.

Michael, dear. Wake up.

A voice—warm and inviting, not the mighty permeating Voice of the Great Entity—pierced his prison, filtering in from the outside. The dream-city melted away as his eyes peeled open, and he was awake in his room. His head throbbed under its bandage.

I did as you asked. The voice again. He recognized it; it was the voice of one of the city's Patrons, the one who called herself Lotus Blossom. *A second bond is broken. He's proved himself against his master.*

The Dark Lion had triumphed.

Michael sat up despite the howl of protest from his injured head.

A sheaf of wrinkled drawings lay on his bedside table. He snatched them up in feverish joy. He remembered. For a few minutes of terrible clarity, everything fell into place, and he understood.

Papers fluttered to the floor as he leafed through them in aimless urgency. He remembered now; he recalled the promise he had made to the Dark Lion a year before the execution of the rebellious slave who would become known to generations of humans as the Prophet of Falsehood.

An unfinished sketch near the bottom of the stack caught his eye.

Michael laid the paper on the bedside table and groped for a black pencil. He added Solomon's Seal to the Dark Lion's outstretched hand, drawing the circle and star from the memory of his own cursed birthmark. A tear rolled down his cheek as he scribbled vague smears where two of the glyphs had once been. Then he began to reach for colored pencils, but he stopped. The Dark Lion's story was just beginning. It seemed fitting that the drawing, too, was unfinished.

The pencil slipped from his hand and dropped to the floor with a dull thud. Exhaustion overtook him, and he began to slide into a mercifully dreamless sleep.

Then another vision came.

Michael caught a glimpse of the Dark Lion himself. He sat cross-legged on the floor of his bedroom with his guitar across his lap. His fingers moved soundlessly over the strings, and a young human girl watched him play. Then the girl leaned in and nuzzled his shoulder. He stopped playing and laid his hand atop her stomach.

The tenderness of the touch exchanged between these two living creatures was such a small thing. Yet it gave Michael hope that all might not be lost after all, that someday soon he would see the rift between their two races mended.

Then, maybe then, I can atone for the evil I brought into the world, he thought.

A sigh of contentment escaped his lips as sleep overtook him. The Dark Lion had passed the first trial.

ABOUT THE AUTHOR

Carly Orosz lives in Kalamazoo, Michigan with her husband. She graduated from Kalamazoo College and went on to earn an MFA in poetry from Sarah Lawrence College. Her poetry has been published in *Wavelength Journal* and *SpoutMagazine*. In her spare time she enjoys cooking, weaving on a hand loom, and studying the art and cultures of pre-Columbian Mexico.

The web comic series starts here!

https://www.devil-music.com/?source=i-read-the-book

You *did* read the book first, didn't you?